The Adventures of Elizabeth Stanton Series

Volume 12 When Worlds Collide

Vic Broquard

Published by:
Broquard eBooks
http://Broquard-eBooks.com
author@Broquard-eBooks.com
103 Timberlane
East Peoria, IL 61611

Artwork by Crooked Willow Studios

For Morgan and L. Ron Hubbard

Table of Contents

Chapter 1 Prelude to a Storm

Forty years of peace has prevailed across Tarra, bringing with it an unprecedented explosion of breakthroughs both in inventions and in medical research. As expected, Velona is leading the way for all of Tarra. In fact, Velona now has the unique distinction of becoming the first industrialized nation in the world, though Barcella and Fortress d'Grange are right behind us.

It's June 1, 822, my new birthday, and we are having a party at our house tonight. My name is now Bethany Elizabeth Bartiana and I am finally of age, fourteen. I'd best try to explain all of our new bodies. Our old group at 42 Hampton Way aged, and as our bodies grew old, we decided to arrange our next baby bodies by choosing our parents once more. Yes, Renzo and I wanted to be together again, as did many of our dear friends. When you know that you are an immortal spiritual being and not a fleshly body, you have a different point of view in such matters.

We decided upon using some of our grandchildren as our new parents, with their permission, of course. We chose our son Nico's youngest son, Tito, and his pretty wife Sofia Bartiana as one set of parents. Dante and Natalie Angela's youngest son Sandro and his wife Marta became the second set of parents. Renzo and I then picked up a new baby body from each of them, hoping to be able to marry once more when our new bodies grew up. Sometimes things never quite work out as planned, especially so with babies. Renzo's new body ended up being female, much to his consternation. This lifetime, we are destined to be very close friends and not lovers as usual. Actually, as we grew up, we both fell in love with each other's brother and sister.

I think that this is getting a bit confusing, so let me try it this way. Renzo, Arsenio, Enyo, Cosima, Len, Bianca, Alessa, and I all decided to attempt to stay together in our next lifetimes. Our other dear friends wished to move onto other locations. For example, Kallisto and Alex felt that they ought to be down in Demokritos to help monitor the situation there. We eight met with Tito, Sofia, Sandro, and Marta and got their agreement on having us as their children when they had them. As a result, the house at 42 Hampton Way now belongs to them and they have become our Forze Segrete, that is, our protectors.

Tito is thirty-two, tall with thick, black hair and eyes to match. He is a foreman at Velona Steel, a company that makes steel in vast quantities. Sofia is a year younger, with wavy, shoulder length black hair and dark brown eyes. She, too, is quite tall and is a musician, playing the violin in the All Velona Orchestra. She also sings, adding her alto voice to the Sunday church choir. We all attend the Church of the Three Holy Roses.

My oldest brother is Sergio, who is tall and fit at sixteen. This is Cosima's new body. She hated to give up being the Chief Detective Inspector, but her body grew too old to keep up. Already, she, I mean he, is in line to be appointed Detective Inspector for Velona, but he has been promised the Chief appointment once he proves that he still has the uncanny ability to find the guilty parties. Sergio has wavy black hair and is growing a moustache, though we tease him about it.

My youngest brother, Giovanni is also tall and fifteen now. He has let his black hair grow longer than Sergio's and it touches his shoulders, barely. Giovanni is not growing a moustache. Oh yes, this is Enyo's new body. She wanted to have a female body once more, but didn't luck out. Now she is working hard to be a he. Yes, Giovanni is still our resident engineer, having been partially responsible for the incredible explosion of inventions during the last forty years. So far this lifetime, Giovanni has not made any actual commitments, though he has a standing offer to rejoin the DAE Enterprises, resuming where she left off last lifetime.

I come next, at fourteen. I, too, am tall, six-one, with very thick and long black hair. Thankfully, mine is not wavy, but lays straight as an arrow down my back, reaching the small of my back now. I look like my mom, everyone says.

My younger sister, Lucianna, is thirteen, and has shoulder length, wavy black hair. She was Arsenio, the inventor who helped Dianna and Enyo found the DAE Enterprises. Both Giovanni and Lucianna often tease each other about having somehow gotten each other's bodies this time around. Like Giovanni, Lucianna has her position waiting for her at DAE Enterprises, should she wish to continue her inventor career. We are all waiting on Lucianna to become of age next year, before we all marry our heartthrobs.

The other father, Sandro Angela, is thirty–one and very blonde! His hair is nearly yellow and falls to his shoulders. His eyes are a rich blue and he is an electrician by trade. His wife Marta is a year younger and has lovely light brown hair and matching eyes. I think that she is even prettier than my mom, Sofia. Marta has taken over the Head Librarian job from her mother, Natalie, who retired several years ago.

Their oldest is Lisa, who used to be Alessa. She is now sixteen and anxiously waiting to marry my brother, Sergio. Yes, Alessa and Cosima are still inseparable. After being sisters last lifetime, they are taking this lifetime's wonderful opportunity to marry. Lisa is blonde like her dad and has her mother's eyes, light brown. She keeps her hair only shoulder length so that it does not interfere with her fighting skills. Yes, she is still the Protector of Sergio strange as this seems.

Their oldest son, Marco, is fifteen and used to be Bianca d'Grange. Marco and I are in love this lifetime. I guess it was inevitable since she and I were so close last lifetime. Marco is not as tall as I am, but has light brown hair and blue eyes. I think he's very handsome, but naturally, I would think so. Marco has promised to be my Protector this lifetime taking Renzo's place.

Next come their twins: Evelina and Valerio at fourteen. Evelina (Renzo) is only five-eight with lovely blonde hair as long as mine is actually. She has light blue eyes and keeps telling us that this lifetime she is supposed to get it right. She means learning how to be a woman properly, since when she, as Dita, and I were married, we didn't have it right.

Valerio has short blonde hair and light blue eyes too, just like his twin. He used to be Len or Ilenakova and is still a Protector as well. Both he and Renzo each took one of the two baby bodies when they were born. We are all very thankful that they did not fight each other for the male baby. Evelina accepted the fact that she would have to be a she this lifetime. For a time, she and I entertained the idea of marrying again as we had when she was Dita and I, Bethany. However, as we grew up, she fell heavily for Giovanni, while I fell in love with Marco. Valerio is waiting for Lucianna to become of age so that they can marry as well. All of us have promised to wait one more year and then have a quadruple wedding.

The morning began with us girls having to clean the house for my party this evening. Eve grumbled, "Now I can really see why I don't like being a girl! We have to clean while the fellows are out doing more exciting things."

Lisa giggled, "Eve, relax, we are going to have fun this evening. Why don't we listen to the radio while we work?"

"Dibs on Two!" she insisted. Fifteen years back, Arsenio had invented this thing called a radio. Velona now has two stations called simply One and Two. One played classical or symphonic music, while Two played the popular dance music. Both had lengthy news hours at eight, noon, and six. The device was in our living room, primarily because it was rather big in size. Soon Lisa was gyrating to the music, while dusting.

"Say, where's Lucianna?" I asked, carrying a large sack of garbage towards the front door. My little sister had vanished once again, as she often did when we had to clean the house.

"Oh, I saw her dash off to the basement with Giovanni a bit ago," Lisa hollered above the music. "She's probably inventing something."

"Will you please turn that thing down?" mom called out as she entered the front room. Sofia would probably not have said anything had we been listening to One instead of Two. As a violinist, she loved the symphonies. Lisa quickly did as she asked. "That's better. Anyone seen Marco, Valerio, or Sergio? I need one of them to crank up the motor-wagon. I need to go to the store, that is, if you want your birthday cake tonight, Bethany."

"Mom, I think they are outside mowing the lawn," I replied. "Want me to go tell them?" I was going to have to take the bag of garbage out anyway. Besides, I also wanted to get outside, if only for a bit this fine spring morning.

I found Marco pushing the mower. His shirt was off and his powerful muscles were glazed with a light sweat. I scooted up to him and gave him a kiss. "Hi beautiful, bringing out the garbage, I see," he said, stopping for a bit. "You get the easy chores," he teased.

"Mom wants one of you fellows to start the motor-wagon for her. She needs to go to the store. Can I watch?" I asked.

"Hey Valerio," Marco yelled over to Valerio, who was doing something with the wall of ivy that seemed to thrive on our brick walls that surrounded the estate. He waved and I headed to what used to be our stables. Here we kept our motor-wagon and motor-cars; both were inventions from the DAE. Now Barcella was the leading producer of both of these. Essentially, a motor-car was a petrol powered engine mounted on an old carriage frame — at least that's what it resembled. The driver sat up front, though another could also sit beside him or her. Inside the carriage, four could sit easily, though six could fit if we were not wearing our fashionable billowing dresses.

The motor-wagon was similar in design with its petrol-powered engine mounted on a horse drawn wagon or so it seemed to my eyes. Still, both of these inventions were terrifically useful and downright practical, though Valerio and Eve deeply regretted that we no longer needed horses. Valerio turned the crank and soon the engine sputtered and came to life, shooting out its smelly exhaust. Mom came out and thanked him, hopped into the driver's seat, and headed off down our gravel path to the entrance gates, where Sergio stood holding them open for mom.

Our two families had one motor-wagon and two motor-cars parked in our stables, along with eight bi-wheels and eight putt-putts, compliments of the Three Mischief Boys Company. We kids got around Velona either by peddling the bi-wheels or more recently by using the putt-putts. They had taken the DAE's idea of a petrol-powered engine and made a very tiny one, mounting it onto a modified bi-wheel. Now we all could scoot around the city effortlessly. Two large baskets were mounted on either side of the rear with a larger one mounted up front. We girls loved the putt-putts because we could go shopping in style and ease. These days, the streets of Velona were teaming with bi-wheels and putt-putts, although there were plenty of the more expensive motor-cars and motor-wagons as well.

Just as I entered the front room, the telefono rang. This was another fabulous DAE invention, which has really caught on and is spreading rapidly throughout Velona. I lifted the heavy earpiece and spoke loudly into the voice cone. "Bartiana and Angela residence, Bethany speaking."

I heard the familiar voice of Chief Inspector Barti West Po. "Hi birthday girl. Happy birthday. Say is Sergio around? I need to talk to him at once."

"Thanks, I'll get him," I replied, raced outside, and yelled, "Sergio! Chief Inspector Barti is on the telefono for you. He says it's urgent." From the way that Sergio dropped everything and came running, I knew that he was very glad to have an excuse to get out of doing the outside chores!

"On my way!" he said into the voice cone. "Lisa, grab your blaster. Let's get going, Chief Inspector Barti needs us immediately!"

Lisa giggled, "Sorry, Bethany. Maybe this won't take too long. I'll make it up to you, okay?" She felt a bit guilty leaving the cleaning to Eve and me, but she just had to be Sergio's Protector, as always.

"We'll take our putt-putts," Sergio said, as he and Lisa, stuffing their Grey Creature's blasters into their pockets, headed out the front door.

"Now it's just us," moaned Eve. "We don't get any breaks at all."

"Oh quite griping and let's get this done in a hurry so we can go play," I chided her.

An hour later, we finished up, and the boys, detecting that we were now done, came inside to clean up. "Good timing," Marco teased me.

"I know you fellows, you just stalled until Eve and I got it all done," I countered. Eve just put her hands on her hips, as if saying this is quite enough! She stormed out of the front room and went in search of her boyfriend, Giovanni, who was in the basement with Lucianna.

"Hi, what are you two up too? You know that we had to do all your chores," Eve chided them. Lucianna looked a bit sheepish.

"We are putting the finishing touches on Bethany's present," Giovanni explained and gave Eve a passionate kiss, completely mollifying her for the time being.

"Think there are enough train lines?" Eve finally asked, staring at the huge map of the dog bone continent. The two inventors kept a very detailed map of all the new lines and spurs. The rail lines ran from Calgary down into Fortress d'Grange and on into Velona. From there, it followed the coastal road built centuries ago by the Centurions of Megalos, passing through all the other Sea Prince sectors. From easternmost Zargarb, it branched. The southern fork went down to New Barq and across to New Xin by the Dakar River, and then on along the shore of the Desert of Desolation into Shansee, Tashien! The northern fork paralleled the Elbe River, stopping at the cities of the Northern Steppes, with spurs heading off to their other cities further to the east. Then, the rail line headed westward into the Greenway, paralleling the old Centurion road there as well, with spur lines branching off to other major cities in the various kingdoms. At last, it entered Calgary from the east, completing the giant loop. Now they were considering running the lines down into the Southlands as well as up into the major cities of Tashien as well.

Arsenio's signaling system paralleled the lines, so messages could be instantly sent to any of these places, changing the nature of communications worldwide. The new telefono system was now citywide in scope, though only about one in ten homes were actually connected yet. Plans were being made to extend these lines to our other cities more inland. However, no one had figured out how to extend this system down to the southern continent and thus to Demokritos and Annelise or even to Dorota for that matter.

However, Eve also noted blue markers pinned onto the map. "Say, Giovanni, what's with these blue markers?" Many were out in the oceans.

"Oh, dear, Lucianna and I decided to keep track of the ocean going steam ships. Velona now has twenty of them; Barcella, five; d'Grange, three. Demokritos has now ten, but many more are being planned," he replied. "You see, these steamships have cut the travel time from here to Demokritos by an entire month and are now handling the mail between us. We think that tracking these ships might be important."

Eve smiled, "I'll bet in another ten years, all the old wooden caravels will be totally obsolete!"

"Yes, then one could buy a used caravel for dirt cheap," Giovanni replied.

"Say, Eve, we'd better go get lunch made. We promised Sofia that we'd fix it while she went to the store," Lucianna suddenly remembered. The two headed up to whip up something for us all.

No sooner had we all sat down to our chicken soup and sandwiches than the telefono rang again. Marco beat everyone to it. He returned and said, "Strange. That was Sergio. He wants Bethany to come down to City Hall at once. Oh, we're supposed to bring them a sandwich or two. Come on, dear. I'll go with you on our putt-putts." He was not about to let me go driving in the city without a chaperone.

We gobbled our sandwiches while Eve wrapped up several for Sergio and Lisa. Marco and I headed out to get our putt-puts out of the garage. He started mine for me and then with a blast of noise, we two sped out of our gates. Small and very fast — those are the chief characteristics of these cool vehicles. Naturally, Marco and I sped along the streets as fast as we dared, arriving at City Hall in just under five minutes.

Lisa was waiting at the door for us, a grim look on her face. "You have to hear this one yourselves," she said avoiding our direct questions about what was going on. She led us to a side room where Sergio and Barti were talking with an older man.

"Ah, thanks for coming, Bethany," Sergio said as we entered. "Luciano here saw something strange in the nighttime sky last night. He's been trying to explain to us what he saw, but it's not coming across clearly. I don't want to bias you in any way Bethany. Could you please Mind Link to Luciano and view what he actually saw late last night."

What a strange request! While I could easily Mind Link to anyone, generally, I only did it with close acquaintances or friends and family. Sergio was asking me to do this to a total stranger, who probably was half-frightened to death already. "This won't hurt a bit, Luciano. Just relax." Very, very gently, I touched his mind. *Okay, just run through your memories of last night and I will see them too.*

"Wow! Don't look at my secrets," Luciano exclaimed, not realizing he didn't have to vocalize his thoughts. Soon, I was seeing what he saw. Now I understood why Sergio had asked me to do this! Luciano had seen a high flying, cylindrical, black object hovering and then flying slowly over the city! A minute later, I broke the link.

Sergio said, "Okay, Luciano, you can go home now. Thank you very much for reporting this to us. You have done very well. Here's a gold for your trouble." He handed the man a gold coin, which brought a smile to his face. Quickly he left before Sergio could change his mind.

"Well?" Sergio asked as soon the old man left. From the strained look on my face, I suspected he already knew the answer. I Mind Linked Barti, Sergio, Lisa, and Marco to me and then replayed what the man had seen late last night. While he had been out drinking at the pub until rather late, still he saw what he saw. Now the others saw it as well.

Barti spoke first, "Well, I'll be! He was telling the truth. I admit when he first came to me with this strange tale, I thought he had just had one too many ales. He was so insistent that I asked Sergio to drop by. I can see why Luciano had such a difficult time trying to explain just what he saw last night. Bethany, there are no words for this. What was or is that thing that he saw? What should we do about it? Does it pose a serious threat to our city? What does it want?"

"Barti, that was an alien flying ship of some kind. Our worst nightmares have returned, I am very much afraid to say. You need to alert everyone in the government. Have night watches setup and have everyone report any further sightings. We need far more data about this thing to have any idea what they want. Whether or not it poses a serious threat to Velona or all Tarra for that matter, I can't say, but I bet you can count on it being bad! Just what they intend to do I've no idea, but it cannot be good for us," I replied.

"Okay. Consider that done. Sergio, I am hereby promoting you to Chief Detective Inspector as of this minute. Your first assignment is to track this thing and figure out what countermeasures we should take," Barti exclaimed, visibly worried. He presented Sergio with his official badge of office, the same badge he had had all last lifetime as Cosima. Lisa let out a stifled squeal of joy for her boyfriend. Now the two were back in the detective business, something they had spent all their last lifetime doing for Velona.

Sergio shook Barti's hand and could not conceal the proud look on his face. "Come on; let's head home. I need to begin work on this at once," he ordered. On our putt-putts, Marco and I followed their motor-car back to our estate.

Mom had returned while we were gone, and the instant we drove through our gates, she and the others came out to find out what this mysterious event was all about. Sergio would only say, "Inside please!" From his deadly serious tone, everyone knew that something critical was happening.

Sergio explained, while we all sat around the dining room table. "An old man, Luciano, saw an alien flying ship hovering over Velona late last night. We believe that it was last night though we cannot be sure since he was quite drunk. The ship moved about for a time before it took off. From the images that Bethany saw in his mind, I conclude that it headed off to the southeast. Bethany, how about showing everyone else those images?" He posed it as a question, but really, I knew it was an order. I Mind Linked us all together and replayed the images that Luciano had seen.

"Incredible!" Marco exclaimed.

"Damn! Here we go again," Valerio commented.

"Shit!" Eve added, but flushed as mom gave her a dirty look. Eve then asked, "Bethany, which ones were they? Grey Creatures? Mantis? Doll Creatures?" She already knew the answer, but was looking to me for confirmation. She and I had both seen a ship very nearly the same as this one many, many years ago out in the Red Desert of the Southlands.

My voice cracked a little, "Mantis."

"Double damn!" Eve replied, growing quite disturbed.

"Let's not jump to conclusions," Sergio admonished us. "We cannot truthfully say exactly when that drunken old man actually saw these images. While he claims it was the other day, exactly what does that mean? We should wait until we get in more observations. Barti will be sending out an alert and will keep us posted. Let's not panic yet, but please, everyone, keep your blasters on your person at all times, just for safety's sake." Sergio enjoyed taking charge. I saw this as a distinctive change from her last lifetime. I guess having a male body allowed her to assume more control over things than before. Still, she was right; we should be very alert, but not jump to conclusions.

"If the mantises return, where do you suppose they will be heading?" Valerio asked. "If they head to their usual habitats in the southern hemisphere, we might not know a darn thing about them and their activities for a very long time."

"Good point, Valerio," I said, running my fingers through my long hair as I thought rapidly. "You know, we probably ought to have one of the new steamships at our beck and call. If they land down south somewhere, we are going to have to go down there after them somehow."

"Yes, but with their flying ships, they can go anywhere in just about no time at all," Eve pointed out. "While we are steaming along on a two month voyage, they could fly anywhere weeks before we got to them."

"Point to Eve on that one," I grinned, adding, "but Eve, you and I

8

could move around and check out their old haunts. We know where they all used to be, well, the ones that we discovered, at least. If we see them setting up shop there, then we can assume that they will be staying there long enough for us to get to them and attack them." Eve liked this idea, so did Valerio. Not so with Lucianna.

"Yes, but what about me?" Lucianna asked, slightly fearful. "I don't know how to do any of the things that you all can do, you know, like telepathy and balls of fire and all that."

"That's why you have me protecting you," Valerio quickly attempted to put his love at ease. "You just keep on inventing things and leave the fighting to me. Now then, I say let's get ready for Bethany's party. After all, it's her birthday, and we shouldn't let this interfere with our fun."

Sofia finally relaxed from the shocking news. Reminded of the party, she spoke up, "That's right. Now you girls need to start getting ready. I've Bethany's cake to bake and supper to prepare. The concert is at seven, but we need to leave by six-thirty at the latest." I grinned. She was taking us all out to hear the All Velona Symphony tonight. I know that she was feeling a bit rushed, since she too had to get ready. She was playing in the orchestra as well, and I knew that she would prefer to leave by six at the latest not six-thirty.

As we broke up from the table, Lucianna asked, "Mom, can I wear an Annelise outfit too? I'm almost fourteen now." The Velona high fashion outfits were still the fancy Annelise ball style gowns that billowed out some fourteen feet around us and required us to wear very constricting corsets and the impossibly high-heeled oxfords. I knew that Lucianna really wanted to start being allowed to wear them, but I knew mom's rule. Only when you are fourteen are you allowed to wear these restrictive outfits.

"You know the rules, Lucianna. One more year. You must let your body mature more. Wear your fancy gown with the ten petticoats. After all, that's what I wear as well as Aunt Marta," mom replied. Lucianna groaned, but knew hers was a lost cause. Since I was now fourteen, I was finally allowed to wear these fancy outfits. I was ambivalent about wearing them, though. While yes, they were the height of fashion still and every woman of means wore them, I found them terribly uncomfortable to wear. Yet the fellows loved to see us in them; our look was enticing. Besides, I knew that Marco really wanted to see how I looked all dressed up.

During the long afternoon of preparations, Lisa, the oldest of us girls, took charge of helping me into my new Annelise outfit. Eve also needed lots of assistance. She was two months older than I was and had only been able to wear hers four times so far. As she got me tightened up to a twenty-inch waist, Lisa explained, "You are going to have to watch what you eat from now on, Bethany. That is, if you want to keep your waist this size. I know. I goofed and had to pay the price."

I had forgotten just how many parts this outfit had, to say nothing of how long it took me to get fully ready. My gown was a sky blue satin, which I thought matched my long black hair rather well. Lisa's gown was a darker blue, which matched her blonde locks and complexion. Eve's gown was cherry red, her favorite color as always. Already, we'd both seen that her outfit drove her boyfriend, Giovanni, wild with desires. We all helped Lucianna into her forest green satin gown, though hers only billowed out some five feet. At least she could walk easily in her Alexa boots. In our extreme Annelise oxfords, we three could only take the tiniest of steps. Fortunately, Lisa realized that this was new to me this lifetime and had Eve and me practice walking for an hour later that afternoon. I hoped that Marco would appreciate what I was enduring just for him. A bit later from the sudden bulge in his pants when he saw me, I knew that I had done just that.

The fellows wore their black silk suits with cummerbunds and fancy twin tails and highly polished black shoes. Marco looked extremely handsome I thought, as he took my hand to lead me into the dining room. Mom wore her black satin gown, the same one she wore to all of her performances. I never did figure out why the orchestra musicians always wore black.

After supper and my birthday cake were done, everyone handed me my presents. Marco got me a blue sapphire hanging on a golden necklace, which he fastened around my neck. "There, now you look perfect, my love," he declared.

Giovanni and Lucianna gave me their newest invention, an image-taker. Shaped like a small box, one pointed it at a scene, pressed a button, which allowed light to enter the tiny lens, and an image was formed on the film inside. They explained that they would then put the film into some chemicals, and presto, I would have a permanent image. The only drawback was that there was only one film in the camera at one time. They also gave me five more film holders so that I could take six images before I needed their help in reloading the holders and developing the six films. They took my image and then I took a group shot of everyone.

Eve got me a new canary yellow Annelise outfit in satin, of course. Sergio and Valerio went together to get me two dozen records of symphonies for my record player. Lisa got me a pair of sapphire earrings, which matched my necklace. I suspected Marco and Lisa had gotten together on this. Mom, dad, and my aunt and uncle got me more clothes, as expected.

At six, Tito and Sandro left to get the motor-cars ready, while the fellows began to escort us out of the house. In our extreme heels, we three most definitely needed the security of our beau's arms. Shortly, we were off to the symphony, and I felt good that we would be getting there early enough for mom to have time to warm up and be ready to play.

The Laird Symphonic Hall was both huge and extravagant. Arsenio's electrical lights brightly illuminated the magnificent hall with its plush red carpeting. We had right side box seats high above the main floor. From here, we had perhaps the best seats in the house for watching the orchestra play. Those in the more distant center box seats had the best sound, though the stage was quite distant.

Marco slid his arm around my waist and I leaned my head on his shoulders, as the lights dimmed and the large one hundred member orchestra took the stage. I closed my eyes and let the music take me away into dreamland.

Sometime later, I had an awful feeling that something was terribly wrong somewhere! I felt a huge emotional shock, as if someone had slapped me violently on my face. I jerked physically. I also felt Marco react, and I opened my eyes at once, glancing around our box and then at the hall. Eve looked ashen; all but Lucianna had a terrified look upon their faces. She only looked a bit strange, so I knew that even she had felt something.

In fact, everyone in the music hall became slightly restless; feet shuffled. Many musicians missed a beat, and the conductor worked his magic to get them recovered and continuing with the allegro movement. Somewhere, something awful had just happened, but I felt helpless to identify who or where or what.

Bethany! Help! I got a telepathic contact that was both full of terror and extreme urgency. Yet, the contact was broken almost as soon as it was made! The contact had only been for a split second, and I fought my increasing nervousness to try to sense who had made the contact. It had been so brief; yet the person was familiar to me, but who? No longer was I listening to the music. I struggled to sense who this was, and yet I couldn't quite do it, for the contact had been entirely too short and my attention had been elsewhere when it was made.

Bethany, something is wrong. Did you sense it? Marco made contact with me.

Something bad just happened! I just know it! Eve's telepathic thoughts entered my mind.

Bethany! Something terrible had happened. Did you notice it? Sergio's thoughts entered my mind.

Did you just sense something bad happening? Lisa's question came into my mind.

Hey, Bethany, I think that something just happened, really bad. Valerio sent to me.

Bethany, I just sensed something awful has happened. Did you notice it too? Giovanni's question came into my mind. I almost giggled; so many nearly simultaneous thoughts hit me.

I joined all eight of us together. *Yes, something awful just happened somewhere. Someone called out to me for help, but they were cut off almost at the very instant that they reached me. It went by so fast that I can't tell who is in dire trouble.*

We chatted a bit, but none of us had any real idea of who or what or where. At last, we sat back and waited for the concert to end. As we rose to applaud, I noticed that mom glanced up at us; now that the house lights were back on and she could see us. She seemed relieved to see us all clapping, so I suspected that she, too, had sensed something.

Once the noise died down, dad, with Sandro's continuous nodding, said, "Kids, we think that something is not right. We must get you home safely and quickly. Sergio, you take my car. I will wait and bring your mother home. Go as quickly as you can." He seemed very worried, and as we began our slow descent, we heard others talking about the weird feelings that they had during the concert.

We put our full concentration on the steps, however. In these enormous gowns and heels, anything less could lead to a nasty fall. Our boyfriends also realized this and kept a tight hold on us. Traffic was a mess and we kept silent so not as to distract Sergio, who did his best to get us out of the jam and back home safely.

As we all entered our front door, we heard the telefono ringing. Sandro dashed on ahead of us to answer it and shortly called out, "Sergio, phone. Important. Here, I'll take Lisa's arm for you." Lisa smiled; she definitely needed his arm. We all did for that matter. Our outfits demanded the secure arm of our beaus.

By the time that we slow moving girls reached the telefono, Sergio had hung up. "Well, that was Barti. He just got a wire message from Shansee, Tashien. Apparently, the easternmost cities in Tashien are reporting seeing an enormous grey mushroom-shaped cloud that is growing rapidly in height far off on their eastern horizon. It's noon there. He said to expect more reports later tonight. What does this mean? Ideas? What just happened?"

"What's east of Tashien?" asked Lucianna.

"Dorota!" I exclaimed, suddenly getting a sick feeling in my stomach. The Guardian and the others were on Dorota freeing spiritual beings. It was my job to ensure world peace so that they could be successful.

Sergio took charge. "Look, Bethany. I think that it is critical that we discover just who sent you that plea for help. I want you to close your eyes and return to that moment when they made telepathic contact with you." He began to run a therapy session on me! I did as he asked. After a couple times through that fleeting instant, I was finally able to detect who had sent the message to me. Now I was really frightened. It was the Guardian himself!

Chapter 2 Pope Pius I

When the Church of Jehosanity in Constanza City, Megalos, finally determined that their Pope Christos and their royal yacht had been lost at sea, another Cardinal Conclave was ordered. This was in December of 782. By now, the world had learned of the treachery of Pope Christos and his Confessore, thanks in large part to Renzo's small publication. As a result, Cardinal Danski of Demokritos easily won the vote and became the next pope of the Church of Jehosanity. He chose the name of Pope Pius I, which fitted in with his plans to rebuild the Church properly.

Already Demokritos was totally under the church's control and would be stable for quite some years. What a stroke of luck that Demokritos had been able to avoid the war of the Second Crusade entirely! Mostly that was because of the change in Emperor and Empress, which occurred around that time. Now Karpos Omela was the young Emperor and his lovely wife, Roxane, was the Empress. Of course, she was a Holy Woman of the Eighth Degree. Both were only in their late teens. Thus, Pope Pius I's first action was to appoint an equally youthful replacement for himself. Cardinal Heli took over control of the vast Church of Jehosanity in Demokritos. He was a protégée of Danski's and was barely twenty. He had matched the ages of the Emperor, Empress, and the Cardinal, and thus he was hoping for a long, undisturbed period of no worries from this huge country.

Rather, Pope Pius I faced serious problems elsewhere in the world, as he was anointed in a lavish ceremony on January 1, 783. The church rulers had been expelled from eight of the ten Greenway kingdoms, and many of their expensive churches burned to the ground. Their two Sea Prince sectors, Vito and Bonito, were lost as well as the city-state of New Barq. Worse, the Church of Jehosanity had to make war reparations to the victors, nearly bankrupting the Church!

He had won the vote of the Cardinals by running on a platform of change — change from the hostile ways of the two previous popes. He kept spouting that the Church had to have change or succumb. Although he never explicitly laid out just what changes he had in mind, his peers resonated with that keyword, change. He spent his first month in his new position studying all the journals and records of the many previous popes. To say that he was flabbergasted at what he found would be an understatement of magnitude. Now the reason that his Holy Church was so widely hated up north was completely understandable, and he found the basis for his Great Change.

What policy worked incredibly well and darn near perfectly in Demokritos was to propitiate to those in power. Thus, his Great Change was centered on propitiating to the leaders of the northern countries. That the overall population in Demokritos was also near propitiation, he did not recognize. For years, he wondered just why his Great Change was not working as well as he had anticipated up north. That the average tone up there was far above propitiation was the actual cause of the slow acceptance.

Still, with constant giving of gifts and words of humility and forgiveness, slowly the Church of Jehosanity began to grow in the north once more. Wherever possible, the Church of Jehosanity created schools for the children. They created safe houses where the afflicted could stay as well as those in dire need. They built many hospitals and staffed them with cloisters of nuns. Here the sick and injured could receive care. More importantly, if the person was unable to pay or to fully pay, their healing was free or discounted. This befriended many a leader, naturally.

Pope Pius I set up a worldwide slogan: In time of need, reach for the Church of Jehosanity. After forty years of these operations, the Church of Jehosanity finally was re-accepted in most northern countries. Even the West Po's, who had suffered so terribly from the Church-sponsored bombings, eventually allowed the Church of Jehosanity back into Velona.

Our new Cardinal Ruggerio Vatore received a cordial welcome when he arrived to begin the reconstruction of his many churches in Velona. Many of us hoped that after forty years, this church had truly reformed. We hoped and prayed that they were now ministering to the needs of people and not torturing, mutilating, and killing people as they had done in the past. On the night of June 1, Cardinal Ruggerio felt odd, as if something unholy was happening. It was just a fleeting feeling, however.

What of the Qaam of Juda Arad and their pledge to bring down this wicked, evil Church of Jehosanity? Initially, some of the messiahs attempted to go after nearby churches and their priests. However, they quickly discovered that because of their skin color, manner of dress, and custom of never cutting their facial hair, they could not become effective assassins. They were spotted immediately and simply could not blend into the population at large. In 783, they wised up and began to follow another path entirely.

Beginning with the towns of Juda Arad, they built Temples of Jehosanity, in which they preached the truth of the Great Messiah, as far as they knew it. Their sermons pointed out the many twisted truths and outright lies being taught by the priests of the Church of Jehosanity.

Now some forty years later, they have established their Temples of Jehosanity all throughout the eight Sea Princes and were moving into the Northern Steppes and the ten kingdoms of the Greenway, as well as West Reach. However, I am growing concerned that with both churches in the same town that strife and hostilities will break out between them — that their followers may begin to lash out at the "enemy" churches. I guess time will tell on this one.

Chapter 3 Thranikansisnestoris, Geneticist

Thranikansisnestoris, very excited about his new assignment, headed for his new ship, eager to get under way. Here on his home world, all was perfectly normal. Their warriors were still holding their own in their three hundred-year war with the greys of Arcturus and the plasticine of Mala. For hundreds of years now, there had been absolutely no change in their coveted, perfect society. Indeed, he thought they had finally achieved perfection. Not a single mantis had to be off-loaded to their penal colony on Planet X, no not for well over a hundred years. Their grand plan for the penal colony was working well.

But to say that there was no change at all would not be totally correct, he corrected his thought. Indeed, he and his fellow geneticist Hammertharmalosis were still working on the necessary genetic modifications that had been suggested by the sire of Thranikansisnestoris, when he had returned from Planet X some hundred twenty-five years ago. Thranikansisnestoris was a direct offspring of this founding geneticist and as such had inherited all that mantis' knowledge and skills, just as Hammertharmalosis had from his sire some fifty years ago.

Indeed, as with all hatchlings, they inherited all that their parent or parents were and knew — a marvel of genetic engineering on a planet-wide scale. Perhaps this was why their people were able to hold their own against their terrible enemies all these centuries. Based on the field research notes brought back, the two geneticists knew that some additional modifications must be made to the mammalian prison cells on Planet X. Studies had shown that given sufficient time, the prisoners may well find a way to escape their cells. Of course, this could not be allowed. If they returned to their home world wreaking and espousing change, their whole society could be destroyed!

Thranikansisnestoris smiled. He spoke to himself as he often did, "Oh My. Our mammalian cells are so much better than our enemies' cells. The stupid greys of Arcturus and the idiot plasticine of Mala must always keep guards in place and constantly intervene with the mammalian prison cells in order to keep the prisoners locked securely in their cells. We certainly do not want to waste valuable personnel, time, and effort on that mundane, thankless task. No indeed, we, the master race, do not. We bred these mammalian prison cells for the sole purpose of keeping our prisoners locked up without the need for constant intervention on our part. A self-running prison is the ideal scene and that's what I aim to guarantee this trip. Yes, it is up to me to make sure that our self-running prison continues to work just fine. Though I do wonder why we have not had any reports from our wardens on Planet X for over a century now. That does seem a bit strange, though perhaps it has something to do with the war. Ah, finally, I have clearance to lift off! About time."

He ignored the basic fact that as a geneticist for the mammalian cells, he had the lowest priority of any ship departing his home world. No, he was a foremost geneticist of these mammalian cells, perhaps even smarter than his rival Hammertharmalosis. Certainly, Hammertharmalosis was too old to make the journey to Planet X to carry out their further genetic enhancements. Why, if he had gone, it would have had to be his offspring who actually arrived and got to perform the work. No, Thranikansisnestoris was very proud that he had been selected over his rival to perform this vital work.

"I'll certainly be able to publish several scientific papers on these latest enhancements to the mammalian cells," he said to himself in a smug manner. That no one but his rival and offspring would actually read said papers he ignored. Slowly, he maneuvered his ship out of the densely packed inner space around home world. Again, he also chose to ignore that he was last to get clearance to activate his main drive.

A month later, Thranikansisnestoris began swearing a blue streak! "Damn them anyway, why didn't they have enough sense to keep the pilot beacon fully operational? Instead of a short trip, this is becoming a long one. Imagine, a whole month! Well, no matter, I will just have to consult my grandparent's memories and find Planet X the hard way. I'll tell them a thing or two when I get there! Why, I'll have them court marshaled or worse. I do have that authority as geneticist." A few days later, he dropped into inner-space drive and began searching for Sol 19342 and the penal colony of Planet X.

Using his ancestral memories, Thranikansisnestoris at last found the star and soon the bluish Planet X. He headed first for the set of beacons in orbit above the planet. "Oh my god! What has happened here?" From his viewport, he saw nothing but twisted metal bits. In fact, after some study, he realized that all three beacons were completely destroyed. Not even the greys and the plasticine could find their own penal colony now. He knew that these inferior races did not pass their knowledge and experiences on down to their offspring. This was a serious flaw in their races' genetic material, of that he was certain.

"Someone will pay dearly for this! Okay, time to find out what the status of the prison is." He turned on his communicator and set it to Planetary Frequency One. "This is Geneticist Thranikansisnestoris calling Warden One. Come in please." He waited for a minute. Hearing nothing, he repeated his message and waited patiently for the reply. Hearing none, he sent a timed message and said, "Geneticist Thranikansisnestoris calling Warden Two. Come in please."

Silence greeted him, although he tried all twenty wardens. "Must be solar flares interfering. I'll switch to Planetary Frequency Two and try again." An hour later, he still heard nothing but silence on his receiver, which truly annoyed him. "How can they all be out in the field monitoring directly our mammalian prison cells? Makes no sense for them to all be out. Ah well, maybe so. We know that some genetic enhancements are truly necessary to make our cells escape-proof. That's why I am here to do this vital work. That must be it; they have to work harder than expected. Well, I'll give them a day to respond back to my messages."

He headed down to his galley for some tasty greens. Quite full, he settled back for a nap, confident that his alarm gong would alert him to any incoming reply messages. He awoke the next day and realized that still none of the twenty wardens had returned his message. Now he became extremely annoyed. Particularly so because now he would have to follow protocol and contact the grey and the plasticine wardens, something that he was loathed to do. His ancestors had carefully engineered these mammalian prison cells. He never understood his leader's decision to share them with their enemies! Yet, they had done so. However, protocol had to be followed. If one could not contact their own wardens, then one was required to contact the other wardens for assistance.

That these were his enemies didn't concern him. Planet X was a neutral planet, and any conflict between the three races here on this world was totally and strictly forbidden. All three civilizations had the very same problem; perhaps the only problem they shared in common: what to do with their undesirables? When the other two learned of the genetic solution being implemented by the mantis, they willingly joined up, sharing the startup costs, and sending their undesirables here as well. Yes, for many centuries now, this had been a most workable solution for all three civilizations.

Thranikansisnestoris switched his communicator to Grey Frequency One and spoke, "Geneticist Thranikansisnestoris calling Grey Warden One. Come in please." He waited a bit and repeated it three more times, before trying the other six wardens. With no answer from any, he sighed and tried Plasticine Frequency One. "Geneticist Thranikansisnestoris calling Plasticine Warden One. Come in please." An hour later, Thranikansisnestoris' annoyance turned into fear. Something was very wrong here!

"Damn, damn, damn. What is going on? Oh My! So much for the formal welcoming protocols. I will just have to go on down and check in personally. Now let's see, which location should I visit first? Ah yes, Dorota. After all, that is our finest, most perfect model and the model on which all our new genetic modifications are based. No wait. As the geneticist, I ought to go to Chichulain first. That's our main genetic research base. Yes, that's my first stop." He began to work the ship's controls and shortly descended through the atmosphere and landed on the three pod legs.

He opened his hatch and crawled out onto the large field. "Hum, no one seems to be around. Well, I will go check on the installation." He entered the massive doors at the base of a tall mountain cliff and went inside the familiar chambers, familiar from his ancestral memories that is.

The dust accumulation was thick and his feet left deep impressions as he walked. "What's going on? Has no one been here since grandfather's day?" He went to the master controls and began dialing the twenty wardens. Certainly, from this land base he could get through to them all. Yet, nothing but a bit of static squawk resulted. Having been cooped up for almost two months, he decided to unload his precious cargo and grab a bite before dealing with the problems on the penal colony.

"Well, okay, I guess I need to go check on the various wardens. Dorota, here I come. I do hope that our perfect society is still doing well." He climbed back inside, fired the liftoff thrusters, and then shot out across the wide ocean at a high rate of speed. Acting on intuition, he decided to come in on Dorota from a high elevation, where he could us his Prisoner Analysis Machine to check on just how well the mammalian cells were holding onto their prisoners.

Thranikansisnestoris nearly fell off his perch as the data began coming in on his device! "Oh hell! We have had a massive, massive prison breakout! What is going on down there? What do I do now? Oh, yes, the protocols. Where did I put the ones pertaining to prison escapes?" He fumbled around and finally found them, carefully opening the sealed document. Just breaking the seal meant something had gone wrong and there would be hell to pay. Somehow, the geneticists had made a terrible error. "Well, it's my job and my duty to set things straight. Now let's see. What actions do I do first?"

A bit later, he began following the ancient escape protocols. His ship flashed from mantis controlled site to site. Next, he shot over the grey's sites and finally over the plasticine's sites. All returned the same data. "What has happened to all the wardens? There is not a single warden on Planet X! This is outrageous, utterly unbelievable. Yet, it is a credit to my ancestor's genetic engineering that this outbreak is so well contained."

"Okay, Dorota is wildly out of control, beyond all normal means of directly re-imprisoning. I hate to have to do this, but there is only one protocol for such a massive outbreak. Velona is next, but theirs is vastly smaller. Protocol One will suffice there. Now I've got only a few other escapees in the other various locations. Those can wait until the two primary infestations are handled. It is to our credit that our mammalian cells have worked so well on these prisoners. Golly, even without wardens, for the most part, all are nicely within their prison cells. I shall have to document these figures. This is incredible proof that our cells are working very nicely indeed. Yes, I can see that our proposed genetic modifications are most definitely needed here. I came just in time, that's for sure. Okay, Thranikansisnestoris. Time to get things ready for operations."

As he made his equipment settings, he mused, "What a crying shame to have to do this to our stellar example of a perfect society. Yet, somehow, so darn many down there have escaped their cells. They leave me no other choice. Well, no matter. We've learned a great deal from Dorota, and I will make the necessary genetic modifications to the others, so I guess it isn't a total loss."

"Let's see, the computer wants to use five. Okay, computer, do your thing. Freeze Chest armed. Beam energy at maximum. Stabilizers on full." He went dutifully down the protocol checklist. At last, he sighed over a fond ancestral memory of Dorota and pressed the Execute button. Just then, a prisoner escapee latched onto his ship, nearly yanking it out of orbit. He felt a twinge of utter panic, but the five bombs dropped on course. He shoved the controls into maximum upwards thrust and broke free of the grasp of the prisoner. Boom! His controls indicated five detonations in the proper sequence. Now his Freeze Chest activated along with the massive energy beams. Giant, high-powered beams swept over Dorota, latching onto the spiritual beings who were now totally dazed by the five atomics that had just exploded. One by one, the dazed prisoners were sucked into the Freeze Chest and properly frozen. As soon as each one reached the proper temperature, close to absolute zero, they were released and fell like ice cubes into the ocean below.

One hour later, Thranikansisnestoris rechecked his readings. "Excellent, all prisoners are accounted for now. According to the fact sheet, that should hold them for the next three months at the very least. Now I can get on with my true mission here, since I obviously need to make some genetic modifications to our mammalian cells. Well, there is nothing in Protocol One that would prevent me from using those mammalian cells for my genetic modification research."

He thought a bit and exclaimed to himself loudly, "Thranikansisnestoris, you are a genius. Yes, I can use this minor prison break here in Velona to my advantage. First, I ought to take a closer survey. I detected some very bad signs during my flyover. Yes, gain more knowledge first. That can then be incorporated into the genetic modifications. Brilliant plan."

A while later under the cover of the nighttime sky, Thranikansisnestoris hovered over Velona. His instruments began a careful analysis of the current culture and state of material existence in this large city. "Oh dear me! They have electricity, steam machines, even a crude radio, and oil based engines. Oh my, this will never do, never. The prisoners are definitely getting far too advanced for safety's sake. Oh dear me. These genetic modifications are very overdue here. I really ought to take some specimens back with me to use to refine the modifications needed here. Yes, I should. I suppose that I ought to. . ." He didn't get to finish his sentence.

Suddenly the ship's automatic defense mechanism activated, sounding the alarm and taking defensive actions on its own. A prison escapee, that is, a spiritual being, had come in contact with the ship's hull. It had perceived the hull with an energy beam, and the ship had activated its primary defense mechanism.

Thranikansisnestoris quickly switched over to manual control and finished the extraction process, adding four to the mix.

Chapter 4 Abducted

"Okay, I will try to contact the Guardian," I suggested. While the others sat around the table watching, I closed my eyes and concentrated, blocking out all thoughts. I focused on him. Nothing. Absolutely nothing, as though the spiritual being was simply no longer existing. Panic struck and I lost my focus.

"What's the matter," Eve whispered. As Renzo then Dita and now Eve, she had been around me longer than anyone else had and could almost sense my mind now.

"Nothing. I got absolutely nothing. It's like he is *not* anymore," my voice wavered.

"What do you mean *not*? I thought spiritual beings are immortal," Eve asked, becoming confused, as did the others.

"I don't know; it's just like he isn't anymore. I'll try some others," I sighed and closed my eyes again. I tried to reach Chaucer and Linda and got nothing. I tried to reach several others that I knew ought to be on Dorota. Nothing. In a panic, I tried to reach De An, who ought to have been in Tashien leading the way there. Nothing, nothing at all. Now I was becoming frantic with worry.

"I can't reach anyone that I know who is on Dorota," I explained to the others. I fought hard to keep my emotions at bay. My eyes wanted to tear up and flow. Good old Eve came to the rescue.

"Bethany, what say you and I go check out what's happening on Dorota?" Eve suggested.

"Good idea. Marco, Giovanni, you fellows watch over our bodies here. Eve and I are going off to Dorota. We'll be back in a bit," I told the others.

"You be careful. First sign of trouble, you get back here pronto," mom ordered. I flashed a fake grin. Eve and I closed our eyes and moved up and out of our house, leaving our bodies below. We both sensed our boyfriend's arms tightly around our body's waists, comforting. We shot over to Dorota, that is, we decided we would appear over Dorota and we were. Only the very instant we arrived, we decided we were back home.

"Oh my god! It's been destroyed, blown up!" I screamed. Eve looked intensely pale, almost ghastly. Still, Eve had the presence of mind to quickly Mind Link to the others, showing them our brief glimpse. We'd arrived and found ourselves in a giant, grey cloud of ash and dust. The entire surface of the giant island was destroyed, as if some giant hand had wiped it clean with a dust rag only to then shake the dust into enormous dust plumes reaching for miles into the sky.

"Are we going to get blown up?" asked Lucianna, her voice filled with a shaking fear.

"Don't know, but I am going to go have a look around here and see if I can see that flying ship," Eve declared. "If I do, I'm going to bring it down!"

Together, Eve and I moved back up out of our house and rose high above Velona, where we had a grand view of the nighttime city. Electric streetlights below us aided our vision. *If we spot it, latch on to it, and let's see if we can bring it down or disable it,* Eve sent.

Together, we began watching. After a time, we spotted a dark, oblong shape moving just below our position. We latched on to it and began to attempt to drag this alien ship down or somehow disable it. Suddenly, a brilliant white light energy blasted into us, taking us by surprise. It was intensely brilliant, so utterly overpowering, that we both flinched. Later, I described what happened as akin so someone suddenly slamming your head into a stone wall at a high velocity. All went completely black for us both. We were totally knocked out by this incredible backlash of white energy beams.

In our house, Marco was holding on to my body, while Giovanni was doing the same with Eve's body. Everyone was sitting around the dining room table, chatting in hushed voices. Suddenly, Eve, Marco, Giovanni, and I — that is to say our bodies — just suddenly vanished! Poof! Gone! Later, we heard that everyone screamed and then panicked.

"Where did they go? What just happened?" Sofia screamed; waves of shock and fear fought each other in the pit of her stomach. Lucianna merely vomited. Eight shocked, ashen faces glanced around the room, as if they might suddenly find the four missing bodies lying in a corner somewhere. Lisa's arms began shaking. Valerio whipped out his blaster and began storming about the room, demanding that the enemy show itself.

Sergio blinked and swallowed hard. He rose, saw the utter and total confusion of our families, and took charge. "Quiet, calm. Let's see what clues have been left for us. Lisa, my detective bag, please. Everyone, stay calm; return to your seats. Observe, yes, observe." Sergio's voice remained normal, though he had to force it to be so. The others now depended upon him and he would not fail them or us, he silently swore to himself. He saw Lisa trying to rush to fetch his bag, but in her extreme heels and restrictive dress, she nearly fell down. Sergio changed tactics. "Lisa, belay that order. I want you to stand guard here. Do not let anyone move from where they're currently sitting. Above all, don't contaminate this crime scene please. I need my black bag." Lisa, fighting back tears both from the sudden loss of us four and from being unable to race to fetch the magic bag for Sergio, slowly walked back to her seat. Valerio helped her sit back down.

Running at top speed, Sergio reappeared with his black bag. He took out his magnifying lens and began examining the four empty seats. Muttering to himself, he then looked at the table and then the floor around the chairs, before he stood up reflecting upon what he'd observed.

"What?" Lisa asked. This was all that she dared utter. She was petrified that if she said more, then she would break down completely.

Nothing like this had ever happened to her, the instantaneous loss of her siblings and dearest friends. To be honest, nearly everyone else was feeling much the same.

"Well, there is some good news. Rather ask what I didn't see, Lisa. I have seen nothing," Sergio replied. Lisa lost it and began crying. Like a tidal wave, Lucianna, Sofia, and Marta began sobbing as well. Only Valerio, Tito, and Sandro didn't, but wiped their eyes, stifling theirs.

"You see, if their bodies had been destroyed, then there would be something left. Dust, bits, fragments, something. We felt no heat so we can rule out disintegration. No smoke, no residue, no flames, no nothing. Their bodies have completely and totally vanished. We all know that if someone were to destroy a body, there would be something that remained, something visible, if only an enormous flash of energy, of which we saw none," Sergio continued his observations.

"But, but what, but what does it mean?" Lisa finally blurted out what her mind struggled to comprehend.

"Assumption: they are not dead; their bodies have not been killed," Sergio explained in simple terms, which he knew would bring relief to everyone. It did.

"But where are they?" Sofia managed to ask, trying to control her weeping.

"Ah, now that is a good question. Let us put our heads together. Let us review what we have actually observed and know already," Sergio continued to control the conversation down his own thought lines. "We know that at least one mantis flying machine has appeared over Velona. We know now that Dorota has been somehow destroyed, probably millions of people killed as a result. We know that the Guardian has asked Bethany for help just before he was likely destroyed."

"Yes, but how does all this help us?" asked Valerio, greatly desiring to have something to attack. "Where does this get us?"

"What did we see here?" Sergio refused to be pulled off his train of thought. "We know that Bethany and Eve have just observed the dust clouds over Dorota. We know that they were floating above Velona and looking for that mantis flying craft. We can safely assume that Eve would desire to attack it. I believe that it is a safe assumption to conclude that a bit ago, the mantis ship did appear over Velona and that Bethany and Eve probably tried to attack it. Further, we can safely assume that they were not successful in their attack and have been very likely captured."

"Why not killed?" Lisa blurted out.

"Because we are immortal spiritual beings, Lisa. We cannot die as our bodies die. You know that the best we can do is to go "unconscious" and stop trying to be aware. That's the closest we can come to death. Postulate: I believe that is what happened to the Guardian, Chaucer, and Linda. When Bethany tried to contact them by telepathy, she said that she got back absolutely nothing — her word, nothing. That would fit with the three of them currently being unconscious."

"Has anyone tried to contact Bethany, Eve, Marco, or Giovanni?" Sergio asked.

"We're a bunch of idiots!" Valerio declared gruffly and he sat down, feeling terribly stupid just now. Such a simple action ought to have been tried the instant we had disappeared! He calmed his mind, focused on me, and reached out to make telepathic contact.

"Nothing! Nothing at all. Nothing from any of the four," Valerio spoke gruffly as he opened his eyes. "This must mean that they too are unconscious?" Though he phrased it as a statement, his voice turned it into more of a question for Sergio.

Lisa backed him up, "I didn't get anything either."

"Excellent, Valerio, Lisa. So we know that the four must right now be unconscious. We also know from our own experiences in giving many others therapy sessions that eventually the unconscious spiritual being will 'wake up' again. Thus, we should establish a routine action of trying to contact them say every hour from now on until they do wake back up." He had just given them something that they could do, but he also remembered that it had been weeks before Bianca had been able to make contact with Bethany and Dita when they had been abducted and kept in an opium daze for nearly a month down in Tashien years ago.

"Okay, now we also know that the four physical bodies are gone. Unfortunately, one was our resident alien engineer, who could better analyze this disappearance than I can. Here goes anyway. With their bodies gone and not disintegrated, we must assume that their bodies were taken for a reason. Look gang, if the mantis merely wanted Eve and Bethany clobbered, that would be one thing. However, in that case, we would have two dead bodies sitting in those empty chairs and Marco and Giovanni would be with us helping to solve this puzzle."

"But they aren't!" protested Lisa.

"Right dear," Sergio replied. "So what does that tell you? The fact that the bodies of Bethany and Eve are missing?"

"Oh, I see. Well, the mantis must have wanted to take their bodies along with them, the beings. They must want to put Bethany and Eve back into their bodies again, or something," Lisa began thinking properly finally.

"But we must then ask ourselves, why were Marco and Giovanni also taken? Those two fellows were here with us, near their bodies. As I recall, wasn't Marco just above and behind his head when this happened?" Sergio asked. Lisa and Valerio backed him up on his observation, though Lucianna and our four parents had no awareness of such matters. These five were not aware of spiritual beings as such. In no way is this a put down of our parents and Lucianna, rather they are what passes for normal on Tarra. Only a few of us who have had many therapy sessions and have had their awareness

24

levels raised now have such perceptions.

"Precisely so. Yet, those two are also missing. Yet, what else did we actually see?" Sergio continued his line of deduction.

"Well, Marco had his arm around our Bethany," Tito suggested.

"Yes, and Giovanni had his around Eve," Marta added.

"Yes, the key thing here is that both boys were in physical contact with the girl's bodies when the girl's bodies were abducted. Conclusion: either they were accidentally abducted because they were in direct physical contact or they were abducted because they were the boyfriends of the girls," Sergio suggested.

"Wait a minute, Sergio," Lisa interrupted him. "I see where you are going with this. The boys were abducted too. So the boys are with the girls. Well, that is a very good thing then because now Bethany and Eve won't be alone with the mantis. They have some help."

"Wait a second," Valerio interrupted the two. "Are you saying that the four have been abducted and not killed?"

"Yes, that is the only conclusion that I can reasonably draw from our observations," Sergio answered.

"How come not killed?" asked Tito.

"There are no traces of the four's bodies here in this room. We all know that if you destroy someone, some traces will be left. In the case of Dorota, there is this enormous grey dust cloud reaching for miles into the sky. In our case here, there is absolutely no trace of the four bodies left in this room. Their bodies have not been slain. The only reasonable explanation is that all four bodies have been snatched from here. How? Well, alien technology must be the answer, which is way beyond me. Lucianna?"

Stifling her sniffles, she replied, "Well, perhaps they used some kind of teleporting mechanism. Bethany, herself, just goes where she desires, so the next logical step is to invent a machine that does something similar with bodies. I don't recall reading anything about that in the various documents that Bethany translated, but then there were none that pertained to these flying ships either, for that matter. Right now, I wish there were, though." At last, Lucianna had something she could focus her mind upon, something engineering oriented.

"Okay, Lucianna. I think that you are right," Sergio continued. "Now we are left with several more questions. Where have the four been taken and why were they taken?"

"What are they going to do to them? Add that one to your list," Lisa added, finally feeling more like Sergio's assistant. She realized that she had been a complete basket case just minutes before, and she felt guilty about letting him down. She steeled herself and vowed never to do that again. Sergio needed her strength.

"Gang, let's think about all this. Bethany translated many of the mantis documents. Their abduction must be somehow related. Perhaps there is a clue in those documents," Sergio suggested.

Lucianna pushed her hands through her hair. "Well, I admit that I was paying far more attention to the device manuals and the wire coils. Let me think. There were these documents that told of the mantis creatures actually creating our mammalian bodies, something about calling them mammalian prison cells."

"Yes, I remember that, Lucianna," Lisa added. "Wasn't there some discussion about them needing to make some genetic modifications to the mammalian bodies in there?"

"Yes, Lisa!" Valerio spoke up, suddenly remembering. "Bethany was so worried about that aspect — that's why she spent all that money funding the Research Foundation. Do you suppose that the mantis have returned here in order to perform their planned genetic modifications, whatever that means?" She had no idea of what the words meant, just that it could not be good for us.

"Gang, I think we are on to something here. I'll bet anything that the mantises have returned to carry out their plans for genetic modifications on us, whatever that may mean," Sergio concluded. "So we have a good guess about why the mantises are back. I think that it is safe to conclude that our four have been abducted and the likely reason is for test subjects. You see, the mantis regards any of us who can move outside of their body's heads as escaping from their prison cell. They believe that our bodies are prison cells, you see. So Eve and Bethany may have appeared to the mantis as being prison escapees and thus had to be recaptured."

"Brilliant! That must be why they wiped out all of Dorota," Valerio concluded. "The Guardian was freeing beings there by the train loads! I bet the mantis freaked out when they saw the sheer number of freed spiritual beings on Dorota! Oh, so they couldn't deal with so many at once and had to blast them into dust. I wonder if the Guardian and the others are still alive?"

"Their bodies certainly aren't, but somewhere I suspect those millions of spiritual beings are lying about knocked unconscious by the explosion," Sergio concluded. "So I believe that it is safe to say that our four have been abducted and are to be used in some kind of genetic modification experiments. Somewhere, they are alive and as well as can be expected, under the circumstances."

"We have to rescue them!" Valerio declared. Tito and Sandro added to this idea with gusto.

"Precisely. Now the next question is just where have they been taken?" Sergio stated.

"They could be anywhere," Lucianna exclaimed.

"True. They could be up inside their flying ship," Sergio pointed out.

"Maybe they were taken to one of their old mantis bases," Valerio suggested.

"But do we know where all of their bases were?" asked Lisa.

"If they are up in the flying ships, how can we get to them?" asked Tito.

"We can't," Sergio replied. "Not unless someone can invent a way for us to fly." Lucianna opened her eyes wide. What a novel idea, she though, flight. Why had she not thought of that before? She resolved to work on this as her next project, well once the four had been safely rescued.

Sergio continued, "There is no way that we can know if we have really located all the old mantis bases of operation. A few have been destroyed, like the one in the lower middle of the Southlands, where the volcano erupted. I suppose that we are going to have to send out expeditions to check on all the known bases somehow. That will take a whole lot of time."

"Time which we don't have," Tito interrupted angrily.

"Right. Besides, we might not know all of their bases. We ought to concentrate all of our efforts right now on finding clues to where they have been taken. That should be our primary focus now. Until we know that detail, there is little that we can do, save to periodically attempt to establish communication with them," Sergio stated dryly.

Tito sank back into his chair, this sounded utterly hopeless to him. Sergio continued. "Now then, let's see what clues we can discover. If the flying ship was here above Velona tonight, then surely some people must have spotted it. We need to interview all of those people and pay particular attention to the precise location of the ship and any direction of movement that the ship may have had. If we can at least determine its direction of travel, then that may lend us some clues to its destination. Gang, we have work to do."

"Well, I am going to change my clothes; I can't work in this outfit!" Lisa declared and headed off to her room to change. One by one, the others followed her lead, all except Lucianna.

She sat there thinking about flying machines. "Aren't you going to change?" Sergio asked her. They were the only two left in the dining room now.

"You know, I've been thinking about this flying machine of theirs. It must have some kind of engine, you know, something to propel it through the air," she said thoughtfully.

"Yes, well go get changed and you can think about that later," he suggested.

"Sometimes I wish I could do what Bethany and Eve can do," Lucianna lamented.

Becoming a little exasperated with the young teen, Sergio asked, "Do what?"

"Oh you know, leave their bodies and go up into the air and look around, you know, like they were doing tonight before they got abducted," she explained.

"Why?" asked Sergio, unable to fathom the reasoning of Lucianna. They were in the middle of a horrible crisis of unimaginable importance and she was lamenting her lack of spiritual abilities.

"So I can look for exhaust trails in the sky. You see, Sergio, all our various motors burn some kind of fuel, whether coal, wood, or the new petrol stuff. All have exhaust byproducts of their combustion; all leave telltale signs of their passing. The trains leave these enormous smoke trails down the tracks, unless the wind blows them. Even our noisy putt-putts leave a smelly exhaust trail behind them. You've seen how those on foot curl up their noses when we pass them by on our putt-putts. I want to be able to look for the mantis ship's exhaust trail, if there is one. I bet there is one, you know," Lucianna declared.

Sergio opened his eyes wide; his opinion of Lucianna changed in an instant. She'd gone from a sobbing little teen to a mature, thoughtful, insightful engineer in a blink. "That's brilliant, Lucianna! I could kiss you!"

Lucianna flushed, "You'd better not. Valerio might kick your butt if you did." She grinned.

"Come on; let's get changed. Maybe we can go look for your exhaust trail, Lucianna!" He led her off towards her room.

Lisa groaned; she couldn't get out of her outfit without some assistance. Normally, Bethany or Eve would help her, but now alone in her room, she struggled, unable to bend enough to even get to her shoes. Marta soon slipped into her daughter's room. "Need a hand?" she asked, knowing that Lisa would.

"You are a lifesaver, mom. Please," Lisa grinned, grateful for her mom's help tonight. "We'll, find Eve, mom. Honest, we will somehow."

"I hope so dear. I feel so awful that we couldn't protect you kids. You were depending upon us and we let you down," Marta admitted her innermost thoughts to her eldest.

"No you didn't mom. None of us could have prevented what happened to them. These mantis creatures are vastly more powerful than we are. Only this time, we got the blasters so maybe that will make a difference somehow."

When Lisa returned to the living room now wearing her casual clothes, she found that everyone had gone outside. Curious, she headed out to join them. The boys were scanning the nighttime sky using their spyglasses, while Lucianna was carefully writing something down. "What's going on? Have you seen the flying ship?" she asked, fearing that somehow she'd been left out.

Sergio answered her, "Lucianna had a brilliant idea. Look for exhaust trails left by the flying ship! She's right. Here, see for yourself," he handed the device to his girlfriend and pointed out where to look. The others continued calling out details which Lucianna plotted on her map of the night sky.

"How long do we keep doing this?" asked Valerio.

Lucianna looked at her watch, a marvelous invention she'd made last lifetime, and replied, "Let's see, they were abducted around ten and it's eleven now. The trail has been drifting for an hour. I need to be able to estimate where it was at around ten, so keep going for another half hour if you can, please."

At midnight, Lucianna sat at the dining room table, charts, maps, and even a globe of Tarra at hand. Marta had made a pot of tea and everyone chatted as Lucianna worked on her calculations. They had spotted a drifting exhaust trail high in the nighttime sky, and she was trying to estimate its path at ten o'clock when it had left, presumably bearing we four with it. At last, ignoring all requests to hurry up, Lucianna taped a bit of string precisely onto the globe, stringing it entirely around the sphere.

"Okay, assuming that the flying ship went straight to its base without any course changes, which is a big assumption by the way, the base lies somewhere along this line," Lucianna sat back, satisfied with her work. Now the rest was up to the others.

All eight gathered around the globe staring at the string line. From Velona, the line of flight led nearly due southwest. It led out over the ocean, passing fairly close to the old Isle of Right, a known mantis base. From there it hit obliquely along the uninhabited coastline of the western continent, cutting diagonally across it and on out into the ocean. In the other direction, it passed through the Appian Way and into the Greenway before slicing across the Northern Steppes. After passing through a bit of the northern part of the Desert of Desolation, it again reached the ocean.

"Possibly the Isle of Right, but if not, somewhere in the uninhabited, unknown western continent," Sergio pronounced.

Lucianna added, "It's not likely to be in the Greenway, because why would you fly completely around the world? It probably is the Isle or the western continent, gang."

"They prefer higher elevations," Valerio added. "We are looking for tall peaks or such. What little do we know about that western continent?"

Marta put in, "Well, we have some field notes from various explorers in the library. In the morning, I can check on them."

While Lucianna sketched out a crude map with the diagonal line on it for Marta, Valerio added, "Okay mom, we are looking for mountains or volcanoes or peaks of some kind along this line. See what the records show. They might give us more clues. Meantime, we need to get our hands on a steamship so we can get there as fast as possible, though that is going to be terribly slow, I fear."

Sergio pulled on his moustache. "You know, once we set sail, there will be no way that we can easily stay in touch with what all is going on. We'll be at sea for several months and a whole lot can happen in that time. I am leery about us all charging off into the southern seas. There are too many what if's to be considered."

Mom yawned, "Well, kids, we've done all we can for one night. Let's get to bed. We have a big day ahead of us all tomorrow." While the teens wanted to pursue the matter further, they too had tired bodies and followed her request.

Chapter 5 Revelations

I awoke with a splitting headache. My waist ached from having worn this Annelise outfit for far too long. I opened my eyes and tried to focus. I was lying on a soft bed. Ah, I was in my body and still wore my fancy Annelise outfit from the concert night. Using my arms, I propped myself up and looked around. On the bed beside me lay Marco, wearing his fancy suit as well. How did he get here, wherever here was? I noticed that he had a strange metal band around his head with a strap going over the top of his head. Weird. I felt my own head. Damn, I too had a band around my head. I tried to remove it only to have it send a shooting pain through my aching head! Quickly, I stopped that action and the pain subsided immediately, leaving my headache intact.

I was in what appeared to be a bedroom, but there were no windows. The walls were beige as was the floor and ceiling. Electric lights provided the illumination. I realized the beige was stone. "Marco, Marco, wake up." I whispered and began shaking him lightly. He moaned a little and then his eyes opened wide; a shocked look faced me.

"What happened? Where are we? Are you all right? Oh, my head! What is that band on your head?" he whispered. "Where are we?"

"Don't try to remove the head thing. I did and got some kind of nasty shock when I tried. I am all right. How about you? You okay?" I replied bravely, but wishing I had answers to the same questions.

"My head aches. Damn!" he just tried to remove his head thing. I managed a smile, I'd warned him, but he had to try anyway.

"I think the mantises have us. The last thing I remember is seeing their ship, and Eve and I began to try to damage it. Then, we got hit with this incredibly bright, super intense white light. Then, everything blacked out. I just woke up here. How about you?" I asked.

"Dunno. I was holding on to you and then it was as if I was flying and bashed unconscious somehow at the same time. Can you get up?" he asked.

"Give me a hand. It's awkward in this overly tight corset and dress, dear." Marco got up. Holding his head with one hand, he pulled me up and supported me as I got to my feet. We both wobbled slightly as we tried to get ourselves oriented. Our headaches were interfering with our senses. At last, our heads cleared.

"Hold on to me, please. Let's see where that door leads. I wonder what happened to Eve?" I suggested. With Marco's steadying arm, we began moving to the door. My heels clicked noisily on the stone floor and I whispered a little curse. Right now, I wanted quiet. The door led to a small hallway; my billowing dress brushed against the stone sides. Electric lights hung from the ceiling. After some ten feet, a pair of doors opened on either side, while the hall continued a long way further. We peered into the room on the left. It was another bedroom and was empty.

We peered into the room on our right and saw Eve and Giovanni sleeping on the bed. Both were in the same clothes that they were wearing to the concert; both had the same metal bands around their heads. "We'd better wake them up," I whispered, though I don't know why I was trying to be so silent.

I moved to Eve's side, while Marco let go of me and went around to Giovanni's side. Together, we whispered and gently shook them. Eve soon moaned a little and opened her eyes. A bit later, Giovanni did likewise.

"Where? What? Bethany? My head. Did we get the ship?" Eve asked. I grabbed her hand and bent my knees for support as I helped her rise. Eve had as much trouble rising as I did, and I could tell that her waist was complaining as badly as mine. We shouldn't have worn these outfits for so long a time. Well, from our previous lives, we knew that this pressure and aching would eventually pass. She was a bit wobbly at first and I held on to her. Giovanni held on to Marco and the two came around to our side, our beaus taking our hands.

"We are in some kind of stone building," I pointed out. Walls, ceiling, floor. All beige stone. At least there are electric lights," I pointed out. "Come on; let's see what else is here."

With Marco holding me and Giovanni holding Eve, we headed out of their bedroom and back into the hallway. Some thirty feet further on down, we again came to two side rooms. One was a spacious kitchen, done in the traditional Dorota style, with everything low to the ground. Both Eve and I grimaced; this was not a good omen at all. The room on the right was a spacious dining room and living room, complete with a large couch. We continued down the long hall another fifty feet where we were completely surprised.

Entering a large room some hundred feet square, we saw a huge garden. A pair of fruit trees offered nearly ripe red apples. Many vegetables were ready to be picked, including beans and peas. A water fountain bubbled in one corner, offering fresh cold water. In another corner was a tall machine with writing that we could read. It was in our Velona dialect. Marco read off, "Beef, chicken, turkey, fish. Push selection. Open drawer and remove. Must be cooked."

"Well, perhaps we will not starve to death," Giovanni whispered. We continued walking around the edge of this huge garden. A large number of gardening tools were stored here. Evidently, we would be tending the garden. We all got the feeling that we were caged prisoners at this point. We continued moving around the garden.

In the middle of the far wall was another door. We entered and saw a number of chairs facing a giant glass window. It was at least fifty feet wide and twenty tall — enormous in size. As we entered, a beeping sound went off and shortly lights came on in the space beyond the window. As we stared out into that huge room with a number of machines and a myriad of buttons and dials, we saw what we most dreaded, a mantis. It walked slowly into the room opposite the window, obviously beyond our reach.

"Oh my. Awake at last, I see. Very good, very good. We should get acquainted. I will be using you and your input for quite some time, you see. What am I to call you?" the mantis said.

"Bethany, call me Bethany. Marco, Eve, and Giovanni. Who are you? Why have you abducted us? Where are we? What are you going to do with us? We want to go back home." I had a thousand more questions, but stopped to see if it would give us any reasonable answers.

To our surprise, the devices on our heads translated its strange speech. "I am called Geneticist Thranikansisnestoris. You probably cannot pronounce my name, so how about just Nestor? I am a mammalian genetic engineer. My ancestors created your mammalian prison cells — what you call your bodies. I have removed you four from your homes because at least Bethany and Eve were escapees, that is, out of their mammalian cells. Such is not allowed, though it is to be expected. Over a hundred years ago, we reviewed the suggestions of the various wardens here and agreed that some genetic modifications were actually needed. I am here to make those genetic modifications. Yet, I will be using your feedback to help fine tune the modifications. As a genetic scientist, my charge is to get the proper modifications made to your mammalian prison cells."

"You see, I can modify them in ways which may have unforeseen complications that could potentially be devastating to the long term survival of this mammalian species. That is unacceptable to both of us. I'm sure that you will agree with me on that point. So I will be using your feedback to help fine tune these genetic modifications. I want very much to get this absolutely right."

"Oh yes. Please do not attempt to remove those helmets. They serve two vital purposes. They guarantee that you will be staying within your mammalian body's heads. No more escapes will be allowed for now. Second, they act as a translator so that we can communicate with each other freely. I am not inhumane. You have probably seen that there are beds, a kitchen, and even couches that you are familiar with using. There are fruits and vegetables growing in the garden, and there is a protein vending machine to help provide a diet that you are used to having. You will be responsible for tending the garden's needs and preparing your own meals."

"As to where you are, I will be telling you that in a little while, once I have things properly prepared. So many protocols must be followed. If you were genetic scientists, you would understand just how important it is to do every step precisely correct. Otherwise, the outcome is under dispute. I hope you will accept my pledge to be more open about where you are at in a short while."

"Is this acceptable, Bethany?" he asked politely, at least the translated voice sounded polite. His body must be at least fifty feet long. He had enormous rear legs and very dexterous upper appendages. Yet his head was so very weird to us, complete with vicious looking mandibles, which could easily cut our bodies in half.

"Acceptable, I guess," I replied. "Are your intended genetic modifications designed to keep us in our heads?"

"Oh yes, bright prisoner you are, Bethany. Yes, this is a penal colony, after all," he replied.

"We know that already. Grey Creatures, Doll Creatures, and you mantis creatures have all been dumping your unwanted spiritual beings here on Tarra for a very long time. We've already taken out all the so called prison wardens from all three of you," I tested the waters to see just how forthcoming Nestor would actually be.

"Ah, so that is what happened. Oh my, I came just in time then. Yes, our researchers over a hundred years ago did suggest that in time you prisoners would find ways to escape your mammalian cells. It appears that you did so sooner than my ancestors anticipated. Fascinating, oh yes, I find that fascinating. Scary too, you know. The Grey Creature's territory where you are living is way too industrialized for safety's sake."

"But then, we mantis knew that the idiot Grey's methods were just awful," he added.

"Certainly. Constant meddling in our affairs, fomenting wars and hostilities — we can't stand for that and we got rid of them," I tested the waters further.

"Oh my, yes, Bethany. We mantis always knew that the Grey's methods would never be accepted. Besides requiring far too much constant intervention on the part of the wardens, such methods are antagonistic to the survival of the mammalian cells. To be honest with you, I never did understand why our leaders ever chose to share our highly developed mammalian cells with our two archenemies, the Greys and the Dolls. Yet, they did. We geneticists knew that the Grey's methods would ultimately fail. I am not surprised that you were able to defeat them, Bethany. Your mammalian forms are a credit to our engineering. Well done, but that's my personal point of view."

Since he was not the slightest bit offended, I added, "Well, we got rid of the Doll's electronic bombardment of our bodies over in Tashien."

"Oh my! You did! Amazing. The resilience of these mammalian cells is sometimes very amazing to us engineers. My compliments, Bethany. Yes, we genetic engineers knew that the stupid plasticine Dolls were totally misusing our mammalian cells. However, we were unable to convince our leaders otherwise. My ancestor actually cried when he learned just how horrible the Dolls were mistreating his magnificent creations. Yet, it is again a great validation to the great resiliency that has been engineered into your mammalian cells to be able to survive this horrid mistreatment. I hope things are going better in their territories now."

"Yes, things are getting better," I admitted. "I don't see why you are so intent upon harming us. We have not harmed you or your race. We don't even know where your world is at nor do we even desire to go there."

"Oh my. You misunderstand me. I have no intention to harm your mammalian forms, only make them better suited to their purpose of keeping yourselves in them. You see, everyone here is an undesirable, on either our world or that of the Greys or of the Dolls. While our three societies are still fighting the war — actually, we've been fighting for over three of your centuries now — we all are facing the same problems on our home worlds. You see, criminals wreak havoc and in war times simply cannot be tolerated. Artists and great thinkers upset the status quo, which is also suicidal in war times."

"So why not just get rid of them? You know, go dump them somewhere else?" I proposed, though I knew what the answer would be.

"Oh my, Bethany, you are highly intelligent and perceptive. Yes, I have made an excellent choice in bringing you here for the research. Well, we tried that at first, dumping the undesirables off in remote sections of space. Ultimately, that failed as they soon made their way back and continued to wreak havoc on our worlds. That's when we came up with this penal colony idea. My ancestors had been hard at work genetically engineering bodies here on Tarra. The mammalian forms showed great promise and were adopted for our use."

"Unlike the Greys and the Dolls, we wish to be humane in this prison. All that we ask is that the prisoners remain in their heads. We do not wish to intervene at all. In fact, I'll let you in on a little secret. You see, if I can get these genetic modifications right, then you all will be perfectly content and very happy to remain in your heads. You can live life as you desire, free from any intervention from any of us, not even the Greys or the Dolls. If all goes as I have planned, we will not even need to station a warden anywhere on Tarra. You will have free will to do as you please, except escape your mammalian cells that is."

"Now doesn't that sound ideal to you? Complete freedom to do as you please with your lives," he ended with what I took to be a smile, if this creature could smile.

"Humane, yes. In many ways, it is ideal, except for one small detail, Nestor," I pointed out.

"What's that?"

"It denies us to be what we really are, spiritual beings, and not mammalian bodies. Some of us prefer to be spiritual beings and not bodies."

"Ah well, prisoners cannot have everything they desire. It is a small price to pay," he justified.

"True, a life of free choice and with no aliens here on Tarra would be far nicer than it has been in the past," I added hastily. I didn't want to antagonize him further. He was being quite communicative with us.

"Oh my, of course it is. Now that the signal beacons have somehow been destroyed, I don't believe that the Grey's or the Doll's will be back here. This place is so hard to find without the signal beacon. I was able to find it by summoning up my ancestral memories and using them to guide me. Still it took well over a month to find Tarra. I doubt very much if the Greys or the Dolls will be able to do so on their own," he explained.

I had an idea and asked, "So do all of your people have ancestral memories of how to find Tarra? Or is it just your lineage?"

"Oh my, such a sharp mind. Why yes, I am very proud to say that it was my ancestors who founded Tarra. No, only my ancestors and my offspring have those memories along with one other geneticist. It is a high honor for us. My line has always been genetic engineers, you see. Of course, the protocols state that I am to rebuild the signal beacons and then notify the Greys and the Dolls that they need to rebuild theirs and even lead them here to Tarra. I have half a mind not to follow that protocol. I always hated the misuse of our marvelous mammalian cells by our enemies. Say, if you cooperate with me, I give you my word that I will forget to rebuild their beacons. What do you say?"

I grinned, "Okay, as long as we are not harmed by your experiments." His huge head nodded. "Say, in the past, mantis creatures used to eat the arms off of women. Why was that?" Eve grinned, thinking this was the best question yet!

The communications device made a strange noise, which I finally deciphered to be Nestor's laugh. "We eat plants and find mammalian flesh most undesirable. Yet, our ancestor's research many centuries ago indicated that further genetic modifications ought to be made to the final forms of your bodies. A number of ideas were tested and having the females of the species have no arms proved the most workable of methods. We conducted a number of smaller, independent tests, before we launched a larger scale model on Dorota. Indeed, the stellar achievements of my ancestors on Dorota have proved that this was a perfect modification. Back on home world for seventy years now, I have been perfecting the necessary genetic modifications to add to that model of Dorota. These changes are based upon those ancient findings from the Dorota experiment."

"Of course, I do not know what happened in Dorota over the last century plus, so I cannot speak of its more recent status," he admitted.

"Well, the Grey Creatures ambushed and killed all the wardens there, something like two hundred years or so ago," I explained.

"Oh my. Well, they are our enemies. Never trust your enemy, I always say. Why our leaders ever thought that Tarra would remain neutral territory is beyond me. Still, when my ancestors ran Dorota, it was indeed a perfect society. No crime, all children were educated, no one went hungry, and everyone had a home. Families were kind and loving — an ideal mammalian society if I do say so myself. Speaking of food, I am hungry and I suppose that you are too. Let's take a break for a while. You will need to prepare your own food."

"When you wish to talk to me again, please come to this room. It will automatically sound an alert for me. Be patient. I may be in the middle of a preparation, but I promise to come as soon as I can. Oh yes, once you are outside this observation room, I have no way to monitor your actions or your talk. The range of those head devices is limited. Thus, you can have complete freedom of life and action when you are beyond this confrontation room."

I didn't know whether he was telling us the truth on that or not. In spite of our tightly constricted waists, Eve and I were hungry and I knew the boys were probably starving. Their strong arms around us, we headed slowly back to the kitchen to see what we had there to eat. We four worked together to see what was what here in the kitchen.

We had a stove and an oven. Numerous pots and pans, along with plates, cups, and silverware lined one set of shelves. Obviously, someone who had no knowledge of their direct usage had placed them there. "Whoa! Will you look at this invention?" Eve exclaimed. She had opened a door only to find cold air coming out. Inside were pitchers of milk, juices, butter, eggs, and some cheeses.

"Wow. I wonder how this works?" Giovanni said, while we began to rustle up something to eat.

"We ought to bake some bread soon. We have to cook everything from scratch," I explained. While Eve and the fellows worked on making lunch, I began to whip up three loaves of bread. I chose three because I found three bread pans.

As we sat down to eat here in the spacious kitchen, Eve commented, "Well, I wish we could find some other clothes. This corset is killing me as well as these heels."

"Yes, but my love, you do look absolutely stunning for me," Giovanni teased her and gave her a brief, but passionate kiss.

After we finished, Marco decided that we needed to explore fully our new prison quarters. "Since you two go slowly, you check out everything in this kitchen and let us check out the rest of the place." This was fine with Eve and me; in these outfits, the less walking we had to do the better. If only we had worn better clothing when we were abducted, I mused.

A while later Marco called out, "We found the bathroom. It's the empty room that we thought was a bedroom. It's got hot and cold running water and a big tub." Eve looked at me and extended her arm. Together, supporting each other, we headed to check out the bathroom ourselves. We both had to use it soon.

Together, we struggled to get the job done. These corsets and giant hoops were becoming terribly annoying. "Why don't we take them off," Eve suggested. Damn societal decency anyway. We helped each other out of the overskirts and then at last got the hoops untied and removed. A bit later, we finally loosened the corsets! What a relief.

Marco stuck his head in and asked, "You need anything? Oh! Excuse me."

"No come on in, Marco. Eve and I simply are not going to torture ourselves with these outfits any longer. You are going to have to see us in our slips and nickers," I replied.

"What about your heels?" he asked.

"We tried to go barefoot, but that's out!" Eve exclaimed. "The floor is very cold. That's what we are trying to figure out now. We are going to have to wear the shoes, but we want to get rid of the corsets, but those are holding up our hose."

"Can you leave the corsets on but make them very, very loose?" Marco asked.

A bit later, we both were comfortable. We put the tops back on to keep our arms warmer, but because the corsets were so loose, we couldn't button them much below our busts. Our white long slips were now our "dresses." "Oh, I do like the feel of you now," Marco teased me, running his hands over my sides and legs. I gave him a passionate kiss.

"Now then, fellows, what have you found? Any way out of here?" Eve asked.

"Nope, we found no door to the outside world. Strange. We both cannot figure out how Nestor got us in here in the first place. But we did find you this," Marco said holding up a hairbrush. I gave him a hug for that one. With our long hair, a brush was critical.

"We can do laundry in some wash basins in the bathroom," Giovanna explained. "We have nearly everything we need to live in here. Yet, I feel like a trapped rat." We all did for that matter.

Marco whispered in my ear at the same time that Giovanna did the same with Eve. "We still have our blaster weapons in our pockets. How about yours?"

Ours were stuffed inside the inner pockets of our billowing dresses. When we undressed, we hid them carefully and told the boys about them. "I also have my new image taker with me and two of those films. I am going to try to take a picture of this mantis Nestor fellow if I can. Let's keep the blasters as our last resort. If we use them now, we might not succeed and he would be sure to knock us out and take them away from us. He obviously didn't search us when he put us in here. Either a blaster would be of no use in freeing us or he simply goofed up. I say let's hold off on using them until we learn more about what is going on here." This the others accepted. As long as we had the blasters, we had a tiny measure of security.

I went to check on the bread and made us a pot of tea. After we all had our fill, Eve and I went exploring, while the boys did so as well. We each hoped to find something that the other had missed.

Bethany. Are you there? Can you receive me? It was Lisa!

Yes, I can receive you. We are being held prisoner by a mantis creature in some underground chamber. All four of us are okay and unharmed. Only we have these metal devices on our heads, which are preventing us from leaving our heads or initiating telepathy. I can pick you up fine.

What a relief! Okay. Sergio wants to come rescue you, we have a rough estimate of where you might be at, but it will take us months to get to you. Thank Lucianna for that one. She explained what she had done, plotting the exhaust trail.

I made a decision. *Hold off on starting to sail across the ocean a bit. Let us see what all we can find out here first. We need to know how many mantises are here and what they are planning. How about making contact with us every day about this time? Say how long have we been gone?*

Two days now. Okay. I'll let the others know. Everyone will be so relieved to hear that you are so far unharmed. Hang in there Bethany. Bye.

"Gang, Lisa just made telepathic contact with me. I can send if she has made the connection. I just can't initiate it, as you also know. She is going to contact us every day about this time. We've been gone two days, and thanks to Lucianna, they have a notion of where we might be at, somewhere on the western continent they think."

"Crap. It'll take them months to get here," Eve complained.

"I know. Besides they will be out of communication with the rest of the world while they sail here. I told them not to set sail just yet. I have a feeling that they may be needed back in Velona. We need to find out more about these mantises. I wonder how many of them there are on Tarra this time?" I explained and asked. None of us knew just yet.

"Bethany, this is one time I am sure glad that I am not the Wid, the leader," Marco admitted. "The decisions that you have to make are mind boggling. If we knew the full picture, then I could make proper decisions, but this way? Well, who knows what will be for the best? Like with the blasters. Maybe we could blast our way out of here. Maybe it would fail and we'd lose them. There are just so many things that we don't know that I am glad you are calling the shots. Whatever you decide, love, I'll back you all the way."

"Yes, you can count on us too," Eve added.

Giovanni put in, "Yes, but do give me a chance to figure out how some of these devices work. In the kitchen, that cooler thing is a terrific invention, don't you think? I don't know why Lucianna or I haven't thought of that before now!" I grinned. Here we were trapped rats in the dungeon of the mantis and Giovanni, or Enyo, was still looking for new inventions and new ideas. Always an engineer, I mused and grinned.

"Okay, let's see what else Nestor has to say," I suggested. We all returned slowly to the observation room, as we began to call this special room. As we entered, the alarm sounded. After a few minutes, Nestor moved before our window.

"Oh my. Busy, busy, busy, so many things to do. Ah, you look different without your apparel, Bethany, Eve," Nestor said.

"Yes, well we only wear those outfits to the dances. If you are so busy, Nestor, why don't you get some of your other mantis to help you with your work?" I asked, pleased with my cleverness at eliciting key information from him.

"I am afraid that I am alone now. Only the genetic engineer was sent to Tarra at this time. However, I am afraid that I am going to need some assistance in a few months. Thus, I am hatching a brood of my offspring. In a while, they will hatch and then I will have all the help that I need to get the genetic modifications made and get all the mammalian cells fully adapted. In the meantime, yes, Bethany, I am a bit overworked. Oh my yes, but then it is so exciting, this genetic work. Fascinating."

"You will be pleased to know that I have already begun the genetic modifications on yourselves. This one is called Version One, which should get us to approximately the right set of changes. Remember, I truly will value your feedback on these experiments, if I am to get them perfect this time. I do, you know, want your mammalian cells to be just perfect for us and for yourselves."

"What? In our food?" Eve screeched.

"Oh my dear. No, no. Your food must be very sterile and clean; no chance of food poisoning can be allowed to alter these genetic experiments. No indeed. Your food is as pure as I can make it. No, I have introduced the mutation into the air that you are breathing. However, don't worry, Eve. It will take several days for your bodies genetically to mutate into the new form. I would advise drinking a lot of water and eating healthy meals though. We don't want to leave things to chance, not in an experiment."

"How long will all this experimentation take?" Marco asked.

"As one scientist to another, though I cannot hope that you would understand, who can say how long it will take? We must get it absolutely correct and right. I do admit, Marco, that I am a little under the gun here, so to speak. You see, I had to apply the protocol for handling a massive prison escape over Dorota."

"What? You murdered millions of innocent men, women, and children?" Marco screamed at him; his veins in his head throbbed. Marco was angry.

"Oh my, well you could put it that way. Yes, drastic action had to be taken, young Marco. You see, there were thousands of escapees there, far, far too many for me to handle alone as I am. I had no other choice than to use that drastic protocol. However, the beings themselves will survive. In three months, they will begin to thaw out from their deep frozen state and will need to acquire new mammalian cells. Unfortunately, that island will take many, many years to regenerate into a life supporting land. However, if you cooperate and all goes as I have planned, before I leave for home, I will use our terra-forming beam on the island, which will make that land habitable in less than a year."

"Will these changes hurt us?" Eve asked. "Are we going to be in a lot of pain?"

"Oh my! Goodness, no, Eve. That would be inhumane. No, you will feel at most some slight discomfort. Probably wearing your clothes is more painful than the genetic modifications that your body will be following. Some stretching and discomfort is about all. However, what I am keenly interested in following will be the ease and ability at which you can adapt to the genetic modifications of your mammalian cells. Oh my, yes indeed. You must realize that I have spent many years working out these genetic modifications, based upon the suggestions sent back so long ago from the Dorota experiment. One of the more difficult aspects has been to reduce the discomfort of the form to the changes, and the ability of the being within the cell to adjust to the new changes."

"The first, I have worked on long and hard and I believe that I can safely say that you will experience little or no pain at all. It will be more as if your body is growing up — that kind of a sensation. However, I have no experience in occupying a mammalian cell or how well one who is currently in one can adapt to sudden genetic modifications. I will be depending upon you for guidance in that arena, you see. So please, for the sake of all your fellow countrymen, be honest with me about how well you actually can adapt to the new forms."

"By tomorrow, your bodies will be well underway with the Version One changes. At that time, I will give you a treat. I will give you a tour of our facilities here at Chichulain. We have the entire history of our genetic creations on file here. You will be very impressed with them, I am sure."

"What are you going to make us look like?" Eve asked. "I like the way my body looks now."

"Oh my, I don't want to spoil the surprise. In fact, I dare not, that prior knowledge would spoil and ruin the adaption aspects of the experiment. As I said, that is the only part in which I really do need your invaluable input, Eve. Now then, I have much to do yet today. Do you have any further questions for me?"

"Yes, I do," Giovanni spoke up. I looked at him and he asked, "The cooling box that has the milk and eggs in it, how does that machine work?"

"Oh dear me, Giovanni, is it? I truly am sorry. I am not a mechanical engineer. I have no idea how it works, only that it does work and that it is needed to keep those items fresh for your needs. Personally, our diet of plants has no such strange needs, but then yours is a mammalian cell.

However, I will see if I can find an operation manual on it, but then how are you to read it? Well, let me think about that, Giovanni. Now, I really must see to the fine adjustments. I will look forward to meeting with you after breakfast tomorrow. Oh my, I almost forgot. An alarm will sound when the dark period comes on your planet, and it will sound again when the sun rises. That way your sleeping cycles can continue in a normal manner. Until tomorrow then." Again, his huge mandible head bowed slightly, and the enormous mantis body moved out of view from our window.

"Do I look any different?" Eve asked us as soon as the creature left.

Giovanni looked her over, "Not yet, dear." Eve seemed relieved and we headed to the kitchen to deal with making supper.

As we finally got supper ready and sat down, I commented, "Boy, my arms are sure feeling awfully weak. How's yours doing?"

"Mine are too! Oh no! Not armless again!" Eve exclaimed.

"My teeth feel like they are loose or something," Marco muttered, as he bit into a piece of chicken.

We all soon agreed with him on that point. Our teeth did feel slightly loose. While we were eating, a low buzzer sounded. We guessed that the sun had set. Marco and Giovanni volunteered to do the dishes for us and we headed off to brush out our hair.

When the fellows joined us, Marco said, "Bethany, my lips are feeling kind of puffy and funny. So are Giovanni's."

We four began looking closely at each other. Indeed, our lips were swelling slightly. Further, my breasts seemed larger, Eve's too. "Well, no sense in panicking, what is going to happen is going to happen," I stated the obvious. "We still don't know what he is going to do with this genetic modification stuff. We need to find that out and determine a proper course of action." They agreed and we four headed to bed. It felt wonderful sleeping with Marco, as if we were married already. I rolled over onto his shoulder and cuddled.

"I love you, Bethany. No matter what happens or what we end up looking like, always remember I love you and will do my best to take care of you," Marco whispered in my ear. I needed his support just now as I had a very bad feeling about all this.

Chapter 6 Disaster's Beginning

Sergio awoke to the telefono ringing. Mom called for him and he dashed into the living room. By the time he finished the short call, the rest of the household had wandered into the room, curious indeed.

"Barti. He has more news. Got to go to headquarters soonest," Sergio explained. "I'll give you a call and brief you as soon as I find out what he's got. Lisa, we best hurry. We'll take the putt-putts."

While they were dressing, Lucianna volunteered, "Marta, I'll go with you to the library and help check on the maps." Of course, Valerio went with her.

A half hour later, Sergio and Lisa pulled into the red brick police headquarters. Many officers who were coming on duty waved to the pair. Already, Sergio had made a name for himself as a Detective Inspector. Now he was a Chief Detective Inspector and many took this chance to congratulate him. Once past the throng, the two headed for Barti's office.

"Ah, come on in. News is still coming in, but I expect more will continue coming in the days ahead. Okay, this dust cloud is of gigantic proportions. It has now reached the edge of eastern Tashien. The word that we are getting from the LDCS system of Arsenio's is that this cloud is completely blocking out the sun! I don't know how that can be, but the reports say that one can barely see that it is daytime there. It doesn't sound good at all."

"Stefano West Po has ordered a steamer which was docked in Shansee to sail by Dorota for a visual inspection. We ought to hear back from them in about two weeks. Again, as soon as I hear, I'll let you know."

"Thanks, this dust cloud has me worried," Sergio commented.

Barti nodded, "Here, the night patrols have assembled these reports of a strange flying ship or cigar as some call it in our night sky last night. I know you are interested in them."

"They abducted Bethany, Marco, Eve, and Giovanni last night. The mantises have them, Barti," Sergio dropped his news on his boss.

"What? When? How? Where? Are they alive still? This is horrible! We must let Stefano know at once," a very shocked Barti said.

"We got back from the concert and were sitting around the table. Bethany and Eve were off looking for the flying ship. Well, they found it and it found them. One minute the four were sitting beside us, and the next instant, all four were somehow transported up into that ship. Poof, like magic. I assure you I did a thorough search and their bodies were not disintegrated or killed. They have been abducted. Why? We don't know yet. Thanks to Lucianna, we have a guess at their direction of travel and are working now to try to figure out where the four are being taken."

"You can still contact them, right? You have that telepathy thing going?" Barti asked.

"Well, we've not been able to contact them yet. However, that may be because they are currently unconscious. I'll let you know when we do contact them. Lisa, let's go over these sighting reports. Maybe we can use them to help refine Lucianna's line."

At the library, Marta led the two to the map section and went to fetch appropriate journals of the various explorers who had ventured anywhere near this remote stretch of continent. "Gosh, there is hardly anything on the map!" Valerio commented.

"Mostly along the coastline," Lucianna pointed out. "That is to be expected. They reported only what they could see from their caravels. Look, here on the eastern side closer to us the map shows thick jungles. That does not sound hopeful."

"Hey over on the western side they have mountains marked, well sort of," Valerio pointed to the hash lines on the map. He watched as his girlfriend carefully plotted her line onto the map very lightly using a thin pencil. She hated to mark up the map, but it had to be done. Not long afterwards, Marta returned with five volumes and the two set to work skimming through them, looking for clues about this western area. By lunchtime, having made an accurate sketch of what little was known on the map, the two headed home.

Sergio and Lisa had already returned and both looked glum. "Sorry, Lucianna, we went through all the reports, but honestly, your observations and ours are far more accurate than any of the others. Yet, they all support your basic direction of travel. You two have any luck?"

"Sort of," Lucianna replied and displayed her map copy on the table, helping herself to a sandwich, as Sofia began bringing in the trays of food. "At least, I was able to get a latitude and longitude for this spot here. That's where we should begin our search. Yet, Sergio, if my line is off even a little bit, by the time it gets to this location, they could be anywhere within a hundred miles north or south of the line. It's like looking for a needle in a hay mow." Lucianna looked very depressed indeed. So did they all.

During the afternoon, Lucianna put her mind onto a different problem. Sergio had reported what had been said about this dust cloud over eastern Tashien. Now she began to calculate what its volume must be to have this effect. Of course, many of her figures were purely speculation, but she finally sat back and didn't like what she had worked out.

"It's going to impact us here in Velona, gang," she said quietly. Now they all stopped and listened. She flushed, unused to so much attention. "Well, given what its volume must be already and that it is moving westward, when it gets here, we ought to be able to easily detect it. I am afraid that if it is strong enough to block out the sun over eastern Tashien, it will be very noticeable here as well."

"Won't it all just fall to the ground?" asked Valerio. "I mean if I throw a ball up, it comes down quickly. Won't that just happen with this stuff?"

"Well yes and no, dear. Dust is very light and it is very high up in the sky. It may take years for all of it finally to settle back onto the ground, but it has me worried. I can tell more when it actually gets over us."

"What will it do? Just block out the sun a little?" asked Valerio.

"Well yes, but if it blocks out some sunlight and it lasts for an extended period of time, it could well have a very bad impact on us. Plants may wilt and die if they don't get enough sunlight. The temperature could also be lowered."

"Plants die? Wait a minute," Sergio broke in. "That could spell disaster for all the crops here in the Sea Princes and in the breadbasket of the Greenway!"

Lucianna replied, "Yes, that's what I am fearful about, Sergio, that and it becoming much colder in the winters."

"How long will it take for this dust to clear out?" he asked. Lucianna shrugged her shoulders. No one had the slightest idea. Something like this had never happened before.

"Maybe my estimates will be wrong," she tried to sound a hopeful note.

After lunch, Sergio and Valerio headed off to visit Vittore West Po, who was in charge of Velona's massive shipping vessels. It was his job to know roughly where every ship of the line was at each day, as nearly as could be determined at least. They knew that if we were to be rescued, they would have to have a steamship to do so.

Gerardo West Po had also retired. For a time, his son Adrien ruled, but he had retired too. Now Gerardo's eldest grandson, Stefano, had become the new monarch of Velona. His second grandson, Vittore, was given the huge responsibility of Shipping Czar, as his title was proclaimed. The two entered his large office around two that afternoon.

"Hi Sergio, Valerio. I just heard about the abduction. Is it true, the aliens have returned?" the young lad asked.

"Yes, they have, but remember, don't tell others about it who are not cleared by Stefano. You don't want to cause a panic. Besides, who will believe in aliens, eh?" Sergio reminded him.

Vittore chuckled nervously. "Well, I don't know what to believe, actually. The radio is reporting all manner of strange sightings over our city last night. I think people know that something is up. Anyway, I am sorry for them, being abducted and all that. We will miss them I'm sure. What brings you here?"

Valerio had never been in his office before and was fascinated with the layout. One huge wall contained an enormous map of Tarra. On it, pins were stuck into the map, each with a little colored flag on it containing a number. Vittore noticed Valerio and explained, "All two hundred sixty-three ships of Velona are on the board there. It is my job to know where, approximately if not precisely, where every ship is at every day of the year. Impressive isn't it? Without this, our extensive commerce would collapse."

"What we are going to need to rescue them is unlimited access to one of the ships. I am authorized to pay any amount to secure a proper vessel for our exclusive use for an indeterminate period of time," Sergio explained. "You see, Lucianna has worked out possible locations where they are being held captive. Unfortunately, it is most likely down there." He pointed out the western side of the west continent, at a point somewhat more than about half the continent's length down. It was below the equator.

Valerio added, "We had hoped to get one of the new steamships that can go really fast."

Vittore said, "See those silver flags on the map? Those are the steamships that we now have in operation. Look at the map where you want to go. Do you see any silver flags around that part of the world?"

Both boys looked, "Er, no," Sergio replied.

"Good reason for it," a victorious Vittore replied, confident that for once he knew something that Sergio, the Chief Detective Inspector, did not. "A steamship cannot travel that distance. You see, they require periodic stops to take on more coal and more water. They make very effective and fast trips over here in our part of the world. However, as you can see, there is nothing but empty ocean for vast distances over toward the western continent. There is simply no place they can stop to take on more coal or water. In short, you have got to use a caravel."

"Rats, there goes speed," Sergio lamented.

"Yes, but a caravel can definitely get you there and back, though you ought to stop for freshwater a few times. How soon do you need the caravel? I ask because we have a brand new one due to be christened in a week or so. It would cause less disruption in shipping if you reserved that ship."

"Hey, sounds good. We won't be ready to sail anyway until we can get into contact with Bethany, Eve, Marco, or Giovanni," Sergio admitted.

"Tell you what. I'll put a hold on that caravel for two weeks. If you don't contact me before that, I'll let her go on her way with her first cargo run. How's that?" Vittore asked.

"Perfect. I'll get back to you as soon as we have worked out our rescue plans," Sergio advised. After shaking hands, the two left.

As they climbed onto their putt-putts, Valerio teased Sergio, "Hey, looks like Vittore knew something that you didn't know, I mean about the steamships."

Sergio grinned, "Ah, I knew that, but I figured if he felt that he had one up-ed me, he'd be more amenable to our request. And he was, a brand new caravel, can't ask for more than that." Valerio grinned and kicked his small motor to life. The two headed back home.

After supper and still no contact with us, the eight sat around the

46

living room listening to the radio and the news. While there was some commentary on the strange night sky sightings, most of the news focused on what had happened in Dorota. Consensus held the opinion that a massive volcano had erupted there. After the news, they listened to the symphonic hour and then turned in.

Eight rose just as glum-faced as they had been last evening, if not more so, especially after Lisa shook her head, indicating that she had still been unable to contact us. Tito and Sandro headed off to work, Marta followed shortly thereafter, leaving Sofia and the four teens to deal with whatever may come up. "I've got a rehearsal to go to at one, so you get to wash the lunch dishes," Sofia ordered.

The four went about their daily chores, pulling double duty to handle those that we four used to do. Then, they sat around and speculated on just what they were going to do to try to rescue us. None had any real ideas, save to open fire with all the blasters at one time on the mantis creature. "That's assuming we can even find this place," Sergio added with a sigh.

After lunch, Sofia took off with her violin and the four finished the dishes and headed back into the living room. After plopping in the sofas, Lisa tried once more to reach me. Suddenly, Lucianna, Valerio, and Sergio stopped chattering and stared at Lisa. From her face, they knew that she had finally made contact with us!

A minute later, Lisa ended the connection and very animatedly exclaimed, "I reached her! She's okay. All four are okay so far. The mantis took them prisoner. They are being held in some kind of underground chamber. However, she says that they all have some kind of metal headband, which somehow zaps them if they try to move out of their heads or to initiate a telepathic connection. She was able to receive okay, though, what a relief!"

Lisa continued, "She says that we are to hold off setting sail a bit. She wants to see what all she can find out for us first. I am supposed to contact her every day about this time for more information! Hurray, we got through."

"Better let our parents know," Sergio advised her. "That will give them some relief at least. Now we absolutely have to work out a method of locating them." The four put their heads together the entire afternoon, but in the end, they came up empty. "We simply lack too much data to solve this problem," he declared.

Chapter 7 Version One

We four awoke when the alarm sounded, but we all let out a scream of shock and surprise! During the night, this genetic modification thing had been steadily working on our bodies. All of us instantly noticed three things at nearly the same time. As I looked at Marco, his two lips had become stretched way out, in a similar manner to the Utu princesses, who slit both their lips and inserted their clay lip plates. Only instead of a slit, some kind of boney material was growing inside his skin. His lips looked as if he wore two lip plates that were both now about four inches around. Yet his actual lips were still as thick as normal, that is they were not stretched thin and tiny as the Utu princess' were.

"You talk funny," he managed to say, though we both had a hard time understanding each other. I too had similar lips the same size as his. I could see the top of the flesh covered boney disk with my eyes.

The second thing that was immediately obvious was my breasts. "Honey, you have some gorgeous knockers now," Marco attempted to soften the blows of our transformations with a little humor. Indeed, they were now triple the size that they had been when I went to sleep last night. Still, they were acceptable in size, I thought.

The third thing caused me the most grief. My arms had withered during the night. Yes, they were still there, but they were mostly bone and skin now. Somehow, they had shrunk in length, as if they were somehow being absorbed back into my body. I could barely move them and only with effort. Marco helped me up and we joined Eve and Giovanni who were just as scared as we were.

"My arms," Eve cried out, but had to repeat it a couple times before we could understand her.

"Come on; let's get some food in us. I feel awfully thirsty," Marco said a few times and we headed to the kitchen. Eve and I were very grateful as the boys immediately took charge and fixed our breakfasts for us. Right now, neither she nor I felt like dealing with only being able to use our feet again.

The next shock came as we four began to eat, with the fellows feeding us. It was just too hard for Eve or me to raise our arms, let alone lift the weight of the spoon or fork. Damn, I thought, but I ought to have guessed this was in the mix; he was a mantis, after all. Damn Nestor anyway.

Double damn! As we four began to chew our toast and eggs, one by one, our teeth fell out! Eve and I had no choice but to spit them out, while the shocked boys removed them with their fingers! Now we truly sounded very funny and strange as we tried to talk to each other! Damn, damn, damn, I thought. I suspected the others felt the same way.

48

After eating, we left the dishes and went to the observation room, where we intended to demand some answers. As we walked slowly there, I noticed that my feet seemed very loose inside my shoes, though the tied oxfords stayed on. However, I observed that both Marco and Giovanni were walking on their toes. "How come you are tiptoeing?" I asked a few times until he understood me.

"My feet don't seem to go flat anymore," he replied, again a couple times until we understood.

As we entered the observation room, the alarm sounded. This time, Nestor arrived quickly. "Ah there you are. A fine good morning to all of you. I see that the process is working well. No pain I take it?"

"No pain, but what is happening to us? Our teeth just fell out! My arms are shriveling up. What's going on with our mouths and lips?" I asked. Miraculously, the translation unit worked in spite of our weird voices.

"Part of the overall genetic modifications. All is going just perfectly. The transformation should be complete in two more days. I promised you that you would feel no pain or major discomfort. I have you know that I spent ten years working out that one detail, you see. Now if we didn't have to genetically adjust all these existing mammalian cells instead of birth adjustments, such care would not be needed you see. However, since the plan is to adjust all of them on Tarra, extreme care is needed. Now hold on a second while I adjust the translators in your helmets. I am having a harder time understanding your language." He fiddled with some dials and then seemed satisfied.

"Have you eaten breakfast?"

"Yes, that's when our teeth fell out," I replied.

"As expected. From now on, please be sure to cook your food so that it is very soft. In three days, your gums will be ready to deal with chewing. Right now, they are too tender and soft. Hazard of losing all of your teeth at once. Couldn't be helped. Now then, are you ready for the grand tour of Chichulain?"

Okay, the Wid in me became very curious indeed. "Yes, we are! How do we get out of here?" I hoped for some clues that we could use later to somehow escape.

"Please remain where you are. This won't take but a minute." He moved out of view and Marco looked at me and winked. I knew that he too was expecting to see some secret door opening and perhaps we could use that as a way to escape.

Energy flashed and we four found ourselves standing beside the fifty-foot long mantis, dwarfed utterly by his huge size. He let go of some controls and bowed. "Welcome. Indeed, you are the first mammalian cells to get such a historical tour of our finest genetic facility, Chichulain! Down this corridor please." He led the way. Marco held onto me tightly, Giovanni did likewise with Eve. Our heels clicked on the stone floor and we moved as fast as we dared.

After a long hall, the space opened up into an enormous circular room. "We begin at the beginning," Nestor explained as we stopped by the first glass case. "In here is where the first form that eventually became your mammalian cells began. Yes, we began many centuries ago with these single cells, imbuing them with a life force of their own. Not much to look at, but then consider the greatness of the act. We built a totally new life form." He moved on to another small glass case.

"Now here is the next phase in your genetic mutation; yes it appears to be a giant clam. I would like to point out that these became your jaws and your teeth, though now we are removing them. This way, you will not need to worry anymore about rotting, diseased teeth. We never could overcome that drawback. So many mammalian cells have extensive tooth troubles that we saw that we needed to rectify that error on our part. You see, we make mistakes, but then we also do our very best to correct them, as any good geneticist would do so." He led us on to the next case.

"Now here was the critical step, where we got your forms to survive outside of the oceans." We saw what could best be described as a sort of fish with legs. "Please don't worry; we never used these as prison cells! These were just our work along the way towards perfection, you see. Let's skip ahead a number of centuries, shall we?" He passed by several other cases.

"Now here is the first of the actual mammalian cells that we constructed. Their bodies were stuffed, put on display here, and their image was burned into the first stone head above us. I will take you there later on." We gazed upon a miniature man and woman. Neither was more than two feet tall with lots of fur and very angular heads.

We moved on a bit. "Now after perfecting that version, we realized that they were too small to survive effectively, and we began genetic modifications to enlarge their bodies. Here in the next ten cases are the main ones on the direct route to the present day mammalian forms. Each of these is also impressed into the stones above us."

"You see, it was mostly trial and error. Some had longer legs; some had longer arms. Some had large brains. Now this group here, Case 1042, these were the first pair who actually worked well on Tarra. In fact, we allowed their offspring to continue live. They inhabit the lower jungles not far from here. Of course, the trouble with Case 1042 is that they are extremely hostile and are prone to hunt people such as yourselves. What was your word for it? Oh my so many facts to remember. Oh yes, head hunter cannibals, that was what your people called them. Well, I don't mean your people in Velona, mind you, but your species, that is. Very vicious, very dangerous these Case 1042 are. Still, we honor them by allowing them to continue to survive here in the nearby jungles."

I didn't like the sound of that. If we were going to be rescued, our rescuers might be in serious trouble from these savages. Eve commented, "I sure hope that you don't intend to stuff me and put me in one of these glass cages."

"Oh my. No, my Eve, I won't do that without your permission. However, when we achieve your ideal forms, I will make a hologram of you to show my genetic colleagues. Have to do that, you see. Now then, let's see the upper level, shall we. I know that it is outside, and at this elevation, it is a bit cold for your mammalian cells. So we won't stay very long. Shall we take this lift?"

We watched him closely to see how he operated this lift mechanism. Obviously, this was at least a way out of this underground prison. We were amazed at how easily it rose upwards and soon we felt a blast of chilly mountain top air. We stood in the center of a smooth stone pit about three hundred feet in diameter. A beautifully worked stone wall some three feet tall rose from the flat floor around the rim. Periodically, stone heads protruded from the rim wall. We recognized many of these heads. We'd just seen the stuffed versions below!

We also got a look at the surrounding countryside. Indeed, we were atop some mountain, though there were many even taller, snow-capped peaks in the distance. I made sure that I looked in all directions trying to memorize the horizon. If I could get these images back to Sergio, perhaps he could find a way to locate his spot! It was my hope anyway.

"Impressive indeed," I finally said.

"Yes, I thought that you would appreciate this view. Now shall we head back down? It is even a bit chilly for me up here." I was shivering and couldn't agree more with this decision.

Once we were back inside, Nestor said, "I know that by now your feet are hurting. They are still adjusting to their new forms as well. I had best get you back. Now then, tonight I will install a new machine for you. It will automatically generate new shoes that will properly fit your feet. No more of this effort to tiptoe, Marco. I want your shoes to fit properly."

"What about some better clothes?" I asked, rather tired of wearing my slip as a dress. It was too thin and chilly.

"Ah yes, I have not forgotten that detail, Bethany. That machine will be installed when the process is complete. Until then, clothing will not properly fit. Just be brave for another three days, please. Then, we will get all things handled to your satisfaction."

As we neared the spot at which we appeared from our cell, he added, "Bethany, Marco, Eve, Giovanni, I must compliment all of you for your accepting attitude in working with me to help perfect this genetic modifications. With your continued help, we will get it right, and all of your species will enjoy the benefits of your efforts. I know that some minor things will need to be altered. I assure you that I will listen and do my very best. I am the foremost genetic engineer that we have. I truly am complimenting all of you. You are a compliment to your whole species." He pressed a button and, after an energy flash, we found ourselves back inside our prison cell.

We headed back to the kitchen, very, very slowly. All of our feet now ached, and I begged Marco to massage mine when we could sit down at last. He and Giovanni did their best and then worked on their own feet. Strange, his feet began to look very pointed, as if he were forcing his toes towards the ground.

I did tell Lisa a whole lot about what we'd learned when she made contact just after we finished lunch. Again, the fellows did the dishes and fixed us some lunch. By then, we all were terribly tired and we napped all that afternoon.

When we awoke, we again observed each other and ourselves. Our lips and their boney circles had enlarged further and were about six inches around. Eve's and my arms were most definitely shrinking. I swear that they were about half as long as they had been before I was abducted. Only now, neither she nor I had the strength to lift them at all, but we could still feel with them.

All of us were terribly thirsty and we drank considerably. Then, the fellows fixed us our dinner, making very sure that the chicken was overly done so that it required little gumming to swallow. All of us felt rather morose about all this and we turned in the second that we heard the low signal that the sun had set somewhere high above us.

The next day, our first action was to observe what had happened to our bodies during the night. Our lips were still as thick as normal, but now our lip plates or whatever they were to be called now were about ten inches in diameter! We had to lower our heads to see the floor before us. Worse, our breasts had become enormous, nearly the size of our heads! Marco, of course, continued to tease me about them in a playful sort of way, trying hard to keep my spirits up, especially when we saw that our arms were now only about six inches from the shoulders to finger tips.

As we rose finally, I noticed that my feet felt strange. Somehow, my shoes no longer fit; they almost slid off our feet. The fellows could not even put their shoes on today. Both of their ankles were rigid, with their toes pointing to the ground, like some ballerina en pointe. The only way that they could walk was on their very tiptoes.

I knew that they were suffering as much as we, but Eve and I were grateful that they still managed to fix us breakfast. After that, we slowly moved down to the observation room. Nestor didn't appear for several minutes today.

"Ah, good morning to all of you. Good news, the process is nearly complete. By this time tomorrow it will be done. When you awake, you will find appropriate shoes waiting for you. There will be another clothing and shoe machine in yonder vacant corner here as well. You can dial in your desires and the machine will make it for you. Now, I have a lot of work to do today. If you need anything, let me know. Keep up the good work!"

What work? I wanted to scream at him. Instead, we hobbled back to the kitchen and remained there most of the day. Although we consumed a rather large amount of liquids, we somehow didn't need to go to the bathroom more than normal. I figured much must be being used in this genetic process. Now, I really didn't care. I just wanted it to be finished.

The next morning came none too soon for all of us. We all counted on and prayed that this process would be complete, as Nestor had promised. Thankfully, it was. Where to begin? Well, our lips were essentially a pair of boney plates covered with our skin, both on the top and bottom sides of these boney disks, which were twelve inches in diameter, top and bottom. Our lips had thickened a little and surrounded the boney inner disks. When we closed our mouths, the two plates made a distinctive clicking sound, much like birds.

My breasts were enormous, so were Eve's — somewhat larger than our heads but yet quite firm. Eve pointed out that our back muscles had definitely strengthened to support such a top-heavy weight. Well that was the only positive aspect. As we had expected, there were no trace of our arms, just merely shallow sockets. No surprise there. After so many lifetimes of this, we took that in stride.

Our feet were now definitely changed. We looked at each other's feet, since with these huge lips we could not easily see our own. "Hey, they are similar to the tiny feet in Tashien," Eve pointed out. I saw what she meant immediately. Yes, our arch was now very curved. While our toes could be flat on the floor, our heels were miles above them. Our new shoes had their heels almost up against the back of our toes, very similar to those we had worn last lifetime in Tashien. At least we could now easily slip into and out of our new shoes. That meant we had the free use of our feet in place of our hands.

The fellow's feet were far worse than ours! Shockingly so. Now their toes would not even bend! They would be walking on the tips of their toes, ballerina style. Their new shoes had the tips of their toes in contact with the ground and an extremely tall heel was right behind the toes. I felt sorry for Marco and Giovanni as they struggled to learn how to walk in on their toes. While Eve and I took small, shuffling steps as we had done in Tashien, the fellows took a beating, wobbling like mad with every step, even holding on to the walls for balance.

Eve and I helped the fellows make breakfast as best we could. However, as soon as we had eaten, we all headed to the observation room. I began to see a possible route out of this mess. Nestor showed up promptly. I suspected he was up early, waiting to see the results of his great genetic modifications.

"Ah, good morning. Yes, oh yes, just perfect, if I do say so myself. I promised you that there would be no pain and very little discomfort. You all look just fine," Nestor said. Even through this translator machine, I detected what must be enthusiasm on his part. Either that or perhaps it was pride.

"Now I want you to learn to adapt to your new forms for a few days. Then, I will ask for your opinions on these refinements. I will be not so available for the next five days. My eggs will be hatching soon, and my children will need my attention for a bit. I promise you that I'll be more than willing to listen to your comments and opinions in five days. Meantime, see how you can adjust. Oh yes, you should check out just how sensitive your lips are now. You ought to find that most enticing, but I do have to run now. Oh my, you all look so good." Before we could protest, he moved on out of the window area, relatively rapidly I thought.

"Five days of this hell!" Eve complained. "Our lip beaks are so big that we cannot even feed ourselves anymore. And you fellows can't even walk except on your toes!"

Marco put his arm around me so that I could steady him, while Giovanni did the same with Eve. Slowly we four headed back to the bathroom, determined to help each other out. Quickly we worked out some arrangements. When the fellows needed to walk, we girls went with them so that we could help them keep their balance. However, we could not carry anything, so they had to deal with much of the cooking activities. We began to all use the long handled spoons, since a regular spoon and fork were too short to get a bite into our mouths. Yes, we uttered quite a few explicatives during those five days.

However, I began to see that my plan might just work. I didn't dare talk openly about it, fearing the Nestor might be monitoring our conversations. I did let the others know that I had an idea, though. Meantime, I asked them to pay extreme attention to our prison. If he somehow got inside here while we were sleeping to deposit the shoes and the machines, then we needed to determine where that secret door was and how it operated. I couldn't accept Giovanni's suggestion that maybe he was just using the same technology that he'd used to bring our bodies from our dining room up into his ship and then to take our bodies in and out of the prison when he took us on the tour. If I did accept that, then there was no way out, something I refused to believe. Why? If that was so, how did our extensive rooms get built in the first place? I knew Giovanni would also likely have an answer for that one too, so I didn't mention it.

With little to do, we spent most of the time lying in bed with our boyfriends. It didn't take us long to discover what Nestor had meant about the new sensitivity of our huge, circular lips. The slightest touch of Marco's lips on mine sent waves of sexual excitement throughout my body, almost uncontrollable sensations. Even Marco had a most difficult time holding back. Now I began to grasp fully what Nestor had in mind with these genetic modifications of his. I began to have even more faith that my plan would work.

By the sixth day, we had a routine worked out fairly well. We all had to cooperate to get nearly any action done, whether it was using the bathroom, bathing, fixing meals, doing dishes, or even setting the table. Hence, we arrived at the observation room fairly soon that sixth morning. Nestor was slow to respond, but he did have a chart and writing tool with him as he appeared.

"Ah, good morning. I see you are all looking fit and well. I do hope that you have adjusted better to these fine modifications to your mammalian cells. I am ready to hear your opinions and comments. After all, we do want these modifications to be absolutely perfect."

"Thanks, Nestor for listening to us. May I ask one question first that is vitally important to our comments and opinions?"

"Oh dear me, yes, please do so. This is so important," Nestor sounded propitiative I thought, if a mantis could be propitiative.

"Once we have these genetic modifications worked out to be just perfect, as I know that you will do so and I have every faith in your superb genetic skills, will you then be treating all the other mammalian cells on Tarra with this final, resultant genetic modification?" I asked innocently. I already knew the answer, but I was setting him up.

"Oh yes, yes of course. Once we have it perfect, then with the help of my dozen children, who by the way have hatched into fine copies of me, we will spread the genetic mutation bacteria through the air above all of Tarra. Within three to five days, all the mammalian cells will have mutated into this fine new form. All babies born after that will also inherit those genes as well. We will only need to let the genetic mutation bacteria loose on Tarra once. However, I plan to do only smaller sections of Tarra at one time. I don't have enough children to do the whole planet at one time."

"Thanks. That is most commendable of you, Nestor. These new modifications that you've done to our mammalian bodies are just perfect." He looked pleased, while my three friends gasped, wondering what I was saying!

"Yes, just perfect, Nestor. You *do* realize what you will be doing, when you mutate all of Tarra into forms such as we now have, don't you?" I asked, setting him up for my punch line. If I had fingers, I would have crossed them!

"Well, yes, the perfect mammalian cells," he replied, slightly quizzical. "What do you mean?"

"Well, all of Tarra will be thanking you handsomely once you modify them all into our new forms. You will be freeing every spiritual being on Tarra! Yes, all of us will finally be totally free of these mammalian cells! You are being so kind and generous to us all. Perhaps they will erect a monument in your honor for having set us all free!"

I'm sure that these translator units were not prepared to handle quite the reaction that Nestor had! He nearly dropped his drawing tool and chart! "What? I don't understand you, Bethany. Free all of you?"

"Why yes, Nestor. You see, once each person sees this result, they will have only one reaction and take only one action. They will simply kill these mammalian cells anyway they can, like drowning them, throwing them off cliffs, anything they can do to kill them."

Nestor looked very confused. I added, "And once each one of us has killed off their new form, we will all be totally free at last. There will be no other mammalian forms for us to use and occupy, so we can then return to the various places from which we originated. I think that they will maybe even elect to call you a god or something for having given them a way to set themselves free finally! Good going, Nestor. Thanks for making it possible for us all to become free beings after these long centuries of imprisonment here!"

"But? How? Why? This is not right! I don't understand. These modifications were supposed to keep you all firmly within your mammalian cells. I don't understand you, Bethany. How?"

"Oh, you see, Nestor, you have made our mammalian forms so ugly, so horrible to use, so unable, that everyone will not want anything more to do with them. The men will be unable to walk much and thus unable to work the fields and care for their wives. Women will be unable to even care for their own basic needs, let alone raise their children and run the family home. You have made the forms so helpless, so useless, that everyone will simply give up and find any available means to kill the body just so that they can be free of it. No one will want to adapt to the new form, because they cannot use it to do the basic actions of life anymore. Hence, we will all simply give up, kill them off, and be free of the cells forever. Wonderful plan of yours, Nestor, genius even! You will be a hero here on Tarra. They might even erect monuments in your honor for freeing all the spiritual beings of Tarra!"

"Oh no! No! No! Something has gone terribly wrong here! Oh dear me! Oh my. Bethany, somehow I must have made a terrible mistake! That is not at all what is supposed to happen. You are supposed to really love these forms, even more than before, and be held tightly inside their heads. Oh, I think I see what you are saying, Bethany. Something is in error in the genetic modifications, something is wrong in the physical results, am I right?"

"Oh, I am terribly sorry, Nestor. I thought that your intention was to set us all free of these bodies. Now I see that you want to make them even more desirable for us so that we hang on to them better. Right?"

"Oh yes, yes, Bethany. Yes, that is right. More desirable, yes, far more desirable. Let me show you some of the proposals that were put forward but which I rejected. Perhaps I erred there." Hastily, he set up a "slide" presentation for us. We watched in amusement at these other proposals for the genetic modifications of our bodies.

Some looked like a cross between a horse and a human, a centaur I believe is your word for it. Some were more snake-like in the lower halves. We saw nearly two dozen crosses between a human form and various animal forms. It was all that we could do to keep from laughing. When he finally finished showing them to us, I said, "Well, Nestor, I can see that you were absolutely right in rejecting all of those. Each one of those would have also produced just the opposite effect from what you desired."

He puffed up a bit. I knew that I had him now. "Nestor, we ought to look at your fundamental starting point, your initial situation and see where the errors in design originated. Then, we can correct them and get this all done right, just the way that you desire."

"I am deeply in your debt, Bethany."

"So your starting point was that our original bodies, the ones that you took from our dining room, the ones that we all had when we first arrived here, those were not working right?" I asked.

"Well, yes, you yourself and Eve, for example, had already escaped the cells. Indeed, you were up in space around my ship when I first found you. That situation we call an escape. That is what we must avoid have happening here, you see," Nestor replied.

"I see. Okay. Then, you must have had a starting point that was different from that, right? You mentioned Dorota once." I hinted, knowing that must have been his or their starting point for this entire genetic mutation sequence.

"Precisely so, you are most observant, Bethany. Yes, centuries ago, quite by accident, my partner's ancestors discovered that when the female mammalian had lost her upper appendages, the male mammalian then devoted far more of his time to her care and needs. They grew far closer and more dependent upon each other. Given this, they performed a number of experiments to see if this would hold more broadly."

"Ah, yes, was the Isle of Right one of those experiments?" I asked.

"Yes, it was. The results were so promising that a full-scale society was established on the island of Dorota, primarily because it was so isolated from the rest of the lands and totally unknown by other peoples. For a century, they had a perfect society created on that island. However, near the end of that time, the wardens detected that, while the forms were nearly perfect, some slight modifications ought to be made."

"I see. Did they suggest what those modifications ought to be? Did they say why they thought the modifications needed to be made?" I asked, more out of my own curiosity than anything else.

"No, Bethany. I believe that you have zeroed in on the crux of the problem. We received word that the wardens thought some slight modifications ought to be made. However, we never heard just what they thought they ought to be or why. We assumed that the why was to help prevent escapes. That's why we decided to give you all those marvelous and highly sensuous beaks. Do you not find them quite stimulating?" We nodded. I was too embarrassed to admit that I had an orgasm just from Marco's kissing my lips.

"Of course, if we gave you such magnificent beaks, then we also had to enlarge the female's mammary glands so that their newborns, who would then have the beaks, would be able to suckle properly. We did very careful studies to ensure that your milk glands would be large enough to handle your babies during their nursing years." He continued justifying his many genetic modifications that he'd made to our bodies.

At this point, I had a decision to make. I knew very well that he would never put our bodies back the way they were, because we had escaped them, from his viewpoint. I made my decision based upon Eve and my experiences growing up on Dorota lifetimes ago as Dita and Bethany. "Well, Nestor, Eve here and I have lived a lifetime on Dorota. We can both vouch for the fact that it was close to a perfect society here on Tarra. It was very true that there was almost no crime among the normal population. All children got a full and complete education. There was a very strong family bond. Men helped women in all ways. Yes, I can see why you have chosen this as your starting point."

"Oh, I didn't know that! You and Eve were there? From my ancestral memories, I know that it was such a good society, so perfect in so many ways, quite unlike Tarra at large as it now is. That you agree with this analysis makes your point of view and your opinion highly valuable to me, you know.

"Thank you for the compliment, Nestor. You know, I am always telling my children when they have a problem to solve to always go back to the original solution and closely re-observe directly what was going on. Then, the real situation presents itself. Only by direct observation can one truly tell what the actual, underlying problem is, you see," I suggested, hoping that he would agree with me.

"Yes, Bethany, that is a solid scientific approach. You have such a scientific mind, you know. Yet, Dorota is no more. I cannot go back in time and observe what the others saw there."

"Well, I don't know anything about your genetic modification science, but if you possibly can undo what has been done to us, my suggestion is to have Eve and myself be as the females of old Dorota were. Then, you can directly observe us four and see for yourself what the true genetic modifications ought to be. What do you think?"

"Bethany, if you and Eve wouldn't mind doing that, why, I would be most appreciative. That would be the very best way actually to determine what the true genetic modifications ought to be! Yes, I can undo what's been done. Again, give me a couple of days to get it started. Once I introduce the bacteria in your air, it should only take three days until it is complete. You don't mind drinking lots of fluids?"

"Oh no. We will eat and drink whatever you suggest. After all, Nestor, it is in our best interests to help you get this right." I hoped that my intense relief did not communicate as such to Nestor.

"Excellent. I will get started on it immediately. I will let you know when the next bacteria are ready to restore your forms. Thank you so very much, Bethany." He quickly moved out of the window area and we headed back into the kitchen. My friends could scarcely believe what I had just negotiated!

While we tried to discuss what had happened, our huge beaks and lack of teeth made this difficult. It would have been nearly impossible without these translator headbands that we wore. I still feared that Nestor was somehow monitoring our private communications. I wanted to put my finger up to my lips as a signal to the others, since I couldn't use telepathy to warn them. I just kept shaking my head "no" as we slowly made our way back to the now messy kitchen. Marco was saying what a wonderful job I had just done, as well as how grateful he was, promising to make it up to me. At last, the three got my message, when I raised my foot towards my ear.

"Overhear?" Marco whispered and I nodded yes vigorously, my lips banging onto the tops of my breasts. God, what a mess we were into this time. Yet, if we held on for a few days, we might have some temporary relief.

I knew that they all wanted to talk about these developments and make suggestions. Lord knows that I needed all the bright ideas I could get. Still, I could not risk breaking my trust bond with Nestor. As long as he held my opinion as valuable, we had a chance. If we broke his trust in us, we and the whole world would be at his mercy! I just could not see the human race surviving with bodies modified as ours now were. I suspected that my doomsday bit might have been quite accurate for a large number of people.

As the fellows volunteered to start to clean up the breakfast mess, Eve and I attempted to wash the dishes using the foot techniques that we'd used so long ago in Dorota. I kept thinking that Nestor had means of overhearing our conversations, and possibly, he even had ways to watch our every action. I was leery of even attempting to write out messages with my feet for fear Nestor could possibly see them as well. Yet, I really needed to discuss everything with them, but how?

After a long struggle to get the kitchen chores done, I really wanted just to sit and sip a pot of tea. Well, that was out for now. About the only way to drink was to have Marco use a long spoon to put some into my mouth. Whatever was Nestor thinking when he thought that having these huge beaks would be desirable? While I knew that Eve liked larger sized knockers, these were ridiculous; we couldn't even see our feet. Still, I could see Nestor's point. If we had babies who had these beaks, of necessity our breasts would have to be large enough for them to be able to nurse. I doubted very much that any woman would chose to continue to live like this.

After an exhausting time in the kitchen, we decided to lie down for a while. Good old Marco. As soon as he got us situated on our bed, he whispered to me and held me tightly. Soon, we were kissing once more and totally enjoying our heightened physical sensations.

As usual, Lisa contacted us in the early afternoon. I suddenly latched on to this as a way for us to communicate without being overheard by Nestor! *Lisa, join we four with you! We have to talk things out!*

Soon, I felt the others with me. *Okay. Thanks for being reserved back there. I do not want to give Nestor any hint that might cause him to change his opinion of us. I am worried that he can overhear what we say and maybe even he can watch what we are doing, so writing is out too. I am willing to take the chance that he cannot overhear Lisa's telepathic connection.* I explained to all of us. For the benefit of Lisa, I outlined what I had done earlier this morning.

You were brilliant, dear, Marco sent. *Honestly, I think you are right. If Nestor turns all of us into what we are now, physically that is, our world will end. Honestly, Lisa, Giovanni and I can hardly even walk. If all men were like us, men would get almost no work of any kind done. Commerce would die off. Heck, I doubt if one could even manage a small farm as we are.*

Giovanni added, *I think you are right. Who knows what all these headbands actually do. We must be careful. Right now, Nestor fully trusts you, Bethany. Let's keep it that way as long as we can.*

Good. Now here's what I am seeing. Correct me if I am missing something. Nestor has come here with the intention of performing some kind of mass genetic alterations on our physical bodies. He is not going to leave until he's done it. Further, I think that he needs his many newly hatched children to help him carry out the spreading of his final bacteria form to all of Tarra. Thus, I suspect he believes that he has at most eleven more weeks to work this all out. I am basing the time line on what he hinted about the millions of people of Dorota that he somehow "froze." Apparently, they will unfreeze, if that is the right term, in three months from when it started.

So gang, we are looking at Nestor turning out some genetic modifications on every human body on Tarra.

Lisa wailed, *Bethany, there is just no way that we can get to you in that time! Even if we knew precisely where to sail to, we just couldn't get there in time to stop him. What are we going to do?*

I don't know yet, Lisa. I am stalling right now.

And trying to minimize the nasty alterations he's making on us, Marco added.

Yes, that is vital. If we cannot stop him from doing this to us all, at least I want to make it as acceptable to us all as possible. The worst part of it is that he is dead set on using the ancient Dorota society as his starting point, where all the women had no arms.

Right! He's made that very, very clear a number of times, now,

Giovanna added. *I doubt very much that we can get him to use any other starting point, Bethany. We are doomed to have to have armless women, if Nestor gets his way here on Tarra. Lisa, let Lucianna know about all this. Look, Nestor is proving to us that his genetic mutation bacteria can be undone. Have her work with the Medical Research Foundation to see if they can somehow figure out an antidote to this bacteria or how it may be undone, once Nestor does it to us all and leaves.*

Good idea. Gang, keep your eyes open around here for anything that we can later use to also attempt to undo whatever Nestor unleashes on us. Also, gang, keep on playing along with me, no matter how it goes. We'll use these times with Lisa to talk things over. In the next few days, be thinking about what modifications we ought to suggest to Nestor, once he has you fellows back to normal and Eve and I just armless. We have to give him something plausible. His goal, remember, is to make these human bodies seem highly desirable so that we are not interested in moving out of their heads, escaping as he puts it. I am now at a loss on what that might be. Whatever we suggest may well likely be implemented on everyone on Tarra.

Wow, Bethany, you are carrying a heavy load on this one! Lisa noted. *I wish we could discuss this with the Guardian. Just do the best you can, Bethany.*

No kidding. Okay, remember; think of all the ramifications of these potential genetic modifications that we can. We must be ready to persuade Nestor as much as possible with arguments that he can understand. He won't be satisfied unless he can recreate a Dorota-like world with some additional modifications. Also, let's do what we can to stall this thing as long as we can.

You got it, boss, Marco teased me.

Now in the meantime, let's all try to see if we can find a way to escape our prison cell. There must be a secret way in and out. Also, see if you can invent a way that we can determine if Nestor is either listening in on our conversations or if he can see what we are doing. If we can possibly use our blasters to get out of this cell, perhaps we can stop him.

Eve pointed out, *Look, gang. We should try to get Nestor to see what may well happen to women when he unleashes these armless making bacteria on us all. Like your mom, she won't be able to play the violin anymore. She will be devastated to say the very least. What about all the women who make a living by using their hands? Seamstresses will be horrified, for example. We all know that on Dorota, women had to help each other out just to get by, but they already had their households and society rigged up for their needs. They had specially made low kitchens, yokes, and such. Think of what will happen if all the women in Velona wake up to find themselves armless? It will be catastrophic to say the very least!*

Yes, Eve, you are right. It is one thing to be born armless into a world, which has been set up for you and where your parents can educate you in alternate methods as you grow up and quite another thing to suddenly find yourself armless. Look at how many of the victims committed suicide in that Dorota expansion fiasco in Velona, Megalos, and Demokritos. We have to find a way to make this side effect real to Nestor. So put your minds on that issue too, gang.

If we cannot, Lisa, I want you to discuss this with everyone and see if you all can find ways to lessen the catastrophe on our women of Tarra. I surely don't know what that might be, but if we cannot stop Nestor from doing this, we must somehow let the world know what is about to happen. Perhaps some of the disaster can be lessened someway.

Will do, Bethany, Lisa promised. The others chatted a bit, while I mulled over another thought.

Hey, Marco, the next time that we all go into the observation room, carry my new image taker with you. Put it down where I can activate it with my feet. I want to try to get an image of Nestor if I can. If he says anything about it, I will say I am just practicing doing little things with my feet. He'll buy that. If he lets us get away with taking his image — I'll use all three films — then we have some idea that he doesn't know about our blasters.

Hey, right. Count on me. If so, then he isn't all knowing! Marco exclaimed. *Also, Bethany, I have some ideas that I want to explore about finding his secret door to our rooms. If I could only walk easily — still, I aim to do some experimenting.*

Giovanni added, *Okay, then for my part, I am going to try to learn all that I can about this alien technology. Lisa, I could use that translation Comm Circle. Make a copy of the Velona letters and the mantis corresponding letters. Next time, I will try to draw them out here as you visualize them and make myself a copy.*

Lisa agreed and we finally ended our chat. We all had much to think about now and I was very glad that we were now all on the same avenues of thought. Yes, right now, I felt a terrible responsibility resting on my shoulders. At least I still had them; I teased myself. If we could not stop Nestor from unleashing genetic mutation bacteria on us, then what I ended up convincing him to do to us would have to be endured by all the women on Tarra and possibly the men as well. In a way, I was like a goddess now, about to determine the fate of everyone's lives. This was a responsibility I wished that I did not have! On the other hand, I was glad that it was I who was in the driver's seat on this one. I swore that I would do my very best to lessen this horrible impact on us all.

Chapter 8 Version Two

After our lengthy chat with Lisa, Marco found my birthday present, the image-taker, and indicated that he would take it to the gardens. I tried to indicate that I would walk there with him so that he could use me for support, but he shook his head no. I watched him taking awkward steps out of our bedroom, carrying the small box and two extra plate attachments, which held the other two films. My heart went out to him, as he worked to walk on his toes.

A bit later, I heard Giovanni doing likewise, walking somewhere on his own. Well, the fellows were definitely not taking this lying down. Neither should I, I resolved. I rose, found Eve, and suggested that we go see what we could do in the kitchen. That turned out to be next to nothing; we were entirely too constrained by our "beaks" and knockers. We'd just have to wait until Nestor got us back to some semblance of normalcy.

Eve struggled to say, "You know, somehow this keep-things-cold machine gets refilled. I wonder how? Thank god for these translators. I don't think that we could even talk understandably without them!"

"Yes, you are right. How are they refilled? Let's see what we can observe, since that's about all that we can do right now," I suggested, wondering if we could really discover something.

After a bit, Eve noticed that there was a small space behind the unit, but with our huge beaks, we had a tough time positioning our heads so that we could see behind it. "I bet it runs on the same energy that powers the lights," she offered. I concurred. Still, we saw no way for the machine to be refilled. Then, we heard the slow footsteps of our fellows coming our way and went to greet them.

Marco nodded, indicating that he had my image-taker in a good position. Giovanni looked glum. Whatever he'd set out to do, he'd not been successful. Eve explained her simple finding with Giovanni and he pointed to his head, indicating that he had an idea. He and Marco moved some things around and made a small hiding place. Now I got the message. He intended to hide out here during the night and see what happened, if anything. I wanted to grin, but of course, could not.

Beginning this night and continuing for several nights, the boys took turns hiding out in the kitchen looking for how the machine was restocked. Just before supper, the alarm sounded, indicating that Nestor wanted to speak to us. Again, I found that it was curious that he didn't have some message to that effect appear in our headband machines. Slowly, with the fellows leaning on us for support, we made our way to the observation room.

"Hi everyone. Good news. I have created retro genetic mutation bacteria. I will introduce it now. It will take three days to complete its mammalian reformation program. Again, you should experience no pain. Do drink lots, especially the white liquid, which contains calcium and other minerals, which your bodies will need in the regrowth process. Again, let me personally thank you for saving me from making a catastrophic blunder here on Tarra. If that would have happened, I would have been utterly disgraced and my entire line destroyed! I owe you my life, Bethany. Now then, I best get to work and get the process started. I'll check on you in the morning as usual."

As we slowly made our way back to the kitchen and the steaming mush, which we were cooking, we attempted to use our noses to see if we could detect any odor or presence of the bacteria which was being introduced. Giovanni kept looking for the insertion point, assuming that it was in the ceiling. As we entered the kitchen, he pointed out a small opening in the ceiling. Later on, we discovered a similar hole in all the rooms. While we smelled nothing unusual, we did conclude that the bacteria were being introduced through these holes. However, lacking any ladders, we had no way to plug the holes. They were way beyond our reach.

During the next three days as the bacteria did its work on our bodies, I did not attempt to capture the image of Nestor. The combination of my beak and knockers prevented me from being able to see my feet without some unusual contortions. I resolved to wait it out.

During that second night of hiding in the kitchen in the dark, a strange whirring noise woke Giovanni from his light doze. He carefully peeked out and saw a most fascinating machine. It had four small wheels and two long metallic arms with several hinges or joints. On its back were a number of replacement pitchers full of the various liquids, milk, juices, and such. He watched as it moved in straight lines, pausing to make turns as it navigated its way over to the cold-keeper machine. He watched the machine as it used its arms to open the door, take out the nearly empty pitchers, and place the full ones inside. That done, it pivoted around and began its return trip out of the kitchen.

Giovanni decided to crawl on the floor and see if he could follow it and see where it went. He managed to see it turn to the right in the garden room, where he lost sight of it completely. By the time he had crawled down the long hall, the machine was gone. Now his curiosity was fully aroused.

The next day, Giovanni carefully copied out the dual alphabets that Lisa was sending us via telepathy. It took all the time that we dared use in one of these secret telepathy sessions to get the whole thing sent, but he was very pleased with the result. Now he had the ability to translate any writing that he discovered. Whether or not such would make any sense was another matter.

Beginning that third night, the fellows took turns hiding out in the middle of the garden. The many rows of the crops provided excellent cover if one laid flat on the ground. Now the fellows were very hopeful of discovering just how these machines entered our prison. We felt that we were getting close to an important discovery. If we could somehow get ourselves out of these rooms and into the larger complex, perhaps we could find a way to stop Nestor.

Relief! Yes, we all felt a huge surge of relief when we awoke on the fourth day. Our lips were back to normal and our teeth were back. In fact, none of us could detect any differences from before this had happened. More importantly for the fellows, their feet were normal and they could walk properly once more. So could we, for that matter. Our breasts were back to their usual size, though Eve and I knew that they would continue to fill out for a few more years. Our bodies were still only fourteen. In fact, we all looked the same as we had when we were abducted, save that Eve and I had no arms.

This morning as we headed to the observation room, Marco brought along the image-taker box, placing it on the floor before my feet as we sat down, awaiting the arrival of Nestor. I fiddled with it and got myself as ready as possible to take his image. Soon, the giant mantis moved before the window as usual.

"Well, now then, you all look just as I found you. How are you feeling? Any ill effects? Do your mammalian forms seem back the way that they were?" he asked kindly.

Marco replied, "Yes, as far as we can tell, all is now back to normal with us, except Bethany and Eve, of course." He was stalling giving me time to attempt to take his image. He did notice me fiddling with the little brown box.

I quickly finished and explained, "Oh yes, this is so much better, Nestor. I am now able to start to do things with my feet that I ought to be able to do. Of course, as you can see, I am going to need to practice quite a lot to get the hang of doing things this way. So is Eve."

"Yes, yes of course. I have given this considerable thought. What do you think of this idea? I would like to give you several days to get accustomed to this form. During that time, please give some thought to what modifications ought to be made. After that, we can discuss them."

"That sounds like a good plan, Nestor. Give us time to see how it goes and observe directly what the situation is or perhaps was on old Dorota," I replied. "We want to make sure that we are looking for the same purpose of the modifications as you are, though. It won't do for us to be looking down one path, while you are looking down an entirely different one."

"Oh, excellent point, Bethany. Oh yes indeed. You are very correct. Yes, well the path we must follow is one in which all of you will greatly desire to remain within these mammalian bodies and not try to escape them. As it stands, Eve and your body are nicely modified; however, the males are untouched. It has long been my supposition that the ancient ones thought that some modifications had to be done to the male bodies as well.

You see, each of you is an individual, not a collective unit. So if the males are unmodified, then there is nothing to compel them to desire to remain in the mammalian cells, you see. That seems the most logical avenue of the genetic modifications. Still, let's give you three days to see how it now goes, shall we?" Why the females would feel that they would really desire to remain in an armless, helpless body Nestor did not consider.

"Yes, that would be fine. If it is not enough time or if we have further ideas later on, we'll let you know, Nestor. After all, we have a vested interest in having our mammalian forms just perfect for us as well." He nodded his head in agreement and then left. Once he was out of sight, Marco picked up the camera, and we returned to the garden, where he switched the plate holders for me.

"Boy you don't appreciate what you have until you don't have it!" Marco exclaimed as we entered the kitchen. "That was the worst experience I can recall. Imagine trying to live like that! How utterly awful. Bethany, thank you for getting us out of that incredible jam. Oops, well, not totally, I forgot about you and Eve." He flushed as he realized that while he and Giovanni were back to normal now, Eve and I still had no arms.

"Well, I can't agree more. At least this way, Eve and I are not so totally helpless. If only we had a pair of those yokes that we used to have, we could carry things around. As we are, I am afraid you fellows are going to have to do the carrying. First thing, I need a pot of tea, and I don't want to sip it by spoon! Ugh."

"Allow me, princess," Marco teased and filled the teapot. I used my foot to reach the box of tea, while Eve used hers to get a spoon for the leaves. As she and I put the loose tea into the pot, Marco added, "Golly, you two are pretty good with your feet."

"Yes, experience. Not ideal, but at least now we can see our feet and reach our mouths," I replied. "Will you add the boiling water for us and fill our cups?"

At last sitting on the reclining chair, holding a steaming mug in my feet, I felt about as normal as I could be, under the circumstances. "Okay, now comes the really hard part. We are going to have to come up with some 'modifications' suggestions for Nestor. I am out of ideas."

"I will make us a list of possibilities," Giovanni suggested, taking up his makeshift pencil and a scrap of Eve's slip on which to write them. "First, I think that we ought to not suggest any further modifications to the women. You are all going to have it incredibly rough as it is."

'Yes, but," Marco interrupted him, "we need to have Nestor realize the huge difference from being born armless into such a society versus suddenly waking up without them. That alone is going to cause a horrible nightmare for the women and girls. He has to address that issue or his whole idea is doomed to failure. There will be far too many suicides. That's what I think. How about you, love?"

"Yes, Marco. I agree totally. We need to make him realize what that mutation is going to cause in the women."

"Good, I have that one written down," Giovanni replied.

"But what are we going to suggest for you fellows?" Eve asked. "It is almost like a symbiotic relationship coming. I mean like this, we are dependent upon you fellows for a whole lot of things now. If this happens overnight in Velona, it will be the men who have to build all the new kitchens, chairs, and yokes that the women will desperately need, starting that very first day. You still have to be able to do your own work, building houses, farming, black smithing, sailing ships, and on and on. From that very first day, all the women are really going to need the help and assistance of the men. Even after you get our houses redone for us to be able to survive, you're still going to have to look after our needs like never before. We can't afford to have you fellows also crippled up."

"Yes dear, but we are going to have to suggest something for the males," Giovanni replied. "Nestor will be insisting on some modifications. We must be clever about this."

"Let's start with what the fellows are going to have to have to support us, Eve," I suggested. "They have to have all of their appendages. How can they get around without legs? How can they do all the things that we are going to need if they don't have hands? No, we cannot allow them to lose any appendages."

"Also, they have to be able to see and hear us," Eve added.

"Communication is a necessity too, we have to be able to speak and be understood," Marco put in. "That means we have to keep our eyes, ears, and mouths as is. None of those beaks please. I don't think that we could be understood without these headband devices."

The more that we chatted about this, the more that we realized that we needed the fellows "whole" and not missing body parts. Then, things took a weird turn. Eve suggested, "Well, they could have tails. That wouldn't interfere." We all laughed. It felt good to laugh for the first time since we were abducted. She added, "They could have greatly elongated ears, but I don't think I would like it if you were totally bald, Giovanni." Again we roared.

Time flew by. Still we had no ideas at all for male modifications. We liked them just as they were; Eve teased us all. Then it struck me. "Perhaps we are looking at this the wrong way. What Nestor wants, his goal, is to have modifications, which make a person *want* to be their bodies. Really, that's what he is saying, if we are honest about it. He wants the spiritual being to stop thinking along those spiritual lines and desire just to be the mammalian body, not themselves. What kind of things make an immortal spiritual being desire to be one of these bodies?"

"Oh that's easy," Eve replied. "Bodies can do things for the person that the person can no longer do directly for themselves, such as moving objects around. With these infernal devices on our heads, we cannot any longer just move things, as we are used to doing — I mean Bethany and me. So now, we are dependent upon our bodies to lift the tea cups up to our mouths. Before, we would just directly lift them ourselves, though we did have to be careful not to totally shock other people's realities."

Now we were off and running in this more hopeful direction. Quickly, we discovered that already the normal person in our world was already using the body for nearly everything. Only those who had had therapy and had discovered their spiritual natures were looking elsewhere. Plus, the Guardian had been really going to town freeing beings, restoring their native skills in this physical world.

Then, I had an idea. "Hey, you know aesthetics plays an enormous role in this. We women like to date handsome men, not pigs."

"Hey, you are on to something, love. We fellows just love it when you gals all dress up in your fancy Annelise outfits! You look, well delicious!" Marco said and then flushed.

"I'll jot that one down, fellows must look handsome, and gals, pretty," Giovanni declared, finally getting something written down. "What do you ladies like to see in men? What do we men like to see in women?" Almost as soon as he said this, he realized that this was a wild variable. "Golly, those will vary from person to person. That insane Doc Yi in Tashien liked to see mutilated women. Some fellows like women with big knockers. Some like women who are shorter than they are. Man, maybe this isn't going to get us anywhere."

"Yes, especially when you ask me about what I like," Eve replied. "Remember, I am really Renzo, and I have yet to get the hang of being a woman. Giovanni is incredibly lucky that somehow I have fallen for him. Last time, as Dita, I just married Bethany here." We all chuckled. I admit, she was doing far better at adapting to having a female body this time. Of course, it was her second one now.

"Jeesh, fat, tall, thin, short — man, we will never get any real agreement on this one," Marco chuckled.

I added, "Big buns, strong arms." We all roared.

Giovanni brought us back to the task. "Well, that was a hopeful approach, but I think we are going to have to approach it slightly differently. Aesthetics is the key, but what about such? That attracts us to each other, but what keeps us coming back for more, so to speak?"

I flushed quite noticeably. My face felt hot suddenly. "Whoa, look at Bethany! Dear, what *are* you thinking of?" Marco teased me. Now my face felt even hotter!

I cleared my throat. "Er, with those beaks that we had, well, Marco was kissing me with his. You know, those thick lips, twelve inches across; they were incredibly sensitive and well so sensual. I kept having intense — well, you know what I mean," I felt too embarrassed just to say it.

68

"Bethany, you are right. I couldn't control my own urges either. We sure messed up our sheets, didn't we? I promise you we'll go all the way just as soon as we are married," Marco promised sincerely.

Giovanni, ever the engineer, spoke up, "Bingo. Now we have something concrete here. Make both bodies extra sensitive to sensual pleasures, particularly intercourse. That would really help keep both sexes focused on their mammalian bodies. Plus, it won't interfere with all the chores and such that they must be able to still perform. Excellent idea!"

"Yes, but won't that tend to get everyone addicted to sex, rather like being addicted to opium for pleasures?" I asked.

"Well, that's Nester's whole point, Bethany," Marco pointed out. "He wants something that tends to keep a being wanting to be a body. That would sure do it."

"Say, it might also be greatly accepted by Nestor," Giovanni broke in. "You see, if that occurred, there would be a sudden increase in the number of babies being born. He has to find new baby bodies for the millions that he wiped out in Dorota. I bet he really goes for that idea. Besides, it would be fun and healthy."

"Except that we would end up pregnant all the time," I added. Everyone roared over that aspect.

Marco added, "Well, larger families will require even more dedication on the part of us males to support them."

"Unless the man just gives up and abandons his overly large family," I added, putting a slight damper on the idea.

Lisa broke in on our discussions. She was checking up on us and was very pleased to hear that our spirits were up and that the fellows were back to normal. Lisa added a few more ideas, promising to query the others and see if there might be some more ideas. She suggested that women's makeup be a part of their bodies. That is, without arms, putting on the fashionable red lipstick would be more difficult. Eye makeup was more problematical, since she preferred different types for different occasions. She also suggested that perhaps women's waists might be small, as long as their flexibility and health was not sacrificed. That way, they would not have to deal with tight lacing corsets.

Lisa also made another startling suggestion. What if women had short arms instead of no arms? She suggested that we would be far better off if we had arms and hands that were long enough for us to hold a cup to our lips. That way, with the tips of our fingers reaching only to our waists, we would still be able to carry out some things easily. We wouldn't be quite so helpless. I had the feeling that Nestor, who was basing everything on the ancient Dorota society, would not go for that idea. Nevertheless, I promised to bring it up. At least we began to have some ideas to share with Nestor, ideas which would not bring utter ruin to humanity.

The next morning, we met with Nestor once more. I again attempted to take an image of him as we began our discussion. "Well, Nestor, we have been coming up with a lot of ideas, but we also have taken a closer look at what we think that you are proposing to do to all the mammalian cells and have some concerns that we ought to share with you. Where should we begin?"

"Oh this is just excellent. Oh my, yes it is. Begin? Well, we should hear your concerns first, since those form the starting point for the genetic modifications," he suggested, wisely, I thought.

"Okay. Let me begin by telling you what we think it is that you are proposing to do. If we are all wrong on that, then we must re-evaluate our considerations." He nodded and I continued. "We assume that at some point fairly soon now that you are going to introduce the perfected genetic bacteria over all of Tarra. At the very least, all female mammalian cells will lose their arms and look like Eve and I look. Is this a correct starting point?"

"Well, nearly so. I cannot introduce it everywhere at one time. I have not the facilities with which to manufacture that much bacteria at one time. Rather, I will be doing sections at one time. I can do an area the size of one globe of your continent."

"You mean that half of the dog-bone continent in which Velona lies, where you retrieved us?" I clarified this vital point.

"Yes, I can do all of that in one shot. Then, the eastern globe. It will take two shots to get the big southern lands that connect to the bone. Another two will be required for the southern elongated continent and three for the western continent. That's nine all total to fully cover Tarra."

"Okay, then Nestor we had better tell you of our concerns and see if we can work them out. There are two very different scenarios in play here. The first one is the one with which you are most familiar, that of ancient Dorota. There, all female mammalian forms are born without arms or they lost them shortly after birth. Thus, they grew up in a society in which no woman had any arms. They thought that this was perfectly normal for their bodies, to have no arms, that is. Their mothers constantly showed them how to carry out the necessary actions of life using their alternative methods of doing things, such as feeding yourself by using your feet. Further, their homes were all adapted for their needs. All men there knew just how to build the proper homes and properly equip them for the women to be able to function in life. Thus, those women adapted well to such a life. Do you follow what I am saying?" He nodded.

"Now in this present scenario, all the female mammalians, well nearly all at least, have grown up with arms and depend upon them utterly. Some women, for example, are dressmakers, tailors, weavers, makers of cloth, and many other things. No one has a home, which is set up for a woman who lacks arms. No home has proper furnishings that will enable such a woman to function in her daily duties. Only a very few people in the world know what ought to be built and done to properly equip or train a woman who has lost her arms. Now suddenly in three days' time, they lose their arms like Eve and I did. Can you envision the utter chaos that will bring to these civilizations and their women and their male folk as well?"

"All four of us are very much afraid that that would bring about many, many suicides on the part of the women as well as many deaths because they had insufficient help to even feed themselves, let alone fix their own meals. We might be facing a catastrophe here as well, Nestor. If too many succumb, the entire race of mammalian cells might die out and we all escape again. What do you think?"

"Oh dear me. Yes, that is a very serious side effect. I had not fully thought this through, but I am so thankful that you have done so. I was planning to install some genetic memories into the female forms that would subconsciously guide them along proper avenues to accomplish things. I admit that I was planning to study just how you two did manage here and then incorporate those ideas into their genetic makeup. Still, I do see the enormity of the problem. Yet, there may be a solution to that. My ship has the capability of mass manufacturing of objects. I could send along sufficient samples for the males to follow to build the proper things for the females, in time. This would slow the overall transformation down somewhat, but we must do everything we can to prevent the females from succumbing and provide enough assistance to allow them to adapt quickly. I just wish that I knew what these alternate ways were and just what objects were needed."

"Perhaps we can help with this, Nestor. Eve and I have spent a lifetime in Dorota. We know all of their alternate ways of dealing with life actions. Only we do not know how we can communicate them to you. If I were not wearing this headband, I could contact your mind and show them to you directly." Oh how subtle I was being. Once free of the thing, maybe there was a way out of this mess.

"Yes, that would seem to be a wise course of action. I could then install those as memories into the genetic modifications. The females would then inherently know how to proceed. Excellent suggestion, Bethany."

Giovanni spoke up, "Nestor, if I had some drawing paper and pencils, I could make you a number of sketches, detail engineering drawings of just what equipment and things the females would need in their homes in order to function normally in life."

"Oh that would be so perfect, Giovanni. Yes, I will acquire some for you right away. Thank you for your kind offer. You are all being so helpful. Now then, do you really want to keep your teeth? I have reports that they decay and become painful and have to be pulled. I could replace them with the boney ridges that you had before if you like."

"No!" we four chorused. I added, "We women often need our teeth to assist us in place of our hands."

He nodded. "Okay. Keep the teeth. What about the large beaks? I thought those looked good on all four of you. Surely, you want them? Perhaps larger? Perhaps smaller?"

"No!" we chorused once again. "Those greatly interfered with our ability to communicate to each other and to even eat our food. Without arms, we need to be able to easily communicate our needs to our men," I explained. "Also, we must be able to feed ourselves, which we couldn't with those beaks. We also couldn't see our feet at all well, which would make the alternate ways nearly impossible to accomplish. No beaks, I am afraid."

"Very well, no beaks." Through the translator voice, he sounded very disappointed. "I have gathered some other ideas. I have observed that your females are particularly fond of wearing such unusual heels. In part, that is why I altered your feet in the first place. However, I have seen that your males had a terribly difficult time with theirs. Perhaps I over did it with them. Surely, you females wish your feet altered, right?"

"No. You see, we need our feet, as they are in order to utilize fully all the alternate ways. However, we also like to dress up fancy for our males and ourselves, especially when we go to dances and for a night out on the town. That's when we don our fancy heels. We women must be given the choice of whether to wear them or not. You see, as we are now, if we were forced to always wear them, we would have extreme difficulties managing everything, except when our males were there at our side. When we dress up and go out, the males are escorting us and care for our needs. Even with arms, in the outfits that Eve and I wore when we came here, we depended on our fellows here to assist us with many things," I explained, hoping for the best.

"Okay, I will accept that analysis for now," Nestor replied. "But how about that apparel you wear which so shrinks your waists?" he asked.

"Ah, now you have touched upon one of our suggestions. If women naturally had small waists, that would be ideal. However, in doing so, we must not sacrifice any flexibility, strength, health or anything. If so, then we would not need to wear those corsets, which we simply couldn't put on ourselves, not without arms, that is," I replied. Nestor wrote that one down, and if a mantis could be said to look pleased with himself, Nestor did.

"Along those same lines, women of Velona like to wear fashionable makeup. Cherry red lips predominate, but we also wear various styles of eye makeup. Perhaps you could visit Velona and observe some fashionable women there, discretely of course. See for yourself what I mean. If women could naturally have such red lips and some variable eye makeup as part of the process, that would make life easier. It is hard to put such on with only your feet. It can be done, but it is hard. The reason for this is that we like to make ourselves look prettier for our men. It attracts their attention to us, you see." He did see and jotted that one down.

"But what about the males? We must do something to them. As it is, there is nothing to prevent them from escaping," Nestor pointed out, just as

I figured that he would.

"Well, we've worked that out too, Nestor. If women have no arms, then we are going to be very dependent upon the males. That means, they must be strong; they must become our arms and hands when needed. They will have to do most all the physical labors necessary to the survival of our species. Hence, they have to have their arms, hands, and feet as they now are. They have to have their eyes to see, their ears to hear our needs, and their voices to speak with us. The way that Marco and Giovanni were with the first modifications, they were totally unable to help Eve or me when we needed it."

"Yet, we also worked out a modification that you might like. It is based upon what you did to our lips in your modifications. Make both our bodies extra sensitive to sensual pleasures, particularly that of intercourse. This would really help keep both sexes focused on their mammalian bodies. Plus, it won't interfere with all the chores and such that they must be able to still perform. Males would become addicted to such pleasures, you see, and not wish to be anything else. I mean, they would not want to escape, finding the pleasures available to them highly intoxicating, if you follow what I am trying to say."

Nestor looked extremely pleased with this idea, again, if our observations of this mantis were correct. "Oh that is perfect indeed. Yes, oh my, yes. That was my personal touch for you in the Version One formula. I had so hoped that all of you would enjoy that. Yes, that idea is a very good one. Thank you so much."

I relaxed a bit; this was going rather well, so far anyway. Nestor then began another line of suggestion. "I have been going over all of our ancient records. Since you also see the need for the sensual stimulation of the mammalian cells, I will tell you what I am also considering. What if your ear lobes were elongated and reached down to your shoulders? Just the lobes, nothing to interfere with your hearing, mind you. I could then make them very sensitive to touch, adding more stimulation as you moved about. That would draw more attention onto your mammalian cells, adding more pleasurable sensations to attract your attentions. What do you think about that idea?"

On the spot, I couldn't come up with any real objections, but I suggested, "If you observe the fashionable women, you will see that we love to wear earrings in our ears, fancy gold and gemstones, usually. Women would hate to have to stop wearing them. Perhaps you can work that into your design." I knew that mom loved to wear her diamond earrings that dad had given her years ago. She'd be annoyed never to be able to wear them again. I also knew that women tended to spend quite a lot of funds on jewelry and would be very upset if they could wear such no longer.

"Excellent idea. I will investigate all of these marvelous suggestions immediately," Nestor replied, preparing to leave.

I took one last gamble, one last parting shot. "Nestor, we have also come up with an alternative scenario. As we've pointed out, there is such a tremendous risk involved with suddenly making all women in our societies armless. So we put our heads together and have come up with an alternative which may bypass much of that, if we cannot solve the very difficult problems we've mentioned."

He stopped and returned before the window. "Please, I would like to hear of this alternative. I do believe that the problems may be solvable, given time. Still, I would be remiss in my duties if I didn't hear of this alternative."

"Our idea would be to have women's arms and hands somehow shrunk to about half their current size. Our fingers would reach only to our waists. Still, we would be able to feed ourselves easily, cook meals, and do most everything without so much help from our males. Women would be able to adapt to such a modification far more easily and with less trouble."

"Ah yes, I can see how that would be. Yet, if we have to go that route, then we must make more drastic modifications to the males to compensate. However, Bethany, I do believe that the fore mentioned problems are solvable. I will see about getting what Giovanni has requested now, and then see about how I can obtain the memories that you spoke of. I will let you know when I have them. Again, thank you all for your kind help in this difficult situation." He then left our viewing window area. Marco quickly retrieved my image-taker and once in the garden, swapped in the last plate. I had one more try to capture the image of Nestor.

Later that afternoon, Nestor appeared in the window and the alarm sounded. When we got there, Giovanni found a stack of paper and a supply of pencils waiting for him. "Will these do, Giovanni?" Nestor asked. They were perfect and he picked them up and headed for the kitchen table.

"I am ready to receive your mental images," Nestor continued. "I will bring you out as I did when I gave you the tour. One moment please." He moved out of our sight. Energy flashed and I stood beside this fifty-foot monster. "Here, you sit in this chair. I will attach this to your head. It will not hurt. Once I have the recorder going, you merely review those images that you think will be most useful for someone to have, when the bacteria has finished its modifications."

I did as he asked. Soon, I was remembering my lifetime as a young girl on Dorota. I was careful to go through the various sequences of memories, which I thought would be most useful for someone who had just lost their arms and was desperate to be able to do something. I began with feeding oneself routines. I spent considerable time dealing with food preparation activities and the use of the yokes to carry things. I even went through the times I had to retrieve a gold coin from a money pouch and hand it to the market man. I added some times when Dita and I brushed out each other's hair. I spent an hour at it before I was satisfied.

"Excellent memories you have, Bethany. See, they came through very clearly. With these, I can genetically engineer them into the bacteria so that the women will inherently know how each of these actions may be performed. Thank you so very much for your kindness, Bethany." With that, he pressed a button and I found myself back inside the observation room. Darn, I had not been able to glean any further information on what was outside our prison cell.

I headed off to find the others, who were watching Giovanni sketching away in the kitchen. Eve and I also gave him some of our suggestions to draw, though he had very good recollections himself, from his previous lifetimes. He didn't finish up until suppertime and left them for Nestor in the observation room.

Eve and I worked on fixing our dinner, with hand-help as needed from Marco. As we sat down to a steak dinner, Marco exclaimed, "You don't know how glad I am that we don't have to eat that mush any longer! A real steak, now this is eating the way it should be!" We all laughed, but honestly, anything was better than eating the soft mush. We were very glad that we had our teeth back.

That night, Marco hid in the garden among the taller plants. This time, he positioned himself to get a better view of just where the machine thing entered the room. While we slept, he dosed, waiting for the moment the machine would enter. Late at night, a low grating noise aroused him and he peered out. The wall close to the gardening tool rack rose upwards about six feet, and the mechanical machine came driving thorough, carrying more milk, eggs, and juices. As soon as its rear cleared the entrance, the stone wall slid back down into place. The low whirring of the machine's motor faded out as it headed down our long hallway.

Since the machine was out of the garden area, Marco decided to move to a better position. He now had a clear view of that wall section and he waited patiently. After perhaps ten minutes, the whirring grew louder as the machine returned to the garden room and angled up before the wall. Marco focused his attention on the wall itself and noticed a small sensor light up, probably from a signal from the machine. At once, the grating noise accompanied the raising of this wall section. All the time the wall was up, the sensor remained illuminating a dull red glow. Once the machine's rear cleared, the red light went out and the stone door came down, sealing us in once more. He waited until he was sure it was not going to return and then slipped out of the garden and headed to our bedroom.

The next morning, he described what he saw, and Giovanni just had to go see the sensor that had glowed red. It was just over our heads, but he could touch it with his fingers. However, he did not do that, fearing that might give away the fact that we had discovered it. Now, he put his mind to the task of figuring out how we might get that red light on and the wall raised. I figured that if Giovanni could figure this puzzle out, he had to be an utter genius!

Two days later, Nestor announced that he was ready with Version Two of his genetic modification bacteria, which would cause our bodies to mutate into the agreed upon forms. I hoped and prayed that only these tiny changes would be made, unlike those of Version One, which had been utterly horrible.

As you might expect, we four sat around all day watching each other and asking, "Feel anything yet?" Well, about all I sensed was my lips, which seemed to be becoming more sensitive to the touch. The next morning, the first thing that I noticed was Marco's ear lobes. They had grown several inches during the night. So had mine and the others, we soon discovered. At breakfast, Eve and I did believe that our waists were a bit smaller, though.

After three days, the minor modifications were complete. Eve and I had cherry red lips, just as though we had put on our lipstick. What fascinated us both was our eye makeup, if that is what it could still be called. The style and color varied with the amount of light striking them. In brighter light, ours looked nearly black. Marco said that they looked enticing, which we both enjoyed hearing. In dimmer light, they changed to a lighter shade of blue, which added to our appearance. Fascinating effect.

Our waists were indeed smaller. Lacking an accurate measuring cloth, Giovanni estimated that they were around eighteen inches around, based upon the fact that the corsets, which we had worn when we were abducted, were quite loose on us now. Eve and I did a lot of twists, turns, flexes, and any other motion that we could think of to do to test out our waists. Indeed, I seemed to have good muscle tone there, perhaps better than before. Again, I was amazed at how effective the result was. We could now wear Annelise outfits, but without the need for the restricting corsets. Well, that was an interesting, but useless effect, I concluded.

All four of us marveled the most over our ear lobes. They reached all the way down, resting lightly on our shoulders. They were thin and unobtrusive, but highly sensitive to touch. As we rolled our heads around, sliding the tips of the lobes across our shoulders, we received wild, exciting sensations both through the lobes and through the shoulders being touched. The fellows really remarked on this strange phenomenon, unsure whether or not they liked it — again, a harmless effect.

Then, we just had to test out our lips and their modifications. Marco and I embraced and both of us experienced wild, pleasurable sensations so strong that we soon were lying on our bed, passionately loving each other before we realized what was happening. "Wow! Now that is a strong one, Bethany. Once we are married, we are really going to have some fun in the bedroom!"

"You are assuming, Marco, that I can hold off that long!" I exclaimed. "Wow is right. Well, that is very sensuous but not harmful. I guess we may have pulled this off. We'd better visit with Nestor soon."

When we reached the observation room, Nestor was there with his clipboard. After asking us about each effect, he then said, "I have a little present for you." A dozen dangling emerald earrings materialized beside us. "Six for each of you ladies. I don't believe your males wear them. Am I correct?" He asked. The fellows enjoyed fastening them on our ear lobes. They soon discovered that there were tiny piercing slits in our lobes ready-made for these. Of course, we wanted to quickly head to the mirrors in the bathroom to see how we looked in them, but Nestor continued.

"I want you all to leave the observation room for a while. I have constructed prototypes of the various items the Giovanni has sketched. The men can transport them to your rooms. I will leave you alone for a few days and let you get used to them. Then, we can discuss any needed modifications to the objects, and how well the modifications are this time. I do hope that these genetic modifications will be to your complete satisfaction."

We did as asked. Well, the earrings certainly added to our looks and greatly added to the touch sensations as the weighted lobes slid across the skin of our shoulders. For once, I didn't regret Nestor's original idea. The only drawback that we had from Version Two was that even the slightest loving kiss sent such passions throughout our bodies that we found it exceedingly difficult to not go all the way with it. I wondered now if that experience would be altered as well, but I was determined to find that one out on my wedding night and not before.

As Marco finally was able to pull himself off of me, he teased, "Well, this will certainly have them making love, not war!"

"And babies too," Eve added, as she entered our room, her hair in a mess and Giovanni, looking forlorn just behind her, unable to take his hands off her. We all laughed. She went on, "We had better get married really, really soon, though! I don't know how long I can hold out."

"Well, it is supposed to be a strong emotion on us. I guess it will be. Still, that is loads better than what we had to endure with his Version One modifications," I replied. We agreed on that one.

After Nestor gave the all clear signal, the fellows began bringing back the newly manufactured items that we'd requested. Yokes! Ah, finally Eve and I could manage to carry something, as long as we kept the two baskets on either side in balance with each other. I found that this single thing gave me an immense relief. I'd forgotten how critical it is in life to be able to carry things around.

Although the low stove and counter top that were originally here in the kitchen were just fine, we now added low shelves, slanted chairs with wheels on them so that we could slide easily around the kitchen, making it possible now for Eve and I to actually do the cooking and dishes. We had writing desks and even a low table from which we could more easily deal with feeding ourselves. We had proper eating utensils and mugs with handles that Eve and I could use easily. Furthermore, we had a number of pots and pans that we could use to fix our meals by ourselves.

I was amazed. Nestor had somehow fabricated every one of Giovanni's sketches, duplicating them almost exactly as he had drawn them. He took pride in this observation. "An engineer is only as good as his drawings are precise." I grinned and gave him a kiss. Oops! That was a mistake, as both of us felt a sudden surge of powerful passions flooding our bodies.

"Well, Bethany, it looks like we are back in business. fellows, you go take care of the garden and bring in the harvest for today and the meat, and we will deal with the cooking," Eve proclaimed, very glad that we could finally fend for ourselves.

The first thing that I did in our new kitchen was whip up my own pot of tea. While I sat back sipping it, I watched as Eve worked on making a loaf of cinnamon bread. "I really have missed my sweets," she explained. "It's certainly oodles harder to do this way, but by golly, I do remember how to do it. That's something anyway."

Later when the whole place was filled with the odor of rising yeast bread, the fellows came back, following the smell. Giovanni was so pleased with the rising cinnamon bread, that he passionately kissed Eve. I watched as the two fought hard to separate themselves! Yes, I thought to myself, he's right. Make love not war will become the new motto, if Nestor has his way.

After three days, Nestor called us back to the observation room. "Well, how are the modifications this time? Any problems?"

I had to be honest with him. He may well have been monitoring us. We had been actually quite happy these past days, even though we were trapped rats. "So far, Nestor, all is simply perfect with our bodies. I must admit that it is terribly hard to keep from, well breeding. One little kiss sets off the most passionate, romantic feelings. I do believe that you have found the right formula."

"Ah, now that is so good to hear. How about all the objects?"

Giovanni answered, "You duplicated my drawings absolutely correctly. Nothing needs to be altered in any way. Incredibly good job of duplication, Nestor. I am impressed with your work." If a mantis could seem pleased, we thought that Nestor was. Determining what a mantis felt was extremely difficult.

"Okay, very good. I will now work on the finalization of the formula. Of course, with the necessity of now providing these necessary objects per household, the rate of conversion will be slowed down. I had intended to make nine batches, but with all the objects to also be fabricated and delivered within the three days, it is going to take considerably more batches. I will have to limit severely the numbers in each batch. Either that or hatch some more offspring to take up the extra workload. Well, I have much work to do now. I won't bother you for a while. When I head off to dose the area where you live, I will return you to your dining room. Of course, I will also see that you and those living there receive these necessary objects. Again, I thank you most heartily for your incredible assistance." He nodded his head, perhaps a bow and then left.

Back in our kitchen, Marco asked, "Okay now what do we do? We cannot stall for more time."

"Do we try to break out and take the mantis out?" asked Giovanni.

"We are going to be darn ineffective as long as we wear these headbands. Besides, perhaps he has an override control built into them. If we attempt anything, he might set off an electronic blast that would knock us out," Eve suggested.

"Gang, for once, I just don't know what is the best course of action to take," I said with a sigh.

Chapter 9 What to Do Now?

Back home, everyone was in an uproar over our abduction and the total destruction of Dorota and the Guardian. As the days passed bringing only more shocking news of the almost unbelievable tortures that we four were enduring, 42 Hampton Way became the house of anger and outrage, followed by a sense of futility.

"What can we possibly do?" asked Lisa. "We have to help them, but how?"

"Dear, better ask what is going to happen to the whole human race," Sergio growled. For the first time in two lifetimes, he had no ideas whatsoever. That some alien mantis creature had returned and was now planning to turn all human bodies on the planet into some kind of helpless freaks was more than anyone could comprehend, let alone attempt to grapple with finding solutions. Overwhelm. That was the key word that described the eight's reactions to the Version One modifications.

The only constructive action they had taken was paying ten thousand gold to have the new caravel stocked for a long voyage, standing by for their orders. Yes, Sergio had informed the monarch of Velona, Stefano West Po, the monarch of Fortress d'Grange, Leroy d'Grange, and even the monarch of Barcella, Miss Barbe Barcella of the abduction of Bethany, Eve, Marco, and Giovanni and the destruction of Dorota. They also were informed of the mantis' plans to turn all of humanity into these horrible Version One creatures. While the three rulers did believe that something terrible had happened to the four, none really believed the rest of it. Alien creatures turning human bodies into freaks were totally beyond these young rulers' reality. It seemed hallucinatory at best, someone's opium fantasy perhaps.

The middle of June came and the situation in the Sea Princes changed markedly. The dust cloud from Dorota appeared on the eastern horizon as a dark grey smoky mass. Each day, people watched the cloud moving closer, covering more and more of the eastern sky. By June 15, half of the sky over Zargarb was totally obscured by the grey cloud. Already word had been received of the cloud's shocking effects over Tashien. Over Arsenio's LDCS system, messages flew from Shansee, Tashien to as far away as d'Grange. We learned that the cloud turned day into dusk and for almost two weeks now, Shansee had been in eternal twilight or night. Days became a thing of the past.

As Lucianna had anticipated, the reports from Shansee now began to indicate that plants were beginning to suffer. Combine that with the visible, ever growing cloud, and the rulers of the Sea Princes began to believe that something awful was happening. The final straw, that convinced them that our story might have some validity behind it, was the wire from the Metal

Petal, one of our new metal steamships. It had been dispatched to check out Dorota the very day of the explosion. It had steamed rapidly to the island, checked it out, and headed back to Shansee to report its findings.

The message that arrived for Stefano was bleak indeed. No, this was not a volcano eruption. The island had been disintegrated, as if someone had unleashed a million bombs on it. The Metal Petal's captain reported that the basic land mass and mountains were still present, though altered somewhat. All houses, vegetation, people, all life was gone, just not there. The land was a barren waste, with massively thick, settling grey dust everywhere. The captain had to leave the area rapidly, because falling dust began causing major problems for the steamship's machinery, to say nothing of the continuous coughing of the crew.

Barti relayed this information to Sergio, who in turn relayed it to the others and Lisa told us about it the next afternoon during her daily telepathy contact with us. At last, Stefano West Po came to our house to consult us that evening. The twenty-two year old monarch looked quite haggard and confused, as Sergio led him into our front room, where the eight had gathered. Thirty year old Chief Inspector Barti came with him, providing security for the ruler. As usual, Barti's thick, handlebar moustache was impeccable, but his countenance was grim.

"One and a quarter million men, women, and children are gone, killed," Stefano said, after taking a seat and accepting Sofia's cup of tea. "It is just unimaginable. Such wanton carnage is beyond all belief, yet the Metal Petal's report stands. I expect additional confirmation from other slower vessels within the next few days. We even lost two caravels, which were docked there. As farfetched as your tales of these alien creatures are, Sergio, I don't know what else to think. No one on Tarra is capable of such utter and complete destruction. An entire island completely gone, reduced to a grey powder dust. What is next?"

Sergio cleared his throat. "Sir, I would be very concerned about the dust cloud that is fast approaching us. Already Shansee reports that plants are suffering with no daylight for almost two weeks now."

"What does that mean? Won't the cloud just vanish on its own?" Stefano asked.

Sergio nodded to Lucianna. She explained, "Yes, in time the cloud will dissipate. But my estimates indicate that it won't be completely gone until sometime next year."

"You mean we will be in a sort of twilight that Shansee is reporting for a whole year?" he asked in disbelief.

"Yes, it could be longer or shorter. As I get more information on the cloud and observe it over time, I will be able to better gage its dissipation rate and its effects. However, the impact is going to be terribly devastating to all plant life, sir," Lucianna attempted to soften her incredibly catastrophic predictions.

"What do you mean? Wilting and such?" asked Stefano.

"Yes, that at first. Sir, we are looking at all of our plants dying off because of a total lack of sunshine. I don't know yet if they will just think that it is winter time and go dormant or if they will actually die and never come back to life when the sunlight finally returns." There, she had finally said it. Disaster of unimaginable proportions was on its way to the Sea Princes.

"Good god, young lady! All plants? Dead?" Stefano exploded. He'd heard just one too many dire reports today.

Lucianna flinched and said timidly, "Yes, sir. All plants. I don't know yet if the Greenway will be impacted or not."

Stefano ran his hands through his hair and then banged his head onto the table, before raising it again. "No food. That's what you are trying to tell me, isn't it?" The thirteen year old girl was fighting back tears. He felt a bit guilty for his outburst. "I'm sorry, Lucianna. I didn't mean to frighten you."

"Yes, sir. There will be no crops this year. Maybe not even next year," she said in almost a whisper. Any louder and she felt that she'd begin crying. She didn't know why she felt so emotional just now.

"Good god!" Images of all Velona slowly starving to death flooded Stefano's mind. No one said anything for a few minutes, as this revelation sank into all minds.

"We should begin to stockpile dried foods," Sergio finally spoke up. "If the Greenway is also affected, we will have an enormous crisis on our hands, unless we act now and quickly."

"Where can we possibly buy that much food?" Stefano asked himself, again running his hands futilely through his hair.

"Sir, I don't think the southern continents will be impacted, just up north here," Lucianna ventured. "We could get food from there, perhaps. Also, sir, I think that this winter will be the coldest winter on record, what with so little sunlight to keep things warm."

Chief Inspector Barti spoke up. "Stefano, if we have a massive food shortage, we can expect food riots and all manner of civil disorders to occur. Starving people will become desperate people."

"Yes, that, Chief Inspector, is a gross understatement, if I ever heard one. What is the answer? What must we do?" Stefano asked.

Sergio took charge. "Normally, in crisis situations, we rely upon Bethany for guidance. However, she's been abducted, and we only have marginal telepathic contact with her. I will step in and fill her shoes for now and bounce my ideas off her whenever we do get the chance. What is the answer? What do we do? The answer is simple, I believe."

Sergio continued, "I would run notices in the newspaper about what our people ought to prepare for; that is, the coming loss of plants, and thus our food supplies. Reassign all available ships to begin bringing in all dried food possible from all southern lands. Lay in a stockpile ahead of time. Make plans for a well-organized food distribution system when the crisis hits. Let our people know how they are to obtain food supplies when the markets are gone. Give them confidence in your ability to manage this food shortage crisis."

He went on, "Since it is going to broadly impact all Sea Princes Sectors, I would meet with the other leaders and work out details on how best to meet this crisis. We don't want wars to breakout over who gets the next food shipment. If this becomes a cold winter, Vito can ship far more coal to Velona to heat our homes in return for more food, for example. I believe that your best avenue to follow will be one of working together with all the impacted countries. Together, you are stronger than as individual countries."

"I fear that if all the countries do not work together, all manner of wars, strife, and conflicts will break out over food, coal, oil, charcoal, and firewood. Our civilizations could well breakdown completely if those kinds of desperate actions take place broadly. In short, Stefano, we are all facing the worst crisis mankind has ever had to deal with," Sergio explained his opinion.

He went on, "Another problem will be that people will eventually be unable to pay for their food and heating supplies, especially if the winter is far more severe than we have ever had. All those who make their living growing things will be without any income and be especially vulnerable. In short, it will be a mess unless some organization is established soon, before the calamity strikes. Here in Velona, few are equipped to deal with a severe winter. We barely get snow, but that may well drastically change. We should try to anticipate the problems, which will develop, and arrange for solutions to them ahead of time. If you wait until the problem develops, you will have an incredible mess on your hands. Personally, I'd be overwhelmed by it all."

Stefano had been writing these ideas down as Sergio spoke, giving Sergio some confidence that his advice may be followed. He certainly hoped that Stefano took immediate action, before disaster struck. At last, Stefano spoke again, "Well, dad always did say that in a crisis situation, look to 42 Hampton Way for solutions. Thanks, Sergio. I will go over these and get in touch with the other monarchs. You know, this will be even worse if the Greenway is impacted. If we lose their grain supply for a year, we will have no choice at all but to go all the way down to Demokritos and Annelise for grain. That's a six-month delay. This is going to take some very careful planning!"

He went on, "All of this because somehow Dorota got blown up. I just don't see how this all happened."

Sergio had been debating whether to let Stefano see the truth of the matter. What the heck, he concluded. "Stefano, would you like to see the face of our alien enemy who has caused this catastrophe and what he is planning for all of us?"

"Sure, but how? Where?" Stefano asked, slightly confused by the Chief Detective Inspector.

"Close your eyes. I will join my mind with yours and show you what Bethany and the others are seeing," Sergio said. He gently touched the mind of Stefano and then replayed his memories of what I had sent to Lisa. There was the fifty-foot mantis, Nestor, standing outside our observation room's window. He also showed Stefano what we looked like in Version One."

"Oh dear god! It's huge! Monstrous! So that's our enemy! How can we ever defeat that thing?" he gushed, shocked beyond coherent words.

As he saw the genetic modification results, he paled and nearly gagged. "Oh my god! What's happened to them?"

"That is what this mantis is going to try to do to us all on Tarra, turn our bodies into those awful things," Sergio explained. "However, take heart, Stefano. Bethany has convinced the alien mantis that we would all perish if he turned us all into those things. She's working to get him to modify his designs for us. I hope that she can succeed. If not, we are all doomed to a fate far worse than mere starvation."

Stefano was white as a sheet. He mumbled something. Sergio allowed him time to recover from this shock. At last, he asked, "Can we defeat this alien? Where is the creature at? Can we stop him from doing this to us?"

"Chichulain, but we do not know precisely where that is. We have a good guess of its general location on the western side of the western continent, an uninhabited area. If some of us could get to him, we might be able to kill him. However, since he has that flying ship, that's going to be very difficult. We estimate that it will take us three months even to get to that general location where it's at — who knows how long after that before we find this actual place. Bethany does not think that we have three months. The alien is already hatching some of its eggs, making more of these mantis creatures to help him in his diabolical alterations of our human bodies. She is doing her best to make those modifications as acceptable to us as possible. Still, she hopes to find a way to eliminate the aliens before he can begin his genetic mutations on us all. I sure hope that she can or what results from that may make this food crisis pale in comparison."

"Damn! Damn! Damn! Isn't there any good news at all?" Stefano growled.

"Yes, the dust cloud is not likely to get into the southern half of Tarra. Food supplies down there shouldn't be affected," Sergio attempted to relay something positive.

"With all our mechanical devices, marvelous inventions, it's a crying shame that we cannot stop one alien creature from destroying all humanity in the world," Stefano lamented. The others nodded their agreement with that statement.

"Yes, we are incredibly frustrated, sir. Yet, we will keep on trying until we perish. You have our word on that," Sergio added encouragingly.

Stefano shook Sergio's hand and then he and a pale Barti left. "I'd rather die than be like that," mom said when they were alone again.

"I know Sofia, I know," Tito consoled her. "Have faith in our daughter a little longer." She forced a smile.

Valerio suggested, "Maybe we could all go hide out somewhere underground while this bacteria thing does its evil on everyone. I sure don't want my love losing her arms." Lucianna grinned back at him.

Sergio countered, "I don't know if that would stop it. Perhaps the bacteria linger in the air for a long time. Besides, how would we keep enough food, water, oil, and firewood underground to survive for any extended length of time? If Bethany is right, this Nestor is planning to release his genetic modifying bacteria worldwide. Nowhere will we be immune to it, not as far as I can see."

"We could hide out in those secret tunnels beneath the Appian Way," suggested Valerio.

"None of us here knows where they are," Sergio pointed out. "The ones who know are all in Nestor's prison." Valerio looked very glum and curled up his lips.

"If hiding is a possible way to avoid it, I'll ask Bethany and Marco for directions," Lisa volunteered.

"Thanks, Lisa. You know the thing I don't like about all this?" asked Valerio. "I'm a fighter, always have been. Yet, we now face this alien, and I cannot figure out any way in the world to fight it! If I could just get anywhere near it, I'd give it my all. I feel so frustrated. All we can do is sit back and take whatever it chooses to dole out to us. There ought to be something that we can do!"

"I feel the same way, Valerio," sighed Sergio. "But what can we do? What do we do now? We can react to the food shortages. We can react to the coming harsh, cold winter. We can react to whatever changes this genetic bacteria does to our bodies. But I am sick of only reacting, Valerio. What can we actually do?"

"Throw a potato at it," suggested Sofia. "At least I will have done something! If that is the last time I have my arms, at least I can say that I threw something at the damnable creature!"

Mom's word rang in Sergio's ears, like a throbbing hammer they struck him. A wave of understanding swept over him, his eyes lit up. "Mom! Brilliant! You are wiser than I ever thought!"

"Son, I think that all this has befuddled your brain, perhaps overloaded it. What's a damn potato going to do to this alien and its flying machine? Not a damn thing!" Sofia exclaimed.

"Mom, that's not the point. The real point is that you *did* something; you fought back somehow! Look, we are facing an overwhelmingly powerful enemy. What is our morale about now? Zero. We are all giving up and becoming victims, total effect. Long term, our emotional tones will be in the utter pits, long after all this is over. The answer is incredibly simple, just as you have said, mom. If we take some actions, fight back somehow, someway, no matter whether or not a potato will cause it any harm, the point is that we fought back! That alone will put us back at cause in life and not at effect! Somehow, someway, we all must remain at cause in this battle. Whether we all stand out on our driveway and throw potatoes at the ship when it comes or throw anything else at it, when it strikes us, we will be being cause. That alone will salvage our long term sanity and well-being!"

Sergio was on a roll, "Okay we won't throw potatoes, except as a last resort. We have cannonae. If we shoot them straight upwards, I wonder how far a ball will go? Maybe we can bounce exploding balls off the ship. Who knows, it might cause it some damage. What's the maximum range of our blasters? Probably not enough to reach a flying ship. We can shoot long guns up at them."

"Hey, now you are talking my language!" Valerio exclaimed suddenly very animated. "Yes, we fight back. We get everyone who has a long gun to fire up at the damn ship. We get people to throw rocks if they have nothing else. Maybe a rock will be caught in its engine or something. We fight back."

"Yes, we should make use of the Medical Research Foundation," Lucianna added, suddenly pulling out of her melancholy. "We get them to store up a bunch of samples of our bodies or whatever. Then, after this plague strikes us and alters our bodies, they can work hard on taking new samples and begin working on a cure. Bethany did say that Nestor had a way to undo whatever he does to us. They did get rid of those awful beaks."

"I'll organize a neighborhood watch," mom suggested. "We'll get folks watching the sky for the first sign of the invading flying ship. Then, sound the alarm. We fire everything we have at it. Maybe it will do some good. At least we will go down fighting! I can live with that."

Finally ideas flowed. "Hey, what about sending the caravel to rescue Bethany and the others?" asked Lisa.

Valerio answered, "We wait. Look, we have to take a stand here in Velona and try to fight this alien. Bethany's group is only four; Velona has millions. We must fight for the millions first, Lisa. I couldn't live with myself if I abandon Velona to the aliens, while I go off in search of our four. If I understand what Bethany has been saying, in the three months that it would take to get somewhere near her, this whole genetic thing may be completely over. Time enough afterwards to get to her, her brother, my brother, and sister. We have no choice but to stay here and put up a fight first."

"I see your point, millions versus four, but I still don't like it," Lisa lamented. She knew logically that he was right. Emotionally, she grieved for us, out there imprisoned and being the genetic guinea pigs for this wicked alien creature.

During the lull, Lucianna spoke up, "Valerio, you know that whatever goes up also comes down. We had better be very careful about firing cannonae up into the air — long guns too for that matter. We might end up causing more harm than good, if we are not careful about it."

"Excellent point, we need to organize the cannonae batteries," Sergio agreed. "We set them up such that their falling balls will miss populated areas. Yes, I can see that we have a lot of planning to do and little time to do it in, so come on. Let's all pitch in and get our defense of Velona on the boards!"

Chapter 10 Decisions

For several days, Eve and I stood near the open doorway between the garden and the observation room, keeping watch for the mantis. Marco and Giovanni were at the secret door trying all manner of things to get it to open for us. Our plan was simple, get the door open, sneak around, and get the hang of the layout. Giovanni suggested that we use the blasters to disable the flying ship or ships, if there were more than one. That way, even though Nestor had the bacteria, he would not have the means with which to deliver it. Good plan. Yet the obstacle remained, the door wouldn't open.

"It has to be done by some kind of electrical signal," Giovanni finally admitted defeat.

"Well, we might possibly blast it open with our blasters," Marco said disgustedly.

"Don't! Not yet," I cautioned him. We all knew that the noise of that would bring all the mantises running here. While we had four blasters between us, Eve and I would be pretty must useless with them. Lacking arms, we'd have to sit on the floor, try to aim, and fire them with our feet, not too practical in a fight I thought. That meant the two fellows would have to do all the fighting. Already we'd seen over a dozen little "Nestors" running around, his offspring. They were already around ten feet long, having doubled in size during the past month. Twelve or thirteen to two was poor odds at best. Way too risky, because without our arms to help us, Eve and I would be in trouble.

"Maybe the next time the machine leaves here, we could stick something underneath the door keeping it open a crack," Giovanni suggested. "Then, maybe we could pry it open." I liked that idea, and we four went in search of something solid to insert beneath the stone slab when it came down and for something with which to pry it upwards later. We didn't find much that was usable. The strongest thing we could find was a thick, metal mixing spoon with a long handle. For prying, there was almost nothing but a few garden tools and those had wooden handles. Nevertheless, we decided to try it.

We had to wait two days before the machine came into our prison in the middle of the night. Giovanni was waiting for it, concealed among the garden plants. Just as it exited, he quietly slipped the spoon beneath the opening as the stone slab was coming down. Quickly, he dashed for the cover of the garden once more. Good thing, as the slab hit and mashed the spoon, an alarm sounded, and the door reopened. The machine backed up, and its mechanical arm picked up the spoon and placed it on the floor inside, then left with the door shutting all the way. The next day, we examined the flattened metal of the spoon.

"Well, based on the amount of flattening here," Giovanni explained, "I guess that the stone door weights at least one ton. Its closing speed was not that great, so the force it applied to the spoon can be roughly estimated. Good thing we didn't try to get our bodies underneath it. That stone door sure has a tight, snug fit with the walls and floor."

Stymied again, we discussed more options. At last, I gave in to Marco's suggestion to see if a blaster could make a hole in the side of our prison. If it was noisy, then all hell might break loose. Yet, if it went undetected, we had a chance of getting out and somehow stopping them. That night, based on what little we had seen of the outside of the cell, we decided to see if we could blast through the kitchen wall. We agreed that there was a hallway beyond that stone wall.

Since the noise might bring all thirteen mantises a running, Eve and I sat down on the floor, and the boys put our blasters at our feet. We prepared to fire them as best we could, if the mantis came charging into the kitchen. Of course, we would be "sitting humans," if they did. Marco took up a defensive position, ready to protect all of us. Giovanni prepared to do the actual breakout firing. We all took a deep breath and Giovanni let loose with his blaster. The setting was to disintegrate.

We waited. Nothing happened. "Hurry up," I whispered. Nothing.

"Damn! My blaster is out of charge!" Giovanni exclaimed.

"Here, try mine," Marco suggested, moving to take my blaster instead. Still nothing. Giovanni quickly checked all four of our blasters. Each had been drained of its charge. "Damn! Damn! Damn! I bet Nestor drained them when he captured us."

"Well, there goes that idea and any way that we have of protecting ourselves," Giovanni said sadly. "Now what do we do?"

"If we could get these headbands off of us, we could back out of our heads and cast balls of fire, lightning bolts, and sheets of ice at them," Marco suggested.

"If we could get out of our heads, Bethany and I could wipe them out. I'll wring their necks, and she can pick them up and bash them into the walls," Eve pointed out.

"And we could also get the overall view of this installation and maybe even damage or break some of their equipment that they need to create this bacteria thing," I added.

For about the hundredth time, Giovanni began examining Eve's headband. Still, he could find no way to remove it, not without killing her body and zapping her with an intense electrical blast. We were stuck and stuck well. Nestor did his prison warden job well.

On July 1, Nestor again contacted us. "Oh my, at last I am nearly ready to begin. I wanted you to know that at each home, a complete set of the needed objects for the female mammalian cells will be placed inside as the bacteria is set loose. That way, when the transformations are complete, there will be one set of objects readily available. Based upon the installed memories that you provided, Bethany, each female will intuitively know what she must do and how it must be done. That should help the transition period enormously. However, this, of course, has slowed the whole process down considerably."

"I have reprogrammed the Dispenser Machine to fabricate these items. My crew is loading them onto my ship at this time. I will hover over the towns and villages, coordinating the dropping of the objects, while my offspring will be handling the bacteria delivery systems."

"Will we be left here alone while you are off doing this?" I asked, hoping for more clues, though I had no idea how I could prevent them from doing this to humanity.

"Well, no. That would not be prudent or efficient of me. I will be leaving two of my offspring to watch over things here. One will appear here by the window if you need anything. They will be running the Dispenser Machine, fabricating more of the requisite objects."

His fore-appendages scratched his huge head. "I know that I promised to return you to your homes. I am going to make the first run on that area where you live. Do you wish to return home at this time as I make my first run?"

Damn. I had only a split second to make this decision. Cooped up in our prison, we had no way to stop them. If I said yes, take us with you, would there be any chance that we could stop him? No, not without our blasters. He certainly would not remove our headbands. Unable to be free, we could do absolutely nothing to stop him. We'd just appear back in our home, watching the horrible changes coming over everyone and unable to be of any real assistance.

"No, Nestor. I appreciate your kind offer. However, I feel that we must take the responsibility to see this through. We should wait until you make your last run on Tarra, in case something does go wrong. If it does, we will be here ready to help you figure out what went wrong and perhaps have suggestions on how to fix it," I replied. What I didn't say was that, given more time, we might be able to figure out a way to stop him. Even if Velona inhabitants were genetically modified, perhaps we could somehow save other countries from falling victim to this atrocity.

"Oh my! That is so very kind of you, Bethany. I was so hoping that you would stay longer for that very reason. Although we have taken every precaution, still, something may go wrong. I value your opinion highly. Thank you for your kindness. I must be off. Tomorrow the process will begin."

Humbly, we four headed back to the kitchen. For once, I didn't even want a cup of tea. We four just sat there, lost in our own thoughts. Much later, Lisa made contact with us, and I relayed the awful news to her. Tomorrow the mantis would strike Velona. Although Lisa did a valiant job of hiding her emotions from me, I could sense her intense sadness, mixed with fear and hopelessness. *I agree with your decision to stay, Bethany. If you were here, there is nothing that you can do for us now, except watch it happen to us all. Maybe you four can somehow find a way to stop the aliens yet and contain the bacteria to as few countries as possible.*

I didn't want to tell her how very slim that hope for us actually was right now. She and mom and everyone else were about to be permanently brutalized. We four felt so utterly awful that we just went to bed. I snuggled up to Marco and we both lay there, tears streaming from our eyes. All four of us were imagining the horrors about to be inflicted on those we loved and our millions of fellow countrywomen. While the sexual addiction aspect would be a societal problem, it could be overcome. The additional minor modifications to our bodies were mostly cosmetic and were not of too great a significance. No, it was the stark reality that all women in Velona and who knows where else would now become armless and that their female babies would be born armless forever more was almost too much to bear. We cried and cried, utterly powerless to stop it from happening. If only our blasters we charged. If only we could remove the infernal headbands that forced us to remain inside the body's heads. If only. . .

I tried to think about what I could have done differently. Was there something that I could have said to Nestor to get him to change his mind about making all Tarra into another Dorota? Should I have contacted the Guardian the very instant that we heard of the report of the old drunken man having seen some strange object in the sky over Velona? If I had, would all of this been somehow prevented? Had I doomed all women to having babies every year until their bodies wore out?

I could not fall back on just saying, "Well, I am only a fourteen year old girl, barely of age, lacking in wisdom and experience. That would be untrue. Yes, my body was a teenager now, but I sure wasn't. No, it had been my decisions that were now being implemented worldwide. Me, my own viewpoint was now being forced upon every other person on Tarra, especially the women. What if, in spite of my actions, women just could not handle the awful, horrible, hideous shock of it all? I could be responsible for the deaths of millions of women and girls, and all because I couldn't stop Nestor. Surely, there had to have been something that I could have done but I just didn't see it. I continued to cry.

Maybe I was to blame. All these years, knowing of the mantis threat, I never scoured the entire world looking for additional mantis bases. Hence, I had not found this one, this most important base of them all! I chastised myself for having been so foolish. I should have gone on a quest to search the entire world, found this place, and destroyed it. I should have done that. I continued to cry.

My thoughts drifted to mom, Aunt Marta, Lisa, and Lucianna. I couldn't bear to imagine their shock and horror three days from now as their whole world came crashing down, turning them into helpless victims, so dependent upon others. I dreaded tomorrow's contact with Lisa, envisioning her shock and terror as she relayed the horrid news to me. Mom had killed herself; she couldn't take it. Lucianna, likewise. Bodies, I saw an enormous pile of dead women and girls sitting beside Velona's dock. So many dead that Stefano had no choice but to cart them off to sea and give them unto the ocean.

Despair. I had reached the utter pits of personal despair, so deep that I could never surface again. I stopped crying and just lay there, all hopes, dreams, and goals gone. I was nothing more than a helpless body, nothing more. I slept.

"Damn! That didn't work!" Giovanni's voice woke me. It was the middle of the night. Marco was not beside me. I sat up and got out of bed to see what was going on. Eve too had been roused and we met in the hallway, just as the two boys came walking back to us.

"Sorry, we didn't mean to wake you," Giovanni apologized.

"What's going on? What didn't work?" I asked, suddenly feeling starved, and I had to go to the bathroom fast!

"I tried to grab hold of that signal thing on the machine. I was hoping to rip it off and then later find a way to use it to open the door," Giovanni said downhearted. "Damn machine just picked me off it gently and sat me on the floor, but not until it energized my headband. God, do I have a headache now."

I dashed to the bathroom, Eve on my heels. "I'm hungry," Marco called out to us. I agreed to eat if they'd fix it.

A somber four ate a late night snack and then returned to bed. Somewhere over Velona, our families and countless other families were facing their worst nightmares, one that would now never be ending for the women, not ever, and all because we four could not stop this alien mantis. I cried myself to sleep once more.

At noon, I awoke to the smell of bacon and eggs cooking. Marco was at it, and I cried again, thinking how well he was handling all this. A few minutes later, I joined them in the kitchen. Eve was just scooping out the scrambled eggs; the boys had everything ready.

"Hi sleepy head," Marco attempted to sound cheery, but failed.

"I have some news, Bethany," Giovanni said, as he propped his head on the table. His eyes were red too. "I chatted a bit with the little one, calls himself Nestor 10. Anyway, he told me that their mother ship uses a teleport mechanism to drop off all the goods into the homes. Apparently, there are five such units on the ship, and they have been programmed to drop off seven hundred thousand units per day. Additionally, Nestor has programmed the buzzers, that's the name of the little scout type ships that actually are delivering the air borne bacteria, to also drop off the units. There are eight of them adding another three hundred thousand drop offs per day. According to Nestor 10, it will take Nestor ten days to service the whole of the Sea Princes. After that, he will be returning to resupply. The Greenway comes next, then the Southlands, then Tashien, then two trips are needed for the southern continent with Demokritos and Annelise. The continent that we are in will be done last. I figure we go home in about fifty days — less than two months."

I nodded and sat down to eat in silence. All this was my own fault. I had failed not only the Guardian, but all the people of Tarra now! I sighed and said, "Okay, after we eat, I want you fellows to kill my body. I will then be free to take off and destroy the two mantis guards and somehow open the door to let you all out. When the ships return, I will set about destroying them."

"The hell you are!" Marco protested. "Bethany, listen to what you are saying. That damnable headband is going to keep you stuck right there inside your head, even if your body is dead. Sorry, my love, that is not a viable answer. Nice try, though. Gang, we just keep on thinking up other ways out of this."

"But I don't deserve to live anymore! All this is my fault! I've failed the Guardian and you fellows and mom and dad and everyone on Tarra!" I began to rattle off all the what if's and things that I should have done differently down through the ages.

"Bethany Elizabeth Bartiana! Will you stop that self-pity drivel?" Marco exclaimed, almost slapping me in the face. "All of us feel absolutely awful about this, but there isn't anything that we can do to change the past. We did what we did with no regrets. After all, we only had the word of an old drunken man whose images were slightly confused at the very best. We didn't have real evidence that the mantis was back until after he appeared over Velona after he had destroyed Dorota. So get real, Bethany. We could have tried our blasters that first day in here, but they had no charge in them and wouldn't have worked then either. In fact, you have done a remarkable job for all humanity. Think about it, if you had not intervened with Nestor, we'd all be Version Ones by now and probably dying or dead."

"But mom," I began to cry again.

"Yes, mom and Lisa and Lucianna and everyone else are becoming victims of the mantis just like us. However, thanks to you, they can still live. Now get your head together and help us find a way to defeat these aliens before they wipe out the whole world. We still have most of the world that we can maybe save somehow. Besides, even if we fail to stop Nestor, after he leaves, we can all begin work on a cure. That Medical Foundation you support — perhaps they can work out a cure for this genetic thing. If Nestor can do it, surely they can do it in time."

"Well okay. I guess I will keep on trying until the world is lost. After that, hang me please." I agreed in part. After we ate, I insisted on doing all the dishes. I wanted time alone and was dreading the coming telepathic contact from Lisa. Never before had I dreaded a telepathic link, but today, I was terrified of it.

Hi Bethany. Lisa here. Well, you should have seen it! Mom was incredible. She got off ten long gunshots at the smaller craft. She thinks she hit it five times! We didn't see anything come out of the little ships, so maybe it didn't work. More later. Gotta run, some commotion in the front room. Back in a bit.

Chapter 11 Fireworks over Velona

Towards the end of June, the grey cloud of dust covered all of Velona. At first, I feared that the cloud would make breathing difficult for everyone in the sector. However, Lisa soon reported that the cloud itself was very high in the sky. Only a tiny amount of dust actually settled on rooftops and the streets each day. However, at noon, Velona looked more as it did at dusk!

Stefano ordered the city's electrical lights to remain permanently on from now on until the cloud left the city. For days, the only talk was about the cloud and what its effect would be. Some said it was only a temporary thing — it'd be gone in a few days. Still, everyone heeded Stefano's call to begin to stockpile food, oil, charcoal, and coal.

The newspaper began carrying the instructions to be followed when food supplies ran low. These notices were repeated on the radio newscasts. At first, few believed that this would really be a problem. It was just a dust cloud and a novelty at that. By July 1, flowers had closed, no longer blossoming. Some plants definitely looked wilted, especially the ivy vines that covered our walls around 42 Hampton Way.

During these days, Sergio and Barti both worked with the twenty artillery field commanders, setting up some three hundred cannonae around the rim of Velona. Per Lucianna's instructions about falling explosive balls, the two made very sure that these commanders had their guns properly setup to avoid collateral damage. Since they knew the precise day of the attack, the second of July, but not the time of the arrival of the alien ships, the hundreds of gun crews were stationed at their guns all day and all night, ready for the word to fire. Actually, Stefano gave them orders to fire the moment they spotted the alien ships, if the attack came in the daytime.

If it came at night, Sofia arranged to have a thousand spotters scattered around the city. If they spotted any flying ship, they were to fire their long guns. That first firing contained only powder and cotton wads, no balls, for fear of hitting someone else by accident.

Stefano, via the newspaper and radio, had issued orders for everyone who had a long gun to open fire at the ships when they heard the signal. He hoped that the falling balls would not hurt too many people. Additionally, he called out the entire army of some fifty thousand men. Part of these was dispatched to outlying towns and villages, with orders to shoot any flying ships that they could see.

Sofia took out a one-page notice that read: If you see the alien flying ships and if you do not own a long gun or gun to shoot at them, please pick up and throw rocks at them. With luck, one stone may land in their engines, causing them to crash. Fight back.

Interestingly enough, that same day, every long gun in every weapon store in Velona sold out. By nightfall, there was not a new gun to be purchased anywhere in the city!

As late afternoon of July 2 came, a shot rang out. Suddenly, long gun shots by the thousands echoed throughout the city, dwarfed by the loud booms of the three hundred cannonae, firing a ball every two minutes! Sofia stepped outside and spotted the fleet of aliens hovering over the city. She picked out the smaller craft and began firing as fast as she could. Lisa and Sergio launched balls of fire and lightning bolts at these smaller ships, as did Valerio.

Tito, Sandro, and Marta joined Sofia, firing their MBGs, multi-barreled long guns at the small ships. Lucianna was kept busy reloading, but she also took several shots herself. For several minutes, the noise was utterly deafening, as all Velona fought back against the aliens. For all their efforts, however, no real damage was done, save one small ship needed some slight repairs to its guidance system. As it spun wildly out of control, hundreds of voices cheered.

About an hour later, the firing stopped; the ships had risen above the grey cloud, which obscured the sun. All around Velona, people yelled and cheered the departure of the alien ships, many figuring that they had beaten them off. Sergio and the others knew better.

Unfortunately, in spite of their best efforts, there was some collateral damage. Ten people were killed by falling bullets, and twenty-three more were treated for bullet wounds from falling objects. Two homes suffered damage from an exploding cannonae ball that had somehow gone off trajectory.

"Well, I think that we showed the aliens that we are not going down without a fight!" mom said as they all headed indoors. The thunder of so many cannonae shots still rang in their ears. "Marta, let's rustle up some supper."

"Do you think that they will be back?" Lucianna asked Valerio.

"Dunno, but I think that they might have been surprised by our stiff resistance," he replied. "That was quite a bombardment. You did well, dear." Lucianna smiled, she had at that, she thought to herself.

"I didn't see any of the ships dropping anything on us," she ventured what was uppermost in her mind, as it was for all the women in our house.

"I didn't either; maybe they never got the chance to let it loose on us," Valerio tried to sound hopeful.

Sergio, ever practical, commented, "Well, according to Lisa according to Bethany, the stuff is invisible and doesn't have any odor. So Valerio, not seeing anything probably doesn't mean anything."

"I — I — I guess we'll know for sure in three days," Lisa attempted to say. "That's how long Bethany says it takes to fully work. God, I hope it doesn't work!"

"Me too," Lucianna squeaked timidly. She was terribly afraid of becoming so utterly helpless. How could she continue to invent new things? Her life would be ruined and Valerio probably would no longer want to marry her.

After they dined, Marta asked the kids to do the dishes. Sofia took out her violin and spent the evening playing. "Look, this may be the very last time in my life that I will be able to make music. Music is my life and it is about to be taken from me." Tito sat beside her all night, listening to her playing and kissing her when she paused. Marta wanted to hold books and read, explaining that without arms, she could no longer hold, read, or even carry books — the things that meant everything to this librarian.

None wanted to go to bed that night. The women were just too afraid of what would happen. However, by midnight, they were so tired that they allowed themselves to be escorted to bed. They slept in, not so much because of their late night as the fact that the daytime was barely dusk. The grey cloud hovered above the entire sector, blocking out the sun.

"Does anyone see anything wrong with me?" asked Lisa the instant that she awoke. "I can't see anything yet. Well maybe my ears are bigger. Anyone?"

Marta, Sofia, and Lucianna also begged others to look at them and tell them what they saw that was different. All four women spent several minutes staring into the various mirrors around the house, before they headed to the kitchen, where Tito and Sandro were cooking breakfast for everyone.

Most concluded that perhaps everyone's ears were getting a bit longer. The women claimed that their arms seemed weaker than usual, though. Lisa kept looking into the mirror every few minutes and swore she could see her ear lobes lengthening. Finally, the hour to make contact with me arrived, and she concentrated and reached out to me.

Hi Bethany. Lisa here. Well, you should have seen it! Mom was incredible. She got off ten long gun shots at the smaller craft. She thinks she hit it five times! We didn't see anything come out of the little ships, so maybe it didn't work. More later. Gotta run, some commotion in the front room. Back in a bit.

Lisa heard some noises and loud talking coming from the front room. Suspecting something awful had happened, she broke off the contact and headed out to see. She found the other seven looking over the large pile of objects now sitting in the middle of the floor. "They just appeared here, Lisa. Magic. Poof!" Marta explained as her daughter entered the room. "One minute they were not there, and the next, there is all this stuff."

"I sort of have some vague idea what this is for," Sofia said, staring at the low writing desk.

"Me too, mom," Lucianna added, picking up a large handled mug and examining it.

"What a weird feeling," Marta said. "Somehow I feel I know what this stuff is for."

Lisa had a sick feeling in her stomach as she spied the slant back chair with rollers on its legs. She too had an innate sense of how it was to be used, and she knew what that meant! Her early childhood last lifetime came flooding back to her. She had her arms removed by the Dorota doktors, when her parents had been deceived into joining that movement.

Lisa sat down and tried to calm down. She reached out to me again. *Hi. Me again. Well, I guess it is going to happen now. All this stuff has magically appeared in our front room. You know — the kind of stuff that we are going to need when we don't have arms anymore. I guess all our fighting didn't stop them. Bethany, find a way to squash them for us all, please!*

I will, Lisa. Somehow, I will. How's mom taking it?

Pretty good. She seems to have some idea how all this stuff is to be used. I sure hope we can somehow manage. The sky is so dark that is seems like dusk and it is noon! I am getting really scared that all the crops are going to fail, and we're going to starve to death. I wish you were here. I miss you. You always seem to know what to do in a crisis. Me, I just fight and protect. Didn't do a very good job this time, did I?

I sensed she was about to breakdown. *Yes, you did, Lisa. Fighting against the mantis with their overpowering arsenal is more than anyone of us can handle. You've done well. I am counting on you to hold the families together until I can get back. Contact me at any time now. Please, keep me up to date. Give mom my love, will you?*

Okay. I better go now and help them figure out what to do with all these things. Bye.

As she broke contact with me, it was all that I could do to keep from bawling right there. "It's happening isn't it?" Marco said very softly. I nodded and he put his arms around me and held me tightly for some time. I needed it and him.

The rest of the day, the telefono at our house rang nearly continuously, as Sergio was kept up to date. Sightings were now coming in to Velona from the outer towns up and down the various spoke roads. The alien crafts were spotted as far away as Alta, our northernmost town. Stefano called to report that a pile of objects suddenly appeared in his house. Barti reported a similar occurrence at his home. Soon, Sergio received reports that hundreds were reporting the same phenomenon as well. By supper, he received a report from Fortress d'Grange that the alien ships were there and being fired upon as well, though he held no hope that the ships would be stopped there.

As he sat sipping a cup of tea, he suddenly remembered how last lifetime, as Cosima, he had manipulated the shoulders of our eight little girls and caused their bodies to regrow their missing arms. He smiled. "If I did it then, I surely can do it now to Lucianna and Lisa. Mom and Sofia are fully-grown. It didn't work on the grownups, just us kids. Well, I'll just have to try it again."

"What's that Sergio?" Lisa asked. "Oh yes, I remember now, Cosima. You did something to our bodies and we regrew our arms."

"I just remembered it. I promise you, Lisa, I'll give it a try if you lose yours this time." She gave her lover a big hug and kiss. Suddenly, both discovered just how incredibly pleasurable their kisses were becoming and continued to passionately make out. Sergio thought that at least this would keep her mind off the doomsday scenario befalling all of them.

By evening, the women's arms appeared to be very thin and weak. Tito and Sandro handled making supper and dealt with the dishes, along with Valerio and Sergio's help. Both boys had spent much of their time, when not called to the phone, on moving the stuff from the living room into the rooms where they would be most needed. Unfortunately, both realized that these items were sufficient for one person only, save the kitchen furnishings.

That night, the four men headed into the basement to see what they could scavenge from all the stuff that we had stored there from last lifetime when so many armless women lived here. Thank god that we are mostly pack rats and seldom discard things! They took an inventory of what was there.

The next morning, Lisa awoke to a shriek. It was Sofia. As she attempted to get out of bed, she added her shriek to the others. Her arms were now half as long as they used to be and so weak that she could barely move them. Sergio rushed to her side at once.

All day long, the men worked on kitchen conversion, removing all the counters, the sink, and stove. Then, the replaced them with either items from our basement or from those that had mysteriously appeared yesterday. Again, Sergio was frequently called to the telefono, receiving updates. However, most of these effects he already knew. They only confirmed to him that the phenomenon was not only citywide but also sector-wide.

By evening, the four men had the kitchen entirely redone and stood back admiring their efforts. "Now that was a fine piece of work," Tito exclaimed. "Well done, boys. Your moms and sisters will be thanking us one day, I hope."

By the following morning, the genetic modification process was nearly complete. Interestingly enough, our parents didn't rise at first light, as they always did. It was not because we no longer had first light because of the dust cloud. Rather, the four teens heard the two couples. They were still in bed and really going to it.

Lisa giggled, "Mom's really doing it, isn't she?"

Valerio whispered, "Yes, let's leave them alone. She needs this, I think."

"What's mom doing?" asked Lucianna, struggling to find a way to wipe the sleep from her eyes. She'd heard noises coming from her folk's room and wandered out of her room, curious.

"Sh," Sergio whispered. "They are making love. Let's let them have this private time, sis. Wow, do you ever look good today!"

"Huh? How so? I've no arms at all now," she asked.

"Come on, I'll show you." He put his arm around her and led her to her bedroom mirror. "See?"

"Wow!" She turned her head from side to side. "Well, I like my lips. Now I look grown up, and I won't have to learn how to deal with eye makeup. Lisa was showing me how, but I couldn't get the hang of it yet. It does look good, doesn't it? Oh, my ears!"

"Yes, I noticed them too. When they rub my shoulders, it feels really — well, I don't know how to say it," he whispered back to her.

"Sensuous, big brother. Now I am going to be moving my head around a whole lot! Way cool. Oh, my waist! Golly, it is really small now!"

Sergio smiled, "Now you won't have to wear those nasty corsets, and you can wear all the fancy Annelise dresses you desire. I bet mom will let you wear them now. She was always hesitant to let you girls start wearing them until you were fourteen. But now, you don't need them. I must say, sis, you look good! If I weren't your brother. . ." he teased her and complimented her as well. She beamed, forgetting about her new condition for a moment.

"I wonder how Lisa looks?" she said. "Come on, I hear them, let's go see." The two headed out to the kitchen where Lisa and Valerio were looking each other over.

"Hi love. Wow, Lisa! You look ravishing!" Sergio exclaimed as he got his first look at Lisa this morning. Her waist was thin; her red lips looked incredibly inviting. He went to her, put his arms around her, and they passionately kissed. Before long, their passions very nearly got out of control.

At the same time, Valerio saw his heartthrob, Lucianna, and gasped. "Wow, Lucianna. You look stunning! So grown up. I like your new looks. Come here; let me hug you!" The two also embraced and Lucianna felt a surge of incredible sensations flooding her body. So did Valerio, who fought hard to keep them under control.

The four teens now realized what was happening with their parents. "I wish we were married right now!" Lucianna exclaimed. "I can hardly wait!" Lisa grinned, her thoughts precisely! Maybe Sofia would allow Lucianna to marry sooner. Then, they could marry as well.

"We'd better fix breakfast for our folks today," Sergio finally said, forcing himself apart from Lisa. They agreed and began deciding what to fix.

"Oh, I seem to know how to do things," Lucianna exclaimed, rather startled. "I've got some kind of strange memories of how to do this. I sit in the sliding chair like this and use my feet like this to stir the pot."

"Well, I'll be! Yes, Lucianna. So do I. But it's not those from my last lifetime! I recognize these. These are Bethany's memory snippets! We have bits of her memory of how she used to do things when she was living in Dorota! Incredible."

Lucianna sighed, "Oh, I feel so much better now! I was terrified about losing my arms. I wouldn't be able to do anything anymore, but now I rather seem to know just how to do some things. I don't feel nearly as scared as I ought to be. I wonder if mom has them too?"

"Has what?" Sofia said from the doorway. She looked very flushed, a reddish color in her cheeks, a sparkle in her eyes, reflecting off the bluish eye shadow, which accentuated her eyes perfectly. Tito stood behind her, resting his arm on her shoulders. He looked incredibly contented this morning, Lucianna thought. Sergio smiled, guessing why they both looked so good this morning.

"Memories of how to do things, mom," Lucinna explained. "Somehow, I sort of know how I am supposed to cook like this, with no arms. I am not so scared anymore. Well, a little bit, I guess. Well a lot actually, but it's as if I somehow know that I can do some things. We're supposed to sit at these low tables, mom."

"Right, Lucianna. We are. Yes, I am sort of remembering that too. We use those mugs with the big handles don't we? And those sliding chairs, we use them to get around as we cook. One foot moves us while the other holds the cinnamon jar. Weird that I should somehow know this," Sofia said, curiously.

"Know what?" Marta asked. She and Sandro had come up behind the two. She too looked radiant and totally satisfied this morning, as did Sandro for that matter. "You know, as I passed the front room, I saw those desks and somehow I just know how I can hold my books and read. I do hope that we can get some of those for the library. You know those two baskets on the ends or the wooden bar with the V-shaped legs; we can use those to carry our books around. Strange that I should somehow know that."

Everyone giggled and began talking at once. Soon, they all realized that they had somehow gotten some old memories of Bethany's, which gave them ideas on how to do the ordinary things of life. The men insisted on making the breakfast today. Meanwhile the four women chatted about this incredible new sense that they had, each pointing out new ideas to the others, who quickly realized that they too had the very same memories.

Sofia asked Lisa, "Say when you contact Bethany today, please give her my heartfelt thanks for what she managed to do to get her memories of how to do things into our minds! Without them, we would be nearly hysterical about now. Even Lucianna is adapting infinitely better than I thought. Tell her that she had somehow given us some hope for life like this. Tell her I love her very, very much!" Lisa grinned and promised to do so.

"Hey, I can't ride my putt-putt anymore!" Lucianna suddenly

realized. She had no memories of how to do that.

"Right, Lucianna," Lisa replied. "They didn't have putt-putts on Dorota when Bethany was there. It looks like we are going to have to figure out some things for ourselves. Damn, I can't ride mine either, Sergio! How am I ever going to be able to go with you now?"

"Sis," Sergio said with a wry smile; Lucianna looked up. "First thing you must design is a modified putt-putt so that my assistant can accompany her Chief Detective Inspector to the crime scenes. While you are at it, fix up one for yourself. Say, and fix one for Bethany and one for Eve too. I expect that they will want them as soon as they get back." She grinned and realized that if she ever wanted mobility as she had, she was going to have to do something about it. Either that, or wait until Giovanni returned. He was the other half of this invention team.

"Well, you know if we had two rear wheels instead of one, we would not have to worry about trying to keep our balance. And if the foot controls were moved up to the handlebars and we had a sloped back seat like our dining chairs, we could do it easily. I'm going to have to get some drawings made first thing after breakfast. Perhaps one of you could take them and me to the DAE Enterprises so I can get the engineers working on it quickly." Sergio promised that he would do so as soon as she was ready. He had a feeling that this engineering design company would soon get quite a workout. He also realized that there would be plenty of profits to be made by small companies building things to help the women of Velona and other countries impacted by the mantis mutations.

After breakfast was done, the women insisted on experimenting with doing the dishes. The fellows continued finishing up the last of the installation work from the night before. They carried more writing desks up from the basement and all the slanted chairs that were in good condition. During all this, the telefono rang. Lucianna called out to Sergio, who was in the basement, "Sergio. It's Stefano, says it's important." He raced up the stairs, very surprised to see Lucianna holding the receiver in one foot, while leaning against the wall. She whispered, "See, I figured out how to use the telefono." He gave her a quick kiss, took the receiver, and put it to his ear. Speaking into the cone, he answered.

"Good to hear that Lucianna was able to get the telefono," Stefano said. "Caresa and little Andrea are taking this rather well, all things considered. They seem to sense how they can do some things. Say, can you come over and lend us a hand trying to assemble all these things?"

"Sure, give me a couple minutes."

"Another thing, I have been thinking. What about all the women who may be living alone or whose husbands are away? I am going to send out my soldiers to visit every home in the entire sector. I want to personally see that every woman is given all the help that they may need in the short term."

"Hey, fabulous idea. Be with you in say thirty minutes. I'll bring my hammer," Sergio jested. When he hung up, seven had gathered around him. Quickly, he told them that Stefano needed help installing stuff and that he was going to send men to every house in the sector to help those who needed help.

"Wow. He's right! Carmela's husband is off on a purchasing trip in Barcella. She's all by herself with her two daughters. I bet about now they are in a panic," Marta exclaimed. They lived two doors down from us.

"Okay, gang. Let's do our part for our neighbors. We're pretty well setup here. So pack up your tools, fellows, we will go door to door around here helping out," Sofia ordered. Sergio grinned. Mom was getting in on the action as well.

Lucianna told her brother, "Say, the putt-putts can wait a day. I'll do the drawings tonight. You had better help Stefano, Caresa, and Andrea. I'll help around here." He gave his sister a big hug. By the time that Sergio's putt-putt fired to life, the other seven headed out the front door, carrying a box of tools with them. First stop was Carmela's home. They came none too soon, the poor woman was hysterical and crying at the same time, unable to do anything for herself or her two daughters.

While Sofia and Marta worked on calming Carmela down, Lucianna engaged the two young girls in a game of hide and seek. The three men, with Lisa helping as she could, began assembling the new kitchen setup. Since this would require the better part of the day, once Carmela had recovered, the women took her and her daughters back to our house. Together, they whipped up a second breakfast, with Carmela now starting to get some ideas in her mind about how she could do these things. Once they were fed, they then whipped up lunch for the three men and themselves.

They experimented with the yokes and proudly carried lunch back for the working fellows. "Honestly, we had the hardest time with the stupid doorknobs!" Lisa exclaimed. "You are going to have to do something about them soon."

"Yes, Tito, it takes us ages of fiddling to get a doorknob turned," Sofia added. Before they left Carmela's, they removed all the doorknobs on the interior doors as well as the exterior doors.

"Don't worry, we will have to get special doorknobs for us all, ones that you can just push down on with your foot to open it," Tito explained. "The blacksmiths will certainly be busy making them in vast numbers, Carmela. As soon as I can get a hold of some, I'll return and fix yours for you." She leaned into him and he gave her a hug.

Our group returned home satisfied, but knowing that now there was a vast amount of work to be done in every building in the entire sector. So much had to be done and quickly. That evening, Stefano, his twenty-two year old wife, Caresa, and their six year old daughter Andrea, came by to thank Sergio personally and to report on the initial findings by his soldiers.

While the women headed off to work on making a pot of tea, Stefano began, "Well, that was the smartest move that I have ever made! Good lord, you would not believe the troubles that my men found so far. I've ordered all available men into an emergency work force. Starting in the morning, I'll have crews visiting every home. We've a list of the ones in which there are no men there to help the women. Those will be done first. Next, they'll deal with those who have men, but who haven't a clue how to install a kitchen or a cabinet. What a mess!"

"Are there any casualties yet?" Sergio asked. He knew that this was my primary concern and why I had worked so hard to get Nestor to do what he had done.

"I am afraid so. We've pulled ten women's bodies from the bay. There are dozens and dozens who have been taken to the Trauma Center. Yet, ten out of nearly a million and a half, that's not bad. I figured the numbers might have been in the thousands, personally," Stefano answered.

"Well, you can thank Bethany for that. If she had not gotten Nestor to implant her memories in every woman and gotten him to fabricate all these necessary objects, you would have had tens of thousands of suicides already," he replied.

His eyes opened wide. "She did that? Those are her memories that Caresa has? Oh my goodness. I had no idea! Bethany is the savior of Velona! Without those memories, Caresa would have likely killed herself! With those objects and with your help installing them, she and I have a good fighting chance to make this somehow work out. Still, I like Tito's idea to remove the doorknobs. I am going to see if the steel plant can somehow start turning out lever style knobs. If so, I will see that every home in the sector gets all of them that they need."

"That will make you beloved by all women in Velona!" Sergio replied. He grinned. He then asked, "Any word from the other sectors? How wide spread has this first attack been?"

"Fortress d'Grange was hit. Actually, I believe that by the end of the week, the entire eight Sea Princes will have been attacked," Stefano answered grimly. "Since we are the first ones hit, I am relaying all the actions that we are finding necessary to the other monarchs. Somehow, we must survive this atrocity!"

Sergio put in a plug for us. "Thanks to Bethany, Eve, Marco, and Giovanni, we stand a good chance of surviving this and remaining strong." Stefano smiled and nodded. Both looked up as Sofia came slowly into the room. She balanced a yoke on her shoulders with cups and biscuits in one basket balanced by the teapot in the other. After she squatted down, setting the yoke's frame on the ground, the men rose.

"Here you go. I think it best if you take them and pour your own tea," Sofia explained.

"Mom, you did great!" Sergio gave her a big, strong hug. She smiled and lifted the empty yoke and returned to the kitchen, where the women were practicing drinking for themselves and chatting about their makeup, ears, and waistlines.

Later after their company had gone, Tito, Sofia, Sandro, and Marta called for a family conference. Sofia explained, "Kids, we have come to realize something that is important. We know what Bethany has said about the addiction side effect that they had to go along with. We know just how strong that is. We've been talking about this and we've decided that you kids should be married immediately, Bethany, Eve, Marco, and Giovanni as well. That way, as married men and women, you should have less difficulties fighting against this new natural urge to procreate." Boy was mom ever being polite about the animal urge that Nestor had implanted in us all. His idea was that this would keep everyone inside their heads. Ha. There were now million plus victims from Dorota who would soon need new baby bodies.

"Even me?" asked Lucianna, who was thirteen, trying hard to become fourteen and of age.

"Yes, dear. We can fudge your birthday a few months, if that is okay with you," mom suggested. Lucianna grinned from ear to ear.

Mom explained, "I talked this over with Caresa and she believes that, if Lisa will make a Mind Link to the four and Stefano's sister, Daniela, then Daniela will marry them telepathically." Daniela West Po was Velona's current High Priestess and co-ruler, though she only handled the spiritual side of the sector's affairs. "What do you think, kids?" Lisa and Sergio, who had been waiting the longest to get married, being the oldest of us all, squealed with glee.

The next morning, Daniela arrived by motor-car. While her husband watched and bore witness to the marriages that he could at least see, Daniela performed a simple wedding ceremony. She too now realized why this was so urgently needed. She and Bernardo had already experience it in their bedroom. Lisa Mind Linked us four and Daniela and took her place beside Sergio, who put his arm around her thin waist, holding her tightly.

"We are gathered here today to unite these four couples in Holy Matrimony. Each of these men and women have chosen of their own free will to join their lives together as one family, from this day forth until death do them part," Daniela began. Some ten minutes later she pronounced, "I give the world, Mr. and Mrs. Stefano Bartiana, Mr. and Mrs. Valerio Angela, Mr. and Mrs. Marco Angela, Mr. and Mrs. Giovanni Bartiana. You may now kiss your lovely brides!" Our parents and Bernardo clapped loudly. Tito and Sandro had to wipe the tears from Sofia and Marta's cheeks, however. All their children were now getting married on the same day, just a bit emotional, to say the very least.

One by one, the new couples gave a hug to Daniela, who was just as armless as the rest of the women. After Sergio hugged her, Lisa came up to her and suddenly realized how she should hug. At the same instant, Daniela also realized this and their legs rose and rather wrapped around each other. Lucianna called out, "Oh yes, that is how we are to do it. I somehow remember it! Strange." Yes, strange days had definitely arrived for everyone in the Sea Princes.

Chapter 12 All Because We Got Married

I have no words with which to express just how I felt that third day after the attack on Velona. I rose dreading the worst, that my mother had killed herself, that my sister had thrown herself beneath the steam train engine. All manner of wild imaginings flew through my mind that morning.

Lisa contacted me earlier than usual. She told me how well things were going and relayed what mom had said for her to tell me. I cried. I just broke down and bawled. Marco feared the worst had happened and held on to me tightly. Hearing how well that mom was coping and that she truly thanked me for having somehow gotten memories of how to live as we now were installed in her and all other women — I just snapped into the present time, my despair and apathy vanished.

"You did it, Bethany!" Marco exclaimed wildly as I broke the news to him and to Eve and Giovanni.

"No, we all did it," I replied. "We all did it." Later, Lisa kept me up to date on all the goings on that third day. I cried again when I heard that they had managed to make lunch for the fellows and even carried it over to them using the yokes! I cried when Lisa told me about how Stefano dropped by and mom insisted that she, Marta, and Caresa make tea for the men and how mom had brought it into Sergio and Stefano.

I told her to thank Stefano for me for his brilliant thoughtfulness of sending men to check on every house in the sector and then sending work crews to help those in dire need. To me, I saw this as a miracle. Instead of our whole country being wiped out by all women committing suicide, only ten had done so thus far. Now I realized that my intervention, while not preventing the mantis from doing what it desired, I had minimized its destruction. I knew from my own experience that most women would have given up entirely had Version One been implemented. I also knew that without the needed objects with which to survive and the memories of how to do things and to use those objects, women would also have just given up and found ways to succumb. Even with them, some, like Carmela, had gone into hysterics and would have died had it not been for my folks and others sent by Stefano to help.

What none of us expected was Lisa contacting us later that night! We had already gone to bed. There was little to do locked up in our prison as we were.

Hi, Lisa here. I have the greatest news for you! You'll never guess what our parents have decided! Are you ready for this? We are going to be married tomorrow morning! Yes! Daniela will marry us at our house. All four of us couples. Even Lucianna! Your mom insists upon her getting married too! I will Mind Link Daniela to you four. Isn't this just incredible?

Just the greatest thing? More in the morning, Sergio is trying to kiss me and oh. . . The connection abruptly ended and I knew why it had!

"More trouble?" Marco asked.

"Yes," I tried to keep a straight face. "Big, big, big trouble for you, Marco," I teased him.

"What trouble is Marco in?" Eve called out from her bedroom.

"Is he all right?" the worried voice of Giovanni put in.

"Giovanni, you are in big, big trouble too. Not you, Eve," I added. I suddenly found Marco sitting up in our bed, a worried look on his face. Eve and Giovanni raced into our bedroom. I couldn't withhold it any longer.

"Lisa just told me that tomorrow morning early that Daniela is going to marry all eight of us at the same time. Even Lucianna and Valerio too. Mind Link for us four. Now Marco, you are going to be in big trouble. You will have me for the rest of your life! You too, Giovanni, you are going to be stuck with Eve for the rest of your life too!"

Eve squealed with happiness, while Giovanni grinned and picked her up and carried her back into their bedroom. He called out, "What a woman to be stuck with!" Eve giggled.

Marco, on the other hand, began tickling me. "You fiend! You had me really worried there for a minute! Now accept your punishment!" The tickling soon ended with a simple kiss. Well a simple kiss now very, very quickly escalated into a highly passionate round of kissing.

The next morning, we four gathered in our kitchen awaiting the ceremony. Lisa gave us a little advance warning, just as Daniela arrived at our home. *Oh, this is so fabulous. So wonderful,* Daniela exclaimed as she found her mind joined with we four and Lisa. She had never experienced anything as intimate as telepathy.

We are gathered here today to unite these four couples in Holy Matrimony. Each of these men and women have chosen of their own free will to join their lives together as one family, from this day forth until death do them part, Daniela began. Some ten minutes later she pronounced, *I give the world, Mr. and Mrs. Stefano Bartiana, Mr. and Mrs. Valerio Angela, Mr. and Mrs. Marco Angela, Mr. and Mrs. Giovanni Bartiana. You may now kiss your lovely brides!*

Thank you Daniela. This means everything to us, I sent her, and the connection was broken. Lisa was experiencing too much to maintain her concentration on the Mind Link. Marco gave me a wedding kiss, while Giovanni did the same to Eve. Within a minute, Marco merely picked me up and carried me back into our bedroom. Giovanni, carrying Eve, was right behind him. Finally, we let our passions run free; our kissing led to far more, far more indeed. I felt utterly and completely satisfied. So did Marco, who whispered, "God, do I ever love you, Bethany."

Much later, we rose to grab a bite. Eve came out, followed by Giovanni. Her face was highly flushed and her eyes sparkling. Eve said apologetically, "Bethany, I have to apologize for all those years that we were married — you know, when I was Dita. Until now, I had no idea what I was depriving you of by your being married to a woman."

"Now wait a second, Eve, er Dita, er Renzo. You didn't deprive me of anything. You gave me very satisfying pleasure and your love. That is what is important. Believe me, what we are now experiencing is a highly exaggerated sensation due in part to Nestor's modifications. Yes, sex is great, but this that we are now experiencing goes way beyond that. So please don't think that this is what we didn't have, dear. In my opinion, our marriage back then was absolutely the greatest!" Eve thought that she understood and gave me a hug.

"All I can say is that sex has become absolutely electrifying," Marco explained to Eve. "Louis and I really enjoyed making love to each other last lifetime, Eve, but what we are experiencing now is many, many time more magnified somehow." Back then, he was Bianca.

"That's it!" exclaimed Giovanni. "Electricity. That's the secret. Come on, gang. I need wire and something that might be magnetic. I may have a way to get that door opened!"

"Huh?" I said, the sudden change of topic took us by surprise. He explained that if we could find the right items, he might be able to make something that would open the secret door. Off we went on a scavenger hunt. Finding the wire proved difficult until the fellows moved the cooling machine out from the wall. Giovanni found that there was quite a lot of extra wire in it beyond what was needed for the short run to the wall fixture. Using a knife, he removed the excess and wired the shortened pieces back together. The two splices were five inches from each other so that they wouldn't short out, according to him.

"I need something metal, like a spoon, but not a spoon." After some searching, we cut one of the heavy metal stays from my now unused corset. Giovanni then set to work. Carefully, he began wrapping the wire around the stay, but one of the wires only went five times around, while the other he wrapped many times. After this point, I rather lost track of what he was doing. I realized that Arsenio, or rather Lucianna, was really the electricity expert and that I knew very little about such.

The next morning, he was ready to begin experimenting. "The wild variable will be the number of wrappings needed to produce just the right level to trigger that sensor there. You two keep watch. If you see any movement out our window, holler." Eve and I stood near the garden's entrance to the observation room. If we actually entered it, the alarm would sound, bringing one of the little Nestors to see what we wanted.

After a half hour, we two tired of just standing there and moved back a ways and sat on the small stone wall around the garden itself. Soon, even this became boring. "Move your head from side to side," Eve suggested. I tried it and received quite an interesting sensation from the tips of my long ear lobes. Thus occupied, we continued to sit and stare out the window. Twice that morning, we spotted one of the little mantises and called out our warning.

Finally, Giovanni called for a lunch break. Eve and I made lunch, though we had them bring us the ingredients. We whipped up a tasty beef stew. Afterwards, we decided to let them deal with the dishes, while she and I sipped our tea. Giovanni was silent the whole time, but I decided to allow him this time to think. If he could just get our door open, we had a chance. A chance at exactly what I didn't know yet.

We spent the afternoon doing much the same. Late that afternoon, I suddenly heard a grating sound. Eve and I turned and saw the secret door sliding up and then immediately down once more. The grin on Giovanni's face was electrifying! Eve rushed over to him and threw herself on him. Of course, he grabbed on to her and returned her embrace. Marco came grinning over to me. "He did it, amazing." We kissed as well. His job had been to plug his end of the wires into an outlet when Giovanni signaled him.

Again, we let the fellows bring us the ingredients, while Eve and I rustled up some supper. We celebrated by having a thick, juicy steak with lots of vegetables. Over dinner, Giovanni explained. "We can now open the door, but from this side only. The only difficulty is that I need Marco's assistance to plug the wires into the outlet when I am ready up by the sensor. My makeshift signal causes it to rise, but then it lowers almost at once. There will be no time for Marco to get over to it and out before it closes again. Worse, once we are out, we have no way of getting back inside. This might be a one shot affair, I'm afraid."

"I wish we could explore around here first. We need to know more about this place, but then there are two mantises out there, and we have no way of handling them," I mused.

Eve suggested, "Bethany, you or I could go out. The fellows can open it and one of us could scamper out and explore a bit. When we need to get back inside, we can tap on the wall or something."

"Wait a minute! I can't let you go out there by yourself, Eve. I mean not as you are now. What if you get into some kind of trouble or something," Giovanni became protective of her.

"I know, Giovanni, I feel rather helpless like this you know, but it is obvious that it has to be either Bethany or me that goes out, if we are to do this. Either that or we all break out and take our chances. I agree with her. We need far more knowledge of this place. Besides, it takes three of us to operate the door, what with one of us watching for the mantis," Eve insisted.

We discussed it further, and at last, Giovanni had little choice but to agree with her. "Okay, let's make this first escape a very short one. I'll open it when Bethany gives the all clear sign. As it goes up, you dash outside. As soon as the door is closed, I want you to tap on the wall, give us the signal. I am very worried that the stone will deaden your signal, and we won't be able to hear you. If that's the case, we must know about it right away. So after the door closes, I will count to twenty and then reopen it. You be signaling during that time. If I hear you, I will open it sooner, but you be ready to jump back inside if I don't hear you. Twenty seconds, okay?" She agreed.

We headed back to the garden room and took our places, while the fellows positioned the wire gizmo once more. Eve crouched low beside the secret door, ready to move under it as soon as it rose enough. She certainly didn't want it to come down upon her! I looked closely for any sign of the mantis pair. Finally satisfied that there was no movement outside our window, I gave the all clear word. Giovanni did a quick countdown and activated his invention. The grating sound came as the stone rose. Eve ducked under it and out into the room.

None of us expected what happened next. Eve cried out in pain and fell down on the stone floor, just inches from the door. Giovanni acted like a hare; he grabbed her leg and pulled her back inside with a mighty jerk. Her head cleared the opening just as the stone shut tightly against the floor! Eve had a most narrow escape for sure!

Giovanni told Marco to bring the device and he carried Eve back to their bedroom. Marco and I followed soon after. When we entered their room, he had Eve lying on the bed and she was coming to. "Oh my head!" she moaned. Giovanni instinctively began massaging her head.

"Oh yes! More, that helps." Soon she'd recovered. I already guessed what had happened. "The second I cleared our room, the headband began sending massive waves of pain through my head. I just collapsed on the ground, unable to move or do anything," she explained. "Guess now I will have a headache all night. Bummer, that didn't work. So close and yet so far, Giovanni."

I added, "Well, we ought to have expected that. He is running this as if he were a prison warden. I'd sure have these headbands activate if a prisoner of mine attempted to leave the prison without my permission."

"Hum, then either we are in some kind of field which nullifies the headband's pain generating unit or there is something outside our cell here which activates it," Giovanni suggested.

"Or the headbands contain something with activates the moment they leave the room," I added. "Perhaps when Nestor takes us out, he turns that off so our headbands don't activate."

"Well, we are at least one step closer to getting out of here," Giovanni said rather glumly. He had such high hopes that were now dashed.

"Let's keep on trying to find a way to get the headbands off of us," I suggested, though not with much hope I admit.

The next day, Nestor summoned us to the observation window. I half expected that he had discovered our breakout attempt and would punish us for it. Well, I intended to explain to him that we had to try.

"Ah, good morning, Bethany. I am back for a few days to resupply. I wanted to report to you that all is going according to our plans. I have swept over the western half of what you call your dog bone continent, from the sea up to the mountain range which divides it in half and all the way over to the desert lands. There are so few people out in the desert that I will pick them up later on. Everything is working well. As I came back over your city, I detected no major change in its population. Conclusion: few have taken their lives there, so your suggestions must be working well. My compliments, Bethany."

He continued, "In two days, I will be ready for the next flight. I'll pick up that big island just off shore from your land and sweep inland through that area that is full of farms and crop lands. I will be able to get all of them, but not on out onto those extensive grasslands beyond there. I have to revise my number of trips. It is taking a bit more time than I estimated. Still, all is going very well indeed."

"I had thought that I could hatch some additional offspring to lend me a hand, but I don't have any more small jumper ships for them to use. That would just be a waste of the eggs. Two of them have been sufficient to operate the machinery here, preparing the next load of needed objects. I hope that you won't be too upset if you remain here for eight or nine weeks instead of the six that I had originally planned that would be needed to cover all the land masses."

"No, that's okay, Nestor. We want to see this through in case some troubles arise. Take as long as you need." He bowed and left, while we returned to the garden to chat over this news.

"The Greenway goes down in two more days. Damn!" Eve said as she sat down in a huff on the side wall of the garden, still frustrated that she had been unable to get beyond the door last night.

"I sure wish that I had been conscious when Nestor put these things on our heads in the first place. That might give me a clue on how to remove them," Giovanni complained. "You know, do the process in reverse."

"Reverse! That's it," it suddenly hit me. "We are going about this all wrong. Nestor is a creature of habit. They all are! His whole race is utterly dependent upon no change. They cannot tolerate any changes from the status quo. You've seen how badly he thinks when something unexpected arises. They simply cannot deal with change when it comes their way. In our case and with our planet, he has been following what must be their standard prison warden control of prisoners. He keeps citing his protocols, which must be nothing but a hard and fast set of rules. If this happens, you do this. Well, his protocols and reactions are all based on predictable actions, where, in their world view, new and novel ideas simply are not tolerated or allowed for."

"Huh? I see that, but don't see where it gets us," Eve interrupted.

"Unpredictable actions, doing exactly the opposite of what is expected of us — don't you see?" I tried to explain my rush of insight.

"Nestor abducted us so he could have someone on which to conduct his original modifications and see the results. We were his prisoners. Yet, we did just the opposite, volunteering to help him get it right. Don't you see, he had no ideas that such could ever happen! Our wanting to help him was not in his predefined protocols. Thus, he was totally on his own and he ended up accepting our suggestions."

"So are you saying that we start acting the opposite of how prisoners would act?" Eve asked.

"Precisely. Force them to have to think, instead of following protocols designed for predictable, uniform, expected behaviors," I replied with a smile.

"Brilliant, madam Wid!" Marco exclaimed, grasping my idea fully. "Ladies, can you manage to survive without our help for a while?" Eve and I nodded. "Okay, I think that we are about to find out a whole lot more about this installation. Come on, Giovanni; let's play helpful. You ladies stay in the kitchen; that will help support our game plan."

Eve looked at me with a funny, questioning look, but followed me. Inside the door, we both stopped and strained our ears to hear what Marco was going to say. They went straight to the observation room, where on the alarm sounded as always. After a few minutes, a harried looking Nestor appeared, if a mantis could look harried. He seemed preoccupied, Marco later explained.

"Hi Nestor. We are sorry to bother you. We know that you are very busy right now, but something you said made an impact on us. Remember, you said something about hatching some more little offspring to lend you a hand, but you said that it would be a waste of your eggs, since you don't have more of those flying ships for them," Marco said.

"Oh my. Well, yes, I said that."

"Nestor, how about using us to help you and your offspring do some work around this place for you. We are just sitting around doing nothing. We are young and strong. Bethany and Eve don't really need us; after all, you have kindly created all the objects that they need. We can follow orders, move boxes, whatever will help you all out and speed up your mission. After all, the sooner you get all of Tarra set up right and properly, the sooner we will feel right in returning home. What do you say? Can you use a couple of strong mammalian cells?"

Nester's strange appendages scratched his overly large head for a bit. Giovanni now saw that my analysis of his thinking was dead on! He had no protocols for prisoners wanting to help him. Such was not in their mind set of experience.

"Well, yes, Marco. That is terribly kind of you to offer to assist me. All right, but you must follow our orders to the letter. One moment please." He disappeared for a minute. Marco flashed a grin to Giovanni, who was already smiling. A second later, energy flashed and the two boys found themselves standing beside Nestor and three smaller versions of him.

"We need the crates of objects loaded into the cargo bays. Nestor 2 here will show you how it is done. Thank you both for volunteering to help with the work load." The two scampered after the ten-foot mantis, taking careful note of everything they saw, memorizing the halls and the layouts.

Left alone for the first time, Eve and I first fixed ourselves a pot of tea for something to do as much as anything else. Yes, we both sort of felt as if we were being left out, but without arms, we knew that there was nothing we really could do to help Nestor. Eve toyed with her tea and finally spoke up.

"Bethany, I know that you told me that the sex with men that we are now experiencing is very different than before, but I am still bothered about us — me, I mean when I was Dita and we were married. I know that we both felt really satisfied, but this real sex — I mean wasn't I still cheating you?"

Poor Renzo still couldn't grasp it. I knew that he had had nothing but male bodies until the Dita one. I still recall how Dita had been so revolted by men attempting to even kiss her. She'd killed Yuen Ming who had actually tried to have sex with her, albeit he was trying to rape her. As Dita, she never had experienced male-female intercourse and was missing a part of what a woman experiences. Now as Eve and a female once more, she had. As a result, she was feeling bad about having gotten us into a lesbian marriage.

There was only one answer. I had to show her. "Come on, Eve," I bumped into her body and herded her to my bedroom. "Remember how we used to pleasure each other?" Eve flushed. A half hour later, she exploded into wild pleasure once more. I knew that she now understood what I meant.

A few minutes later and still quite flushed, Eve said, "That was far beyond what we experienced when we were under the heavy influence of the opium addiction! So Nestor really has greatly heightened it, hasn't he? At least ten fold! Okay, I get it at last, love. Thank you. I can see now that while not the same, it is nevertheless quite satisfying. Love is what really matters isn't it?"

"Yes, love is all that really matters, Eve. Now I am hungry once more." We chuckled and headed back to scrounge up something in the kitchen. A bit later, we decided to try our feet with some baking. Our fellows had not had a wedding cake. Unfortunately for Eve, we couldn't find any chocolate and had to settle for a white cake.

As suppertime approached, the fellows returned quite pooped from their physical labors. Both were in high spirits, they'd seen and learned a great deal about this location. "Hey, Eve, something smells really good," Giovanni said as he hugged Eve, while Marco put his arms around me.

"Wedding cake, no chocolate though," she replied. "Okay tell us all about it. What did you see?"

"You two finish making supper and I'll start drawing it out. A picture is going to be better than my words," he replied.

Later as we ate, Giovanni explained his sketch. "This complex is basically a giant oval cavern affair, nearly a half mile long and half that wide. Our cell here is this rectangular area here in the middle of the bottom of the oval. The machines that service us are in this little room just beyond the window area. The genetic lab part is at the far right end of the oval. We didn't get to see that, though. We were mostly at the opposite end. There against the wall is some enormous machine, floor to ceiling, which fabricates things. We have no idea how, though. Not far from there is an opening to the outside world. Along the top wall is his main flying ship, huge. It covers three quarters the whole inside length."

"Anyway, this machine pumps out boxes of the stuff and we spent the day moving them into the hold of the huge ship. There are some more machines here against the back area behind our cell, and there are ten tiny little flying ships behind the machines. One doesn't work, Nestor 2 said. We think their living quarters go down the middle with the last room being the one where they had all the display cases with the stuffed bodies. We done good, didn't we?" Giovanni teased us. We both gave them a passionate kiss as thanks. Now we did know tons more than before. Still, until we could get these headbands off our heads, the knowledge was not too useful.

The next morning, Nestor summoned us. He thanked the boys for their help, saying it had cut an entire day off the resupply time. He was now off to deal with West Reach and the Greenway and would be back in five days. There was nothing that the two could do to help out until his return, however. As before, two small Nestors remained here at the complex, working the fabricating machines, and building up the supplies for the next run.

As we walked back to the kitchen once more, Marco said, "You know, I don't think that Nestor actually found our blasters and de-charged them. I've been thinking about something that Nestor 2 said yesterday. This place has some kind of defensive energy protection system in place. I think that the machine automatically discharged our blasters as Nestor brought us in here. If we could somehow get them outside into the sunlight, we could charge them back up again. I don't think the little Nestors are going to let us go outside though."

Having little else to do and being extremely bored with our captivity, we spent the afternoon in bed, making love to each other. After a very passionate time, Marco and I lay beside each other nearly exhausted from our frolic. He said the magic words that I longed to hear, "You know, love, I think I know how we can get out of these headbands."

I sat up like a rocket, "How?"

"While we were doing it, my attention went so wholly down there that I actually slipped out of my body for a time. I don't think that Nestor expects any being to attempt to move out of their heads by way of their lower organs and feet. It's rather an unexpected move, actually. Usually, I just move back of my head and up. In fact, I can never recall my moving straight down," he explained.

I needed no further encouragement. I sailed down and found myself looking back at my body from my toes. Finally, I was free of my body! *Come on out! You did it, Marco!* I sent him telepathically. A second later, he joined me, free at last. *See if you can now lift the headband off our heads.* They slipped off easily; nothing was now holding them in place. I realized now that it was us, ourselves, who were somehow electronically holding them securely around our heads. Two minutes later, Eve and Giovanni were out, and their headbands lay on their bed.

I decided to take a tour of the complex, and we four floated through the stone walls, which had for so long imprisoned us. The layout was pretty much as Giovanni had drawn it, and we spotted the two little mantises working the controls on the fabrication machine. Before the rest of us could react, Eve had latched on to their heads and twisted their necks. Two dead ten-foot mantises lay on the floor.

Never mess with Eve, fellows! She thought angrily.

How would we explain this to Nestor, I wondered. Then, I had an idea. I moved a bunch of the heavy crates and placed them over the dead creature's bodies, as if they had had some kind of unfortunate accident. Crates had fallen on them. We studied the layout closely and at last shot up through the cavern's roof, high into the sky. From such a viewpoint, we could tell finally just where this place was located on Tarra.

We were all very surprised indeed. Yes, as Lucianna had estimated, we were in the mostly unpopulated western continent, about two thirds of the way down from the northern edge along the western side. A set of tall mountains rose commandingly from the ocean. The cavern complex lay atop a high arid plain, probably a hundred miles long and a little less in width. What so shocked us were the ten monster-sized, whitish drawings down there on the arid brown surface. Someone had carved a likeness of the mantis. In order for it to be this large and visible from the height that we were at, the drawing had to be gigantic. Several other stylized figures represented other animals; one was some kind of cat, perhaps a jaguar. We all took careful note of the cavern's entrance in relation to the drawings as well as the coastline. One day, we all knew that we needed to return here, explore, and learn what we could. As darkness descended, we headed back inside and to our bodies.

Marco carefully placed the headbands back on our body's heads, and we four slid back into them from our feet. We only experienced a slight jolt of energy discharge as we took our positions squarely in the middle of our heads. "Well, Marco, I could kiss you, but I won't. My body can't take another round in the bed," I teased him.

"Yes, but mine can. Are you sure, dear?" he teased me back.

Eve, on the other hand, started singing. "Thirteen little Nestors

116

walking the halls, one fell down. Twelve little Nestors walking the halls, one fell down. Eleven little Nestors walking the halls." We all laughed.

The next morning we were very startled to hear the summoning alarm go off. Hastily, we four dashed down the hall to the observation room, very worried that somehow Nestor had discovered that we had gotten free and had killed two of his children. As we looked out the window, we saw another little Nestor. For an instant, I feared that perhaps Eve had not actually killed the two!

"Sorry to bother you this morning, Nestor 10 here. Nestor 8 and I ran into engine trouble and had to return for repairs. I am sorry to say that there has been a bad accident in the fabrication storage area."

"Oh! I am sorry to hear about your engine troubles. Can you fix them? I do hope it won't delay Nestor badly. Has the accident damage the machines somehow? That would be just awful." I plied it on thick.

"Nestor 1 and 2 were killed by falling crates. They must have gotten careless in handling them. No, I am very thankful that the fabrication engine is operational. We will stay here now and continue their work. That way, the accident will not delay the project. I am to ask you, if we need your assistance, can we count on your help?"

"Oh by all means, yes, yes, you most certainly can," Marco replied, slightly overdoing it, I thought. Nestor 10 nodded and then left the window area.

Back in the kitchen, I mused, "Well, I bet that Nestor 10 has already notified Nestor about the accident, and it was Nestor who ordered the little one to ask for your help, Marco, if he needs it."

"Eleven little Nestors," Eve began to sing again, but Giovanni put his fingers to her lips.

"Sh! No clues, dear."

That night, Eve got her wish. Eleven little Nestors became nine. I put their bodies beneath their small flying ships, as if they had been crushed while trying to fix them. It looked realistic enough, I thought. Now we again waited.

However, Nestor didn't return for three more days. By the third day, we realized another significant detail. Our machine, which kept our cooling machine stocked with perishables, still came, but left us nothing new! Obviously, the little mantises had been somehow keeping these robotic machines supplied with new milk, eggs, and such. Without their assistance, we had no new supply. Still, we were not going to starve. There were plenty of vegetables in the garden, and the meat dispenser seemed well supplied. At least it had not run out yet.

When Nestor did return, he seemed very agitated. "Oh dear me. So many bad things seem to be happening to my offspring. Terrible, just terrible, Bethany. Two were crushed beneath the object crates, and two somehow got themselves crushed beneath the small ships. Probably trying to fix them. You heard that two of the little ones had engine trouble?"

"Yes, Nestor 2 was kind enough to tell us. He said that he would ask for our help, but he never did ask. Now we know why. We wondered why we stopped getting more milk and eggs there for a couple of days. Nestor, this is horrible!" I replied, exaggerating it a bit, I suppose.

"This must be going to definitely slow everything down, isn't it? How awful for you and for all of us on Tarra! Is there anything that we can do to help you in this crisis?"

"I will need the boys' help in a short while, loading more cargo. Again, thank you all so much. I ought to report, Bethany, that everything has gone very well indeed over that small island and the green farmland belt. No problems encountered at all, save for the engine troubles on two of the little ships, but that was not a major problem at all. The remaining ones were able to compensate nicely."

"Bethany, since these accidents have happened, I can no longer place my full trust in these babies. After all, they are really still just babies. I am growing very worried about your safety here, while I am gone. If something needs immediate attention and the silly babies don't handle it properly, why, your bodies could be killed. Your air supply must never be allowed to fail, you see. I apologize about the food shortage."

"We understand; it couldn't be helped."

"Yes, that has me very worried. I owe you so much for your kindness and assistance in the extremely vital project. I've decided that since everything is going so very well, when I head off for the lower half of the other side of the dog bone continent, I am going to return you four to your home. Please, don't protest. I know how much you want this project to succeed. I give you my word that if I detect even the slightest of problems, I will fetch all four of you at once, so that you can lend your observations to the problem. Will that be agreeable with you? I just do not want any accidents to happen to you four."

Once more, I had to make an instant decision! To go or to stay? If we stayed and eventually killed them all, we would be stranded here. It would take Sergio at least three months even to get to the coast. Who knows how long it would take to climb those tall mountains to get to this high arid plain and us. Without food and water, we would be long dead by then.

"Yes, under these extenuating circumstances, Nestor, I believe that is the wisest course of action to take. But do please get us the very instant that you sense something has gone wrong. We do not want to have our mammalian cells dying off somewhere."

"Oh my. Yes, very good indeed. Yes. I promise to fetch you the very moment something is amiss. However, Bethany, you and I have done such a perfect job of it, that I can foresee no problems at all. Except for the accidents of the babies, all has gone extremely well indeed."

"Okay. You are sure that there will be no differences in Tashien? I mean there they were under the plasticine Doll's control, right? Maybe we could be dropped off on your return trip from lower Tashien after we both make sure all is still going well there." I wanted to be able to attack them right after we were set free and the job was finished. If we were set free and then attacked while the mission was ongoing, we could be dooming millions of women who would not then be able to get their required objects with which to survive. Chairs, mugs, spoons, low kitchen equipment, yokes, the list was lengthy. Without them, the women were doomed!

"I thought about that, Bethany. However, there is one insoluble problem. I don't have the facilities on my ship to support your lives for so many days. If I take along enough to sustain you four, that will drastically reduce the objects I can carry, and I cannot omit some homes from having the needed objects."

"Okay, you are right. It would be a complete disaster for some women not to have their needed objects, Nestor. You are right as always. Thank you." I complimented him. Again, he bowed his head. A bit later Marco and Giovanni again disappeared, transported off to load crates.

Eve and I sipped tea and pondered how and when we could eliminate the mantis. "We simply have to wait until their return trip. We just cannot chance taking them out before they deposit all the objects for the women they are altering," Eve stated. We agreed on this. "Yet, they can fly awfully fast back here. How are we going to get them? The last time that we touched his ship, we got zapped instead."

"That, my dear Eve, is what we have to figure out and soon!" If we had our blasters with us, fully charged, then perhaps those Grey Creature devices would damage the huge flying ship. I suppose that we could wait until they return here and then take them out one by one."

By evening when the exhausted fellows returned, Eve and I had really not yet worked out a foolproof way of destroying the mantis, though we had several workable ideas, based upon what actually would be happening at the time that we made our attempts.

"We leave in the morning, ladies. So unless you want to arrive home in your slips, we will have to get you dressed in your fancy Annelise gowns again," Marco explained, while we ate diner.

After dinner, I had Marco experiment with my fancy dress to see if we could leave off the monster hoop. Lacking scissors, the outer skirt dragged the floor, making walking impossible. Eve and I would be stuck wearing them once more. Since I knew that it took some time to get us in them, I made sure that we rose early so they had time to dress us.

While both Marco and Giovanni teased us about having so many parts to don and in the right order, we all laughed. Both of them had worn dresses like these last lifetime, some sixteen years ago. With all of us, we had full access to our memories, and the fellows dressed us rapidly and properly. Had they not had those memories available, then yes, it would have been most humorous.

We both discovered that the dresses didn't fit at all well. Designed for a twenty-inch waist, the dresses were loose fitting around our now eighteen-inch waists. However, neither of us really enjoyed having the extreme Annelise heels back on our feet. While forced to take small steps, we no longer had the use of our arms and depended upon our mate's arms around our waists just to walk safely. Still, Marco thoroughly enjoyed my fancy look and said so several times.

A bit later, energy flashed once more, and we found ourselves standing outside the cell, hopefully for the last time. Nestor nodded, and we followed slowly behind him, our heels clicking noisily on the stone floor. In these outfits, we could not manage to get into the ship ourselves, and the fellows had to carry us on board. All the while, Nestor was chatting away.

"Again, I thank you all for your kind help in this vital project. I expect that all will be completed in about two of your months. If something does go wrong, I will get you immediately as promised. I decided that since I will be at the eastern edge of the dog bone continent and a short distance from Dorota, I will use the Terra-former on Dorota just before I return here for the next load. Once I finish this whole project, I still have that signal beacon to repair before I can go home as well. Now here is the room in which you must stay during the trip home. It will only take a few of your minutes. I will transport you directly down from this room. So I guess this is goodbye. You have been extremely helpful. I won't forget you."

"Thanks for accepting our suggestions too, Nestor. Good luck and bye," I replied, as Marco sat me down in a strange looking chair. I braced myself for some sudden movements, as did everyone else. "I hope I don't get knocked off the chair," I whispered. In fact, we felt nothing — no motion of any kind. Then suddenly we were no longer in those chairs with the headbands around our heads. We were standing in our own front room, minus the headbands. Lucianna let out a shriek; our sudden appearance startled her.

Our families came at once and more cries and hollers echoed, as one by one, we were all hugged by our parents first and then by our brothers and sisters and friends. Well, the women couldn't hug us, of course, but we managed a loving contact anyway. It did feel wonderful to be home again and out of prison finally.

"Mom, you look really good," I said as we leaned into each other.

"I owe you my life, dear," she whispered in my ear. "You've made surviving possible."

"Hey, I need a hug too," dad grinned as he put his arms around both of us. "You've worked a miracle for us all. How are you doing? Any ill effects? You look healthy. Was the alien food okay?" Good old dad, still protective of me and us all.

Lucianna squeezed in. "Wow, sis, you look gorgeous. I swear you look all grown up," I told her. She beamed as I added, "I can see married life agrees with you." She giggled.

"You look really good yourself. I was afraid the mantis would have you looking dreadful," Lucianna replied.

"Hey, my turn," Sergio joined in. "Well, big sis, you really did it this time. I don't know how we are ever going to be able to thank you enough."

"Hey, big brother, we are not done yet. We have nine mantises to kill real soon now."

"Where are they? How? Need a hand?" Sergio asked. With the mention of the mantis, suddenly everyone was interested to hear what I had to say. Eve spoke for me.

"Hey, I killed four of the little ones already. Bethany made it look like they met with an accident. Now we have to get Nestor and the remaining little ones when they are on their way back from southern Tashien. We don't dare get them while they are in the middle of their run. Too many women might not get the things that they are going to need to survive. We're going to take them out on their return flight in a few days," Eve pronounced. Everyone cheered.

"But how are you going to do that, Eve?" Lucianna asked, her voice quite worried. "I cannot even hold a blaster anymore."

"I twist their necks. Don't worry; you are supposed to be inventing things, not shooting blasters. That's our department," Eve did a marvelous job of handling. "Say, I want to see this grey cloud that you have all been talking about."

We four were escorted outside. It was around ten on July 23. Yet, it seemed like dusk. Overhead we saw nothing but a dull grey glow. As I gazed at our lawn, it had already turned brownish. The many vines on the stone walls had lost their leaves. "Oh dear god! This is far worse than I expected," I exclaimed, becoming far more worried than before. Well, cooped up in a prison cell, I had only been imagining what the real situation was. Now I knew that we were in for a very bad time of it.

Back inside, we found that they had moved Marco's things into my room and Giovanni's into Eve's room. With the four of us couples married, they had rearranged the rooms to suit our new needs. The first thing that Eve and I did next was to change out of these Annelise outfits and into something we could manage. Okay, we also took a long bath first.

Although Lisa had kept everyone pretty well informed of our adventures, everyone insisted that we four retell our story. Our moms made a pot of tea, and they had baked a chocolate cake especially for Eve, to welcome us back home. We spent the rest of the day going over the details. "So you see mom, your brilliant idea to have us get married was the key to our being able to finally strike back and stop them before they modify the whole human race here on Tarra," I explained. Mom certainly looked proud, though she had suggested we marry for entirely different reasons. Hers had been a practical one.

Each day, Eve and I took off to go monitor where Nestor's ship was at over Tashien. We observed that he stayed south of the Lian River that divided Tan Loc Province from the rest of Tashien. He was only able to do the lower third of this densely populated country. Further, we soon estimated that he would need seven days to make his run, not five.

On July 29, Eve and I waited for the returning ship. We were high over the Helios Grande mountain range which formed a natural barrier between Tashien and the Desert of Desolation. Our problem was that we didn't know whether the ship would begin its return beneath the obscuring dust cloud or above it. Consequently, we Mind Linked to each other, and she went high, while I stayed low. We still had no concrete plans exactly.

My idea was to hit the ship with a huge boulder, as if it were an incoming meteor. Consequently, I spent quite some time finding just the right stone chunk. It had to be large enough to damage the ship, but not so heavy that I could not pick it up and give it a good throw. After two hours of searching and experimenting, I had my rock. Eve was going to try to hit it in one end, causing it to begin a wild spin. Then, while the mantis was attempting to regain control and thus preoccupied, she would strike a death blow, though she was not yet sure what that would be exactly. She had the idea that she could appear inside the ship and twist necks.

We waited and waited, as patiently as possible. Once more, I began to think about their slavish following of predetermined protocols. The way to defeat them was to go counter to what they would expect. I began to realize that they would certainly have a protocol for incoming, falling stones, in other words meteors. Those would be rather a common occurrence. So my grand idea of throwing a boulder down on the ship would be playing according to their usual protocols!

It struck me then that meteors always fall down from the sky, never up from the ground! I changed my tactic at once, lowering the huge bolder to the ground. Still we waited, and then I spied the ship zipping along at a fast clip towards us. Eve, via me, saw it and began to dive down to my position. I gaged its velocity and energized my tractor beam, which I had fastened to the boulder below. Zoom! The huge boulder flew up in the air, flying by me at a high rate of speed.

Wham! It hit the cigar shaped ship squarely in its middle. I was completely right about their protocols. They had good defenses for meteors, but no meteor ever came flying up from the ground! The huge ship lurched, and I saw it buckle and bend in the middle, as if someone had broken the cigar in its middle! Just after that, Eve smashed her presser beam squarely opposite the damaged spot, only from above. The ship cracked into two halves. As if in slow motion, the two halves slowly began to descend, gradually picking up speed. A huge pair of explosions flared back up at us as the two pieces hit the granite of the Desert of Desolation!

Take that you dirty bugs! Eve thought. *That'll teach you to mess with Eve and Bethany! Nice shot, Bethany!*

Hey pretty good punch yourself, Eve, I thought back. *We best zoom down and make sure that there are no survivors. We don't want a mantis walking the face of Tarra.* Together, we headed down to survey the burning wreckage. As we looked, I felt a little sad for Nestor. He had come to trust us and me in particular, and now I had actually killed him. Yet, he had just totally altered the genetic makeup of millions and millions of humans. He'd doomed millions of women to horrible lives. Untold problems would now be raising their heads and for generations to come! I knew that women would dread hearing the words, "It's a baby girl." That could only mean here was another one of us who had to face an impossibly hard life.

We watched for some time and saw no life at all, just smoldering ruins. At last, Eve sent, *Well, that takes care of that. Shall we head back now?* Satisfied that the job was finished, I agreed, and we headed back to our bodies, which were sitting in sofas in our front room.

We arrived to cheers with everyone begging to know what had happened. I let Eve relay the sordid details. I still felt a pang of sadness for having used Nestor. Still, it had to be done. Now we had to face the consequences, which only grew worse by the day.

Chapter 13 Dealing with the Beginning of the Aftermath

"Bethany, I am so glad that you are back safe and sound. I don't know how to say this properly, but I owe you everything for what you did for us all. I mean, you have saved the loves of my life: my wife Caresa and my little girl, Andrea! Thanks to your intervention, both of them seem to know what and how they must do basic things. Without that, I am sure I would have lost them both! And for all the women in not only our country but all the Sea Princes and the Greenway and even southern Tashien, please accept my humble thank you. Words cannot express my undying gratitude, Bethany," Stefano West Po exclaimed. He'd come by the very evening that Nestor had returned us to our home.

Caresa and Andrea came along with him, but his wife broke down into tears, unable to deal with trying to explain how she felt. So much had so overwhelmed her. I just hugged her as best I could.

After the emotional moment passed, Stefano continued, "I know that your life, like all the millions of other women, is now going to be so utterly difficult that I don't know whether or not I should ask more of you. Do I dare ask for your advice any longer? If this is all too much for you to bear, please, please just say so."

"Look Stefano, I've lost my arms not my head. I would be horribly offended if you did not continue to use me as always. It's just that I am not so good with my hands anymore." My attempt at levity brought a delayed round of outright laughter from the whole room. Even Caresa managed a smile and giggle.

I went on, "Although Lisa has sort of kept me informed about what's been happening, I admit that I was preoccupied with the mantis. Now, you have my undivided attention. Can you brief me on what the situation is and what actions have already been taken?"

"Bless you child! You are as close to a goddess or a saint as anyone I know. Yes, well, as I see it, we have two horrendous problems facing us all: the destruction of our whole society because of this horrible mutation of our women and this infernal dust cloud which has turned day into night for over a month now," he answered.

"Yes, two separate ones. Let's deal with the women first, shall we? This is the most critical immediate problem. Without assistance, some may die," I pointed out the obvious.

"Yes, very true. I realized that the third day. I sent out fifty thousand soldiers to check on every home in the entire sector. Almost at once they discovered that there were some homes where men were absent — either the women were not married for various reasons such as widowed or their husbands were away, often at sea, or on a business trip. I immediately ordered the soldiers to assist these women in getting their kitchens properly setup. Almost at the same time, the enormity of the problems facing our women began to surface. It's crazy, something as commonplace as a doorknob has become an almost insurmountable barrier to Caresa and Andrea as it has to all women now."

"Tito, here, gave me the idea: make lever operated latches to replace the knobs. I issued orders to the Velona Steel to begin to turn out lever replacement doorknobs by the thousands. At this point, there isn't a man anywhere who is not acutely aware of this barrier. Already they are turning out thousands of replacement latches and I am having my soldiers go from house to house installing them. I received an estimate yesterday that within a week they expect to have manufactured enough to fulfill Velona's basic need for replacement outer doorknobs. Still, they plan to increase production by several orders of magnitude and ship them to the other sectors and countries. We'll deal with internal doors later on. I have been keeping everyone informed with daily newspaper columns and by radio newscasts for those few who have the radios. I took Tito's advice and told everyone to simply remove the interior door latches for the time being."

"Yes, I also issued a number of Official Laws. The first law states that as of now, anyone harming, harassing, stealing from, cheating, raping, or simply failing to help a woman or girl will be executed on the spot. No trial. No Isla la Roca. Shot immediately. I am afraid that I had to issue that law. Our women are suddenly horrifically dependent upon men. We have to help them or our whole society is doomed utterly."

Sergio broke in, "Hey, so far no one has been shot and crime has fallen to nearly nothing. Everyone is pitching in to help. It's amazing how this calamity has begun to pull everyone together like nothing before."

Stefano added, "Well they damn well better! Any idiot can see that if we do not react with everything that we possibly can do and immediately, our women will die off and there goes our whole world. Our whole society is being forced to change drastically almost overnight. Now where was I? Oh yes."

"At this point in time, I believe that someone has visited every home in our entire sector and made sure that the new kitchens have been installed and operational. Yet, as you might guess, there is a drastic shortage of what Caresa calls yokes, which cleverly allow women to carry things. I've ordered the shipwrights to begin massive construction of yokes. No more caravels for the time being. Each day, they are making several thousand and once more, I'm using my soldiers to visit every house in the entire sector. Their job is to ensure every female in that house has a yoke and one that fits her height, I might add. I'm afraid that it may take several more weeks before I can check that one off as a done."

"I've met with your mothers and Lisa several times and we've gone over all the necessary items that you women need. Such things as special cups, spoons, slanted chairs, ones with wheels on them, low tables, low writing desks, special clothes drawers, all those things which until now we took for granted — I've compiled the extensive list and have assigned various manufacturing companies throughout Velona to begin mass production of those items. I know it'll be at least a couple of months before every woman and girl in our sector has their own items, but I'm determined to make it so no matter how long it takes."

"Once more, Bethany, with each of these, I've taken out newspaper columns explaining what we're doing and the time scale that they may expect the actions to be accomplished. I dare say that I've had a column in nearly every day's paper since that third day, that'd be July 5."

"Daily I'm in contact with the other monarch, kings, and rulers that have been affected by this disaster. I'll be getting in touch with those in Tashien soon, I expect. I've shared the precise details of what I've been doing here and how I'm getting it accomplished. Of course, many of the other sectors don't have our manufacturing capabilities. In those cases, I've promised to send them the appropriate goods in the quantities that they need, for remuneration to be worked out later. I do feel sorry for poor Barbe Barcella. She is unmarried and the sole ruler of Barcella now. Not only does she have to face the same widespread problems that I am, but she has to deal with no arms as well. She is eternally grateful for my help, I will say that."

"Before we get into the longer range ramifications of all this, I need to discuss how we have been presenting the calamity to the world and our people. As you know, I roused Velona, following your family's advice. When the flying ships appeared, we put up one hell of a good fight. Don't think it did anything to them, but now long after the fact, I can see the results. I swear that you folks here in this home are true geniuses! After fighting back, our people in Velona were in a fighting mood and were immediately ready to begin helping all women everywhere, the moment it all happened. And we still are all working as hard as we can every day."

"However, not all the other sectors followed our example, neither did the Greenway. The results there compared to here are as different as night and day. Even their rulers are in apathy! Succumb might be a better term. I have had to work very hard in my communications to those rulers to get them back to battery as much as possible."

"Anyway, I'm digressing again; there is so much to tell. I know — I was telling you about what has been told to our people. Here in Velona, we saw the flying ships and knew that they had to be some alien race attacking us. Thanks to you, Bethany, we also knew that they were releasing deadly bacteria on us that has caused these genetic mutations to occur. I decided to keep it in simple terms. My article in the paper explained what had happened this way. Aliens had attacked us with horrific bacteria, a plague that permanently alters our bodies in various ways. I described the main effects that we all are experiencing. This has been accepted uniformly as far as I can tell. I would like you four to dictate a report to appear in the paper just as soon as you have dealt with the remaining mantis creatures. Our people will have an immense satisfaction in knowing that the aliens have been slain. It will make a huge difference in their attitudes, I am certain."

"Now then, I advised the other sectors and countries to also announce that a deadly plague has been unleashed on their country and to outline the permanent alterations being made to their people. I just forgot. I also took out a lengthy article explaining to all women everywhere to go with this intuition or strange memories on how to do things. I admit that I used Lisa here for most of that information, though your mothers also greatly helped in that article as well. I sent along that article to the other leaders and told them to spread those words to all of their women. I trust that they did so."

"Since it is a plague or bacteria, I've temporarily quarantined all docks and advised the other leaders to do so as well. We simply do not know how this plague is spread, how long the bacteria will live, and so on. I don't want a caravel to set sail to say Annelise and then bring this plague to that country. We are still under quarantine."

"Now knowing that this is a plague, I took the liberty of informing the Medical Research Foundation of this and put them on notice. This bacterium is their one and only priority. While they claim to be an independent research foundation, after that third day, they all came around. They have taken, pardon my medical ignorance, Bethany, numerous samples of some men, but mostly women. They have preserved those. After the massive effects were complete, they then took samples from the same subjects. They also collected air and water samples from before and after. Their director assures me that he has every doctor and researcher working on the bacteria. Well, he ought to — there is nothing worse than what we now have. I know that you are funding them heavily. I would appreciate it if you could visit them and check on how they are doing." I agreed to do so tomorrow.

"The most critical fact that I must know soon is when is it safe to resume shipping without fear of transmitting this plague to other lands. Now then, let's see. Oh yes, nearly forgot. I've also issued an order that every public building — well every building that is not a home where folks live — every building must be made accessible to women. That means door latches not knobs and wide enough doorways so that they can get their yokes through carrying their whatevers. With all the higher priority actions that must be done quickly and since most shopkeepers are home dealing with their own homes and families, I have given them until the end of September to make every building accessible to women and their yokes."

"There, that about sums it up. I've attempted to identify the emergency actions that just had to be accomplished immediately before disaster really struck. Of course, Bethany, now I want to talk with you about the long-term social reorganization that will be coming no matter what we do. I have promised in the newspapers to give guidance and hope for the future to our millions of women. I have delayed because I honestly don't know what to say. What do you say to your mother who was one of the most talented violinists of Velona? What can I possibly say to her? She can never play again. I'm truly sorry about that, Sofia. The world has lost your immense talent forever. Nothing can replace that. I am truly sorry. You are not alone, dear. Velona has lost one half of their performing and working artists, a staggering loss for us all."

Of course, all eyes turned toward mom, who fought hard to keep from crying. Tito put his arms around her and leaned his head against hers.

"With your family's help, and that of mine and Barti's, I have compiled a rather extensive list of occupations that women in Velona have had in the past. However, before we go into that, I ought to tell you that I issued another temporary order. Until I come out with answers, no employer is to fire any woman. They must give her the opportunity and time to learn an alternate way of accomplishing that task, wherever possible. Of course, in Sofia's case, such is no longer possible by any means that I can see at this time."

"Now some jobs that women held can very likely continue to be handled, since their tasks did not require the use of their arms necessarily. For example, a singer can still sing just as easily as before. Yet, in the long run, Bethany, I must address this issue. Do you realize that fully one third of our entire workforce is women? If we do nothing, we've lost one third of our whole workforce. And that we simply cannot afford to lose and still thrive."

I interrupted him. "Say, I've been meaning to ask. How many women have died already?"

"Oh, I neglected to mention that. As of today, one hundred six have died in our sector. In Barcella, the count is double that. In Vito, it is triple that and rising. The Greenway kingdoms are reporting counts as high as three hundred, but it is still a bit early to know the final numbers there. I'm told to expect more as time goes on, and the women discover that they cannot adapt to their new life. That's why I have to get this article written soon to give them some hope and guidance, Bethany."

"Can I see your list of occupations, please?" He handed me his exhaustive list. I counted more than sixty! I felt a bit sick. "Stefano, would you permit me to write a series of articles on these occupations for you? You can put your name as the author if you desire. I think that I might be able to offer some suggestions on how some of these may continue to work at their trades."

The relief that Stefano had on his face was incredible! "Oh, thank you,

Bethany! That is the best news yet! Please do so; only try to do it as soon as possible, please." I understood.

"Now then, there is this damnable dust cloud that Lucianna tells me is going to be around a long while. Giovanni, can you please look over her estimates? Tell me some good news about this infernal darkness," Stefano rubbed his face with his hands, exasperated. I could see definite signs of intense stress in this young leader. He was well-intentioned, and I intended to do all that I could to help him through this crisis.

"I already have," Giovanni replied with a solemn face. "I agree with her estimates. As time goes on, we will have more data and can make better forecasts. This cloud is very likely to be over us at least through the winter, maybe on into next spring. I've never seen anything as thick as this. It is so high in the sky, that's the main problem. If it were lower, the rain and snow would more readily clear it out."

"Damn! Damn! Damn! We're going to lose all of our crops this year, the Greenway breadbasket too," Stefano pointed out. "You know what that means?"

I answered for Giovanni, "Yes, we are all facing starvation and a long cold winter. Stefano, I've given this some thought while we were sitting around in the prison cell. West Reach, the eight Sea Princes, and the ten kingdoms of the Greenway absolutely must have sufficient food imported or we die. It is that simple. I figure that you can encourage as many folks who have boats to go out fishing. We should put up as much fish as we possibly can."

"Okay, I'm taking notes," he grinned, writing that one down.

"We should begin to make arrangements for the Northern Steppes to begin sending hay to the Greenway and us. You will need to find out what they greatly desire in exchange and make it happen. The hay will help keep the animals alive. We dare not lose all the herds. Next, I say that it is high time that the Church of Jehosanity steps up to the counter. They keep claiming that they have reformed and that they want to succor mankind. So contact them and get them to start bringing in food supplies and probably blankets, coal, charcoal, and lamp oil. If the winter is excessively cold, the Sea Princes are not prepared for such. Let's see if they will play ball with us. If they do, fine. If not, they have once more shown the world that they are hypocrites."

"Duly noted."

"Okay, the only real source of sufficient grains and food that I can see is Demokritos and Annelise. As I see the situation, we are at their mercy. Somehow, someway, we must get them to begin massive shipments of everything edible, except fish. Honestly, they have us over the barrel on this. We have no choice but to give them what they desire. If we don't, many people will simply not survive this dark period."

"I have already sent my cousin Flavio and another down there, based on Lucianna's initial estimates. For once, I am a little ahead of the game," Stefano declared.

"Well done! Further, we should explore what food might be obtained or grown in the Southlands. Vast reaches of it are uninhabited, but perhaps we might find some additional sources there," I suggested. Again, he noted that one down on his list.

"Stefano, my next suggestion is to make Velona the shipping hub for all the effected countries. With our train system, we can transport supplies to all the countries faster than caravels can get there through the Med Sea. Calgary will ice over, probably sooner than it ever has and remain so far into spring. So Velona has to take the responsibility as the food distribution center; send it out to all the needy countries by train."

"Of course, the other countries are going to be hard pressed to cover all these costs, particularly the ten Greenway kingdoms. A burden is going to fall on us. If we allow the Greenway to die off, then when the sun returns, there goes the greatest single source of grain production on Tarra. The farmers will eventually become desperate. If they cannot feed their animals, they will want to use them for food and trade. If they kill off too many, they may never be able to recover. If they lose too many horses, there go their future crops. No horses, no plowing, and so on. They do not have much in the way of gold mines, gemstones, or even coal there. Their choices for trading are severely limited. That is why I'm suggesting that we may have to allow them to repay us over an extended period of time, several years perhaps."

"Hey, I like that idea. It is very saleable!" Stefano smiled and wrote that one down in large letters.

"As far as Vito goes, convince them that they have 'black gold.' That is, coal. We are going to need vastly more coal than has ever been needed before, especially if the winter is as cold as is being suggested. All the countries are going to need coal in quantity. Convince Vito to quadruple their production and make a large profit off its sale. While you are at it, mention to the other Sea Prince monarchs to do what they can to greatly expand their coal production as well."

"I think the most important thing is to have all these rulers using the telefono or the LDCS to communicate their needs to you and your staff on a daily or weekly basis. Having one focus, one central point that services all the impacted countries will make this run as efficiently as possible."

"Yes, I can see that now. Brilliant idea, as always, Bethany. I sure see why granddad always said that you could count on Bethany to come through in a crisis. I now think that is an understatement!"

"Thanks, I try to, anyway. Now that also means that you are going to need to acquire a rather large staff to organize and deal with all of these countries requests and needs, not to mention the multitude of shipments and coordination needed. That gives me an idea. There are going to be many desperate women out there who can no longer do the work that they used to do for a living. Keeping ledgers, accounts, all these things, they can do, if they have the low desks. I suggest that you hire as many of these women as you possibly can. I'll know more once I finish those articles for you in the newspaper." I had gone too fast for him to keep up, and I paused to allow Stefano to catch back up.

"What about Tashien?" he asked.

"For now, let's assume that the northern provinces there can make up their food shortages. If not, add them to the bundle, but let's see if they can deal with this on their own. The travel distance is vast and costly from here." He agreed.

"Say, I have another idea, Stefano. How about setting up a telefono and LDCS hot line, which anyone can call or send a message requesting some help? I know that everyone doesn't have one, but many do. Put a big advertisement in the paper and on the radio saying if anyone knows anyone who needs some help, please call this number or contact so and so. That way, there will be a fast way for those in trouble to get help. I think that may become vital for the women of Velona."

Sergio broke in, "Hey, that is another brilliant idea, Bethany. We could use the police headquarters as the repository of these requests and send them out as first responders to the scene. Our policemen could then call in whoever was needed to resolve the issues."

"Great and great, duly noted. I will see Barti about this yet tonight, get it in the morning paper, and have it run daily from now on, well at least for several weeks, until people get familiar with it. Gosh, it is getting late. I didn't mean to take up so much of your time, this being your first day back home."

"No problem. Glad that we could talk. Let's talk as often as we need to, Stefano. Honestly, Stefano, I think you've done a stellar job in your handling of these crises. I'm very proud to have you as my monarch." He grinned and his wife broke into a very big grin, the first time I saw her smile this much.

Mom walked in, "Well, you positively can't go just yet. You must stay a bit longer and have some of Eve's welcome home chocolate cake. We have plenty. Tea's about ready as well. Please, you must stay for a bit yet."

"Well if you insist, but you must let us help you, then," Stefano agreed and suggested, rising from his chair.

"Oh no. You all stay seated. Caresa, why don't you come lend us your shoulders," mom requested.

"Well, I'm not very good at it yet," Caresa answered, but rose and followed mom into the kitchen.

I heard mom's reply, "Well, dear, who is, eh? None of us, but we must practice and get it right sometime." A few minutes later, Caresa, Sofia, and Marta came slowly into the living room, yokes balanced on their shoulders.

Mom did allow Tito and Sandro to pour and serve the tea as well as cut the cake.

"Um, chocolate," Eve muttered, her mouth stuffed with a huge bite of chocolate cake. She always did love chocolate. Well, I did too, but not as much as she did.

After they left and the house quieted down, I headed to my room to see if there was a writing desk there. I grinned. Sergio had brought my old desk up from the basement. I was very glad that we had not discarded all that stuff that we had needed last lifetimes. I sat down and began to think about Stefano's request for hope and guidance for the women of Velona. Marco came in, saw me sitting there, and said, "Okay, love, I'll leave you totally alone for one more hour. After that, I'm going to kiss you, and you know that you simply cannot resist my kisses!"

Grinning, I replied, "Oh dear! I am *so* sorry! You have it completely backwards. You cannot resist my kisses!" He laughed and left me alone, though I knew that he wanted to give me a hug and kiss right then, but we both knew what that would invariable lead to, now that our bodies had been genetically modified. Those urges were very strong indeed.

I began writing, <u>Bethany's Guide for Plague Survivors</u>. I liked that title. It put us in the proper perspective. We had survived. If Stefano wanted the credit, he could scratch out my name and insert his. What to say? Words began flowing faster than I could write them with my feet.

"The first and foremost rule for all survivors of the plague is to practice **patience**. This applies to both sexes. Men, you absolutely must give women time to perform their actions in their own unique way. Never, ever rush them. Women, do not fret about how long it is now taking to perform an action that you used to do in a short time. The only thing that does matter is that you get the action performed and get it done right. This should now be your mantra: forget about how long it is taking, focus only on completing the thing done properly." I sat back and reread it. I thought that was a good start.

"Prior to the plague, we all had one or more occupations, whether it was a housewife, a nanny, an accountant, a mother, or a violinist. Many of us had more than one role to play in our lives. While the plague has deprived us all of so very much, it has not and will not deprive us of our lives. We still have most of our bodies and all of our minds intact. Now we must use our minds and what we have to find and use Alternate Ways of doing what we used to do. True, it takes vastly more time and infinitely more patience than before, especially as we are now just beginning to adapt to our after-plague lives. In time and with practice, our speed of execution will increase, that I promise you. It will not be easy, expect to become frustrated frequently, but always keep at it until you do succeed. Never just give up. If all else fails, call the hot line and ask for some guidance."

"As I sit here looking over this extensive listing of all the many and varied occupations that we women survivors have had in the past, I am amazed that we have done so many, many things. I admit that lacking our arms, as we now are, many of these occupations seem at first glance wholly undoable any longer, such as playing the violin. On the other hand, singers are only slightly inconvenienced by their missing arms. You see, there is a vast range in between these two extremes, and we all lie somewhere along this line, usually in more than one place, since we women do so many different things in life."

I thought that this was a compassionate and effective start, but I needed to instill more hope. I continued writing.

"Nearly anything is possible for us, given enough time to do it, the right equipment such as our sliding chairs or yokes, and the proper setup as in our new low to the ground kitchens. Additionally, some skills require much practice. Can you recall how long it took you to learn to write well with your hands when you were a little girl? Well now that we have to write with our feet, you must expect that it will take quite some time to gain skill writing this way. Do not become discouraged because you used to write well and swiftly and now it's just scribbles. Time and practice cures much. Never give up, just keep at it until you have mastered it. In the end, all that matters is that you have gotten it done and done right."

"Over the next many days, I will give you many hints on how to accomplish various tasks in life. I intend to cover every occupation that we women used to perform. However, I will save some of the more difficult ones until later on. Right now, we all need to be able to fix our meals. So today, let's look at some useful hints on how to accomplish this task. Let's say that we need to have supper prepared and ready to serve at five. You are used to timing everything just right so that everything is done about the same time. Who wants to eat cold steak with boiling potatoes, eh? Now the amount of time that food takes to cook is not going to change just because we don't have arms. No, the cooking time remains the same. What changes is our preparation time. Let's say that you used to allow a half hour to prepare everything and start the actual cooking. My suggestion for today is to multiply that preparation time by a factor of five. In this example, allow yourself two and a half hours to get everything prepared and ready to start cooking."

"In fact, you can use this as a very, very crude rule of toe. (We don't have thumbs anymore.) Take the time that you used to perform some action and multiply it by five and that is how long you ought to allow yourself to do it now. Yes, with practice you will most definitely speed that way up, perhaps even becoming as fast as you once were with it. What I am saying is to always allow yourself sufficient time to accomplish the task at hand. As we are at this moment, we simply cannot speed things up. Everything is incredibly awkward for us to do. So slow down and give yourself enough time to get it done. Okay, I admit that it took me over an hour to get this much written. I promise to write longer and provide more hints and advice tomorrow."

Marco read over my shoulder as I finished up. "Very, very well done, love." He kissed my neck, I turned, and our lips met. Shortly after that, we were in bed!

I slept in the next morning, well to be honest, we awoke, kissed, and then, well you can guess what happened next. When we came to the tables for breakfast, I saw the pages I had written last night were now on the tabletop. Evidently, everyone had already read my first article. Marco whispered, "I had to use the bathroom last night, and I brought them out for everyone to read."

Mom came in from the kitchen to ask how many eggs we wanted. "Take them while we have them. One day there might not be more eggs for a long time. Oh Bethany! You're up. I read your article. Honey, you've really given me some hope for the future. You are so right about the time factor: five times as long to do anything. I sure am glad that Tito helps with breakfast, otherwise you would get it around ten and not eight!"

From the kitchen, Marta heard us talking and called out to mom, "Tell her it's a fabulous article and I want more, more, more!" We both grinned.

"More what?" Eve walked in, her long hair as disheveled as mine. We both knew what we both had just done in bed and grinned at each other. She sat down and read it too.

Sergio entered nicely dressed. "Say, great article Bethany. If you want, I can drop it off at the newspaper on my way to the police headquarters. I'm going to help Barti setup the new hotline. Lisa will help us too." I agreed, one less thing that I had to do today. First thing after breakfast and getting myself presentable, I intended to visit the Medical Research Foundation.

"Morning sis," Lucianna came out of her room, Valerio trailing her. "I almost can get my own pants on now, sis, almost, anyway. You rather do this jumping thing, while wiggling your butt to raise them. Now if they would only fit me properly. I guess we are all going to have to wear clothes that don't fit right now. I mean, all the dressmakers are like us and can't sew anymore." I cringed. I knew what she meant on both accounts. The waistlines on all my clothes needed to be tucked in at the very least.

"Hey, you'll have to show me how you are doing it, sis," I replied. She giggled and gave Valerio another kiss.

She agreed. "I am going to drop by the DEA this morning; they said that they have my putt-putt done. It's going to be called a T-putt-putt, all fixed up so we can ride them, sis. Once I have any last minute changes made, I'll get yours and the others fixed too," Lucianna explained.

"Wow! That's great. You're right. I miss my putt-putt — so easy to get around in them. I can't wait to see how they will work for us. Good thinking!" She gave me a big smile. I also realized that we youngsters would be adapting far more easily than older women would. I vowed to consider that in my next article.

After breakfast, I had Marco help me with my hair first. It needed a good brushing, and I was, frankly, too lazy to spend time right now doing it myself. Next, we tried on nearly all my clothes. I saw now what Lucianna meant. Nothing fit well at all. Then I remembered all the dresses that we had gotten so many years ago, gift dresses from the princess of Annelise, back in the Demokritos days. I had Marco follow me into the bowels of the basement, where we stored everything in a tight, compact wall of stuff. Unfortunately for him, the boxes I wanted were at the very back against the wall.

Panting, he declared, "Next time, dearest, you can levitate them yourself. I'm pooped already." I gave him a kiss as a reward, and we almost couldn't pull ourselves apart. Several minutes later, I had him open the crate.

She had everything very clearly marked, and I picked out a sky blue ball gown marked as having an eighteen-inch waist. A half hour later, Marco had me dressed up perfectly. I wore my old Alexa boots, the ones that I could easily slip off myself when I needed my feet. This dress billowed out only about ten feet and I asked, "Well, how do I look?"

"Ravishing, my love, positively stunning. Go look in the mirror and see for yourself," he insisted. A bit later, I had to agree, I did look well dressed. I figured that would only add to my credibility.

Marco insisted on driving me to the foundation in our family motor-car. As we drove, I saw several women walking along the streets, yokes over their shoulders. I took that as a good sign. As we parked outside the large single story stone building, I wondered how long we would be able to get the petrol needed to run our vehicles. Marco helped me out of the car, as I quickly realized that opening the door was going to be challenging.

"Say, I probably will be quite a while here. Why don't you take off and do what you want for a while. I'll let you know when I need you to pick me up." He agreed and left to check if Sergio needed more help setting up the hotline. I walked up to the front door. It did have a lever handle, but it opened outwards. A bit of balancing on one heel and I had the lever down and struggled to open it. That took an annoying bit of time to do; I almost broke down and just pulled it open myself, ignoring my body entirely. I cast that notion aside for the minute. I thought to myself, "Look, I need to maintain the reality that all our women now are facing. No fair cheating just yet." At last, I entered and headed to the main desk.

A young woman whom I knew was still the receptionist. "Well, hi Bethany. Wow! You look good in that dress. Mine don't fit well at all. Who do you want to see today?"

"Thanks, Constantina. You look very good yourself. I am glad to see that you are hanging in there and holding your own as our receptionist. Good going."

"I have to. I need the paycheck, but it is so incredibly difficult. Isn't it hard for you too? How did you ever manage to get yourself in the dress?"

"Yes, we all are experiencing the same things, Constantina. Everything is a challenge to do, but we just take our time and get it done. I had Marco get me dressed today. Boss man. I'm supposed to see Doctor Benigno, please." I noticed that she now sat in a sloped chair. I watched as she ran her toes down a list of names and locations where they were at today.

"He's in room five this morning. I'll buzz him and let him know that someone is coming. Good to see you again, Bethany."

I thanked her and walked down the hall looking at the numbers as I went. When I got to number five, I paused. The doorknobs had been removed so I could push it open. I knocked on the door with my shoe. Hearing the familiar voice of the doctor, I pushed the door open enough to slide on through.

"Ah, it's Bethany! Well, this is a pleasant surprise. My, you look good today. Come on in. You remember my nurse and assistant, Donatella?" he said, looking up from some papers that he and she were going over. He was thirty, tall and thin, with a slight twitch around his left eye that always kept one wondering what was going on. Doctor Benigno was perhaps the best research doctor that we had at this time. His assistant and nurse was a gorgeous blonde, Donatella. She was twenty-three, with platinum hair and pale blue eyes. With the modified permanent red lips and eye shadow, she looked very attractive now, I thought.

"Bethany, so glad to see you. My, I do like your dress. Yours actually fits, unlike mine. Doctor Benigno here claims that fairly soon now someone will figure out how to modify our clothes to fit us better, though I still have no idea how I could ever get myself into a dress like yours."

"Thanks, Donatella. You look good yourself. I'm so glad that you are still working here. Thanks for keeping her on, doctor. Honestly, Donatella, I had my husband dress me this morning." She grinned.

"Of course, I'm keeping Donatella on. Why, she's the best darn nurse and assistant around the entire foundation. Keeps very accurate records. I keep telling her that she is now very like our original records keeper, Selene, the Holy Woman of the Eighth Degree from Demokritos, who was married to the original founding doctor. Yes, Bethany, I know things are now so terribly hard for all of you, but I keep telling her, if Selene could do this work, so can she."

"Well, records maybe, but nursing, well, hardly! I think my nursing days are over now. How can I possibly wrap a bandage around someone's wound?" she admitted, though I sensed grief just barely hidden from view. I didn't press her.

"Doc, I've come to discuss the bacteria," I decided that the best thing would be to get us all on the key topic.

"Ah excellent. Come both of you. Let's duck into my office behind this room." He led the way.

"You are wearing heels?" Donatella whispered. "You can manage them now?"

"Yes, these are the old Alexa boots style, you know, the kind that you can easily slide on and off. This way, I can get my feet free when I need them. I admit that when I tried my old Annelise extreme heels, I had to have Marco holding on to me the whole time. Tricky to keep your balance now." I was honest with her, I sensed that she wanted to wear her heels again, perhaps to the dances and such.

He pulled up a slanted chair for the both of us and then pulled his in between ours. He pulled out a large stack of notes. "Ah where to begin," he mused.

"How about I tell you what I do know for starters?" I suggested.

"Excellent idea, since you were right there with this nasty alien. My, that must have been absolutely awful for the four of you," he replied.

I began to relate all that I knew about the genetic modifications done via some kind of bacteria, which somehow mutated our bodies. When I discussed the results of the Version One bacteria, I Mind Linked to them both and replayed some of my memories of how we looked. They reacted wildly.

"Oh my god! That's what the alien was going to turn us all into?" gasped Donatella.

"Yes, it was particularly awful. If he'd actually done that to us, we probably all would have succumbed to it and died. Now then, I managed to get him to see how devastating this modification would be to us all."

"Wait a second. Your bodies really were so altered? No teeth, those beaks were really real, not just some illusion?" he asked.

"Oh, I assure you our bodies were really turned into just what you saw! It was beyond awful. Our bodies really were permanently altered that way. When he realized that this would likely cause the extermination of the whole race, he then concocted other genetic bacteria that totally reversed all the genetic modifications he had made, except that he did not restore Eve's or my arms. Everything else evolved back to the way that we were before he unleashed Version One on us, except our arms."

"Then, he set about designing a Version Two, which is the way that we all are now. I am certain that he could also have created other bacteria, which would have undone this result as well. So we know that his genetic experiments, while permanent, can be reversed with other bacteria. However, doctor, all this genetic stuff is beyond my knowledge."

"Well, don't feel bad on account of that, dear girl. Here at the foundation, we don't understand it either. However, we are beginning to understand some basic bacteria that cause illnesses and are working on cures for them."

"I took some samples from some test subjects before and after the plague hit. Since we don't know what we are looking for exactly, it's too early to say much. However, Donatella and I have been spending our time studying the bacteria that the aliens unleashed on us. We managed to isolate a large number of them for study. They are airborne in nature."

"Now here is Donatella's sketch of the bacteria on the first day of the attack." He showed me her meticulously drawn sketch. "She used our most powerful tiny-scope to make this drawing. Now I will lay the next one down beside the first one. Here are the bacteria on the third day. Please excuse the relative crudeness; she had to draw it with her foot. I am afraid that I draw with my hands even worse than she does with her feet." Donatella blushed, but appreciated the compliment.

"Gosh, I bet you spent hours making this first drawing with your feet."

She smiled, "Yes, I was crying frequently. I wanted to give it up, but Doctor Benigno kept on insisting that I finish it, no matter how it looked. So I did."

"Honestly, this is a great drawing compared to any that I do," he explained. "Now notice that there are apparently no differences present." I did.

"Now here are the bacteria after one week. Compare it to the others, please."

"Say, it looks all sort of shriveled. What does that mean?" I asked.

"I believe that it is either dead or dying. That was the theory that we decided upon. Now here are the bacteria after two weeks. Its shriveling is even more pronounced. In this latest one at three weeks, it has definitely expired. These past few days, Donatella and I have been introducing various human secretions directly onto the bacteria in hopes that we will see it come back to life, so to speak. Yet, it has not. We were just looking over the results when you came in. We can see no change from these dead bacteria here."

Donatella added, "You see, Bethany, we want to be absolutely certain that it is both dead and that further human contact will not in any way bring it back to life once more. As horrible as this bacteria is, we do not want to infect other women in other countries. Stefano will not lift the quarantine until we say so."

"I am behind you completely on this. I wouldn't wish what has happened to us on any other woman," I stated factually. "Well, this does fit in with what Nestor explained to us. He said that the bacteria lifetime was only three days, although he did not say that after that the bacteria died. Not outright, that is. He implied it. Since it is airborne, have you tried introducing someone's nasal fluids onto the bacteria?"

"Donatella, wouldn't she make a marvelous researcher?" he

answered. "Bethany, that is precisely what Donatella here suggested that we do yesterday. Those were the results that I mentioned that we were examining when you entered. Would you like to see the bacteria yourself through the tiny-scope bought with the funds that you provide us?" How could I turn that offer down?

They led me back into the lab room. In one corner, they had the scope set up. I looked through the tiny lens. It looked very much like Donatella's sketch. Well, hers had lines that were rougher, but she had drawn a fair likeness with just her feet. I told her I thought that her sketches were very accurate, which pleased her and aided her own self-confidence. All we women needed our self-confidences boosted these days! We returned to his office once more.

I asked, "Knowing what precisely this little critter did to our bodies, is there any way to figure out how it did that to us?"

He shrugged his shoulders. "If I did, I would be a genius, which I'm not. I'm afraid to say that these aliens are miles ahead of us at this point. Now my next action is to discover whether baby girls are born with these modifications as well. I know that we received word from you via Lisa that supposedly, all our babies will continue both the male and female alterations, but I need proof of that, before we go public with that news. I'm sure that you can appreciate the highly sensitive nature of such news."

Donatella whispered, "I'm pregnant, so one day I will find out, won't we?" Wow, here was another hot potato!

I defused it. "Look, Donatella, if it is a little girl just like you, I'm certain you'll love her just the same, perhaps even more. I know I'll love any children that Marco and I have." She braved a smile, though I know she felt badly about bringing another into the world just as we were.

Doctor Benigno cleared his throat and continued. "I have alerted all the doctors in Velona. When any mother gives birth, they must report it to us along with what they can observe about the child. We are certain that they will be able to tell if it has been affected, even if it is male. We now have these ear dangles, kind of sensuous things. Not good for anything."

Donatella glanced at me and I grinned. She did too; the doctor didn't realize how we women used them at least to be able to feel our shoulders and even our breasts. He continued, "I believe that there are ten women who are due any day now, so we ought to have our first results in sometime this week. Would you like us to keep you notified?"

"Absolutely, from now on, I want to be notified of any and all findings. We know where this alien research lab is located now and one day we will launch an expedition there. Perhaps we can find something there that we can use to reverse this catastrophe," I hoped so anyway.

"You know, I know nothing about these bacteria creatures. Do you have time to educate me a little so I have a better understanding about them?" I asked.

"Well, I have to make my rounds and see what all the other researchers have discovered, if anything. Donatella here knows as much as I do. Will you be so kind as to educate our benefactor?"

"Love to, doc," Donatella replied proudly. She and I spent the rest of the morning educating me. She showed me twenty slides of various bacteria that caused illnesses. "The very first one ever identified is this one which causes cholera. Have a look at the beast. Our first director, Doctor Gasparo Flavio, found it." She adjusted the slide in the instrument for me and I took a peak. Fascinating. She explained that they had found the ones that caused our lung rotting disease, the skin rot, and even food poisoning. As she put slide after slide in for me to see, I saw that she was becoming rather expert at using her feet to operate the tiny-scope instrument. I told her so as well.

Time flew by and lunchtime came. "Say, Bethany, would you like to come eat lunch with me? I always dine over at Becky's. It's just a few blocks from here in Eastside. You just have to meet Becky; she's one of us, you know. I mean she has always been like us, one of those whose parents came from that southern place, Hieras Anubis, some forty years ago. Honestly, Bethany, I owe her everything now. We've always been friends, ever since I came to work here seven years ago. We met my first day on the job when I dropped into her diner for lunch. When this all happened to me, I was so scared, so helpless, and so freaked out. Not even Doni, my husband, could calm me down. Becky, she saw that I wasn't there for lunch for a week and came and found me hold up in my house, frightened out of my mind."

"She took me under her wing right there, showed me how to do what I just had to do, and even helped me figure out how I can do some of the things that I had to do if I was going to be able to continue to work here. Honestly, Bethany, you just have to meet her, though I know she will be busy at lunchtime. It's her busiest time of day, but she will want to meet you I'm sure."

"Okay, let's get some lunch at Becky's." I had forgotten all about Eastside and the tens of thousands of women Renzo had rescued from Hieras Anubis some forty years ago. I suspected many had already passed away and probably quite a few were now senior citizens. Still, some of the younger girls back then ought still to be around and perhaps in their forties now. I sent a telepathic message to Marco and followed Donatella.

She was adept at opening the main door, I discovered, and I realized most of my difficulties came because I was years out of practice, and I was wearing heels, not flats. "I still can't get used to it being so dark at noon time," Donatella commented as we walked along the street, thankful for the glowing street lamps. It seemed more like five o'clock and yet it was high noon. Quite a few people were on the streets, and I noticed many small shops along the way. While originally built as a subdivision of duplex homes, where two families could assist each other with daily living chores, many had converted a front room into a small shop. I wondered how well all

140

those twenty thousand folks had been all these years.

The walk was short, only five blocks. A sign over the duplex home's front door read simply Becky's. Two other women were ahead of us as we neared the door, which I noticed was double hinged, making it easy for us to enter and leave. "I have a standing reservation here, but I'm sure that she can find a place for you," Donatella whispered as we entered. The odors of several soups and entrees greeted my nose as I set foot inside.

What had been a spacious front room was now filled with small, square tables, large enough to serve four people. Three quarters of those I saw at a glance were low to the ground. Only a few were usual sized, and I saw several men crowded around them. A vivacious blonde woman of forty-three walked up to us. "Doni, you are looking good today. Usual seat? I see you have brought a young one with you."

"Hi Becky. This is Mrs. Bethany Bartiana Angela, *the* Bethany!" she emphasized with a proud grin. "Bethany, this is my savior and good friend Becky Lumano."

"Well, I can't believe my eyes! The Bethany! Wow, I'm so very pleased to meet you finally!" she leaned into me, and I felt her leg giving me a hug. I reciprocated as best I could. She then picked up two menus with her foot and tucked them securely against her neck while holding them by tilting her head. She led us to a back, low table and deftly placed the menus before our places. As we seated, Becky exclaimed, "My mother told me all sorts of wild tales about you and Renzo. I had you pictured as an old lady, but Donatella has been telling me about your new body, and I just didn't believe her. Golly you are so young! Such long black hair. It does look good on you. Wow. I can't believe this. And your dress, Annelise is it?"

"Yes, a really old one. It was all that I could find that would now fit me this morning. My last body got old and passed away on me, but I still remember all that happened back then. Renzo sure did a wonderful job of rescuing all of you. Say, I can see that you are busy now, but perhaps I can stick around until the rush hour is over. I'd like to chat with you, if you have the time later." I suddenly had an inspiration.

"Wow! You bet I would! What an honor even to meet you, Bethany. You and Renzo are a legend here in Eastside. My daughter, Kristina, will take your orders in a minute. I have more folks to seat. In case Donatella hasn't told you, I am the chef here; spent all morning in the kitchen. Please, stick around until one or if you prefer, drop by later this afternoon. Oh, they are waiting to be seated; please excuse me." She rushed off to handle another five women who had entered.

I slid off my boots and began looking at the menu, though Donatella didn't. She knew the menu by heart. Shortly, a young blonde girl, a splitting image of her mother, though only twenty-three, came up to us. "Hi Donatella. Who's your young friend?"

"Hi Kristina. This is *the* Bethany Bartiana Angela. Bethany, Kristina is our waitress, but she's like me and you, I mean, she's only just learning how to do everything without her arms." She was giving me a heads up hint, but I already suspected that she too was like us, valiantly trying to cope and keep from emotionally breaking down at every moment.

For a moment, Kristina forgot about everything. "Wow! The Bethany. This is so incredible! Everyone knows about you; well, we thought you were an old lady. Honestly, we didn't believe Donatella and her stories."

"Yes, my old body passed away and this is my new one. I just got married too, and I have to learn new ways to do everything now, just like everyone else. What's for lunch?" I asked, trying to shift the focus off me.

"Oh, I'll have my usual salad and chicken soup, please, Kristina, and your mom's special oolong tea. Bethany, you ought to try the oyster soup or the chicken soup. They are Becky's specialties, unbeatable anywhere in Velona," Donatella suggested.

"Okay, I'll take the same thing that Donatella is having, especially the tea," I ordered.

"Okay, give me a minute here. Gosh, this is still so darn hard to do," Kristina's gay demeanor vanished, as she fumbled to get her order pad out and a pencil from her low pocket on her dress. "Can't even write anymore," she complained and clumsily sat down on the floor and began to jot down the order. Then, she rose and fumbled with the pad and pencil, struggling to get them into her pocket again, all the time fighting to keep from breaking down before us.

As she finished and tried to pick up our menus, I whispered to her, "You did it. That's all that matters. You did it." She flashed a fleeting grin and tucked the menus onto her shoulder, holding them tightly with her head. "Back soon — well you know what I mean." We both did.

Donatella chatted, "It's so crowded in here that using a yoke would be terribly difficult. Before all this, she had several girls serving the orders. Now they really aren't able to do that, not unless she removes half of the tables and restricts the number of customers. The other two girls who used to work here have quit, just unable to cope at all. Kristina's husband, Pedro Zuni, runs a small grocery store nearby. Since all this happened, he's been coming in at lunch hour and doing the serving for Kristina and Becky. Becky's husband is Rudolfo, a butcher. She has an inside track on the very best cuts of meat, you see." Donatella chatted away, and before long, a harried looking Pedro brought us our lunch. From his eyes, I could tell how sympathetic he was to not only his charming wife but also all us women.

By the time that we were eating, the place was packed. I counted nearly fifty customers crammed into the large room. When we finished, Donatella had to return to work, but I stayed to chat with Becky. Around one, most all the customers had left, including Pedro. A small boy, around six years old, walked in. "Hi grandma, mom." I learned this was Kristina's son Dan. Since the disaster, he had been coming in to help clean off the tables for the two women who ran the diner.

"Dan, take this pie over to Bethany there, please. Then we can get to work," Kristina said. The small lad brought me a piece of chocolate pie. Kristina hollered over to me, "Mom's famous for her chocolate pie. Donatella is still watching her weight though I don't know why any of us do now. Our waists are so small. Mom's lost twenty-five pounds."

"Kristina!" Becky called out, slightly exasperated with her daughter's frankness.

"Hey, so have I. My waist has lost a bunch too. Now I can indulge my taste buds. Thanks." I ate the most delicious chocolate pie that I have ever had!

As I finished up, the two women appeared with their yokes, and Dan began piling the dishes onto them, though Kristina kept reminding him to keep the loads balanced. Once they had cleaned up half of the place, Becky finally came and sat across from me. "Well, I can take time out now. I have so many questions to ask you that I don't know where to start. I can't get over how young you look, and your hair, so long and thick. Were you really abducted by those evil alien creatures? Donatella told us about it, and she heard it from her boss who heard it from Stefano who heard it from Sergio I think." My, how fast and far word had spread!

We began chatting, with Kristina listening in, while still clearing off the tables. Sometime later, I said, "Well, one of the things that Stefano suggested is that I write a series of articles in the newspaper telling women how to now accomplish things, give them hints on how actions might be performed."

"Yes, I read your first article late this morning. Honestly, Bethany, it brought tears to my eyes! It is so very much needed around here. With me, well, I've been like this my whole life. Mom taught me how to do things, and I just accepted our unusual ways as normal. But my heart nearly burst when Kristina lost her arms. She was so helpless those first few days! I even lost my two other waitresses; they just gave up entirely. I noticed my friend, Donatella, hadn't been in for a week, and I checked at the foundation and learned that she had not been to work for several days. That's when I went to visit her. She was as bad off as my daughter and nearly everyone else. I took her under my wing for a couple weeks there. At least I have them both back at work now."

"Thank you, Becky, for doing that. We all have to help each other now as we never did before."

"You have that right. Please, do write more articles. Some of us can share a lot of ideas if you are interested."

"Yes you bet I am! That's why I am here. I need to divulge as many hints and ideas as I possibly can and as rapidly as I can. I'm sorry that I had forgotten all about Eastside. I rather figured that most all of you had grown old and passed away by now."

She grinned, "Many have. That's true. Mom passed away three years ago now. Yet, there are still some of us around. I'm sorry. We all are armless now, but I meant that there are still some of us who have been this way for forty years. Precisely two thousand three hundred and six of us."

"Wow, that many? You know the exact number?" I exclaimed very surprised at the accuracy of her count.

"Yes, but that's all Kara's doing. Kara Lata. She's a midwife and nanny. When this all happened, she got the notion that we should somehow lend a hand, figuratively that is," she grinned at her own pun. "She made the accurate count of all of us who remain. Yes, some are not doing so well and are rather old, but that's the number."

Crash! A pile of dishes shattered on the floor. "I'm sorry mom!" Kristina called out, barely able to keep from crying.

"That's all right, Kristina. I've broken hundreds of dishes in my time. Just keep on practicing, dear. Remember what Bethany's article said this morning. It doesn't matter how long it takes you to do it, only that you get it done and done right."

"Honestly, Bethany, you are so right about that. At first, it does take an exorbitant amount of time to do the simplest of things, but after forty years of it, it's as simple to do as you used to doing with your hands. It just takes time and imagination to work out the how and then lots of practice. Kristina, remember how long it took you to learn to walk and then to learn to ride that bi-wheel of yours?"

"I know mom, I know, but now I cannot even ride my putt-putt anymore," Kristina almost broke down again.

"Hey, Kristina. Hang in there a bit longer. I can't ride my putt-putt either, but my sister, Lucianna, has made a modification to hers so that we can ride them again. I think she's calling it a T-putt-putt. Once she has it worked out, then we all can take our putt-putts in and get them fixed up so we can ride them. I can't wait to get mine back. I miss it." She broke into a small smile, and a tiny bit of hope returned.

"Well thanks for telling her about that; she was addicted to driving that noisy thing everywhere. Me, no thanks, I'll walk."

"Mom, you are too old fashioned. You can carry lots of things on a putt-putt," Kristina explained.

"I know," I added. "I'll make sure that Lucianna puts a notice in the paper when the conversion is done and ready for all the rest of us."

"Way cool! Thanks."

"Say, Becky, could you arrange a meeting with Kara for me? I would love to meet her and the rest of you and have you all help me with relaying tips and hints for all us women. Is that possible?"

"You bet. Kara will be ecstatic about that. We all have been utterly swamped with helping our own daughters and granddaughters these past three weeks. I know Kara really wanted to find a way to share what we know with everyone else. Lord knows you all need it."

"You can say that again! Let's plan on the first meeting on say the 30th. I have to go kill the aliens on the 29th. Where shall we meet?"

"What? You are going to kill the aliens who did this to us?" Becky exclaimed, her eyes looked like they might pop out of her head. Kristina nearly dropped another load of dishes, but quickly lowered her yoke and scooted closer to us to hear better.

"Yes, Eve and I already have killed four, well Eve mostly. She used to be Renzo, you see. We did it while we were being held prisoners. Now we know where they are going to be on the 29th and are determined to kill the last of them." I felt that she ought to have some hope that justice was being served.

"But how? You are like me," Kristina protested. "I can hardly do a damned thing anymore."

"Like this, Kristina." I lifted her body up off the floor and set her back down. Her mouth opened but made no intelligible sense. "Only I won't be gentle with the aliens. I like to smash them, but Eve or Renzo simply snaps their necks. You see, we are not our bodies; we are immortal spiritual beings and as such we command far greater powers that mere bodies, if only you allow yourself to use them." I began to launch into my religious fervor once more, but caught myself.

"Anyway, will the 30th work for Kara?"

"Yes, that's perfect. How about meeting here? I'm closed on Saturdays anyway, but I can provide refreshments, as I expect that you all will want to talk a long time."

"Perfect, the 30th it is; say around ten?" We agreed and I finally left. Cleverly, I had already contacted Marco, and he came walking into the diner right on time. I introduced him, had him pay my tab, and also carry out an entire chocolate pie for me. I intended to treat Eve to this delight.

Chapter 14 Kara Lata's Assistance

The next few articles of mine featured around the home hints that I remembered, including how to brush out long hair. I soon learned that these articles were a smash hit! The newspaper circulation had almost doubled in the last few days. Daily, they had to make extra print runs so great was the demand for these articles. Lini's Publishers sent a representative to my house, begging to be allowed to combine all of these articles into a book or pamphlet when I had finished them. I agreed on condition that they printed enough copies to send to all the other countries as well. This they eagerly agreed, seeing a huge profit in the outcome.

The second night, Giovanni and Lucianna cornered me. "Bethany, will you please follow us into the basement? We have something to show you." Although I couldn't get them to elaborate, I followed them down. "Ta da. Here are your first five images from your new image-taker," they said in unison, having worked together on this development process. There was a four by five inch image of our whole family, less me, and one of me in my new dress at my birthday party. I got an emotional pang seeing us women with our arms. The other three showed Nestor. One showed mostly his bottom half. I was unable to aim it and only got his lower half. Another one showed the top half, but the third had captured most of him.

"Wow! These are cool. Thanks."

"We are going to work on an alternative way to use it. Lucianna thinks that it will be easier for you to use if you can somehow look down and see what will be on the image instead of holding it up to your eyes and looking straight through it as we originally thought," Giovanni explained.

"We've loaded up five more so it's ready for you to take more images," Lucianna added.

"Has everyone else seen these yet?" I asked.

"Nope, you are the first," she answered. Carefully, I slid the five into a pile, picked them up, and cradled them against my neck.

"I'll bring the image-taker and the extra films. Let's go show everyone," Giovanni suggested. My thoughts precisely. Of course, everyone was delighted to see the image of Nestor, but the ones of our family brought instant tears, as I suspected they might.

"Well, dear, you are the luckiest woman around. You have a treasure there; you can always see what we used to look like before the plague," mom said, wiping her eyes with her foot. I flashed her a smile.

The third evening since we got back, I had some unexpected visitors. Marta answered the door and called for me. I was off writing the next article. "It's the three mischief boys for you, Bethany."

"Huh?" I said to Marco, who was reading today's newspaper article. I had not heard that term for ages. I headed out into the living room. I was very surprised to see the three mischief boys, as we had called the trio of youngsters some forty years ago. There stood Luigi, Pietro, and Nicolo, looking as mischievous as ever, though they were now fifty-seven years old and greying fast. Beside them were their wives and I remembered two of them. Queen Ann and Queen Mary Beth had lost their arms to the Confessore, and we had rescued them. Both women were now sixty-three, but still had sparking eyes and the same sense of playfulness that the boys had brought out in them way back then. The third woman I didn't recognize, Nicolo's wife, Lu Ann, an exotic dancer, I soon discovered and the same age as Nicolo.

"Wow! It is you fellows!" I exclaimed, very happy to see them once again.

"Damn, Bethany, you are one hot young lady! Oh, if I were only forty years younger!" Luigi teased me. I flushed, remembering how he used to tease us all, especially his wife Ann.

"Oh you had better watch it buster," Ann teased him playfully. "If you are not careful, you can sleep in the dog house tonight."

"Oh no! Anything but that, my love," he faked a begging attitude, and the trio chuckled. Same old mischief boys, only now they were old mischief fellows.

"Hi, Ann, Mary Beth. Come on in and have a seat. It is great to see all of you."

"Lu Ann, Nicolo's exotic dancer and wife," the third woman greeted me. "He's told me a lot about you, though he didn't tell me that you were so young. I had the idea that you were now an old lady. Touché, Nicolo. Now you are most definitely in the dog house tonight." He faked a wounded puppy dog look, and she cracked a smile.

"Well, that's Nicolo for you. My body obviously passed away fourteen years ago. And don't go getting any wild ideas, mischief boys. I am very happily married to Marco here. Just then, Eve and Giovanni walked in. The three mischief boys all whistled at her. Indeed, Eve with her long blonde hair cut a striking figure.

"Boys, control your accentuated urges. Eve is Renzo. So if you value your necks, I would stuff your whistles in your bulging pants," I teased them back. All three women laughed.

"Good one, Bethany!" Ann said. "It's been a long time since someone got them that good!"

"Ah, come on boys, whistle again. I haven't twisted any necks yet today," Eve demurely teased them.

After more introductions, Ann spoke up. "Bethany, the reason that we insisted that the boys bring us to see you is that we want to help you out if we can. We both remember how you really worked with us when we lost our arms some forty years ago. You literally saved our lives, and now that it's happened to you, we want to help, if we can. We apologize for not coming sooner, but we've been quite preoccupied helping our daughters, granddaughters, Nicolo's wife, and their kids cope with all this. It has been absolutely horrible everywhere and this infernal darkness isn't helping at all."

Lu Ann added, "They have been a life saver to me. I mean I have been close friends with Ann and Mary Beth for almost forty years, but I never dreamed that this would happen to me or my kids. I feel so utterly helpless at times, but Ann and Beth Ann are always there for me, as are the mischief boys. We still call them that; they haven't changed, thank goodness for that."

We women began chatting, and the fellows headed for the basement to try out the torque ball court and to throw darts. All three women had been reading my articles and wanted to share their ideas as well. Their ideas included an admonition to keep your body fit, get out, and run a mile each day. Above all, according to Ann and Mary Beth, life should be fun and lighthearted, even in these dark times.

Ann suggested, "Do all that you can to generate levity around you; tease someone; play pranks on someone. Don't take life seriously, but have fun and enjoy the life that is within you. It helps enormously if your husband has the same attitudes, and if not, work with him to start playing pranks on you and to tease you playfully." Well, I concluded that these women hadn't changed either; they and the three mischief boys were still not only madly in love with each other, they still made life a fun game to play. I took heart from their visit.

The next morning, Lucianna called out to me from her bedroom. "Bethany, come and watch me, I can now put on my own pants!" This I had to see, I dashed over to her bedroom.

"See, Valerio and I worked it out. He fastened these strings to the front and back, a couple of large loops. Now I lay them out on the floor." She sat down and began wiggling her legs into the pant legs. Once she had them fairly well up, she took one loop in her teeth and wiggled about until she had that loop over her shoulder. Then, she got the other one over her other shoulder. She got up and taking first one loop in her teeth and pulling up that side by lifting her head and then the other side, and with some added wiggling, her pants were up. Now it was a matter of using her toes to close them. "I am still working on a way to fasten the front buttons all the way, but the belt is easy," she said proudly. After hugging her, I promised to put that hint in the next article and to get Marco to make me some string loops.

He did better than that. He and Valerio sewed four buttons, front and back on the waistband. Now we could easily attach the loops when we wanted to put pants on and then take them off once we were dressed. Our fellows were getting clever, I thought. We needed all the cleverness we could find, that's for sure.

At ten, Marco pulled up to Becky's restaurant and helped me out of the vehicle. I told him I'd let him know when to come get me. This time I was better prepared and wore a simple dress and flats. I got the door open and headed inside. "Hi, Bethany," Becky called out. "Come on in and join us."

She had moved a number of tables back and put two of the low tables together so that we could all sit around one table. Kristina sat beside her mother along with four other women, in their forties and fifties. Kristina awkwardly poured my tea and then I sat down. Introductions followed.

Lia Dana was a fifty year old quilter. Carmina Lotella was a forty-five year old dressmaker. Tamara Porto Flavio was a forty-six year old weaver, who followed her mother's example, making highly artistic rugs and tapestries. Finally, Kara Lata was a forty-eight year old midwife and nanny and the leader of this group of women.

After the introductions, I began, "Well, I guess the first thing that you need to hear is that yesterday, Eve and I finally killed the remaining alien creatures. We brought down their flying machine. It broke in half, exploded, and burned up. At last, we are free of these monsters. There will be an article in the paper about it soon, I think." They cheered and looked very relieved, not so much for themselves, but for their daughters and granddaughters especially.

After that, Kara spoke, "Well, Bethany, it is a real pleasure to meet you, though I did not expect to see one so young, fourteen is it?" I grinned and nodded.

"Well, your articles are coming none too soon. My daughters are both reading them every day. It's one thing to grow up without arms as we all did and quite another to be an adult and suddenly lose them. We all agree that it is hard for us to relate to them and their intense feelings of helplessness and inadequacy, which we've not really had. Stefano has also been a huge help in getting assistance out to everyone."

"Becky has told you that there are two thousand three hundred and six of us. We all want to see if there is anything that we can do to help others learn our ways. After all, it was you and your friends who saved our parents and us some forty years ago and even built this whole subdivision for us. It is long past time that we repaid our debt to Velona and you."

I explained, "I am sorry that I took so long to get in touch with you. To be honest, I had so many other worries, that I completely forgot that some of you were likely still alive. Yes, I am afraid that all women in so many countries now are desperate for the guidance that only you can provide us. Tamara, I knew your mother, Mara. She sent us the secret message plea for help that started the whole rescue operation. We still have those fabulous rugs that she made. Simply gorgeous rugs. We use them as wall hangings." Tamara smiled proudly.

"Well, as you probably have guessed," Kara continued, "I am the ring leader of our bunch. I asked Lia, Carmina, and Tamara to join us today, because their crafts are some of the more difficult ones to do as we are. I wanted you to realize at once that almost nothing is impossible for us, once you set your mind to it."

"And have some help getting the *right* equipment made," Carmina interrupted and added. I got the impression that she felt this was a very important, extra detail.

"Well, Carmina has made all the dresses that we are wearing," Kara pointed out.

Carmina added, "Well, I don't make the fancy ball gowns, just simple, everyday dresses for women like us. Actually, it is far simpler than making dresses with sleeves. There is no easing that has to be done to fit sleeves to the bodice top."

"Makes sense. I do like all of your dresses. Carmina, you do wonderful work, that I can see," I complimented her. I did like the style and fit. "Stefano compiled a list of over fifty occupations that we women used to do. I aim to see if I can find helpful hints and tips for every one of them. However, I am prepared to accept the fact that perhaps my mom can never play the violin again. Some things we just might not be able to do anymore by any means."

Kara consoled me, "I've heard your mother play a few times. She was a gifted performer. Unfortunately, Bethany, none of our group plays a musical instrument. I checked just to be sure. We will be unable to help her with that, I am very sorry to say."

"Thanks. I had another idea. It is so hard to describe how to do some of these things in writing. What would you think of the idea of holding training sessions for those who are interested? I was thinking that if a woman used to be a dressmaker, maybe Carmina could hold some training sessions showing her how it is now accomplished. That way, the woman could get back to her trade, perhaps."

"Great minds think alike," Kara grinned. "That's what we all have been talking about. Becky here has been working with her daughter, training her on how to continue being a waitress. The hands-on approach does seem to be working out rather well. Kristina is actually performing her old job."

"Well, not very well. I am so terribly slow and I still break dishes and have accidents," Kristina pointed out.

"Dear, that is to be expected. You have only been doing this for two weeks. How long did it take you to learn to ride your bi-wheel? At least that long," Becky countered her daughter's dismal report.

"Hey, Kristina," Tamara broke in, "my first few rugs were a total failure. We had to junk them and recycle all the yarn and start over."

"Kristina, my first few dresses were so bad that we turned them into rags! They were complete failures. It takes time to learn any new craft.

Kristina, we think that is *really* what is going on; you are learning a new craft. The confusing part is that you think you *already* know the craft from before, yet you have to approach it from the very beginning all over again, as if you know *nothing* about it." I thought that was a wise observation and decided to use that tip in my next article.

I asked, "Okay, Carmina, if you were going to run a dressmaking class for former dressmakers, how many students could you handle at one time? Where would you be able to conduct the classes? How long should they be?" We all began to work out the details. Each craft or occupation had different requirements.

We decided to begin the experiment in education with just these five women, who volunteered to conduct classes for women who used to practice in their fields. Quilts, dresses, handling of young, rugs, and waitress type actions were sorely needed, especially since the weather was getting colder every day that the sun didn't shine. I suspected that warm "everythings" were soon going to be in great demand everywhere. Each decided to try to handle two women at a time for either two or four hour classes each day. They would train them at their shops or place of business, in the case of Becky.

Additionally, we decided to try a one-week pilot program to see how it worked out. In the meantime, Kara and I would work out details to bring the other women who wanted to help with this into the program. Kara said that with the right organization and scheduling, she could have all two thousand three hundred and six women training others within a couple of weeks. To assist us, I suggested that we use the new hotline and let Barti add as many women schedulers as he needed to handle the traffic volume. This would give some more women jobs that they could do, as only minimal writing was needed.

I was about to layout the lengthy list of occupations and go over them with Kara, when Becky said it was time for lunch. "Ladies, I've had my specialty stew steaming all morning. I figured that we would need to have lunch. Kristina is going to serve us. This is sort of her final exam kind of test. Her husband has been so very kind to drop by every noon to dish and serve for us, but it is high time that Kristina is able to do this for herself."

"But mom! What if I spill a bowl all over Bethany and ruin her dress?" Kristina protested. I could tell that she was terribly nervous and very frightened about being put on the spot before all of us.

I said, "Kristina, who cares if you spill a bowl? It's only food. Relax and do your best. Take your time and all will be fine. We won't starve if you take an hour serving us. Giving up is just what the aliens want of us, give up and succumb. Well, we will show them that we're not about to give up without a fight!"

She brightened up and agreed to give it a go. Now I saw why Becky had moved the tables aside. There would be more than ample room for

Kristina to use a yoke and carry in our lunch. She would have to sit on the floor and use her feet to set the bowls from her yoke baskets onto the table before each of us and that needed space as well.

"If this works out," Becky said after Kristina went into the kitchen to begin, "I will buy the adjoining duplex and have the wall there knocked out, expanding my serving area two-fold. Of course, I won't be adding tables, just putting enough space between tables for the waitresses go get around and serve the customers. I used to have only half of these tables in here when I was running it by myself. When Kristina grew up, she wanted to help out, and she and some of her friends took over the serving duties and convinced me to squeeze in more tables."

"I know that I have been pushing her hard these past three weeks, but we are in a crisis now. She has to begin to help. We have to get millions of women productive again or we are doomed," Becky said what she deeply felt.

"Well, I agree with you completely, Becky. We have nineteen countries in the same situation, not counting part of Tashien. Except for you folks, not one woman in all these countries is able to function well in life yet, with many struggling just to stay alive somehow. If we cannot get ourselves back into some kind of production, the men will have no choice but to somehow continue what we should be doing. With that kind of overworked stress, only disaster awaits us all."

Kara complained, "Well, if the damnable sky doesn't clear up, we may all die anyway. The farmer's markets are all but dried up now. It is getting more and more difficult to find enough food variety these days."

"Except fish," put in Lia, with a grin. The women wrinkled up their noses, but I am afraid that we all will be eating a whole lot of fish in the near future as this dust cloud continues to dominate and destroy.

Kristina passed her final exam. True, she was painstakingly slow at it, especially serving us. Try sitting on your butt and lifting a bowl with your feet and setting it before someone. At least the tables were low to the ground. I know that I could not do that with a regular tall table. Twice, she misjudged the distance from where she sat the basket of the yoke to the table and just couldn't reach the bowl over that far and had to readjust the yoke's position and try again. Yet, she did it and that was what all of us told her several times. She was also exhausted when she finally finished up, physically and emotionally. She had been terrified of making a blunder the entire time.

"Very well done, dear. You have passed your test. Now it looks like I have to get busy and buy the adjoining door duplex and start having someone knock out the walls."

Kristina grinned. "Don't rush on my account," she teased, very relieved that she had succeeded.

After lunch, we began going over Stefano's extensive list. Just about all the women could teach classes on homemaker type activities. That would be no problem and was the least of our worries now. Six women were dressmakers while five others made quilts, for example. Ten made rugs or tapestries. Five were teachers at the Eastside School and four others often did private tutoring. Ten others besides Becky had either their own diners or teahouses. Four more worked as chiefs at various other establishments around Velona. Six worked as janitors, some doing the nightly cleaning at the research foundation. Ten had their own grocery shops.

Large numbers worked as maids, laundresses, receptionists, secretaries, accountants, and gardeners primarily raising crops. I was surprised to hear that two worked in factories, running some of the machinery. Two were weavers. Three ran their own general stores, while two others had their own specialty shops. Several women actually worked with training horses; one trained birds. Several raised small animals, while dozens dealt with the raising and care of the usual farm animals, working on farms just outside the city limits.

Two women were fashion designers at a large firm in Velona, which intrigued me. Ten worked in the fishing industry, assisting the drying of catches. A dozen had raised and/or sold flowers in their own shops or worked for other floral shops in Velona. One woman worked for the Laird Library restocking books, which I thought interesting, as I tried imagining how she could reach the higher shelves. Five women served as midwives and often as nannies to babies or very small children. One woman had her own local pharmacy, filling prescriptions for various remedies. Three women were shepherdesses for their local flock, that is, the Eastside flock. Three still worked as waitresses at another local diner and inn. Two made cheese, and there was even one woman who was famous as a vintner.

Two women were painters, portraits mostly. One was a ballerina, while a dozen were singers in various chorales, some church related. Two women were authors; one wrote mystery stories, and the other wrote children's tales. Ten worked as linguists, translating both spoken and written words.

On the other hand, there were none who played musical instruments; no cloth makers, no tailors of men's suits, no general servants, no hosiers, no doctors, no nurses, no street sweepers or street light maintenance women, and no beauty parlor owners or workers, including hair dressers, manicurists or similar jobs. There were none who worked as actual fisherwomen, domestic workers, innkeepers, matrons, policewomen, or sail makers. None worked in the telefono or related industries, and none served as train stewardesses.

Once we finished the analysis of this list, Kara brought up another issue. "Can I ask about something entirely different?" I agreed and she explained, "When we were still down in Hieras, a number of women came to us from Dorota. They performed a therapy on all of us. I remember well how fantastic I felt when it was done. That feeling has never left me. At that time, they suggested that we could or would be getting further therapy from those on Dorota, who were achieving spiritual freedom. Unfortunately, we never found out more and nothing ever came from it. Now, Dorota is no more, as I understand it. Was there anything to that? Is there any way to get more of that therapy for ourselves and in particular for our daughters and granddaughters?"

"Yes, I knew those people on Dorota, Kara. They were working to achieve total spiritual freedom for us all. Unfortunately, the aliens disintegrated their bodies just because they were indeed succeeding, and the aliens could not tolerate us achieving that. I and a few others here in Velona know how to perform that therapy. Yes, it would be more than ideal if every woman could get it now, but there is only one of me. I will do everything I can to figure out some way of doing it, but as of this moment, I don't know how I can. I will let you know if I can ever work out some way to make it possible. I am truly sorry that we cannot give therapy sessions to every woman right now."

"Thanks. I do hope you can find a way. I know that I was personally helped greatly by it and would love for my kids to experience it as well."

It was late afternoon before we finished up. Kara promised to have things ready for the first pilot program, set to begin on Monday. I placed the notice in the newspaper that very evening. By Monday, all the first set of classes was full and a waiting list had already been started! When Kara evaluated the results on Friday night, she was enthusiastic about the results.

Stefano then placed an announcement in the paper and over the radio, explaining that the cost of retraining of women would be paid for by himself. He then began payments to Kara and her ever-growing group of volunteers. He donated ten gold per each woman trained. He explained to me, "I am willing to bankrupt our country in order to get our women back to battery in some way. If I do nothing, our whole country is doomed." I asked him to relay what he was doing to the other rulers as well, though at this time, I had no idea how they could retrain their women. The only link those women would have would be through my newspaper column, which was now becoming lengthier with each new article.

During the ensuing weeks, Sergio, Stefano, and Barti had to hire on fifty more women to assist in the scheduling of these classes, giving them a job that they could do, as well as some income. The second week in August, the newspaper now ran a full page of retraining classes and their availability.

Beginning on Monday, my personal task was to track down how many women (and their names) who used to play musical instruments or worked in the arts, such as sculptors. I also had to find out those who had been cloth makers, tailors, general servants, hosier, doctors, nurses, street sweepers or street light maintenance women, those who worked in the beauty/hair dressing industry, fisherwomen, domestic workers, innkeepers, matrons, policewomen, sail makers, those who worked in the telefono or related industries, and train stewardesses. None of these was in the skill sets of these women, and these special women I really needed to find ways to assist. I knew that they would be scanning that list of retraining classes and would be very depressed when theirs was not listed.

To my surprise, most all the cloth was now being made in our new factories powered by steam motors. I could find no women tailors, doctors, or those working in street maintenance areas. None made sails, which surprised me, and none was working for the police either. As I expected, there were a large number who had worked in the various arts, and very substantial numbers who had been servants, nurses, and beauticians of one kind or another. There were only a few in the other occupations. I presented my findings to Stefano and to Kara.

I explained, "Well, the women who are going to be the most at risk are those who worked in the arts, like my violinist mother, those who worked as general servants, nurses, and the thousands who dealt with the beauty industry, doing hair, nails, and the like. These women are not going to be able to easily return to their livelihoods." In fact, only our toenails now need handling, since we had no long fingernails to manicure and polish any longer. I wondered how we could possibly handle scissors now.

As I expected, neither had an answer for this group of women, but both promised to give it serious thought.

During this time, specifically on August 1, Rachele Madella, a reporter for the Velona Times, our big newspaper, came by our estate at 42 Hampton Way looking for me. Marta answered the door and called out for me. I was unfortunately in the middle of trying to work out Lucianna's new method for getting our own pants on. I at least got mine pulled up and one button fastened before I headed out into the living room.

I saw a thirty year old woman with raven hair that fell below her shoulders. Like all of us, her lips were bright red, and her eye shadow was bluish because of the lower light levels. She had an oval face, quite pretty I thought, with dark, all seeing kind of eyes. Her low alto voice had a penetrating quality to it. She wore a bright blue chiffon dress, whose waist was far too large for her current eighteen-inch waistline — the same problem that we all were facing. She wore three inch pumps easily removed when needed. She was only five-five, short compared to me.

"Hello, Bethany Bartiana Angela, I presume? I am Rachele Madella with the Velona Times. I would like to interview you for an article in our paper."

I gave her a hug — well, I leaned into her and wrapped one leg around her waist. "Sorry that I look like a mess. I am just figuring out my sister's invention enabling us to put our own pants on. Gee, my hair is a mess."

She laughed, "Well, I'm not here to draw your image, though probably many of our readers would like to see a sketch of what you look like. So she's figured out a way to pull our pants up? Now that *is* good news. By the way, we all just love your articles with hints and tips. Honestly, we all so desperately need them now. My job is so terribly difficult to do now. I have to write, but where?"

"Say, come on into my bedroom. You can use my writing desk. That has to be loads more comfortable for you. Has it been hard for you to learn how to write with your foot?" I led her into my room, which was a mess this particular morning. If I had hands, I would have made a quick dash around the room bringing some order. I sighed; she'd have to report that my room's a complete mess. She sat down at my desk, took off her heels, and prepared to write.

"Yes, it's been really tough for me. The shock that first week nearly killed me and our two daughters! Poor Tomasio, my husband — he didn't even go to work until last week; he had to take care of all of us. I do admit that it was so strange, sensing those memories of yours on how to do some things. When he finally got the desk out of the pile of things, I rather knew what I had to do to write again. It's still just awful, even after all these weeks. I mean we had a nanny who looked after the girls while we worked during the day, and she had suppers waiting for us. She hasn't been back yet, and I doubt that she ever will be able to return to us. Tomasio is now working every other day, as am I. We both hope that we will not be fired from our jobs because we can't work every day. Someone has to be with the girls. I still cannot cook hardly anything, so we all depend on Tomasio, but he is looking very haggard these days. I don't know how much longer we can continue like this. But here I am dumping my problems on you, and you have the same ones that we all do."

"Hey, not a problem. We all are doing all that we possibly can to help each other out. I am sure that neither of you will be fired. Honestly, if you are, let me know, and I'll tell Stefano West Po, and he'll make it right. So what did you want to interview me about, my lengthy articles?" I asked.

"Well, not exactly. We know that you and some of your friends here were actually abducted by these aliens and held prisoner. Rumors abound about how you had something to do about all of us women losing our arms. Today, I heard rumors that you have killed these aliens. Of course, none of this is actually true, now is it? I mean, you cannot even hold a long gun."

"Look, I can tell you the whole story, but it might scare the pants off of you. Are you really sure that you want to know the whole story? When you do, you might not want to publish it."

"Well, I am a reporter. I report the facts, and what is really going on. Our readers, all Velona, want to know the truth. Bring it on. Let me be the judge of it all," Rachele said defiantly. I suspected she had her own personal reasons for wanting to know the truth, probably because she and her daughters lost their arms. I sighed and began.

Part way into the story, I stopped and Mind Linked to her and showed her just what Version One looked like. "Yes, that is what the aliens wanted us all to become. I couldn't live like that, and I had to try to convince the alien not to do that to us. His whole premise was that we had to be like the perfect society on Dorota. Apparently, the aliens thought that was the best civilization on Tarra." I continued with the story, ending with Eve's and my attack, which finally destroyed the ship. I also replayed the images of that short final attack which destroyed the flying ship.

When I was done, Rachele was white as a sheet. She had seen far more than she could handle, as I knew would likely happen. "Then, then it is all true! You are a goddess among us!"

"Of course I am not a goddess; don't be silly. I have just had many therapy sessions and have regained some of my spiritual abilities, that's all. I don't think that it would be wise for you to publish some of those details, like the actual description of what the aliens looked like. It would frighten too many people. Right now, we need less fright and drastically more help. If this dark cloud doesn't go away soon, we are in for real trouble. However, people ought to know that the alien enemies who did this to us are all dead. That will give them some comfort, but we all need real help right now."

"I have to learn to put my own pants on. I never thought that I would ever have such a hassle putting on my pants! Making a bed is quite a challenge, don't you think? We absolutely have to learn how to do things or our husbands are going to suffer horribly. How long can they keep all this up, constantly helping us with everything? Eventually, they have to get back to other things. We are going to have to have lots of food imported as well as coal. Workers are going to be needed to handle all that and run the trains. You've heard how Stefano is making Velona the central hub for all nineteen affected countries? Mountains of supplies will soon be funneling through here and that takes scads of workers, who cannot be at home putting our pants on and cooking our meals. I for one am not going to lie down and cry over this. We must somehow get back on our feet once more, get our lives going again."

"So go ahead and write your story. Please do not call either Eve or me a goddess; that's ludicrous, and don't give out a description of the alien bodies, because that will scare too many people badly. Okay?"

She agreed. Her foot was aching from so much writing, so I suggested, "Say, you might try writing the article tomorrow when you are home with your girls." She grinned, agreed, and left. I finished fixing my pants.

Valerio and Lucianna came inside. "Hey, Bethany, time to learn how to ride your new T-putt-putt. It's all working out perfectly," Lucianna exclaimed very excited to have her wheels back. Now she could get around

Velona rapidly and not be dependent upon others to drive her.

Outside, I looked at my revised vehicle. It now sported two rear wheels so that I did not have to worry about maintaining my balance. The seat sloped back so that my feet could control the front steering and the various controls. She had added a kick-start lever replacing the pull string, since that would be next to impossible for us to manage. The right foot controlled a shifter lever and a speed pedal. The left foot controlled the rear brakes. By pushing with either foot, we could steer it. Kick starting was easy; getting used to the new controls was not! An hour of driving around our spacious yard and I finally had it down. She had also put two large front side baskets on it and a larger rear basket so that we could carry even more things with us. I gave her a big hug and kiss and a pile of thank you's. She also placed an article in the newspaper notifying every female owner of a putt-putt that they could bring it in to DEA Enterprises, and it would be retrofitted with these new modifications at no charge to the owner! Lucianna was picking up the conversion costs herself. What a sister.

The next day, I got a telefono call from Donatella. "Hi Bethany, just wanted to report that we've had six births now. The three boys all have long ear lobes and the three girls have no arms as well. However, Doctor Benigno says that this may well be due to the fact that the mothers were carrying their babies at the time of their exposure to the bacteria. Conclusive proof, he says, will come when we get births sometime after next March. Those babies will have been conceived long after the plague, you see." I thanked her and wondered what our babies would be like next year. If this bacteria had really somehow altered our genetic blueprints, then we still see no change. There was always a distant hope that after March, our babies would be normal and with arms again. I didn't hold out much hope of that. Nestor was too thorough to make such an error.

Chapter 15 August Nightmares

"Notice anything at all?" Sergio begged us four girls. It was August 5. For days, Sergio continued to work that magic he'd used last lifetime. She was Cosima back then, and she had touched the energy shell around our then young armless bodies, somehow convincing them to re-grow arms, as if we had been still babies in our mother's wombs. Her technique worked until the person was fully-grown. Thus, it had no effect on the adults, only we children. Now, he had been faithfully attempting to repeat it with our bodies, since we four were only in our middle teens and our bodies still had some growing to do.

"Nope, sorry, Sergio, nothing at all. It is not like last time at all," I replied, knowing how hard he was taking this. He wanted so badly to help Lisa and the rest of us, but his technique just was not working. "Look, your approach worked before, Sergio, because our body's genetic blueprint indicated that our bodies had arms. Now our blueprints must not contain that information. That's probably why it isn't working. Still, we four thank you very much for trying. We all have to try everything that we can think of doing." He still looked downcast; he hated to fail, and Lisa snuggled up to him to comfort him.

Mom walked in, "Well, kids, that's the last of the milk for us. The supply is almost completely gone. Stefano is now rationing what little is now being produced to the mothers with very young infants. Cheese will be imported or so I have heard. We're all going to have to tighten our belts around here. I won't be surprised if Stefano has to implement some form of rationing fairly soon."

"Any apples left mom?" Sergio asked.

"Nope, no apples or the usual fruits. Trees produced nothing before their leaves fell off. We've used up all of last year's supply, and there won't be any more unless they come in from overseas. We still have some dried vegetables yet. Honestly, we are really missing the farmer's markets now. Things are getting grim. Hardly anything can be found at the local markets, and the grocery stores mostly have just dried items. Grim."

The telefono rang and Lucianna, as usual, was the first to answer it. "Bethany, it's for you. Stefano." We all heard her call out. I was writing my next column for the newspaper.

The call was brief and when I hung up, everyone was behind me. I chuckled, "Okay. He wants me to go with him to meet with Cardinal Ruggerio Vatore."

"Why?" asked Sergio.

"He thinks that having a woman facing the Cardinal when he asks for their aid will be a visible reminder of our precarious position and dire need.

Do I look all right like this?"

"Dear, why don't you wear your blue Annelise dress and heels this time," mom suggested. "After all it is the Cardinal, and he is the most important church figure here in Velona. Good first impression."

"Okay, Marco, need dress help quickly," I teased him. Actually, I did need his help even to get into that complex outfit. By now, he was an expert at getting me dressed up, and we headed off in the motor-car in just over twenty minutes. I had him drop me off at the monarch's government offices, telling him I'd let him know when to come pick me up. As I walked up to the main double doors, someone was just coming out and they kindly held the door for me. Inside, my Alexa heels announced my coming, long before Stefano actually saw me.

"Ah, so good of you to volunteer to accompany me," he said, picking up a folder of papers to bring along with us. "I'll drive, if you don't mind." He was teasing, of course.

As we walked out, I replied, "What? You don't like my driving in these high heels and billowing dress?" We both laughed. I know, times were becoming a nightmare, but he and I both had to create a little levity. Things were entirely too serious these days and only promised to get worse.

The rebuilt Church of Jehosanity stood where the old one once stood before it had been burned down. It was not far from the governmental offices. Stefano helped me out, and with his arm around my waist, we walked into the church. This was the first time I was in the newly rebuilt church, and the thing that impressed me most was the change in grandeur. Before, everything was as gaudy and lavishly over done as possible. The new church was more subdued in tone.

"Ah, there you are Stefano, so pleased to see you once again," the forty year old, portly Cardinal Ruggerio exclaimed in a fake enthusiasm. I disliked his greasy, slicked back, black hair as well. The two men shook hands.

"This is my close advisor, Mrs. Bethany Bartiana Angela." Thankfully, he bowed to me and made no attempt to hug. I noticed that his ear lobes were as long as Stefano's. He was suffering as our men were, probably worse, since as a celibate priest, he had no sexual outlet. I did a curtsey, minus the arm motions of course.

He led us into his private meeting room. Plush red carpeting and ornate gold fixtures reflected the wealth of the church. His desk was enormous, designed to make us feel vastly less important. Once Stefano helped me seat properly with my large hoop skirt, he sat down and opened his folder.

Cardinal Ruggerio spoke first. "This plague. Stefano, is it really over? Are we entirely sure that we can no longer spread it to other as yet not infected lands?"

"Yes, Your Holiness. The bacteria that caused the plague in twenty countries, if you count the Tan Loc Province, are dead. Verifiably so. Actually, it was dead three days after we were infected. The Medical Research Foundation has verified it and has positive proof that the bacteria are now completely dead, not just dormant. I brought some sketches that you can send to your Pope Pius I as proof." He pointed out the various drawings nicely labeled by days after infection done by Donatella, though her captions were very wiggly, done with her feet.

After examining them, the Cardinal seemed satisfied. "Thank you for providing these. You must understand the great fears that the other countries now have of this horrid plague. The world has never seen such an evil plague as this one has been! I will do my best to use these to help convince the other lands which have as yet not been affected to resume trading with those countries that have borne the brunt of this unholy plague."

"Yes, this is absolutely critical. We must begin importing all of our food, not just for Velona, but all other countries. This year's crops have all failed. Rapidly, we are using up all that was stored from last year's crops. Soon, there will be no food to be had anywhere in these nineteen countries, unless we make it happen immediately," Stefano stated, getting to the point.

"Yes, yes, but what I want to know most importantly is just how soon we may expect our women's arms to reappear, to heal up from this wicked, evil plague? How much longer will it be?" the Cardinal asked.

I wanted to burst out laughing! The man had no idea of what was really going on. Stefano was completely taken aback by the question and muttered, "Why?" I think that he meant, "Why haven't you been paying any attention to the newspaper reports and radio newscasts." The Cardinal took it differently.

"Well, we here at the Church are suffering as is everyone from this awful plague. As you know, we are trying to provide assistance and aid to those in dire need. It is our Holy Nuns who perform much of this work for the needy, to say nothing of preparing our meals and caring for our physical needs so that we priests can attend to the spiritual travails of our flock."

Oh god! I had an image of this man having to cook his own supper and change his own dirty sheets. How horribly awful. I fought hard to keep a straight face.

He continued, "Our poor nuns, as other women of Velona, are now completely helpless and are able to do almost nothing for themselves. Indeed, we priests have had no choice but to step in, temporarily put aside our vows, and assist these poor women with their physical needs and grooming. We've had to take on all the many duties and chores that they have always done for us. We find now that we have almost no time left over to perform our own duties and obligations. So I was hoping that you and your research foundation would have an estimate of when the health will return from this plague. I, for one, do not like these silly ear growths. Yet, I am not complaining. Our nuns and indeed all women have borne the brunt of this wicked plague."

Stefano, fighting hard to keep from laughing, replied, "Your Holiness. I hate to tell you this, but the plague's effects are permanent. It has altered our body's genetic makeup. Even our newborn babies are born as we are — girls without arms and all with these dangling ear lobes. I am afraid to say that the plague's effects are indeed hideously permanent, Your Holiness. I would suggest that you might see if you can acquire some replacement nuns from the countries and lands that have escaped this awful plague. Your nuns will remain as they are for the rest of their lives, as will all women in all these impacted countries."

"Oh dear me! I had so hoped that this was not true. How do you know this for certain?"

"The doctors at the foundation took samples of people from before the plague struck and then samples from the same people afterwards. Their bodies are permanently altered. Of that, there can be no doubt, whatsoever. I didn't bring those documents with me today, but if you like, I can have the foundation send you a copy of their findings."

"No, that will not be necessary. This plague is even worse than I ever imagined. No cure? It is hopeless then, for our women." He slumped visibly in his chair, as he finally realized that all of his nuns were permanently helpless and that he would have to beg the Pope to send complete replacements for all the nuns in all of these countries and soon.

"Your Holiness, I came by today to ask and to beg for the help of your church."

"Yes, please, how may our Church of Jehosanity be of assistance in this our most desperate hour of need?" he finally looked up, having made some kind of decision.

"In two ways, I hope, Your Holiness. First, many poor in Velona are in the direst need of food and helping arms. I know that your Church has said many times that is wishes to assist those in need. Well, now our need is great. We have thousands who need help with food, clothing, blankets, and even shelter, to say nothing of hands to help them with daily life chores, much as your nuns. I beg of you: if you have such places where they may seek shelter and aid, open them wide. Allow me to publish their locations in the newspaper and over the radio so that those who are desperate may have a place to come to for immediate assistance."

"Granted. I will see that my assistants provide you with that yet today. We will open all our shelters at once. Of course, they were run by the nuns primarily, so service will be often a bit slow as parish priests step in to fulfill these unfamiliar roles."

"That will be more than acceptable. Next, because of the infernal dust cloud, crops have failed this year, and food of all kinds, except fish, is becoming scarce. If the church has any reserve supplies of food, I beg you to donate them to our rationing group so that we can give the basics of life to those who are in the most need."

"Granted, we have a small reserve. I will send word to you later today where they may be found. However, I will let you provide the means to transport them to wherever you desire."

During these talks, I noticed that the Cardinal continued to eye me and not so much Stefano. I sensed a deep, sickly, pity emanating from this portly man. Perhaps Stefano was right in bringing me along. He was apparently getting all that he desired from the Cardinal.

"Is there anything else that our Church can do to assist you, Monarch West Po," he asked formally.

"Well, if you have any connections, we are becoming desperate for shipments of any kind of food items, preferably dried — anything except fish, of course. Perhaps Megalos or your extensions in the Southlands could be persuaded to begin massive shipments to Velona. I am setting Velona up as the central service hub for the nineteen countries around us, you see. Using our extensive rail line, we can move the supplies faster overland than by caravel or even stream ship."

Stefano added, "As you can well imagine, there is a big profit to be made just now for those who can supply food items in large quantities to these affected northern countries. Within a month, our nineteen countries are going to be very desperate for just about anything edible. I have sent a delegation to Demokritos, but even if they respond immediately, it is three months down there and three months back. We're talking December before we could possibly get any relief from down under. Of course, if Demokritos does start sending vast amounts of dried food our way, the profits for things more local to us than down under will be lessened." I saw that he was trying to suggest that Megalos and the Southlands should start sending food right away, because after December, they may not get as much money for their produce. I thought this a clever way of enticing supplies from them quickly. Well, we needed them that was for sure.

"I'll see what I can do. It is really going to be that bad then?" he asked.

"It may be far worse than we can even imagine, Your Holiness. Nothing on this scale has ever happened before," Stefano pointed out. After a few more perfunctory pleasantries, we left.

His arm around me, we began to walk back to his office. "Well, a few people are starting to come back outside, but most of the shops are still not opened. The open-air farmer's markets have all but dried up. I can't seem to find much at the grocery stores anymore, except fish. No eggs, no milk to speak of. Honestly, Bethany, this is starting to scare me."

"I expect that soon some farmers will be dumping their livestock onto the market," I added. "If they can't feed their cows, chickens, and sheep, sending them to market may be their only alternatives. Now if hay will start coming in from the Steppes that may help a little. I wish I had better answers."

"I guess I had better start work on some way to ration what we do get. Based it on the number of people per household?" he queried.

"Makes sense, though young children ought to be given some consideration. We don't want to stunt their growth."

Stefano pointed out, "Even we teens are still growing, Bethany. What a mess."

"If we have to ration, will everyone have to go to a certain location to pick up their allotment of food?" I wondered.

"Ordinarily, I would like to do it that way, but with you women as you are, that would be pure sadistic torture to make you walk for miles carrying food back in your yokes. I can't have only the men making the trips as that would take them away from their jobs. I have to come up with more localized pick up locations. However, if I do that, I have to make sure that someone does not go to more than one location and get double or triple rations."

I suggested, "You might assign some of your soldiers to specific blocks. Have them survey each house and log the name and number of occupants. When rationing occurs, have the soldiers make the deliveries, based on those logs. That is, if you have enough soldiers to do all this."

"I like that idea, Bethany. Thank you for coming with me today." We returned to his office and Marco was there waiting for me.

"Hi gorgeous, you ready to head home?" he called out. I grinned and he helped me get inside.

"Rationing is coming soon, I am afraid."

"Not surprised, everything is dead now. Lost all crops, probably lose all the livestock and chickens too, before long. They have to eat as well. We could all hop a caravel and head south," he suggested, but not seriously, though.

Once home, I had another message from Donatella. Apparently, three more babies were born; all had our mutation. I was not surprised, though.

A week later, a soldier came by our estate and logged our two families and how many were in each. He explained that once rationing was underway, he would be bringing our weekly allotment. That put a very sober look on everyone's faces at the dinner table that night.

"Look, I can't do anything about the food situation, but maybe I can continue to help the women with our new needs," I explained. "From now on, I am going to devote even more of my time and resources to helping in that arena.

"We're swamped working the hotlines," Sergio added. "Lisa and I are kept busy helping Barti. Do you realize that we have a hundred working on it now? Three quarters are women, who are doing a marvelous job with all the record keeping."

"Lucianna and I are working on the design of more machines that will be able to help mass produce some of the basic things women need," Giovanni explained.

Lucianna added, "We hope to be able to make a machine that can create the various cooking utensils, pots, and pans that we can handle. The big handles are a problem, but we're working on it."

"Hey, we are sticking around here to help whoever needs it," Eve said. "I used to grumble about having to do chores around here, not anymore. Valerio takes care of the heavier things. If any of you need a hand or foot, just ask Valerio or me." Both of our mothers really appreciated Eve's help now. Marta still had not gone back to her old job at the library. Hardly anyone was visiting it, and with so few yokes available, there wasn't any point in her returning. Eventually, the library would need to acquire a large number of them for their patrons and their staff, which had mostly been women.

The third week in August, food rationing began. I learned that Stefano's men had scoured the few markets that still had a little and all the grocery stores, buying their remaining stock. Having collected it all in warehouses down by the docks, they sorted and prepared weekly bags. As I suspected, well over half of each bag contained dried fish. Yes, one could still get fresh fish down at the docks, but few women dared to make such a long walk trying to carry the fish back in their yokes. Even fewer men had the time to spare in doing such.

At this point, mom and Marta had to work out how to make the bag last us a week. Fortunately, we still had some dried food stock left to ease the pain. "Well, if this keeps up much longer, we women will have a sixteen inch waist," mom teased us at dinner.

What scared us all was the snowfall that occurred on August 20! We knew that it was getting colder each day, but it had never snowed in the late summer before! We women now had the additional misery of trying to find ways to keep warm. That is, how do we bundle up when we only have our feet to do it with? Worse, we needed to keep our feet available to be able to do anything else. Misery upon misery, that's how Eve put it.

Near the end of August, Stefano finally closed the book on the deaths from the plague, that is, the number of women who died, some by their own means, unable or unwilling to face what had happened to them. In Velona the official death toll was one hundred-ten, sector-wide. In Barcella, the numbers rose to one hundred ninety-three. In Zargarb, two hundred five women were lost. The other sectors had counts between six and eight hundred.

Only much later did we have estimates for West Reach, which suggested the death toll was closer to nine hundred. The Greenway kingdoms reported figures that ranged between seven and nine hundred women. The counts from Tashien were still coming in, however. The figures there were alarming, five thousand plus and climbing each week. I made a guess that the reason for so many taking or losing their lives there was the fact that as a whole, the people were so low in emotional tone. It wouldn't take much of a shock to send them down a short way to body death.

As the month wore on and I continued my investigations and research, more and more uplifting stories began to appear — tales of ordinary folks reacting to un-ordinary and shocking events.

Chapter 16 A Woodworker's Tale of Hope

Aldo Tolio was a tall, thin eighteen year old woodworker. He had curly, light brown hair that draped almost to his shoulders; he cut it himself, unable to afford a barber. When his father was killed in a construction accident at the docks two years ago, Aldo inherited his father's small carpentry shop in Velona. Unmarried, he still lived at home caring for his mother, Rubina, who was forty-one, and his sister, Rosario, who was just sixteen. While his father had always managed to scrounge up some business to meet the family's desperate need for funds, Aldo seemed fully to lack that skill, or perhaps his father had yet to teach him that aspect of his craft. As June approached, their coin box was very low, and his sister had begun making trips to the countryside outside of town, picking wild flowers and then selling them on street corners to bring in a few more coppers.

"Times will get better, you will see Aldo," his mother constantly encouraged him each morning as they ate the same porridge day after day. It was cheap and filling.

"I'll get more flowers today, you'll see, Aldo," Rosario added, trying to encourage him as well.

"Maybe I will get a commission today," he finally admitted, if only to shut the two women up. Now that his father was gone, he knew that commissions were rare.

When the plague struck, Aldo had just finished a set of cabinets and came home with ten gold, the largest sum he'd made all June. When the massive gunfire and cannonae barrages broke out late that afternoon, Rubina said, "We're supposed to fight them, Aldo." All three went outside to watch. They saw the huge cigar shaped craft hovering above and a number of smaller ones flying a crisscross pattern. Above the noise, Aldo yelled angrily and began throwing rocks at the little ships. Shortly, Rubina and Rosario joined him, ignoring the fact that their stones didn't even come close to reaching even the lowest little ship. Anger seethed in all three as it did in so many others.

Three days later, Aldo panicked as he responded to the screams coming from his mother's bedroom and that of his sister. Ordinarily, the shy man would never have entered their rooms when they had their doors closed. Their hysterical screams cut through his modesty, and he dashed into his sister's room and stood motionless, shocked utterly.

Rosario was sitting up in bed, screaming wildly. Her lovely white, soft arms were completely gone! He stood frozen for what seemed like an eternity. Then, he rushed to her and held onto her tightly. She laid her head on his shoulders and began crying; her screaming subsided. He literally pulled her out of bed and carried her alongside of him to their mother's room. She, too, was sitting up in bed, screaming hysterically. Aldo moved his sister, who he still held tightly to him, over to his mother. With his other arm, he cradled his mother around her waist, and then pulled her on out of the bed. The three stood there for a long time, while his arms held onto both of them, each one crying, sobbing uncontrollably on his shoulders.

He said nothing, he could think of nothing to say. "I'm sorry" seemed utterly pointless; of course, everyone was sorry. Magic had removed their arms, and he knew of no magic that could put them back again. He knew of no magic at all. He wanted to give them hope, but could see no hope at all. At last, he joined them and began crying as well.

Time passed, and finally Rosario whispered, "I've got to go pee. Oh god! I can't even go pee anymore!"

This shocked Aldo. "Huh? Has something else gone too, sis?" He couldn't imagine what else they could have lost besides their arms, though he had never seen a woman's lower private parts. He was far too modest ever to attempt a sneak peek.

"No, I can't get my pants down. All I can do is pee in my pants!"

"I have to go too, Aldo," his mother complained. "You have to help us, son." Thus, shy Aldo began the first of many embarrassing actions, learning rapidly their anatomy.

After helping them use the bathroom, he decided that they should at least be dressed in something other than their nightgowns. Once more, he spent a long half hour, red-faced in embarrassment, as he tried to follow their orders getting them into their simple day dresses. By now, all three were starving, and Aldo, still holding one in each arm as if they might somehow fall down if he let go of them, led them into the kitchen.

More sobbing and crying followed immediately, as both women realized that they could not make breakfast. At last, he figured out why they were crying and suggested that he make it for them. Alas, he'd never cooked anything. Rubina, who had been a creative cook, making do with so very little, and yet producing a meal that filled, found no other way than to start giving Aldo step by step orders, which so frustrated her that she kept breaking down and crying between orders.

Once he had the porridge ready and ladled out into their three usual bowls and the tea steeping, he carried them to the table where the two women sat. Now they began crying again, and Aldo now realized that he would have to feed them himself. "Mom, Rosario, please stop crying. I am here and I will feed you. I will take care of you. I won't ever abandon you, I promise. Here, try to take a bite, mom."

Later, with the women fed, he gulped his down and began holding their tea cups so that they could somehow take sips. Waves of deep sympathy flowed over him as he watched their awkward attempts even to sip from the cup that his inexpert hands tried to position so that they could even sip it.

"Oh Aldo! Whatever are we going to do now?" Rubina finally asked as her body's metabolism finally kicked in.

"Mom, sis, I don't know. I am going to have to take care of both of you somehow. Come on, let's go into the living room, and get you both onto to the more comfortable sofa. Then, maybe we can figure this all out." He held no hope of figuring anything out now. He only knew that he needed to get out of the kitchen.

"I can walk okay, Aldo. You don't have to keep holding on to me," Rosario said, and Aldo finally let go of the two. "What's all this stuff?" she asked, as they entered their front room.

"Where did all this come from, Aldo? Did you bring some of your work home with you last night? You didn't tell me that you were. We might have tripped over this stuff in the night, since you didn't tell us it was here," his mom chided him a bit.

"I didn't bring anything home, mom. I don't know where it came from. Seats, they look sort of like bent seats. That is a desk, perhaps, but someone made it for a midget or something. Do we need more kitchen wares?" Aldo asked.

As the three stood there staring at the pile, the Bethany genetic memories began stirring in the two women's minds. Before long, both began trying to tell Aldo what these things were and that they were somehow supposed to use them. Aldo began unpacking the pile, sorting everything out. Now he began to see the larger picture. Half of the larger items formed a replacement kitchen. Once the three began to grasp the picture, Aldo finally made sense of it all.

"Mom, this is supposed to be your new kitchen somehow. I don't know who gave it to us, but I can install it all for us. Do you think I should, mom?"

"Somehow, Aldo, that seems like the right thing to do. Can you do it?"

Aldo spent the rest of the day reworking their kitchen. He was a good carpenter and woodworker. He took his time, salvaging the old, while making a perfect installation of the new items. All the time, the two women stood out of his way and continued having ideas about how the things should be arranged and how they might be able to use them, well somewhat anyway.

Late that afternoon, he had the work finished and decided to hold off on the plastering and painting until tomorrow. He carried the old sink, stove, and cabinets outside, making a nice pile by their door. Later, he decided to take them to his shop where he would salvage all that he could. Perhaps, he could sell the metal as scrap and get a few coppers for it.

Again, he followed his mother's directions and tried to make their dinner. He was so ill equipped to cook and made such a mess of it, that the two women began to butt in, until at last, Rubina was sitting in the chair with wheels and attempting to use her feet to do the cooking. At last, she just gave Aldo an order to get her this and that — orders which he could actually follow. "Men! Honestly, they have no idea how to cook!" she declared, and Rosario giggled for the first time this day.

Aldo set the table, but complained, "Mom, your half is almost on the ground! Are you two sure that you are supposed to be sitting there?"

"We think so," his sister called out, while she stood beside her mother watching and offering ideas that somehow came into her mind as well.

Aldo prepared to feed both women again, but as they sat down in the strange new chairs, more strange ideas began to appear in their minds. While he sat on the floor and tried to help them, they began to experiment some, using their feet and toes. "Maybe it's this way, mom," Rosario suggested, trying to hold onto one of the special forks.

Later that night, he got them undressed and into their nightgowns. All three suddenly realized that the doorknobs had to go. After helping tuck each into bed, he got his screwdriver out and dismantled all the dozen doorknobs and latches, ending with those on the outer doors. Again, he saved all the parts, figuring that he could perhaps get a little something for them at the pawnshop.

He kept his door open that night, insisting that they should call out for him, if they needed anything. He slept fitfully. The next morning, he again fetched the things that his mom asked for, while she struggled to figure out how to make their usual breakfast.

Around eleven a soldier knocked on their door, "Ah, I see that there is a man in this house. Good. Stefano West Po has ordered us to check on every house and report any in which there is not a male adult living there. Good, I see that you have replaced your kitchen. Not many have as yet."

"Well, I am a carpenter. It was easy to do. Say, what's going on? My mom and sister have lost their arms. What's happening?"

"Haven't you seen the newspapers or listened to the radio?"

"No, we can't afford the paper or a radio."

"Okay, I will see that you are sent a newspaper everyday now, no charge. Stefano's orders."

All three eagerly began reading the newspapers each day. Aldo usually read them to the two women at first, until they at last thought that they could do it for themselves, turning the pages with their feet.

Later the second day, two of their neighbors came by to ask Aldo for assistance with their new kitchens. He was rather unwilling to leave them alone, but his mom insisted that they needed the extra money that he might make. For the next five days, Aldo was kept busy helping his neighbors get their kitchens fixed up. While most were also poor, Aldo did receive the equivalent of a gold for his efforts.

As the days in July progressed, slowly the two women began to be able to take care of more and more of their needs, until at last, they insisted that Aldo return to his shop and attempt to drum up some business. Their funds were rapidly vanishing. "Honestly, Aldo, you have to do it. I can't pick wild flowers anymore. I don't know what I can do to make a few coppers anymore. Please, we will be all right. You have to make us some money or we will starve soon," Rosario pleaded with her brother. She was scared to be so alone without him around, but they had to have some more income and soon.

Aldo opened his shop, but hardly anyone was on the street. Absolutely no one came into his shop all day. He spent the day cleaning up the shop, although it really didn't need it. He had a goodly supply of wood, but no customers came ordering anything. He was not one to go door to door begging for a contract. He was entirely too shy. Perhaps that was also why he had never had a girlfriend either. Glumly, he headed home when he thought it was dark enough. This infernal dusk from the grey cloud was horribly depressing, he thought. Of course, they chided him for not having made a copper that day.

That evening he sat around and watched his sister. She was using that low desk to reread the newspaper. "Listen, Aldo," she said, "Stefano is offering to pay anyone who can help build more of these things that we need, like this desk I'm on. Surely you can do that. We only have this one and mom needs one too. Plus, there are all the kitchen cabinets and chairs too. We ought to have another one with rollers on it for me and another one with the sloped back so we can both have one at the table."

"Okay, I will make some tomorrow. Only I ought to take this desk to my shop and use it as a model. Can you get by one day without it?" he asked.

The next morning, Aldo began building another desk. At the end of the day, he stood back and admired the first of these low writing desks. It was a duplicate of the one that had mysteriously appeared. He carried the original home with him, confident that he could produce desks. Over dinner, he said, "You know, if I had some workers, I could make a lot of these desks."

"See if you can find some, Aldo. Stefano put an ad in the paper today calling on all who can to begin making more of all these things that we need. He says that every woman should have her own chair, desk, rolling chair, and other things. There must be thousands of us who need them, Aldo," his mother explained.

"I'm on it, mom. I can do this. Tomorrow I will see if I can find some workers. Maybe we can make enough money to really get ahead this time." Indeed, this appeared to be their salvation. Stefano was covering the construction costs, a sure paycheck.

Aldo tried everywhere he could to find workers to assist him. He came home dejected. "Mom, there just isn't anyone who can lend a hand. If only we could get some workers, we could build many of these desks. I myself can only make one a day."

"Aldo, Stefano is almost begging for carpenters to get going. Why don't you put an ad up on the street lamppost? Surely someone will see it and apply for the work," his mom suggested. He wrote out an ad and posted it right after supper.

He spent the day making one more desk. However, no one had answered his ad at all. "If only I could hire some workers, I could really make some money. Besides, all these women need these desks and soon," he said to himself, though he began to realize that almost all men were in the same position as he. They had families who needed so much of their help during the day that they just couldn't do much work. That night, his mother told him that the newspaper had an article, which said that only about a third of Velona's men were even part-time back on their old jobs. Of course, none of the women were.

The next morning, he again opened his shop, hoping that some workers would finally answer his ad and be waiting for him as he opened up. Sadly, there was no one. Well, that was not exactly true. He did see four teenage girls, dressed rather poorly, standing against the store wall across the street from his shop. A tear formed as he spotted the four standing there, they reminded him of how awful a time his sister was now having, unable even to do the one thing that she had ever worked out that she could do to make some money, her small wild flower business. He went inside and began to lay out another desk.

He heard footsteps and looked up. There were the four teens standing meekly in his doorway. "Hello. I'm Aldo. Do you need some help?" He put his pencil down and rose, figuring they needed a hand with something, though he had no idea what it was, only he hoped and prayed that it was not help going to the bathroom. He was still horribly embarrassed when he had to assist his mom and sister.

"We saw your ad. We want to work. We will do anything you ask, sir," the eldest girl said very softly. She was nearly as tall as he and about his age, he thought. Her hair was a mess, long and blonde, but then whose hair wasn't these days? He had been very thankful that his mother and sister had not asked him to help them with that! He'd never touched their hair and knew nothing about that at all!

Aldo couldn't believe what he'd just heard! "You, you want a job?" he muttered, running his hands through his hair, unable to grasp the concept. Women, girls were now completely and utterly helpless, almost unable to do anything for themselves. He needed workers to build desks so that they could at least sit down and read the paper or write something. He'd seen sister practicing writing last night, pitifully. He had cried silently to himself, trying not to disturb her.

"Yes sir. We will work hard and not ask for much. Please, sir. Our parents are dead. It's just me and my three sisters. The soldiers came and fixed our kitchen, but now we cannot work at our old jobs for the dressmakers. We are almost out of money. Please, sir. We will do anything."

Aldo's heart nearly broke as he looked at the four sisters, each about a year younger than the other. "Wait a minute! Don't I know you four? Aren't you the Prudentia sisters who live just down the street about four houses from us?"

"Five houses, sir," the eldest replied. Aldo's eyes clouded; he fought back tears. He knew their story of how they had lost both of their parents. Yet, they had good jobs working for ABC Dresses; he remembered his mother telling him that.

He found himself saying, "Okay," before he realized what he was saying. The four teen's faces lit up with giant smiles, and he knew that he could not possibly deny them a job!

"My name is Pia," the eldest said. She had long brown hair and blue eyes; her face was pretty, but today her face needed a good washing, and her hair was a mess as were those of her sisters. "This is Nena; she's seventeen. This is Rosana; she's sixteen. This is Savina; she's fifteen."

"Well, I am very pleased to meet you," Aldo said, extending his hand and instantly regretting it! His face went red as he realized his horrible gaffe.

"That's all right, sir. We keep trying to raise our arms only they aren't there anymore. It is weird you know. We try to reach for something and find that there is nothing there reaching. It is really a strange feeling. I think that we are supposed to now lean towards you and put a leg around you, like this." She leaned into him and her leg arced around his back. He found his arms going around her, giving her a hug. He felt a strange sensation doing that, one that he liked. One by one, he hugged each of them.

"Well, now that I have workers maybe we can make some desks," Aldo explained. "I am trying to make as many desks as possible. Stefano is paying good gold for as many as we can make. By myself, I can only make one a day. I hope that we can make many more and earn a good bit of gold. We need it so badly that it's not funny."

"So do we. We are down to our last copper," Pia explained. "What are we to do?"

"Oh!" Aldo exclaimed. He sat down and ran his hands through his hair. He'd just hired the four of them, but they wouldn't be able to do anything!

"The paper said that if we have the right tools, that we can do things. Do you have the right tools for us? We will try to learn whatever you need us to learn," Pia said softly, already guessing what was going through Aldo's mind. He grinned.

"Well, I have an idea. Why don't you four watch me do all the steps to make a desk today? Then, we can put our heads together and see where you can help. We are working with wood, and often we can make our own woodworking tools. I want these desks to be very well made. After all, I am making them for others like yourselves and my sister. We want them to be perfect."

They agreed and watched him measure out the distances on the lumber. They watched as he sawed the lines, making the individual boards. They watched him drill small holes for the dowels and then watched him apply the glue and finally hold the different subassemblies together with clamps. While the parts were drying, he explained, "Now we have to sand them and get them really perfectly smooth. Then, I glue these three pieces together, and we have a writing desk."

A bit later, when the glue was sufficiently dry, he began to sand. "Hey, we can do that, sir," Pia exclaimed. "If you can put the desktop on the floor, we can do it!"

"Aldo, please, not sir. Okay." He put the top on the wood floor and prepared four sanding blocks. He watched as the girls eagerly sat down. Using their feet, they began to sand. He realized that using strong leg muscles, they might well be able to handle the sanding. Hence, he began marking a second set of boards.

When he was about ready to start sawing, Pia interrupted him. "Aldo, we could saw too, if somehow you could make some kind of strap that we could put our foot into. See?" She extended her foot and laid it against the handle. Her foot extended well past the edge of the handle. Aldo saw that instead of gripping the handle with hands, if she had a sort of socket around the handle and in which she could insert her foot, she could indeed saw.

"Time to invent, Pia. Let's see what I can make here." A half hour later, he had a five-inch leather band looped through the saw handle and the ends laced together. Pia slipped her foot into the loop, and Aldo adjusted it so that it fit her foot firmly. He fixed up a low bench and put the lumber to be sawed on it. He also saw that she was definitely going to need some back support and rigged up some boards that sloped back at about a forty-five degree angle. After a little experimentation, the idea worked.

Now Aldo realized that he was actually training an apprentice woodworker! He took on his new role with vigor, explaining how to saw and how to properly sand. By suppertime, they had the wood for three desks cut, one completely assembled and ready to be sold, and one gluing.

"Pia, you and your sisters are doing a fabulous job! With more practice, why I bet we can make four desks a day. Stefano is paying two gold each, so we can make eight gold each day. That means I'll give you four a gold each, use three gold to purchase more wood and supplies, and still have a gold for my mom and sister! This is going to work out well!"

"Four gold! Wow! Are you sure?" Pia asked, wide-eyed. If they could somehow earn this much, they could survive.

"Sure, you are earning it. Look at what we made today and you're just learning. We wasted lots of time trying to figure out how to make those saws work for you. I'm sure that we can figure out even more each day. Say, what are you going to do for supper? We didn't even have lunch today and I am starving myself."

Pia looked down and shuffled her feet; she didn't reply. Her sisters were equally silent. "You don't have any more food in your house, do you?" Aldo suddenly realized. Probably even if they had some money, how could they even carry the groceries home? Already it was suppertime and even if they had food at home, it would be way past bedtime before they could have something ready to eat.

"Okay, my four new employees. You are all coming home with me for dinner. I know that mom doesn't know that I'm bringing four guests home for dinner, but we will make do, even if I have to do some more cooking myself."

"But Aldo. Are you sure? We really don't have much left at home to eat anymore. When we finally get some gold, we can then go to the markets again, if we can somehow figure out how to get stuff carried back home," Pia explained.

"Sure I'm sure. Come on, follow me." The four teens followed him out and down the street to Aldo's family home. Their house was five more houses on down the street. Already it was nearly dark, due mostly to the dust in the sky.

"Hi mom. Here are my four new workers! I brought them home for dinner, because I worked them very late tonight. We got quite a lot done today. I think that we will be grossing at least eight gold each day, once we get my girls all trained up. But tonight, they haven't got any food at their house, so I've invited them home for supper. I'm sorry mom; I should have let you know beforehand. I'll have to do some cooking, if you tell me what to do."

"I know you kids. You're the Prudentia girls aren't you?" Rubina asked.

"Yes, ma'am. We are. He's right. We are desperate right now," Pia answered meekly. "It's just us at home, and we're out of money, and there's no food. Until today, we couldn't even find a job. After we get paid, we will make this up to you somehow."

"Lordy, lordy, oh no you won't! We have to stick together! That's just what Stefano's been saying in the newspaper and that's what this Bethany lady has been saying in her very helpful columns each day. Now we don't have much, but we sure can share what we do have, can't we, Aldo. Lordy, these kids don't even have anyone to look after them! Aldo, can't you tell? They are wearing their nightgowns, not even proper clothes! I bet you are having the same problem that we are having, dears. Rosario here and I, we have a devil of a time trying to get dressed, don't we?"

Aldo's face crimsoned. He'd not realized that the four were wearing nightgowns.

"We can go to the bathroom this way, ma'am. When we had our dresses on, we just couldn't manage. We just don't know how to do it anymore, and there is no one to help us at all," Pia explained.

"Rubina, dears, just Rubina. My daughter, Rosario. Aldo, you are simply going to have to help them as well as us. That's all there is to it, Aldo. We all have to help each other as we can. Kids, after we eat, I want Aldo to help you all bathe and then get into some clean clothes. Whatever are we going to do about our hair? Now Rosario and I have been trying to figure that one out all day. We think that we have it, so after your baths, she and I will see if we can do it. Now, Aldo, you go start serving up what we got. We can sit on the floor if we have to. Come on girls; kitchen is this way."

"I'm Pia. This is Nena, Rosana, and Savina. We are ever so grateful, Rubina. We know that we are in big trouble, but now that Aldo has given us a job, maybe somehow, someway we can make it."

As they sat around the low table, Aldo began dishing out the stew. He realized that his mother had made extra, figuring on having it the next two days. Well, he'd get the gold for the two desks tomorrow and then get in some supplies, he thought.

"Honestly, Pia, what can my brother possibly be having you do? I used to pick and sell wild flowers, but I cannot pick them anymore. I cannot imagine what you four could possibly be doing. I know that he is making desks like the ones that we all need," Rosario asked, very curious indeed.

"We all did a lot of sanding at first," Pia answered. "We can get the table tops really smooth. Then, he made us a leather handle and taught us how to saw the lumber into the right pieces. Nena and I both did a bunch of sawing. Once he gets more things made for us, we can do lots more. It's rather fun to sand. When it's finished, it feels so smooth to our feet. We owe Aldo everything for giving us a chance. No one else would hire us or even give us a chance to try. We are actually down to our last copper. I don't know what we would have done if Aldo hadn't given us a job."

"Wow. Sawing? Sanding? Is this true, Aldo? They are really helping you build desks?" Rosario asked in disbelief.

"Yes, sis. You know that I was only able to make one desk a day. Well, today, we got one done, one drying, and three more cut out and ready for gluing. And that is just the beginning; we wasted a lot of time trying to figure out how to fix up the saws so they could learn to cut. Once we had that, they are becoming good at sawing, square and on the line."

"Hey, if they can do it, how about me? Then you would have five of us," she asked.

"Okay, sure sis. One more is always welcome. At two gold a desk, we can make even more each day," Aldo replied.

After they finished, Rubina insisted that Aldo follow them home and bring back some clean clothes for the girls. Meanwhile, she and his sister would get the bath ready for them. As the five walked down the street, Pia said, "Aldo, you have been incredibly kind to us. Your mom and sister too. How can we thank you?"

"I don't know. Honestly, my heart aches every time I look at mom, my sister, and you four. I hope they kill the monsters that did this to you. I guess just help me make all the desks that we can. Lord knows that we all need the money desperately, Pia." She smiled; he didn't know why, but he felt tingly. Inside their house, he noticed that the soldiers had installed the girls' new kitchen, but their cupboards were almost completely empty.

In their bedrooms, clothes lay about in disarray. They had been unable to get the hang of keeping house and had spent most of their time desperately trying to find a job. When he followed them into their large bedroom, he became embarrassed again. He spotted undergarments lying around, the ones that they had been unable to don themselves. The four asked him to take this dress and that one, but Pia then asked, "Aldo. What about panties? I mean, when we have to go, can you help us? If not, we will continue to go around without wearing panties. We just have no idea how we can take them off once we have them on. Why is your face so red?" Of course, Aldo's face got even brighter.

"I, ah, I haven't done, ah, I mean, I don't, I ah, well, yes, I will certainly help you, but you will have to tell me what to do, what needs to be done. Sorry, I don't know anything about such matters."

"Don't you have a girlfriend?" Pia asked, baffled by Aldo's reply.

"No, never had one. Guess that's why I don't know anything about girls. I am sorry, but I will help anyway that I can," he answered sincerely.

"Okay, we will take panties," Pia declared. Aldo, arms full of cotton dresses and panties, followed the girls out of their house. A bit later, he allowed Pia to use her foot to open his front door. Now Rubina and Rosario took charge, much to Aldo's relief.

However, that didn't last very long. Soon, Aldo was asked to wash their backs and help out with their bathing. Although his mother and sister continued to try to help wash the teens, Aldo was really needed to get the job done properly. "Just bear with us Aldo. One of these days, we will have it figured out somehow. That's what this Bethany keeps saying in the paper. Practice and it will come, she says."

Aldo grinned, "Yes, that's what I told Pia and her sisters. Practice and soon we will be making many desks. Maybe this Bethany knows what she is talking about."

Aldo was further embarrassed as he soon found himself having to dry each of the teens off, since his mother and sister just couldn't quite get it done well enough. "Thanks, Aldo," Pia whispered when he finished drying her off. Again, Aldo didn't know why he felt so tingly.

At last, the six women sat around with hairbrushes and dismissed him. He headed to the kitchen to make a pot of tea and relax. Finally, an hour later, the four teens came into the kitchen followed by his mother and sister, each of which looked extremely pleased. "Well, how do they look now, Aldo?" is sister asked proudly.

"Wow! Pia, you look, well, really great. Pretty. Nena, Rosana, Savina, wow, you all look good. Sis, you did a good job."

Pia smiled coyly, her red lips catching Aldo's undivided attention. Now that the dirt was off her face, her eyes looked so attractive! "Thanks, Aldo. We haven't had a proper bath since we got the plague."

"Aldo, they are going to spend the night here tonight. There is no point in their going home. In the first place, they need some help getting changed into their nightgowns. In the morning, they need help getting changed again. You simply cannot have them working in your shop wearing their nightgowns! Hardly civilized at all. Besides, there is nothing in their house for breakfast. At least here, they can have some porridge. First thing in the morning after you open up, take the two desks, and go get some gold for them, and spend the lot on food. I am going to try to see if I or Rosario can write you a readable list to get from the market. If they are all going to work for you, the least we can do is provide them their meals to help."

He smiled and headed off to make four makeshift beds. Later, he helped all six change into their night gowns. As he finished helping Pia into hers, she leaned over and kissed him. Both were very surprised at how electrifying their kisses were! Aldo now paid far more attention to Pia than he ever had!

The next morning, after opening the shop, Aldo left Pia to show his sister what to do, and he used his pushcart to transport the two desks. Indeed, he got his four gold plus a standing contract for as many more desks as he could produce! Elated, he then visited the markets, carried a large bag of food supplies home, and helped his mother put them away, before dashing off to his shop.

"Hey brother, I can do this too!" Rosario exclaimed very excitedly when he entered. Already the teens had made substantial progress. By day's end, they had five more desks ready to be delivered the next morning! In the days that followed, Stefano's purchasing men arranged to have a wagon drop by Aldo's shop each morning to pick up the new desks that were ready and to pay him for them. Stefano was desperate for as much product as could be obtained and was doing everything he could to facilitate those who were making the desperately needed products. All that Aldo needed to do was see that raw lumber was delivered in a timely manner.

One day in late August, Aldo heard a knock on his shop's door and went to see who was there. He blinked, there was a young teen wearing a beautiful gown, one of the wealthy of Velona, he just knew it.

"Hello. I'm looking for Aldo Tolio," I said.

"That's me, how can I help you, ma'am?"

"I'm Bethany Bartiana Angela. Maybe you've heard about my columns in the newspaper? Well, I heard something that intrigued me and I came to see if it is true."

The teens heard me identifying myself, and they all stopped working and came out to see if this was for real. "Er, mom and my sis have said something about a Bethany writing hints or something." He didn't quite know what to say, I could tell.

"Well, do you have women in your employ? I heard that your workers are indeed women?" I asked.

"Yes, of course. Ah, my sister, Rosario, my girlfriend now, Pia, her sisters, Nena, Rosana, and Savina. They are my workers. Why?"

"Hello. I'm Bethany, I write the helpful hints column in the newspaper." The five teens giggled and realized who I must be. "Do you really help make these desks? Really?"

"Sure, we do most of it," Pia explained. "Aldo does the measuring and marking of the lumber. We do the sawing, and we all help out on the drilling and gluing. Mostly he lets us do all the sanding. Why?" Pia asked.

"Well, I just wondered how you did all this. Could I possibly watch you and maybe I can pass on some tips that may help other women?" A few minutes later, I watched fascinated as the five teens went back to what they were doing. I saw the novel way he'd fixed up the saws for their use. After a half hour of watching and seeing for myself the quality of their work, I was truly impressed with them.

"Well, no one said that we could not possibly do this," Pia explained when I asked her about it. "I read that you said with the right tools, so I had Aldo make us the right tools. We can do this work, can't you see that?" She was being defensive, I noted.

"Pia, I can see that you make a really top quality desk! I admit that I just could not believe this at all. Aldo, would you mind if I shared with others how you have adapted the tools of your trade with others?"

"Er, no. Especially if it can help other women find a job," he answered.

"Thanks, it certainly will. Now then, Aldo, I have a proposition for you. I will buy the vacant shop next door to you here, give it to you, and see that any needed modifications to its interior are done to your specifications immediately. In return, I want you to hire on as many young women as you possibly can, train them, and turn out as many high quality desks as you can. Velona and the nineteen other countries need many, many more desks as rapidly as we can build them. The other shop is twice the size of this shop, so you ought to be able to make far more of these good writing desks. What say you?"

"But, I, ah, okay, but how much am I to pay you? Will you then be my boss?"

"I will not be your boss. You are the boss, unless you want to appoint one of your girls here as the boss. No, Aldo, I am doing my part. I have the finances to make things happen. You owe me nothing but to continue to produce as many of these fine desks as you possibly can. We women everywhere are dependent upon having them. So my part is to help people like you produce as many as possible and hire as many willing women as you can without sacrificing the quality of your products. There are so many women who are desperate for work."

"Okay, Bethany. You have a deal. That's why I have hired these four; they were almost starving to death. I had to help them earn a living, but it was Pia who showed me that she could do most anything if she and I can figure out a way to make her the proper tool. She's the greatest woman around!" Pia beamed with pride, as did her sisters.

"Oh, Pia, he is paying you a fair wage, isn't he?" I asked, but I felt confident that he was.

"He pays us more than he pays himself! Honestly, I keep telling him that we are being over paid," Pia replied.

His sister added, "And I keep telling him that he needs to hire an accountant to keep track of all the money his shop is making."

"Hey, I know a woman who is a trained accountant and is looking for a job now. It has taken her all this time to learn to write her figures well enough. With this expansion, you will need her services to help you keep this much larger venture running smoothly."

"Okay, send her by. I am tired of all that tedious bookkeeping anyway. Wow, we are going to triple our size. Pia, you and your sisters are going to make even more money! Thank you, Bethany! We'll do our part," Aldo insisted. Pia planted a passionate kiss, and his arms flew around her before he realized that they were embracing in public. He pulled away, red faced, but I understood fully.

"Okay, I will go make the arrangements. See you later on. Thanks Aldo, Pia, Nena, Rosario, Rosana, Savina. Bye." I left them, heading off to take care of the details. They were making six desks a day, so I hoped that now they would be making closer to twenty. I also intended to double their operation in about six months after they had the new women working up to speed. We had to meet the incredible demand for the items that we women needed and time was not on our side.

"I cannot believe our luck, Pia! We are going to be rolling in money now," Aldo exclaimed once I had gone.

"Aldo, we are already rolling in money," she teased him. "So what now?"

"Will you marry me, Pia? I am now confident that I can support you and raise a family. Please say yes. I love you so," Aldo begged.

"Of course, silly! I've been waiting for you to ask me for ages!" she moved close to him and they embraced again. Of course, the other four teens giggled and whispered among themselves.

By the start of the new year, Aldo Desks was turning out a hundred desks a week and employing twenty women workers. While this was still a small operation, I intended to keep on working with them to increase their size and thus output.

Chapter 17 Beppe's Wickers

182 Water Street is the location of Beppe's Wickers, a shop that specializes in wicker baskets, chairs, seat coverings, chests of drawers, and many other household items. Chairs, however, have made the shop famous in this area of town, as they make ideal lawn or patio chairs. Indeed, nearly all the surrounding homes and shops have at least one Beppe chair in them. Yet, Beppe is also known as the "luckless man."

Now thirty-six, Beppe Bonaventura is not unlucky in his business, far from it. His wicker products are topnotch, and the wealthy are sometimes seen shopping here at his combined storefront, workshop, and home. No, it is not in business this short, blazing yellow-haired man is luckless, rather is it his misfortune of having had six girls in a row without a single son! Capping it off was the premature death of his wife some six years back. The many other small shop owners around the area occasionally felt a touch of sympathy for him, for fathers usually left their businesses to their sons and poor Beppe had none.

Beppe ignored their infrequent sympathetic comments; he was still full of life and vitality, and he dearly loved his six daughters. Since the death of his wife of the lung rot six years ago, Beppe took over her duties as best he could. He regretted not that they had had no sons. Each of his daughters he treasured, all of whom had the same yellow hair as he, plus his wife's deep blue eyes. His eldest were twins, Carla and Celia, now sixteen. Then came Adriana at fifteen, Elisabetta at fourteen, Gabriella at thirteen, and finally Marcella, who he still called his little baby though she was now twelve.

From the time that the girls could walk, they spend long hours in their dad's shop. He always found something that they could do to help him. To say that he doted on his brood would be correct. He dearly loved them and spent as much time with them as he could, which is why they were always helping him in his shop, even when his wife was alive. Upon her death, little changed for this family. Celia, who wore her hair just barely long enough to touch her shoulders, took over the cooking duties for the family, filling her mother's shoes. The laundry duties fell to their youngest, Marcella, who chose to have her yellow tresses long like her sister Adriana. Those two refused to have their hair cut short, in spite of Carla's often insistence.

Carla knew well that her father ought to have had a son to take over his wicker business one day. Thus, when Marcella was born, she was determined to fulfill that role for her papa. Now sixteen, Carla knew everything about the business and really was Beppe's right hand man. She dressed the part, wearing her hair cut very short, even shorter than Beppe's. She always wore pants and took charge of the business, as well as doing her share of the actual construction of the many wicker products. Beppe often said that she was as good as any son could possibly be, which pleased her immensely. Customers often mistook her for a young lad, so careful was she to fulfill that role which she saw society requiring.

Her twin sister, Celia, on the other hand, wore her hair a bit longer and fluffier, as she remembered her mother had. Of all the girls, she had always been the one sticking close to their mother. Upon her mother's death, she naturally assumed many of the family chores of her mother, most importantly the preparation of their meals. Celia now did all the shopping and all the cooking for the brood, nearly a full time occupation for a family this size. However, she too lent a hand in the workshop as well.

In fact, in June of 822, all six teens spent their days helping their papa in the shop. All knew well the art of wicker and were quite good at it. Carla, however, was always the second in command, behind papa, claiming that she wore the pants. She always accompanied him on his trips to acquire more supplies and tools. She handled his banking and doling out the funds to Celia for their daily needs, thus freeing papa from such tasks.

Around this area of Water Street, they were widely known as a very happy family. Often on a summer evening, they could all be seen sitting on their back patio beneath their wicker awning sitting on comfortable wicker chairs chatting merrily or listening to one of papa's tales of high adventure, which he was always making up for his "little girls." Carla remembered how he had begun making up these stories for her when she was five. Even to this day, he was always drilling into their minds that anyone could do anything in life, if only they set their mind to it. There was always a way to win. This became the usual theme buried within his tales of high adventure that he invented for his daughters.

Of course, four of his daughters were now of age and ought to be seeking a husband and a life of their own. However, Beppe somehow just could not let go of his daughters; they were so precious to him. Carla had no such thoughts of boys; she focused her full attention on the wicker business. "One day, papa is going to need me and you to run it for him," she always told her sisters, who believed her. Well, all except Celia, who did have a boyfriend, who lived two doors down, Durante Pachino, the son of a keg maker. Often on Saturday nights, Durante and Celia went to the local dances.

This intrigued Adriana, Lis, Gabriella, and Marcella, who always demanded to know all about each night out that their older sister had. Celia was eager to tell them as well, filling in for her mother. Carla merely poo-pooed such nonsense, preferring to continue to keep their banking records up to date on Saturday nights. Carla knew that their business was very profitable, and that they had over a thousand gold saved up in the bank, a fact of which she was very proud.

Each Sunday, Beppe insisted that they all dress up and attend services at the Holy Rose Church. On these days, Beppe wore his fine black suit with twin tails, but always stood grinning and smiling as his six daughters dashed around their rooms taking forever to get dressed up and ready. Beppe also cut their hair when needed. He kept his short, and Carla insisted on having hers done the same way, though he always managed to cut hers a bit longer than his in spite of her orders. He was all thumbs when it came to the very long locks of Adriana and now Marcella. Celia deftly handled their long hair for him.

Also on Sundays, Beppe and his daughters always took their next-door neighbors with them to church. Mona Doran was a thirty-three year old widow, whose husband had been a soldier and had been killed in the line of duty. Her older son Piedro was eighteen, married now two years, and living in the northern town of Alta. Twice a year, Piedro came down to visit them. Mona still had her twin daughters living with her, both sixteen, Nora and Pina. All three women had long brown hair. Mona took in laundry for the neighborhood, since her husband died some three years ago. Her daughters were a big help to her as they struggled to get by.

Beppe liked Mona and he most definitely sympathized with her situation. Beppe had already donated a set of lawn chairs to her and was always fixing things around Mona's house when they broke. Carla always said to her siblings, "It's our duty to look out for the Doran's, who are less fortunate than we." Celia and Nora and Pina were best friends, which only helped.

"Papa, this dust cloud is going to make the willows die off, don't you think?" Carla asked Beppe when the cloud finally turned day into night.

"Oh, maybe it will just blow away," he tried to sound hopeful.

"But papa, what if it doesn't and there are no more willows?" she countered. "We could run out of branches. Then what would we do? Take in laundry like Mona?"

"Well, I suppose that it wouldn't hurt to take in an extra-large load, just in case," Beppe went along with her. She was more often right and quite bright. "Okay, let's see what we can get."

"Okay, papa, I'll take care of it. You keep on working on the chairs for Mrs. Wiggens." Later that afternoon, Carla returned with the largest supply of willows that Beppe had ever seen! It took all seven of them the rest of the night to get them properly stored in every conceivable location within their large shop.

Over a late supper, which Celia grumbled had gone cold on them, Carla said, "The paper is suggesting that we store up food, oil, charcoal, and coal. I think that they think that we are in for some very hard times. What do you think, papa?"

He chuckled, "Well, we have all this willow. It would be a shame if we didn't have enough charcoal to run the heater to warp and shape them. Okay, I think that it might be wise. Carla, see what you can get us tomorrow.

Celia, lay in a goodly supply of dried food. We don't want fresh things because they would spoil. I suppose that I ought to suggest that Mona stocks what she can afford to as well."

"I'll tell them, papa," Celia volunteered. "I'm going to go play cards with Nora and Pina after I do the dishes."

Some days later, Beppe tried to calm his daughters down. "Maybe the paper has it wrong."

"But papa! Stefano is telling everyone to get a long gun and to be on the lookout for these alien flying ships tomorrow!" Carla exclaimed, terribly worried, as were all his daughters.

They were interrupted by a knock on their back door. It could only be their neighbors. Celia let Mona and her daughters into their kitchen. Beppe quickly brought three more chairs for them. "Thanks, Beppe," Mona said. Her face showed signs of fear and worry. "What do you make of all this talk of aliens and flying machines? Should we get us a long gun? Will we be safe? What would aliens want of us?"

Carla stated, "Stefano is telling us to get long guns and shoot these things. Look, he is the monarch, and if he says it is so, then it is so!"

Nora added, "Throw rocks into their engines. It said that we are supposed to throw rocks if we can't get a long gun."

"Long guns aren't safe. You can get hurt or even killed by them," Beppe cautioned, looking sympathetically at Mona, whose soldier husband had been so killed.

Mona sighed, "I know what you are thinking Beppe, but maybe we should. What if these aliens land and try to harm us?"

Beppe looked at all the women around him and sighed, "Perhaps you are right. I will go and see if there are any to be had. You all stay here until I get back, please." They agreed. He knew that tonight Mona really did not want to be alone.

An hour later, he returned empty handed. "I just don't believe it! There's not a long gun to be had at any of the nearby stores! I even went all the way over to High Street. No luck. They are saying that they've been sold out since noon!"

"Well, that settles it, papa! We have to go scrounge up as many rocks as we can find!" Carla took charge. "Come on; let's go outside and lay in a pile." The eight teens dashed out, leaving Mona and Beppe sitting at the table.

He took her hand and said softly, "Mona, it will be okay. I'm sure that this will all blow over soon. Please, I want you and your girls to stay here with us until it is done."

She took his hand in hers and gave a good squeeze. "Thank you Beppe. I don't know what I'd do without you." He smiled and they chatted. A while later, the teens came back inside, having made a large pile of stones on their back porch. All were excited that the Doran's would be spending the night with them, especially Celia. The teens dashed off to their rooms with Nora and Pina in tow.

"You take my bed tonight, Mona. I can sleep on the couch in the front room," he suggested. Mona tried to refuse, but he wouldn't hear of anything else.

When the first gunshot sounded, the eight teens made a dash for the porch door, Beppe and Mona followed along behind them. "Papa! Look! Flying ships! Come on! Throw our rocks at them. See if you can hit their engines!" Carla ordered and yelled. Soon, even Beppe and Mona were tossing rocks! The cannonae sounds were deafening, as well as the multitude of gunshots. All ten of them soon were lost in the frenzy of the battle. Only when they ran out of rocks and were also out of breath did they stop and watch.

"Look, papa! I think someone got that little one. It is wobbling around! Come on; crash into the ground!" yelled Carla. The other teens joined her in encouraging the small ship to crash. It didn't, but that didn't stop them from continuing to yell for it to fall out of the sky.

Wham! A stray bullet fell down and smashed into the patio deck, startling them. "Come on, kids, get inside! We might get hit by a bullet!" Beppe ordered. A bit startled, they obeyed. A short while later, the guns fell silent, and they all headed back outside once more.

"Papa! I think we won. I don't see any more of the ships," Carla proclaimed victory. The grey dust cloud was the only thing visible, though the smell of gunpowder drifted by their back porch.

By nightfall, the excitement died down, and at last Mona felt that all was now safe. She and her daughters returned to their home next door. The next day, Beppe began to notice subtle changes in all of his precious daughters. They seemed to tire easily while working in the shop; their strength was just not there today. He chalked it up to all the excitement from the previous afternoon. Still, he felt ill at ease the whole day.

The second day, Beppe knew that something horrible was wrong! All six teen's arms were so terribly thin and had shortened somehow. They could barely move their arms, and all six were quite frightened, begging him to tell them what was happening to them, what was wrong with them. He felt very sick and had no answer. However, he had the presence of mind to go check on Mona and her daughters. All three were scared out of their wits, and he brought them over to his house so that he could look after them all.

All were extremely scared by nightfall. Beppe had to do all the cooking; Celia could no longer move her matchstick arms. None of them could! He did his best to feed all nine of them, and he helped each one get into bed and tucked them in. Beppe just could not say to them, "It will be better in the morning."

As he finally tucked Mona into his bed, she begged him, "Beppe! I am so scared. Please, please will you sleep beside me tonight and maybe just hold me. I am terrified, please?" He could not resist her plea, crawled into bed beside her, and comforted her as he could. He finally fell into a troubled, fitful sleep.

Screams! He awoke to terror screams coming from his girl's bedrooms! He sat up only to hear a startled scream from his side! Mona had wakened and sat up as well, only she was now screaming as loudly as the eight teens! Beppe turned to see what was wrong with Mona; he felt his overly long ears flopping around; strange sensations came from them, but such was dwarfed by his tense stomach. Mona had no arms now at all and was screaming hysterically.

He got her up on her feet and then dashed for his daughters two bedrooms! He saw the girls also sitting up in their beds, armless and screaming wildly. He glanced into the second bedroom and saw the others were the same way, shaking and screaming uncontrollably. Beppe vomited in the hallway and nearly collapsed himself.

He recovered and went inside the door and opened his arms, beckoning his girls to come to him. He watched as they wiggled out of bed and came rushing to his arms; even Nora came to him as well. He put his arms around all four of them, moved them down the hall a few feet to the other bedroom, and repeated his gesture, tears nearly blocking his vision. At once, the four in here ran to him, and he tried hard to hold onto all eight of the crying, sobbing teens at one time.

"Got to get to Mona," he tried to say, but nearly choked on the words. With bumping and stumbling, he got the mass of eight teens to his bedroom door and motioned for Mona to come to him too. Still crying hysterically, Mona struggled to get out from under the sheets and came over to join the pile up around him. Beppe managed at least to touch her, which began to calm Mona a little. For some time, they all stood there in the hallway sobbing and crying.

Finally, Carla whimpered, "Papa, I have to go pee." A bunch of me too's echoed. "I can't get my panties down, papa! I'm scared!" she added.

"Okay, Carla. Be brave. I'll help each one of you. Let's line up at the bathroom. Carla's first." He led them down the hall to the bathroom and began to help them go, one at a time. "Let's leave your panties off for now, Carla, shall we? Maybe then you won't have to have me with you. I know that this is embarrassing for you." She managed the tiniest of grins.

Twenty minutes later, he finally got to Mona, who was determined to go last, allowing her daughters to go before her. She stopped crying hysterically and was rather subdued. Beppe observed that they all were wearing their loose fitting nightgowns, which fell to just below their knees. All their sleeves were drooping — no arms present any longer. He felt sick once more.

Carla whimpered, "Papa, what's happened to us? Where did our arms go? We are so helpless like this. Please, find our arms and put them back on." A bunch of "yes, please" followed.

"Kids, I don't know what's happened to all of you. I really don't. I am as scared as you are."

"Papa, I'm hungry," Marcella whimpered forlornly.

"I know honey, I know. We all are. Why don't you all head to the kitchen and papa will fix us some breakfast?"

"But papa, how can we even eat?" Gabriella asked, tears still trickling down her cheeks.

"There, there, Gabi, don't cry," Beppe said softly. He grabbed handkerchief and dabbed her cheeks dry. One by one, he did the same to his teens and then did Mona's twins as well, finishing up with Mona. "There, we must be brave. I can feed you as I did yesterday, but Celia is going to have to tell me what to cook. You all know how lousy a cook I am," he tried to tease them a little.

"I bet the aliens did this to us," Carla declared. Now they all began agreeing with this idea and headed off to the kitchen, Beppe bringing up the rear, blowing his nose on the soaked handkerchief.

"Well, what will it be for breakfast?" he tried to sound a cheerful note, but mostly failed.

Celia said softly, trying desperately to avoid another bout of sobbing, "Bacon, eggs, rolls, papa."

"I want pancakes," Marcella added hopefully.

"Pancakes it is for my little angel," Beppe tried to sound a more cheerful note. Celia began giving him suggestions and Beppe, unused to cooking, was thankful for her directions. It took nearly two hours for him to get breakfast made, the nine women fed, and the dishes cleaned up.

While he was trying to cleanup, Carla said, "Papa, we are very late opening the shop. What if a customer has come?"

"Well, I'll open up after bit." Running his shop right now was the furthest thing on his mind.

"I'll go open up as usual, papa," Carla declared. She often had been the one who opened up their storefront of a morning. A bit later, she came crying back to him. "Papa, I can't open the doors. They've got knobs and I can't turn them." Beppe broke down and cried himself. His back was to the nine and he allowed himself to cry.

Once the dishes were done, he sniffled to clear his nose and turned to face the nine. "Well, first thing, all the doorknobs have to go. I can't have my angels locked in, now can we. Mona, you and your twins are staying with us for the time being. Eventually, I fix your doorknobs too. Okay my little workers, to the doors."

"But papa, we aren't your little workers anymore, we are all grown up," Marcella protested.

Carla began to cry again. "We can't work anymore! None of us can help papa run the store or make wicker things. Nothing. We can't do anything anymore!" Now all nine began wailing once more, as her words stung them like a barbed whip! Beppe felt like his heart was being wrenched from his chest!

His youngest, Marcella, spoke up, her voice piercing through the sobbing, "But papa is always telling us, Carla, that anyone could do anything, if only they set their mind to it. There was always a way. We have to find it, that's all. Right papa?"

Through his tear-clogged eyes, Beppe looked down at the bright blue eyes of his youngest daughter with her pretty long yellow hair, so like her mother. He wiped his eyes on his shirt sleeve and managed to back her up. "Yes, that's the spirit, Marcella. Anyone can do anything; we just have to find a way. Come on. We have to get rid of the doorknobs. I can't have all of you trapped in a room. How can we get any work done if you get stuck in some room? You wait here while I get some tools."

He ducked into his huge workshop, grabbed a screwdriver, and headed back in time to hear Marcella say, "Gabriella, papa is going to get rid of our doorknob first." The two shared a bedroom along with Lis and now Pina.

"Right angel. Now papa needs your help, yours too Gabi. I want you to sit here and put your feet on the door. Marcella, you sit on this side of the door and push against Gabi. You two hold the door steady while I undo everything." Both girls sat down and pushed against the door, holding it relatively still. Soon he had removed the knobs and the latching mechanism.

"Okay, there you go. Now you four experiment and see what else we need to do so you can get in and out easily. Carla, yours is next. You and Celia hold it for me, please." Both teens sat down and did as Marcella and Gabriella had done. After that, Carla insisted on following him to each door and holding them still for him. Adrianna joined her as well, since it took two.

An hour later, they finally had removed the last one, the storefront's lock. However, they saw almost no one out on the dimly lit street, and it was getting close to noon! This had never happened before. Beppe guessed that everyone else was home in the same mess as they.

"Papa! Come quick!" Elisabetta called out from the front room. Everyone dashed to her and stopped short. There in the middle of the floor was a large pile of objects. "Papa, what are all these things? Where did they come from?"

"Well, that's a teapot and that's a cooking pot, only they have such strange handles," Celia pointed out. "That's a sink and stove, right papa?"

"Hey, what's this stick with four legs and two baskets for?" asked Marcella. "The stick is bent in the middle. Somebody used a broken stick, I'll bet."

"No, Marcella," Adriana suddenly spoke up with a curious note in her voice. She walked over to it, bent down, and moved under it. "See, the bend fits our necks." She stood up, and the yoke rose, the two baskets were now off the floor. She walked a bit and exclaimed, "Hey, we can carry things around in the basket! I bet that's what this is for, so we can carry things."

Thus, the implanted genetic memories began to surface in these nine women. As Beppe began to sort through the items, more and more strange ideas appeared in their minds. Finally, Beppe realized that here was a replacement kitchen, one that would help them deal with cooking and such.

"Say, I'd better go check on your house, Mona. At least I need to remove the doorknobs so you and the twins can get what you need. You are still staying here until further notice," Beppe insisted. Mona leaned into him to give him a heartfelt hug, and his arms found their way around her and pulled her tightly to him. "I know. I am here for you, Mona," he whispered in her ear.

"Okay, I need two assistants to help me with Mona's doors. Meanwhile see if you can carry the cooking stuff into the kitchen." Carla and Adriana volunteered to help and Nora and Pina came along too. As they left, Beppe heard Marcella and Gabriella arguing over who got to use the yoke thing first. He smiled, for once it was good to hear them arguing.

An hour later, the five returned. "Mom! We've got the same pile of stuff in our house," Nora exclaimed.

"Okay kids, while Celia and Mona and I fix some lunch, you kids see about carrying the pots, pans, cup, and stuff over here to our kitchen. There's another yoke thing over there. Some of you will have to hold the doors open. Hop to it," Beppe ordered, giving the teens something to do while he butchered lunch.

"Papa! You are making a complete mess of it!" Celia chided him and his pathetic efforts to fix a hearty stew, figuring they could eat it for supper too.

"She's right, Beppe, you put that in last, not first," Mona agreed with Celia. Pina, who was watching, giggled.

Two more hours later, Beppe finally got the nine fed and the mess cleaned up. He groaned, for it was almost time to start thinking about supper!

"Papa! There is a soldier at our door," Carla called out. She'd gone to see who was pounding on their door. Hastily, Beppe joined Carla.

"Hello. Stefano has asked us to check every house. Are there any adult males living here? Well, that's obvious." He checked off the address on his list. "I got no answer next door. Do you know if anyone is living there, sir?"

"Yes, a widow and her two daughters. I am having them stay with us for now."

"Very good sir. Okay, I will mark that one as needing a man. Oh yes, have you received a complete replacement kitchen plus a number of other items?"

"Well, yes, we finally figured that the stuff is supposed to replace nearly everything in the kitchen."

"Right on that one. Are you qualified and capable of installing all those kitchen items yourself or is there someone else here who is?"

"Well, I think so. I haven't gotten to it yet. I could use some help. We need to do Mona's kitchen next door too. I don't suppose that there is anyone who could lend us a hand is there? I mean this calamity must be citywide, eh?"

"Yes, sir. Citywide. I will see if someone can assist you tomorrow. Until then, make do as you can. Good day." He left and the two returned to the front room.

"Hey papa, look at me. I am brushing Marcella's hair with this fancy new brush," Gabriella called out. Beppe watched, as Gabi was indeed being successful with Marcella's long yellow hair. The brush had a leather handle on it that fit her foot rather well.

"Papa, we need more brushes like that one," Elisabetta added. "We only got one, Nora's got one too. We need seven more, papa."

"Six, I don't need one," Carla added. "See, if you cut your hair short like papa and me, then you wouldn't have to worry about brushing it." Beppe grinned.

Two days later and with the help of a soldier, the two kitchens were finally redone. However, Beppe insisted that Mona stay with them, and that they merge her food supplies with theirs. They also brought over a number of other items and clothes as well. No way was Beppe going to have Mona attempt to get by on her own! Of course, the girls giggled a lot when they found out that from now on Mona was going to be sleeping in the same bed as their papa.

That next morning, Beppe finally got a break. Tired of his slightly burned eggs and rolls, Celia and Mona began to attempt to figure out how they could now cook in the new kitchen. With the counter so low and with the new items that had handles that they could manage with their feet, combined with their two chairs on rollers, they actually got breakfast made. Beppe had cut off the legs of their main table, adding it to the new low table, which made enough room for the ten to eat at once. He joined them by sitting on the floor. By now, they were all experimenting with valiant attempts at feeding themselves, though he was there to help as needed.

As they finished their tea, Beppe couldn't help saying, "See, I told you that you can do anything, if you just set your mind to it. There is always a way somehow. I am so proud of all you girls! You and yours too, Mona. You are all doing very well indeed." The nine women all grinned and began to believe what he was saying.

"Celia, I must compliment you on your foresight in laying in such a good supply of food for us. Very well done, dear. You too, Carla, well done. I think that we will have a hard time getting more willow in the near future. I promise to always listen to you both!" The twins grinned.

"Papa, we need more of these desks. With nine of us, we each ought to have one," Adriana explained. "We are supposed to use them to be able to write again."

"Papa, I want my own yoke," Marcella broke in. "I can't carry anything without it, unless I use my teeth."

"We need more of those mugs, papa," Celia added.

"Okay, family council time; Mona, you and your twins are now officially family too, if you don't mind," he grinned.

She teased him, "Beppe, is that a proposal I'm hearing from you?" Beppe flushed, resolved to speak of that later when they were alone.

With the eight kids sitting on the sofas and he and Mona sitting opposite them on soft chairs, he began. "Kids, we need to make some plans so that we can all survive better in the future. What things do we need around here the most? I am going to make us a list. Then, we'll see about doing the most urgent ones first."

"We need more yokes papa," Marcella spoke before anyone else had the chance.

"Yes, but papa, I've been thinking," Carla added, "the two yokes are bulky. We could make them from willow and put soft pads where they meet our shoulders. Also, for carrying lighter things, these are way too bulky and awfully wide. We need some that are thin and lightweight, plus some ones that don't stick out from our sides so far. We can carry around lighter household things easier that way. Then, when we need to carry heavier loads, like more charcoal, we ought to have stronger yokes. I think that we ought to have a variety of them for different uses."

"You know," Mona broke in, "she has a point there. Some really lightweight, small ones would be idea for things around the house."

"Great ideas. I got them written down. What else do we need around here?" Beppe asked. Of course, they wanted more desks, mugs, fancy spoons and forks, and many more things. They wanted the doors to swing both ways so that they could enter easily from either direction. Carla suggested having a sliding latch at the bottoms of the doors so that they could shut them. Plus, she suggested that they could then be somehow locked to make their store secure once more. She was worried about always having their shop door unlocked and with no doorknob.

"I hate to bring this up, kids, but what about clothes? You've been going around in your nightgowns since this all started. Am I looking at always having to dress you?" Beppe asked. He got an earful.

That night after Mona and Beppe tucked the teens in bed and entered his bedroom, Beppe finally got up the nerve to ask. "Mona, I really do love you. Would you consider marrying me?" Mona wanted to throw her arms around him, but couldn't. She whispered yes, leaned into him, and gave him a passionate kiss. Both soon found themselves in bed!

The next morning, both rose very contented. At breakfast, Beppe explained, "Girls, Mona and I have an announcement. Mona has agreed to marry me. However, girls, I want you to have a say in this too. She can never replace mom, but. . ."

"Yes, papa! We thought that you'd never ask her!" Celia interrupted him. All six of his teens cheered him.

"Now let's don't get too excited yet. I mean, Nora and Pina have a say in this too, since I'm marrying their mother," Beppe cautioned.

"Of course we approve, mom!" Nora giggled excitedly. "We love Beppe too. Are we going to have a big wedding, mom?"

She didn't get a chance to answer as the teens began talking at once, congratulating Beppe and Mona and saying how they knew it all along.

Later that day, Beppe finally got each of them dressed. While the women loved the fact that they had such marvelous figures — Mona claiming that somehow she'd lost twenty pounds — none of their dresses fit at all well. Hence, uniformly they all chose to wear pants and a shirt. However, the sleeves were annoying, but since they were short, they agreed to manage for now.

Now looking presentable for the first time in a long while, Beppe finally headed into his workshop determined to deal with the yoke problem. He saw this as their number one problem. Yes, he could be interrupted to help the nine use the bathroom when needed, but their inability to carry or move anything around was pivotal. Carla and Adriana followed him into the workshop.

"Well, kids, we have lots of willow here. Let's see what we can do for yokes, shall we?" he suggested.

"We want to help, papa. Before, we could do everything, but now we can't, papa," Carla said, fighting back tears of disappointment. "If only you had a son. . ."

"Now cut that out, Carla. I love every one of my angels. I don't need a son, not when I have all of you pretty ones. Remember, we just have to figure this out. You both know well what has to be done. Let's just figure out how you can now do it, okay? Now we'll start with some lightweight ones for around the house use. Those are most critical, don't you think?" They agreed.

"See if you two can find us some inchers." He meant willows that were an inch in diameter. "I'll start the steamer going."

The two teens soon found some willows of the right size. Using their feet and teeth, they managed to extract them from the pile and brought them over to the workbench. "How are we going to use the saws, papa?" asked Carla, staring at the saw, which she had used nearly every day before this had happened.

"Well, first thing is that your workbench needs to be lowered," he mused. A half hour later, he'd sawed off the legs, and now she could sit on the floor and deal with her bench effectively. She tried to hold the saw between her feet, but that was ineffective.

"If only it could fasten to my foot, I could saw, papa," she suggested. He wrapped a bit of soft willow around the saw handle and her foot, and she experimented and was effectively able to make her first cut. Seeing this as a successful action, he rummaged around, found some leather, and made a foot loop on two saws, one for each girl. Elated with their success, they eagerly set to work. Both knew well what had to be done, they'd helped in the shop since they were six. Adriana and Carla worked as a team, designing a lightweight yoke for each of them, fitting their body size and shape.

When they had the willows cut properly, Beppe had the willow branches steamed and ready for wrapping. An hour later, the two V-shaped poles were secured to either end along with a crosspiece. A bit of thin rope would hold the two baskets. Now the two worked on how the baskets ought to be shaped.

That decided, Beppe began handing out strips of steamed wicker, allowing the girls to do the weaving themselves. He knew that they totally knew the process; they'd done this hundreds of times before. Now he wanted to see if they could somehow manage to do it with their feet. The first thing he noticed was that it was back breaking for the teens, leaning as they constantly had to do in order to use their feet. He quietly remedied that by fixing up some slanted backstops for each. Both felt instant relief!

When Celia and Mona called for supper, the two teens proudly carried their new yokes into the main part of the house. From the excited squeals that Beppe heard as he shut down the steamer, he knew these would be an instant hit with all the women. He was right!

During the next few days, Beppe converted all the other workbenches to a low height and fixed up four more saws so that the other teens could help make their own yokes as well. Soon, the kids and Mona each had three different yokes, fitted perfectly to their own heights. One was a lightweight one that they used to carry the newspaper, dirty clothes, towels, and other things around the house. One was a heavier, very sturdy one that could carry ten pounds per basket. The third was intermediate in size.

"Papa, we should put up a sign advertising that we make yokes," Carla insisted. That night, she worked for hours making a sign that would have normally taken her a few minutes to whip up. She was determined to make it look professional!

Mona and Beppe discussed what to do with Mona's house and laundry shop. She and her twins used to make their living taking in laundry. "Look lacking arms isn't going to stop people from having dirty clothes that need washing. I think you can still run your business."

He and the three spent another couple of days redoing Mona's shop. Because women were the ones who usually dropped off the laundry, they would now need to use yokes to carry them. The front door was too small, making it terribly difficult for them to negotiate. He removed the door and enlarged it double-wide, saying that whenever carpenters returned to work, he'd have them make a better doorframe. Now it was wide enough for easy access. Mona and her twins then began to work out what changes they had to make to be able somehow to deal with the laundry.

The biggest change was lowering everything close to the ground and re-stringing the numerous clotheslines so that they could reach them with their feet. Two days later, Mona put up a new sign advertising that the Mona's Laundry was again open for business.

By the first week of August, Mona began to have all the laundry business she and her twins could handle. Folks had been storing up their dirty things for weeks now. On the other hand, the yoke business blossomed almost the very day that Carla posted her new sign! With the three models on display, orders began coming in until after a week, all five teens were constantly busy making yokes. Only Celia didn't, she was kept busy in the kitchen cooking for everyone. Business was booming, and at last, money was coming in once more, although they really didn't need the money. Food was fast becoming the problem as it was for everyone.

On the eleventh of August, wearing my pants and driving my T-putt-putt, I arrived at 182 Water Street to check out the report of someone making excellent yokes of wide varieties. The sign read: Beppe's Yokes — All Sizes Made to Order. I knocked on the door with my foot and a young woman called out, "Come on in. You don't have to knock."

I pushed the door open and stepped inside. Whoa! Yokes were everywhere. Made from willow and with soft cloth wrappings where they would lay over our shoulders and necks; these yokes did come in all manner of sizes and a wide variety of baskets too. A teenager with very short, very yellow hair and an infectious smile came walking in from the backroom workshop. She too wore pants and was a bit sweaty, having just arisen from working with steamed strips. "Hi, I'm Carla. Looking for just the right yoke?"

"Hi, I'm Bethany Bartiana Angela. I am truly impressed with the incredible variety of yokes that you are making."

She grinned, "Say, are you the one who's been writing all those articles in the newspaper?"

"Yes, that's me."

"Excellent! Keep them coming. We are all finding them so useful you know. So you need yokes? We have them. We can make them to fulfill any need. Now these smaller ones are ideal for around the house, lightweight with low sides on the overly large basket, perfect for carrying laundry, sheets, and such. The big ones are for carrying heavier loads, like fetching more charcoal or a bunch of groceries, that is, if you can find much besides fish these days."

"These are incredible. How did you ever figure out how to make them?" I asked as the lights began to go off in my head. These would be incredibly useful around our house!

"Necessity. We have nine of us women here, and only one man, papa. So you see these were very necessary for us to invent right away. Now we always make them just the right height to fit each woman or girl."

"Well, I'd like six of the lightweight ones, six heavy ones, and six sort of in the middle. I can tell you the shoulder height of each of us, will that do?" It did. She scampered around the store assembling them for me. I felt a little guilty, for I was buying nearly half of her stock!

"Oh that's no problem, Bethany. You see, this is Monday, and all these we made over the weekend when we were not open. We make quite a few of these each day. They sell for a gold each. Is that okay?"

"Sure is! Say, can I possibly see how these are made? I take it that you run this store?"

She giggled. "No, it's papa's store. I run the storefront so he can keep us all busy in the back making them. Follow me." She led me into the next room, and I realized their store section was only a very small part of the whole building. I entered a stream bath, more or less.

"Hey, everybody. This is the Bethany. She's the one who is writing all those great articles in the paper each day. She wants to see how we make our yokes," Carla called out. I looked at four other yellow haired teens sitting on the floor busily weaving baskets with their feet and toes. Nearby, a tall man with just as yellow hair was trying to keep up with the demand for more steamed wicker. Sweat dripped from his forehead as he looked up. At once, the teens stopped and got up to come over and say hi. Beppe rose, wiped the sweat from his brow, and followed.

"Beppe Bonaventura, pleased to meet you. Your articles are an inspiration for my nine angels here. This is my youngest, Marcella." He introduced me to his five teens. "Marcella, go fetch your sister Celia, and then get Mona and the twins." Turning to me, he explained, "There's more. Celia is Carla's twin sister. I just got married to a wonderful woman, Mona. She's got twin daughters too. All told, I have nine of the best women in Velona, that I do. Carla here will one day take over my shop. She is a super wicker maker. Heck, they all are good at it. Ah, here's my other twin, Celia. She's been assigned permanent cook for this large outfit."

We had just got introduced when Marcella ran back with Mona and her twins, Nina and Pina. They were doing laundry next door, I discovered. All were actually very pleased to meet the woman behind all the highly encouraging, useful articles in the paper.

"Beppe, Carla, besides getting some very much needed new yokes, I've also come for another reason. As you well know, thousands upon thousands of yokes are now needed, countless beyond number. I would like to make you a business offer."

"Well, papa, you should invite her for some tea," Carla pointed out. A bit later, I sat in their kitchen sipping tea and outlining what I had in mind. Two blocks away was Stan's Warehouse, currently empty. It would quintuple their workshop space. I offered to buy the warehouse and all the equipment that Carla and Beppe would need to fill the warehouse and begin a larger scale production of yokes. In return, I wanted them to hire mostly women who needed a job. While he would need a few men to handle the purchase and transporting of such a large volume of willows and charcoal and a few to handle the steamers, women would make up the vast majority of his workers. This he was very willing to do.

Later, Marco arrived with the motor-wagon to pick up our eighteen new yokes, and I said goodbye, but promised to drop by later on and chat. As I left, I heard Carla exclaim, "Papa! We're going to be millionaires!" I grinned, not likely millionaires, but they would be well rewarded, that's for sure.

Within a few months, they were producing nearly a thousand yokes per week. At last, we began to start having yokes for the desperate women. I did an article on how the wicker yokes were made. These, we all soon discovered, were a vast improvement over the old ones based on those we had had in Dorota.

Chapter 18 Engineer Rinella

When Marcella Rinella was five years old, her parents took her to see the passenger train, the Coastal Comet. From the moment Marcella saw the train, she knew that she wanted to be an engineer and drive one of these mammoth steam engines! She begged for train rides and often got them as her birthday presents while she grew up.

When she was twelve, she began studying everything the Laird Library had on steam engines and their adaption to the trains. When she was fourteen and of age she was highly knowledgeable on the whole subject and eagerly went to apply for a job as an engineer.

"I'm sorry, miss. Only men are accepted as engineers. It is a rough job, very demanding physically. They must know vast amounts about the mechanical operation of the engines. They have to be very strong to shovel all that coal into the burners. I'm sorry miss," the man had said.

Devastated. Devastated beyond all reason, Marcella went home and cried for days, refusing even to eat. Her parents tried to get her to see reason and perhaps to put her knowledge to use in other industries, which were making use of steam, such as the cloth making factories. Marcella refused even to consider them. One day, she reached a decision. She told her parents that she was moving out to get her own room and a job at a factory downtown.

She did so, got a small room, but not the job. Alone in her small room at a boarding house, she looked in the mirror at her lovely, long black hair. Marcella took a deep breath and began to cut. A half hour later, her hair was now very short. She slipped into some pants and donned an old shirt of her dad's that she'd swiped before she left home and headed to the store. When she returned, Marcella now had five men's shirts, underwear, pants, and heavy work boots similar to those she had seen engineers wear, along with more casual men's shoes. Eagerly, she tried them on and stared at her appearance in the mirror. Her small bust was not that noticeable, and she felt confident that she could pass as a young man and began calling herself Marcello Rinella.

She began working out and building up her muscles, intent upon being able to shovel coal as the man had suggested. She hung around the train yards near the docks, lending the engineers there a hand. Slowly, she picked up even more knowledge about their maintenance and learned the key datum: next month, they were hiring a number of young men into a training pool. Marcello immediately went to the station master and put his name in for the pool. The following month, he joined twenty other young men in their on-the-job training.

Carrying his duffle bag of clothes, he reported in and was assigned to room five. "Hi, you must be my bunk mate. Luca's the name. Luca Cellino, a lad about her own age cheerily said as he entered and looked the small room over.

"Marcello Rinella. Hi." The two shook hands and thus began Marcello's official training as a railroad train engineer. For ten weeks, they shoveled coal, pulled down the water tank's funnel to fill engines, and greased pistons and valves. Although both were filthy at the end of the day, the bunkhouses had private shower stations, and with a combination of luck and clever use of time, Marcello was able to continue his disguise.

After the ten weeks were up, half of the men had already dropped out, because the work was too demanding and dirty. Marcello loved every minute of every day, except the cleanup hours. The next ten weeks were spent on the diagnosis and repair of problems that routinely befell any engine on a long haul. Here, Marcello excelled above all other nine students. Luca constantly needed Marcello's help in working out the many problems that they were presented. Many were real problems.

That is, engines would come in for inspections or with troubles, and the students were given an opportunity to fix them, before the actual engineers would step in and handle them. By the time these weeks were up, the team of Luca and Marcello were known as the hot shots who never needed any assistance in either diagnosis or repair of the problems. Both graduated with honors, and at fifteen, Luca and Marcello were presented with their official engineer coveralls and paper documents stating that they were qualified, certified engineers.

Both were hired at once and began working as a team. Each engine always carried two engineers. Not only was this done for safety's sake, but also in case of injury or breakdown, there was always a backup. Besides, on the long runs, one could sleep while the other ran the train. They were assigned the freight train called Coastal Run #1, which routinely ran from Velona across the Sea Princes to New Barq and back again.

The happiest day of Marcello's life began when he and Luca first climbed aboard their very own engine. As long as they didn't goof up, this would be their train for life or until the engine wore out. "We did it, Luca! We really did it! We're engineers!" Marcello exclaimed, slapping Luca on his back.

"Best day of my life, Marcello. All because of you, you know. If you hadn't tutored me in school, I'd never of made it! I owe you big time, buddy!" Luca returned the back slap. "Let's get this train a'moving!"

For five years, these two best friends ran their freight train up and down the thousand mile run. Yes, they had many adventures with routine breakdowns and engine problems, but always, the keen mind of Marcello rapidly uncovered the problem. The two had a spotless record, almost unheard of among the many other engineer pairs.

The two shared their lives together. In New Barq, for instance, they went to the barbers and got identical haircuts. Then, they toured the sights of the city and visited the pubs. During slack times, they played cards, with Luca running up a tab of losses, but both only considered such to be play money.

They did make money, but had few chances to spend it in ordinary ways. Mostly they saved it, but often splurged when visiting some of the more exotic towns and cities. They picked up a strange brass Arad teapot, which they rigged up to their engine so that they could have a hot cup any time they desired. In Zargarb, they discovered the incredibly soft and warm paca wool and had two identical heavy coats made especially for them, keeping them warm on the colder night runs.

After five years of eating, sleeping, and working together, these two, Marcello and Luca, knew each other extremely well. They always knew what the other was thinking and when the other needed some help. On the job, they were a model of efficiency and had already received a pay raise five times from their station yard boss in Velona, Manlio Rossi, a gruff, no nonsense retired engineer. He'd been forced into retirement from active duty, put into management because he'd shattered his leg on the job, and now walked with a terrible limp. Manlio, though sounding rough, actually respected those engineers who performed their jobs well. Thus, as the five years went by, his respect for the Luca and Marcello team only rose higher and higher.

Now they were both nineteen, and Marcello began to worry a little. Luca now had to shave every day or else his blonde stubble looked awful. Yet she, of course, didn't, though she did occasionally shave just to keep up appearances. Worse, her breasts were finally beginning to fill out and were becoming more and more difficult to hide. Sometimes Luca would tease Marcello, "Of all the luck, you don't have to shave every day." Marcello always felt her face heat up, but brushed it off.

Sometimes during their layovers, Luca took Marcello out to party with the ladies, as he put it. Those times, Marcello hated the most, but played along with Luca, even kissing some of the women. The two shared a small house back in Velona, but were there only for a few days every month. Several times, Luca wanted to bring back some of the ladies that they were partying with, but so far Marcello had been lucky enough to convince Luca that they would be offended by how dirty and messy they kept their place.

In early July, the two were on a three-day layover in Zargarb. Their twenty rail cars were being loaded with a number of sheep destined to be divided between the other Sea Prince sectors. Already the dark days were taking their toll, and the shepherds of Zargarb Sector were thinning their flocks as the grass died off. The station master knocked on their two bunkhouse doors. They each had a tiny, private bunkhouse during layovers, which Marcello greatly appreciated.

"Horrible news just in from Velona! Strangest thing I ever heard tell of — they've been attacked by some alien flying machines turning some kind of plague loose on them. Least that's what the message says. Who ever heard of flying machines anyway? Now plague, that sounds bad fellows. You be careful when you get there."

"What do you make of that, Marcello?" Luca asked.

"Dunno. I never heard of flying machines before. What's an alien? Must be some plague going around. Hope we don't get sick," Marcello replied honestly.

Later they heard a wild commotion going on outside and both headed outside to see what was up. In the sky, they saw this enormous black cigar, as Luca later called it, and a bunch of little ones flying or hovering over the city. Long guns sounded sporadically over the city, but the two just stared up in awe. Neither had ever seen anything like this before. An hour later, the flying machines rose up above the dust cloud, which had been turning day into dusk for well over a month now. Just as they were heading off to get some supper, the station master hailed them again.

"New message. You are to lay over here another day. Vito is going to be loading your empties with coal for Barcella and Velona. Go get some grub fellows." They waved at him and headed off to eat at the station house with the other rail yard hands.

The next morning, Marcella didn't feel very well. Her arms felt very weak, but when Luca knocked, she headed off to eat breakfast with him. They played some cards that afternoon, but increasingly Marcella's hands weakened, until at last, she dropped too many cards, and they decided to do something else. After supper, the two hit the sack early. All this talk of aliens and plague had upset both of them.

The next morning, Marcella nearly screamed when she awoke! Her arms were now almost matchsticks, so thin and so short! What's happening to me? She wondered. Luca knocked on her door, and she began to panic. "I don't feel well, Luca. I think I may be getting ill. Maybe you can bring me back a bite and leave it for me."

"You got it buddy!" Luca called through the closed door.

Marcella wiggled under the covers to hide what was left of her arms, hoping that Luca wouldn't suspect anything. Later, Luca knocked and left him a tray; Marcella pretended to be asleep and Luca quietly left. Only with the greatest of effort was she able to manage to eat, eventually just eating it with her mouth, because her arms simply wouldn't work anymore. Luca kindly left her some dinner that night as well.

The following morning Marcella awoke and truly panicked! Her arms were completely gone! Shaking like a leaf, she struggled, got out of bed, and noticed her ears had strange appendages that touched her empty shoulders. When she looked in the mirror, she almost fainted! Her lips were full and cherry red, and her eyes had a beautiful blue outline. Her waist was very thin, eighteen inches around. She knew that her disguise was blown forever!

Even if she had arms, she had no idea how she could hide all this! Marcella stood there shaking and trembling, completely shocked.

Just then, Luca knocked on her door and opened it quickly, "Marcello! I've got the plague too! Oh!" He'd come in to show his best friend his strange, dangling ears, but saw instead a young armless woman with gorgeous makeup standing there in a total shock, unmoving.

Slowly Marcella lost it and her body slumped to the floor. Luca, stunned, stood looking for a moment before his mind began functioning from the sudden surprise. He carefully picked her up and laid her back on the bunk. Now he did notice her bosom and very small waist. As he looked at her, so many things about Marcello, or whatever her name really was, suddenly began to make sense to him. What to do?

He poured a glass of water, wetted a rag, and began swabbing her forehead. At last, she responded and roused. As soon as she awakened, Marcella began sobbing uncontrollably. Luca sat on the edge of the bed, lifted her up, and held on to her, comforting her. He said nothing; what could he say? This plague was utterly unimaginable in its effects! At last, he said, "Want a drink?" She did and he had to help her drink it.

"Kill me, Luca, please! I'm done for now. I can't do anything like this. I can't even go pee by myself."

"Here, I'll help you. Tell me what to do," Luca suggested, suddenly having no idea how his friend could go to the bathroom.

"Pull my underpants down and hold me so I don't fall over." Marcella nearly filled the chamber pot. Hastily, Luca pulled up her pants, which were identical to his, he noted.

"Okay, now go ahead and kill me, Luca. Please, I can't live like this," she pleaded.

"But I don't even know your name," Luca fumbled around for any ideas at all.

"Marcella silly. I just changed one letter. Now hold that pillow over my head, please, old friend."

"Marcella? Great. Why are you a she? I thought that you were a he," he asked what was on his mind the most.

"Cause they don't hire women engineers, and I just *had* to be an engineer! All my life, all I ever wanted to be is an engineer. Luca, these past five years have been the best five years of my whole life. I'll never forget them or you."

"They don't? Well, that's stupid. You are the best damn engineer on the line, Marcello, I mean Marcella."

"Not anymore! I can't even put my pants on, go pee, or drink a glass of water. Please, just kill me now. I am ready. I've had the best five years that anyone could ever want with you, Luca. I love you. So please put me out of my misery," she begged.

"No wonder you didn't want to make out with all those ladies!" he said instead, as he began to understand more.

"Of course not. I wanted to kiss you, but of course, I couldn't. You'd think — well you know."

"Yes, right. I would have thought that. Still, I loved you like my brother, Marcella. I owe you everything still, you know. If it hadn't been for you, I'd never be an engineer now. I can't kill you; I love you too much. I know. I am going to go get us some food and see what I can find out about this plague. You stay put. Here, I'll cover you up in case someone sticks their head in the door." He put the sheet completely over her face. Her makeup would give her away instantly now. Hastily he left, headed off to get some answers, and some food.

An hour later, he returned; knocking, he called out, "It's Luca." Then, he entered, carrying what food he'd managed to scrounge. "God, this plague is really bad, Marcella! All the women around here have lost their arms like you! Even the cook! Everyone's sort of making their own out of whatever they can find in the kitchen. All hell has broken loose! None of the stores is open; hardly anyone is on the street. Zargarb is mostly deserted, like a ghost town! Here, I got us something to eat. Lean up and I'll feed us both."

As they ate, Luca continued chatting, "You know, I always did have some suspicions about you. I just never could quite figure them out. You know, how you always took your baths after everyone else was done. Now I understand. You have been incredibly skillful. Brilliant even."

"I know. I couldn't risk anyone seeing me."

"God! Remember those times when I came into your room stark naked?" Luca laughed, remembering how she'd reacted.

Marcella flushed. "You don't know how often I wanted to kiss you either. I'd be sleeping or dozing while you were sitting there running the engine. I wanted to badly to reach out and kiss you, but I dare not. All would be lost utterly. Well now all *is* lost utterly. Please, after we eat, will you please put the pillow over my head? If you can't do it that way, then how about using my big wrench over there? I can't lift it anymore. One good swing to my head ought to do it. God, you've dangling ear lobes too. Are you ill? Anything going wrong with you? Are your arms getting weak? That's what I noticed first."

"They are really strange, feels really funny whenever they touch anything. My lips feel thicker than normal, but that's about all. No, my arms are not weak. I'll stay alert for that, just in case. Gosh, what happens if I lose my arms too?" Luca looked slightly scared now.

In spite of her dire predicament, seeing Luca afraid was more than she could bear now. She leaned into him, wanting desperately to put her arms around him and comfort him. Almost automatically, he put his around her and held her tightly to him. Before long, their lips met in the gentlest of embraces. That triggered their passions long withheld. Before long, they were lying in bed passionately kissing and making love to each other.

202

Sometime later, both lay beside each other. Luca made up his mind. "Marcella, will you marry me? I really love you, and I want to be with you always. I don't care if you don't have any arms. I've been I love with you for five years now, only I didn't know it. Every time I see you, my heart beats faster. Please, will you?"

"But I am completely helpless now, Luca. Surely, you can find someone far better than me? I love you too, but what use am I to anyone like this?"

"You are not completely helpless Marcella. If you believe that, I'm going to have to kiss you again and show you. Come on, will you?"

"But Luca, surely, you don't want to marry a hopeless cripple."

"You look like a gorgeous woman to me. Besides, you have all your parts except a couple. Come on, say yes."

"But Luca — well okay, but you must promise me that if it doesn't work out for us, you will put me out of my misery. Promise me that, and I'll give it a try."

"I promise, but it isn't going to happen. Come on; let's get you dressed and see if somewhere in Zargarb we can find a priest to marry us right away." He got her pants, shirt, socks, and shoes on her. She did look a little unusual dressed as a man, but with a now very womanly shape and makeup that no one could mistake. He slid his arm around her waist, and the two began to walk into Zargarb proper.

"You are right; there is almost no one around. All the shops are closed. Luca, what's going to happen if all the women lose their arms?"

"Love, I surely don't know. It's awful, but you are one lucky woman. You have me now to help look after you. Say, I think that we can use the Church of Jehosanity there. They have male priests. Come on."

A half hour later, the two left the church, now Mr. and Mrs. Luca Cellino. They headed back to the station yard. Because the sky was so dark anyway, they didn't have to sneak in, hardly anyone was around. Once inside, they began to make some plans.

"Look, at least until we get back home to Velona, we are still the number one engineer team!"

"Yes, but now I can't do anything. Well, maybe I can so some things," the genetic images began coming into her mind now.

"That's the spirit. Obviously, I get to shovel the coal, but you can probably run the engine with your feet, I'll bet. It's just a throttle lever. The ones, which have a pull switch — I'll handle those. Game to give it a try?"

"Yes, if this is destined to be my very last run as a train engineer, I aim to enjoy it!" She leaned over and kissed him. Quickly, their passions escalated, and they found themselves in bed once more.

The next morning, Luca raced off to grab them some food and returned just as the station manager was walking to fetch them. "Your train is all set to go anytime you are ready. Schedule says you should leave in ten minutes. That okay?"

"Sure, we'll get our things and eat breakfast on the line." Luca waited until he turned his back before slipping into the room. Hastily, he dressed his bride, making sure that she was as presentable in her engineer coveralls as possible. Holding onto their bag of food with one arm, he led her outside with the other. Together, they walked to their beloved engine. As they approached it, the station manager spotted them and did a double take when he saw Marcella. Luca just waved, hoping they could get onto the engine immediately.

Marcella looked at the behemoth engine and knew that she had to climb up there on her own. Using her chin to help balance herself, she slowly and carefully climbed the five steps, finally setting foot on her familiar engine's cab. Luca was right behind her. Rapidly, they went through their checklist. Some Marcella could do, such as verify gauges; some she could not, such as shovel in a bit more coal. Luca released the main valve and nodded to Marcella. She used her foot to push the throttle lever, and the loving chug-chug sound began once more as the large pistons began moving slowly. She used her foot to pull the whistle rope, sounding the three blasts with told all yard hands that the train was in motion and leaving the yards.

Before long, they cleared the yards and hit the open line. Here, she opened the throttle up and treasured the wind now blowing on her face as she leaned out the window to observe the track ahead. Meanwhile, Luca spread out what food he'd been able to acquire. "Slim pickings this morning my love. No cooks. Hope you like dried fish sandwiches. Have a bite." He leaned to her, holding it for her to take a bite and then he took one himself. They looked at each other and smiled.

"This is the life for me, Luca! We're free when we are sailing along like this. I never ever wanted this to end, but I am sure to be fired once we reach Velona. Besides, I am probably going to be useless to you now. I think that you are a crazy man for marrying me, but I love you anyway."

"Crazy and free. Love them both! If this is our last run together, let's make it last forever!"

Later that day, they pulled into Solamina and had to stop to take on coal and water. Additionally, they had to wait for one car to be unloaded. While Luca supervised the hands refilling the coal bin, Marcella climbed on top to deal with the water. What used to be fun and simple, removing the lid, pulling down the water tower's tunnel, and watching the water flow into the engine boiler, now was a total challenge. She managed with effort to get the lid open. Now to get the funnel pulled down. It had a pull cord. Standing on one foot, she raised the other high and got her toe over the rope. She pulled and thankfully, the funnel lowered. Soon she was able to lean on it, keeping it down, as the water gushed into the boiler. When it was full, she merely let it go and the funnel swung back up. Sitting down, she pushed, shoved with her feet, and got the lid back on. Carefully, she made her way back down into the cab.

"Hey, you did it. See, I told you that you are not completely helpless, little lady."

She smiled, "Yes, but there are a whole lot of things I can't do, buddy."

"Hey, I bet you can pull the release lever. I know that we grip it with our hands to cause the catch to release, allowing us to pull the lever. I bet you can do it; come on, try it. Sit here and push that way."

Marcella grinned as his idea took form in her mind. A bit of fiddling, she succeeded in releasing the level, which then allowed the throttle to operate. "Say, you wanted me to do this so you could drive!" she protested, as a grinning Luca opened the throttle, and the engine began its slow chug-chug once more.

In rural Bonito, the engine ran into difficulties. While Luca attached the signal device to the LDCS system and signaled their delay, Marcella climbed down and began seeking the cause of the loud, scraping noise. As usual, she spotted the trouble. "Lost a bolt here; lost grease. I'll find a bolt; you grease her back up." Twenty minutes later, Luca signaled that they were again on their way.

Seven times, they had to stop to take on more coal and water. Each time, Marcella got better and better at operating the water shoot, though she knew that there was little chance she could deal with the coal. "I wish the sun was shining on my last trip," Marcella mused as they neared Velona. Luca just put his arm around her and kissed her neck as she controlled the throttle, perhaps for the last time. Luca couldn't imagine life without being her in the cab, and he felt for her. A half hour later, the big engine pulled slowly into the Velona yards. Although it was early afternoon, the sky was more like dusk.

Luca hopped down and turned to catch Marcella if she should slip. Climbing down was the most difficult part for her. The only safe way was for her to go down backwards, reversing how she climbed up, using her chin to help keep her balance on the vertical bars. Once down, she knew that the time to face the music of her deception was at hand. Their boss, Manlio, came walking up to them.

"Good run. What the?" he nearly dropped his clipboard. "Marcello?"

"Yes, boss, it's me, only it's really Marcella. You wouldn't hire women, so I pretended to be a guy. It worked didn't it? It's just this damnable plague, but on the way back, I still was able to do my part. Just ask Luca. I drove it into the yard just now, if you didn't see it."

"This is highly irregular. You know damn well women are not allowed to be engineers! It's too damn dangerous, and it's too hard of work for a — well, ah, you are probably fired, you know." Manlio growled; nothing like this had ever happened. All this time this woman had been setting a top quality example, perhaps the best engineer on the line.

"We are going home for our rest break. You'd be a fool to fire her; she's the best one we got. Besides, we just got married," Luca stuck up for her. He pushed her on, and they left the fuming boss behind them.

"Well that's the end of my engineer career," Marcella sighed as they walked to their small quarters where they stayed, their only "real" address. Once inside, they found a compact pile of objects occupying most of their living room.

"What's all this?" Luca asked. "Pots with strange handles? That looks like a desk but the top is far too low. What's this thing on legs with the two baskets? Ever seen anything like this?"

The genetic memories kicked in. "You know, I think I can use this thing to carry things. I get under it like this and lift with my shoulders. Oh, I see myself sitting on that desk and writing with my feet, though I certainly don't know how to write with my feet," Marcella mused.

Later, a soldier came by and asked if they needed help setting up the kitchen. Since neither had any idea what he was talking about, the soldier began bringing the two engineers up to date. Both accepted help installing the kitchen in their small place, since neither had any idea how that was done.

While Luca headed off to try to find them some groceries to last them for the theoretical three-day rest layover, Marcella sat in the desk and began catching up on all the newspaper articles. She came across the first Bethany one and began reading. Soon, she began to understand more and more of what had been happening all across the Sea Princes. More importantly, she began to understand how she could possibly adapt to the horrible mess in which she, like all women here, found themselves.

Luca returned an hour later with what few groceries he could find, mostly fish and some dried vegetables. They stayed up late that first night, reading the many articles. Luca was as fascinated as she, reading about alternative ways and hints. When they finished, he whispered, "See, I told you so. You can do things, only differently than before."

"Can't take my pants off," she teased him.

"That's what I am here for," he teased back. Not long after, they were in the bed once more.

The two enjoyed themselves and worked together to try to figure out how Marcella would be able to do things now. By the end of the three-day layover, she was finally able to fix their supper mostly. "Well, in the morning, we'll find out, I expect. If I am fired, I'll stay here and wait for you, Luca," Marcella finally decided that she could accept being parted from the man who had been her constant companion for five years now, day in and day out.

"I can't stay away from you for that long, Marcella. If you are sacked, we'll have to figure something else out. Maybe we can just always buy you passage on my trains or something. I won't leave you here for weeks at a time. I can't bear to be away from you. Look, you've been by my side for five years!" They kissed and quickly went to bed.

In the morning, Luca got her dressed in her coveralls and tied her boots securely. They packed their few things and took a last look at their small place. "Well, this is it. I guess it's time to face it, Luca." The two walked out and headed for the station yard, a short distance away.

"Ah there you are. She's loaded and ready for you," Boss Manlio growled. "Leaves in ten for New Barq."

"What do you mean? I thought that you were going to fire me?" Marcella asked, not daring to believe her ears.

"If it were up to me, I would fire you, if only for the deception. But I can't. Monarch Stefano's orders. No woman can be fired from her job unless she simply is unable to perform her work at all. You are one lucky woman, Marcella. Now get going before I lose my temper with you two."

Marcella was so happy that she leaned into Manlio to hug him. The best she could do was to press her body to his and wrap one leg around him. "Thanks, boss." The two jogged to their engine, eager to get behind the throttle once more.

Chapter 19 L'Eleganti

Mario Cenza unlocked the teakwood doors of their two-story red brick shop. He gazed up at the large sign, as he did every morning when he opened the shop. Mario, who just turned forty last week, was a man of habit. He read his sign, L'Eleganti, in large black letters. Just below it in smaller letters his eyes continued, Cenza Makers of Fine Suits and Dresses for Three Generations. Mario felt a surge of pride, as he always did when he read the sign. He and his extended family were still carrying on the family tradition handed down to him from his grandfather through his now deceased father. He stepped inside and unrolled the red carpet, making sure that it went under the front doors properly.

Satisfied, he turned on the many first floor lights and stepped into the back office where several full-length mirrors lined two walls. He paused and looked at his reflection, as he always did. His black hair was nicely oiled; his moustache was straight. He adjusted his grey suit jacket and picked a tiny dust mote off his sleeve. Perfect, he thought. Now he walked up the red-carpeted stairs and turned on all the lights there. How wonderful these new electric lights are, he thought. It was the same thought that he had every day since their installation some fifteen years ago.

He heard the bell sounding as someone entered. It would be the others, he thought, as he glanced at his gold watch, another of the great inventions coming from the DAE. On the off chance that it might be a customer arriving extremely early, he quickly descended the stairs and headed for the door. Ah, the others were arriving, right on time, as they always were.

His son, Gino, escorted his young wife Milana inside as well as Mario's wife, Silvia. Gino was twenty now, a splitting image of his father or so everyone said. His hair was jet black and he too wore a moustache. His wife Milana was a year younger with long brown hair, slightly wavy, that draped perfectly down her back. Her blue eyes accentuated her oval face. Mario thought that his son chose well. While Gino also wore a grey twin tail suit, Milana wore an elegant Annelise style ball gown, whose hoop flared out nearly ten feet. Hers was a light blue satin.

Silvia was the love of his life. A year younger than he, she had very long blonde hair that fell to the small of her back, a lovely accent to the pink satin ball gown that she wore today. Again, the style was an Annelise copy, though with the smaller hoop of ten feet. Her eyes were blue and bright as always.

Right behind the three, his other two daughters were following, with their husbands escorting them inside. All the women preferred to be escorted, since they wore the extreme Annelise heels that were so the elegant fashion of Velona. Their older daughter Susana, was nineteen now, and their youngest at eighteen was Vanna. Both women were splitting images of their mother. Both wore their blonde hair long, draped down their backs. Susana's ball gown was a pale green satin, while Vanna's was blue. Susana's husband, Gustavo Rosa, had immaculately cut brown hair and was tall, matching Susana's height in her tall heels, a perfect match, Mario thought. Indeed, in his eyes, a woman in her elegant dress should not be taller than her husband, oh no. Vanna's husband of some nine months now was Jovanni Arcaldo, who had brown hair and eyes to match. He was short and Vanna, in her tall heels, was at least two inches taller than he was. Jovanni had rejected Mario's hint that he use platforms in his shoes. Ah well, Mario thought, Vanna is happy with him, and he does good work.

L'Eleganti was one of the most elegant tailors and dressmakers in all Velona, for three generations now. Mario, Gino, and Gustavo were the three master tailors, while Silvia, Milana, and Susana were the master dressmakers. Vanna and Jovanni were their purchasing agents and handled the payroll and accounting for the firm. They excelled at finding only the very best in materials and accessories. Indeed, their reputation depended in a large measure upon these two always finding top quality cloth bolts.

As these eight took up their positions on the main floor, their other workers began arriving, including sixteen tailors and twenty seamstresses. While these thirty-six did much of the actual layout and construction work, the other six also did so when they were not busy with assisting a customer. Unless they were very busy, these six always did the measuring and final fittings, since their names were on the products. Perfection was the only result allowed. Indeed, in the second story workshop, every workstation had a sign over it, which read: Only Perfection.

"I say, father," Gino made polite conversation. "I do believe that business will be slow until this strange dust cloud goes away. Honestly, it has turned day into night."

"Dad, our petunias have all died, and it is only June!" Susana added her observation that she made this morning when she went to water their outside flower box.

"Surely, this dust will blow away soon," Mario replied, though if pressured, he could not say why he thought that might happen. Such matters never concerned him, only the construction of the very finest suits and dresses held his attention — that and of course Silvia.

"Dad, why do you suppose that these aliens, whatever they are, wanted to blow up Dorota? It's such a small, isolated island," asked Vanna.

"Aliens? Bah, rubbish! I tell you it must just be some kind of cover up, that's what I think," Mario blurted out. Who ever heard of aliens? Someone had to be hiding something. No matter, they had no trade with that small, far distant island.

"But sir," Jovanni stuck up for his wife, "it was in the newspapers and on the radio casts. It came from Monarch Stefano himself."

"Well, maybe Stefano is in on the plot too. You never can tell with these politicians. He isn't the best dressed monarch, you know. I always say that you can tell the cut of a man by the clothes that he wears."

Vanna and Susana giggled. Susana said, "Yes, we know, dad. You've been telling us that since we were little girls. He seemed to like this compliment and the subject was dropped.

Time passed, Mario pulled out his pocket watch and checked the time for the thousandth time today. Five o'clock on the dot, closing time. "I don't believe it, Silvia! Not a single customer all day long. This dust cloud must have everyone utterly spooked!"

"Yes, dear, it is most strange, and to be honest, dear, I am a little frightened of it. Our lovely flowers are all dead now, and it is only the start of summer," she replied.

"Jovanni, how about closing up today? I feel out of sorts. Not one customer, humbug. Come, Silvia, I'll walk you home." He gave her his arm and they left the store in the hands of their children. Outside, if it were not for the streetlights, which had been burning continuously now for weeks, it would be pitch black. Mario made sure that he had a good grip on Silvia's arm and together, they began their short stroll home.

In her extreme Annelise heels, Silvia moved very slowly but elegantly, and Mario, the perfect gentlemen, adjusted his pace to match hers. The Cenza Estate was four blocks from their store and easily walked, just not swiftly by the women. As they reached the ornate wrought iron gates, Mario pulled a key from his waistband and unlocked them. The two then walked up the paved drive to their mansion's front door, where upon he produced another key and escorted his wife inside.

Their mansion was large enough so that all four families could live here with their own separate wings. However, they all had long ago decided to share one kitchen. Tonight it was Silvia's turn to fix supper for the four families. There was no time to change out of her ball gown, not if they wanted supper by six. With an expert hand, she began getting things ready, while Mario sat down with the morning's paper. He never read it in the morning, oh no. His attention was always on dressing perfectly and getting the store opened, just as his father and his father before him had taught him. "Holler, Silvia, if you need me. Just reading the paper," he called out.

When they were not cooking, the kids didn't usually return home until close to six, when traditionally the extended family would dine together. Mario expected peace and quiet for at least an hour. He heard the radio turn on; Silvia would be listening to the symphonic music cast as usual. Peace. He began reading.

"Silvia! Stefano is asking that all stores be closed tomorrow!" Mario yelled angrily as he read the announcement, warnings, and suggested actions to be taken by the citizens of Velona on the morrow. "Aliens again!"

He crumpled the paper and headed to the kitchen. He was just in time to hear the broadcast being interrupted by a similar announcement.

"Aliens are going to attack Velona tomorrow? I just don't believe it, Silvia! Honestly, if they are aliens, how can we possibly know that they will attack tomorrow? Tell me that if you can! Preposterous, I say."

"Well, dear, the announcer did say these are Stefano West Po's orders. We don't have a long gun, now do we?" she sounded a little frightened by all this talk of an attack.

"No, someone would just get hurt if we had one of those infernal things around here. Honestly. We are civilized, not some back country hicks. Well, tomorrow I bet that we see this hoax shown for what it is: a hoax. That's what I think, dear. Don't worry your pretty little head over all this nonsense." He kissed her on her neck. She smiled and relaxed a bit. If Mario thought that this was just some hoax, then perhaps it was after all.

"Fish again?" he asked, peaking at what she was cooking.

"Yes, dear, there is hardly any other meat in the markets anymore, though I can still get eggs and milk. Perhaps we ought to lay in a supply. What do you think?"

"Hum, you may be right, dear. We should see to it in the morning, before all this hubbub is supposed to happen. I'll set the table for you, my love."

Mario set the six place settings around their elegant, mahogany table, placing the plates, cups, silverware, and napkins just perfectly. Then, he returned to finish the paper, after pressing it back out.

As six approached, the three young couples came in talking among each other, quite animated. "Dad, did you hear? The aliens are attacking us tomorrow! It was on the news," Susana asked her father the moment she saw him sitting in his easy chair.

"Rubbish! How can they know that, I say? Preposterous. Mark my words, tomorrow this hoax will be revealed for what it is: a hoax. Now don't scare your mother with these stories," Mario chided his daughter, though he doubted that she'd heed his admonition. She seldom did, not even as a child. None of his children had, for that matter. Still, he couldn't really complain; all were excellent tailors and dressmakers, the best of the best. At least, he'd instilled that into them. Always look your best; never settle for less than perfection. His father had taught him that, and it had served him well. They had more money in the Banca del Dio that they could possibly spend if they retired from the business now!

As he expected, the topic of discussion over dinner was the coming alien attack. Jovanni said, "Mario, we stopped at some gun dealers on the way home, just to see if they had any long guns, like Stefano suggested. Don't worry; they are completely sold out. I guess if the aliens come, we are to throw rocks at them, according to Stefano."

"Lot of good that will do," Mario grumbled. "Rocks don't stop our soldiers. How are they going to stop an alien anyway? Besides, what do aliens look like? Answer me that?"

"I heard that they think the rocks might clog their engines and make their flying ships crash," Gino explained.

"Just so they don't fall down on our estate," Mario grumbled again. "Flying ships! Who ever heard of flying ships? What are these aliens? Birds or something?"

"Dad, since we are supposed to be closed tomorrow, I put up a temporarily closed sign in the door and gave our workers the day off. We don't want to raise the ire of Stefano. Probably this will all blow over in a day. Maybe then people will begin dropping in to get new suits and dresses," Gino suggested, trying to sound a more cheerful note. It wouldn't do to get his dad all riled up.

Mario glowered, but nodded affirmatively. Gustavo spoke up, "Bet they don't start coming back until this damnable dust cloud goes away." Many agreed with his statement.

Changing the subject, Silvia said, "Girls, in the morning we are going shopping. Your father and I think it best if we lay in a good supply of food. It is becoming terribly difficult to find much besides fish in the open markets."

"Say, Mario," Jovanni changed the subject again. "If this darkness continues into the fall and winter, the weather may become quite cold. We know where we can get our hands on a good deal of paca wool. What do you think about laying in a stock to use to make warm, colder weather coats? Women love the feel of the soft paca wool."

"Hum, I do believe that you are on to something, there, Jovanni. This damnable dust cloud doesn't seem to be letting up. Already it is the chilliest June on record. Go ahead, son, lay in what you can. Silvia and I will begin designing some outer coats that are both fashionable and yet warm. Best be prepared, I do believe. If we don't need the heavier coats, then I'm sure that in time we can make use of the paca wool."

The next morning, Silvia, Milana, and Susana left in the motor-car to search out more food items, while Jovanni and Vanna took the motor-wagon to purchase the load of paca wool that had just arrived from Zargarb. By one, all had returned, though they had mostly dried food items to show for their long morning out. Still, their panty was now well stocked, far more than usual.

They had just finished their late lunch and were about to clear the table, when a gunshot rang out, a small popping sound. Within minutes, the noise of the hundreds of cannonae encircling the huge, sprawling city drowned out much conversation. "My god, we are under attack!" yelled Mario, quite shocked. His arm around Silvia, they headed out into their spacious front yard, followed by the others. All gazed upwards and saw the huge cigar shaped object hovering above the city. Ten smaller ones darted about in zig-zag patterns. Long guns fired rapidly.

Anger flooded into Mario. He reached for a stone and gave it an upward throw. "Damn aliens, take that!" he screamed, though he didn't know why.

"Dear, hand me a stone too, please," Silvia asked. Before long, all eight were throwing stones upward, all the while the cannonae and long guns nearly drowned everything out. Susana even tossed a flowerpot with a dead petunia high into the air. All eight were fuming mad. Sometime later, the noise subsided, and the flying ships vanished.

"Well, I guess we showed them a thing or two," Mario said hostilely. "The nerve of them! Attacking us!"

"Hey, dad. I didn't see them shooting anything at us. You know, like guns or bombs or such," Gino said curiously.

"I read that they were going to dump some kind of nasty plague on us. That was in this morning's paper," Gustavo added.

"A plague? Oh dear, that's horrible. People will get sick and die from the plague!" Silvia began to become a bit afraid once more. Her anger gave way to fear now.

"They could have been dumping the plague things on us while they were zig-zagging around," Jovanni added to Gustavo's theory. "That pattern did look like they were somehow blanketing the whole city. Did any of you see anything coming out of those little ships?" No one had and they headed back inside in dire need of a cup of tea or perhaps a little something stronger.

Mario got out a bottle of expensive plum brandy and poured everyone a small glass. "I think my nerves need this about now," he explained.

"If they did dump a plague on us, I wonder how long it will take before we start showing symptoms?" Susana asked.

"Better ask if there is a cure, dear," her father pointed out. "I believe that I will use the telefono and call that medical research foundation. Perhaps those folks will know." A bit later, he returned. "No answer. Guess everything is indeed closed today. Perhaps tomorrow."

Early the next morning, Mario called the foundation and asked his question. He hung up and looked very glum. "Well dear, what did they say?" asked Silvia. The other six were also sitting around the table just as curious as she was.

"They said that they know of no cure, but that they are taking samples of the bacteria and will be working on a cure. They wouldn't say just what symptoms we should expect. I guess it is an unknown alien bacteria or something. I feel just fine. How about you, dear?" he asked Silvia.

"Oh I seem to be okay, just perhaps a little weak this morning," she replied. Vanna, Susana, and Milana also felt a bit weak, but no one had any other symptoms. By evening, the four women's arms were very weak, and the men did the dishes for them. All went to bed early.

Mario rose early as always, but for the first time in ages, he didn't immediately dress. Silvia looked awful. Her arms were thin and somehow shorter than he remembered. Indeed, all four women's arms were suffering. Gustavo whipped up some breakfast and a very somber eight dined. All four men hovered over their wives that day. By nightfall, Mario knew that something awful was happening to the four women; their arms were almost matchsticks! None could raise them any longer. He had changed Silvia's clothes and dressed her in her loose fitting nightgown so that she could manage better. Likewise, the others followed suit.

Three times that day, Mario called the medical foundation asking for assistance, guidance, or what he should do for the ailing women, but only once did anyone answer, and he was a janitor who had no idea at all. "What good is the foundation if they don't have any answers?" he growled.

The next morning was the worst morning and day in Mario's life! Silvia's high-pitched screams of stark terror woke him up; he nearly wet his pants so startled he was! Silvia sat up in bed beside him screaming at the top of her lungs. He saw why and his stomach tightened into a tiny, compact, painful ball. Her arms were completely missing! Bits of her ears dangled down and touched her shoulders. All he could think of doing was to put his arms around her and hold on to his wife of twenty-three years. Now he heard the wild screams of terror coming from the other three wings of their mansion and he felt horribly sick. He felt helpless, unable to do anything for his loving wife or their three children. He just sat there holding her while she screamed and cried.

How long the screaming lasted, Mario couldn't tell, an eternity perhaps. At last, her screaming turned into a low continuous sobbing, and Mario finally woke from the shocked trance that he'd been in all the while. All he could think of saying was, "Dear, you forgot to take off your makeup last night." It seemed utterly lame.

"What's happened to me," Silvia finally was able to speak.

"The alien plague, I think. Are you ill?" Now that was a stupid question, if ever there was one, he thought to himself. "Your arms, they are completely gone. I hope more of you doesn't go away too." Damn, that sounded even worse, and Silvia began bawling again.

Soon, she calmed down a bit. "I have to pee," she whimpered.

"Come on. I have my arms around you. I won't let you fall or anything." Slowly, he got her up onto her feet, but she was trembling awfully, he noticed. Carefully, he led her into their large bathroom. He saw at once that he would have to help her raise her nightgown and then lower her panties as well, bit embarrassing, but he did so.

That handled, Mario said, "Okay dear. I'm going to take off your nightgown. I want to see if there is anything else that we need to know about, like welts or red spots or open sores or whatever a plague does." She whimpered and nodded and he removed her nightgown. She instinctively moved to the full-length mirror to see for herself, while Mario began looking her body over carefully.

"I do look like I have my makeup on, dear. I don't remember putting it on and I don't wear red anyway," she finally put a longer sentence together. "My ears, look. Gosh, yours too!" They both stared at their long dangling, but thin, ear lobes, which now rested on their shoulders. Her long blonde hair was a mess. He carefully pulled it back and out of the way, continuing to look for other awful signs.

"I've lost at least ten pounds! My waist is so much smaller."

"You look as trim as you were when I married you, before the kids, my love. I guess there's nothing wrong with that. I don't see any red spots or anything on your back. Good sign, I think. Your legs look normal. Except for your lost arms, I think everything is there. Do you feel ill, sick? I don't think that you are hot or anything," he continued his observations.

"No, just hungry is all. I don't feel ill. Mario, what about my arms? I can't do anything, not even get dressed like this. I feel so completely helpless!"

"I'm here, love. I'm here. I'll take care of you always. You are sure there is nothing else going wrong?"

"No, but your ears are long too. Take off your clothes and let's see if there's anything on your body. What if your arms go away too? We will be lost utterly!"

"Oh lord, I hope not! We'd better check." Hastily, he stripped as well, and she looked over his backside, while he looked over his front. "I don't see anything amiss, how's my back?"

"Seems okay. It's just my arms. Whatever am I going to do, Mario? I cannot live like this. I am as helpless as our babies were."

"I just don't know, dear. I love you always. Except for your arms, you look more attractive than you have for years. Er, that didn't come out like I meant it," he flushed. "You look stunning, except. . ." Silvia leaned and gave him a loving kiss. Suddenly, she felt electrified and Mario as well. Passions swept over them, and they could barely make it back onto the bed.

A bit later, the contented couple lay on their backs. "Mario, that was fantastic. It has never been so good for me," Silvia admitted.

"Me either. I feel twenty years younger! Again?" he suggested.

"The kids are calling. You have to get me dressed, and we have to eat something. What if the kids are affected too?" she answered, growing fearful once more.

"Nightgown?" She nodded. For once, Mario didn't get fully dressed. He wrapped a bathrobe around himself, and with his arm around her, they headed out of their private wing into the main hall and then into the spacious living room.

"My god! All of you?" Mario exclaimed as he walked in and saw the three couples sitting on the couch. The three women appeared to be wearing similar makeup as his wife, but their arms were nowhere to be seen. They too were in their nightgowns. Their eyes were bloodshot from their crying. Their husbands looked a bit greenish, Mario thought.

"Daddy!" Susana cried out and ran to him; Vanna was right behind her. He put his arms around his wife and two daughters and pulled them as tightly to himself as he could.

"I love you," he whispered to them. Both began sobbing on his shoulders.

"There, there, Susana, Vanna, it will be all right," Sylvia found herself saying as she had so many times when they were young and ill.

"Mommy!" Susana sobbed.

"Dad. What should we do? I tried calling the trauma center, and they said that nothing could be done at this time. Everyone is being affected, at least that's what the man said," Gino asked.

"I, I don't know. I just don't know. Your mother is hungry. I suppose that we ought to try to get some food in them and see if it will stay down. Maybe if they eat, then something will start reappearing. Lord, I don't know," Mario replied more frustrated than he'd ever been.

"Hey you stay put. Gustavo and I will go fix something for us all," Jovanni suggested. Finally he had something that he could actually do. Besides, their wives were being comforted by their father now.

Later, the eight sat very solemnly around the dining room table, the men feeding their wives who looked simply pitiful, valiantly trying to keep from crying once more. "We are so utterly helpless like this, Mario. I don't know how we can even survive. We can't even eat like normal people. We have to be fed like babies. It is so humiliating! We can't even dress ourselves, cook, shop, or even sew. Oh my god, Mario! L'Eleganti is going to be utterly ruined! We can't sew anymore!" Silvia cried out in shock at this last revelation. "I've let you down horribly, Mario! I'm the ruin of three generations of the finest dressmaker shop in Velona!" She began to cry again, as did the three others, who now realized that she was right — their whole lives had just ended; they could not do what they loved to do, sew and make only the finest of dresses.

"Well, dad, it looks like I won't get to hang up a sign saying fourth generation now, once you retire. We're ruined. Maybe we can just turn it into a tailor's shop," Gino suggested. They four women bawled all the harder now.

"Son, my shop is the very last thing on my mind now. Your mom and your sisters and Milana are what we must focus on. I don't care if I ever open the store again. We've got to help them son; time enough to worry about the store later on," Mario chided his son. Strange, he never in his life had ever thought that he would say that about his shop. Until now, the shop had been everything to him, besides his wife and children, that is. Faced with a choice of them or his store, the choice was clear.

"Now then, they seem to be keeping the food down. I still don't feel

216

that her head is getting hot, no fever. Good sign, I trust. I don't see anything else appearing on their faces. I suggest that we take them to our bedrooms and inspect their whole bodies carefully for any additional signs of trouble. If we don't see any, then, I suggest that we get them dressed. It is no good sitting around here in our bathrobes and their nightgowns all day. Whatever else we may be in this household, we are civilized. Let's meet back here once we are all presentable," Mario took charge.

Back in their bedroom, Mario carefully checked every inch of Silvia's body for signs of any further abnormalities. "Oh, Mario, rub me like that again," she said and kissed him. Once more, their passions overwhelmed them.

A half hour later, they rose and Mario asked, "Okay dear, what dress would you like to wear today?" She decided to wear her everyday blue dress, which had five petticoats and no hoop skirt. The one benefit these men had came from their work at L'Eleganti. The all were intimately familiar with women's dresses and undergarments. Thus, Mario had little trouble dressing his wife.

"Oh dear, Silvia, your dress no longer fits properly!"

"Let me see," she became alert from her brooding and examined her figure with the acute eye of the dressmaker that she was. "Oh, Mario, this is just awful! My waist is so much smaller now. I'm going to have to take in the whole bodice and waist! Oh!" She began to sob once more. Mario was surprised by her sudden grief, but then realized why.

"Oh sit back and relax, dear. I can take it in for you. Won't take but a few minutes." He removed the dress and left her sitting on the bed in her slip and petticoats, sobbing softly to herself. Her life was ruined utterly. A half hour later, her dress fit far better, and he finished dressing her.

"Dear, what shoes do you wish?" She chose her Alexa heels, terrified of now wearing her Annelise extreme heels. Finally, Mario took the time to brush out her long, lovely hair, arranging it perfectly across her back. "There, my love. Have a look. Allow me to adjust what needs to be." She looked at her image and was satisfied mostly.

"The sleeves look funny, but there's nothing that can be done for them now. Thank you, Mario." She kissed him, and he passionately returned her kiss. Both were barely able to pull themselves away, grinning sheepishly. "Mario, if we keep this up, we'll never get me dressed. Okay, let's go see how the girls are doing. I feel so awful that I cannot even be there for them anymore. Oh Mario, what are we going to do?"

"Well, maybe we could hire some servants to assist, if there are any women left who would be able," he suggested. She liked this idea and they headed to the main family room. They found that they were there ahead of the kids.

"Mario, what on earth is all this stuff doing lying in the middle of the floor? Did the kids pick up stuff and forget to tell us?"

"Surely not, dear. This looks like a sink to me and that's a stove, only they are way, way too short."

"Hi daddy," Susana broke in on their cursory examination of the pile of stuff. She too wore a similar blue dress with petticoats. "Mom, you look really good, if it weren't for your arms."

"How's my little girl holding up?" Mario asked, opening his arms wide to hug her.

"Terrible, but Gustavo was kind enough to take my waist in for me. I can't ever do that anymore." Tears came into her eyes once more.

"Oh, I see you got a pile of stuff too," Gustavo said as he walked into the room, wearing an around the house suit. "We have one that's similar in our living room."

"Hi all, say we got a pile like that too," Vanna said as she and Jovanni walked into the room. "Mom, you do look good, excepting the arms of course." Silvia managed a slight grin.

"Did you boys bring this stuff in without telling us about it?" Mario asked.

"Hi dad. Say, you got a pile too. Ours looks just like this. Strange stuff. Sink and stove and tables for midgets, I figured," Gino commented as he led Milana into join them. "I do hope that we do not all turn into very short people!"

As they eight began looking through Mario's pile, now relatively calm and feeling at least more civilized, though utterly helpless, the four women began having the genetically installed memories surface. Several hours later, the eight now realized that somehow these objects were going to be critical to the survival of the women.

Just as they were about to go fix a late lunch, a soldier knocked on their door. Mario answered it. "Good day sir. I see that there is a man in this house. Stefano is having us visit every house in Velona checking on whether or not there is a man present to assist any women who may be living here."

"Yes, we have four men. How bad is it? I mean our women have lost their arms, no less. This is unacceptable. It's beyond horrible," Mario just couldn't find the words to express himself now.

"Widespread, sir. I believe that Stefano is anticipating that all of our women are similarly affected. Stay tuned to the radio, if you have one." He left Mario standing on his porch, his mouth open.

"Who was it dad?" Gino's voice brought him back to the present. He returned to the group. His face had lost its color. "Dad?"

"Stefano sent a soldier to see if there is a man in this house. Apparently, this has affected all the women in Velona! Turn on the radio; maybe there will be something on it."

All eight crowded around the large radio and listened. "Again, this is Captain Dante of Velona's First Division. I am filling in for the regular folks who run this station. The plague has utterly devastated on our whole city.

Stefano is asking that any woman who still has her arms to please contact the police station immediately. Our soldiers are in the process of visiting every home in Velona. Be patient. If you do not have any able-bodied men to assist you, help is on the way. Stefano is asking that all men who do not have a wife or other women to assist to please report to the police station to assist Velona in this unparalleled crisis. We are receiving scattered reports from outlying towns and villages. The plague situation is pretty much the same there. This just in from Barcella, the plague has struck there as well with the same viciousness as here. More as it comes in. Tune in at six tonight for a special address by our monarch and leader, Stefano West Po. Again, this is Captain Dante of Velona's First Division, filling in for those who normally run this station." He continued to repeat what he had just said.

"Damn, this is hideous! All women? Oh good lord!" Gino exclaimed.

"I guess that this is the beginning of the end for us all. I have truly enjoyed my few years with your firm, Mario." Gustavo sighed, figuring the end of the world was upon us.

"Oh don't be silly, we are not dead yet," Mario retorted. "We men are mostly okay. Our women seem okay except for their arms. It could be a whole lot worse. Let's wait and see what Stefano has to say before we all go jump in a lake or whatever."

That evening, the eight heard Stefano's radio broadcast. "Stefano West Po here. Today, all Velona is suffering from the effects of this most hideous alien plague unleashed upon us three days ago. It is with deepest grief that I have to report to you that the alien plague has struck our women so very hard. There is no easy way to say this. I'll be frank and candid and hope for the best. There is no woman in our sector who retains her arms. This is beyond all hideousness, viciousness beyond description. Yet, it has happened. The question facing us now is how do we survive, for survive we must. I ask that all men and boys everywhere to pitch in and do everything they possibly can do to assist our women in this, their darkest hour, their direst need."

"We have discovered that the aliens have left each home with some objects with which our women may better survive this unimaginable ordeal. It appears that some of it is a replacement kitchen, one that is low to the ground. I will be sending the soldiers around to every home tomorrow. If you or those in your home do not have the skill to install these replacement kitchens, then let the soldier know. I will be sending assistance to those who need it as quickly as possible."

"My wife has told me that she is now having some kind of images in her mind that are telling her how she might be able to use these things. For example, she believes that she may be able to learn to write with her feet using that strange, very low desk. The stick with two baskets on it we are calling a yoke. She believes that, using it, she can carry things again. I urge all women, if you begin to sense such things, do not discount them, but see if they might hold some secrets to aid your survival."

"I have heard from the other Sea Prince sectors. We are not alone. All are reporting the very same plague effects. We are all in this together. As long as we do all that we can to help our women, I believe that we can somehow survive. I will continue to keep you abreast of the latest developments. Thank you."

They turned the radio off. "Damn, so we were right, that is a kitchen. What are we supposed to do with four kitchens?" asked Gino.

"Keep three back. Maybe there will be some who did not receive theirs," Mario suggested. "Are any of you skilled enough to install our kitchen?" The three said no. "Okay, when the soldier comes, tell him that we need someone to install ours. I suppose that we ought to carry the pots, mugs, and such to the kitchen now."

Three days later, their kitchen was installed. As anticipated by Stefano, the four began dealing with their unique situation. All four began with learning to use the yokes. That was simple enough. As the week stretched on, they began to use their feet more and more, catching on to what they now must do. The articles began appearing in the paper and were avidly read every morning by the women and then the men. Slowly some semblance of normalcy began to return to the Cenza household.

By the end of July, the four women were confident enough to begin taking over preparing their meals, following closely all the hints in the paper. They had the men cut them out and paste them on the kitchen wall for their ready reference. After diner on the last day of July, the extended family met in the main living room. A family council, Mario called it.

"Well, our wonderful, brave wives are able to do many things now. Let's take stock of where we are and what must be done still," Mario began.

"We cannot dress ourselves in anything but perhaps nightgowns, totally unacceptable," Silvia suggested.

"We need help with our hair and going to the bathroom," Susana added.

"Hey, at least my writing can now be sort of read. That's a good sign, isn't it?" Vanna asked.

"It certainly is, Vanna, yes indeed. Well done," Mario complimented her.

"Dad, what about the shop?" asked Gino.

"I am appalled, as all of you are, at how ill-fitting all women's dresses now are. I say that we, as the Cenza family, must take it upon ourselves to bring elegance back to Velona and to our wonderful and brave women. Further, I have been watching you, my love, and you dear daughters, these past many days. It struck me that you are now learning new and different ways, methods, to cook our meals, carry things, and such. You are using, for want of a better term, specialized tools to accomplish what otherwise would be impossible or exceedingly difficult."

"What struck me today is that all of you are the finest dressmakers in Velona, in my opinion."

"*Were*, dad, *were* is the key word here," Susana interrupted him.

"True, Susana, true. Yet, you all know what must be done. Silvia told me precisely how to tuck in her blue dress. You have not lost the knowledge of dressmaking and fittings, rather the means to accomplish it. What struck me watching all four of you is that perhaps we can work together and figure out some new tools or methods by which you can continue to turn out only the finest dresses in Velona. Who better to take on this enormous challenge but we, the Cenza family, the finest in the city? I propose that starting tomorrow, we finally return to the shop, and all eight of us work on the problems that our wonderful and beautiful dressmakers are facing. Let's show these hideous aliens that the Cenza family may be down, but we are not yet out of the fight!"

"Hey, dad, I like that! We are a team. What say you, Milana, ready to give it a try?" She grinned and nodded.

The next day, for the first time since the alien attack, the eight got properly dressed in the morning. They kept careful records of how long it took them to deal with all that was needed, getting breakfast prepared, getting the women dresses, their hair brushed, and themselves ready. The women opted to wear the Alexa heels for two reasons. One, they could take them off when they needed their feet, unlike the fashionable Annelise oxfords, which had lace ties. Two, they could walk far better in the lower heels; balancing was far too difficult to manage while wearing the extreme heels. Likewise, they opted for the petticoats and not the Annelise style gowns with the enormous hoop skirts. Later, if things worked out and they became more skilled, they could revert to the height of fashion. Just now, they had far more important issues facing them.

As the eight entered their store for the first time in weeks, all felt a surge of pride in themselves and were more determined than ever to somehow make a go of it. Quickly, the key questions that all were asking of the women were: "How might this be done differently?" "Could someway we make a tool that would enable them to do it?" The latter question became a close second. Soon, it became a grand game to play!

After the first day, Silvia suggested, "You know, while we are working out the details, it would be vastly easier on us if we wore pants and not these fluffy dresses and petticoats. They interfere too much. Once we get everything worked out, then perhaps we can deal with them as well."

They began at the beginning of a dress, the selection of the materials and the measurements that needed to be taken. The fellows brought the three unused desks over and this simplified their jotting down of measurements. Taking the measurements turned out to be quite doable, though many awkward motions were needed. Yokes were a necessity, and they moaned the fact that the ones that were provided were far too big and bulky for their needs. However, later in August, they learned of some new lightweight willow yokes that were being made and bought four for starters. Later, they bought three dozen.

Laying out the pattern pieces was more difficult. The thin paper pieces were not easily handled, and pinning them to the fabric was impossible for the women to do. Mario came up with a brilliant idea of making a thin board pattern with a little bee's wax on the underside to keep the board from slipping over the material while the women held them down with their feet — sitting on the floor, of course.

Now they faced their greatest hurdle to date. Scissors were unusable by the four, wholly. For several days, the men tried various approaches until they hit upon two solutions. The women were adept at pushing forward with their feet. By using a leather bootie attached to a knife with a very short blade, they were able to guide it around the pattern cuts. It took several more days to get this fully worked out to everyone's satisfaction. Still, scissors were a necessity. Gino finally hit upon a brilliant idea. By attaching two booties to the scissors, the women were able to get their feet in them and thus operate the cutting action. Again, they spent several more days refining this as well.

All four women were amazed that the actual sewing was doable. "Bethany's right, it is taking us five times longer to do one stitch now than before," Silvia pointed out. Still this they could do, pricked toes became the order of the day instead of pricked fingers. Occupational hazard. Next came the fittings and their challenge was how to get a woman into her new dress. By working in pairs, they discovered that even this was doable and soon put this into practice at home, finally being able to deal with some of their own dressing.

The many bodice pinnings and pinning up of hems were again most difficult. Still, they had no solution for pinning. However, after much experimentation, they worked out how they could pin up a hem. Yet they could not replace their old actions of pinching a bodice tight and inserting a pin to hold it.

"Looks like we need to step in for the fittings," Mario finally conceded.

"Dear, if that is all you need to assist us with, I call that a miracle!" Silvia replied. This was in the morning of August 20.

"Hello? Is anyone here?" I called out. I had been keeping an eye on the various dressmakers around Velona for some weeks and finally noticed that L'Eleganti had its lights on brightly and decided to investigate.

"A customer?" Mario asked, confused. It had been over seven weeks since he had a customer in the store. He rushed out to meet me.

"My apologies, we really are not quite ready to open our doors yet. Oh dear, you must forgive my messy appearance. We are working out how our women can continue to make and modify dresses. Dear me, yours is in dire need of some tucking."

I grinned, "Duh, you can say that again. Millions of us are in dire need of your services. I am Bethany Bartiana Angela."

"Oh my, the Bethany who is writing all those articles in the newspaper each day?"

"Yes, that's me." He called the others to come at once and many introductions followed.

All eight were elated to give me a demonstration of the various techniques that they had worked out. Initially, I put them in touch with the dressmakers of Eastside and for a week, they learned from these other armless women who had been making dresses all their lives. When I returned, they had their tool modifications fully ironed out. I agreed to get them duplicated in a large quantity for them at no charge.

"If you will begin retraining all of your women workers, I will cover their pay while they are relearning their trade. Once you are finally open for business, I will pay the costs of every woman who brings in a dress to be altered to fit her new form. Plus, if you will begin teaching other dressmakers of Velona how to do it, I will pay you the cost of their training as well. Look at it this way, Mario. L'Eleganti is known for the finest in suits and dresses in all Velona. Now you get an opportunity to train the other dressmakers so that they can produce far better quality dresses as well. Your establishment will become even more famous." He and his extended family could not resist such an offer.

"All I ask is that when you are ready for business, there are six of us at my place who are in desperate need of having piles of dresses altered."

He chuckled. "We altered our wives' dresses that first day. Honestly, it grieves us so to see such fine dresses so ill-fitted, such as yours." I grinned, so did I.

Silvia spoke up, "Our real problem, Bethany, is just what to do about our sleeves. They serve no purpose anymore and to be frank, they look strange on us now. We want our dresses not only to fit perfectly, but also to be visually perfect. Sleeves have to go, but as yet, we don't know exactly what to do. We do not set the fashion trends; rather we only give our customers what they desire in the way of fine apparel."

Susana, who had been listening to all of this added, "Mom's right, but Bethany, we women need some new designs for everyday clothing that we can actually relatively easily put on ourselves. While we love fashionable dresses, we must have our husbands dress us. Plus, we've discovered that we will be unable to really work here and do our jobs if we wear dresses such as yours, old style Annelise, isn't it?" she asked.

"Yes, very out of date, but it's new and it fits me mostly. My other dresses are way loose," I admitted. "Okay, I will see what I can work out for us all. Lord knows that we need clothes that we can put on ourselves. My husband dressed me this morning. He's not always going to necessarily either be there or have the time to do it for me." Susana smiled, knowing that I understood her point exactly.

Chapter 20 Tatiana Torellini

The next day, I went in search of a good dress designer, wondering why I had not thought of this much earlier. I made some inquiries and learned of several possible candidates, of which Miss Tatiana Torellini was at the top of the list. I used my T-putt-putt to drive the two miles to her studio, but found it closed. A neighboring grocery storekeeper told me that her studio had been closed since the day of the alien attack, nearly two months ago now. I didn't like the sound of that at all.

I spent a half-day tracking down where she lived. Interestingly enough, she had a manor house at 340 Hampton Way, just three blocks on down our own street. I cranked up my T-putt-putt and headed home. Of course, everyone wanted to know what I'd found out, and mom chuckled when I told her where this designer lived.

"We really should get to know our neighbors better," she teased me. I gave her a hug and headed down the street, glad that the early snowfall had melted. Still it was chilly, and I dreaded the coming winter.

As I walked up to her manor house, the shades were all pulled down. From the leaves and ground, I surmised that at one time, they had many flowers and shrubs adorning their front. Now, as everywhere else, the landscape appeared as though it was the dead of winter, not late summer. Worse, the ill kept grounds suggested no one had been caring for them, not since all this began. I walked up to the door and knocked with my foot.

No answer. I knocked once more. Just as I was about to give it up for today, I heard an alto voice call out, "God damn this anyway. Come in, if you can." The doorknob had been removed. I observed that the door opened inward, making it easy for me to push it open and step inside.

"Hello." The smell of ale was strong, as was the distinct odor of human wastes. Red flags went off in my mind.

A woman with a butch style haircut, short and black with matching eyes walked up to me. I guessed that she was around thirty-eight. She had the alto voice that I'd just heard, and she wore an extra-large man's pullover shirt, perhaps a pajama top. I caught a glimpse and noticed she wore no panties — no shoes either, for that matter. Clutter littered the hallway, which I later recognized as simply garbage. "What do you want?" she asked gruffly.

"I'm looking for Tatiana Torellini. Are you her?"

"No, I'm her mate, Vanda Vincenza. Who are you and what do you want with her anyway?" Her tone was definitely hostile.

"I'm Bethany Bartiana Angela. I live just down the street at 42 Hampton Way. I want to talk to her about dress designs. May I see her, please?"

"Oh all right. Follow me. Ignore the mess; we can't do a damn thing about it. No one can anymore. It's all hopeless anyway. Wanna ale?"

"No thanks." We passed through their living room, which was littered with empty bottles, miscellaneous wrappers and discarded articles of clothing. Obviously, they no longer used this room much. We passed a side room where the remains of the old kitchen had been just dumped on the floor, making the room unusable. Their dining room was a shambles of filthy plates and glasses. Dried spills dotted what was once an elegant carpet. We finally walked into their kitchen, the only room whose lighting was at all bright. Off the kitchen was their bathroom, and the awful smells were coming from there.

A woman, who I estimated was a year younger, sat at the table. She had her head down even with the table, her lips sucking ale from what was left in the bottle, which lay on its side. Tatiana Torellini had very long blonde hair with natural waves, though now it was a disheveled mess. She had light blue eyes and one of those faces that are highly attractive to both sexes. She too wore only a grossly oversized men's pull over, again I suspected a pajama top, and nothing else. Both women were dirty, and some of the stink came from them.

Behind her, their new kitchen had been installed; however no one had plastered the old holes in the walls or painted it. Their low panty shelves were almost empty, but then these days, whose weren't?

"Wanna ale? Bout all we got 'til Bosco shows up and who knows when that'll be," she said.

"Hi, Tatiana. I'm Bethany Bartiana Angela from a couple blocks down the street."

"You are all dressed up. Going to a party? Must have a fellow dress'n you." She sounded slightly drunk. She was also hostile, but not necessarily towards me. Vanda sat down in the only other chair close to Tatiana. I sensed that she was somehow protecting Tatiana. "Can't even drink a bottle anymore." Holding it between her teeth, she threw it onto the piles of trash behind her and looked at me. "What?"

"I'm told that you are one of the foremost dress designers in Velona," I decided to get straight to the point and see what happened.

"Was. That's the key word now. Was," her tone dropped towards grief.

Vanda quickly spoke up defiantly, "Yes *was*. We had it all, fame, glory, money, respect, even love. Hope we don't offend you with that. Our designs were the hottest topic in the fashion circles, though hers were better than mine were. Now we've lost it all. We still got money, for all the good it'll do us."

"And love. Don't forget that, dear," Tatiana added, turning her head and planting a kiss on Vanda. "That's all we've got now: love. We can't do a damn thing anymore. Have to have old Bosco bring us stuff when he can.

We're just waiting for the end to come."

I could see that I wasn't going to get anywhere until I had run a little therapy on these two. I spotted another chair, pushed it over to the table, and sat down. "Okay, when did this all start?"

"With the alien attack. We were perfect before that," Tatiana answered.

"Okay, I want you both to close your eyes, go through all that's happened, and tell me what you are seeing, feeling, hearing, touching as you go through it." Yes, I had little choice but to attempt to run them both through a little therapy and at the same time. My guess was that they had not been apart since that day. I was right about that. Their stories were the same as they began to tell me about it.

The two lived alone here in the manor house. They did not take the newspaper, primarily because prior to the attack, they had far too busy a lifestyle to have time to read it. Besides, others always told them the latest news. When they awoke armless and the shock and terror struck them, they had no one to comfort or assist them in any way. While a soldier did come around and then some workers returned the next day and installed the new kitchen, no one actually helped them.

After a couple of days, they were starving and had eaten all that they could readily eat without cooking. In fact, both had gotten a touch of food poisoning and had vomited all over the bathroom. After a week, an acquaintance of theirs, Bosco, had come by and had begun to bring them some food supplies, but even those deliveries had tapered off. They'd given him the rest of their cash to bring back a lot of ale because it was easy to open and drink. Besides, they now sought refuge in being slightly drunk. There was nothing else to do, after all.

They had tried to dress themselves in many of their designer clothes, but all such attempts had failed. Originally, they had been unable to get their pants down to even use the toilet and had soiled their clothes. Bosco had changed them twice but now they just wore the only things that they could get on themselves, these old pajama tops. The house was chilly because they had no way to turn on the heat. They couldn't do the dishes, so they used all their dishes until they were all dirty and stacked or thrown into the piles here in the kitchen. Obviously, neither had any ideas how to cook anything.

Vanda, I learned, used have strong arms and served as Titana's protector, when they were out and about, which used to be all the time. Now, she couldn't protect her lover from much more than a cockroach, but only if it was on the floor.

They didn't have a radio either. They received the usual pile of objects, and the workers had used some when they installed their kitchen. However, the two had not yet figured out how effectively to use any of them. Why? They were in the depths of self-pity all this time. Now I had an idea why so many in Tashien chose to kill their bodies or allow them simply to succumb.

I thanked them and had them go back over it all once more. After recounting it three more times, both women became rather angry about it. "Why the hell didn't someone come here to help us?" Vanda spitted out her anger.

"Bunch of ass holes!" Tatiana added her anger to the pot. I thanked them and had them go through the events again. A couple more times through and both began yawning heavily. After another pass, both women brightened up considerably. I decided this was a good start and not to press my luck. After all, sitting behind this was the shocking loss of their arms. I wanted simply to get the edge off their trauma.

"God, Bethany, I am starving! I am so hungry. I've never been this hungry ever," Tatiana observed.

"Hey, me to love, me too," Vanda added.

"Well, times are changing. Will you both please come over to my house now for a good hot meal?"

"A real meal? God, Bethany, you are an angel!" Tatiana exclaimed.

"Yes, but we can't go looking like this, love," Vanda protested. "It's too damn cold outside."

"Are there any clean clothes about? Any shoes? Flats?" I asked.

"Clothes are everywhere, probably dirty or soiled by now. We can't do any laundry any longer," Vanda answered.

"Hell, we can't even open half of our clothes drawers and chests anymore," Tatiana added.

"Okay, okay, I can take a hint. Here's what we are going to do. I'm having my husband and my brother come over here, wrap you both in blankets, and carry you over to our house. A bath, hair wash, clean clothes of some kind, and then it's a good hot meal for you both!"

"Safe to enter, Bethany?" Marco called out from the open front door.

"Huh?" Tatiana exclaimed, surprised at how fast Marco showed up.

"Follow the light; we're in the kitchen, dear," I called out. Shortly, Marco and Sergio walked in, each carrying a blanket.

"Marco, Sergio, this is Tatiana and her mate Vanda. Please wrap them up so they don't freeze and carry them home at once. Straight into the bathroom, mind you, fellows."

The two didn't protest as the strong arms lifted them up. A couple minutes later, I pushed open our door and led them into our large bathroom. After setting them down, I nudged the fellows outside, while Lisa, Eve, Lucianna, Marta, and mom came in to say hi and help. Together, we gave them a good hot bath, got their hair washed, and patted dry.

After a bit of trial and error judging their sizes, we got them into a pair of simple cotton dresses with panties and a couple of flats, but no socks. We wanted them to have full use of their feet. Once dressed, Eve and I worked on their hair, well mostly on Tatiana's, showing Vanda how to use the special hair brushed that had been left at their place, though they had not known it.

When we were done, we had them stand before my mirror and see how they looked. That's always a good thing for a woman's self-respect. "My god, Tatiana, you look ravishing, love!" She gave her lover a passionate kiss and the two had a difficult time breaking it off.

"Yes, no kidding. Our passions are definitely enhanced," I teased them. Tatiana grinned.

"Thank you, all of you. We feel like human beings again," Tatiana said.

"Really, thanks," Vanda added.

Mom called for supper. "Oh hell, how the hell are we going to eat? We'll just get ourselves filthy again," Vanda complained.

"No you won't. We're going to show you how to eat. Come on." I led them to our dining room and had to go through a lengthy set of introductions as our fathers had returned along with Valerio and Giovanni.

"These low things are tables?" Tatiana said rather surprised.

"Oh yes, I'm beginning to see. Kind of got images or something in my mind," Vanda said. I relaxed, at last the genetic memories were surfacing.

It took some coaching, but soon the two were mimicking our motions with their feet. Both caught on rapidly and ate as if they were indeed starving. After dinner, I had them sit down on a pair of writing desks and, using my yoke, I brought them a stack of the finished and already published articles that I'd done. I had them in order and got the two of them reading the pile.

Many, ah ah's and so that's how it can be done's later, the two finished up. "We're a bunch of dopes, Vanda," Tatiana exclaimed when they finished the last one.

"Duh!" Vanda added.

"No, you were both all by yourselves with no males with you to help you through that awful beginning. Now tomorrow the fellows here are going over to your place, and it's spring cleaning time. We're going to work on doing your laundry and, together, we'll get you all setup. Mom's going to try to see if she can get you some additional food supplies from Stefano's emergency fund. I think that you qualify for sure. Now I do need to write up my hints for tomorrow's article so I need my desk here back. Tonight, you get to sleep in our spare bedroom, but first, we'll help you get ready. Takes many feet to dress us now," I jested and they grinned.

"God what a mess," Marco declared as the boys got their first look at the women's manor house. We let the fellows do the picking up and cleaning, while we helped each of the two get used to using the yoke to gather up their dirty clothes scattered about the house. Then, we showed them how to use the low buckets to do the wash. By the time we were done,

Marco had strung the low clotheslines for us. I sat back and watched them sitting on the floor, raising an article, and hanging it onto the line to dry. Both had a look of satisfaction by the time we were done.

Mom and dad showed up with three large bags of food from the emergency reserves and we women now worked on getting the kitchen operational, with the food on the low shelves where we could reach them. The chair on rollers was a revelation to the two women, who now saw that it might be possible for them actually to prepare a meal. Again, I cautioned them to allow five times longer than they would have allowed getting an action done.

Around five, we all headed back to our house for dinner, leaving their manor house completely redone and clean. We even had changed their messed up, filthy sheets. After they ate, we allowed them to return home and spend their first good night in their place as human beings once more. Around ten the next morning, I went to check on how they were now faring.

They were ecstatic. They had fixed their own breakfast and even made their bed. Donning proper clothes was still a bit beyond them, however. "How about some tea?" Vanda asked.

I even let them use their yoke to bring the pot and cups to the table, and pour one for me. Yes, they were terribly slow at it, but then I had already had a lot of practice. Over tea, Tatiana said, "Bethany, we don't know how to thank you and your big family for all that you have done for us. We owe you more than we can ever pay."

"Well, there is actually something that you can do for me, yourselves, and for all we women," I said coyly, finally able to ask what I originally desired.

"We need a whole new line of clothes designed for us women. I know that you are some of the most respected fashion designers in Velona. If you come out with a design, it will very likely be accepted everywhere. As you are acutely aware, we need some everyday clothes that we can actually put on ourselves somehow. That trick with the pants works well, for example. If our panties had loops we could hook our toes on to pull up or down, then that would be fabulous. You get the idea. We need them to accentuate our figures and look elegant on us. After all, Tatiana, you look gorgeous. Vanda chose well." Vanda beamed.

I continued, "We will still wear our fancy Annelise outfits on occasion, when our fellows dress us up for a ball, but then it is their responsibility to look after our every need. We need something that looks elegant, stunning, is easy to put on, and in which we have full use of our legs. Topping that off, we ought to have some fancy, easy to put on cloaks that are warm. It is going to likely be the coldest winter yet."

"When you have the designs worked out, I have several dressmakers who will be ready to begin making them."

"What? Have some guy who knows nothing about the fall of women's clothing make the dresses?" Titiana protested.

"Oh heavens no. These are women. Yes, they are re-learning how to sew again. I've got several top shops ready to begin production, such as L'Eleganti."

"What? The Cenza's can still make dresses?" Tatiana asked in disbelief.

"You bet. Took a lot of re-learning, but they are on their way back into full production with all of their women dressmakers. If you don't believe me, drop by their shop. By the way, Lucianna has taken your two putt-putts in to get them re-fitted. By tomorrow you will have T-putt-putts, ones which you can easily operate."

Vanda exclaimed, "Wow, love, you are back in business! She was utterly devastated when she realized that she could no longer design. There is hope now, something we didn't have before, Tatiana."

I chalked up another victory, but hoped that the new styles would begin appearing soon. I then decided it was high time to see about shoes and boots. I dropped by the Alexa Heels company. Wow! I'd not been here for over a century, when Alexa founded her company to replicate the incredible Grey Creature's boots. I just could not believe how large this company had grown. Occupying an entire city block now, Alexa Heels was the largest shoe and boot manufacturer in the world, specializing only in women's foot apparel.

I entered their main display and sales building, which was quite small, since they usually shipped their products to smaller shops around the city as well as the world. A middle aged woman rose to meet me. "Hello, welcome to Alexa Heels. How can I assist you?" She was wearing a brown dress with Alexa boots, the kind that we can slip off without too much trouble. Her fluffy dress, decorated with contrasting scallops, used petticoats not hoops. Again, I saw this as highly practical.

"My name is Bethany Bartiana Angela. I'm here to see what kind of practical, warm boots we women can get for the coming cold winter."

"I'm Zeta. Say, are you the one writing all those articles in the paper?" I grinned and nodded. "Wow. Pleased to meet you. Your tips are a true lifesaver!" She chatted for a bit about just how valuable they were to her. "You know, you are the first customer since the attack. Actually, I think only a few men have returned to work so far. I had to; we need the money badly. I can see why we've had no customers. Honestly, things are so hard for us now. I only returned to work this week because my husband has been staying home to help me all this time. Of course, I really did need him to be with me, especially for those horrible first few weeks. He still has to dress me and fix our supper. If he didn't, we'd be eating closer to eight not six. Oops, here I am telling you all about my problems when you likely have the same ones too."

"Yes, I have to have my husband dress me, if I am to look presentable like this. I'll have a look around your displays."

"Sure, don't worry about the sizes. If you see a pair that you are interested in, I can measure your foot and get them from the warehouse. We only keep one size of each kind here on display," Zeta explained.

For a woman, this was shoe heaven! From the extreme Annelise oxford knock-offs to the sturdy Alexa boots, for which the company was originally founded, to pumps and mules, hundreds of styles and colors lined the shelves. The smell of quality leather permeated the room. However, none was quite what I had envisioned for us during the cold spell ahead of us.

Zeta quickly returned with Mr. Leandro, the company's top executive. After introductions, he explained, "Since the catastrophe, most all our workers and cobblers are off taking care of their own families. I insisted. We had a skeleton crew filling orders for overseas shipments, but those were single men with no obligations to any woman. Right now, I have about a tenth of the men back on the job, again dealing with overseas orders. Only Zeta and one accountant woman have returned. We usually employ one hundred men and twenty-five women. Yes, they are in charge of shipping, records, orders, accounts, payroll, and Zeta handles our small storefront."

He continued, "Business is bad, but then it is much as I anticipated, when the plague struck my wife and kids. Awful. Just terrible beyond words. You have my deepest sympathies, Mrs. Angela. I wish that there was more that I could do for you and all of our women."

"Well, actually there is, Mr. Leandro. As you know, I am writing the columns on all the tips for us. Our next big unsolved issue is with proper footwear, that is, footwear that we can more easily manage, especially with the coming extremely cold winter that is forecast."

"Please, do go on, Mrs. Angela," he said becoming interested.

"I have two suggestions to make and one is a small modification to your existing lines. First, what about adding a small rear extension, perhaps less than a half inch where the heel joins the sole? With a little stub sticking out there, it will be easier for us to push off the boots. The pump styles are easy enough as it is, but the boots are more difficult. If we had a little bit of a bump thing there to push against, it would make it easier."

"Excellent idea. I will see to it at once." I liked his accepting attitude and continued.

"Second, what about a new boot that is designed to keep our feet really warm in the winters? No high heels, just flat, perhaps up to our calves to help keep our legs warm, since we no longer wear socks as that inhibits the use of our toes. They need to be soft and warm, yet easy to slip off. I was kind of thinking of either lamb or paca wool for the lining."

"Now that is an excellent idea. We have been putting nice linings in our Alexa boots, but in snow, those can be treacherous for women. Yes, that is perfect. I know my wife will love to have them. She's been complaining of cold feet already and it's only August, such a weird August. I believe that I can have a prototype for you inspection in say two days."

"Wow, that fast. Excellent. Now here's the deal. Once we get the details worked out, I want you to bring back all of your employees and begin mass production of the boots as well as flats. Our goal is to donate one pair of each to every woman in the nineteen plague stricken countries as fast as humanly possible. I will pay for the entire cost myself, though I may be able to get others to help donate to the cause. You have millions of boots to produce before our feet freeze," I teased him.

"What? You are going to cover their cost? This is unheard of generosity! On behalf of all women everywhere, thank you, Mrs. Angela!"

"If you can find a way to temporarily enlarge your production facilities and hire more workers, then that will be covered as well. We are under a bad time crunch, what with this strange weather. Anything that we can do to get warm footwear to the needy women must be done. I know that many of us have warm Alexa boots already, but with the predicted heavy snow, walking will be treacherous for us. We can't even grab on to something if we slip."

"I get the picture. You are an angel indeed. I'll get on it immediately. Do you have a telefono so that I can contact you the moment the prototype is ready?"

We exchanged numbers; he measured my feet and I left. Now I was off to see about additional financing. I spent two days visiting the wealthiest of Velona. I knew who they were via the Banca del Dio account records. When I explained my plan, all agreed to assist with the financing, as long as their family name was somehow mentioned as one of the benefactors. I then had Stefano relay our plans to the other rulers, asking them to see if some of their wealthiest might help offset the costs to provide footwear for their country's women. By mid-September, the financing was worked out. I ended up spending only ten thousand gold; the others covered the rest. I now had a very comfortable and warm pair of black boots, lined with paca wool, heavenly to slip onto my feet.

As promised, Mr. Leandro quintupled his cobblers, tripled his women shipping staff, and began meeting the tremendous demand. Quickly, other cobblers around the city began duplicating his new product and helped to fill this huge need.

Chapter 21 September's Hope

Dockhands yelled and cheered as the first of many caravels bring desperately needed food supplies began docking at our two large harbors. Our old harbor could handle thirty caravels at one time and the new Eastside Docks could handle twenty more. Rapidly, the fifty slips began filling up. With the news that so many ships were arriving, Stefano put out a call for all dockhands to report to work. If they needed someone to watch after their families, they were to contact the hotline. Barti added another dozen women to help handle the increase in volume there. Even Marco and Valerio now spent a good part of their day helping with hotline calls for aid.

These supplies were coming in from the Arad, New Barq, New Xin, and the Northern Steppes to the east and from various locations in the Southlands. Of course, now more manpower was needed to go through what was arriving and divide it up into nineteen lots, one for each of the affected countries, based on their projected needs and population. To this end, he set up nineteen different warehouses, each labeled with the country destination. His soldiers did the initial dividing of each caravel's load, based on his estimates.

At least twice a week, Stefano and I had been going over the employment statistics for the women of Velona. Our task was to find those who needed work some appropriate job that they would be successful at doing. As September came, I still had been able to do nothing for the three thousand or so women who worked in the beauty industry, doing hair, nails, and such. None of us had any great desire to visit such shops. Besides the cold weather and constant dusk, we all were more concerned in just somehow getting by and somehow having enough to eat. With the five times longer rule in effect with most women, they had little time for beauty parlor visits.

Even so, now unable to use scissors and barely able to handle the modified hair brushes to say nothing of needing special chairs built high off the ground so that their feet could even reach a woman's hair, these women had all but closed up shop. I had no helpful hints for this large group of women. Thus, Stefano adopted my suggestion to put as many of these women to work on the creation of ration packages from the food supplies in the warehouse labeled Velona.

Each week, more and more of these ex-beauticians were hired. We had a distinct shortage of yokes, but compensated by forming them into teams of three. Two would sit and load the two baskets, while the third manned the yoke, carrying the selected items to a packing station.

At this station, thousands of shelves lined the walls. One wall was labeled "City" while the others held the names of our many outer cities such as Alta in the far north. Stationed here was another identical trio, one of whom swapped yokes, giving the first team an empty one to carry back, while the other two put the items onto the lower shelves. One man was also part of this team to handle the higher shelves.

Rationing went this way. Soldiers did the actual home deliveries of the week's rations per home. They each were given an assigned route to follow, dividing their blocks into six equal parts, one for each day of the week. Each day, they would report to the shelves, take the ration items from the shelves, and deliver them to the homes on their list. Transportation was a major headache. Some were able to use motor-wagons or motor-cars, but those were very few. Often they would use horse drawn wagons. Even carriages were pressed into delivery service. Some had little choice but to use a simple pushcart, much like street vendors.

At home, our rations began arriving on every Tuesday now. Whatever came had to be carefully allotted to last for seven days. This drove mom and Marta half nuts trying to work it out so that come Monday we still had something to eat. One could still purchase fresh fish down at the docks, if you had the time. Few women did at first and even fewer men. The few grocery stores that remained open carried dried fish products and some dried seaweed, which we avoided, believing that it tasted more like glue.

At the height of the rationing, five thousand women found work along with eight hundred men and young boys. Yes, Stefano had no choice but to ask children twelve and up to pitch in as well. Barti and Sergio's biggest fears were that food riots might break out. They didn't because the deliveries were made by a soldier who always carried his long gun over his shoulder. Stefano had a wise idea there.

By the end of September, we were barely holding our own. We all knew that when the weather turned bitterly cold, much more food would be needed. Stefano hoped and prayed that Demokritos would come to our aid. By mid-September, our bargaining group would finally arrive way down south. Even if they responded immediately, the caravels would not arrive before late December at the earliest. Could we hold out that long?

September 3 became a pivotal day for us all. I was struggling to get into my pants that morning, just after finishing breakfast. I faced a morning of cleaning for mom.

Bethany. You there? Help, please, it's me, the Guardian.

Jes! Thank god! Are you all right? Now that was a stupid question to ask. His whole world had just been blown up, and all the spiritual beings, including himself, had somehow been zapped unconscious for three months.

I need you to help me recover very quickly from that traumatic blast. Get very clear of your body. Then, hold your position. Whatever you do, don't move, and keep clear of your body. I will discharge against you. It's a two terminal universe, Bethany. Two poles held apart generate electricity and electrical flows. Can you do this?

Okay. All set. I am high above Velona. What's going to happen?

Energy discharge. Just don't move and all will be fine.

Wham! I spotted Jes out over the ocean. Enormous energy flows arced between us and then on into the earth and waters below. Whitish in nature, I was reminded of the blast, which Nestor had used to entrap me when he abducted us. Curious. The terrific discharge lasted less than a minute before it was done.

Okay, that's better. Wow, what a sock that one was. How long have I been out of it?

Three months. Jes, the mantis blew up all of Dorota! There's nothing left.

Yes, there is. One and a quarter million spiritual beings are left. Chaucer and Linda are just now waking from it. Bethany, I need to know rapidly what all has happened and what the current situation actually is. They will be rousing shortly. I will need to deal with all of them.

Okay, shall I start at the beginning and tell you?

It will be faster if I just take control of your memories and play them back at a speed that I can assimilate them. Just focus on the very beginning times, and I'll take it from there, unless you do not wish me to see all of your last three month's memories.

It's okay. I am focusing on the beginning. Now what?

I'll take it from here. What a new and novel experience I underwent! My consecutive mental images for the last three months, beginning with the old drunk's suggestion that a flying ship had appeared over Velona began flying by at a speed that was about two thousand to one. That is, for every two thousand minutes that had elapsed in my life during the last three months only one minute of time passed as he viewed them. I found it interesting too. When Eve and I had touched the ship, we had been blasted with that same whitish energy beams, and we both had gone unconscious. Now I was yawning and seeing what had actually taken place during that supposed "unconscious" period. I was far from unconscious. I saw and heard again, albeit at a high rate of speed, everything that happened and was said. I could not understand anything that Nestor was saying to himself or our unconscious bodies. Once he had placed us inside that stone prison cell and placed the headbands on our heads, only then did I finally understand what Nestor was saying. By then, he had little to say except, "They will be out of it for a time."

One hour later, Jes had finished viewing all that had happened with me for the last ninety days. *Thank you for allowing me to catch up rapidly. Hug.* He floated to me and enveloped my beingness with his. What a feeling! As he separated, he sent, *Bethany, on behalf of all we beings on Tarra, I want to personally thank you for saving our world. If you had not done precisely as you have, I would have no world in which to return and continue freeing beings. Honestly, the mantis' solution, Version One, would have done precisely what you said it would, the annihilation of all women and thereby our species in a very short amount of time. I can find no fault in any of the choices that you have made for us.*

While your current situation is precarious indeed, we, as a race, still have a chance to make it all the way as free beings. Many others and I will soon lend you a hand in setting this right. Please hang in there a little longer. I must help all those who are now beginning to awaken. I will get back to you as soon as I can. Again, Bethany, you have my heartfelt thanks for all you and your companions have done. Please relay my thanks to them for me. I had better go now. Chaucer is arising and is highly confused.

Quickly, I telepathically let everyone know that the Guardian was back in operation and the vague idea I had about what he was now doing. *What a relief. Maybe he can help us,* Marco sent. The excitement over, now I faced cleaning the house by myself. I grabbed a yoke and headed for the bathroom first. After filling a wash bucket and adding some soap, I got out rags and the short handled mop with the two leather foot holders on either end. Darn, I forgot, the load has to be balanced. I filled a second bucket and put it on the other side. Carefully balancing my load, off to the kitchen I went. Scrubbing the floor normally would have taken me a few minutes, but now I spent a good hour on my butt, scooting along, using my feet with the brush. So went the whole morning, but by lunch, the house had been cleaned and things picked up.

I know, I kept expecting the Guardian to contact me any minute. Instead, the others of our household all showed up close to noon. "Tell us what all he said!" Eve demanded to know, "Marco and the fellows are going to fix lunch so we can get back to the hotline work soonest." Indeed, today, they were all lending a hand or foot; so many were calling in asking for various kinds of assistance. I complied, half expecting the Guardian to interrupt me. He didn't.

I will say that with our men fixing the lunch, we were able to eat in short order. By one, they all took off once more; only this time they left all the dishes on the table for me to wash. Ah well, more practice I thought. The longest time was spent alternating sitting on my butt so I could get my feet to one of the dirty objects, whether it be dish, cup, plate, spoon, and lift them down and into a basket. I began to see that with enough practice I would naturally sit down at the right spots, without having to reposition my butt. When the baskets were full, it was a simple matter to use the yoke to carry them into the kitchen. Well, that killed an hour and a half before I had them dried and put away. I smiled to myself as I realized here was yet again my five times rule in operation. What used to take me at most twenty minutes to do from start to finish now took five times longer. Yes, while I could have just used my native spiritual being skills to lift them, I firmly decided to continue doing things the way the normal women had to do them.

I'd finished when a very loud thunderclap jarred the house. Wow. It was loud. I peeked outside and saw that the weather looked threatening, if one could really tell in the dim dusk light of midday. Just then, the telefono rang.

"Bethany? Oh hi, it's Tatiana. We now have a telefono too!" She gave me her number, and I hastily scratched it onto the wall, unable to write it down otherwise.

"The reason I called is that they just delivered the first of my new dress fashion prototypes along with the shoes. I wanted you to be the first to see the outfit and tell me what you think. It's a prototype, so we can change anything we want. Are you free?"

"Great. Yes, I'm free. Say, how did you get it made so fast?"

"I remembered all that you've been saying, especially about the Eastside subdivision dressmakers. I had one of them make this first work up. Alexa Heels was also interested in a new line of heels to go with it," Tatiana replied.

Five minutes later, I knocked on their door, just as another round of low rolling thunder jarred me. Well, it had not rained in a while, and I suppose that we needed it. Vanda opened the door, as I expected. She was the protector, adopting the male role in this household. "Hi, wait til you see it! Even I love it. Come on. This way to the living room."

I found Tatiana in the living room sitting at the low desk, surrounded by many charcoal drawings of dresses. On the couch were a white silky slip and a bright yellow dress. Matching yellow five-inch pumps sat beside them. "Hi Bethany. I rather used your measurements for this first one. You and I are about the same sizes, I think it will fit you. Come on, let's try it on you, and see how you look in it." She was more animated than I'd ever seen her.

Between the three of us, we quickly got my slip-on shirt and pants removed. "Okay, now notice the bottom inside of the slip," she pointed out, sitting on the floor before the couch, pointing at it with her toe. "I followed your tips." I saw immediately what she meant. Four discrete toe loops had been sewn on the underside bottom. "See, now you can use your toes to help pull it down. We always had to pull our slips down before anyway. Now we can do it very discretely with our toes while we are sitting. Go on, see how well it works."

I laid the slippery slip out and began to wiggle my head into it, and then stood up and shook a bit and my head poked through. Vanda was right there to ease my long black hair out for me, making it a whole lot easier. I easily found the loops with my toes and exclaimed, "Wow, this is super easy to pull down. Fantastic idea. We should put these loops on all our apparel."

"Yes, I have already got that one written down for the dressmakers," Tatiana said with a wry grin. "Now the dress. I wanted it to outline our figures. After all, they are smashing now, don't you think? And without

238

needing a corset. You wiggle into it and find the pull loops as with the slip." Again, I wiggled my head inside and then stood up and jostled it on down until my head poked through. My bosom rather held it from slipping further down. I found the lower loops and soon pulled it on down. To my surprise, the whole front of the dress, from just below my bust line down to my hips, was one open slit.

"Okay, here comes the really cool part," Tatiana eagerly began to explain, pointing with her toe, "On one side are the hooks, like the ones which we used to use to hold up petticoats to the waist bands. On the other side are small grommets. Start at either the top or the bottom. Oh, yes, sit down first. One foot pushes one side toward the other, while you use the other foot to push the other side. When the hook hits the hole, it slides in." I had some twenty hooks to fasten, but once I got the hang of it, it went rapidly. I stood and used the loops to pull it straight once more. I slipped into the pumps and followed her to the full-length mirror on the wall. She had six of them here in her living room. I suspected that she used to do quite a bit of designing in here.

"Hey, this looks fabulous on me. I like the way that the flap automatically folds over the hooks and holes, hiding them. Wow, it sure does show my figure off!" The dress followed the curves of my hips as they widened from my waist. Then, it fell straight to the floor. A huge walking slit allowed me still to use my feet to eat. The high back ensured that the dress would not slip off my shoulders because of the large U shaped front that showed quite a bit of skin, discreetly, of course. Even more enticing, she had a scalloped band that hung over my bosom and straight down a few inches, drawing attention to my form, highly accentuating our small waistlines. I knew at once, this style of dress would catch the fancy of a great many women. It was perfect for everyday and about the town use. It was not a party dress or one you would wear on formal occasions that was not its intended purpose.

"I love it! I cannot wait to get some of these! How soon?"

"Next week, if we don't make any changes. What's interesting is that they can use some kind of a machine to drive all the grommets in at one time. A press, I think they said at L'Eleganti. The shoes, however, will be delayed until they get the boots and flats made for us all. Bummer."

Vanda added, "Hey, it looks so good on me that I will actually wear one. I hate to wear hoops and petticoats; I don't like to look like that at all. So I always wore men's outfits, but this is another story entirely."

I laughed, "No kidding. Well, Eve also always liked to wear men's outfits last lifetime. Sometime, you two ought to chat about it." Vanda's eyes rose most curiously. I added, "I wore the fancy dresses and Dita, that was her name then, she wore the fancy twin tails suits."

Vanda said rather quietly, "You were with her?"

"Yes, we were actually married in the Church of the Three Holy

Roses. Say, the second these are available, I know six of us who want them immediately!"

Vanda grinned; even Tatiana smiled knowingly. Then, Tatiana gave me a coy look and whispered, "It's *so* much better after the plague."

I grinned and nodded. She got back on the subject at hand. "Okay, I promise you that when L'Eleganti is ready to start making them, you will get the first six they make! Here are my other designs that are based on this shell. I keep getting more and more ideas. I know that we will still want to wear the flaring skirts to formal affairs, but these are vastly more practical for all else. Besides, we can get into them in short order." I began looking over her colored sketches and became lost in her dream world of dress designs for quite some time.

"Mark my words, Tatiana, a year from now, your designs are going to be all over these entire nineteen countries! Incredible work!" Boom! A very loud blast of thunder shook the house, and the rain began falling down hard. I hated to get out of this fabulous dress, but did so. Finally, I decided that I had better get back. I was supposed to get supper going for the others tonight.

By the time I got back, I was soaked completely and wasted another half hour drying off and changing my clothes. Immediately, I wished that all my clothes had those loops. They made dressing easy. The choices for dinner were slim; it was Monday, and we'd get our next week's rations tomorrow. It was fish gumbo or fish gumbo tonight with peas on the side.

It wasn't until two days later that the Guardian contacted me. For two days, it continued to rain. Initially, a deluge of water came down, but now it was a constant, steady rain that showed no signs of letting up. It was the early afternoon. Once again, everyone was out helping deal with the calls to the hotline. My task was to have supper ready when they all returned home around five. At least tonight, I had a little choice; the week's ratios had come yesterday, though mom had already divided them up into seven parts. At least I could choose which part to use. Five were fish based, with one salted pork, and one salted beef. The only thing that we had in abundance was tea.

Bethany. Good time to chat?

Jes! Yes, totally free.

Good. We're working on blowing off that powerful energy trauma charge that all of us received. Chaucer and Linda are off supervising others. We've quite a lot of beings to handle now. That's our first task: to remove this most recent trauma from all the million beings. However, you needed drastic help here, so we put our minds together and came up with a solution.

You see, Chaucer and Linda firmly believe that your attempts to acquire vast food shipments from Demokritos are going to fail. I'll let you discover the why for yourself. We also observed that this dust cloud will take almost two years for it to settle out on its own completely. Your coming winter will be akin to living in the Axemen's world of bitter cold with mountains of snow. With no food production for two years, grim is an understatement. We worked out a solution and now it is being implemented. We are making it rain. Actually, it's going to rain for about an entire week. After it stops, all the dust will be out of the sky; sunlight will return.

With the ground soaked and soft, we want you to convince farmers everywhere to plant quickly. The dust that is coming down with the rain is exceedingly rich in nutrients. We think that you will find that it is rather like a miracle plant grow, probably for two seasons. We will be delaying the onset of winter until late December. Combined with the miracle grow, it is our belief that you will be able to get one quick crop grown and harvested or nearly harvested before we can delay the winter any longer.

In addition, the northern half of the three northern kingdoms of the Greenway has not been impacted severely by the dust cloud. You should be getting word from those three kingdoms that they will have some products to send your way as usual in early October. Things will still be tight until sometime in January, when food supplies should become more available everywhere.

Thank you! We were dreading starvation here, honestly.

I am very well aware of that, Bethany. We had to take action or lose all of you. Now tonight, will all of you be home? If so, Chaucer, Linda, and I want to drop by and perform a thorough examination of your bodies, if we may.

Please do! Yes, we'll all be done with supper by seven. It takes us a while to do ordinary things now.

I know. I am sorry about the conditions of your bodies. Truly, these bodies were meant to have two arms. Okay then, we will appear around seven. I have more beings to rescue. Bye.

This was the best news in a very long time. I called Stefano and we talked for nearly an hour. I made sure that he would take every available means to convince the rulers in the Greenway kingdoms to plant a crop as soon as the rains ended. I knew that he would so order it here in our sector. Undoubtedly, the other sectors would follow suit.

That done, I then contacted the others, giving them the brief version. Finally, I knew that I had to get started on supper — the old five times as long rule was kicking in fast. As I slid about the counter top space and the stovetop, I marveled at how easy the chair on rollers actually made cooking doable for us. Without it, the task was tedious at best. I even turned on Radio One to listen to the symphony while I worked on fixing dinner for everyone.

The fellows kindly did the dishes for us so that everyone was ready for the coming visit. All were excited and greatly relieved about the food situation. "See, I told you that we were going to have a long, cold, nasty winter here and that the dust wouldn't go away for at least a year," Lucianna declared. The Guardian had proven her theory was mostly right. "Now when this is all over, we've got to have our own flying machines, right Giovanni?"

"True, but a machine to make clothes fast and easy would also be a great help, if we cannot get your arms back," he replied, pointing out another serious problem in our altered economy.

We all sat around in the living room waiting. Promptly at seven, three ghostly images formed before us and then solidified. They remembered that we preferred it when their "bodies" looked solid to us and not like thin gossamers.

"Greetings savors of half the world," the Guardian spoke as soon as he sensed that his form was sufficiently solid enough for us. "Again, I want to personally thank all of you for the incredible job that you have done and are continuing to do. I certainly picked the right people to watch over the security of the planet for us. Bethany, incredible job under the most trying of circumstances."

"Well, we are really grateful for the rain and getting rid of that dust cloud," Giovanni replied.

"Say, is the reason the dust is going to act as a miracle plant grow because it contains bits of all organic life that was on Dorota?" asked Lucianna.

"Precisely so, Lucianna. Wise deduction on your part," the Guardian complimented her and she beamed.

"Now then, to the business at hand. We have millions to deal with, but we must see for ourselves just what this genetic modification actually is. With your permission, we three will examine your bodies." We all agreed.

For an hour, the three rather merged with our bodies — that's about the only way that I can describe it. He called it more like a blanketing effect, but I didn't know what that meant. Each one merged with each of us and then compared their observations. We were not privy to that, however; they used telepathy between themselves, maintaining a smile on their "body's" face all the while. Valerio suggested that they would make terrific card players. No one could tell when they were bluffing.

At last, Jes spoke for them. "Well, Bethany, this Nestor actually was a genetic engineer. He has indeed somehow totally altered the genetic blueprint of your bodies, male and female. We agree, it is an incredible feat of work, far in advance of anything that we have ever encountered in our long past, but then we three were never in the mantis society. We were in the Grey's."

"Can you fix it? Put us back to the way we were? There are millions of us now. Probably too many to handle, right?" I asked.

"For once, Bethany, I admit that I do not have the skill to reverse what has been done. We three agree that if we restore your arms, they would not last, as your body would reject them. Such is not in the body's blueprint

242

of operations. Perhaps if we restored them, you would not even have any feeling in them before the body reabsorbed them. If we reduced your ear lobes, for example, we believe that the body would slowly regrow them. You might try cutting them off. That might work, but long ear lobes are the least of your concerns and not worth the trouble."

"We also agree that for a while, your increased sexual drive will be useful. We are going to need a million and a quarter baby bodies soon. Yet, we feel that perhaps once that number has been reached, there is some evidence that the drive may subside somewhat."

"We also agree that your conditions will be inherited by your children, just as Nestor suggested it would. He has altered the genetic makeup of your bodies, in essence, creating a sort of new subspecies of humans here on Tarra. Had you not stopped him, one species of human bodies would have completely replaced the other in but three months or however long it took him to get around to everyone."

"You mean that as of now there are two different human forms permanently in our world?" asked Sergio.

"Precisely so. Number wise, your new species represents one third of the human forms on Tarra. What concerns us is what will happen when one of you joins with one of them: male to their female or female to their male. On this, we've decided that we cannot predict what will occur. In time, this will become clear."

I decided to ask what I had often thought about. "What about us taking a trip to Chichulain and studying what is there? Nestor did say that these genetic modifications could be undone. Might it be possible for us to find a cure that way?"

"I believe that 'undone' is a poor choice of words. I suspect that to 'undo' what he had first done, your Version One, he just re-engineered your bodies, not erasing what he had done. That is, he made more modifications, which to you appeared as though he had erased what he'd done to your bodies. That being said, it might be worth a try someday in the future when our knowledge is sufficient to actually understand his. If my idea is correct, you would need to rebuild arms into the genetic blueprints, but only on female bodies."

It sounded farfetched and way beyond anything I could do. I had hoped that one could just push some kind of undo button and that would be that. He continued, "I am truly sorry, but it is my belief that a third of the human race is destined to be as you are now for years to come. Perhaps one day your science will gain the necessary knowledge to reverse what has been done. I cannot say. Already, your devices in Velona are beyond my knowledge. My compliments to Giovanni and Lucianna."

Yes, we six found this a little disheartening. I know that in some small corner of my mind I had held out hope that with a wave of a magic wand, all this could be undone. Jes was being very gentle with us on this point.

He went on, "I am thinking now that Nestor intended for those beings whose bodies he destroyed on Dorota to take over new baby bodies here. I can see his line of thought. Here in Velona, life is now more difficult for everyone, making the beings far less likely to have thoughts of their true natures. However, on Dorota, we have found that to be a factor in our advantage. In actual fact, with a little therapy, the beings quickly realized their true nature and become much easier to spring out of their heads and begin to make true progress towards their own spiritual freedom and ability."

I broke in, "Jes, what about all of us? Women here have undergone a nasty shock and trauma with all this. Although we experienced no pain or unconsciousness per se, nevertheless the shock and terror caused some to give up and die. I did a little emergency therapy on a couple of women and it was really making a difference. I know we all could use the lift that therapy sessions can give, but we're so many. It's not like it was when Dita and I were on Dorota. . ."

I paused; you know it is somewhat similar after all. On Dorota, everyone either had former lives in which the mantis had removed their arms or in which their doktors had done it or they in turn had done such to infants. Here, we all had undergone the massive shock, terror, and humiliating loss from the plague within days of each other. Still, could I possible train so many women to give therapy sessions as I had done before?

As if reading my thoughts, the Guardian said, "Not likely, Bethany. Here there is emotional shock and loss, but no pain and unconsciousness. Each person will have their own underlying painful traumas upon which this huge, catastrophic loss hangs and depends upon for its continued impact on their lives. Skill will be needed to reach the real pain and unconsciousness, which lies in back of this event. That's where we will need to step in, Bethany."

"We have not yet decided upon the optimum path for us to follow to continue our work of freeing all beings on Tarra. It is obvious that most all of us will need to obtain a new baby body and get it grown up to where he or she can then resume their path to personal freedom. Dorota was actually an ideal location and its people were ideally suited. We made great progress with a large number of them."

I spoke up, "Major problem. As I see it, you can't just materialize over a million adult humans and suddenly repopulate Dorota. You need a quiet, remote area where interruptions are seldom, as you first had in the Red Desert and then Dorota. Honestly, I don't know of any new such places, Jes. What can you do now?"

"That my dear Bethany is precisely the problem. We have arrived at a point in time and evolution of Tarra in which there is no isolated, safe, secure location, save somewhere out at sea. Mankind has yet to develop the technology for us to live out our lives wholly upon the sea without ever touching land. While there are still a few relatively untouched areas of the large western continent, we have also the problem of needing to find new baby bodies for a million people, whom we simply cannot desert in their hour of desperate need."

"The only solution that I can see is to take advantage of the perhaps gift given unto us by Nestor, although for completely different reasons. I feel strongly that one of the reasons that he went along with your ideas of having increased sexual sensations was not as you presented it as a means of making a person more solidly attached to his body, which I will admit it will do just that, making our task more difficult, but rather he needed to generate rapidly new baby bodies for the prisoners whose bodies he had just eliminated on Dorota. I believe he went along with your suggestion because it also fulfilled his need for a swift repopulation effort."

"What he could not know is that as each spiritual being 'awakens' from the traumatic shock that he gave them, we are going to immediately discharge that electrical trauma. Each person will have that trauma totally gone before they pick up their next baby body. Yes, we have quite a few sessions to give in the very near future, but as you saw with me, Bethany, the electrical discharge can be quick."

"This should then have each person, each spiritual being, whose body was destroyed, resuming their therapy sessions right where they left off when this all happened. In other words, Bethany, wherever they were at along the road to spiritual freedom, in their new body, they will be at the same spot, ready to continue moving on down that road."

"This is diametrically opposite to Nestor's plan, where each one of us would be so utterly confused, so wiped out, that in essence we would be back at square one, nicely imprisoned within these bodies. Still, with a bit of therapy they could resume their road. Only they would first have to rediscover that there was a road on which they could walk, having lost all knowledge that there even was such a road."

I looked a bit confused by all this. What exactly was he planning? Where would be his new "base of operations?" "So where?" I finally asked.

"The Sea Princes. No other choice is possible at this time. Zargarb is an ideal land in which to make our primary base of operations, but it has a serious drawback. It borders with the Arad and the Northern Steppes, both of which may be unsettling in the future. Zargarb is more difficult to protect. Enemies have many overland routes by which to attack the sector. So while I would prefer the secluded inner lands of Zargarb, it is too risky. We need a buffer zone around us, where you and others can protect us and keep the peace."

"I think that the ideal location now must be in Barcella. However, we will have secondary bases of operations in the other seven sectors, at least until we have re-acquired all those who were on the path and who wish to continue to walk it. We will once more be dependent upon you and your people to keep us free from distractions as you have been doing for quite some time now. With luck, no more aliens will be returning until after we have finished our work here."

"There are twelve of us now who can materialize a body, so we will take it upon ourselves to prepare the way. We create permanent identities and set up the bases. When the others have their bodies grown and are ready to continue our work, we will allow these identities to disappear, for we twelve really no longer have need of bodies in the sense that you perceive."

"You will find that as time passes, more and more of you will be receiving therapy for the shocking losses you have suffered. It is my hope that all of those who have been affected will eventually be released from that trauma and what lies beneath it. We just need time to make all this happen. Again, we are counting on you to help give us that time, Bethany."

"The identity I will have in Barcella is Macario Ines. Linda will be known as Raffaella Ines and will be here in Velona. Chaucer will be known as Lucio Ines and work in d'Grange. All twelve of us will use the surname of Ines. Within a few weeks, Raffaella will come here looking for a place to establish our base in this sector. But first, we have to finish assisting the others who are still awakening from the trauma."

I replied, "This sounds like a really good plan. You can count on us. Drop by when you are ready, Linda, I mean Raffaella."

"It will be fun working with all of you once again, Bethany. I have missed all of you, but really, we had better get going. I sense hundreds have awakened and are very confused, Macario."

We said our farewells and watched as their forms turned from solid looking bodies like ours into a thin, ghostly image and vanish. Marco said, "Well this is going to be interesting. We're going to have them nearby now. I'm grateful that we don't have to stop everything and dash off to Chichulain right away."

"No, I think that we have a lot to learn before we can make that attempt," I replied. "Say, the Guardian has just told us more in this visit than in centuries! Great!"

Sergio rubbed his moustache. "I didn't like the sound of what he was saying about there now being two species of humans and how the southern folks will react to our plague. I sense real trouble developing, Bethany. Be on your guard."

"Maybe we shouldn't have any children, Valerio," Lucianna spoke up. "What if we have a little girl and she is doomed to be like us?" She voiced what many of us were thinking, though just not saying.

"Oh, you and I will love her all the same, Lucianna. Stop fretting. She'll be just as pretty and cute as her mother. Besides, by then, it will seem normal to be the way that we are. You'll see. Have faith, love, and keep on inventing things." She flashed him a grin. The other fellows quickly added their support to us as well.

"Hey, I figure that there is something like four million women in all the Sea Princes. If even a quarter of us have a baby within a year, all those from Dorota will pretty much have a new body. I bet that all these new babies that will be appearing in the next year or so will have come from Dorota," Marco pointed out.

"Hey, some of us may have some really intelligent and precocious children," Eve added with a sly grin. We all chuckled at that prospect.

Right on schedule the torrential rains ceased and that morning all Velona celebrated! The sun finally appeared bright in the morning sky. All around town, the coming of the sun was the sole topic, until Stefano's urgent plea came. He encouraged everyone to plant any and all kinds of crops. The newspaper and the radio newscasts all carried the same message.

"Beginning tomorrow, all shops and stores and plants will be closed for three days. Take this time out to plant whatever you can, wherever you can. Use your backyards for garden plots. I am opening up our reserve seed bins countrywide. If you need seed to plant, drop by. I am encouraging all women to lend a foot to all farmers. If you will assist them, I will see that you are paid three gold for each day that you help. Carry their seed bags across your shoulders, anything. Please, everyone, we have an opportunity to get in one quick crop before the winter comes. Let's all take these three days to get our farming industry back on its feet. I am encouraging the other countries to follow suit."

"Finally, there will be some grain arriving soon from the far north of the Greenway, where in spite of the dust they have been able to grow some crops. Have faith, soon our food shortages will be a distant memory."

"Have we even got any seed around here?" asked Marco as soon as we all heard Stefano's announcement. We eight kids looked at our parents, who shook their heads. "Okay, fellows, come on, we're off to the seed bins." We laughed and all began telling them what to get.

"Hey, how about some pumpkins?" I called out. "Pumpkin pies?"

Mom and I remained home, while the fellows went off to get seed, while Lisa and Lucianna headed for the hotline once more. Meantime, mom and I headed outside to see where we could plant all the seed. "Will you look at this?" mom exclaimed. "I do believe our rose bushes are starting to get leaves again. Do you suppose that we will be able to have a few roses at the dinner table once more before winter comes?"

Eventually, we went back inside and began to fix lunch. The four fellows didn't get back for two hours. "Hey, you wouldn't believe the long lines that we had to wait in," Marco complained. "We got a little of a lot of things. Yes, got you a few pumpkin seeds, dear. Now we have to plant everything after lunch."

"Hey, we are going to have to plow it up to get rid of the grass,"

Valerio pointed out with a groan.

"Glad I don't have arms now," I teased him, as they would have to do that hard chore.

That afternoon, mom and I helped the four boys begin our new garden. We chose to plant most everything along the south side of the estate where the plants would get the most sunshine. The four dug up the sod and mom and I, sitting on our butts, planted the seeds. While we were very slow at it, that didn't matter because it took the four even longer to get the ground ready for the seeds. All six of us were quite tired come suppertime. Thankfully, dad and Sandro fixed dinner for everyone.

After dinner, Vanda came by. "Hi, I hate to ask you all for anything after all you have done for us."

"Hey, dear, not a problem. What do you girls need?" I asked.

"Help with putting in a garden. We don't know the first thing about it. I stood in line for four hours to get the seed. Do we just dump them on the ground? Tatiana thought that I should come by and ask you folks. We don't want to waste this precious seed."

"Great. You have to dig up the grass and then plant the seeds in the ground," Marco explained. "How about if some of us come by in the morning and help you two get your garden in?"

A big grin formed. "That would be really great! Thanks. I'll tell Tatiana the good news."

After she left, Valerio groaned. "Oh my aching muscles. Another day of it ahead." We all laughed.

I added, "Well no sense washing my muddy pants until after tomorrow." Mom smiled; the seats of our pant were incredibly muddy having sat all afternoon on the still soggy ground.

It seemed strange that "springtime" came back to Velona in late September. Yet it did. The days became warm and balmy. The seeds sprouted, and daily we all swore that we could see the plants growing. Miracle growing now became the topic of conversations each day.

Chapter 22 Barbe Barcella

Barbe Barcella turned eighteen in May of 822. She'd inherited her father's throne only a year ago when her parents, Gervaise and Alli, had been accidentally run over by a motor-wagon. Gervaise was the son of Andriano and Adelina Barcella. In fact, Barbe was proud of the fact that she could trace her lineage all the way back to the famous freedom fighter, Jovanna Barcella, who had restored the former glory of Barcella, wrestling it from the control of the Megalos Centurions back in 640.

It was early June, and Barbe stood looking at the many portraits hanging on the palace walls. She was staring at Jovanna in fact, the woman who had been tortured by the Centurions and had lost her arms. Well not all of them, Barbe noted. It appeared from the portrait that she still had maybe six inches of her upper arms left. She wondered how her famous ancestor could possibly have done all that her history books claimed. Barbe tossed back her long wavy brown hair, which fell just below her shoulder blades. She had hazel eyes and her looks, while not stunning, were at least acceptable for a ruler, she felt.

Barbe was unmarried. She was an only child and her parents had been very careful about the boys that she met. When they had been killed last year, Barbe still did not have a steady boyfriend. She did have a steady girlfriend, best friends since childhood, the long blonde haired Tina Perez, the eighteen year old daughter of the palace stewards, Jacopo and Tecla Perez, who were in their late thirties and who Barbe's late parents had complete trust in running the day to day affairs of the palace.

As she stood reflecting on her ancestor, she heard the rapid click-click of high-heeled shoes. Their rapid pace could only mean Annelise oxfords and that meant Tina. Barbe turned and saw Tina, wearing a bright blue Annelise style billowing dress, gracefully, but very slowly coming her way. In contrast, Barbe's similar dress was pink. Both dresses had hoops that billowed out nearly fourteen feet across. As she watched her dear friend moving towards her, she rubbed her waist hoping to relieve the pressure slightly. Both she and Tina were working hard to reduce their waists to what was considered proper in the most fashionable circles of Barcella, an eighteen-inch waist. Down to twenty inches now, she knew that they had to endure this awful discomfort for quite some time yet. However, most of these fashion conscious women also thought that Barbe ought to be setting a proper example for them and have an even smaller waist size. After all, that's what was routinely found down in Annelise, where a fourteen-inch waist was considered ideal.

"Here you are, Barbe. Dad sent me to find you. You have an LDCS message from Monarch West Po. Dad says that it is very urgent," Tina relayed her message. "Looking at them again?"

Barbe giggled, "Yes, it kind of reminds me of who I am or rather what I am supposed to be, you know ruler and all that."

"Yes, but you have kept all of your many cousins at their old jobs. They do most all the real work." She was referring to the fact that when her father died, she had allowed all her relatives who her father had working underneath him to continue in their positions. She had not made a single change yet. To be truthful, she had no idea what to change and did the wise thing of changing nothing. After all, Barcella was thriving and her many cousins were handling everything properly, as far as she could tell.

The two joined hands, making walking far less treacherous in their extreme heels. As they headed for the main office where the LDCS system was located in one corner of the huge room, the two chatted, mostly about Tina's boyfriend, Manfredo. "He's asked me out to the symphony tomorrow night. Why don't you come along too, Barbe?"

"I don't want to spoil your date, Tina. He is rather cute, isn't he?"

Tina giggled, "Sure is, such strong arms. He wants to be a soldier now, but I expect he'll change his mind again. Only last month, he was talking about becoming a sailor and before that one of those train engineers. Wish he'd make up his mind."

Suddenly Barbe felt a slight stinging on her cheek as if something struck it. She saw a small pea drop onto the floor, followed by a chuckle. She turned to see Mariano holding his pea shooter. "Ah ha, Barbe. Got you!" Mariano was Tina's brother and a year older than the two girls were. He too had blonde hair, but cut it just short of his neck. He was the Perez's mischief boy, as Barbe often heard Jacopo and Tecla call him. Always he was into something that he should not be messing with, always joking around, and frequently playing tricks on others. Of late, Barbe was his favorite target.

"Mariano! You stop this right now! I'm going to tell mom!" Tina chastised her older brother.

He ignored her. "Barbe, you didn't see that one coming did you? A monarch has to be able to know everything. I'm just helping you expect the unexpected you know."

"Well, it is pretty easy to hit women dressed as we are you know," Barbe replied somewhat annoyed. "We can hardly breathe or move in these dresses, and with these heels, we can barely walk. So I think that you are just taking advantage of the situation. Besides, I don't have time to mess around. There's an important message waiting for me. Grow up, Mariano."

He ignored her too. "Tina, heard that you are going out with Manfredo tomorrow night. That true?"

"Yes," Tina curled up her nose a little. "We are going to the symphony!" She said it as if this was a very significant and fashionable thing to do, something that would be way above her brother.

"Hey, Barbe, how about we go out tomorrow to the big dance?" he asked.

"Mariano! You know the monarch should not be seen going to the local dance halls! She needs to be seen in all the right circles and attend the symphony like real adults," Tina continued to chastise him.

Barbe was torn between the two. She'd love to just forget everything and dance to the popular tunes like ordinary folks. Yet, she was the ruling monarch and had to be seen at the important cultural events, such as the symphony. She knew that she ought to go to it, but she didn't want to interfere with Tina's date.

"Mariano, I can't go to the dance, but you can take me to the symphony tomorrow night, if you can dress up properly," Barbe replied.

"Oh, I am your ever humble servant," Mariano gave a fake low and sweeping bow. "It will be my high honor to accompany Your Highness to the Symphony tomorrow night," he added in a characterization of high nobility. Then he grinned, satisfied with his performance. Barbe smiled; it was humorous. So many of these noble men and women were so stuck up and snobbish, she thought.

"You best be on your very best behavior, Mariano," Tina scolded him. "We leave at six. We won't wait if you are late."

"Aye, aye, Your Majesty," he replied, making another fake, grandiose, low bow, spilling his peas onto the floor. Both girls giggled and continued their slow walk down the hall.

Jacopo was waiting for her in the main office. "Ah, here you are. I don't know what to make of this message from Stefano, Barbe."

She read the deciphered message. "Barbe Barcella. The aliens are back. A strange flying machine was spotted over Velona last night. Suggest you keep guards watching the sky. Let us know if you see any flying machines over your city. Best, Stefano."

"Flying machines?" Barbe said in disbelief. "Well, I suppose that we had better follow his suggestion. I'll go talk to the captain of the guards and have him post some men to keep an eye on the sky." The two left and headed to Barbe's private quarters to chat about what to wear to the symphony.

The next afternoon, the two began to get ready. First, though they experimented with their new corsets, which when closed properly would produce a fine eighteen-inch waist. "Oh, this is impossibly tight," Tina complained when Barbe finally got it fully tightened. It took her a half hour to get it completely closed and tied off. "Maybe we shouldn't rush it so."

"Well, do me and then let's see," Barbe suggested. She had a brand new bright blue Annelise gown with an eighteen-inch waist that she was dying to wear. It would be perfect for the symphony. A half hour later, Tina finally managed to get hers fully tightened. "Oh my! I can scarcely breathe in this one. Maybe you are right."

"Well, I haven't fainted yet. Maybe we can do this after all. It will be good if we can. Everyone will notice that our waists are smaller," Tina suggested. Thus embolden, the two continued donning their new outfits, whose hoops were sixteen feet across this time. Finally, they got into their satin bodices and struggled to get the matching overskirts on over their enormous hoops. Then, they did each other's makeup, which killed another hour, and it was time to dine.

Manfredo arrived, dressed in a blue suit, and at last, Mariano appeared, dressed in a fine suit as well. Barbe was relieved to see that he looked very presentable when he chose to do so. "May I have your arm?" Mariano said in a swashbuckling, overdone manner, but grinning.

Barbe gave him her arm. She had little choice. In these heels and such a billowing dress, she depended upon him all the way. Her feet were eight feet from where her eyes last saw the floor. Scarcely able to breathe, she wished that they had not been so impulsive and stayed with their usual dresses. She whispered a stern warning to him as they slowly glided down the long hall towards the entrance and waiting motor-car. "I can barely move in this thing. I am depending on you utterly."

During the concert, she, like we in Velona, felt that something awful had happened somewhere in the world. The day after the concert, she asked her cousins to find out if something had happened that she should know about and maybe handle. Alien flying ships were in the back of her mind, though she had never seen one.

During the next few days, more and more alarming information began to arrive. Stefano's top advisors were abducted by the aliens. Dorota had been somehow destroyed; millions of people were vaporized. A giant dust cloud was drifting around the world. Mid-June, the cloud appeared over Barcella, and Barbe began to be very worried about its impact. She listened to her cousin who was in charge of their agricultural programs and to Stefano and decided to act.

She issued an order to have all available caravels to be sent off in search of additional food supplies. By the end of June as day turned into dusk, she had fifty caravels on their way to various ports in search of whatever could be found. As Stefano continued to discuss actions to take, she followed up on them. Orders for increased coal production went out to their middle tier cities, the region of their coalmines. Her fears grew daily as she watched the many flowers that adorned the exterior of her palace wilt and die off, along with trees and even ivy vines. She too issued orders for the electric streetlights to remain on all the time, which required additional coal supplies to keep the steam engines running to produce the needed current.

Day by day, the young woman began to take more of an active role as the leader of her country. Tina was always with her, but now they met with her eight cousins on a daily basis. They gave her updates and she relayed what Stefano reported or suggested. She realized quickly that her cousins, while they loved their jobs and loved the influence and control over their areas, none of them wanted the awful responsibility that she now had to accept. Her decisions, good or bad, affected everyone. If things went south, it would be on her head, not theirs.

As the end of June came, one evening when they were dining in the palace back dining room, reserved for the stewards and the royal family, she asked, "Jacopo, how is the palace fixed for food? Do we have enough? Are we running low on anything? The crops are lost this year. The markets are almost dried up."

"Hey, we can withstand a siege," Mariano spoke before his dad could answer and in a jesting manner. "After all, your palace has to be able to stand if we are attacked."

"Mariano, these are serious times," he chided his son. Turning to Barbe, he answered, "We are well stocked. Assuming that you do not host any grand dinners, we have enough to last us six months, assuming that no additional supplies are brought back by those fifty caravels that you sent out."

"Well, that is encouraging. See princess, we aren't going to starve," Mariano jovially pointed out. His father glared at him.

"What about our subjects? I bet most depend upon the neighborhood markets," she asked.

"Aye, that they do," Tecla advised.

Barbe was worried. "What are my people going to eat if the markets are empty? We have to do something fast. Some of the caravels will be back soon. We should see that everyone gets some part of it — spread whatever we do get around equally."

"Ah, let the soldiers do it; they have guns," Mariano jested. Again, he father glared at him.

Jest or not, Barbe wondered what lay behind his suggestion and asked, "Why the soldiers and guns?" Jacopo thought she was just asking for more of his antics.

"Well, if people can't get enough food to eat, eventually, they will become desperate and do just about anything to get something to eat. You can't blame them for wanting to keep their families alive, you know. Ergo, soldiers with guns." He had a smug, told-you-so look on his face as he looked at his dad.

The next day, she told her cousins that food rationing was going to be established. Some fifty thousand soldiers were stationed around the sector. These men were then given the assignment to work out how they could deal with the delivery of food rations to every household. Her cousin Fredo was given the enormous task of establishing the actual rationing process from the arrival of a caravel with food supplies up to the point where the soldiers took delivery and began passing them out. Thus, Barcella was the first of these many countries to implement food rationing. She ordered Fredo to write an article on how the rationing would work and get it widely circulated and into the newspaper as well. This key information then appeared four days after the alien attack on Barcella.

On July 1, Barbe nearly fainted when she read the latest message from Stefano. True, her corset was tight, but that wasn't the reason. Via his abducted advisor, Stefano had learned that sometime tomorrow the alien was going to begin attacking Velona and the Sea Princes, unleashing some horrible new plague on them all. He also suggested that she and her countrymen take a stand when the alien flying ships flew over their cities. He told how they were ringing Velona with all of their cannonae and how he'd issued orders for anyone who owned a long gun to fire at will at the attackers. If one had no guns, they were supposed to throw rocks at it, hoping one might get caught it a ship's engines and thus bring it down.

After recovering, she reread it thrice more and then acted. Barbe called in all of her generals that were in Barcella and told them what was going to happen tomorrow or perhaps the day after. Then, she sent out an urgent special edition of their newspaper outlining the actions that she expected her people to follow. Finally, she sent out dozens of town criers disseminating the information. Using the LDCS system, she sent similar messages to all of their outlying towns and villages as well.

During the next morning hours, she received back disturbing reports that over half of their cannonae were in armories and could not be activated so quickly. She glared at these reports. Jacopo found a small arsenal of long guns in the basement of the palace, and he and Mariano spent the morning loading each one. All told, they had fifty of them lying against the hall walls just inside the main doors of the palace, ready for action. For once, Jacopo was thankful that his son kept his mouth shut and did as he was told.

Later that afternoon, a final message came from Stefano. It read: Aliens are attacking Velona. "Damn, it is really happening," Mariano exclaimed. Until this instant, he presumed this was all some sort of elaborate hoax. "Don't worry princess, I'll protect you."

Barbe glared at him; she hated to be called a princess. She was a monarch not some silly princess. Yet, she was glad to have his support. She and Tina were still keeping up appearances, wearing their Annelise outfits. Tina insisted that they look their best to instill confidence in the many visitors who came to make their reports or to ask for assistance in some manner. She always reserved the afternoons to meet with petitioners. This afternoon, everyone was on edge, looking up at the dusk sky, just a little fearful.

Now the dusk began to darken, as somewhere above the thick dust cloud, the sun was getting lower in the sky. While it would not set for another two hours, the dim daylight began to fail. "Damn! It is a flying machine!" Mariano exclaimed, pointing out the huge cigar shaped object that was moving towards them just below the bottom of the obscuring dust.

All four of them headed outside and began firing the long guns. Even Barbe, who had never fired one before, got into the action herself. "Damn these aliens. I'll show you!" she exclaimed.

Mariano handed her a loaded long gun and showed her how to use it. She fired off ten gunshots herself. Within a few minutes, they had fired all the loaded weapons. Jacopo and Mariano began to reload them. The three women had no idea how to do this, so they just stared up at the sky. Twenty of their cannonae were firing, though the reloading time between firings was several minutes. Hundreds of long gun shots, much like popping sounds, echoed from all directions. While their barrage was only a small fraction of what occurred over Velona, they nevertheless fired back at the enemy ships.

By seven, the ships were last seen moving northwards toward their outlying towns and villages. "Well, I guess we showed them a thing or two," Mariano declared. "Dare you to come back here and fight it out. Probably they are cowards."

"Don't call them back!" Tina exclaimed.

"Why cowards?" Barbe asked, curious as to why he chose that word. To her, it seemed that all their firing had no effect upon these flying machines.

"Cause they have left heading north, kind of like they are fleeing the battlefield. They didn't shoot us or blast us as they did Dorota. We're all standing here just fine. I think that we scared them off," he declared convinced of his notion.

"But Mariano, Stefano said that they were letting loose a plague on us," Barbe pointed out.

"Oh, well, I don't feel sick or any different. Besides, I didn't see them doing anything but moving around. I bet they forgot all about it, seeing all our fire power," Mariano tried to sound a cheerful note. He had forgotten about this plague thing. "Besides, you look just a pretty as ever." She flushed.

"No, I stink of gunpowder. Now I have to take bath and get this dress cleaned. Come on, Tina, let's go get cleaned up. Nothing more we can do here."

The next day, her cousins came by for a conference. More LDCS messages came from Stefano and many from their outlying towns and villages. Frequently, Barbe and Tina looked over each other's faces to see if there were any red spots or signs of illness. They saw none, but by evening, the women were more tired than normal.

The next day was frightening! The three women's arms were incredibly weak, nearly skin and bone. Jacopo sent for the court doctor, who arrived rather late. He took one look at them and said, "It is the plague. I've seen a hundred cases of it so far. Always, it is affecting the women. My ears are getting longer. All men's ears are, as well as all women too. There is nothing that I can do except suggest that you continue to eat well and hope for the best. We have never seen anything like this anywhere. I have to get back to my wife and daughter. They are also ill with it."

After he left, Mariano exclaimed, "Well, that's a fine how do you do! He's the doctor. He's supposed to know how to cure you!"

"Mariano, this is an alien plague. How's he supposed to know how to cure it?" Barbe pointed out. "Come on, I am starving. Somehow we have to eat, Tina."

"I'm horribly sorry, Barbe, but my arms are so weak I simply can't fix you girls anything," Tecla said and began crying. This was the first time in her life that she had really felt that she had let them all down.

"There, there, dear," Jacopo said kindly, putting his arm over her shoulder. "Let me and Mariano fix us all something." Together, the five headed for the kitchen.

The third day the plague had finished its work. Tina and Barbe were sleeping together in Barbe's bed, down the hall from Tina's parents. While Tina and Mariano each had their own bedrooms near their folks, Barbe had asked Tina to sleep with her the last couple of nights. The two were awakened by wild screams coming from Tecla. Tina tried to sit up, but her arms failed her. She looked down and saw that now they were completely gone. She panicked utterly and began screaming at the top of her lungs, which startled Barbe, who was just coming out of a deep sleep, recognizing the screams of Tecla. Now Tina next to her was also screaming. She tried to push herself up to see what was going on. Was an alien in their room? Her arms didn't react. Barbe looked down and saw hers were completely gone, and she too added her voice to the wild reactions.

Mariano came running into their room, frightened to death. All the color was gone from his face. He burst in the door and stared at his sister and Barbe who were sitting up in bed now, wildly screaming. They too had no arms. Already he had dashed into his parent's room when his mother's screams woke him. He saw her sitting up like this, his father holding her tightly, but she had no arms. Then, he'd heard Tina scream and dashed down to her room, just as Barbe's voice added to the cries.

The captain of the palace guards came running up behind him and stood looking to see some assassins, believing the worst. "Oh my god!" he exclaimed and quickly backed off and headed back to the other guards.

Mariano saw two hysterical women and did the only thing he could think of doing. He sat down beside them and pulled each of them onto a shoulder, putting his arms around both of them, who buried their heads into his shoulders, crying uncontrollably. How long he sat there, he couldn't say. Eventually, Barbe stopped bawling, and Mariano tried then to comfort his sister, "Tina, it will be okay."

"No it's not! I don't have any arms at all anymore! I can't do anything. I got to pee and I can't" she wailed.

"I do too," Barbe whispered. "You have to help us. The pot is under the bed."

His ashen face now began to flush. "But," he tried to protest. He stopped short, realizing that neither was in any position to be able to do this for themselves. Since Barbe was at least not bawling or quite so hysterical, he decided to assist her first. He raised her nightgown and pulled down her panties. Though he tried not to look, he had little choice.

"Wow, you've got to see your waist, Barbe. I thought girls took off their makeup when you went to bed." Barbe looked very confused, but relieved herself, grateful for his help.

"Thanks. Tina, come on. Let Mariano help you too," she said very quietly. At last, Tina had no choice but to let her brother see her privates and help her use the pot. Either that or make things worse by wetting her pants, nightgown, and the bed.

While Tina was going, Barbe got up and walked over to her full-length mirror. "Oh my god! My lips look as if I'm wearing bright red lipstick! My eyes are done too, how did that happen?"

Now done, Tina got up and came to stand beside her. "Me too," whimpered. "My ears are touching my shoulders now."

"Mariano, come here, I need you to take my nightgown off," Barbe decided that she just had to see how badly the rest of her body was doing. "I might as well know the worst of it now and be done with it."

"But Barbe, I'm a guy," he protested.

"Well, that's rather obvious isn't it? I can't do it myself, and I need to see what else is wrong. Please?" Barbe asked.

He realized that she was right. She and his sister were helpless invalids now. He bashfully removed her nightgown and then Tina's too. Both young women stared at their naked forms in the mirror, as did Mariano, who was as surprised as they were.

"Our waists! What's happened to them?" Barbe exclaimed. "They've shrunk."

Tina stared at her form and said, "I wonder how small our waists actually are? Mariano, get us a tape measure from her sewing basket over there. Come and measure our waists, please. Then you can help us get something on besides nightgowns."

"Eighteen inches sis. Isn't that what you two were trying to achieve with your tight corsets?" Mariano remembered some of their chatting from a week ago. "You both do look really stunning. I just wish your arms were there, though. I don't know how to dress you."

Tina now began crying again. While she had one of her wishes, a small waist, she felt utterly helpless to dress herself. Barbe took charge, "Come on, try that drawer there. Yes, those get two, one for me and one for her. Slip them up. I am going to have to lean on you to get my foot in there." A bit later, both women had panties on. Before long, Mariano had them both into a white long slip and he felt more relaxed now that they were not standing naked beside him. Tina continued to cry almost endlessly, but Barbe kept on giving him directions that he somehow managed to follow. A few minutes later, he had both women into a simple day dress. He was just getting their flats out when Jacopo came to their door, holding on tightly to a sobbing Tecla.

"Good, you are taking care of them. Come on down to the kitchen. I need a very stiff drink!" he said. Mariano agreed with that. With an arm around each woman, he followed them.

In the kitchen, Jacopo poured all five a tall glass of wine. Fine red wines were Barcella's specialty, unrivaled anywhere. Mariano held a glass up to each woman who took a hefty sip. "Dad, we better get something solid into them. Perhaps if they eat enough, their arms will come back." He wanted to sound hopeful, somehow.

An hour later, with a good breakfast in them, the three women felt a little better. Still Tina and Tecla continued to have outbursts of crying as they continued to discover things that they couldn't do anymore. Barbe grimaced at each new thing that arose, but kept from crying somehow.

The captain of the guards came in. "Your Majesty, if you can, you should come to the main office. The LDSC system is going nuts. Messages are flooding in, ma'am."

She sighed, "Coming." As she moved to the door, she realized that she could not now open the door. The knob stared back at her like an immovable mountain. "Mariano?" she said, fighting from breaking down.

"Shit! The damn doorknobs! Coming, dear," he replied, his mind instantly recognizing the difficulty. His dad said he'd bring the other two along in a few minutes. Jacopo continued to wipe their eyes and cheeks as best he could. By now, his handkerchief was soaked.

"What's this pile of stuff doing in here?" Barbe asked as she entered the main office room. On the floor was a large pile of things. She recognized what some were: a stove, a table, and some kitchen gear.

"Sorry, Your Majesty. They were there when we came in. Here. Have a look at the messages. There are over fifty of them now!" the captain said.

"Shit, I can't even hold them. Mariano, will you. . ."

She didn't get to finish her question. He saw what her problem was after the explicative. He picked up the oldest one and held it up for her, reading along with her. They went through message after message. "Damn, this plague is everywhere. All our women are being horribly disfigured," Mariano exclaimed so that the others could know the gist of these messages.

"Mariano! We are not disfigured; we've just lost our arms!" Barbe corrected him testily. "There is a big difference, you know. Our arms have like vanished, but the rest of us are okay."

He flushed. "You are right, you are still a very beautiful woman," he whispered to her.

Barbe added, "Stefano reports that it's done this to the women all over Velona too. Say, this latest one says that doorknobs are a huge barrier. He says that we ought to send soldiers around to every home and see if there are any women who are there alone with no one to help them. God! I can't imagine what it would be like if you were not here, Mariano, you too, Jacopo. Captain, will you see to it. Send word to all the towns and get the soldiers on this fast. Women could die if they don't have someone around to help them."

"Yes, Your Majesty. On it. This is the worst thing that I have ever seen!" He left quickly.

"What do we do now?" asked Barbe. She went to a chair, shoved it a bit, and then sat down. "Women of Barcella seem to all be like us. We are now really helpless." Hearing that, Tina and Tecla began crying again. Her words rang true in their minds. Barbe wished that she hadn't said that. "What is all that stuff doing there anyway?" She and Mariano got up to take a closer look at the things lying on the floor.

"Well, much of it looks like what one might find in a kitchen, only for gnomes," Mariano suggested.

"Gnomes don't exist, silly," Barbe replied.

"I know — very short people then. God, I hope your bodies don't start shrinking next!" That brought on another wave of crying from the two, but Barbe glared at him.

"That looks like a writing desk, only it is way too short, and in comparison, the seat is way too tall. What the devil is that thing standing on four legs with baskets hanging from it?" she asked. Mariano shook his head. He had no idea at all.

Suddenly, Barbe began having strange images appearing in her mind. She saw someone cooking dinner using these objects, sitting in the strange chair with wheels on it. She saw a woman carrying food from a market. The yoke was across her shoulders and the baskets were filled with bread and cheese. "Hey, these are for us. This is a kitchen that somehow or other we are supposed to be able to use to cook. Yes, I see it; we use our feet. And we are writing with our feet, while sitting at that desk. Hey, we can carry things around in those baskets. It fits across our shoulders. Weird. Where did all this stuff come from anyway?"

"This is getting stranger by the minute, Barbe," Mariano replied. "I can see what you mean. I think it might work, that yoke thing." Tina and Tecla continued to cry, however. Neither were interested in these weird things on the floor. At the mention of carrying anything, both broke down once more. Poor Jacopo continued to comfort his wife and daughter.

Another message came through and Mariano and Barbe read it together. "Guess you are now my Official Message Holder, Mariano," Barbe managed a slight tease.

"Hey, that's the spirit, kid."

She smiled. After reading it, she called out, "Stefano reports that he has ordered everyone to remove all doorknobs and associated locks. Otherwise, women can be trapped in a room or house or cannot get inside.

We should do the same. Come on, Mariano, we need to find one of the palace guards and get him to start spreading the word."

"Shouldn't we send a message to all the other towns about this first?"

"Okay, do it. I can't anymore."

After getting the word out, Barbe said, "Okay, Mariano, let's start getting the doorknobs off the ones here in our living quarters."

He found a screwdriver and set to work on the main office's doors. "Man, this it is hard on the arm muscles."

"Hey, don't complain, Mariano. At least you have them to ache."

"Okay, there this one is done. Looks weird with the hole where the mechanism was at."

"Let's see if I can open it now." She put her toes partly into the hole and was able to open it, hopping back on one foot. "Hey, Stefano was right. Okay, on to the next one."

"Are we going to do all the doors? There must be over a hundred in the palace!"

"Probably, so let's get busy. We have a lot of work to do."

"What do you mean we? I seem to be doing all the screwing around here," he teased her.

For the first time this morning, Barbe giggled.

"Now that's better. I like it when you smile."

"Okay, I will sit down and hold the doors steady while you unscrew them. Okay? Just don't go looking up my dress, buster."

"But I have already seen you naked."

She flushed, but felt playful. "Well, did you like what you saw?"

Mariano acted on an impulse. He leaned over and planted a passionate kiss on her lips. Both felt an explosion of sensual desires, and she returned his passion. His arms held her tightly to his body. Only with sheer will power did they manage to separate. "Wow! I guess you did," she replied, quite flushed.

"I really do love you, you know, Barbe. I always have, but our folks wouldn't let me say so. You know that you can count on me to be here for you, don't you?"

"I know. I like you a whole lot too. Always have, but mom and dad were so darn picky about what fellows I dated. I don't think that they approved of you."

"Yes, but the only thing that matters is what you think." She flushed and gave him another kiss, a little afraid to say more.

Soon they began on the next door. When that one was done, Jacopo joined them. "I have them calmed down some. They are still in the kitchen. Both are taking this terribly, I'm afraid. How are you holding up, Barbe?"

"So far so good. I'm at least being a little useful holding the doors from moving while Mariano takes them apart. Stefano was right; I can open the closed doors now."

An hour later, twenty guards took over for the two, who headed back to deal with making lunch. On the way, they stopped by the wing that the Perez family lived in, only to find a second pile of stuff sitting in their living room. After that find, Barbe asked the guards to be alert for additional piles of these things elsewhere in the palace. No more were found, however.

As the two men began trying their best to make lunch, Barbe watched them, unable to do more than offer suggestions. She became more and more frustrated with her predicament. "You know, I think that those kitchen things need to be installed in here. Perhaps then, I could do something useful to help. I feel so helpless this way."

Of course hearing this, the other two women began crying again, and Barbe wished that she'd not said anything. She went over to Tina to comfort her, laying her head over Tina's shoulder for moral support at least. Soon Tina calmed down again.

Later that afternoon another message arrived from Stefano, explaining that most of the homes in Velona had received a replacement kitchen. He was sending his soldiers around in the morning to find out which homes needed assistance in installing the replacement kitchens. Once more Barbe had Mariano relay that message off to the other towns and the two then headed off to find the captain of the guards and have him arrange for something similar in the morning here in Barcella. Then, she realized that work crews were obviously going to be needed, and she issued orders for any man who was so skilled and free to report to the palace to help those in need.

"I can see that we are going to need some kind of hotline, which those in need can contact to get help. We're going to have to set that up somehow, Mariano." Her mind was now beginning to envision the multitude of problems facing her people.

After supper, her six cousins finally came by to meet with her. All six looked awful, having spent the day dealing with their own family crises. Phillipe asked what they all needed to know, "Cousin, are you going to want one of us to take over for you now?"

"Of course not. You fellows have your hands full with your own families and your areas of our government. I could not possibly put even further burdens on you now. I don't have a family to take care of, so I will do what I can to take care of our country. Phillipe, how are your wife and two daughters taking this?"

Fighting back tears, he replied, "Thank you cousin. None of us can handle any more responsibility. This is all so utterly overwhelming. Not good, I'm afraid. God, their screams this morning — I'll never forget the terror in their eyes and screams as long as I live! You are holding up extremely well, cousin. How are you managing it?"

"It's hard, Phillipe. I have to fight off tears, but we simply have to move forward or we all end up dying off. I will not let Barcella die as long as

I have breath in me."

The seven talked about what plans were needed for the morning. All six loved the ideas she had ordered to be implemented by the following morning. They agreed to lend a hand in the overall organization of this new hotline. "We need to find single men who do not have the responsibility of women at home to care for. Those could man the hotline and go out and deal with those in need," Phillipe said. The greatly relieved cousins all agreed to work together in the morning to get the hotline established here in an unused section of the large palace.

After the cousins left, Manfredo came by to see how Tina was doing. "Oh Manfredo!" Tina called out when he entered the living room where everyone had gathered. She rose and ran to him, beginning to cry once more. He put his arms around her and held on to her. "Sorry I couldn't get here sooner. I had to help dad out around the house with mom and my sister. Now I am free."

"I am so helpless now. I didn't think that you would want me anymore, not like this."

"Everyone is in the same mess. I can't stop loving you just because of this, Tina. Now stop crying. Things will somehow work out; I just know they will somehow. I don't have a clue how, but we just have to have faith. What else is there? Lie down and die? I won't let you. I love you too much to let anything happen to you. Let me see how you look." He wiped her eyes on his shirtsleeve. They began to chat quietly among themselves.

On the other side of the room, Barbe decided to give Tina some space. She nodded to Mariano and the two quietly left and began walking the halls. He slipped his arm around her waist and she didn't object. "How come you have a cool head when everyone else is going to pieces? I love that about you, you know that Barbe? I mean just look at Tina and mom. Basket cases. Yet you, here you are running the whole darn country still! Making all the decisions, issuing the orders, everything, like nothing has happened."

"If I don't, then think what is going to happen? Besides, it helps to keep me from crying too; you know, kind of puts my attention on other things besides my pathetic self now."

"You aren't pathetic, Barbe."

She smiled. "Wait until you have to wipe my bottom. Then, you'll sing a different tune," she teased him.

"Hey, it can't be worse than my sister's messy diapers. You are grown up now," he teased her back. She bumped into his body with her hips playfully. He responded by tickling her.

"Hey stop that," she laughed, trying to wiggle her way out of his fingers. Soon the two were dashing around the long halls of the palace, laughing and enjoying their romp. At last winded, they stopped beneath the wall of portraits.

"It's good to see you laughing again. I missed that the most. Your eyes light up so."

"It's probably this strange makeup that you are seeing," she replied demurely.

"Ha. You know, you remind me of old Jovanna Barcella there." He pointed to her favorite painting, one that she had spent hours looking at over these many years.

"Well, she at least had some arms left," Barbe pointed out.

"Somehow, I don't think those would have done her much good, Barbe. Still, you are a lot like her, even before this alien plague, I mean. I think that's why I've secretly been in love with you for years now."

"Really? I've always liked you a lot, but my folks didn't it was right that I do, and I thought that you didn't like me because you were always being ornery to me, like shooting me with your pea shooter."

"I'll show you," he whispered and gave her a passionate kiss. Once more, their senses were flooded with passions.

When they finally separated a little, she said, "Wow, you sure know how to kiss! I feel like ripping your clothes off and hopping into bed with you right now!"

"Better not or my folks will cream me. You're the monarch and I'm nothing much."

"Hey, buster, I can love whoever I please and I love you." There, she'd said it, and the relief that she felt was huge. How long had she been suppressing her feelings towards him she didn't know, but it must be years.

"Really? You do?" She gave him a passionate kiss this time.

A bit later, Barbe said, "You know, Mariano, if we got married, then we could always be together no matter what more awful things happen here. Would you consider marrying me now, when I am like this?"

Mariano has a sheepish grin on his face, "Barbe! Are you proposing to me?"

She flushed. "Well, I guess that I am, Mariano. After all, I am your monarch, and I do give the orders around here. How about it, marry me?"

"Incredible. You bet I will marry you! The sooner the better, before anything else bad happens around here." She giggled and suggested that they go announce this to his folks and Tina.

"What? Barbe, are you sure?" a very surprise Jacopo reacted to her announcement. "He is so immature, joking around all the time."

"That's part of what I love about him. In spite of all that is happening to us all, he can still find a way to make me laugh again. You bet I am sure."

Tina shrieked, "Oh, Barbe, this is so wonderful." She tried to hug her best friend but was frustrated to find that was no longer possible. The two just pushed hard into each other's bodies instead.

"Mom, maybe we can make it a double wedding. Manfredo still wants me, though I don't know why now. I am so helpless this way. Can we?"

"Under the circumstances," Barbe spoke up, "I think that it should be a really simple, short, small wedding. Everyone is hard pressed to take care of their own families to mess with a formal wedding. Maybe we can just get Father Bartoli to drop by and marry us here. What do you think, Tecla?"

Tecla cautioned them, "Barbe, we have been your surrogate parents for a year now. I do think that we all should sleep on it and not make hasty decisions. After all, look what you both will be saddling your men with now. We are all so completely and utterly helpless. Manfredo and Mariano will have to devote so much of their time to just caring for your everyday life needs. I think that we all ought to sleep on it. Let's talk about it in the morning and see if you kids still feel as you do now."

This was the most that Tecla had said all day. Barbe had forced her to assume the role of surrogate mother once more. While the teens didn't like what she said, they agreed to sleep on it. Manfredo explained that his father had given him permission to spend the night at the palace, in case Tina needed him.

Mariano helped the girls undress, get into their nightgowns, and then tucked them in. The next morning, he knocked and entered. Once more he assisted both with using the pot and getting dressed. "Tina, mom and dad are really going to it this morning. I heard them through their door." Both grinned.

"Mom needs the support now," Tina observed. "We do too, for that matter. I feel so incredibly helpless like this. I keep reaching out with my hands only to see that they are not there. What a weird sensation."

"Hey, me too, Tina. It is weird. Come on, you and Manfredo can fix us some breakfast. I'm starving."

"Okay princess," he teased her and she attempted to butt him with her hips as he darted out of the way.

The four were eating when Jacopo and Tecla finally joined them. She looked flushed, but contented, Barbe observed. Tina just grinned at her mother. "Well, we still want to get married," Barbe declared.

"We give you our full approval," Jacopo replied. "But son, if you don't treat Barbe right, I will shoot you myself! You do right by her, you hear me?"

"Yes father," he suppressed a laugh.

He continued, while holding a roll for Tecla to eat, "I think that you are wise to keep it as simple as possible. Everyone is engrossed with their own families right now. After we eat, I will see if Father Bartoli can come by and perform the ceremony."

"Thanks dad," Mariano said, civil and respectful to him for the first time in ages.

Later that day, the two young couples were married. Barbe found that her cousins were greatly relieved to hear that she had. Between them, they feared for her well-being and survival, living alone as she was, with only the palace stewards to look after her fundamental needs after this horrid plague had struck.

As the days went by, Barbe continued to depend upon the messages from Stefano, following them as best she could here in her own country. When the articles of Bethany began appearing, Stefano sent them to her. She had them reproduced in their newspapers and in flyers, having the soldiers, who were now doling out weekly rations, hand the flyers to the homes as well.

Quickly, Barbe became known as the "prima woman," the one who was in tight control of the country and with the well-being of its people as her uppermost concern. While chaos and confusions swarmed around her, she stood resolute and steadfast, calmly pointing out the optimum direction they should follow and seeing to it that it was followed. Lead by example became her motto. While she rapidly picked up new ways of dealing with life, she never failed to pass these on to others.

For example, the night of their wedding, she began to attempt to feed herself using the new utensils and her feet, shocking the other five. Once she got the hang of it, she insisted that Tina and Tecla also try it. By the end of the dinner, she even held her mug of wine up for Mariano to sip. He laughed so hard that she nearly spilled the wine. "Does nothing stop you, my love," he jested. Daily, Barbe continued to lead by example.

Once the hotline became a lifeline for her people in very early July, she began to spend three hours each day handling some of the calls for help. With Mariano at her side, she went to the homes of those who'd called to show them personally how something was done and to work with them until they could do it themselves. By the end of September, Barbe had visited some two hundred women and aided them in grasping these new ways, endearing her even more with her people. Even the men now held her in extremely high regard, and none more so than the husbands and relatives of those she'd visited and personally assisted.

On October 1, Barbe had just returned from another of her personal trips to help a woman work out how to dress herself. Barbe had had her husband sew some loops into the bottoms of her slip and dress. The joy on the woman's face was all the thanks that she needed, as the woman was finally able to get into her own clothes, freeing her husband of constantly attending to her needs. She and Mariano sat down on the couch, taking a moment to embrace each other while waiting Tina and Tecla's call to dinner. The palace captain called out, "Your Majesty, a man has come to the front doors asking to speak with you. He claims that it is important. Shall I show him in or shall I ask him to come back in the morning when you normally see petitioners?"

"Oh what the heck, send him in. Supper's not ready yet. Guess I can see one more before we eat. It would be a shame to make him come back."

Presently, a tall man, who otherwise looked completely non-descript, entered. However, he had a presence that made her sit up and take notice, listening intently to his every word. "Greetings Your Majesty. I am Macario

Ines, a Holy Man. I have come to Barcella to assist everyone in this time of great spiritual need." He looked like he too had suffered the plague, at least as far as she could tell. His ear lobes were long and thin, touching his shoulders as Mariano's did.

"Well, we certainly need all the help we can get. It is a miracle that the rains came and got rid of that infernal dust cloud. Already our late season planting appears to be working. I may yet have a rose to smell this year. What is it that you need of me?"

"I came to assist you, Barbe Barcella."

"Dinner's ready," Tina called out from the kitchen. "Guys, how about carrying things in to the table for us?"

"Well, how about dining with us? After diner, we can talk more," Barbe asked. He bowed and agreed. "Mariano, quickly go set a place for Macario, please. Sir, if you will follow me, I'll lead you to our table. Mind you, it's not the greatest. I have the whole country still on food rations, trying to make sure none of us goes hungry. Sure do hope that Stefano is right, and we get a crop harvested before winter comes. Otherwise, it may be very grim around here." She chatted away, as she led him into their private dining room here at the back of the palace.

She introduced Macario to the others, including Manfredo who was now always with Tina. "Hope you don't mind the strange ways that we women have to eat now. You sit there on the taller part of the tables," she explained, unsure if he was familiar with the way things had to be done now. That he had just arrived echoed in the back of her mind, which led her to suspect that he might not be familiar.

"Thank you all for your generosity. I hope to repay you after dinner," he said quietly. All six of them noted that this man, whoever he was, had more "presence" than anyone they had ever met. Once the dinner was finished, Barbe promised to do the dishes the next two nights. "It's my night to wash up, but since you are here, I'll meet with you and make it up to them later on. Do we need to talk in private?"

"Private is best, Your Majesty, if that is acceptable to you," he replied.

She led him into her own private office, which she now seldom used. She sat down in her comfortable sofa and he sat in another one opposite her. "Okay, Macario, you have my undivided attention."

He smiled. "Okay, Barbe. Close your eyes. Good. Now I want you to return to the first moment that you heard that there were aliens and that they might threaten you. Good." Before Barbe knew what was happening, she was right there reading that message from Stefano. Now she began re-experiencing all that had happened to her, most significantly the morning of the shocking discovery of the loss of her arms and her terrible feelings of helplessness.

He had her go over it several more times, each time she added a bit more detail that somehow revealed itself to her. At last, she could discover nothing more that was new. She heard his incredibly confident voice say, "Barbe, is there something that is similar to this that happened earlier in time?"

"Well, I've never lost my arms before. I don't see how."

"Okay, take a look there. What's that that you are seeing?"

"Oh, I'm in the hallway where we have all the portraits of the Barcella line hanging on the wall. I'm looking at the pictures there."

"Very good. Go through that one and tell me what you are seeing."

"Oh, I am standing there looking at the portrait of Jovanna Barcella. She was our most famous ruler back around 640. She'd lost most all of her arms. I think that hers were about six inches long or there about. I had this feeling of empathy for her, like I could feel her loss." Barbe went through this light incident a couple times before Macario asked for something even earlier. She yawned and looked at the images in her mind, then yawned even more.

Suddenly, Barbe opened her eyes wide and exclaimed, "Oh! Oh! Oh!"

"Yes, did something just happen?" Macario asked.

"I — I — that was me! I was her, Jovanna! I've lived before and I was her and I — I got this very same kind of therapy from someone called Bethany back then. God, that was fantastic in how it helped me! Wow! You are doing the same thing now. This is a therapy session, isn't it? Just like Bethany did for me back then! Well no wonder I have been adapting faster than any other woman in Barcella! I already know how to do all these things for myself! I did it all back then! Wow. This is fantastic! Oh my god! Back then, I had to rescue and save my people and here I am again rescuing and saving my people once more. I seem to be the monarch when my people need me the most. Strange how that works out. This is incredible. You aren't Bethany, are you? No, you don't feel the same as she. Wow. This is something else. Can you give this therapy to Tina and Tecla and everyone else here in Barcella? If not, can you teach me how to do it so that I can do it to the other women? It'll take me a long time to get to perhaps two hundred fifty thousand women though." At last, she wound down.

"Our therapy session is over now. Very well done, Barbe. No, Bethany is in Velona still. You have been reading and publishing her articles in the newspaper and in your flyers that you send to every woman in Barcella. I am sure that one day later on you will get the opportunity to meet her again. As I said, I have come to help you and all of your people. I began with you because you are their ruler. Before I leave your palace, I will do your five companions. In time, I and others who follow me will get to all your people. I give you my word on that. It is good that you wish to learn how to deliver this most special spiritual gift to others. I will be happy to teach you, but now is not the time. Your skills and talents are needed to continue to lead your people out of this disaster. In time, when things are back to normalcy, then we can take the time to do this."

"Incredible. Thank you. Thank you. What can I do to help you and to thank you for this?"

"I would like to have a building which has a number of small rooms in which we can safely and without being disturbed deliver our therapy to your people. Later on, I would like to be given some land much further inland where I can establish a permanent location where all those seeking spiritual enlightenment may come and receive therapy. But of that, we can worry about much later on. For now, a place to deliver is all that I ask of you."

"You got it, but are you sure that you don't need some workers, someone to cook meals for the folks that you are helping? I am sure that I can find some willing helpers," she asked.

"I am sure that others will come to me soon. No, you need your willing workers helping you with your plans for the survival of your country. There is so much work to be done now and so many fewer hands with which to do it. Yet, I know that you and your women are lending your feet as best you can. In time, all will have relearned how to do things and to do them swiftly. That will be more than ample for Barcella to recover fully from this disastrous alien plague. I am very confident of the outcome, though there will be hardships yet to come. You have the inner strength to see it through."

"Well, okay then. Let me see if I can find a suitable building for you, might take a few days as things are still pretty chaotic around here."

"That is fine. I will need several days to assist your five companions."

"Would you like to stay here in the palace with us until you finish with them?"

"That would be most convenient and most efficient of our time." Thus, the Guardian began his ministry in Barcella.

Chapter 23 Survival

Back in 812, three young, close friends, who lived in Uru, kingdom of Karka, Greenway, grew tired of working on the village communal farms. They and their wives dreamed of owning their own farmsteads. For months the three, twenty year old men, worked on plans for how they could make this come true. All lands surrounding Uru were now owned by either more wealthy farmers or the community. They knew that to achieve their goal, they would have to move far out into the wilderness. As their wives pointed out, they'd be totally on their own, and the three families would have to work together to make it. Each knew that they ought to be able to farm forty selions each, that is, forty acres. (A selion was the amount of land that could be plowed by one man in one day, six hundred sixty feet long and sixty-six feet wide.) The cash crops were wheat, corn, oats, and barley, though some of each would be needed for their own use and that of their animals. After careful planning, the three families decided to take this big gamble. If they succeeded, in time, they would become wealthy and independent farmers.

The key word for these men and their wives was independent. None of them liked the communal style living arrangements of Uru. While such gave all inhabitants real security, these six saw it as limiting their freedom and wanted out. Thus, in 812, the Whitefield, Johns, and Weston families struck out on their own.

Some twenty miles north of Uru, they found an ideal isolated valley. A ridge line formed a natural western barrier; forested hills covered the northern edge and part of the eastern side of a fertile valley. A small creek came down from the northern hills passing below the eastern forest. Tall grasses covered the valley floor and swept off far to the south. Near the eastern edge of the forest, a small hill rose from the gently sloping valley, large enough to support three homes, barns, and various outbuildings.

The Weston family built their home and barn on the northern side of the hill and farmed the northern forty selions. The Johns family built their home and barn on the eastern side of the hill and farmed the forty selions south of the Westons and east of their communal hill. The Whitefields built their home and barn on the south side of the hill and farmed the forty selions due south of the hill. They fenced in another forty selions of prime pastureland east of the Whitefield's crop fields. Here they kept their many horses, sheep, goats, cows, and oxen during the summer months. The creek, which ran past their hill, cut through the pasture, providing a source of water for their herd. Their orchard was above the corral, adjoining the forests on the eastern hills.

All three families also planted extensive gardens, drying and preserving fruits and vegetables for the long winters. Yes, this far north in the Greenway, winters were long and cold with snow depths sometimes reaching a foot. Blizzards were also not uncommon here. This was a rugged life for hardy adventurers, certainly not for the faint of heart or those ill equipped to handle everything that life could throw at them. If something went wrong, they had to be able to fix it. Uru was a two-day journey by wagon, with no inns along the way. These were pioneer souls who moved out here some ten years ago.

In June of 822, the three pioneering families had most definitely succeeded in their venture. Each year, they harvested close to 3,600 bushels of corn, 960 bushels of wheat, 1,500 bushels of oats, and 1,400 bushels of barley. Of course, some of this they kept for their own needs, while the rest was hauled to market in Uru, bringing the three families over six thousand gold each year, a very handsome sum indeed.

On farms this size, everyone had to pitch in to get the multitude of chores and field work done. Springs and falls were particularly hectic as you might imagine. Summers were lazy times, but the harsh winters were fun, family times, especially for their many children, who loved to go sledding on the many hills west and north of their crop fields. The three families were close, even their three homes on the hill were but a hundred feet from each other.

Tom Whitefield was now thirty and his rugged wife Elaine was a year younger. She had long fiery red hair. Their oldest was Betsy, now fourteen and with her mother's red hair. James was thirteen; Tim, twelve. Their father cut their hair using a bowl over their heads. What stuck out was trimmed. Next came Marge at eleven and finally Lilly who was ten. All but Betsy had black hair.

Bill Johns and his wife Jean were both thirty. Their family had brown hair and Bill cut his son's hair the same way. Their girls emulated their mother and never cut theirs. Able was their eldest at fifteen. Then came Mary who was fourteen. Martha was twelve and their baby was Hank at ten.

Henry Weston and his wife Allie were both thirty-one and had rather blonde hair. Again, he also cut their boys' hair in the same manner, but their girls never cut theirs. In fact, none of the women here ever cut theirs, only the men. Their eldest was Fran who had turned fifteen last month. Their twins, Billy and Jim, were fourteen now. Sally was thirteen and Mark was twelve. All were very blonde.

All twenty were strong, able, and loved the freedom of their lives. Yes, they all worked hard and as a team, lending a helping hand whenever needed. Yet, there was one problem that these three families faced, one that kept the adults up at night when they thought their children were at last asleep.

Henry whispered, "Fran, Billy, and Jim are of age. We both know that they ought to be out looking for their own families."

"Well, we are so isolated here, Henry, what do you expect?" Allie replied. "Fran has a crush on Able, you know that. Billy has his eye on Betsy and Jim is always hanging around Mary. What do you expect? They are of age."

"I know. I know. The nearest place around here is the Williams place, but that is seven miles south. I'd hoped that at our barn raising last year, the kids would hit it off with some of the fifty who came to help us get the barn up."

"Well, they didn't. Have you talked to Bill and Jean about Able?"

"No, I was kind of hoping that they'd say something first."

"Well, you should, Henry. Think of Fran; she's fifteen now and ought to be starting her own family. Of course, we can build another home on the hill for her, assuming that she still wants to be so close to us," she suggested. They continued to chat, resolving nothing before they gave up and went to bed themselves.

The three homes were almost identical. A huge kitchen, dining room, and living room occupied most of the front half of the large farm home. A bathroom and pantry adjoined the kitchen. The back half of the home held six large bedrooms and two more bathrooms. In their basement was yet another bathroom, but this one was for muddy times. Clean off here, before you track it into the house was the cardinal rule that they all followed. Most of the basement held their preserved food and many bags of grain, both seed and that for their consumption.

Now you might think that these three families were rugged pioneers, eking a bare living from the land. This is only partially true. Each home had a coal-fired furnace in the basement and each fall they received a delivery of crushed coal from Uru. The main bathroom off the kitchen had a wood-fired water heater in the basement. Saturdays were bath days for everyone. The families would heat up the water heater and take turns bathing in the hot water. The boys went first, in and out in a flash. The women took their time, languishing as long as they dared, even putting various scents into the water. This was their only pamper time, as their mothers put it.

What of water? When they first arrived, they dug a group well centrally located between the three houses. Today, one could still use the rope and bucket to draw water. During the less hectic summers, they worked on farm improvements. Here in 822, they had built a small water tower to provide water flow under some pressure to the three homes. It delivered water to the kitchens and the bathrooms now. Cold water only, that is. Once a month, they hitched a team of horses to the pumping screw and refilled it.

Yes, they still needed six cords of firewood each winter, collected during the idle summer months. Some of this was also used in their three drying houses in the fall. Here, they dried and smoked much of their produce and meat for the winters. The rest of the wood was used for cooking. The littler children were in charge of bringing the day's firewood from the woodpile up to the front door, where their mothers could get easily get at it.

The next morning as the Johns family sat down for breakfast of leftover fried chicken, eggs, pancakes dipped in honey, and milk, Bill outlined the day's project. Already the children had handled the early morning chores. All rose with the sun. While Jean made their breakfast, the others milked the cows, gathered up the eggs, milked the goats, and fed and watered all the many animals, after which most were led out to the south pasture to graze.

"Today it is sheep shearing day," Bill announced.

"Darn, this will take all day," Able complained. He had promised to take Fran for a long walk in the woods today.

Bill already suspected what was really on Able's mind. "Able, you and Mary will assist me. Don't worry. Henry's going to be there along with Fran, Billy, and Jim. Tom's helping too, so are Betsy and James. The rest of you kids get to herd them up to us, as we need them. Hey, don't gripe. Tom, Henry, and I have to do the hard work of shearing."

"Hey, can I do some too, dad? I'm old enough," Able asked, thinking how great it would be if Fran could see him doing a man's work.

"Sure son. You're old enough. Probably Billy and Jim will get a chance to try as well. Now let's finish up. We have fifty sheep to shear. Your mom needs the wool, if you kids expect to ever get any new clothes."

"But dad, why can't we get some fancy dresses when we are in Uru next?" asked Mary.

"Yes, me too," Martha spoke up.

"Of course you can. It's just that we all need heavy, warm winter clothes. You keep growing like weeds," he replied.

Around nine, the families gathered outside their barns and got setup. From across the lawn, Fran kept glancing over at Able. Mary watched Jim as he moved the benches out and then waved to her. Billy called out a greeting to Betsy as well.

Suddenly, Able looked up and called out, "Hey dad! Look at the southern sky! What is that?" He spoke loudly so that Fran could hear too, but the whole clan heard him. All eyes turned to the south. There was a dark grey cloud hanging across the entire southern sky!

"What is that?" Bill asked. "I've never seen anything like that before. Hey Tom. Ideas? Henry?" The three men walked over to each other, meeting at the center of their hill, and naturally, all the kids came too. Fran and Able snuck a quick kiss while everyone was staring at the southern sky.

"Kind of looks like a dust storm, sort of," Henry suggested. Although they chatted, no one had a better idea and no one had any clue from where such a huge amount of dust could have come. Since nothing else was happening, they all headed back to their barnyards to begin the long day's work of shearing. Each family had three feed sacks full of wool when they were finished. For the next many weeks, their wives and girls would spend evening hours carding it and spinning it into bobs of wool string. During the long winter, they would begin to weave cloth from it, dyeing it with various herbs to add a bit of color to the cloth. Later, their wives would make heavier clothing from the cloth. Nothing went to waste here in this farmstead.

The next day was an idle one for the kids. While their dads headed out to walk their fields, the kids headed off to the orchard to play. Apple trees, pear trees, and peach trees stood in long rows, with soft green grass and wild flowers beneath them. In one tree at the edge bordering on the forest, Able, Bill, and Jim had built their younger brothers a tree clubhouse and a small teahouse for their younger sisters. This had been a very clever plan of Able's. Their younger siblings headed into the teahouse or climbed up into the tree house to play, leaving the six older ones alone.

Fran spread out a blanket and she and Able lay down beside each other. Not far away, Billy and Betsy did the same thing, while Jim and Mary followed suit. "This is such a wonderful life out here, Able. Space for miles around us. Beauty everywhere. I love it, don't you?"

"You bet, Fran. I would hate being all cramped up in Uru. How can they live in all those houses so close together? Here, we have everything we could ever want!"

"Indeed. Say, I promised mom that we'd pick her some wild berries, if any were ripe yet. Raspberry pie sounds good, doesn't it?"

"That sounds good," he teased, and the two stole a quick kiss.

"Hey, Able, that cloud is still here. Hasn't moved any," Billy called out.

"Weird," Able replied. The June day was warm and sunny, a perfect idle day for a change. Not like April and May. Oh how they had to work those months! The forty selions had to be both plowed and planted as rapidly as possible. Topping it off, their mother's large garden also had to be plowed and planted as well. During those months, it was dawn to dusk work. No one had any thoughts of play; all were exhausted at the end of the day. Now, summer was finally arriving, bringing with it idle days.

True, it was time to build new things, repair harness, and do general upkeep around the farmsteads, chop the next batch of firewood, and handle the yearly butchering in August, but mostly for the kids, it was idle days when they could relax and enjoy the freedom of the land — also, each other, in the case of these six. Later in the summer, the gardens would begin producing. Then, they had to pick the peas, beans, and such. The girls helped their mothers put up the produce for the coming winter. Still, the kids were left with substantial free time.

Come fall, it would be harvest time, and once more, the heavy work would begin again. The fields had to be harvested and the grain hauled into Uru. The stubble was then cut and stored in the hay mow for the winter. At the same time, the gardens also had to be harvested, and the food dried or preserved as well. Also, the orchard's yields had to be picked and stored in barrels in the basements. Autumn was once more a dawn to dusk proposition.

"Well, we have eight more sunny weeks of relaxation," Able pointed out. "I was thinking that perhaps you and I could take a couple of horses and make a day of it, riding in the northern hills, Fran."

"Hey, that would be really fun. Maybe we will see some deer. Dad says that there are lots of them around," she replied.

"Hey Fran, Able," Billy called out, "you want to go swimming after lunch?"

The kids in the tree house heard that and began yelling that they wanted to go swimming. Then the girls in the teahouse stuck their heads out and agreed. Able laughed, "Okay, okay. After lunch."

After lunch, Able told Jean what they were planning to do. "Okay, the day is warm, but you and Mary look after the little ones. No accidents, you hear me?"

"Sure mom," Able replied with a grin. Hank had almost drowned last year and his mother wouldn't let him forget it.

A half hour later the fifteen gathered at the swimming hole north of their hilltop homes and at the eastern edge of the Weston's wheat fields. Here the creek rounded a bend of a steep hill and formed a deep water hole, six feet deep and about thirty feet across. Although shallow for the most part, the center was deep. Swimming was one of these children's favorite summertime activities! They took every opportunity they could to come here and splash, swim, or jump into the water. The boy's favorite activity was jumping in and splashing the girls.

Today, Fran and Able sat with their feet in the water, watching the younger ones have a ball. They discretely held hands and occasionally stole a kiss when no one was watching them. Able said, "Fran, if you got married, would you still want to live close to here or would you want to move away from this place?"

"All depends on who I marry, Able. I like it here. There is so much to do. Why? Do you want to move away and get away from your parents?"

"Oh no! I love it here too. I rather wondered how you felt about it. That's all. You know that I love you, don't you? I want to do right by you," Able explained.

"I love you too, Able. I wonder if our folks would let us get married? Would they help us build another house on the hill? Or would they want us to move away to maybe the next valley?" she asked.

"Dunno. There is plenty of rich land below your dad's fields and our fields. Heck, there is so much land out here that we could never farm it all!" She giggled. That was an understatement.

"Well, Fran, what do you say if I come over tonight and ask your parents for your hand in marriage? Let's do it!"

She gave him a big kiss. "Come over after the dishes are done. Mom's in a better mood then. Dad too," she hinted and squeezed his hand.

The hours seemed to move excruciatingly slowly for Able. At last, the dishes done, he said, "Mom, dad, I'm going over to the Weston's for a minute. Back in a bit."

"Here, take this fresh loaf of bread over to Allie, please. I owe her one," Jean asked him.

The loaf under one arm, Able took a deep breath and knocked on their door. "Hi Allie. Mom sent me over with this for you," he said handing her the loaf. He headed into their living room where Henry was sitting and relaxing. Fran was on the couch apparently sewing some patches of cloth together that would eventually become another quilt. He waited until Allie joined them and his nerves almost failed him.

Henry looked up, "Did you want something, Able?"

"Well, yes sir. I came over to ask you for your daughter's hand in marriage, sir. I love her and she loves me and we want to get married." He wondered if he ought to say even more, but wasn't sure what.

All eyes turned to Fran, who blushed. "Fran?" Henry asked.

"Yes, we do dad. Please?" she said softly, her finger's crossed.

"Allie?" Henry asked. She smiled and nodded. "Well, Able, you have our permission. Congratulations, son!" He shook his hand. Pandemonium broke out. Her four younger siblings began all talking at once. Some congratulated their big sister and Able; this was the biggest news in days.

Embolden by Able's sudden move, Billy and Jim asked if they could go ask Bill and Tom now too. Five minutes later, the fifteen children and six parents met outside on the lawn separating their houses. All parents were heading to the other parent's homes to discuss these surprise requests of their oldest teens. As they met, all six began laughing.

"This was bound to happen, Henry," Tom said.

"But so soon?" Elaine added. "She's still my first little girl."

"Mom! I am fourteen now! I am of age!" Betsy protested.

"I know dear, but I remember when you were just my first little baby. Now you are so grown up," Elaine explained, calming her daughter's worries. The littler kids all giggled and guff hawed, trying to tease their older siblings.

"We should hold a family council, Tom, Bill," Henry suggested. "We certainly cannot stand in their way. Yet there is much to discuss and decide." Their wives agreed and they all headed into the Weston home. Quickly, the three wives whipped up some tea and the six adults sat down at the dining room table to discuss this surprise event.

"We all saw this coming," Jean said with a wry grin.

"I'm surprised that Able took this long to ask Fran," Allie added.

"Well, we should find out what their plans are, first off. You know, if they want to move back to Uru, that's one thing," Henry added. Shortly, they summoned the three couples before them. Their younger siblings were told to stay out of the dining room, but they all snuck up close to the doors so that they could hear too.

"Well, I guess the first thing we need to know, boys, is where you wish to make your new homes," Henry asked. "Were you considering moving into Uru? Carving out your own spreads somewhere?"

Able spoke first, since he felt guilty by having started all this. "Fran and I like it here. We want to stick around here, if that's okay with everyone." Quickly, Billy and Jim agreed with him. All three fathers seemed very pleased and visibly relaxed. Able finally did as well, once he saw their relief.

"Well, boys, looks like we need to allocate a good deal of this summer to felling trees and making the lumber needed to build three more homes. As you three know, it took us two summers to get enough to raise Tom's barn two years ago. When we have enough, we'll have a house raising again, calling on the neighbors to lend us a hand," Henry proposed.

"Meantime, we have extra rooms," Jean suggested, "Fran and Jim are welcome to move into our house with Able and Mary. That will give you more room, Allie."

Allie chuckled, "Well, we haven't got a guest room now. Perhaps Billy should move over with Betsy. That way we'd each have another 'man' in the house." This went over well with the six adults.

"Now then, what kind of a wedding did you gentlemen and your brides have in mind? A priest from Uru?" asked Henry.

Able grimaced. "If we do that, we're going to have to wait all summer until late fall when we haul our grain to the Uru markets."

Tom and Bill laughed. Bill teased them, "Our boys are hot to trot with their fillies!"

"Bill!" Jean exclaimed, rather disgusted with his brazen teasing of the three young couples. "You were hot to trot too, if you can even remember those days." His face reddened.

Allie suggested, "Well, you could have a traditional country wedding or even a simple nature wedding."

Fran spoke up, knowing that Able was a bit out of his league with such formalities. "Mom, I'd like to keep it simple, just a nature wedding is fine with us. We hardly know the neighbors anyway. We only see them at barn or house raising events anyway."

"We do too," Betsy added and Mary agreed as well.

Fran then asked, "Mom will you perform our ceremony, please?" Allie could not turn down her daughter and agreed to perform the Nature Wedding, an age-old rural wedding ceremony handed down from the earliest settlers centuries ago. Elaine and Jean suggested that Allie wed all three couples at the same time. They set the date for this coming Saturday, that way the three brides would have their baths and be fresh for their husbands on the wedding day.

Since Allie would do the ceremony, Elaine and Jean took care of cooking the wedding feast and the combined wedding cake. The rest of the week took on an air of festivities. Able worked hard to clean up his bedroom and make room for Fran's things. Mary began moving her things over to Jim's room, once he had his room in some semblance of order. Likewise, Betsy adjusted her bedroom and Billy began moving his things over to her room.

Saturday afternoon, the three brides, bathed, smelling of lilacs, their long hair brushed and dressed in their nicest white cotton dresses purchased last year in Uru, took their places beside their beaus on the lawn beside the water tower, beneath a giant white oak tree. The boys wore their best brown cotton pants and white linen shirts, also purchased last autumn in Uru. Each held the arm of their bride.

Allie stood before the three couples and the other family members gathered around in a semi-circle behind the couples. Allie began, "We stand here before Mother Nature recognizing the Eternal Cycle of All Life. In the spring, Life begins anew and grows and multiplies throughout the summer. In autumn, Life ripens and we partake of the Bounty that Nature gives forth to one and all. Yet in Winter, life dies, becomes dormant, as the cold winter snows cover the once grass-filled lands. We have eternal Faith in the Grace of Nature, for in time, Spring comes once again, bringing forth New Life and the Eternal Cycle of All Life begins once more. Through death comes resurrection and new life. Such has it been since the dawn of time."

"We are gathered here today to join and welcome three loving couples into the Eternal Cycle of Life. Each has pledged themselves solely and only to the other for all time, until death do them part. In sickness and in health, in bad times and in good times, each pledges to support and assist the other that they both may grow and become fertile, bringing forth New Life to continue Nature's Eternal Cycle."

Several younger girls giggled, realizing she meant that their sisters and brothers would be having babies soon. Allie continued, "Able, do you take Fran Weston to be your Holy Wife, to treat her always with the honor and respect that she deserves, to be faithful to her, to assist and provide for her needs, to love her and cherish her in sickness and in health, in good times and in bad, until death do you part?"

Able squeaked, "I so promise, always, Fran." She grinned. He was nervous; she could tell.

"Fran, do you take Able Johns to be your Holy Husband, to treat him always with the honor and respect that he deserves, to be faithful to him alone, to assist and provide for his needs, to love him and cherish him in sickness and in health, in good times and in bad, until death do you part?"

Fran said stoically, "I so promise, Able." There, she said what her heart had for so long desired to say.

Similarly, Allie asked Billy, Betsy, Jim, and Mary the same questions. The vows finished, she announced the three couples, and everyone clapped and cheered, while their sisters tossed wild flowers over the three couples. Now the festivities began.

Bill got out his fiddle and played country dance tunes, accompanied by Tom on guitar and Henry on percussion. Allie and Jean sometimes added vocals, while the three young couples danced on the lawn. Soon all the younger ones joined in as well. Later that afternoon, they feasted on roast chicken and finally cut their wedding cake. As the sun lowered, the three couples, arm in arm took a stroll around the hill, before heading into their rooms.

Able led Fran into his room, now their room. Of course, she had been in his room before, but not like this. She had butterflies in her stomach. "Hey, we had better be careful here, Fran. I'm sure that Mary, Martha, and Hank have been up to no good. I saw them sneaking in here a while ago." They looked around but saw nothing amiss. When Fran pulled the sheets down, she giggled. They had spread dried peas on their sheets.

To say that these extended families were completely isolated from the world at large would be an error. Once a month, the Uru Rural Postman came by the settlement, bringing any accumulated mail, picking up any that they wanted sent, and dropping off the Karka News. On July 2, Hank rode up on his bay mare as usual. The arrival of Hank was always an event, for seldom did visitors come here to this remote hill settlement. Everyone dashed outside to greet Hank.

Sally gushed, "Fran and Able got married. So did Billy and Betsy and Jim and Mary!"

"Well, looks like congratulations are in order around here," Hank grinned. "Say, won't be long before it's your turn, young lady." Sally grinned; she had her eyes on James. Another year, maybe, she thought.

"Hi Tom, Bill, Henry. Got some letters for your families and the kingdom's news. Men, I fear that the news is, well, unsettling. I don't know whether to believe any of it. Mine is not to question, just to deliver."

"Well, Hank, come on in and sit a spell. We've got some wedding cake left over and some honey mead or ale, if you prefer," Allie offered.

"Don't mind if I do, ma'am. Been a long ride — still got to get over to the Williams yet today."

While the women opened the letters, many from their sisters and brothers back in Uru, the men gathered around the one page Karka News, reading over each other's shoulders. Tom called out, "Aliens? In flying machines? Going to attack us? What on earth for? A plague? I don't believe a word of this. I think King John has lost his rocker. Bill?"

"What?" called out the women, looking up from their letters.

Bill explained, "King John in Karka says that he's received word from Monarch West Po down in Velona that some aliens in a flying ship are going to be attacking us and unleashing some kind of plague on us."

"Preposterous!" Tom growled. "Who ever heard of aliens?"

"Wonder what they look like?" Able asked.

"Who cares? There ain't no such thing, that's what I think," Tom answered.

"So what are we supposed to do?" Allie asked, ignoring Tom.

"Says here if we see them flying about, we are to shoot them with long guns or throw rocks into their engines," Bill answered.

"When are they supposed to be attacking us?" asked Jean, becoming worried.

"Sometime next week maybe? King John is a bit vague about the when, sometime after the tenth he is suggesting. We're supposed to be on the lookout for alien flying machines," Bill answered.

They chatted nervously about this the strangest news yet. "Hey, there's more, turn it over," Hank pointed out.

Bill began relaying the second half of the news. "Says some island called Dorota was blown up back in early June. That's where that southern dust cloud is coming from. I guess that we can be very thankful that we are way up north. Down south, the dust is blocking out the sun, turning day into eternal dusk. All the crops are dying. King John says that we may lose all the crops this year. Same thing down in the Sea Princes. He says that we should husband all that we have and he is trying to get food supplies imported from far to the south. Wow! Incredible."

Tom spoke up, "Well, now we have something that we can deal with here. We had better lay in our meat supply early. Bill, we ought to get on to the butchering now, get the meat drying."

After Hank left, the three men met and agreed upon the direction that they should follow. Tom, Henry, and Billy would begin their annual butchering, while Bill would take Able and Jim out to the woods and begin to chop their needed eighteen cords of firewood, six for each family. Sally would take the younger children out to pick all the berries that they could find, while the other women would assist with the butchering process, preparing the meat for salting, drying, and smoking.

By the end of the week, their three smoke houses were releasing curls of smoke into the summer sky. Ten of the eighteen cords of wood had been dumped near the three woodpiles, but not yet stacked. As the tenth approached, the three men cleaned up their long guns, preparing them for a battle, if such things as aliens existed. Between them, they had fifteen long guns. Mostly they were used for winter hunting and to drive off the occasional predator that wandered near their corral or barns.

Everyone looked forward to butchering time. "Oh, this is delicious!" Able exclaimed as he sunk his teeth into another bit of a juicy steak. Fresh meat abounded but only at butchering time. True, they would have chicken and an occasional duck often, but fresh steak was had only at these special times. Later, it would be dried, salted, or smoked beef, usually softened in a stew.

On July 10, Tom placed his five long guns and their accompanying powder horns and small bag of lead bullets and wadding close to the front door. At least, he ought to be prepared, he figured. Tom still thought this was a hoax or some trickery. In his mind, such things as aliens didn't exist.

The girls had picked a large quantity of berries. Now that the butchering was finished, the women worked in their kitchens preserving the berries for the winter. Jams, jellies, and preserves predominated, along with a few berry pies. It was afternoon on July 16. Bill, Henry, and the older boys were out in the eastern woods chopping the rest of their needed firewood. Tom was out in their fields, chopping weeds from his large cornfield. Sweat poured from his head in the summer heat. The children were outside pulling weeds from the three garden plots.

Martha looked up, wiping the sweat from her forehead when she saw the cigar shaped object moving through the sky towards them. She screamed. James screamed to the other children, "Run to the houses fast!" The many kids raced towards their homes. Hearing the scream, Tom looked up and saw the impossible. Bang! A long gun fired, bringing him back to his senses. He raced towards his home.

Elaine fired off the first long gun shot at the ship, while her children came running in from their garden. Bang! Betsy fired another one, standing beside her mother. Both dashed inside to get another pair of guns. Billy had the fifth one with him out in the woods.

Jean and Fran fired off a round from their front yard, while Allie and Mary followed suit. Sally and Mark also fired the remaining long guns. Martha and Hank handed the other two to Jean and Fran, who fired a second round. Now they all had to reload. Tom rushed up in time to speed up the reloading process at his house.

Out in the woods, the men heard the gunfire, looked up, and saw the alien flying ship. At once, they grabbed the three long guns that they had brought with them and fired a volley as well. Jim was forced to throw a rock instead.

Bang! Bang! Tom fired off two more rounds, while Elaine and Betsy fired the other two long guns. Meanwhile, the little children began tossing stones at the ships. At the Johns home, Jean and Fran worked feverishly to reload the four weapons, handing one to Martha and Hank as soon as two were loaded. At last, they too fired off a second round. Allie, Sally, and Mark reloaded their four and headed outside to fire their second volleys.

After that, the whole group just stood and watched as the ship flew off to the west, leaving them alone and apparently unharmed. "Well, we did it; we drove them off," Tom yelled. Everyone shouted and cheered now, the little ones jumping as well. Never had they seen such excitement.

Not long after that, the others came running from the woods, yelling to see if anyone was hurt. "Everyone okay?" Bill asked, out of breath. The woodcutters were greatly relieved to see that no one was injured at all.

"I'm proud of you, Fran, you got off shots and did swell on reloading," Able complimented his new bride.

"Of course, silly, dad taught me to shoot when I was eight. I think that we have run them off. Will they be back?" she asked.

That was the topic for the next hour. The men got the guns reloaded and ready, but after an hour, nothing had appeared. At last, the woodcutters returned to finish up for the day. When they returned near suppertime hauling another large load of firewood, everyone was talking about the alien ship and the attack, except Tom continued to insist that it had actually not attacked them. No one was hurt. Nothing got shot or blasted. He insisted that they check on all their animals, in case the aliens ate cows, horses, or sheep. No one could find anything amiss.

Over dinner, the aliens were still the topic of conversation among everyone. Allie pointed out that the Karka News had said something about an alien plague. Hence, Henry had to reread that section of the news to everyone once more. Now Allie began to become worried, as did the other two mothers. All three insisted that the children disrobe for a full body inspection. "We are looking for red splotched or bumps or anything unusual," she explained.

Finding none, the adults also checked over themselves. At last, they were satisfied that all was well with everyone. As the sunset, the families headed off to bed. At dawn, the families rose. While the children headed outside to do the morning chores, the women began to make breakfast, glad that Fran, Betsy, and Mary were now fully helping them, making the job go much swifter. All three complimented their daughters for being so grown up and mature now that they were married women themselves. They, of course, giggled.

As they ate breakfast, Allie asked if anyone had any symptoms. Was anyone feeling ill? They checked everyone's foreheads, if only to satisfy themselves no one had a fever. However, Fran pointed out, "My arms seem awfully tired this morning." Once said, the other women began noticing it as well, even the younger girls.

The older women began to worry, and the six men did likewise. Tom suggested that today they all stay close to the homes and hack weeds out of their fields. All suspected that the aliens might return and kept their guns at the ready. No aliens appeared however. By suppertime, all twenty of them were extremely worried and anxious. All the women's arms were extremely weak, as if they had lost all strength in them. Allie was now convinced that they indeed had come down with some plague!

As pioneers, they had to depend upon their own skills when it came to illness and accidents. Hence, they had brought with them simple books on first aid, remedies, and cures. For hours, the men searched through the three books for any clues that might tell them how to treat their women and girls. Yes, the men had fixed dinner and dealt with the dishes afterwards, but it was well past dark when they finally gave up. Nothing in the medical books dealt with what their women were experiencing.

Henry, Tom, and Bill tucked their children into bed, giving each a good night kiss, suggesting that they probably would feel better in the morning. Then, they tucked their wives in and crawled in beside them. The three young couples had already done so. All six couples talked worriedly for quite a while before sleep finally came.

"Tom! Wake up! Tom!" Elaine called out. Tom opened his eyes; it was not quite dawn yet. "Tom. Help. Something's really wrong with my arms, I can hardly move them!" He got up and lit the lantern. He nearly fainted. Her arms were nearly skin and bones now and somehow half of their original length. He helped her to use the chamber pot, but his hands were shaking wildly.

"Are yours getting weaker too?" she asked, fear growing rapidly.

"No, I am just scared out of my wits!"

"Go check on the girls. Try not to panic them. Oh god! What's happening to us?"

"Will you be all right?"

"Yes, I feel fine otherwise, just scared to death! Hurry up."

Soon, her worst fears were confirmed! All of her girls were similarly affected by this plague! It is a compliment to these hardy pioneers that none of them screamed wildly, but somehow took this in stride. While they were terrified and very frightened, they kept their heads about themselves.

Elaine called out, "Tim, James, run over to the Johns and Westons. See if they are up. Tell them what's happened to us. See if they are all right. Hurry sons." She fought hard to keep her voice from sounding panic-stricken. "Kids, to the kitchen now," she ordered.

Tom and Billy had all the kitchen lanterns going when the rest filed in, scared looks on the women's and girl's faces. Billy was frantic with worry over Betsy, hovering over her as if she might break or die at any second. The men felt helpless.

As the sun rose, the frightened Westons and Johns all joined the Whitefields in their large kitchen. "What's happening to us?" asked Martha, their twelve year old. Everyone was examining everyone else, shocked and almost speechless.

Jean answered her daughter, "We have the plague. That is the only possible answer, dear. We must be brave. Daddy will figure something out, I hope."

"But I can't move my arms anymore," she complained. Sally, Marge, and Lilly added their "me too's." The older teens were quiet, fighting hard not to panic and scream, looking to their mothers for support.

Tom was badly affected and sat staring at nothing. Bill took charge.

"Okay, boys, go take care of all the morning chores. Henry and I will fix breakfast. Now hurry along. Elaine, what's where?" he asked.

At last, Elaine had something that she could do and began telling him what to fix and where she kept it. Meanwhile, Jean and Allie ushered the others into the dining room and had them use any means possible to get a chair and sit down. The two women tried to answer their daughter's questions, but could only really say, "We must wait and see."

An hour later, the twenty crowded around the table. Bill suggested that the men and boys sit between their wives and girls. "Look fellows, we have to feed them all."

"But we're not babies, daddy," Martha complained.

"We know that dear. Just eat what Hank gives you, honey."

Once fed, Bill suggested, "Okay kids, why don't you go outside and play a while. Let us adults see if we can figure out what's happening. Boys, help your sisters."

"But they are in their nightgowns, Bill," Jean protested.

"Better let them play. Who is going to dress them?" She flushed, realizing what he meant. Now full, the younger kids headed out to play. Doors were not a problem anywhere here; they all had sliding slats with a dowel used to move the slats. Doorknobs were a luxury and wholly unneeded out here. A simple sliding slat was sufficient to hold a door closed, usually indicating that the occupants desired privacy, normally the adults and now the three newlyweds.

The twelve began closely examining each other's bodies. "Tom, you are affected too, your ear lobes are getting really long," Elaine pointed out. Indeed, all twelve had lobes that now dangled about two inches down from their ears. Tom nearly vomited up his breakfast when he felt his ears.

"Mom," Able said, "it's like the trees in autumn. Your arms are sort of dying off."

"Son! That is exactly what it looks like!" his father praised him for the best observation yet. "Wilting like a plant, sort of."

"Yes, but the leaves eventually die off and fall to the ground!" Allie said growing more worried by the moment. "Do you suppose that ours will completely fall off, like leaves?"

"If they do, maybe they will grow back in the spring, like trees and grass do," Fran suggested the only hopeful thing that she could think of now.

"We're all doomed," Tom ranted. "Lucifer's work! Devil's work at play. I say Doomsday has come upon us all!"

"Oh don't be silly, Tom. It some kind of hideous alien plague, just like King John said," Elaine tried to silence such upsetting talk.

"I tell you, Elaine, it's Doomsday come. Mark my words; your arms will be completely gone. Then bit by bit, the rest of all of us will die off until we end up in Lucifer's Hell!"

"Daddy, I don't want to lose my arms! I don't want to go to Hell. I don't want to lose anything else. You got to help us daddy!" Betsy pleaded, becoming even more frightened.

"Tom, stop that nonsense talk!" Bill chided his friend. "You are scaring the women. Brace up; we have to find a cure or something."

"Yes, can it Tom! We need helpful suggestions. Why don't you go over the medical book one more time, Tom," Henry insisted, tossing the book at him to shut him up.

Fran timidly asked, "Able, are you feeling any effects in your arms?" She realized that if somehow she could get her attention on him and not herself, then she might feel less scared. Her stomach was very tense, knotting in fact. She couldn't move her arms even to rub it.

Able rubbed his and replied, "No, so far they seem normal. Can you move yours at all?"

"No, but I can barely feel them now. Able, I'm scared. What's happening to us?"

"I don't know, but I won't leave you. Remember, in sickness and in bad times? I'm right here and I'm going to take care of you," Able declared. The two younger twins thought this was an excellent thing to say and repeated something similar to Betsy and Mary, who most definitely appreciated hearing it.

Jean finally said, "Bill, why don't you and the boys go finish stacking the firewood and take care of the garden and fields?"

"But dear, we can't leave you alone, not like this," Bill said, highly worried still.

"We can call if something else happens or we need something. Right now, I think that it is best if all of us stay together, for moral support if nothing else," Jean suggested. "Keep an eye on the girls too."

Unable to do anything useful for their wives, the six men headed outside to stack the wood and see what else ought to be done. Able checked on the smoke houses and adjusted the drying meat. The younger kids were running around. James had convinced the girls that they could still run about and all were now into a game of kick the beanbag.

As they sat down for supper, their arms were at most a foot long and very withered looking. Yet they didn't have any other symptoms appearing. There was little else to do but go to their respective homes and to bed. As the Johns approached their home, Bill said, "Let me get the door for you, Jean."

"Oh, I can manage the door, Bill," she used her foot to slide the bar and pushed her way inside. "I'm not a total invalid just yet." She kept biting her lip, though she felt that she very nearly was, but she had to hold up and set an example for the many children. There was so little else that she could do for them just now.

"Come on, kids. Time for bed, wash up" Jean insisted, before she realized that none of them could wash up themselves. She fought back welling tears.

"Hank, wash off your sister now, while I do your mother," Bill added, she leaned her head on his shoulders.

"Our hair ought to be brushed out too, Bill," she whispered as he was drying off her face. Bill, Able, and Hank did their best with this chore and then tucked them into bed, crawling in after they blew out the lanterns.

Bill slept fitfully that night and awoke at twilight. He slipped out of bed and lit a lantern to check on Jean. His fears came true. His love lay sleeping soundly, but her arms had now vanished completely. He sighed to himself and decided it best to wake her now and then see to Martha. He leaned over to kiss her and his long lobes brushed against her face, sending wild sensations through him. He kissed her on her forehead and Jean began to rouse.

"Something wrong?" she whispered as her eyes opened. "Bill, your ears are really long now!"

"Let me help you sit up, my love. They're completely gone now. How do you feel?"

Jean sat up and saw that it was true, but her lobes brushed against her shoulders and sent strange sensations throughout her body. "I feel okay otherwise, Bill. How are you doing? Are your arms getting weak now too?"

"No, I feel okay. Jean, get up. There's something else going on with you!" He helped her get up. "Look," he pointed to her reflection in the mirror.

"I swear that I look like a courtier or something. Is that makeup? Bill, see if you can rub it off, please." It didn't come off.

"Well, I do like your lips and eyes; you looked really good, Jean," he put his arms around her and had a second shock. He pulled her nightgown off her, and she stared at the rest of herself.

"Bill! My waist is going away too!"

"I don't think so. It's curvy. You do look really good, though." He pulled her close and they embraced. The electricity flew and it was all that they could do to pull themselves apart from their passionate kissing.

"Wow, Bill, your kissing is, well I don't know what to say," Jean said slightly out of breath.

"I had better go check on Martha. Be back shortly."

Bill quietly entered Martha's room, hoping not to wake her. Instead, she was squatting over her chamber pot. "Hi dad. They are all gone today, just like the trees. I guess now I am like a tree. Maybe they will come back in the spring. I had to go pee."

"That's my brave little girl, well done, Martha!" he praised her. She too had red lips and the same blue eye shadow. From the fit of her nightgown, he thought that she looked thinner around her waist as well. "When you are done, go wake Hank and tell him I said to get a start on the chores, please honey."

Able and Fran heard the low voices and roused themselves from sleep. "They're gone!" Fran whispered. Quickly, Able rose and got the lantern burning brightly. Indeed, all traces of her arms were gone. Yet that didn't startle him as what else he saw.

"Come on, get up, and look in the mirror, my love!" He didn't know what else to say.

"Oh! My lips, my eyes! Say, it does look good, doesn't it? Like some of those wealthy women in Uru," she moved her head from side to side, which caused her to experience a wild sensation at the tips of her ear lobes. Then, she noticed her waist and had Able remove her nightgown. "Am I shrinking there too?" she asked, becoming worried once more.

"I'm here. I love you, Fran. You do look gorgeous, but I wish you had your arms back." He kissed her on her cherry red lips. She returned his kiss with a wild passion. Both fell back onto their bed and didn't get up for some time, not until they heard the others starting the stove to fix breakfast.

Over at the Weston home, Allie, after looking herself over, made the mistake of kissing Henry. Before either of them knew it, they too were on their bed, passions overtaking them. Likewise, Jim and Mary found themselves kissing most passionately and rose a bit later extremely satisfied. When Henry finally went to check on Sally, he discovered that she had managed to use the chamber pot herself and was looking at herself in the mirror. "Look at my lips, daddy! Don't I look good? You think James will like me like this?"

"Darling, I think you look absolutely beautiful. Go wake Mark and have him start in on the chores, please. Daddy has to get breakfast started."

At the Whitefield home, Elaine rose first. She was not too surprised to find her arms had vanished completely. All signs had pointed to that yesterday. As she rose, her ear lobes ran across her shoulders and sent wild sensations through her body. She got up and wiggled out of her nightgown to see if anything else had happened. In the dim early morning light coming in through her window, she looked at her reflection. "Tom! Wake up. Look what's happened to me today!"

Tom rose and saw her facing him. Her waist was shockingly small; her lips, red; her eyes had a pastel blue shadow about them. He panicked. "Elaine! The devil has indeed come again. You are shrinking into Hell! Doomsday is upon us now for sure! My god! What can I do? Lucifer is coming to take us all!"

His loud outburst woke all the others in the house. Billy and Betsy woke up, heard the commotion, and got up. Each noticed the other's changes and she stared into the mirror trying to grasp the changes in her appearance. Billy forgot about Tom for the moment and the two checked her over for any ill effects. Finding none, they headed out into the living room, where they could hear Tom now yelling wildly.

There in the middle of the room was a pile of strange things, items that neither had ever seen before. James and Tom were cowering in a corner; Marge and Lilly were pressing themselves up to Elaine's body. "The devil has come into our house! See, he's left his hellish things here! I swear, Elaine, the devil is taking you over, all the girls! You are all going to be the devil's maidens! Look at your face; the devil's work, I swear it. I cannot let the devil take you and the girls!"

Tom had a machete corn blade in his hand. Billy didn't like the way that Tom was ranting. It was as if the man had gone crazy or insane. "James, Tim, go get Henry and Bill fast! Betsy, stay behind me." He pushed Betsy behind himself and edged closer to Tom, who continued to rant and rave about the devil taking brides, whatever that meant.

Marge and Lilly were crying now, their dad was scaring them. Elaine kept trying to calm Tom down, but he heard not a word that she said. He kept stomping around the room, kicking his foot at the stuff piled on the floor. "Aliens, bah! It's the bloody devil himself. Can't you see? He's moving in; you are all to be his brides! I can't let him get you! I can't let him get you!" he lunged towards Elaine and the two girls. She fell back and Marge lost her balance and fell off to Elaine's left, while Lilly continued to press close to her mother, following her as she backed away from Tom and his threatening blade.

Billy afterwards said that it all happened lightning fast. Screaming, "I won't let the devil get you, my precious," Tom swung the machete onto Lilly's back. She screamed and blood began flowing. Billy tried to grab Tom's arm, but Tom swung his arm back, hitting Billy in his nose, knocking him backwards, blood gushing from the teen's nose.

"Run, Betsy, run," Billy screamed as Tom's blade hacked a second time into the back of Lilly.

"No! Tom! Stop!" screamed Elaine. She threw her own body over that of her youngest daughter, trying to stop her bleeding and her husband's insane actions.

"I won't let the devil get you either, Elaine. I promise you, he won't lay his filthy hands on you or any of our daughters!" He swung the blade down on her body, cutting her deeply in the back of her neck. She screamed and tried to roll over. Billy struggled to get to his feet. He saw the blade coming down again; he would be too slow. He lunged for the man anyway. The blade cut deeply into the side of Elaine's neck. Her gushing blood flew onto Marge, who was still trying to get up. Marge began screaming wildly. Tom raised his machete again as Billy tackled him. Just as he was about to bring the machete down hard onto Billy, Bill raced into the room.

Bang! The long gun fired. Tom jerked, the weapon slipped out of his hand, and his dead body slumped to the floor. Billy landed hard on the floor from his tackling fall. Bill dropped his gun and ran over to the two bleeding women; Henry was right behind him, dropping his gun beside Bill's. In fact, the entire group followed the two men inside.

"Oh my god!" Allie screamed.

"Damn!" Jean added.

As Bill leaned over Elaine, trying in vain to use pressure to stop the massive blood loss, Elaine whispered, "Save my baby. Save my baby." She exhaled and slumped limply in Bill's arms. Henry moved her off the young girl, who was bleeding from two back wounds. He clamped his hands on one, while Bill did the same to the other wound.

"Boiling water fast! Needles, thread, towels, wash rags. Brandy, fast!" Bill yelled loudly. Jean, Allie, Fran, Able, Betsy, Mary, and Jim all dashed out of the living room, yelling orders among themselves, saying who was getting what. Meanwhile, Tim helped his sister get up and took her with him to get the blood washed off her.

"My god, my god," Bill kept saying.

"Keep the pressure on it, Bill. We can't lose her too!" Henry exclaimed, blood oozing between his fingers.

He looked up and Jean held a towel in her teeth for him. Allie had a washrag in her teeth. Betsy had brought an entire pincushion of needles, holding it carefully between her teeth. Fran had a spool of thread in her mouth. Mary said, "The fellows are getting the stove going. It will be a few minutes, and they'll bring the boiling water. Will she be all right? Is Elaine dead too?"

"Yes, she is. She wants us to save Lilly. Thanks everyone," Bill replied. "Honey, can you drop the rag over my hands? If I let up, she'll bleed badly." She did so.

"Why don't you let me and Allie hold the cuts together while you fellows stitch them up? We can to that much to help," Jean suggested.

"Okay, but wait for the boiling water to come." At last, the boys dashed into the room carrying two pots of hot water. "Great, but we are going to need even more, boys." They dashed off again.

Allie and Jean sat down beside the now unconscious Lilly and carefully got their feet in position. First, Henry released his hands. As the blood began oozing out again, Allie got her feet into position and pressed hard with her toes, slowing the blood loss. Then, Jean was able to free up Bill. Now the two men began sterilizing the needles and thread as well as the washrag. The others gathered around to watch how this was done.

Slowly, the two men got Lilly's two back wounds closed, and the blood ceased oozing out. Carefully, they wiped her clean and removed the tattered remains of her nightgown. Finally, the two men made a bandage out of strips of the nightgown, put a clean cloth over the two slices, and wrapped the strips around her waist and chest securing them.

"Okay, Able, Jim, lift her up carefully and carry her to her bed. Fran, see if you can find another nightgown for her," Bill ordered. Now they washed off the two women's feet, and at last, Allie and Jean got to their feet and stretched.

James said, "I got Marge cleaned up. She's unhurt, just scared. She wants her mother. What should we tell her? I have her in her bed right now. Dad went crazy, didn't he?"

"Son, I am so sorry about this. Yes, this plague has been too much for him to handle. We should have seen something like this coming. Your mother died trying to protect Lilly and Marge, and she was successful and in part due to you two boy's fast actions in getting us. Well done, boys," Bill complimented to two lads, attempting to lessen the tragedy for them.

Henry then said, "Okay, Able, Billy, Jim, get some shovels and dig two graves south of the corral. Bill and I will wrap them up and bring their bodies there shortly."

"One of us ought to sit with Lilly," Jean said to Allie.

"Mom, I'll sit with her while you get changed. Your gown is really messy," Sally offered.

"Okay, Allie, I'll come help you," Henry said. "I guess this can wait."

"No dear, you clean up here. I can get myself into something. I'm not completely helpless yet. I still have my teeth and legs," Allie replied determined not to make Henry stop what he was doing.

A half hour later, in clean gowns, the two women checked on their kids and then headed over to relieve Sally. Henry and Bill had the bodies wrapped in two old sheets, lying on the grass just outside the front door. Inside, the two stopped and looked into the living room, where this had taken place. Both were surprised. Bill and Henry already had most of the blood wiped up and now the younger kids were finishing the scrubbing. Marge, Martha, Mary, Betsy, and Fran were sitting on their butts, using their feet to push drying towels over the places that the boys had just scrubbed. They were working as a team, which brought smiles to their two faces.

Allie relieved Sally. She sat on Lilly's chair and smoothed out the girls hair. In doing so, Lilly roused. "Sh. Don't try to get up. You've had a narrow escape, Lilly. Just relax and try to rest. I know it hurts, but in a few days, you will be just fine. I promise."

"My mommy, I want mommy."

"I know you do, Lilly, but your mommy really, really wanted you to live. She died making sure that you would live. She loved you very much. Now we get to look after you. Will that be all right with you? If Jean and I look after you?"

"Okay. It hurts. Why did daddy hurt me and mommy?"

"The plague honey. It made him lose his mind. We lost our arms, but he lost his mind and that is much worse than a little hurt." She accepted this and sighed.

"You won't go away will you?"

"No, I will sit right here as long as you want me. How about a little kiss? I always kiss Fran and Sally right here on the backs of their necks." She did and Lilly relaxed even more.

About an hour later on, Henry poked his head in the door. He whispered, "We're going to bury them now. Is she doing okay?" She was, but Allie insisted on staying with her.

The clan gathered around the graves. Bill had put both bodies in them and then had the boys cover them up a little, before he allowed the younger kids to join around the graves for a simple funeral. Jean performed the ceremony.

"It is with the saddest of hearts that we now lay to rest Tom and Elaine Whitefield. Both are victims of this alien plague. While Elaine, like us, lost her arms, poor Tom fared even worse. The plague destroyed his mind. We can live without arms, but no one can live without their mind in one piece. Elaine, Tom, we will miss you terribly. We promise to look after your children and help them through their lives, as you would have wanted. Elaine, know that Lilly will be fine in time. You have saved her life."

"All of us loved you both. All of us will miss you both. You can now be at rest and at peace, free from this awful plague. Our lives have been enriched just by knowing you and having you as our dearest friends. If I say any more, I will be bawling like a baby. Goodbye, dear friends." She then used her foot to slide token dirt into the grave. One by one, the others followed her lead, casting a bit of dirt into the holes. She led the children back up to the homes, while the older boys and men finished covering the graves.

"Okay, while Henry and I fix breakfast, all you kids go take care of the morning chores. The chickens are raising a stink and the cows are baying. Girls go along with them and make sure that they don't miss doing one of your chores," Bill ordered.

Marge spoke up, "But I wanna do my chores myself. I can feed the chickens if only someone will put the feed sack over my shoulders. Please." He agreed and off they went. A bit later, he peered out the kitchen window. There she was with the shoulder strapped feed sack around her neck, using her foot to toss grain out for the chickens. Well I'll be, he said to himself, very much surprised.

Over breakfast, Henry said, "Okay, here's what we should do. Billy and Betsy are already living here, but I think that it would be wise if Jim and Mary also moved in over here. The four of them can look after the nightly needs of the four younger ones there. After we eat, we'll go clean out their room." Everyone agreed with his suggestion.

After many wet eyes, they had the parent's things removed and put into storage. Jim and Mary brought their possessions over and stowed them, though both felt weird now that they would be sleeping in Tom and Elaine's old room. Finally, they all returned to the living room once more. all the new stuff now got their attention and they attempted try to figure out what is was. They had no idea where it came from and gave up even trying to guess.

Slowly, the genetic memories began surfacing, after Henry pointed out that much of it looked like it belonged in the kitchen. Hearing the women and girls suddenly having some ideas about how these things could be used, they wisely kept silent and listened to them as they made small discoveries after discoveries.

Allie commented, "That thing on sticks, I think it is called a yoke, because I can see me resting it on my shoulders carrying bread. Hey, we might be able to better carry things with it." One by one, they tried it, and the revelations came flooding into their minds. Quickly the men got the idea that this contraption was perhaps the most greatly needed of all that was in the pile. As the group discussed the yoke and its potential uses, all realized that they needed lighter, smaller ones for carrying things around in the house, and that the ones that were here would be better suited for outdoor carries.

"Able, Billy, Jim, go over to the forest and see if you can find smaller saplings or some of those branches we left. We need to make a bunch of smaller yoke things. In fact, use your imaginations, fellows. See what you can invent for the women. Bill and I and the other boys will see what we can do to install these kitchen things," Henry suggested.

"So what do we do?" asked Fran.

"You girls carry the pots and things into the kitchens of all three houses. After that, you can be our go-fors. Let's get cracking; lots of work to do now." The eighteen sprang into action, except Lilly and Sally, the latter now sitting beside her sleeping girlfriend.

By evening, the boys had made twenty-seven of the yokes, coming in a wide variety of sizes. Some were quite narrow so that one could more easily navigate doorways. A few were quite sturdy, able to carry at least thirty pounds, maybe more. Henry thought those might be over doing it a little, but time would tell.

They had the kitchen installed in the Whitefield kitchen. Instead of removing the old items, they simply added these onto the back wall. This way anyone could use the kitchen. Allie insisted that until further notice, everyone would eat together as one large family, alternating homes each day. Only at nighttime would they return to their individual homes, though Billy and Jim were under strict orders to come get Bill or Henry if anything amiss happened. However, for the next few days, Allie and Jean took turns watching over Lilly.

A week later, Lilly was free of her stitches and feeling much better. Henry and Bill were very much surprised at how well the girls and women were somehow adapting to the results of this horrible plague. Marge, Sally, and Martha insisted on returning to their egg gathering chores for each family. Using their new yokes, they gaily went about it, enjoying pushing the hens off their nests with their feet. The only problem was that they got very dirty sitting on the ground each morning. With a little help from Mark, Sally was able to return to her morning milking of the family cows. Catching on,

Mary had her brother Hank assist her and returned to milking the Johns' cows. Tim had always done it for the Whitefields.

By August 1, the two mothers and the older teens were back cooking the family meals once more. As Allie put it to everyone, "Well, we can't sit around here and do nothing. Harvest will be on us before you know it. We have to be ready for the wintertime. So we will do whatever we can do. Bear in mind that it might not be quite what we were used to doing and need the men's assistance. Perhaps there will be some things that the boys and our husbands used to do that we can now do, freeing them up so they can pick up some things that we are unable to do." That became their guiding principle in the weeks to come. Pioneers survive by adapting their environment to meet their needs.

On August 5, the Uru Rural Postman, Hank, rode up, he was three days late. They had no mail this time, but they did get a lengthy Karka News flyer. Plus, Hank was dying to relay all the news. The extended family groaned when they heard that all the women in both the Sea Princes and all the ten Greenway kingdoms had gotten the plague and lost their arms. In a small way, this brought them a little comfort, knowing that they were not alone in this.

What scared the older men the most was that down in the Sea Princes, all crops were lost; fruit trees bore no fruit this year and lost their leaves. Worst, the same thing had happened to all the Greenway except north of the latitude of around Uru. Hank said, "If you can get your crops to the market in Uru, they will fetch a really good price! Millions of people are starving and your grains will help save lives."

After Hank left, the women read over the published tips by someone called Bethany of Velona. While they thought these most interesting, here, they had already worked out far more ways to do the things that had to be done. However, she at least had one thing right. Initially, they spent five times longer doing some of the things that they used to do.

As harvest time came, all took to the fields as before. Allie insisted that they still could help. Indeed, the women and girls sat on the ground shucking corn, filling their baskets, and when full carrying them to the waiting wagon. There, one of the boys would empty the baskets for them. While they were all thus engaged, twenty wagons pulled up at the south end of their fields, along with forty men from Uru. Indeed, they were very surprised to see the women hard at work in the fields.

The king had sent them to help these three farmers harvest their crops and get the corn, wheat, barley, and oats down to Uru as fast as possible. Henry and Bill were shocked to learn that they were being paid triple what their crops brought them last year. Within a day, the wagons began making the four day run to and from Uru. By late September, a whole month earlier than normal, their three forty selion fields were harvested, though several men stayed on to help them put up the straw portions in their mows.

On October 1, they had their own three wagons loaded with their garden produce and fruits that they could spare and the families headed down to Uru to drop off this last load and collect their wages. This also meant that they would do their annual shopping as well. The girls would get new dresses, while the boys, pants. All would get some chocolates. The annual fall trip into Uru was one of the most exciting times for the kids and adults as well.

With so much gold earned this year, they returned home with their wagons fully loaded with many new items for their farms, including three new wagons with six young draft horses to pull them. However, they all knew that a whole lot of worked remained to be done. They had yet to preserve, dry, and handle that portion of their garden produce that they had set aside for their own winter.

What Allie and Jean found interesting was the reporter who insisted on hearing how they had handled the plague and on relating all the tips and tricks that they used to help on the farm. He said that he was going to relay all this to the Bethany person in Velona. In turn, she would then relay these on to the Sea Princes farmer's wives and daughters. Hearing that, the two spent several hours relating their story of plague survival.

Chapter 24 Arad and Megalos Respond

July 20, 782, the Qaam Oikoumen met in Jerilum, Juda Arad. Qaam is the only sect of the ancient Jehosa religious order that survives today in the Arad. As always, they are staunch believers in the old ways, though there are no new ways any longer, not for centuries. Oikoumen is an ancient word that means the entire inhabited world. The Qaam Oikoumen is the highest religious authority of these people.

Jerilum was chosen as their place of meeting, not because it was a larger city in the Arad, nor because of its ancient traditions, nor because of its strategic position on the old north-south Centurion paved roadway. Rather the high altitude dust cloud that turned day into night began here at this city. Began is misleading. The southern edge of the cloud lay over Jerilum, reaching northward to the Dragon's Teeth and a bit beyond into the Northern Steppes. Within this zone, high noon appears as dusk and has done so since the first week in June, when Lucifer's Tongue, as the superstitious locals called it, first appeared. Now over a month later, all plant life below it had either died or gone dormant, further convincing them that this could only have come from the devil himself.

Via the only port city in the Arad, New Barq, the messiah leaders had heard the truth of the situation. The island country of Dorota had been disintegrated, presumably by some alien forces in flying machines, and that this dust was all that remained. True, New Barq had acted quickly to pleas from Velona and the other Sea Princes, sending all of their extra food supplies. They had even gone so far as to send word to some of the nomads of the Red Desert, telling them of the crisis and great need for food in the stricken countries. Already figs and dates began arriving in New Barq and hence loaded onto waiting caravels.

Juda Arad and Velona have been staunch allies ever since the First Crusade for Religious Freedom centuries ago. With the startling discoveries of Messiah Bani el Marina and his wife Tamina some forty years ago, these alliance ties were even stronger. Indeed, within Velona and the Greenway lived the direct descendants of their Great Messiah Jes Amir himself. Of course, the wicked, evil Church of Jehosanity denied that Jes was a man, claiming instead that he was immaculately conceived as the Holy Son of God, come to redeem all mankind. One day, these ardent followers of the true Jehosan religion would rise up and reveal the utter lies of the evil Church destroying it forever. However, as was said back then, as now, "Now is not the time."

Rather this supreme council was called upon to meet the latest, most startling and shocking news from the Sea Princes and the Greenway. A plague had struck, sickening all the inhabitants. All now had long, dangling ear lobes. That in itself was not shocking. All their females, both adults and children, had mysteriously lost their arms, had their waists shrunk — to that of a wasp some said — and their lips were bright red. Even their eyelids held some magic, changing colors from blackish to bluish depending upon the light. Some even claimed that because of the plague, their sexual drives were greatly enhanced as well. Not only were the native peoples of these lands affected, but also the Arad religious leaders who had gone there some thirty years ago, establishing Temples of Jehosanity designed to counter the evil Church of Jehosanity in those lands. That their own people had been affected was what had so deeply concerned the Arad religious leaders.

The many prophets and messiahs of the Arad called for this special session of the Qaam Oikoumen to rule on the meaning of this horrific plague, which so altered all life in some twenty countries. Three old, wise men made up this group. Badar Tunis, sixty, was the eldest. His long bushy hair and enormous beard was nearly grey now. (No males of the Qaam sect ever removed their facial hair.) Hamir el Wad was the youngest member at fifty-five. Yaz Madi was fifty-nine, with a hint of grey in his brown hair.

For three days, they had listened to the arguments presented by dozens of messiahs and prophets and even concerned followers. Now here in Jerilum, with the stark contrast in the sky above their heads, the three met in private to reach their important decision, which would dictate how the entire Arad reacted to this catastrophe of unparalleled proportions.

As the eldest, Badar took charge. "First, let us review nothing but the absolute, provable facts — that which is directly observable by our people. Correct me if I mis-speak or have an omission. The island country of Dorota has been destroyed by some massive explosion. Only dust remains. One and a quarter million people lived there at the time of the destruction. This plant-killing dust cloud is all that remains of what used to be on that island. This dust cloud blocks the living sunlight, which all plants must have to live. Beneath its canopy, all plant life is or has died, but perhaps has only gone dormant. In turn, animals and mankind are now threatened with extinction via starvation. Pleas for food have come from all the twenty impacted countries; millions of people are affected at this time. This Cloud of Death shows no signs of going away, having been over us a month. Correct so far?" The other two nodded.

"What of the supposed alien flying ships which attacked these lands and spread the plague? Have we seen such things? Such impossible things? Can we now see such things? The answer is no, we cannot. We cannot show this to our people or any people for that matter. We and they must accept this on faith, for we cannot view this as a verifiable fact. Yes, we do have countless eyewitness accounts from every Greenway kingdom and the eight Sea Princes and even West Reach. All tell the same story, even unto the firing of cannonae and guns against these flying machines. Yet, it is only their stories that can be heard as testimony; there is nothing that the rest of the world can use or see to lend solid, believable fact and certainty to these tales. Further, no one has yet reported seeing these things casting the plague upon them. Indeed, no account has yet indicated that these machines in the sky did anything more than appear and move around. Are we to then count this as believable and provable fact?"

Yaz spoke up, "We should consider that our own messiahs and prophets who run our Temples of Jehosanity in the Sea Princes and the Greenway have also been victims of this plague and have born witness to these accounts of the alien machines which moved through the air. We have their sworn statements of the massive defense of Velona to these ships. Can we discount the sworn words of our own prophets and messiahs who are there and bore witness?"

Hamir responded, "In open markets, does not a rope maser work his magic upon all who watch his show? All swear that his limp rope becomes a solid pole and that he does climb the pole and disappear, only to then reappear before them, his rope nicely coiled. Men and women can be convinced that they saw what was not there. This we know as true. While it pains me to say this because they are our hand-picked chosen messiahs and prophets whom we sent forth from the Arad on this Holy Mission to establish Temples of Jehosanity, I say unto you that we cannot accept as provable fact what they have reported to have witnessed."

The three men agreed on this point. Badar continued, "Thus, we must strike from the facts all such ideas of flying alien machines attacking these lands spreading some unknown plague upon the people. We can, however, rank among the facts how all of these people, our own as well, are now. This is observable fact. All men and women and children who were in those lands, whether native or foreigner, now have elongated ear lobes that rest upon their shoulders. Observable fact. Vastly more horrible and destructive are the results upon all women of any age within those lands. We cannot accept as fact that their arms were seen to wither as though leaves upon an oak in the autumn, withering and falling off. Rather, we can accept as visible fact that they have no arms, merely empty arm sockets. We can accept as fact that their waists are uncommonly small, some say uniformly eighteen inches. Again, that would be measurable, if we so chose."

"Observable fact, all female's lips are bright red, all female's eye lids vary in color from black to light blue depending upon the amount of light. In other circumstances, such was called makeup, though many of us believe such is only used by the common whore to lure men into their domain. Still, we must accept these as facts. Reports say this 'makeup' cannot be washed off or removed."

"This then brings us to the assertion that all this was somehow the result of a plague. Certainly, we have no words to describe adequately such a horrific alteration of human bodies. Yet, our messiah and prophet in Velona have sent us word that this Medical Research Foundation there in Velona has claimed to have found tiny bacteria, which has caused this plague. First, this bacteria thing cannot be seen by our eyes, but only by using one of their machine inventions, which greatly enlarge tiny things. While I am inclined to suspect that something tiny can be seen by this machine of theirs, as witnessed by all the unfathomable inventions we've seen already coming from Velona, our people cannot see for themselves these tiny things. Further, we again only have their word that it was these tiny things, which caused the 'plague.' Had they taken some of these tiny things and put them into a person who showed no signs of this plague and then that person became ill, that would be proof, though our people would not likely insist on many such demonstrations because of the horrific outcomes from it. Rather, they would like to use it on our enemies, the Church of Jehosanity, if they could. Opinions?"

Yaz answered, "I do not believe that we can at this time accept as provable fact that these tiny things directly caused the observable results upon these millions of people. Something has done this to them, we just cannot prove that it was this unseeable thing."

"Accepted. Are there any other directly observable facts that I have overlooked?" Badar asked.

Hamir spoke up, "Yes, by all reports, many strange, alien objects appeared in nearly every home in the affected countries. Our messiahs report that among these are replacement kitchens, desks, kitchenware, and even something which enables women to carry things. Should we go there, we could observe these things for ourselves. I believe that we should log them in the observable fact category." This was accepted by the other two.

Yaz added, "Some women have given birth since the infection struck. Their babies are similarly affected; baby girls have no arms. This is observable." This too they accepted.

"I know this is relatively minor, but the wives of the messiahs in our temples in those lands report that they can no longer fulfill their wifely duties to protect their messiah's back, fight with him in his battles, prepare his meals, or serve him or his guests, as dictated by our Holy Scriptures," Yaz explained. This was accepted.

"Okay, let us move on into the realm of direct conclusion and speculation supported by the facts," Badar continued. "We can accept that some explosion wiped out Dorota, though we did not see or hear such. We can accept as speculation that some plague has caused this catastrophe to their bodies, since we have no other word for it. We can conclude that these people are now mutations of the human race, since their offspring carry on their deformities. We can accept as speculation that these tiny bacteria things may have played some role in causing the infection, if infection is the proper term. We can accept as speculation that they fired their weapons at something in the sky. We can accept as speculation that they believed that they saw strange alien flying machines. We can accept as direct speculation that these infected countries are no longer contagious."

"How can these speculations be supported by the direct, observable facts? The one thing that has impressed me the most are the countless reports of the alien objects, which apparently appeared in every home. Not of any traceable origin to human hands, these must come from an unknown maker, hence alien, meaning foreign. This lends some credence to the possibility of alien flying machines. If this is accepted, it also lends support to the suggestion that the aliens destroyed Dorota by some horrific weapon unknown on Tarra. Since no outbreaks have been reported in lands bordering upon these infected countries, we can conclude that they are no longer contagious. Yet, time may well tell a very different story on this point."

"May I add another supporting idea?" Yaz asked. Badar nodded, "It is reported that the infected women somehow had some notions of how these alien objects ought and should be used to help them recover life actions. Again, while not an observable fact, it does lend more credence to the alien speculation theory. Why should they have such thoughts? Would any of us have such thoughts if we suddenly found a pile of alien objects before us?" That was added to the supporting ideas.

"Before tackle the realm of mere speculation, let us address the known fears that we have," Badar requested. "We fear that without sending them as much food as we can spare, millions of them will starve to death. Yet, we fear that contact with these infected people will in turn infect us. We fear that a merging of people will result in catastrophe for us. If an infected person mates with one of us who is not infected, will they then become infected? Even more importantly, will children born from such a union be also infected? If so, over time, the entire remainder of the world may become infected with this horrid affliction. Do we have other direct fears?"

"Velona and its inventors are bringing new and valuable inventions to the world. We cannot discount the metal trains, which has so shrunken our world. We cannot discount the value of their long distance means of communications, without which we would know so little of what has been going on in the world. If these contributions are considered valuable and worthy, we fear that the loss of Velona and its inventors would be a terrible tragedy, especially if by our hands it could be prevented," Yaz suggested.

"Fear taken, Yaz. Others?" Badar asked.

"An indirect one," Hamir spoke up. "Our people are in total confusion over all this. Wild speculation and fears are rampant everywhere. I fear that if we do not act to establish for our people just how this disaster is to be viewed and handled, if we do not do our assigned task, then our society will break apart, infighting will inevitably result among those with so wildly differing views of all this."

Badar smiled, "Duly noted. Okay, then let us outline these wild speculations. Perhaps now we will be able to assign some basis for such wild speculations. Some say that association with these infected people will result in our becoming similarly infected. Some claim that this is the work of the devil, casting out the unholy from our human race, reforming their bodies that we may be able to identify the unholy. Many claim that they are the Unholy, that Lord Jehosa is now punishing them for their earthly sins, and that Lord Jehosa has cast them out. Some say the Lord Jehosa has marked them so that all can tell at a glance the Unholy and thus avoid all contact with them, allow them to starve. Some believe that Lord Jehosa has passed judgment upon them, that the Days of Judgment have arrived and that we should pray and be prepared for his Holy Judgment upon us, which could happen at any time now."

Yaz commented, "It is hard for many to accept that Lord Jehosa would not have intervened with his children, if this was an alien attack upon his children, as witnessed by his holy messiahs and prophets in these lands also being infected. This, they claim, proves that it was not some intangible aliens, but the work of Lord Jehosa himself. Yet, this does not explain why our holy messiahs and prophets were also infected, for they are the humble servants of Lord Jehosa, as we are. Yet, they then claim that this shows us visible proof that Lord Jehosa wants us to have no contact with them at all, showing us that if we do so, he will infect those who make such contact."

Hamir chuckled, "So we are left with the ideas that the Days of Judgment have arrived or that they have not arrived. That Lord Jehosa saw all these infected people as truly the Unholy and has thus struck them down or that he had no part in it. That Lord Jehosa has acted marking the Infidels with the infection that we may know them at a glance and thus avoid all contact with them or that he has marked them so that we know whom we must help, as our hearts go out to those women whose lives had been made so utterly horrible. That Lord Jehosa is challenging the infected people, forcing them to adopt more holy ways or he has done no such thing. Others are saying that it is the Church of Jehosanity that has infected these countries in order to get back at them because they lost the Second Crusade to these people. Truly, the notions of our people in trying to understand what has happened here stretch imagination to its limits."

"How are we to counter these arguments and suggestions?" asked Yaz.

Badar answered, "Look, one thing has been on my mind from the beginning. While these infected people, with the exception of our holy men and women running our Temples of Jehosa, are in dire need of learning more holy ways, they are not the worst enemies that we have. Not by a long shot. No, it is this vile and wicked Church of Jehosanity that is corrupting our very foundations! To my way of thinking, Lord Jehosa, if he indeed caused this plague, ought to have struck only those who lead this Church, spreading such lies, deceit, and vulgarness across all Tarra. It is as the man who has a viper biting at his hand and who has stubbed his toe. The man cuts off his toe, the viper then kills him. It seems to me that if we accept Lord Jehosa as the force behind this, then he has struck at the wrong target. Indeed, we know the Holy Descendants of his son Jes Amir, our Great Messiah, now live and multiply in those lands. This suggests to me that these speculations are untrue. Why would he strike down such Holy Descendants, unless it is for their failure to step forward and lead the world back into Lord Jehosa's realm?"

"Very true," Yaz replied. "Yet, are we to ignore that now, for whatever reason, the infected can be spotted with a mere glance? It seems to me that this is a significant and important detail that we must address."

Hamir added, "It could be that Lord Jehosa is testing these infected people somehow." They discussed theories and ideas for another hour before they reached a consensus.

Badar stated, "Our primary concern must be to address the fears of our people. Thus, we agree on the following. All people in the Sea Princes, West Reach, and the Greenway have had a horrific bout with some unknown plague. While at this time, they believe that they are no longer infectious to others, we will restrict anyone who has been infected from entering our lands for a period of another three months. If no other signs of an outbreak occur, our quarantine will then be lifted."

"Because of the horrid aftereffects said plague and because children now born from these infected people are also deformed, we hereby declare that it is both unholy and illegal for any non-infected person to marry an infected person or engage in any sexual relationships."

"We feel that Lord Jehosa is in some way testing their strength of character and faith. As such, it is our duty as the Holy Leaders of Lord Jehosa to do all that we can to support them. Specifically, in their time of great need, we will send all the extra food supplies that we have to Velona, there to be distributed among the needy. We will continue to multiply our Temples of Jehosanity in their lands, once the risk of contagion is passed. It is our duty now more than ever to attend to their spirituality."

"These infected people are not to be condemned, defiled, criticized, or belittled, for they too are children of Lord Jehosa. Instead, support them so that they may too achieve the true grace of our Lord Jehosa and at last enter his Holy Realm."

"As for the rumors of this being the work of alien creatures or the plague being devised by the Church of Jehosanity or coming of the Days of Judgment, we have no proof of any such things nor do our prophets so predict. Remember, we cannot know what the Holy Plans of Lord Jehosa might or might not be. Do not be so arrogant to presume to know such."

The three men agreed on the wording and set them forth onto paper. Quickly, they were copied and sent to the many messiahs and prophets around the Arad. In turn, these men spread the word to those that they served. Caravels still docked and the trains still ran down to New Barq, picking up all the vital food supplies that could be had.

Pope Pius I learned of the devastation of Dorota in late June when word reached Megalos from the Sea Princes and New Barq. Not long after that, some returning ships from Shansee brought words of confirmation. That over a million people were annihilated in one blast staggered his mind. Almost at the same time, he learned of the dust cloud, which was slowly expanding around the world, resulting from the destruction of Dorota. All reports stated that alien creatures in flying ships were responsible, this he doubted totally. There were no such things.

Only days later, he began to receive pleas for immediate food shipments. The dust cloud was not going away and all vegetation was dying off. All food crops in the Sea Princes and the Greenway were going to be lost this year, a staggering loss, far worse than a mere million people. Tens of millions were now involved.

Hence, in late June, he ordered all the Church's vast emergency supplies in Constanza City to be sent up north, as their caravels came down to pick them up. He met with the Senate of Megalos and requested that they too agree to send all that could be spared to assist with this unholy disaster. The Senate approved massive sales to the afflicted countries, seeing a tidy profit on some of their older grains, some of which ought to have been pitched and not eaten any longer. Pope Pius I chose to donate the Church's reserves, anticipating the huge rewards such kindness and generosity would ultimately bring the Church. He was still fighting to get the Church of Jehosanity re-accepted in these two lands, after the debacle of his predecessors and their total loss of the Second Crusade.

The third week in July, all this changed utterly! The first of many Church caravels arrived at Constanza City, bringing back the many helpless nuns and wild, wild tales of aliens and plague! The many cardinals up north begged him to send replacement nuns as soon as possible. The only good news in this mountain of bad news was the letter from Cardinal Ruggerio Vatore, who went so far as to indicate that the plague had run its course, that the inhabitants were no longer infectious, and that it was safe for others to be in these affected lands now. The pope didn't understand the Medical Research Foundation's proofs, but accepted them. None of the men on the various caravels who had not been in port there when the plague stuck had yet come down with it.

The pope himself had met this first caravel returning with this news and the thirty nuns from Velona. He looked on in horror as these pitiful women struggled across the gangplank. Unable to care for their personal needs, their habits were filthy and covered with their own body's waste products. Their hair, a tattered mess. Even more shocking, they all looked in his eyes as harlots of the night, what with their cherry red lips, eye shadow, tiny, tiny waists. Couple that with their utter helplessness and by now half-starved condition, they shocked the pope completely! These once holy sisters of the Church were now in a complete apathy, not even caring that they went to the bathroom in their underclothes or that their bottoms were now red with sores.

He watched in utter dismay as the nuns of Constanza City greeted their sisters and ushered them off to receive the care that they now needed. He sat in his office a half hour later, listening to the horror stories that the captain told him and then read the very lengthy report from Cardinal Ruggerio. "All women in all these countries? All look like harlots of the night? All are utterly helpless, not an arm on any female anywhere?" he asked in shocked disbelief.

It was one thing for a woman to choose to become a Holy Woman of the Eighth Degree. Here in the Church, such an armless woman was given the highest of honors. She had many servant women to assist her in her daily needs. What was happening up north was entirely different! No woman would have any servants to help them! Worse, the Cardinal wrote that his priests had to break their vows and help their nuns with their very personal parts, dressing, undressing. Dealing with their bodily needs had been most humiliating both to the priests and to the poor nuns, who had to endure a man seeing their privates, wiping and cleaning them!

Word of the plague striking the northern lands spread like wildfire throughout Megalos. Within two days, everyone was talking about it. His priests reported their parishioner's fears and concerns to the cardinals and they, to the pope. Even before he could act, the Senate issued a strict quarantine of all contact with these northern countries. Only a few caravels were allowed to dock and their crew was not allowed to leave their ships. Centurions enforced this with a strong presence at the docks.

Daily, his cardinals begged him for answers. What were they to do? Was this God's Holy Wrath? How many more countries would be infected? He listened to them, but said nothing. What could he say? He merely prayed for guidance for hours each day. As the weeks went by, more details came to Megalos. Now all the countries of the Greenway were infected with this plague, their women becoming armless harlots. He learned that those affected now had some kind of wild sexual drives, not present before they got the plague. Even the island of West Reach became infected. Just when he thought he could hear nothing worse, caravels returned from Shansee, Tashien, reporting a massive outbreak of the plague there, thousands of women had died. The survivors were once more armless harlots, with painted faces and tiny waists.

By August 1, no caravel from these infected lands was allowed to dock, and no further food supplies were being sent northward! Then he learned one additional fact. Cardinal Ruggerio now reported that children being born from these infected women were also infected, that is their little girls were born with no arms, bright red lips, eye shadow on them, and with abnormally small waists! This finally convinced him that he just had to take action, but what?

He pondered this for quite some time. By the middle of August, he began hearing the best news in months. No further northern countries were becoming infected. Indeed, it appeared that the plague had finally run its course. All Megalos breathed a huge sigh of relief as word of this notion spread throughout the island. Somehow, Megalos had been spared, as well as their people in the Southlands. Now he relaxed a bit and decided the best thing that he could do was listen for what the ordinary person thought of all this. After all, his whole motive of operation was based solely on giving the parishioners what they needed, as long as it was spiritual in nature, of course. Up to the present, this had worked fantastically well in the largest country in the world, Demokritos. Until this plague, it had begun working well in the north lands which they had lost during the ill-fated Second Crusade.

Besides, he needed time to hear from the rest of the world, specifically Demokritos. Were they infected? Annelise? He thought little about the native savages on the Western Continent; they mattered not. No, the Southern Continent was critical. Did they get the plague too? It took a caravel three months to get to Demokritos from Megalos and another three to return. Due to this hideous crisis, he had sent two empty caravels down to check on their well-being. The two captains were under strict orders to make all possible speed there and back! With luck, he might know by December. In the meantime, he kept watch for other caravels who were returning with cargos from down under. Any that docked, he had questioned for news. As August drew to a close, all seemed normal in Demokritos, as of May, when these ships had set sail from there. This was hardly newsworthy, he mused, since the first infection in the north had not occurred until the first few days of July.

On August 31, Sister Melina, who ran the Constanza City Nunnery, came to meet with him. "Welcome, Sister Melina, you look well. How may I assist you in your ministry to our needy?" He sat back in his enormous chair, while the nun in her heavy habit sat on a small chair before him.

"Your Holiness, I have come about our poor sisters from the north, the victims of the plague."

"Yes, how are they doing now?"

"As you know, we have taken one hundred forty-nine of them under our care. It is indeed most trying for us. They are so completely helpless in all things. One of us must constantly attend their earthly needs, Your Holiness."

"Yes, that is to be expected. Ordinarily, Holy Women of the Eighth Degree hire servants to handle their personal needs. Are you suggesting that we do such with these nuns?"

"Oh no, Your Holiness. It is not about their care that I have come. I am so embarrassed by this. I am not sure how to explain it to you." She looked terribly embarrassed as well.

"Please, Holy Sister, you may be frank with me. I do understand all," he replied, knowing that he had not a clue about this whole mess. His words had the effect he desired, putting her more at ease.

"Your Holiness, you know that our poor sisters now have the look of harlots about them, what with their permanent, seductive makeup and their wasp waists only achieved by wearing the restrictive clothing of the Annelise."

"Yes, yes of course. Such is impossible to miss," he replied, not yet grasping what her concern actually was.

"Your Holiness, it goes deeper than that. They all are acting as harlots. Well, I don't mean that they are out walking the streets looking for men. Rather we are routinely catching them doing whatever they possibly can do to pleasure themselves! Rubbing bedposts! We've even caught some using their mouths on others! Horribly disgusting, but they simply cannot stop. They claim that they have such overpowering urges now, urges that they cannot control. We nuns find this horribly embarrassing, that some of our own sisters would so lose their faith!" She attempted to put a lighter spin on the situation.

"Oh this is awful, Sister Melina. Let me see what can be done about it." She thanked him and left. Pope Pius I knew that he had to take action now, but what? He sent for his Supreme Prelate and discussed this embarrassing matter with him.

"Your Holiness, you cannot allow these harlots to subvert your Holy Sisters any longer. As I see it, you have two choices here. One, you can defrock the harlots and turn them out onto the streets of Megalos, there to seek their pleasures. Two, you can allow your Mano del Dio to, shall I say, dispose of these women in a manner in which they will never again come to your attention."

"You mean to kill them?" Pope Pius I asked rather startled.

"We could, but I think that is a bit drastic. I know of a way that they can disappear for the rest of their lives, troubling the Church no longer."

"I can't just turn them loose on the streets of our towns. Such would become a huge tarnish on our Church. Make them disappear instead." He smiled; the problem would soon be solved!

The next day, all one hundred forty-nine women were taken aboard a caravel. Sister Melina was told that they were being transported to a location, which could better serve their needs. For this, she and her many other nuns were most grateful! These women ranged in age from twenty-one to sixty, with the majority in their thirties. Two weeks later, the ship arrived in Shansee. There, by wagons, they were transported to a seedy section of town and given to a man who ran a number of whorehouses. We learned of this sometime later from one Sister Natasa, but more of that later on.

In late October, more caravels returned with cargo from Demokritos and Annelise. Still all was well down under. No signs of the plague were present whatsoever. Estimating back, the pope figured that they left Demokritos around early August, more than a month after the massive infections here in the north. Since there had not been any further infections since July up here, he took a gamble that all would remain well in the south. Besides, he could not delay any longer outlining the Church of Jehosanity's position. Every day now, he received dozens of pleas for the Church's position. Even the Senate begged him for guidance.

On November 1, 822, he issued Papal Proclamation 52. This was copied and widely distributed as fast as possible, satisfying his many critics and pleas for the Church's position.

1 November 822

Long has the Church of Jehosanity sought to bring the Holy Word of Jehosa unto the heathens, heretics, and ignorant of our world that these people may have their souls receive the Holy Redemption and rise unto Lord Jehosa's Holy Realm of Heaven upon their body's death. Alas, we have been unsuccessful in the north. I take responsibility for our failures there. Instead of seeking the Holy Path of Righteousness and Salvation, they have spent their time and efforts building new devices, new machines. Mechanistic they have become, against all of our many teachings.

Lord Jehosa, upon seeing how hard that we have tried and how little these in the northern realms have listened, has acted. Lord Jehosa has sent unto the Sea Princes, the Greenway, and even part of Tashien, this horrible plague that has left all women there armless. He has instilled in both sexes an Unholy, Unnatural Sexual Drive, and has reformed their women's bodies into that which they so greatly desired, that of a painted harlot with tiny waists. Further, Lord Jehosa wants us all to be able to recognize one of these inflicted at a glance, and thus he has elongated their ears that we may recognize them even from afar.

Why? Why has Lord Jehosa done this to these northern people? Long have I prayed for guidance in this matter. My prayers have been answered finally. These people have for centuries now refused to hear his Holy Words and to follow his Holy Decalogue. At last, Lord Jehosa has smitten them with this plague, turning their fleshly bodies into mutants. Yes, I said mutants, for even their newborn babies carry on their gross deformities. Why?

Lord Jehosa has made their physical lives vastly more difficult, vastly more challenging in the hope that they will now recognize his Mighty Power and change their evil, wicked, sinning ways! He is challenging them with a wake-up call to change before their time of Redemption is at hand. This is Lord Jehosa's way to try to reach the Unholy and the Unreachable, to bring them back into his fold, before Lucifer gains total control over their souls. Yes, these mutants now have two feet squarely in Lucifer's Realm. Lord Jehosa is giving them a small taste of just how horrific Lucifer's Realm actually is, with the hope that these sinners will see the Holy Light and seek Holy Redemption before it is too late and Lucifer takes away their souls forever!

How are we, the Holy Faithful Followers of Lord Jehosa, to interact with these Unholy Mutants?

First, none of us should ever mate with a mutant, for such is an Unholy Union and is despised by Lord Jehosa. Children of such an Unholy Union would themselves become mutants and be themselves halfway into Lucifer's Realm.

Second, we must not attack them, belittle them, kill them, or harass them, for Lord Jehosa has already done that by changing their fleshly bodies into utter mutants. It is not our Holy Place to judge these people. Lord Jehosa has already done that and found them wholly unworthy!

Third, we must recognize that Lord Jehosa has done this to them in a last ditch attempt to get them to cease their sinning, wicked, vile ways and to turn back unto the Holy Light, to begin to follow the Holy Decalogue, to worship and pray and support our Holy Churches of Jehosanity. We must recognize that Lord Jehosa wants these mutants to understand the errors of their ways and to change before Lucifer takes total control of their precious souls for all eternity.

Fourth, given Lord Jehosa's Holy Plan of Salvation for these wicked, evil mutants, it is our Holy Duty to assist them in achieving what Lord Jehosa has challenged them to do. We must do all that we possibly can to help them renounce their wickedness and to adopt and accept and follow the Holy Decalogue. We must help get them into our Churches. We must help them rise above the Unholy Pit into which they now have been cast by Lord Jehosa. Our Holy Duty dictates that we do all that we can to help their precious souls finally attain Holy Salvation and receive the Grace of Lord Jehosa finally. That is our Holy Duty, one that every one of us must act upon at every possible turn each day, even if it is only saying a daily prayer for the Holy Redemption of their souls. We, as the Holy Chosen Ones of Lord Jehosa, must continue to perform our Holy Duty to these unfortunate mutants of the north. We are the Holy Chosen Ones, for has not Lord Jehosa spared us from this plague?

As your Holy Pope, I will do all that is in my power to help these pathetic mutants turn their lives around before it is too late. All that I ask and all that Lord Jehosa asks of you is to do your part.

Pope Pius I

By year end, he had replaced all the cardinals who had become mutants, with new volunteers. Replacing the many priests took much longer. Those mutant cardinals who returned to Constanza City were quietly put out of their misery by the Supreme Prelate. That their cardinals, priests, and nuns of the north had become mutants as well was kept secret from the public.

Chapter 25 Demokritos Deals

The Le Envoy, the private caravel of the West Po's, finally pulled into the docks of Patri, Kingdom of Thrace, Demokritos on August 25, having made very good time. "Damn, it's summer and it is freezing!" exclaimed the twenty year old Flavio West Po, a cousin of Stefano's.

"Hey, the seasons are backwards down here, Flavio," Fino Rello teased the young lad. Fino was thirty and a skilled negotiator that Stefano sent along with Flavio to help ensure that somehow they could get massive grain shipments from the Emperor of Demokritos. He also spoke the Demokritos language and taught Flavio on the voyage down from Velona. "Hey, Patri is a quaint looking port. Things look strange here. Look at all the white marble columns everywhere." Neither had ever been here before.

"First thing, we get some warm clothes," Flavio added, shivering beneath the blanket that he had wrapped around himself so that he could stand being on deck to watch the docking.

An hour later, they entered a tailor's shop. After explaining that they were on their way to meet with the Emperor, the man knew just what they needed. Two hours later, the two men walked out dressed in matching black suits, with white silk shirts, cummerbunds, and twin tails. They also wore an elegant but warm cloak with a paca lining and hood that could be pulled up over their heads if the weather got too cold. Their shoes were highly polished and black. Moreover, each now carried a mandatory mahogany walking stick. Their finances were three hundred gold less, a small price to pay for a good first impression.

They had expected to travel by coach from the port of Patri to the capital of Thrace, Axos, and then on to Kefall and the Emperor's palace. The tailor gave them a pleasant surprise by telling them that there was now a stream train that ran from Patri to Kefall.

A half hour later, the two boarded the Emperor's Express, a four-car passenger train that made round trips to and from Kefall. Their conductor was very eager to chat with them, as the train began its chug-chug. They learned that ten years ago the Emperor bought the rights from Velona's DAE Enterprises to manufacture their own steam trains. Now, there were five engines in the country. This one made the passenger run to and from Kefall. The other four hauled freight cars.

"You are very lucky men to have just caught the Emperor's Express. It takes twenty-four hours to make the four hundred fifty mile journey. Had you missed us, you would have had to wait two days for us to return. When we stop in Axos, you will have a chance to get off and grab a quick supper at the station there. We arrive in Kefall at one in the afternoon tomorrow. We will make a number of short stops for more coal and water. At those stops, I encourage you to step off and relieve yourselves." Both men grinned, glad that they didn't have to try to hold it so long.

"Maybe someday they will have restrooms on here," Flavio jested.

"And beds to sleep in and food service too," Fino added. "We ought to suggest such to Giovanni when we get back."

Around three the next afternoon, they arrived in Kefall, delayed by a minor breakdown. Since it was too late in the day to see the Emperor, they took a room at an inn within walking distance of the palace. At least they got their first look at this impressive combination fortress and palace. At the inn, the men learned that the Emperor and Empress took visitors and petitioners during the afternoons.

Promptly at one, the two men, dressed in their fine new clothes walked through the palace gates, where a guard met them. "We wish to speak with the Emperor, please," Fino explained to the guard. The man was rather bored and said little, but he led them deep into the palace courtyard and then up to a well-dressed doorman.

"Audience with the Emperor," the guard said. The doorman bowed politely and opened the extremely wide doors for them.

As they stepped inside and onto a fine red carpet, the doorman indicated that he was staying outside. "I'm the Empress' doorman. This is my post. You go down the hall and take the first door on your right. That will be the waiting room. Someone will come and get you when it is your turn," he said politely.

As they walked the short distance, Fino whispered, "Remember, the Empress is a Holy Woman of the Eighth Degree. She has to have someone around to open the doors for her." Flavio nodded, he had forgotten about her. Another perfectly well dressed doorman stood beside their door and opened it for them as they approached. Again, the doors were about fourteen feet wide and Flavio began to wonder why their doors were so wide.

"I will get you when the Emperor is available. You are the first this afternoon. It should not be a long wait," he said formally and shut the doors. The two men saw some thirty plush chairs lining the three walls. Over half of the chairs were extremely wide. They chose to sit on ones that seemed to fit them, normal chairs, as far as they were concerned. Both found the chairs very comfortable and guessed that they were quite expensive.

Some minutes later, the doorman opened the doors. "The Emperor will see you now. If you will follow the Announcer," he bowed and the two young men hopped up. "You may leave your coats here, if you like," he added.

As they stepped outside the waiting room, another man, also dressed as well as they, said, "I am the Announcer. As we enter the Royal Throne Room, I will announce your names and country of origin." They told him their names and followed him on down the hallway a short distance, where another doorman stood who proceeded to open yet another set of enormously wide doors. As the Announcer stepped in, two trumpeters blew a short fanfare and the man spoke loudly, "Fino Rello and Flavio West Po of Velona, Sea Princes." He then whispered to the two men. "Walk straight ahead and bow."

They did so, their eyes taking in the incredible splendor of this throne room. At least fifty oil lanterns provided the illumination. The whole floor was covered in an emerald green carpet. Against the far wall were sixteen thrones; the two in the center were raised higher than the other fourteen. Ahead, they saw three men, dressed as elegantly as they, and four women.

The Emperor and Empress were both sixty years old and sat on the taller thrones. The Emperor wore a diamond crown and allowed the two men an opportunity to glance around as they slowly walked the thirty feet up to his throne. The Empress wore an emerald green satin Annelise style dress. She had a huge green emerald around her neck and a pair of large emerald earrings. Her dress was at least sixteen feet across at the floor, which only accentuated her incredibly tiny waistline of fourteen inches. She sat stiffly, though, as if unable to bend much, Flavio thought. She had bare shoulders, which drew their attention to her missing arms. She was a Holy Woman of the Eighth Degree. While his hair was mostly grey, hers was still long and very blonde, though it had been fading the last few years.

Neither of the men had ever seen a Holy Woman of the Eighth Degree before, and they were more than a little surprised to see that all four women here were just that! All of their dresses had similar sixteen-foot Annelise hoops, and all four had nearly identical waist sizes of fourteen inches. All four proudly bared their armless shoulders to the world.

After bowing, the Emperor spoke. "Welcome Fino and Flavio of Velona. I am Emperor Karpos Omela, my lovely wife, Empress Roxane. To my right is my eldest son, Akios and his wife, the lovely Diona." He appeared to be around thirty-five, while she was perhaps four years younger. Her hair was brown and very wavy and full. His was blonde like his mother.

Emperor Karpos continued, after allowing the two men to bow to his son and daughter-in-law. "On my left are my youngest son, Alexio, and his lovely wife Io." Alexio had his father's looks and hair. Flavio suspected that he might be thirty-three while Io was barely thirty. She had very curly, long black hair. Again, they bowed respectfully to the pair.

"On my far left is my youngest, our unmarried Alexa." Flavio did a double take; Alexa was the most beautiful woman that he'd ever seen. She had pale blue eyes, rich, long, straight blonde hair that fell almost to her knees. Her bronze complexion was complimented by immaculately done makeup. She wore an enormous emerald necklace and a set of emerald earrings the likes of which Flavio had never seen. They dangled in what appeared to be tiers, five layers; the bottom five gems resting barely on her naked shoulders. Her smile was infectious, and he could not help but grin as he bowed low to her.

Introductions done, the Emperor Karpos asked, "How may we help you this afternoon?"

"Sire, it is a long story and a most desperate one. We have come to beg to purchase vast quantities of grain. May I begin at the beginning?" Fino asked. After a nod, he began to outline what had happened on Dorota. As he began, Karpos asked him to relay every detail that he could. Somewhat surprised, Fino did as asked, complete with the data that an alien had returned to Tarra and had blown up the island country. He described how the dust cloud had appeared and now its terrible consequences. He explained how the DAE Enterprises predicted that the crops would all fail in some nineteen countries. Tens of millions of people would starve unless substantial grain shipments and other dried vegetables, fruits, and meat could be secured and very soon.

He ended, "We are prepared to immediately transfer one million in gold to you and to negotiate absolutely anything else that you might prefer to acquire in lieu of gold, if gold is not desirable. Truly, the nineteen countries will be most desperate for food, probably by now, since it has taken us three months to get here."

Emperor Karpos grinned, "Anything? My, in all my life I never thought that Velona, of all countries, would be making me such an offer! Still, I am sure that we can make some arrangements. You realize that it is winter here. Spring comes later next month and with that, the spring planting season begins. I believe that we can make some arrangements satisfactory to us both. However, we already know about the destruction of Dorota. One of our caravels arrived only yesterday bringing us this most terrible news. A million people were killed or so the captain says. Such a tragedy. My sons and I wish to confer and discuss this news that you have brought us. Where are you staying? When we are ready, we can send for you?"

Fino told him about the inn. Just then, Alexa spoke up, "Father, why don't we have our esteemed guests from Velona stay in our palace guest quarters? That way they will be right here when you need them. I'm sure that your men will have lots more questions for them."

He smiled. "You are right, dear. Gentlemen, please accept the hospitality of my palace. The Announcer will show you to your quarters. You will dine with us at six." The two bowed.

"Father, why don't I show Flavio here around the palace?" Alexa asked. Her father smiled and agreed. While Fino followed the Announcer out, the others rose. He watched as the men stood before their wives and held their hands out to the women's sides, gently helping them rise.

Alexa whispered, "That's how it's done. I need a little help rising in this dress." Flavio reached out and found his hands partly encircling her tiny waist. She smiled as he gently lifted while she got to her feet. By now, the others were heading out of the door, leaving the two alone. Flavio was uncertain what needed to be done, if anything.

"Now you put your right hand around my waist, but please, beneath my hair so you don't pull on it. Yes, like that. I need your support as we walk. It's these tall Annelise heels, you see. We take very small steps and glide across the floor," she explained.

"Thanks for the tips, Alexa. I've never been around a Holy Woman before. We do have some in Velona; it's just that I've never met one. You are an incredibly beautiful young woman. I am surprised that some lad has not scooped you off of your feet before now."

"Thanks, I try to look my best, though I am very particular. Way too particular my dad says, but mom thinks I am doing just fine," Alexa chatted as they finally reached the door, which the doorman held wide open for the pair. Now Flavio saw why all the doorways were so wide; it allowed the women in their extremely wide hoop skirts to pass through them more easily.

"Those are some earrings, you have, Alexa. Incredible as the woman who is wearing them," he said what his pounding heart felt.

She smiled, "Yes, I had them specially made for me so that I can bend my head and touch and feel my shoulders. Let's go this way, and I'll show you the Royal Dance Hall first. Do you like to dance?"

"Love it! You see in Velona, we have the symphony concerts on Friday nights. Regal affairs — you would wear what you are now wearing to those. Then, on Saturday nights and Sunday afternoons, you have your choice of formal dancing, where again we both would be wearing what we now have on, and popular dancing, which is far less formal. I try to alternate each day from one to the other. I can't make up my mind, which I like the most. I can say that we all have far more fun and laughter at the popular dances. I think that you might like those, if you like good old plain fun, that is. Yet, if you prefer slow waltzes, those are common at the formal dancing halls. We have around ten of each type of hall in Velona; dancing is very common among the young and old alike."

"Oh, both sound delightful. And so many to choose from and two days even. You take your wife there often then?" Alexa asked coyly.

"Oh no. I am not married, Alexa."

"I'm sorry. I just assumed that a handsome man like you would be. You take your girlfriend then," she added.

"Okay, okay, Alexa. You have me. No, I don't have a steady girlfriend either. I take some of my cousins, and sometimes I just go and meet anyone that's there who is available for a dance or two. I guess that you can call me particular too," Flavio admitted, feeling a bit embarrassed to have to admit such to a very beautiful young woman.

"Here we are," Alexa said as the doorman quickly opened the huge ballroom doors. "A thousand can dance at one time in here. The band is up on that low balcony over there. Refreshments are served from those tables against the far wall."

"Wow, this is a spectacular dance hall."

"We are having a winter ball on Friday night. Would you care to take me to it, Flavio?" she asked.

"Alexa, I would be delighted to take you. Er, only I don't know what all would be expected of me, I mean escorting a woman such as yourself."

"Don't be silly, I'll tell you what you need to do. Then it's settled. I'll send a Fetcher to bring you to my quarters when I am ready to go."

"What's a Fetcher?" Flavio asked.

"Oh, sorry. When I need something, I use some of my servants who are called Fetchers. I tell them what I need, and they go and fetch it for me, you in this case. It's a century-old tradition around here. It gives many poorer women well paid employment, and it helps us Holy Women with tasks that we cannot do for ourselves, obviously," Alexa explained.

"That makes sense. Say, how long have you been a Holy Woman, if it is not impolite for me to ask, Alexa?"

She giggled, "Ever since I was born, really. Mom and dad insisted that all of their daughters be given this highest of honors in our country. That way, according to them, we stand the greatest opportunities for success in life. You didn't get to meet my older sister, Airla; she's thirty now. She married a handsome and very successful nobleman. I think she's now very rich indeed."

"I hope that money has made her happy. I'm not much interested in making a lot of money. Yes, as a West Po, I have inherited probably more than I can ever spend, but Alexa, there is so much more to life than making and having money. At least that's the way I feel — probably why I am so picky about women. So many are looking at how much money I have — as a West Po, that is."

"Interesting man you are, Flavio. So what does interest you if it isn't money?" Alexa asked, once more rather coyly.

"Fun and traveling to all sorts of exotic, exciting places. Seeing the wonders of the world. I guess that I just like to play and have fun too much. That's why Stefano, he's our monarch and ruler, sent me on this trip. He knew that I'd love to see the sights. I was really taken with how quaint and pretty your port of Patri is. All those white marble pillars and red tile roofs — really quite pretty."

She smiled, "You should wait and see it in the spring and summer, when the flowers are in bloom. Ah, here is the dining hall where we will be dining tonight. I sit over there on the far right. I would be honored if you would sit beside me and assist me with my diner, Flavio."

"Sure, that'd be great. Er, wait. I have no idea what you are asking me by 'assisting.' Sorry that I am so ignorant of you Holy Women."

She giggled. "Oh don't worry. All you have to do is hold up my cup so that I can drink, and use a fork and spoon to feed me. Surely you can use a fork and spoon," she jested, but watched his reaction carefully.

"Oh, what's spoon? Is a fork a thing that you use to sip your soup?" he teased her, watching her smile appear. "Sure I can do that. Only I am not sure about your manners and customs in Demokritos, let alone anything that is special for you. I won't embarrass you if I don't do something quite right?"

"Of course not, Flavio. Then that's settled. You sit beside me tonight. I will arrange it."

"Okay, it was at six?" he said pulling out his gold pocket watch that Arsenio had invented. He checked the time. "Three hours."

"What's that?" she asked. Flavio explained about the watch — how it kept time so that he always knew what time it was.

"I hate to be late for things. I am always nearly the first to arrive at the symphonies and dances."

"That is a marvelous invention. I am going to tell dad about it. I'm sure that he will like to see it. Ah, here is a small waiting room." The doorman immediately opened the door for her. "Thanks. In here, please, Flavio." They stepped inside a small room perhaps twenty feet square. It had a wide chair, which Flavio now realized was made for these women and their wide dresses. She headed for the chair and he helped her sit down.

"Ah, that's better. My feet get a bit sore with all that walking. Would you be so kind as to remove my shoes and massage my feet a little? After a little rest, we'll continue with the tour. Actually, Flavio, we could spend days touring this whole palace. It's huge, but then perhaps not if I could walk faster."

"My, these are high heels. Annelise oxfords, right? Many of our women wear them. That's why I was used to walking at your speed. How's this?" He began to massage her feet. From her moans, he knew that he was hitting the right spots. She wore thin black silk hose, very expensive and imported from Tashien. After a few minutes, he put her shoes back on and made sure they were properly tied.

They continued their tour for another hour before she explained that they had arrived at his guest quarters. "Should I walk you back to wherever you are heading?" he asked, realizing that she was going to be walking alone.

"No, I have a Fetcher nearby. She will assist me now. I need to get my hair brushed out before dinner. See you in an hour. Bye, Flavio."

He went inside and found Fino lying on a very fancy bed. "I see you kept the princess happy. Knock out blonde."

"Yes, got a nice tour of a bit of the palace. Any news?"

"Nope, just lying here in total luxury. I think that the contents of this room would probably fetch five grand back home. Incredible. Gold wash basins and golden chamber pots. Unreal. Your bed is over there. I warn you, once you lie down, you won't want to rise!"

In her private quarters, Alexa sat on her bench while Selene brushed out her long blonde tresses as she did every afternoon about this time before dinner. Alexa's heart was pounding as she reflected upon her life.

Her fondest memories were when she was five years old. In these very halls where she just walked, she saw her father, mother, and sister Airla. They were in their nightgowns, but Airla and her mother still wore their tight corsets and tall heels. They were laughing and playing kick the bag. Then, came hide and seek. She smiled. To make it fair, her mother kept saying that dad had to wear tall heels too. Such fun and laughter, every night. She never wanted it to end, but then when Airla was eighteen, she stopped coming to play their nighttime games.

Alexa sighed. Now she was ten. She remembered her mother explaining that she was now allowed to wear a corset and heels just like her. "You must start training your waist, for then it will be so much easier for you as you grow up. We must have fourteen-inch waists if we are to be perfect. From now on, you must always wear these heels too. That way, you will be smooth and graceful when you become a young lady." Alexa hated both at first. No longer could she run and play; she fainted frequently at first, over doing it and unable to breathe. Yet, they still played their games, and she still treasured these times at night, never wanting them to stop.

Stop they did, when she was fourteen. "You are a young lady now, Alexa," her mother said. "Time for you to find yourself a loving, kind husband." She longed for the games, but was not allowed out in the hall, though she still heard the laughter of her father and mother late at night, when they thought that she was asleep. For a time, she felt that her parents were rejecting her. That also passed, as her father now allowed her to sit on a throne and listen to all the visitors who came to see him.

During the last six years, she had learned a great deal, far more than she had expected. All of it centered on this magical place called Velona, somewhere in the far north. All manner of incredible inventions poured out of this place. She tried to imagine what kind of people they could be to be so imaginative. Her first train ride down to Patri and back convinced her that she just had to go visit Velona and ride the trains there. A visitor told the Emperor that the train lines covered such a vast territory. The man even showed her and her father all the lines on a big map, impressing her even more.

Then came the marvelous long distance communications systems, which were still being installed all over Demokritos. That one could communicate nearly instantly to anywhere in their entire seven kingdoms was incredible, even more incredible was that someone in Velona dreamed it up and made it work.

Last year, some traveling musicians came to the palace and performed what was called a symphony, written by a woman who had moved there from Demokritos. She had married a wonderful man from Velona and moved back there with him. She too had been a Holy Woman like herself. It was not that she found the music so moving, rather it was that the composer of this symphony had been just like her. Alexa swore that somehow, some way, she too would find a man from Velona who would take her there with him. That's why she had been rejecting all suitors that her father had sent her way. Now after six years of trying, her father had given up all hope of finding a husband that suited her.

Today, as she listened to the two men from Velona. They were ready to do anything to obtain large food shipments over the next many months, absolutely anything. A plan formed in her mind. She began its first step by having Flavio accompany her under the guise of showing him around the palace. True, she had done just that, but she had used the occasion wisely. More than that, she detected in him that same spirit of play that she so treasured from her childhood. Could this be the one chance that she would ever have? That's why her heart was pounding so, as Selene carefully brushed out her very long, blonde hair, arranging it perfectly across her shoulders and back.

"There you go, my little princess," Selene said, finally laying the hairbrush down. "See how pretty you look?" The two gazed at her reflection in the mirror.

"How's my makeup, Selene? Is it okay, perhaps my lips need a retouch, do you think?" Selene grinned and touched up her lipstick. "Now, it's off to your room; supper will be called shortly," Selene said. Alexa rose and her Fetcher assisted her back to her private sitting room. Once seated properly and her dress adjusted, she sent the Fetcher off to bring Flavio to her.

"Hi again, Flavio. I do hope that you are hungry," Alexa said charmingly as her Fetcher brought to her and quietly left them. "Assist me to my feet, please." She really didn't need any such assistance; she just wanted to feel his strong hands around her waist and be rather close to him.

"Ah, there you go," he said and slid his arm around her waist once more, providing support for her, but being careful not to disturb her long tresses.

As they walked slowly towards the Royal Dining Hall, Flavio said, "I have to admit, Alexa, you are the prettiest young woman that I have ever had the pleasure of dining with!" She grinned; so far so good, she thought, but would he be able to handle feeding her? Ah, now that was a question to ask. She'd heard all manner of stories about how badly men were at such. So few of them ever assisted their Holy Woman at the table. No, servants usually did so. Not her father, though, he was an expert at it. This she'd known since childhood.

As they entered, Flavio saw that five children were now with their parents. Although Alexa pointed them out, he was more worried about making sure he got her properly seated and such. A bit later, he noticed that each of her brothers had a teenaged son. One was perhaps sixteen and the other thirteen at best. Both were dressed in suits as their fathers. Akios had two teenaged daughters; one looked to be a year younger than her brother was, and the other was perhaps two years younger. Both were Holy Woman and both wore the constricting corsets and billowing dresses, only slightly smaller in diameter. Her younger brother also had a younger daughter, perhaps twelve at most. She too was a Holy Woman dressed similarly to the others. Flavio now saw that in this royal family, all the women were expected to be Holy Women of the Eighth Degree.

Fino was seated close to Emperor Karpos, on his right, while Empress Roxane sat on his left. He also noticed a number of servant women taking seats beside the two younger wives and their daughters. Five of them to be exact. Flavio carefully got Alexa seated and then took his seat on her right. They were off to the far left once more, and he got the impression that they chose this order deliberately once again, probably reflecting the importance her brothers had to the throne, she being the least important one.

Next, a band of six musicians entered and struck up some quiet background music and the feast began. Alexa kindly told him what she desired on her plate and he served her and then himself. From the corner of his eye, he noticed that Karpos was doing much the same for Roxane. "You are eating like a bird," he teased her, noticing that his plate held twice as much as hers.

"You would too if you wore such a corset as I do. I will be fine. Bite of the roast first, please," she said daintily. He complied and soon they were chatting and eating, in a very relaxed manner. He had no qualms about assisting her; of this, she was very much aware. For his part, Flavio saw that Karpos was also assisting Roxane, while chatting with Fino. On the other hand, the five servant women fed the two wives and their daughters. Evidently, her brothers didn't like to do this. He wondered why that was, but dare not ask her, figuring such would be a private matter.

Finally, sipping a red after-dinner wine to wash away the grease from the meal, she said coyly, "Flavio, you handled that expertly. Are you sure that you've never done this before?"

"Nope, never. Sorry. Glad I didn't embarrass you."

"Not at all. My brothers are an embarrassment. My father always assists mom. I think that is the way it ought to be, don't you?"

"Of course. Why wouldn't a man assist his wife with absolutely anything that she might need? I wasn't going to say anything about it, but yes, I think they're being a bit rude to their wives by not assisting them or their daughters, for that matter."

"So do I. Do you know my brothers don't even play in the halls with their daughters? When I was a little girl, both my mother and father played games with me every night. I think parents ought to do that," she tossed out a hook to see what she might reel in.

Flavio chuckled. "You bet they should. In Velona, we always treat our children well. My dad always played with us kids — girls just as much. We used to play hide and seek when I was very little. I once got stuck in a commode and couldn't get out. I was scared then, but now I think it was rather funny."

She giggled. "We did too — play hide and seek around the palace at night. Did you ever play kick the bag?" He had her describe it briefly to make sure that he understood.

Grinning, he replied, "Oh yes, we call it kick the beanbag back home. I hate to admit it, but I played it up until I was sixteen. Stopped then because no one else wanted to play it anymore, claiming they were too grown up. Ah well. Say, did you ever play dodge ball. You don't need arms for that, just kicking." She hadn't and had him tell her about it.

When he finished, he looked up and noticed that the others had left the room. "Oh, don't worry; it is everyone's private times now until morning. If I know mom and dad, they are off doing something together in their quarters. My brothers are with their families, though I don't really know what they do together. I think that a Fetcher took your partner off for a tour of the palace. Would you care to accompany me back to my drawing room and light a fire for me? We could sit and chat a bit, if you like."

"Sure, doesn't look like I have anything to do until the morning. Allow me," he leaned close to her and assisted her to rise once more. Some ten minutes later, the doorman opened the wide doors to her sitting room. Flavio set the fire and joined her on her small two-person couch before the crackling fire.

"Tell me about Velona. What's it like there? Are there a lot of West Po's?" The two began to chat. Flavio was more than happy to talk about Velona. At least, he knew what to say. He was afraid that he would have to ask rather dumb questions about Demokritos, of which he knew very little at all, only barely able to speak their language basics.

The fire had turned to embers, when Flavio suddenly realized that it was getting late. He looked at his watch. "Oh my goodness, Alexa. I didn't realize it was getting so late. It's ten o'clock, way past bed times, I'll bet!"

"Don't fret. I loved every minute of it. Can you find your way back by yourself now?" He could and her Fetcher entered and helped her into her private bedroom, where a servant was ready to help her change into her nightgown.

The next day, Emperor Karpos sent for the two. "Good news, men. I believe that we may be able to help our Velona friends. Of course, this is going to take some time, as it is still winter. Can you both stay for some weeks to help us plan how to best fill your needs?"

"Thank you Emperor Karpos. Yes, we are at your service. We can stay as long as we are needed. However, Flavio and I ought to visit a tailor's shop and purchase additional clothing. We were not prepared for winter. It's summer back home," Fino replied. That agreed, the two headed off to find the recommended tailor shop.

"I think that his youngest daughter has her eyes on you, old boy," Fino said when they were alone.

"She is a gorgeous woman. I figure that if she likes me, then that might help sway her father if we need it. We must not fail in our mission. She is charming too." Fino grinned.

For several days, the two met with the Emperor's advisors working out the details of exactly what was needed and how best to provide it. For example, apples could make the long journey and still have enough shelf life to make it worthwhile. Pears and peaches could not; these would have to be dried before shipping. So it went. However, each evening they continued to dine with the Emperor and his family. Fino got a work out telling Karpos about all the latest inventions and marvels of Velona. Flavio now became Alexa's constant dinner companion, assisting her at each dinner. Afterwards, they continued to return to her sitting room and sat before a crackling fire chatting for hours.

The dance went very well, Flavio thought, although he was not familiar with many of their dance steps. He followed Alexa's lead and tried not to look too clumsy at it. She was a most graceful dancer and he told her so. When they finally played a three beat song that he could waltz to, he then taught her how the waltz was done in Velona.

The next evening when they sat beside the fire in her sitting room chatting, she decided to take a chance with Flavio. That he had not resisted the slightest bit in accepting her control at the dance made a solid impression in her mind. So many of the men that her father had attempted to foist off on her simply would not accept a woman controlling anything. Yet, Flavio thought nothing of it. Right then, she decided to take a chance, though she didn't get up her nerve to do so until this next evening.

While Flavio was relaxing at her side, his arm over the top of the couch, she leaned over and gave him a passionate kiss. At first surprised by her sudden action, he willingly slid his arms around her and returned her kiss. When their lips finally parted, he whispered, "Wow. I do like you too."

At last, Alexa knew that this was indeed her first real chance. "Flavio, soon something is going to happen with us. I want you to really, really go along with me on this. You have no idea how very, very important this will be for me. Later on, I promise you that I will explain everything to you. Then, if you decide that you don't want to continue, I will understand and not hold it against you. But please, if you like me even a little bit, please, please go along with me on this."

"Sure, Alexa, but I don't want anything to interfere with our obtaining food supplies for Velona and the other countries. If it doesn't harm that, sure I'll go along with you. But what is it that you want of me?"

"It is best that you do not know just yet. I have some things that I must first work out. Believe me, when it happens, you will know. Please, when it does happen, please play along with me on it, I beg you." She was so earnest, so sincere that he could not refuse. Besides, he liked this gorgeous young woman. She had an awful lot of spunk in her. He agreed.

The next evening after their meal, Flavio was surprised that Alexa left with her parents. No matter, he headed back to his room with Fino. They had many figures to go over. The cost of such quantities of food supplies was increasing by the day. Stefano had given them pretty much free rein to make what deals they could, but there were limits to how much gold they could realistically spend down here.

Alexa followed her parents into their private sitting room, taking seat beside her mother and facing her father. "Okay, my dear little girl, what do you want to talk to us about this evening?" he asked with a wry smile on his face. He had a notion but dare not mention it.

"Dad, I know how hard you have tried to find the right husband for me for six years now."

"Yes, dear, you are awfully picky, I'll give you that."

"Well, I have found him, but I am going to need your help in netting him."

"What? You have?" Roxane perked up. Wonders of wonders! Her daughter was finally interested in finding a husband. She was nearly sixty-one now and worried that she would never live to see her youngest daughter marry.

"You know that I will do all that I can to help you. What do you need? A little friendly persuasion from the Emperor?" he teased her.

"Yes, that's it exactly. I am madly in love with Flavio from Velona. He is the right man for me; I just know it. Mom, like you knew that dad was the one for you. He likes me too; he said so last night. Of course, I would be moving to Velona with him, but just think of all the things that I could send back to you. I could be your eyes and ears in the country of inventions!" Oh, how she played her father, knowing how much, how eager he was to gain more knowledge of the latest inventions and how he might acquire such for Demokritos. His greatest coup had been acquiring the steam train technology! Yet there was so much more there in Velona.

She went on, "You remember what they said the first day we met? They said that they would do *anything* you asked to get food supplies for Velona. Daddy, for me, could you please insist that Flavio marry me and take me back to Velona as part of the trade deal? I know that he really does like me, but this will ensure that he will. I do love him, and I am sure that he will love me back. He is kind and is always assisting me at dinner, not like Akios and Alexio. He is perfect for me. Please, daddy?" she poured on all the charm that she could muster.

"Honey, you won't mind being in a strange country so far from home?"

"No, daddy. There are Holy Women in Velona too. I'm sure that I can meet with them and they can assist me too. Please."

He looked at Roxane and then replied. "Darling, we both love you so. Yes, I will do as you ask, but on one condition."

"What's that?" she asked, holding her breath.

"You must write us a letter every month. Tell us all that you can about how you are doing and what you can learn of their marvelous technologies. Will you promise me that you will do this?"

"I promise daddy. I'll send you a letter every month! Thank you!" She got up, leaned into him, and gave him a kiss, as his arms went around her and held her tight. Then she leaned into her mother, and they pressed the sides of their heads together. She then left them alone, heading back to her room, scarcely able to breathe. Her dream was about to come true; she dared hope so now.

"Well, what do you know, our littlest angel has finally found someone," Karpos exclaimed.

"I am so surprised, but he seems like a nice fellow. Have you noticed that he assists her with supper? In fact, every dinner so far, quite unlike our sons. He reminds me a little of you, dear. I do know that she has been fascinated by this Velona place. I suppose that having her in Velona would be a good thing for our country," Roxane replied.

"Yes, if it makes her happy, I am for it; besides, it will help our country to have her there."

The next morning, Fino and Flavio were summoned to the Emperor. Neither had expected to meet with him this morning, only his aides. Both were a little surprised to see only the Emperor, Empress, and Alexa present when they were led into the throne room.

"Good morning, gentlemen. I have reached a final decision about your request for food supplies. As you and my advisors have suggested, we should break this into two portions. Since it is a three month voyage and you have already been gone some three months, we will have four caravels ready to sail in five days. That may help hold starvation at bay. During the next two months, fifty-six more caravels will set sail with the balance, scattered over time. It will take a month to get word to some of the more outlying kingdoms. Beginning in September, the second wave will begin, spread out over three months, bringing a total of one hundred twenty more caravels of grains, vegetables, fruits, and dried meats."

"Thank you, Emperor Karpos, you will be saving thousands if not millions of lives," Fino replied, very much relieved to have been able to obtain a rather large amount of food supplies on such short notice. Payment would be the sticky point — he knew and braced himself for the amount.

"Now then, for the cost of doing business, my price is a little unusual. I know that my aides were talking three to four million gold all told. I find that a bit much, especially between friends and allies in a life-threatening situation. I will propose another deal, unless you really wish to fork over four million."

"Please, we are all ears," Fino jested, wondering what he would have to sacrifice and if Stefano would agree to such a demand.

"One million gold will barely cover the costs of packaging and shipping of such a vast amount. I will agree to this exceedingly low amount under one condition: that Flavio marries my daughter Alexa. Of course, she expects to return to Velona with him. I believe that such a union will bond our two countries closer together. Flavio is a cousin of your monarch and Alexa is my daughter, so our ties will be closer. Besides, Alexa is used to getting her way." Alexa held her breath; this was the moment that she hoped Flavio would recognize and hold to his promise to her.

Fino didn't quite know how to respond to this highly unusual request. His thoughts had been on having to give away the new radio technology or more, but an arranged marriage? He looked at Flavio, who broke into a smile.

Flavio realized now what Alexa was wanting. This was the moment that she'd begged him to support her action. He replied, "Emperor Karpos, I am overwhelmed with your generosity and most honored indeed. Before I can answer, it is the custom in our country to first ask for a woman's hand in marriage — okay," he grinned widely, hoping his gesture would not be misconstrued, "in this case, a woman's foot in marriage. With your permission, I would first like to ask Alexa." The Emperor chuckled at his humor; he liked this man's style.

Before anyone could change their minds, Flavio went over to Alexa, got down on one knee, and asked her, "Alexa, will you marry me?"

"Yes, of course I will!" she burst out, hoping that she wouldn't faint. Just now, her corset felt like it was cutting her into halves.

"Okay, Emperor, Empress, I will be high honored to marry your daughter. I have been smitten by Alexa since we first met. She is witty, bright, charming, intelligent, and fun just to be around. I give you my sworn word to always treat her with nothing but the highest respect and honor."

"Very well then. Shall we shake on our bargain then?" The three men shook hands. Fino could scarcely believe what had happened: vast food supplies for barely shipping and packaging costs and one marriage.

Emperor Karpos added sternly, "Son, if I ever hear that you have mistreated my young daughter here, I will go to war with you. You treat her as promised; she is a Holy Woman and deserves nothing but the very best."

"Sir, if I ever mistreat her, I deserve all that you can throw at me and then some. She is an angel," Flavio tossed out, hoping that he was not overdoing his part.

"Now then, I believe that Flavio and Alexa will want to accompany these first four caravels back to Velona and announce our deal, bringing hope to the millions of starving people. However, Fino, it would be wise if you could stay a little longer to help iron out any minor problems that may arise, unless you feel you need to also return at this moment."

"Glad to stick around, Emperor Karpos. I think that is a very wise decision. Flavio can take our caravel back to Velona. I can hitch a ride on one of the others bringing supplies later on when there is nothing else needed of me here. Again, on behalf of Velona and all the other eighteen countries, we thank you for you incredible generosity in our most desperate hour of need."

"Good, good. Then, we have a wedding to prepare and on short notice, but such matters are best left to my beloved Roxane. Dear, if you will accompany our young couple and work your magic for the fourth and final time, I would be most grateful. You know that I am all thumbs in such matters," he teased his wife, who grinned. Flavio guessed that Roxane had handled the arrangements for their two sons and older daughter. While the Emperor helped Roxane rise, Flavio took this hint and put his arms around Alexa's waist, helping her rise as well.

Fifteen minutes later, Flavio found himself in Roxane's private quarters for the first time. The elegance and splendor of her quarters dwarfed that of her daughter's. "Now then, the caravel sails in five days, so we don't have a lot of time to prepare, Alexa," Roxane began.

"Mom, we should keep this a simple wedding, perhaps have the Cardinal marry us here at the palace, with just our families present. I'm going to need to pack as well," Alexa suggested, still struggling to catch her breath, but trying hard not to show it.

"Yes, that seems appropriate and easier to handle. Now then, I will have the dressmaker here this afternoon to get your gown made. We should have a tailor come and deal with Flavio as well," Roxane began planning.

"Excuse me. I'm not familiar with your wedding customs here. Back home, it is customary for the bride and groom to exchange wedding rings during the ceremony. Is that done here? If so, I must fulfill my obligations," Flavio asked, feeling a bit rushed and on unfamiliar ground.

Alexa giggled, "I have no fingers on which to wear a ring, silly. Holy Women exchange wedding triangles. Mom, show him yours, will you?" Roxane leaned forward. "See on her neck." He saw a small pair of golden interlocked triangles on a thin gold chain around her neck. Until now, it had been totally dwarfed by the enormous emerald necklace that she wore. "You see, the triangles represent us, one for each of us. They are interlocked, showing that we are bonded, joined together, married. Get it?"

He grinned, "Okay, I see it, that's really a good symbol, full of real meaning. Say, do we need to go to a jeweler to pick out ones that we like?" he asked.

"No silly, they are all the same. We can just order us a pair."

"What about wedding presents?" he asked, relieved that the triangles would be easy.

"Oh you don't have to worry about that either. We'll probably get some things from my family, but not to worry. You just have to dress properly for the ceremony," Alexa was making this as easy for him as possible. They chatted over a few more details and set the date for the afternoon before the day the caravels would set sail. Roxane then shooed the two out of her room, while she set to work making the arrangements.

A few minutes later, the two entered her private sitting room, alone at last. After getting her seated, Alexa began, "Flavio, I don't know how to thank you for going along with this. I promise that if you want out of this, we can get it annulled in Velona at the Church of Jehosanity. I will make up some plausible reason for the cardinal there. This means so very much to me, to get to Velona."

"You'll do no such thing. As I said, Alexa, I'm smitten with you." He kissed her passionately and she returned his passion as well.

A bit later, she said, "The only real problem is how many of my servants I ought to bring along with us."

"Darn, I forgot about that aspect of your life, Alexa. You know, it seems almost criminal to force these young women to abandon their lives here and move thousands of miles away to a foreign land, where they don't even speak the language."

"I see what you mean, but how will I manage?"

"Well, you have me. Honestly, there is nothing to do but sit around for three months as we sail to Velona. Once there, I am sure that we can find proper servants to help you. After all, there are Holy Women in Velona and they must have the right kind of help as well. We ought to be able to find plenty of assistants for you there."

"But Flavio, are you sure that you want to be this involved with me? I mean you would have to dress me, brush out my hair, and even handle my private, personal needs. Diona and Io say that their husbands never do these things for them."

"Well, I admit, Alexa, I haven't the faintest clue about women's dresses or how you do your hair, but I sure can learn, if you are willing to instruct me. I will feel very bad taking a young woman away from her home just to handle things for you that I should be doing. After all, I am about to be your husband."

"I feel badly about that too. Okay then, but you must realize my position, Flavio. If I don't bring along any servants, then I am utterly dependent upon your assistance with everything."

He smiled, "You will be in good hands." She smiled and consented, hoping that she would not regret this. Without even one servant around, she felt more than a little intimidated. Never before in her life had she been without even one around to help her when she needed something. She decided to take a gamble on Flavio, though she knew that her father would object and take some convincing.

Four days later, Flavio, dressed in an immaculate white suit with a black tie, walked into the throne room, accompanied by a musical fanfare. Cardinal Heli, a sixty year old man, stood before the Emperor and Empress, who sat on their thrones. In his scarlet robes with real gold trim, he caught Flavio's eyes first. Besides her older brothers, their wives, and five children, Alexa's older sister, Airla and her husband, son, daughter were also seated on the thrones, the children standing beside their parents. All wore their finest suits and dresses. He walked up and stood before the cardinal.

Now the music began playing the tradition music of the bride. In glided Alexa, radiant in her white silk gown. It was strapless and her hoop skirt billowed out the usual sixteen feet. Her five tiers of emerald earrings that just touched her shoulders accented her carefully brushed out, long blonde hair. Likewise, the enormous emerald that hung around her neck and resting just above her dress caught one's attention. For an instant, Flavio did think that she was an angel!

Gracefully, she glided slowly up to him and stood beside the cardinal as well. At last, the Holy Matrimony ceremony began. Flavio was so nervous that he scarcely caught the words that the cardinal spoke. Towards the end, as he fastened one of the golden interlocked triangles on a gold chain around Flavio's neck, he said, "Accept these interlocked triangles as a symbol of your love and Holy Union with Alexa. As the triangles show, may you always be locked together in life. Be faithful unto her alone. Treat her always as you would yourself, for now she is of yourself." He said more, but again, Flavio was too nervous to pay close attention. The cardinal repeated similar words as he placed the second one around Alexa's neck. He then blessed both and to the sounds of more music, he proclaimed them officially married.

A feast and party followed, along with an evening of dancing. Flavio got the opportunity to dance with Airla, Io, and Diona as well as his new bride. Indeed, her sister and sisters-in-law all wanted to chat and dance with him. He realized that they anticipated that it would be a very long time before they saw her again, Velona being so far away.

Her parents gave her a present of a half million gold in a Banca del Dio account in her name only. They were still concerned that Alexa's hasty decision might not work out as she had planned and they wanted her to have something on which to fall back upon, if things didn't work out for their little angel. Her brothers and their families got her four new complete outfits, one of which was a maternity outfit just in case, and two sets of satin bed sheets.

Flavio received four large oil paintings, each a portrait of the respective families done last year. One was of Alexa alone, one was of her parents alone, and the other three showed her two brothers and sister and their large families.

However, Alexa was completely taken by surprise with her sister's gift. "I know how you love your tier earrings, so I am adding another layer for you." Her husband fastened another five emeralds making six layers. Now they draped upon her bare shoulders. Airla whispered in her sister's ear, "I know why you love them, sis. Enjoy and think of me often. Do write when you can."

Later that night, the new couple entered Alexa's private bedroom. Most all her things had been packed away. "Are you sure that you want to do this?" she asked timidly.

"Well, I am not about to wait around while someone gets you out of your wedding gown! Where do I start?" She giggled.

A bit later, she explained, "No, leave the corset on. I wear it all times, except when bathing, of course. Undo my emerald, but the earrings always stay on, even when I bathe. I haven't ever taken them off. I'll show you why in a bit," she said coyly, with a twinkle in her eye.

The next morning, while a servant got her dressed in her traveling blue dress, Flavio saw to her last minute packing. After a tearful breakfast and many farewells, a coach took the two to the train, along with thirty-six large chests, containing her many dresses and personal items. A long train ride later, they arrived at Patri, where several more hours passed while her many chests were transported and loaded onto the West Po caravel. Finally, in the late afternoon, Flavio, his arms around her waist, guided her up the gangplank and onto the Le Envoy. His arms around her to keep her on her feet on the gently rocking boat, the two watched Patri slowly shrink away from them. By the morning, the caravel would join the other four slower moving, heavily laden caravels bound for Velona.

Chapter 26 Demokritos Reactions

Starting in the middle of October, Demokritos caravels, arriving with their routine cargos, began to report on the devastating news of the alien ships and the massive, horrible plague sweeping across the Sea Princes and the Greenway. News came in bits and pieces, shocking everyone.

"What horrors have we sent our youngest daughter into?" wailed Emperor Karpos. Roxane was white with fear. Soon, his advisors pointed out that all their seamen were at risk of catching this plague and bringing it to Demokritos!

"My god! Are you saying that they could bring it back here and infect us all? Tens of millions of us? All our women? Armless as Holy Women? All of them?" Karpos yelled in anger, though he didn't realize he was shouting. Fino looked incredibly pale and felt sick, slumping onto the palace floor.

"Good god!" Fino exclaimed. "Sir, may I suggest a quarantine?" he ventured. Although he knew that the ongoing food shipments were vital, now perhaps even more so, the mere thought of infecting everyone here was too much to bear.

"Yes, that is the only possible answer! Quarantine. No more ships are to go anywhere near these countries until further notice! Any returning from these countries could be bringing the plague with them. We must somehow keep those seamen from bringing it ashore," Emperor Karpos ordered. Soon, his aides worked out preventative measures, with dozens of arriving caravels finding themselves now placed into quarantine, until their captains got clearance from the harbor masters, and only then after they provided proof that they had not been anywhere near the affected countries. Gunships ensured that the quarantine was strictly observed.

For two weeks, the Emperor continued to receive all manner of wild accounts of the plague and its effects. Now the Greenway was infected. A bit later, he learned that even the south of Tashien had been infected as well. For two weeks, panic spread throughout Demokritos, many fearing that they would be next. Some said that the end of the world was upon them. Soldiers were needed to keep order, as people flooded the markets, stockpiling literally anything they could find. Why one would need to stockpile a year's supply of lamp oil was beyond Karpos' logical mind.

Fearing that this breaking news might jeopardize their extremely critical food shipments from Demokritos, Stefano took preventative action. By September 1, he had sufficient proof that the alien bacteria were indeed now dead, that there was no further risk of anyone else contracting the plague, and knowing that we had killed the aliens responsible, he wrote out a very lengthy letter to the Emperor. Although he would not hear back from Flavio and Fino until December at the earliest, he could not risk jeopardizing any possible arrangements they had made. He hated how slow communication was, now being totally used to instant communications all the way to Shansee, Tashien.

He summoned his cousin Vittore, who handled shipping for Velona, his fifteen year old son Gasparo, and me to his office. "Bethany, this is Gasparo West Po, Vittore's eldest son. I've asked you here for a critical mission. By now, the Emperor and probably all of Demokritos have learned of the plague. While we have no way of knowing how successful Fino and Flavio have been in acquiring continuing food supplies from there, I have to assume that they have lined up something."

"Use your imaginations. When news of this disaster reaches them, especially considering it's being called a plague, what will be their reactions? If nothing else, I would expect them to end all shipments to us. We absolutely must have their food shipments. Demokritos is the only country on Tarra that has the potential to supply us with enough food to make it. So I have written a very extensive letter to the Emperor, outlining all the details, all of them, Bethany. I am giving young Gasparo the mission to get this letter to the Emperor. He can answer many questions that they may have down there."

"Of course, with his ears, Gasparo runs a real risk of not being allowed to meet with the Emperor. Fear of plague can run all manner of courses. Hence, Gasparo is given free rein to do whatever is necessary to get this letter into the hands of the Emperor. You may have to be very creative, son. Just get it to him somehow."

"Communications are extremely trying, Bethany. I would like to ask you if you can take time out each day and use your telepathy on Gasparo here to find out what is happening. He can let you know if he had major problems. Maybe there will be a way that we can help. I want you to keep him up to date on the changes that are occurring here. When he arrives, I want him to be fully briefed on our exact status here. He should get there around November 1."

"It may well be that the Emperor may need more convincing than my letter gives him. In that case, Gasparo can let you know, Bethany. I beg you to use your powerful skills somehow to help the young lad here out with the Emperor, though I have no idea what that might involve. I'm sending him down there in that new caravel that Vittore had reserved for Sergio to use to come and rescue you from the mantis prison. He ought to get there in just under ten or eleven weeks."

I didn't know Gasparo well. "Let me make contact with you now so that I can more easily do it with you later, Gasparo," I explained. A moment later, I had him found. *Hi. Now I can reach you no matter where you are.*

This is incredible! He sent back, very startled and very much awed. After a bit more discussion, Gasparo was off to the docks.

By October 20, Fino came up with a grand plan to somehow keep the supplies moving northward. "Emperor, why not change the caravel's destination to Megalos. Have them stop there and see if New Barq is still free of the plague. If it is still okay, have the caravel go on to New Barq and unload there. Our steam trains can get the food over to Velona in just a few days from New Barq. On the other hand, if the plague has gotten them, they could unload either in the Southlands or Megalos, and Velona caravels could then pick up the supplies from there."

"I believe you have something there, Fino. Yes, I fear that in spite of all our efforts, we are going to be too late and people will be starving. It is more than I could bear to see my lovely Roxane starving to death. She has had to endure so much as a Holy Woman. If she didn't even have enough food to eat, well, I just would be out of my mind over it. Yes, we'll attempt to use New Barq first. Southlands, if New Barq is infected. Megalos , if the Southlands is also infected. However, Fino, if Megalos is infected, then I just don't know what we can do. We would be watching the death of a third of our whole world!" Emperor Karpos said with a heavy, heavy heart.

Roxane, still pale with worry about her youngest daughter, asked, "What about poor Alexa? If all the women in Velona are as she, where will she ever get servants to help her? How will she ever be able to manage?"

"Mom," Akios, her eldest son spoke up for a change, "look, if all the women in Velona are as she, then who are they going to get to help them? There must be millions like sis now. I am sure that she will find a way. Flavio seems like an all right guy; he certainly didn't mind assisting her at dinner."

"Well, that's true; he did, but how unimaginably awful for all those other millions of women. Honestly, Akios, without my servant staff, I would be completely helpless and unable to do nearly anything," Roxane admitted what she very rarely ever acknowledged and then only in the privacy of her room and Karpos.

During September, I kept Gasparo updated on the ever-changing events. I told him that the rains had come and finally the sun appeared finally. Now we were doing a rapid replanting, in hopes of getting some produce harvested before the winter came. Then came the news that the very northern part of the three northern Greenway kingdoms had still managed a harvest. By mid-October, small amounts of grain and produce began coming into Velona. As expected, Stefano had it divided into portions for the eight Sea Prince sectors and sent those off by rail line. Even though it was small quantities, we relished our relatively fresh peas, carrots, and green beans. Gasparo was glad for the update, and he began to relax a little. When he left, he had envisioned everyone would be starving shortly, the supplies from New Barq and the Southlands were totally insufficient to support so many countries and so many people.

By the time that Gasparo docked in Patri on November 7, I was able to give him the most encouraging news yet. Based on our gardens and the amount of crops that were planted in the Greenway and the eight sectors, Stefano was able to estimate that if we could get a substantial input of Demokritos' fall harvest, which would come during our next spring and into summer, then that would do it. We could make it then until our own fall harvest occurred. We all found this a highly encouraging prediction, one that Stefano was finally elated to divulge. So much had been doom and gloom.

"Why are we stopping out here?" Gasparo asked the caravel's captain.

"See that gun ship? That's why; the port is flying a quarantine flag." He gave the orders to heave to and drop anchor, about a half mile from the docks. The gun ship came along side, but kept a good distance between ships. After the captains exchanged information, Gasparo decided to act.

"Sir, I have an urgent dispatch from Monarch Stefano West Po for Emperor Karpos Omela. How can it be delivered, sir? It is vital that the Emperor gets this immediately," he yelled to the gun ship captain.

I chose to hover over the ship as it came into Patri, just in case Gasparo needed some assistance. I suspected something like a quarantine would be in effect, I would have done so if I was the Emperor. After quite a lot of yelling back and forth, it was obvious that the gun ship captain was not amenable to any arrangement for getting the waterproof pouch transferred between ships. All this way and yet so far.

Gasparo. Tell him that you will throw the dispatch to him.

Bethany! Wow. Cool. Hey, I can't throw it that far.

Just give it a good toss and I'll take it from there.

Okay, here goes. He gave the dispatch bag a mighty heave. It probably would have gone perhaps a hundred feet, but far short of the other ship. As it fell towards the ocean, I picked it up with a beam, moved it over, and dropped it in the captain's hands. The man was shocked. "Damn, that kid sure has a throwing arm on him! Hey kid," he yelled, "I got it. I'll get it to the Emperor."

"Wow, some toss, Gasparo!" the ship's captain complimented him. He grinned. How could he explain that an unseen Bethany had really done it? Now came a long waiting game.

I decided to keep track of that pouch, ensuring that it made it to the Emperor's hands. It wasn't until around dusk that the gun ship finally headed into port. I stuck to the dispatch bag like glue. Chain of command played a role. He gave it to his boss, who gave it to the harbor master, who gave it to a general, who gave it to an aide, who gave it to a captain, who gave it to a soldier, who finally headed to the train station and sat down to wait for the train to Kefall. I overheard someone saying the next train would not be leaving until tomorrow morning. Ugh. I decided that I'd come back then.

The next day, I hung around and finally saw the dispatch on its way to Kefall. Yes, the soldier was incredibly bored, but was following orders to take the bag to the Emperor. The train, I noted, was one of the older designs from the DEA Enterprises, perhaps five years behind our current models. Nevertheless, it would get the dispatch to the Emperor in twenty-four hours. Now I had a choice. Do I hang around the moving train all that time or do I appear at the palace in a day and hope for the best? I chose the latter.

Around one, the soldier reported to the Emperor, stating that a caravel had arrived, claiming to be sent directly from Monarch Stefano West Po with an urgent message. "This was given to our gun ship's captain, sir." The soldier saluted and left.

Emperor Karpos handled it as if it might somehow be poisoned. "Here, why don't you let me handle it, Emperor. If there is any chance of contagion, let it be on me," Fino volunteered. Although he had no idea of the contents of the message, he assumed that it must be highly important and critical. The Emperor handed it at once to Fino, wiping his hands on his suit coat. Clearly, he was ill at ease over even touching the dispatch pouch.

Fino declared it was still sealed with Stefano's Velona seal and then he opened it. In it were a letter and a number of drawings. He proceeded to read the letter to the Emperor and his other family members. I eavesdropped on the reading, curious about what Stefano had to say. I soon realized that Stefano was a very sharp lad. He did not know this Emperor, who was a total stranger. Hence, instead of using the word alien, he used the word perpetrator. He outlined the details of the bacteria, which had been identified by the Medical Research Foundation as being responsible for the horrid plague. Via the attached drawing copies, he outlined the key datum that the bacteria shriveled up and died after three days, a very short-lived creature. The subsequent drawings made after several weeks clearly showed that the bacteria was vastly different than it was on that first day.

Stefano pointed out that there had been no further outbreaks of the plague anywhere since southern Tashien back in late July. The date on the document was September 1; two months had gone by without more infections appearing. He also discussed how his agents had tracked down the location of the perpetrator who was returning from having infected Tashien. Further, his agents had then killed the perpetrator whose remains could be found in the Desert of Desolation.

He outlined the horrific alterations that the plague had caused on us all, particularly women. He pointed out the critical need for food supplies for the nineteen countries, and how Velona was acting as the distribution point for the other countries. All countries had implemented some form of food rationing. He ended by saying that he did not know how the negotiations were progressing, but prayed that the Emperor would send food supplies as soon as possible. He indicated that his cousin, Gasparo, would be able to discuss more recent events and findings.

"Dad, if I was in his shoes, I'd say anything just to try to get food deliveries. I would not break the quarantine just because of some funny looking drawings," his youngest son, Alexio, advised. "Once it's broken, all hell can break loose. Every other ship is going to want to dock as well."

Curiously, his eldest son, Akios, said nothing. Emperor Karpos was definitely feeling his age. He lowered his head and rubbed his temples for a bit. He rose up, "You are right son. We dare not break the quarantine on such scanty evidence. However, your sister is on her unsuspecting way straight into this maelstrom. If I had known that all this would be happening, I would never have listened to her or allowed her to marry Flavio. Still, I cannot abandon her."

"Fino, our agreement still holds. We have all the details worked out now. Shipments will go to New Barq, as long as they remain free of the plague. We will honor our commitments. Our humanitarian aid will continue to flow and we will plant more crops this spring. You may expect further deliveries as you have planned with my advisors."

"Thank you, Emperor Karpos. Since there is really nothing more that I can do here, I believe it prudent that I take advantage of this caravel, return to my Velona, and aid my people as best I can. It has truly been an honor to have met you and your family. Your kindness and support of the northern countries shall never be forgotten."

"May Lord Jehosa look after you and your people. I fear what you will find upon your return," the old man said. Fino left and the others followed suit, leaving the documents lying on a side table. As I watched and was about to take off, I noticed that Akios quietly picked up the documents and read them. He stood there thinking for a moment and then acted as if he had just decided something. Quickly, he too left. I later learned what happened next.

Fino packed his new possessions into a large trunk and headed for the train station. He was in luck; the train was scheduled to leave in four hours. He took a seat on the wooden benches to wait. Three hours into his wait, Akios walked up to him, dressed for traveling.

"Hello once again, Fino. I've read Stefano's letter and looked at those strange drawings myself. I've decided that I want to question this Gasparo West Po myself. I've figured out a way to do it without risk catching the plague myself or violating the quarantine. Here's what we're going to do."

Late the next day, the train pulled into Patri. The two men went directly to the docks and hired two small skiffs to take them out to the quarantined Velona caravel. Akios' craft stopped several hundred feet from the ship, while Fino's skiff drew alongside. A rope was lowered, and soon Fino and his chest were hauled on board. The skiff returned to the docks.

A short while later, the caravel lowered one of its dingy craft, and a sailor rowed Gasparo out towards the waiting Akios, being careful to maintain sufficient distance and yet be able to talk well.

"Sorry that dad is still maintaining the quarantine. You are this

Gasparo West Po mentioned in the dispatch?"

"Yes, you are Akios Omela?"

"Yes. The letter said that you would fully brief us. I ask you to brief me fully instead. Dad is old and unable to make this kind of journey. Please, withhold nothing. What is meant by this perpetrator? How could anyone on Tarra know how to create such a horrific plague? Indeed, his letter did specifically say that the perpetrator did manufacture the bacteria that caused the plague. I wish to know all that you know," Akios asked.

The two men sat in their bobbing crafts for over two hours. Gasparo told him all the details, including all that Stefano knew about the aliens. He even mentioned that I had captured the image of the alien on our newest device, the image-taker.

When Gasparo finished, Akios commented, "Well, now I know why Stefano said perpetrator. This tale sounds utterly fantastic. However, I have a plan that I wish you to carry out. It will benefit both of our countries in the long run. My sister is on her way to Velona. Alexa has married your Flavio West Po. I believe that they are to arrive around mid-November. I want her to meet this Bethany person and see for herself the image that she has of this alien creature. Have my sister then write directly to me and tell me what she has seen and learned. This is vital; tell her to say nothing about aliens to dad or mom. Send her report directly to me personally. Will you do this for me?"

"Absolutely, sir. Consider it done! Glad to be of service. Sorry that I couldn't relay all of this to the others," Gasparo replied. "I do understand. Honestly, unless you actually saw these flying machines of theirs, you wouldn't have believed it yourself. But then I do now have these weird long ear lobes, so something happened."

"Yes, I admit, you do look weird now. Thank you and give my love to my sister for me." With that, the two crafts pulled away, and shortly thereafter, the caravel set sail for home.

I conferred with Gasparo the next afternoon to let him know that I witnessed the Emperor hearing the contents of the letter. He then told me of his secret meeting with the Emperor's oldest son, Akios. This, I thought rather odd. However, I told Gasparo that I would see that Flavio and Alexa heard about her brother's request once they arrived, saving a three month delay.

Sometime later, the Papal Proclamation arrived in Demokritos. Cardinal Heli immediately had it widely circulated throughout the entire country, starting with the Emperor. Now Emperor Karpos felt convinced that he had done the right actions with the total quarantine and yet sending all the food supplies he could. His only regret was that his daughter was heading straight into all this. However, as Roxane pointed out, if this plague was truly over, then neither Flavio nor Alexa had contracted it. Thus, they were not mutants, although they may now be in the lands of the mutants.

"Dear, think how useful her monthly reports will now be to us!" He smiled, realizing once more what a wonderful and clever wife she was.

I now began to see that our world was slowly being divided into the mutant lands and the normal lands. I hated being called a mutant; however, the term actually fit our bodies now. There was no denying that point. Still. .
.

Chapter 27 Flavio and Alexa

"Le Envoy is a fine ship. It belongs to all of us West Po's really, though our Monarch Stefano usually has control of it," Flavio explained as he walked Alexa into the poop deck cabins. "It's set up for passengers, not for carrying much cargo. Below there's a large area for playing games during long voyages, so you have something to do. The best cabins are these here on the poop deck. We're in the one that Stefano uses when he sails." He opened the small door and the two struggled to get her enormous dress inside. "Sorry, it wasn't made for such dresses, I'm afraid, my love."

"Wow, this is nice. Mahogany furniture. I expected it would be much smaller," Alexa commented as she got her first look at the spacious cabin, three times the size of normal ones. "You know, since we are going to be at sea for three months, I guess there is no real reason that I need to wear these fancy gowns. It's going to be difficult to manage in them."

"I'm glad you suggested that. I agree, next to impossible. What say we find you something more suited?"

"Wow, I can't believe that I am free at last, but I suppose that I will still need to wear these gowns when we go out in public in Velona. You know, I am terribly sorry, but I didn't think this far ahead, Flavio. I don't have any dresses except all these fancy ones. Oh!" She nearly lost her balance as the ship rolled a little to port. Flavio caught her and held on. "Thanks. Golly, these heels are not made for being on a ship either. I am practically standing on my toes and it is too hard to keep my balance."

"Well, we have to see about shoes too. We'll get you fixed up somehow." He removed her overskirt and eventually her giant hoop skirt off, leaving her standing in her slip, which covered her corset and nickers. With her top bodice of the dress still on her, she did look a bit strangely dressed. Chatting and experimenting with clothes, bearing in mind it was still chilly winter, the two finally got her more practically dressed. Although she still wore her undergarments including her corset, she now wore one of Flavio's shirts with the sleeves tucked inside and hidden from view along with one of his warmer pants.

Embolden by the more manageable clothes, Flavio took her on a tour of the rest of the caravel, lifting her down the stairs into the cargo hold. Here there were ten more normal sized cabins, a large play space with dartboard, a dining room area, and the galley, where the cook was busy working on their next meal. Several more times, she nearly lost her balance, and the two decided to next deal with her heels. She had worn these Annelise extreme heels ever since she was ten, that is some ten years, day in and day out. Her calf muscles had adapted, and now when she took them off, her feet would not go flat on the floor any longer, meaning she was still having to stand stretched up on her toes without the extra bit of support from her heels.

"Well, let's see if they will eventually stretch back out to normal," Flavio suggested. "We've got three months to work on it." This they did, though for weeks, Flavio always had to have his arm around her whenever she stood, especially in the rougher weather.

At first, the two spent hours in their cabin laying side by side on their bed chatting about their lives. Alexa began the explanation that she had promised him. "You see, mom and dad used to play with me every night, so did my brothers and sisters. I've always been like this," she shrugged her shoulders, unwilling to come right out and say armless. "As far back as I can remember, I just couldn't do anything for myself. Someone was always doing the things I needed done for me. All I can do really is walk, and when I was a little girl, run around. That's why I so looked forward to the nights when we would run around and play. That was the only times during the whole day that I felt, well normal and free. The rest of the time I felt, well, helpless really."

"I mean, I saw all my servants doing so very many things with their hands and I couldn't do anything. I felt trapped, if you can possibly understand. Only at night was I free and truly happy. Then, when I was ten, they put me into my first corset and those Annelise heels. I cried a lot when mom wasn't around. Now I could hardly breathe anymore and walking was very hard. I had to take such tiny steps and watch my every step to keep from falling or losing my balance. I can't grab on to anything to keep from falling if I do. I felt like I had just lost the only freedom and fun in my life."

"Still, they continued to play with me at nights, only now I could barely walk and was out of breath constantly. Most of the fun was gone. All that was so hard for a ten year old girl to understand. Anyway, now I know why they did it. I have a proper waist size that is easy to maintain, and I can walk fine on level ground, that is. By the way, going down a slope is still murder on my knees! Anyway, like mom and my sisters, I am a good role model for the Holy Women of the Eighth Degree. Everywhere I go, people treat me in the highest regard. You wouldn't believe the number of men that have tried to ask me out. So I do understand now why mom did this to me back then."

"Yet, Flavio, there has to be more in life than just sitting around looking perfect and pretty, able to do nothing at all except talk."

"You dance divinely," Falvio teased her. She grinned.

"Okay and dancing. These last six years, I've heard so many exciting things about Velona that I decided long ago that I had to get away from Demokritos and see this magical Velona. Then I thought what could I realistically do when I am there? Honestly, Flavio, I really am mostly just a helpless wallflower. Anyway, I got this idea that I could find some fun of some kind in Velona. Plus it hit me one day. I could travel the world and see all the wonderful sights. I decided five years ago that's what I was going to do: escape and see if I could possibly find fun and see the sights of the world."

"Yet, how remained my challenge. My parents would never, ever let a Holy Woman do either of those. Honestly, both would chide me horribly if they saw the way that I am dressed right now! No, I had to find a way to leave being a Holy Woman behind me. I waited and waited. Then, I met you. I'm sorry that I have used you so, but I saw a chance to escape, get to Velona, and seek out some fun and somehow see the world. I do love you, though, but I will understand totally if you wish to go your own way when we get to Velona. I am sort of trapping you, since I have to have you do everything for me now."

Flavio gave her a passionate kiss. "Don't talk silly. I married you because I've fallen in love with you, you playful rascal." They embraced and took a long time out from chatting.

Later on, she asked him about his family. "Well, mom and dad are now both fifty-six and have retired from their old jobs helping to run our country. Jules and Daniello. I think you will like mom; she's really nice. I'm the youngest. They always say that they thought that they were all done having children, then I popped up. First, there is Jovanni, he's thirty-eight now. His wife is Sandra and they have four kids. Next is my sister Silvia, she's thirty-five. Her husband is Geraldo and they have three kids. Then comes my brother Lazzaro who is thirty. His wife is Tonia and they have three kids too. Last is my sister Tina, who's twenty-five. She and Gustavo had two kids. Then, there is me and I have the prettiest wife of them all!" She gave him a loving kiss.

"Where does Stefano fit in all this?" she asked next.

"Well, I have three old uncles and aunts. Uncle Adrien and Aunt Elaina have five children. Both of them are fifty-six now. Daniela is twenty-eight, I think, and she is Velona's High Priestess of the Church of the Three Holy Roses. She and Filberto have three children. Uncle Adrien's youngest is Stefano, who is twenty-two. His wife is Caresa and they have an adorable little girl called Andrea. She's five now. You see, Elaina used to be our High Priestess and Adrien, our Monarch. Now they've passed those top leadership positions on down to two of their children."

"Then, there is Uncle Felix and Aunt Justine, they are fifty-six too. Uncle Gervaise and Aunt Juliane are fifty-five. Both of them also have a bunch of children, all are married and have kids of their own. Actually, I'm the youngest of all my cousins and Stefano is next. Now there are a whole lot of second cousins."

"Interesting. What about your grandparents? It sounds like you have quite a large bunch of West Po's."

"Actually no. The Church of Jehosanity in one coordinated set of attacks murdered thirty-three of the West Po's back at the start of the Second Crusade. That one day, the Church very nearly wiped out the entire

West Po line! Only my four uncles and aunts and a couple more who have passed away recently survived that evil assassination. Can you believe this? The Church of Jehosanity sent suicide bombers who blew up men, women, children, and even babies! Thirty-three of us. Only a handful survived and only because they were not at home at the time of the bombings."

Alexa looked very pale; her face turned white as a sheet. "My, my Church of Jehosanity did that?"

Flavio realized that he had struck a nerve. After all, she was a Holy Woman of the Church of Jehosanity. "Not your Church in Demokritos, dear. Your country was totally neutral during that whole war. No, it was the Church of Jehosanity in Velona and other Sea Prince sectors who did it, following orders from Pope Christos in Megalos. Your country didn't have anything to do with trying to wipe us all out."

"Why? Why did they do this?" she asked, still quite shocked. Her orderly world was definitely crumbling. For hours, Flavio talked about their history, and slowly she began to get a better picture of just what her Church had been doing elsewhere in the world. For over a half century, Demokritos had been quietly on the sidelines, taking no role in these world domination plans of her Church. She took a little comfort in that.

Much later, he got to the story of Hieras Anubis, which took nearly an hour to relate. However, in doing so, Flavio suddenly got a brilliant idea. "Say, you know all those twenty thousand women, they were like you, armless. Yet, they all did nearly everything in life for themselves! You know, feeding themselves, dressing, everything. None of them ever had a servant, though they did have loving husbands. I once ate at a restaurant in Eastside, that's the subdivision where all of those people settled down after Renzo rescued them. My waitress kind of shocked me. She had no arms, just like you. Yet, she took our order, brought our food, and sat it before us, all proper like. I tried hard not to stare at her, figuring it would embarrass her."

"You know, Alexa, what if you could learn how they do these things? What would you think if you could feed yourself, brush your own hair, dress yourself, even carry things, just like anyone else?"

"I'd be free! But I don't see how any of that is even possible, Flavio. I don't have any arms at all, none. Surely, you have to have some arms left to do all that. Do you really think that any of that is possible for me? I wouldn't be helpless any longer. Flavio, that would be an absolute miracle!"

"Alexa, I promise you that as soon as we get to Velona, the first thing we're going to do is find some of those women and see about having them teach you. You know that waitress actually wrote our order down. She used her foot somehow, but I tried not to look. That's going to be our first thing to do."

"Wow, that would be fantastic, though completely unbelievable, Flavio."

"Oops, sorry, the first thing we are going to have to do is get us our own place to live. I have been living at my folk's house. We won't fit in my bedroom." Both laughed at that.

Then, Flavio realized that Alexa had to learn to speak and read the Sea Prince dialect. During the rest of their voyage, they spent hours on language lessons as well as history lessons. He also described all the major sights that they just had to see. Then, he was sidetracked on all the many cultural events.

After a month at sea and going around in her bare feet, one day the two discovered that finally her feet went flat on the floor once more! Quickly, Flavio put some of his shoes and socks on her. For the first time, she was able to maintain her balance while walking on the rolling ship. Now the two began to make use of the play area. Several times a day, they played kick the beanbag. He taught her how to play kick ball too, though they really needed more players. Laughing and having a ball, Alexa suddenly realized that she as having pure fun for the first time since she was ten! Only she continued to lose her breath because of her tight corset. At last, Flavio convinced her to take it off for a time. She could always get back in it when they docked and she needed to dress up again. After that, Alexa felt a freedom that she began to cherish utterly, she felt like she was ten again!

It was at this point, Alexa finally realized the underlying consideration, which until now remained neither viewed by her nor voiced. "Flavio! I just realized that I didn't have a say in whether I wanted to become a Holy Woman. No one ever asked me if I wanted to lose my arms! They just did it when I was a baby. Wow. A woman is supposed to desire and want to become a Holy Woman, but only when fully supported by her husband in this church ceremony. I didn't have any choice to be like this! I've been fighting against this ever since I was a very little girl and saw other women who had arms! I was never allowed to say that I wished that I had arms! Oh no! Mom and dad always insisted that I was special. I was a Holy Woman. Flavio, I don't even feel holy! No wonder I wanted to get away."

"Wow, Alexa. I think that is a very important thing to have realized. Well, I think that you are a holy angel to me." He put his arms around her and gave her a loving kiss, which she returned in kind. This was on the morning of November 10 and at the exact point in time when I finally made contact with Flavio.

Oops. Bad timing. Sorry, Flavio. Bethany Bartiana Angela here, Stefano's friend.

"Whoa! Someone's talking in my head!" Flavio said, breaking off their passionate embrace. "Where are you? You're in my head somehow." Alexa looked confused and startled. "A friend of Stefano's is talking to me inside my head somehow."

Sorry. Telepathy. She must be your new bride, Alexa? You don't have to speak. Just think what you want me to hear. I'm in Velona.

Wow! This is incredibly intimate. Can you bring Alexa into this too?

338

Hi Alexa. I'm Bethany Bartiana Angela, Monarch Stefano's friend. Telepathy. Just think your thoughts and I'll pick them up.

Unbelievable! Flavio! So intimate! I feel you too. Incredible! I've never felt anything like this before. Where are you, Bethany? Are you a goddess or something?

No. I'm in Velona. Stefano asked me to contact you and share some very urgent information that you need to know before you get to Velona. He sent your cousin Vittore's son, Gasparo, to deliver a critical message to the Emperor. Gasparo's just left Patri on his way back now, and I promised him that I would contact you and bring you up to date. I think that it would be wise if you both were sitting down. I have terrible news to share. Alexa, your family is fine. It has to do with us up here in the north.

Are you all starving now? she asked.

No, thanks to all the other countries who are responding, including Demokritos, we are making it, although food is still being rationed here. I have an awful lot of news to tell you, most of it will be horrible, though, Flavio. Stefano asked me to tell you the complete, whole truth, because you selfishly went on the mission to talk Demokritos into sending us food supplies, which we so desperately do need.

Hey, does this mean Stefano is bringing me into his inner circle now? Flavio asked boyishly.

Yes, Flavio, consider yourself part of his inner circle. I began to relate all that had gone on here in Velona since Flavio and Fino left in the middle of June to convince Demokritos of our plight and secure extensive shipments of dried food. I replayed my memories of Nestor and his Version One plan for the whole world. It brought a similar reaction to both, total dismay and horror. Then, I went into all the negotiations that we had done with Nestor to attempt to get him to not do Version One on us all.

God! You are right! None of us could live if we were like that! Flavio interrupted. *I'd have killed myself too!*

I got them to see that Nestor was not going to accept anything other than a Dorota style society, and I went through our attempts to try to change Nestor's mind. I showed him Stefano's images that he later shared with me of their defense of Velona when the flying ships came, delivering the plague. That certainly made the attack real to both. Then I went through what happened to us all because of the plague.

What — what — what do you all look like now? Flavio finally was able to focus and ask.

I shared some images of me and my extended family and even Caresa and Andrea, figuring he would relate to Stefano's wife and daughter.

But, but if all women are now Holy Women, who cares for all of your needs? We are so helpless! Alexa asked, becoming afraid that she was sailing into a world where she would have no one to help her at all except Flavio.

I continued the story, showing them the piles of Nestor fabricated objects based on what I had used back in old Dorota. I began showing them some examples of how everyone was learning to cope and to begin to start doing some things for themselves.

Flavio! I have to learn how to do some of these things! Look, they are actually feeding themselves! Bethany, I just have to learn how to do things! I've been trapped like this for my whole life. I have to learn how so I can get my freedom back, at least a little of it!

We know, Alexa. Stefano has already guessed that you would want to learn. Flavio, Stefano has talked to your folks and they agree. When you get back to Velona, you are to move in here with us at our estate for a while. Stefano thinks that Alexa will have the easiest time learning how to do things from us. He considers us here the experts. I can't convince him otherwise. We have lots of room, and we'd love to have you.

When you dock, your folks and your brothers and sisters will be there to meet you. They are dying to meet your new bride. Stefano will be there too. You will all come over to my estate for a welcome home and welcome new bride party. I want to show you my image-taker birthday present and the images I took of Nestor. Lucianna and Giovanni invented it. Pretty great. Oh, tell Alexa that she will be getting a putt-putt that she can drive around, only Lucianna has modified them for women to use, called a T-putt-putt. I showed them some of my memories of Lucianna driving hers around the estate.

I can drive myself around? Alexa was flabbergasted! *Who are Lucianna and Giovanni?*

My little sister and brother. Have you heard of the DEA Enterprises?

Yes, they are the famous inventors. Dad got our steam trains from them about six years ago now, Alexa replied.

Yes, Enyo and Arsenio started that company along with Dianna West Po. Hence the letters, DAE. Their bodies grew old and passed away. Now they have new bodies. Arsenio is Lucianna and Enyo is Giovanni. They are still inventing and still running their company. Lucianna is working on a better way for us to talk to others over long distances. With it taking six months to get a message to Demokritos and the answer back, she is determined somehow to make talking with the Emperor almost instantaneous. I don't know if she'll be successful or not. They both are determined to make us some flying machines. Now wouldn't that be something! I don't know if it's even possible, but you know those two. Anyway, you both have lots to discuss now. I'll see you both in a few days when you arrive. Flavio, have you told Alexa about our dances and symphony concerts? They are supposed to start back up again in December. See you in a few days. Bye.

"Flavio! Who is she? That was the most incredible thing that I've ever heard of in my whole life! She and they have to be gods and goddesses, right?" Alexa exclaimed after I broke the connection.

"I remember now. Great Uncle Gerardo always used to talk about the amazing things that went on with those people at that estate! Wow. Now we are going to be privy to some of the most interesting things going on in Velona!"

On November 12, I got quite a surprise. I had finished my morning chores and had sat down to work on the next article for the newspaper. All of a sudden, from my mom's bedroom I heard a familiar childhood song, "Twinkle, twinkle, tiny star!" Slow, single notes on the violin, the tune was impossible to miss. I dashed into mom's room. She looked up sheepishly at me.

"Your father fixed this up for me. I am at least able now to make a sound on it again. Sorry that it's a total beginner's first tune," she apologized.

"Mom! You are able to play again!" I leaned into her, and we cradled our heads together. She began crying, though.

"I have to try somehow. I am lost without my music."

"Mom, you are doing it! I heard it."

"I know that I'll never be able to play like I used to play. Maybe I can sort of pick out some really simple, slow tunes, and remember how it used to be," she said, but then broke down. I comforted her for some time.

"Mom, you keep this up. Practice, practice, practice," I teased her, remembering how often she'd told me this bit of advice. She managed a slight grin. She was sitting in a chair; the violin was on the floor pointed away from her; the neck was closest to her feet. Dad had made her a leather strap, which helped her hold the bow in her right foot. Her left big toe was fingering the notes.

"I don't know if this will ever amount to much, but at least I can make a little sound this way. I really don't want to join a choir, unless there are no other alternatives," she explained.

"Hey, at least you are able to do this much. The flutists and such — they have it even worse, no fingers to cover the holes. Go for it mom," I encouraged, though I was again reminded of the terrible sacrifices so many women were now enduring. While her playing reminded me of a six year old hashing out their very first notes, nevertheless, I was uplifted.

Around one in the afternoon of November 14, I got a call from Stefano, who had just received a call from Jovanni West Po, who was our harbor master. Flavio's caravel was spotted making its way into the Velona docks. He was giving us a heads up. Flavio and Alexa would soon be arriving, and his whole family would be dropping by our place after they arrived. I let everyone else know. Telepathy is often faster than using the telefono.

On board, Flavio had gotten Alexa dressed up in her fancy blue satin gown. While she didn't appreciate having her corset on or the extreme Annelise heels again, she wanted to make a good first impression on his relatives. Besides, she didn't want them to have their first view of her be while she was wearing his clothes. Holding her steady on the deck, the two watched the immense city grow larger and larger as they slowly drifted into the bay and docks.

"It's so huge!" Alexa exclaimed. Indeed, the port of Velona was more than double the size of Patri, discounting our newer Eastside Dock expansion. Before long, they could make out the group of people waiting for them. Flavio began pointing them out to her. Besides Stefano and Caresa, his parents were there along with his brothers and sisters and their spouses. The women all wore their Annalise style gowns, but with Alexa heels, in deference to Alexa. I had relayed to them that such were the only outfits that she had.

With great care, Flavio helped Alexa down the gangplank and made sure that he had her well balanced, as they moved slowly toward the smiling group. When they were at last close, he called out, "Hi mom, dad. Everyone. This is my wife, Alexa." The many introductions began at once. Although he knew what to expect, he was extremely shocked by what he saw. All the women were as armless as his wife was, yet their permanent makeup was identical. It was impossible to miss their long, dangling ear lobes.

Alexa, who had been feeling very nervous about meeting all his relatives, now felt very relaxed. They looked so much like her, even to the style of gowns. Somehow, she felt that she fit in well with them, a comfortable kind of feeling. She suddenly realized that if they all had their arms, then she would have not felt the way that she did.

Everyone exchanged hugs, handshakes, and welcomes. Jovanni, his oldest brother, teased him, "Well, little brother, you do know how to choose them. Wow. Alexa is a beauty queen to beat all beauty queens. It is my pleasure to welcome you, Alexa, to our big family." She flushed slightly.

"So I'm not pretty eh," Sandra, his wife teased him playfully.

"Oh Jovanni is in big trouble now!" his other brother, Lazzaro, teased. Everyone laughed.

"Honestly, Alexa, don't pay these over active boys any mind," Silvia, his older sister, added. "Welcome to our family." A bit later, she whispered to Flavio, "You chose well. She is gorgeous."

"Okay, let's get going," Stefano broke in. "Flavio, we are all heading to the Angela and Bartiana estate. They are hosting a welcome home and wedding party for you two. I want you both to ride there with Caresa and me."

"What is this thing?" Alexa asked as they neared the strange looking vehicle.

"A motor-car," Stefano explained. "It runs on a petrol engine. We also have motor-wagons, which carry lots of cargo. No need for horses any longer. Latest inventions from the DAE. They are a bit expensive still and not too many can afford them yet, particularly since this plague struck. We are all still coping and recovering and trying to put shattered lives back together somehow as best we can."

Stefano helped Caresa get inside and Flavio followed suit, allowing Alexa to see how Caresa managed it. "This is something else," she exclaimed as they began driving through the streets. It was a short drive to 42 Hampton Way. Stefano asked if Flavio had anything urgent to tell him. Since he didn't, he asked them to give him a full report later after they were settled in.

Soon, introductions flew once more as Stefano brought the young couple into our home. His parents and siblings followed them in, and our celebration got under way. "This is Bethany Bartiana Angela and her husband Marco," Stefano introduced us to Alexa.

"Gee, you are so young. I do like your dress, so unusual looking," Alexa said to me.

"Yes, fourteen now. This is the very latest design from Tatiana. I can dress myself in this one. When I wear ones like yours, I have to have Marco here dress me. Say, I do love your earrings!"

"Thanks, I can feel my shoulders with them." I understood completely.

"This is my little sister, inventor Lucianna, and her husband Valerio."

"I'm almost fourteen now. Please to meet you, Alexa. Welcome to Velona," she said.

"Wow, you are the one doing all of this incredible inventing? How can you possibly do it?" Alexa asked quite surprised.

"Giovanni is my partner as always. I have to use my feet now plus my mind. Bit challenging at times. Right now, I am trying to adapt my radio invention into a kind of communication device that can reach from here down to Demokritos," Lucianna chatted away.

I interrupted, "If you let her, she will talk all day about inventions. This is my brother Sergio and his wife Lisa. He is our Chief Detective Inspector, a solver of the most baffling crimes. She is his protector."

"Hello. Pleased to meet you, Alexa," Sergio said, giving her a hug. Lisa gave her our usual kind of pressing hug.

"But how can you protect him? He should be protecting you," Alexa asked, becoming confused. Here was an armless woman just as she.

"Oh I certainly can. I once killed a man who was trying to kill Sergio with a sword," Lisa attempted to explain.

"Did I hear my name mentioned?" Giovanni walked up with Eve around his arm. I introduced them.

"Welcome to Velona, Alexa. I'm sure that you will find many new and strange inventions here. Lucianna and I are still at it. Why, we've decided to see if we cannot make our own flying machines. Now that would be something, flying in the sky between here and Demokritos."

Eve interrupted. "Yes, dear. Honestly, Alexa, if you let him just talk on, he'll never stop. He and Lucianna are quite a pair. Wow, Alexa, you are one very hot woman! Flavio, you'd best keep your eyes on me or I may steal her away from you!"

I explained, "Alexa, Eve here used to be Renzo. This is only his second female body, and he still is looking at you from a male perspective. I ought to know. A while ago, she was Dita. She and I were married. Don't worry. Eve is finally in love with Giovanni. If this all sounds confusing, well it is, but you'll get used to it around her." I then introduced our two sets of parents.

The party got underway. His parents bought him a small home not far from theirs and had it equipped properly, using an extra kitchen that one older woman didn't need. His brothers had pooled their resources to buy the couple their own motor-car. His sisters helped furnish the home, linens, sheets, blankets, and such. Lucianna gave Alexa a T-putt-putt, promising to teach her how to ride it safely tomorrow. The rest of us decided that Alexa really did need more manageable clothes and shoes. So we went together to arrange it. Since they are made to fit, tomorrow we planned to take her to the various shops for fittings, including L'Eleganti and Alexa Boots.

Around four they left, and I knew that their suppers would be later than normal, unless the men took over for the women in the kitchen — the usual five times longer rule still applied to us all, though we were getting more skilled at it and a bit faster.

"Come on, Alexa; let's see if we can find some more comfortable clothes for you to wear around the house. You are about my size. Flavio, I'll let you help her out of her fancy gown. No way can I manage that one." I took them to my room. While Flavio undressed her, I showed her some possibilities. She liked one of my blue new dresses that Tatiana had designed.

"Okay, I've got her this far," Flavio said. "What else comes off?"

"Well, you don't need to wear your corset, unless you have to, Alexa."

"Oh, please, remove it if I don't need it. I have had three months of freedom, Bethany, and I love it. I want to learn all these new ways. I don't want to be helpless like I am now. Please, can you help me with it all?" Alexa asked.

"That's why you're here. All of us are going to work with you as long as you need it. Yes, Flavio, off with the corset and even her nickers too. We'll use the new style slip with the dress. Okay, now leave us alone, please. Take her things to your new room. Marco can show you where it is. Alexa, see these loops at the bottom of the slip and the dress? We use our toes in them to help pull them down." I began showing her what needed to be done, allowing her time actually to do it for herself. This was rather a little test for her. I needed to see just what her attitude was toward learning new ways.

An hour later, we two walked out and joined the others. Alexa's face was radiant; she'd completely dressed herself for the first time ever in her life. Plus, in this new style dress, she looked good as well. (Well, I did brush out her hair for her.) Thus began the education of Alexa in our unique alternate ways to do the many things of life. I had them both read my many newspaper articles after supper to prepare the way.

As we all sat down to eat, I explained how we women managed, though Flavio would be feeding her tonight as usual. "Look, Alexa, from now on, I want you to carefully watch us and how we do it. No fair just taking a discrete peak at us." I wanted her to feel comfortable staring at us as we used our feet. She definitely appreciated this suggestion. To say that her eyes were opened is an understatement. Alexa saw routine things during the rest of the evening that she had never dreamed were possible. A real hope blossomed in this beautiful young woman. I intended to help it flourish.

Chapter 28 December Bounty

During the next few weeks, Alexa made rapid and swift progress learning to care for her own needs. As the first weekend in December approached, she was able to dress and feed herself. Already, she was nearly able to write legibly. I discovered an interesting skill that she had developed. Treated all her life as a Holy Woman, that is to say a completely helpless woman, unable to do anything for herself, her mind had attempted to compensate. Alexa had a terrifically good recall. Though not quite eidetic, she never forgot a face or the name that went with it. She was good at doing math problems in her head, complex ones at that, I thought.

She was so good at math, that Lucianna and Giovanni wanted her to consider coming to work at the DEA, at least part time. Now, both were heavily involved with mathematics, trying to work out their new inventions. She was pleased with their offer and eager to try it, once she was more independent.

On Friday night, the All Velona Orchestra was finally going to hold a performance. Until now, all dances and other artistic events of which we are so fond had been cancelled for obvious reasons. With the food crisis somewhat at bay and with our women becoming more independent, Stefano at last allowed the arts to reopen with one stipulation. If women found it still too difficult to manage, they would have to remain closed longer.

After lunch, I explained to Alexa about the evening concert coming up. "We ought to wear our fancy Annelise outfits and make our men look after our every need for a few hours." We giggled a bit. "Of course, our fellows will have to dress us. Expect them back around two. You know how long it takes them to get us all ready. They are all thumbs." Again, we giggled.

Later, while we were chatting as Marco and Flavio worked to get us dolled up, Alexa made a comment that not only impinged upon me, but also bounced around my mind for days afterwards. "You know, Bethany, someone ought to find this Nestor fellow and make him make all this right."

I wore my light blue Annelise dress and matching heels, though I wished I'd not put on the corset. While I really didn't need it, since it was part of the outfit, I did. Oh well. All we women were similarly dressed, though Alexa cut the most striking figure of all of us. Her fourteen-inch waist caught even our eyes. The fellows were dressed in their finest suits as they helped us to the dinner table. Okay, I did enjoy letting Marco feed me, though Flavio put all of our men to shame. He had it down pat, something that Alexa noted.

We left the dishes for later. Escorted to the many motor-cars, we soon were on our way. As expected, this first performance in five months was sold out. Still, we had our usual box seats and our beaus proudly escorted us there. We could not help noticing the hundreds of women here were just like us, armless, dependent upon the men at their sides. Yes, all had dressed up for the occasion, as had we.

The conductor walked on stage, but only the men were now able to applaud him. The volume was noticeably less I noted. He spoke loudly, "Welcome to the All Velona Orchestra. Tonight's concert is dedicated to all the women of our orchestra and of the many other arts of which they are now denied. It is with the greatest respect for these brave women that we, the remaining members of our orchestra, dedicate our evening's performance to them. All of us on stage truly miss the incredible talents that have been lost to us forever. Three quarters of a century ago, an armless woman from Demokritos immigrated to Velona. Here she began her study of music and has left us with a vast legacy of symphonic music. Tonight, in honor of all our women, we are proud to present Alekto's Symphony Number 1."

I had chills as I remembered that first performance so long ago. A loud driving rhythm began on the lower instruments and drums; gradually their theme was picked up by the violas and then the violins and finally the woodwinds. So compelling was the music that many could not keep from tapping to the beat. In stark contrast, the second movement depicted a springtime pastorale. So moving was the theme, so realistic the melody and sound, so moving, that at times, I alternated between having shivers all over my body to tears trickling down my cheeks. The third movement was an orchestrated set of variations on Lyneth's Lament. I cried throughout it. I couldn't help myself; her music just pulled the emotions out of me! The rousing fourth movement again brought the house down, though we women just yelled and cheered.

Alexa had never heard anything so rousing, so moving; tears of joy covered her face, forcing Flavio to have to wipe her off discretely. "That was so beautiful. She was from Demokritos and armless like us and yet she wrote that!"

"Yes, she wrote a whole bunch of symphonies, actually. No one has since equaled her works, though many have tried. A few equal hers, but not many," mom answered her. Dad continued to wipe mom's cheeks; she'd cried through the whole thing.

The next night was our formal dance night. Once more, the fellows dolled we women up in our fancy dresses and heels. Then it was off to an enjoyable evening of fine dancing. Again, more than half of the women were dressed in our Annelise style dresses, though many opted for the lower Alexa heels. The remainder wore some of the new sleek fitting dresses that Tatiana had designed for us, far more practical for the dance, I thought.

Alexa had a ball at the dance. Poor Flavio, he barely got to dance with his new bride half of the time. Others kept cutting in on him. Even Eve cut in. "Excuse me, Flavio. May I have this next dance with the gorgeous Alexa?"

"But how? We have no arms," she whispered.

Eve pushed her body close to Alexa's and rested her head on Alexa's shoulders. "Follow my head lead." She explained the system that she and I once had used. I thought that they did very well.

Even Marco took her on the floor for a dance. He returned flushed. "Wow, can she ever dance! What a knock out!"

"Cool it buster," I teased him as I pushed myself closer to him. He grinned. At least Alexa was getting a good introduction to our formal dancing, I thought. The radiant look on her face told us all that she was loving every minute of the dance, in spite of all those who wished to share a dance with her. If I am to be honest, she was perhaps the prettiest young woman here.

The following week, we began to harvest our garden. The outside temperatures began falling dangerously low at night, and Stefano issued a countrywide alert to harvest what could be done at this point. None of us wanted to risk what produce we had growing. Again, we all pitched in to help. Even Alexa used a yoke to help carry pumpkins inside. She joined us sitting on our butts attempting to work out how to pick the green beans with our toes. We all had a good laugh over our pitiful struggles. Yet, we managed somehow to get the job done. Finally we had plenty of fresh vegetables and some fruit. Still, this would have to last us until next fall's harvest, a complete impossibility. We most definitely needed the continuing shipments from Demokritos.

As we were struggling to carry a load of beans into the house, Alexa reminded me of something she'd said earlier. "Someone ought to make that Nestor fellow make all this right. What an annoying pain it is to be like this anyway." Well, we were and I could see nothing I could do about it, except make the best of our lives as we could. Once food became plentiful once more, I hoped things would become much better everywhere.

During the last week of December, our front room became the headquarters for Lucianna's latest experimental invention. She had strung wires seemingly all over the place and hooked them up to her new apparatus that she'd been working on with the help of some hands from the DAE. An even bigger apparatus was now in our basement. Giovanni operated the controls there, while from the front room, Lucianna kept yelling orders for him to follow. I thought it a bit comical. So did Sergio and Lisa who came home from work only to find our front room one big wire mess.

"What's going on, Lucianna? Mom's going to have a fit when she sees this mess," Sergio complained.

"No she's not. I already asked her. Giovanni, I'm ready up here. Power yours up," she yelled. Flavio and Alexa stood by watching. Like us, they had no idea what was going on either. Hearing a faint okay, she hollered, "Dial to one. Sweep to one." She sat down before the box-like electrical thing. I call it a thing because I had no idea what it was. Her feet flipped a switch, and her toes moved a dial to where I saw a number '1' located. She leaned forward and pushed another button down on what looked like a telefono cone on a pole and called out loudly, "Testing, testing. Lucianna here. Can you hear me? Can you hear me?"

Suddenly, we all nearly jumped out of our pants. From inside the box, we heard Giovanni's voice boom out, "Loud and clear, Lucianna. Testing. Can you hear me? Giovanni here."

"Woo hoo! Yes, I hear you loud and very clear. Great! It works! Yahoo," Lucianna yelled, turned it off and jumped up. Valerio latched on to her jumping body and kissed her passionately just to calm her down. Just then, Eve and Giovanni, wearing enormous grins, came up from the basement.

"It's my LD radio modification," Lucianna finally began to explain. "Our regular radio transmitters only have a relatively short range of some fifty miles. We need to have a voice signal reach all the way to Demokritos, if it is going to be worth doing at all. Now we don't exactly know what frequency will transmit the best or at what angle the sender must be positioned to. That's what we have to determine next. You just heard it work on the first of the frequencies I've built into the sets. Of course, that one ought to have worked, cause we're only a hundred feet apart. Any frequency would transmit that far, you see. So now that we have the sets working, we have to conduct rigorous field testing to determine which frequency will transmit the farthest and with the best reception on the other end and at what angle works best. Lots of testing to come. We need to test it over some long distances, once we prove it works over shorter ones. Now I've worked out a plan for that testing. . ."

I interrupted her fast flow, "Valerio, kiss her please!" He laughed and planted a smooch on her lips; that shut her up if only for a moment.

As soon as their lips parted, she went on, "So we have to get these two units thousands of miles apart. In small steps though, so that we don't go out of contact long. What?" she asked, looking at our smiling faces.

Alexa began to laugh. She stopped and said, "I think that's fabulous, Lucianna! I know I sure could not have even thought of it." Lucianna gave the rest of us a girlish smirk, as if to say "so there."

Later over supper, Lucianna explained everything all over again to mom and dad, though I admit, I got no more sense out of it the second time through it all.

Good old dad, though said, "Say, dear, why don't you use the stream train that goes all the way to Shansee. Isn't that a long enough distance to test this all out?"

"Brilliant, dad! Perfect! We can get the engineers to stop it at regular points and conduct our tests. Perfect. Giovanni, you need to calculate how far Shansee is from here for me." She and Giovanni left the table to continue their work.

"Come on Alexa. Let's get our yokes and clear off the tables. That way, we don't have to wash or dry them," I suggested. She giggled and complied. In truth, she was not yet very expert at either. Together, we sat on our butts and lifted the dirty dishes from the table, placing them into our yoke baskets. It took us a half hour to get them all off and into the kitchen, where mom, Marta, Lisa, and Eve took over from us. Eve glared at me for having usurped her chance to clear off the tables. Tonight, I got to it before she did and she was stuck drying them.

By the time that we finished, Lucianna and Giovanni were still experimenting. "Shansee will be a good test," Lucianna told me as I walked into the living room again.

"Wait, so you are actually planning to take a long train ride there?" I asked.

"Yes, though I suppose it will take some coordination with the train lines," Giovanni replied. "I am going to check on that tomorrow, while Lucianna explains what we are proposing to Stefano."

"Say, can I tag along? I've always wanted to travel and see the wonders of the world," Alexa asked. She'd followed me into the room.

"Sure, why not? We will need some help with all this testing," Lucianna answered.

"Thanks! I'll help all I can." She headed off to find Flavio and tell him the news, her earrings bouncing on her shoulders — she was that excited about it. So many of her dreams were coming true. Again, I noticed her earrings and decided to see if I could find that old pair I had when I lived on Dorota.

Some of the fellows were playing darts in the basement. Marco came over and asked me if he could help and I told him what I was looking for — my old earrings. It took me an hour to find them, they were still in the nice mahogany box in which I'd stored them so long ago. As we found them, Flavio and Alexa joined us. He wanted to thank us for letting Alexa tag along on this long train trip.

"Oh, wow! Look at those gorgeous earrings, Bethany! They are even bigger than mine. I bet you will look fabulous in them. Try them on. Don't you think she will look terrific in them, Flavio?" Alexa asked.

"Let's take them to where we have better light, dear. It looks like these will fasten on, but are not easily removed. I may need some small pliers," Marco suggested. A short while later, he had them once more secured to my ears. Emeralds and rubies and diamonds dangled in six tiers, many of which held a dozen each. They draped down onto my upper shoulders and felt stimulating as they touched my skin. However, I'd forgotten just how heavy they actually had been. "You look stunning, love," he said as he stood back and took in my new look.

"They feel like they are pulling my ears off," I jested. However, mom and the others also suggested that I looked good in them, so I decided to wear them for a few days and see if I really did like them.

Naturally, as soon as Eve saw them, she remembered her set and had Giovanni fetch hers and fasten them to her ears as well. Now we two were a matched set once more and Alexa really complimented us both. That night, I showed Marco an additional property that they had when we went to bed.

By the next afternoon, the testing plans were moving along rather well. Stefano thought Lucianna's invention and testing request merited his full support. Of course, I knew that it would. Being able to converse with the Emperor of Demokritos nearly instantaneous was vastly more survival oriented than waiting six months for a round trip of only one question and answer. Obtaining the needed clearance from the train master was more problematical.

A dozen steam trains regularly ran these southern routes and there was only one main line along the coast of the Sea Princes. Of course, there were rail yards with sidings where cars could be loaded and unloaded. Here, at precise times, one train would layover, while an oncoming one passed by. Considering what Lucianna and Giovanni wanted, the various train masters would carefully have to control the trains to avoid running into each other. In which case, one of the two would have to back up until they got to a siding somewhere.

"Well, I hired us their best engineers, but we will be traveling in freight cars. Using the one passenger train is out. Had to pay double rates to get their best engineers for this venture and a dedicated train. I think it will be worth it, especially if Lucianna's invention actually does work. Listening to someone talking is preferable to the dots and dashes of the Arsenio LDCS code that we now have — not saying it is bad or anything, just hearing a voice is lots easier to understand," Giovanni said.

"Until you get familiar with the code," Lucianna countered. She'd invented the LDCS system last lifetime. "When do we leave? We need to finalize our plans and get the equipment installed in the car."

"How's the first sound to you, sis?" he asked.

"I think that we'll have enough time. We best sit down and work out the exact sequence to be followed at each test point and the records that we need to keep," she suggested.

Giovanni and Eve would run the tests from our spare bedroom, where he set up the transmitter. Lucianna and Valerio would go on the train to conduct the tests. Marco, Flavio, Alexa, and I would accompany them to look after them and assist them with anything they might need.

However, this very afternoon, I had a second reason for wanting to make a quick trip to Shansee. I held it in my toes and reread the LDCS message just delivered from Stefano's office by a courier on a putt-putt.

26 December 822

Monarch Stefano,

Many years ago, a band of your highly skilled and able personnel came to Tashien in our hour of need and helped us set up our new form of government. Their leader was a Bethany Bartiana.

While none of us can doubt that this plague is by far our darkest hour, that is not totally why I am sending this. Something most strange has come up. If those people are still alive and are able to travel, it would be of great assistance to me if they could take the train to Shansee.

We have in our custody a very unusual woman. I say unusual because of her ranting and ravings. Sometimes her words sound utterly alien to our ears. None of our linguists recognizes the dialect, which she speaks. Occasionally, she says the phrase "mammalian cells." This reminded me of your messages from last July. Perhaps it is nothing and the woman is merely insane. There have been numerous such cases here since the plague. She was reported near death some time ago, but made a miraculous recovery. The ranting began after her recovery.

If this seems like it warrants your attention, please let me know. I will make my palace available to them and cover any of their expenses.

As always, yours truly,

Princess Pian Ling Wu

Shansee, Tashien

Okay, the phrase definitely got my attention. I had not really heard it spoken for five months or more. Perhaps as she said, it was nothing but the ranting of an insane person. Still, since we were going there anyway, I rang up Stefano on the telefono and told him that we would check it out when we got to Shansee. Why not? We would be in her city and it would only take a few minutes, I figured.

Mom and dad insisted that we take along both long guns and our blasters for protection. Eve insisted too. "Remember how badly we got mutilated the last time we were there, Bethany." Images of Doc Yi came to mind as well as Yuen Ming. "Whatever you do, don't go into any Purple Palaces this time!" We both chuckled.

Obviously, we women couldn't use a blaster anymore. Giovanni took Flavio aside and gave him a thorough education in the device and its use. He was astounded to learn about these powerful alien devices. Now he was certain that he was in Stefano's Inner Circle! Marco, Valerio, and Flavio each would carry a long gun and a blaster. For insurance, we stowed a spare blaster in my bag.

Since this was a working trip and since the weather was chilly now that winter had finally come slightly late, we women decided to wear heavier pants and shirts. I explained that if we needed dresses for some reason, we could purchase them when needed. Mom pointed out that while that was good logic in the past, since the plague struck, new dresses might be hard to come by, especially outside of Velona. I took her advice and we packed two dresses each as well. One was our fancy Tatiana designed slim dress and the other an Annelise style dress.

Chapter 29 Of Experiments and Shansee

On January 1, 832, we were dropped off at the rail yards in Velona, down near the Eastside docks. Giovanni drove the motor-wagon carrying the equipment that we were taking and parked it near the shack where the yardman Manlio had his office. The older man stepped out, a cane in hand. He leg was giving him trouble as usual in the colder weather.

"Ah, Giovanni. Here on time. If you will follow me, I'll show you to your train." We followed his slow walk. "Well, you asked for the best engineers. Here they are." He stopped by an engine with white stenciled lettering saying Coastal Run #1. A man with short curly hair hopped down from the tall cab. I did a double take as I saw the second one carefully backing backwards down the vertical steps, using a chin for support and balance. No doubt, the second engineer was a woman!

"Luca, here's your passengers. I'd like you to meet our two best engineers, Luca and Marcella Cellino," their boss introduced the husband and wife team. Both engineers were dressed in their bib overalls, though her top had no sleeves. They were tucked inside her heavy work shirt. Her bright red lips and thin waist were impossible to hide. She had bushy black hair no more than four inches long, while his was cut rather short. Both were all smiles. Luca shook Giovanni's hand and then Marco's and Valerio's. He gave Lucianna and me a hug. Marcella stood back, unsure of what to do, but smiled and nodded to us.

Manlio added, "Show them to their car, Luca. You are scheduled to depart in one hour." He turned and hobbled off to his shack.

"You must have pulled some strings," Luca said. "You've got a work crew car and one box car. We've stored some food in the boxcar along with extra charcoal for your heater-stove. That way we will not have to put in for more charcoal on the way."

"This will do fine, Giovanni," Lucianna said, looking over the size of the work crew car. "I'll let you fellows install the gear for me."

While the three fellows headed back to start bringing the gear and our supplies over, Marcella walked quietly behind us. "We were surprised that you wanted us and double pay for this really special trip. You must have some real pull. What's this all about anyway?"

"Oh, it is my great experiment in LD radio," Lucianna began to explain. "You see, Giovanni will stay here in Velona, and at precise times, he will operate my special transmitter, while I will attempt to pick him up here with my smaller version and send back a return message. We have to figure out which frequency will travel the farthest and at what transmission angle. My goal is to be able to have Stefano chat in one LD radio here in Velona and talk to someone in Shansee. You know, hold a real conversation, not like my LDCS code signals. While that system works well, it cannot go over the ocean. Ultimately, I hope to get my LD radio to reach all the way to Demokritos, so Stefano can chat with the Emperor there. Pretty cool, huh?" she finally wound down, as the fellows arrived with her equipment.

Marcella was impressed, but as the fellows walked up with their arms completely full, Marcella acted. "Here, let me get the big side door for you." She swung her leg up, hooked it on the latch, pulled it down to unhook it, and then slid the door open, while hopping on her other foot. I smiled, nice move, I thought.

Marcella replied, "Lucianna, you must be one of those DAE inventors that we've heard so much about."

"Oh yes, I was Arsenio last lifetime. Giovanni there, he was Dianna and Enyo last lifetime. We're at it again. Careful with that transmitter, fellows!" Lucianna left to make sure that they didn't drop it.

"She sure can talk," Marcella said to us, a grin on her face. "If you two want to follow me, I'll show you the usual entrance and show you around the work crew car." She led us to a set of easily negotiated steps that led to an entrance to the car. She slid the sliding latch aside and pushed her way inside. "Now way up front are six sleeping bunks and the charcoal-fired combined heater and stove. You'll probably need the men to light it for you. You'll find some cups and things in the cabinets there. One small washroom comes next. Here are two large benches. You can see out the windows on either side. Now back beyond that door is the work room where she's setting up her experiment things."

"We've only got one rule that you must follow. When the train is moving, do not try to get off it. Wait until we come to a complete stop. Otherwise, you can really get yourselves hurt. Now if you need to communicate to us — see this thin rope line here? Just give it a pull. It will sound a whistle up in our cab, and we'll take it from there. Okay?"

"Got it. Say, you actually drive this train don't you?" I asked.

She flushed. "Yes, of course. Oh, I see what you mean. Well, they don't allow women to be engineers. I always wanted to be an engineer, so I had to pretend that I was a man. It worked perfectly until I got the plague. I still pull my workload, only obviously now there are a few things that I cannot do, like shovel the coal and use our heavy wrenches to tighten bolts. Luca does those. I can do almost everything else. Would you like to ride up in the cab later on? We're not supposed to let passengers do that, but since you are paying double and this is your special trip, Luca and I won't mind. Just don't tell our boss, Manlio, please."

"Thanks, that would be quite an experience!" I replied. Alexa was very excited about this possibility and chatted a bit with Marcella. I went to see how the fellows were coming along with getting things set up. Giovanni had already left; he needed to get the first transmission done before we left; there was very little time left.

After stowing our personal bags and chests in the front part, we congregated in the workroom. Even Luca and Marcella stood near the door watching curiously. "Marco, start cranking the generator. Let me know when the gauge reads in the red." Marco began cranking the handle, but I saw that I could also do it with my feet, if needed. I realized that this provided the electricity to run Lucianna's set. She sat down in front of it, flipped switches, and set her dials. Valerio had a check sheet on a clipboard and began to take notes, checking his gold watch.

"One minute warning," Valerio called out. "Are you about ready, dear?"

"Yes, there. That should do it," she replied.

Valerio soon counted down, "Ten, nine, eight. . ."

"Giovanni calling Lucianna. Come in please. Can you hear me. Giovanni calling Lucianna." He repeated. Marcella and Luca gasped as they heard his voice loud and clear.

"Lucianna here. You are coming in loud and clear. Switch to band two now." She moved a dial and they repeated their tests. She went through a whole series of tests. I did see that in some of them, Giovanni's voice sounded weak and there was a lot of static. "Okay, Giovanni, all tests complete. Next scheduled test is in two hours, mark."

"Got it, Lucianna. Giovanni signing off."

"Okay, all set. Everything is working perfectly. We must make our next set of tests in precisely two hours, but we will not need to stop the train to do it. At least I don't think so," she explained, struggling to get back on her feet.

"Okay, then, we'll get this train on the go," Luca announced. He and Marcella left, walking to their beloved engine. Before long, we heard three whistles sounding and then the familiar chug-chug followed by a slight jar as the train began moving. We all headed to the bench seats to watch.

No one was more excited than Flavio and Alexa. "This is incredibly fantastic, Flavio! My dreams are coming true!" He gave her a loving hug. He'd never been on any kind of long train ride either, just some short ones here in Velona and the ride up to Kefall down in Demokritos. She was off to see the world.

Every two hours during the day, Lucianna conducted her tests. Every four hours or so, we halted to take on more coal and water. We followed their suggestions and relieved ourselves at these stops, though our husbands lent us a hand with it to speed us along. Twice, I saw Marcella standing on the very top of the tall engine, using her foot to pull down the water tower's spigot, filling the engine with more water. Gutsy woman, I thought.

At the last stop towards evening, Luca notified us, "We have to layover four hours in Barcella's yards to allow another train to pass us. I just got an LDCS message from Barbe Barcella. She wants you to visit with her and have supper while you are waiting. A carriage will be waiting to pick you up. You must have connections! She's the monarch here in Barcella." We smiled. That we did.

Around six, we pulled into the Barcella train yards and parked on a siding. There was a carriage waiting for us and we six soon found ourselves entering the Royal Palace of Barcella. Luca and Marcella stayed behind to service their engine. Barbe stood waiting for us, tossing back her long wavy brown hair so that it fell just below her shoulder blades nicely. She had hazel eyes, I noted, and wore a brown ball gown with petticoats. Her husband, Mariano, stood proudly at her side and her best friend Tina, who had long blonde hair and a blue matching gown stood behind her with her husband, Manfredo, at her side.

"So glad that you could stop and dine with me. I do so want to thank you for all that you've done for us," Barbe said after the brief introductions and as we followed them to her private dining room. There we met her stewards — Tina's parents.

"Wow, this is an occasion," Barbe said as we began to dine, allowing our husbands to feed us, since Barbe and Tina were doing just that. "I've never played host to the Emperor of Demokritos' daughter before. I do love your earrings, Alexa. I hope that you like our simple fare; we are all still on food rationing, and I believe that I must set a good example and take rations just as my people must do."

"This is excellent, Barbe. I am living my dream of seeing the world," Alexa confided. "I just which we could spend more time at it, but Lucianna's doing her experiments. Later on, Flavio and I would like to come for a longer visit, perhaps in the spring."

"Oh do so! It is so pretty when all the flowers are in bloom. We have concerts and dances here too, just like in Velona. I'd love to have you both come to a ball with us. By the way, Bethany, I wanted to personally thank you for all that you and Marco and the others did for us. Stefano kept me fully briefed. I know that if you had not convinced that monster to fabricate all those things for us and install your memories of how to use them, most all of our women would be dead by now. Still, we lost far too many for my wishes. On behalf of all of us, thank you!"

After we dined, she gave us a short tour of her palace, pointing out her hallway of portraits. She whispered to me, "Bethany! I got a therapy session from this fellow and discovered that I was her! Jovanna Barcella! You saved my life and country way back then, and you did it again now!" She gave me a big hug, women's fashion. I grinned.

"Now I recognize you. I thought you seemed very familiar to me. Terrific. We should get together later on when this mess is finally resolved," I suggested. She agreed. Soon, we had to leave to be sure that we were aboard when Luca and Marcella were ready. We made it with a half hour to spare.

"Are you going to drive all night?" I asked them before we climbed aboard.

"Sure, do it all the time. One of us naps while the other drives," Luca replied.

"Where can you nap up there?" Marco asked. "You are welcome to have a bunk with us."

"Thanks, but we have to be close by in case of trouble," Marcella replied.

As the train got underway again, we got ourselves ready for bed. The bunks were narrow, serving only one person. Hence, we had the fellows tuck us in, let them climb up, and use the upper bunks. What a peaceful sleep we had!

We awoke and found that we were stopped in the Vito rail yards, delayed for two more hours while another train passed by. As usual, Lucianna continued her tests promptly at eight o'clock and then every two hours afterwards. I began to notice now that there were enormous differences in sound quality between the many settings. Some produced no reception at all. "This is why we are doing the tests," Lucianna patiently explained to me, when I commented upon this.

We had other layovers lasting from one hour to four hours in the other major sector capital cities. On January 4, we pulled into Zargarb for another two hour layover. At this point, over half of her settings didn't yield any trace of Giovanni's voice, and I grew a bit anxious about it. What if we couldn't hear him at all when we got to Shansee?

The next day, we pulled into New Xin. Here we had a five hour delay, and Marcella came back to explain. "We are about to head out on the long Desert of Desolation run into southern Tan Loc Province. We have to carry enough coal and water to make the crossing, as there are no way stations along the way. Poor Luca has to really shovel in extra coal this time and load on a dozen water barrels, just in case we run low. When we leave the station behind, we will stop and let you all come up front. We can have two of you up front at a time. The view is spectacular, and it will be daylight for our crossing.

Sometime later, it was my turn to ride in the cab. "Whoa, this is a climb!" I exclaimed as I looked up at the vertical steps.

"Use your chin for balance," Marcella called out. I was determined to do this if she could, though I knew that I could just cheat and levitate myself up. Soon Marco and I were standing beside her. Luca was lying down near the coal mound, wrapped in a blanket. "I'll wake him if we need him. Here we go." She sat down and used her feet to release the safety lever, then rose and used her feet to release the brakes. At last, she gave a whistle and hooked one leg over the throttle lever, while leaning to watch out of her front window. Chug-chug, we began to move once more.

I took her advice and leaned out the other side, peering down at the thin rails moving off into the distance far ahead of us. The ocean waves crashed upon the shore to our right, while the shimmering heat waves distorted our vision of the desert on our left. She was right; the view from the cab was exhilarating.

"I see why you love this job," I told her. She grinned.

"There is nothing better in life than to sit here and run this engine. Honestly, there isn't. I was ready to have Luca kill me when I got the plague and figured my life as an engineer was finished. He helped me figure out how to run it on our last run from Zargarb to Velona. Yet, I wasn't fired. So I'm the luckiest woman in the world."

"No you are the smartest train engineer in the world," Luca called out from his bedroll. "Best troubleshooter anywhere. Hasn't been anything yet that she cannot diagnose." Marcella grinned.

We learned that this crossing of the Desert of Desolation was the worst run of all the lines in the world. Since we were not heavily loaded, we finally pulled into Station One just inside Tan Loc Province after fifteen hours. We'd used every bit of extra coal that Luca had brought and all the water as well, pumping it into the engine by hand. Luca explained that freight trains hauling heavy cargo often ran out of water or coal on this stretch and had to be rescued by the mini-engines, which brought more of each out to the stranded train. The LDCS was the train's lifeline, especially when such occurred.

Their monsoon season was nearly over, though it rained heavily for the next two days, letting up as we finally pulled into Shansee late on January 7. Incredible. Less than seven days to get from Velona to Shansee, Tashien. Simply unbelievable, unless you traveled it for yourself.

Now, Lucianna's experiment seemed to me to be in dire trouble. At the designated hour, we heard nothing. Still, she continued to go down her usual settings, each about a minute apart. Finally, we heard Giovanni's voice once more! "Testing. Giovanni calling Lucianna. Come in please. I am still not receiving you. Can you hear me? Giovanni calling Lucianna, come in please."

"Can you hook up the LDCS for me?" she asked Luca. He got out their small ladder and climbed to the top of the pole. There he put a clip onto the wire and then stuck a metal pole into the ground. He fastened the other clip to it, leading the wires inside the work car. Here, sitting on the floor with their sending unit, Marcella struggled a bit to get the two clips onto the two poles. Now the wires carried the current flow.

"Okay, I'm ready. What are the destination city and the person?" Marcella asked.

"Velona, Giovanni Bartiana," she replied.

I watched fascinated as Marcella rapidly tapped out a series of dots and dashes with her foot. "Message as follows. Lucianna in Shansee. Am picking you up clearly on band 5, setting 3. My power too low for you to receive. Otherwise, it is working fine. Mark these settings. Will try to boost power here. If so, I'll send another LDCS message with date-time. Sign it Lucianna Bartiana Angela. Thanks, Marcella. You are darn fast with it."

She grinned, "Lots of practice." She unhooked her end, and Luca undid his end. "Honestly, I can do all that Luca is doing, only the darn ladder is really hard for me to get down, carry, and then raise. Also a bit tricky hooking the clip while not falling off the ladder. So I let him do that unless it is an emergency," she explained.

Luca came inside. "Well, we're here. According to Manlio, we are going to be here a few days? Right?"

"Yes, we need several days to check out something for their princess," I replied.

"Okay, we'll need at least two days' notice when you want to leave. It all has to be scheduled, you see. Don't want to run into any other trains," he jested. "We'll be staying in our usual yard bunks. The yardmaster can show you where, if you need us."

"Don't you want to see the sights of Shansee?" I asked.

"We've seen them before. This is our private time together, if you know what I mean," Luca explained, giving Marcella a gentle squeeze. I got the picture. For days they had to be alert and on the job. At these extended layovers, they had time for themselves. We waved goodbye and headed out of the train yards.

"I can't speak their language!" Alexa suddenly realized. Neither could Flavio or Lucianna.

"Don't panic, Marco, Valerio, and I do. This is a new section of the city. I haven't been here before. Well, first thing, we find us a rik to get a ride to the palace." I then had to explain to them that a rik was a hand pulled two-wheeled carriage. It was anyone's guess which way we should go, so I eventually asked for directions, and soon we found a main street and shortly after that, hailed three riks.

"Good god, Bethany!" Marco whispered to me, quite shocked at our rik driver. "Ours is a woman!" In spite of my intentions, I did stare. The armless woman wore the poorest of clothing, rather filthy and soiled. Her hair was long as I expected, but sorely in need of a wash and brushing. Her waist was tied to the rik much as a horse, with no way for her to undo herself. Her waist was tiny and her lips as red as ours. A coin pouch dangled in front of us and a crude sign read, "Deposit fare in bag."

"Hello. What is your name?"

"Bei Lin. Where to go?" she replied.

"Pian Ling Wu's Palace, please. I thought only men pulled the riks."

"Bei Lin must work. Not do anything now but pull rik. You see." We were off heading out into the streets of this huge city. The streets were still wet from the rain, though the clouds had begun to break up for a while at least. Now I recognized where we were at, the far southwest side, the slums. Before long, the streets were packed with people. Many women were attempting to negotiate the mass of people, their yokes hanging precariously from their shoulders. Often they would be bumped and have to quickly set their loads down and reposition themselves before continuing. I held my breath, mostly, until finally, we cleared the slums and reached the main north-south street called Tiger Street. We were about a mile north of the docks and the Santi Inn with which I was familiar. Now I knew where we were at and relaxed.

We had just started up Tiger Street, which was even more densely packed, when a loud gong sounded. Actually, there were hundreds of gongs sounding at nearly the same time. To our surprise, Bei Lin stopped. So did all the other riks on the street. So did all of those who were walking. All forward motions ceased. Bei Lin turned her head as much as she could towards us.

"Please, it is pleasure time. Come pleasure me."

"Huh?" Marco replied. "I don't know what you mean. We are strangers to your land. Why has everyone stopped? What's going on?"

She was undulating from one foot to the other trying to rub her privates. I looked around and could find no words to describe what I saw! Everywhere, men and women were rubbing private parts, either theirs or someone who close to them! I was shocked and dumbfounded.

"Please, it is the law here. When gong sounds, everyone stops and takes pleasure. We have to; we cannot stand it any longer. Please, Bei cannot stand it any longer. Must be released. Please." She sounded pathetic. I just could not believe what was going on here.

"Bethany, what's happening here?" Flavio called out from the rik behind us.

Just then, a passerby came up to Bei and began using his finger on her. I turned away, trying not to see this display, but it was happening in all directions! At last, Bei moaned, and the man bowed to her and went his way. Not long after that, the gongs sounded, and Bei resumed pulling us along. Suddenly, the whole street was alive and in motion once more. "What the hell just happened, Bethany? Did we see what I think we just saw?" Valerio called out from behind our rik. He was just as shocked as I was. "Good lord! They all did it!"

Well, now I did have something to discuss with Princess Pian Ling Wu! What was going on in Shansee? It was beyond shocking. I was so disturbed that I forgot to point out some of the sights as we pass, such as the huge Central Gardens on our left. At last we reached the Princess Path and turned right onto this major east-west street. Ahead, I spotted the walls of the palace, and soon the rik halted before the main guest entrance, where two guards armed with swords and long guns stood. Marco kindly put the two coppers into her money pouch and we stepped out.

"I am Bethany Bartiana Angela. I believe that Princess Pian Ling Wu is expecting us."

The guards bowed and one asked us to follow him inside. We entered the public throne room where the Princess met with her subjects. Incense was burning on two side tables, adding a distinctive fragrance to the air. We could easily tell which of the three women before us was the Princess.

Princes Pian was tall, with the same red lips and dark eye shadow as the rest of us. Her thin waist matched ours. Indeed, all three women had the same characteristics. We all did, for that matter. However, Pian had very long, lustrous, and shiny black hair, straight as an arrow, draped over her bosom and falling nearly to the floor. Her dress was sky blue silk, and I saw immediately that she wore the shiny black, tiny, high heels so popular when I was last here nearly a half century ago. A large emerald hung from her neck. Her two handmaidens also wore fine silk dresses, but were reserved and didn't rise when we entered. As she rose, her hair fell to three inches of the floor.

She began the familiar sort of shuffling walk, taking a step no more than three inches at a time, as she moved towards us. "Bethany?" she called out questioningly. Her feet appeared extremely tiny, though Marco, Valerio, and I knew that her feet were the same size as ours, only hers had been altered to have an extreme arch. Her feet could no longer lay flat on the floor. Her tall spike heel nearly touched the end of her toes in the back, making walking challenging; hence the sort of shuffling gate.

"Yes, I am Bethany Bartiana Angela. You must be Princess Pian Ling Wu." She smiled and said that she was. One by one, I introduced the five others. I leaned into her and we pressed our heads together, Lucianna and Alexa followed my lead, while the fellows put their arms around her and gave her a warm hug, which we all knew that she would appreciate.

"How was your train trip?" she asked politely. After a bit of chat, she said, "Will you please come with me and take tea? We can discuss things in private."

While we walked as slowly as we could, she shuffled along as swiftly as she could. Still we has to pause so as not to get ahead of her. After many steps, we entered a beautifully done tearoom, with bamboo walls and a huge window that opened onto the gardens. Although winter here, the gardens still showed some green and were very pleasing to the eye. Marco assisted her with a chair, which brought a smile to Pian's face. We sat around a teakwood table. Soon, four servant women came shuffling in with teapots in their yokes, along with cups. I noticed how hard it was for them to manage, yet manage they did. Just as they sat the yokes down, the gongs around the city rang out again. The four looked at Pian.

"Leave your yokes. You may leave now," Pian said quietly. The four bowed and left as fast as they could shuffle.

"Will you allow me?" Marco said to Pian. She nodded. I wondered how well he remembered the art of serving tea. He didn't do a bad job of it, pleasing Pian. A bit later, with tea before us, we all shed our shoes and began to sip.

"Pian, what is this gong thing? It sounded on our way here and everyone stopped, even those on foot." I wanted an explanation for this strange, bizarre, and shocking behavior.

Pian sighed. "Bethany, it has to do with the emotional tones of the people. When you were last here, the tone of so many was so low: dying, useless, apathy, hopeless, victim, abasement of one's self, undeserving. Well, after the plague struck us, any man or woman who was emotionally at undeserving or lower found the vastly increased sexual urges impossible to control. Those who are higher in emotional tones, such as me, are able to keep them at bay and release them with our husbands in our beds at night."

"Almost from the beginning, we found that those people simply have to cease everything and satisfy or pleasure themselves to a release. It got so bad that almost no work was being done anywhere in the entire province! Personally, I found this utterly disgusting and debasing; yet, those who were so low emotionally simply had to get a release somehow. My four servants here — they would rub against anything to get the satisfaction that their bodies craved. It is the wildest thing that I have ever seen, save for all the other effects of this abominable plague."

"At last, the High Parliament made it a law that every two hours throughout the day, when the gongs sound, everyone who needs a release are allowed to stop everything they are doing and achieve it. Honestly, I would suggest that you time your travels around the city accordingly, unless you wish to see such a grotesque display. Mind you, they only pleasure themselves. We do not allow actual sexual intercourse in the streets, although plenty of that now goes on inside virtually any building, especially down in the slums. After the law went into effect, we finally were able to get some work out of the men and women."

"You will find that many of us simply tolerate it. Obviously, I do not need to pleasure myself when the gong sounds. However, my servants will writhe around and begin rubbing against anything possible to achieve their craving for pleasure release. Incredible, but true. After the person achieves such, they seem to be fine for up to a maximum of two hours, after which the drive begins to utterly overwhelm them once more."

"But enough of such disgusting talk. I should more fully introduce myself, Bethany. You knew me last lifetime. I was called Jemma, Kali's little girl," Pian said.

"Wow! I thought that you were very familiar. Jemma! Well, your new body does you justice! Has everything gone well for you? Kali and Ania took off for Demokritos this lifetime. I think that they felt they would be more useful down there. I haven't heard from them in a long time." We began to chat about old times, and I introduced her to the others, explaining a little about who we used to be, body-wise. Marco was Bianca back then. Valerio was Len. For an hour, we chatted like mad, not having seen each other for almost a half-century. I did learn that she was hesitant to use her telepathy to contact me, not knowing what my current situation was or where I was now living. I gave her permission to contact me anytime, and we promised to come back for a long visit when this crisis was finally over.

Alexa asked to see her feet and was shocked to see their extreme arch and how her foot no longer would lie flat, far from it. "I can only walk on my toes. You see, in our society, having small feet, such as I have, is a sign of great honor and respect. We are called Great Ladies by the common folks. Our tradition is much like yours in Demokritos, Alexa. In your country, is not having a tiny waist seen as being the height of fashion among the wealthy and noblewomen? Here, women of power and the highest of social standing all have tiny feet. Actually, as you can see, my feet are about the same size as yours. Only my shoes, which are the only kind that I can wear, make it appear as if my feet are very tiny."

"But how can you walk in them? Your walk is so unusual. Isn't walking terribly difficult?" Alexa asked.

"We must take very tiny steps, so it looks more like we are doing a tiny shuffle. We simply cannot take a larger step. Someone once told me that we move slowly so that we can truly see the world around us. Before the plague, it was not much of a problem. Now, it is very tricky, since we have so few ways to keep our balance. Anyway, Alexa, in your country, don't you find that wearing those impossibly tight corsets terribly uncomfortable and restrictive as well? Yet you all do it." Alexa saw her point at last. It was a cultural difference.

"Now then, I suppose we must talk about the reason that I sent for you. I've discovered two very upsetting things within the last month. First, our old Church of Jehosanity is at it again," Pian began. Alexa flushed slightly; it was her church once more coming to the fore. She wondered what they did this time.

"Apparently, you have Churches of Jehosanity in the Sea Princes." I nodded. "Well, as you know, they have a lot of holy women who take vows of celibacy and become nuns, serving the needs of others, usually the less fortunate. Some, I believe, cook, clean, and do laundry for the priests. Anyway, those women also got the plague. Can you visualize a nun in her holy habit, yet with bright red lips, our fancy eyeshadow, and tiny waists? I find that a most curious image. Anyway, I digress. When they were afflicted and unable to perform their regular duties as nuns, apparently, the cardinals shipped them back to the pope, asking for him to take care of them and to send them new replacement nuns, since they could no longer obtain any from your countries after the plague. Well, the pope shipped them over here to Shansee. They put them in beggars clothing and dumped them on the streets known for prostitution, down in the slums. Can you believe that? Anyway, they were suffering from the same uncontrollable urges to be pleasured as so many of our own people. As you can imagine, Bethany, they found themselves in dens of iniquity and craving it. Most have now passed away, thankfully. However, I have found one who desperately wants to change, and I promised her that you would speak with her. She is from Velona originally. Her name is Sister Natasa."

Alexa was rather pale, but didn't say anything. Pian continued. "The second thing is this insane woman, Lin Zu. I've done a bit a research, and part of her story is clear. She is twenty-two now. Before the plague, I believe that she was down around an emotional tone of victim. She worked in the rice fields at that time, some twenty miles from Shansee to the east. After the plague struck, she sank all the way down to dying. According to her villagers, she, like many others, just sat around in a complete stupor, refusing to eat or even care for her bodily needs. Her husband tried his best, but honestly, men have no clue about how to help women with their needs. Anyway, she apparently passed away or at least that's what the villagers claim."

"The next day, some of the men were getting ready to bury her and several other women who had passed away from the plague, when she awoke from her sleep, shocking them all. She ran around shouting in some unintelligible language. Not long after that, she began to submit to these powerful sexual urges that we all have. She went crazy trying all manner of motions to pleasure herself, just as countless thousands now do. That was not surprising to the villagers, as most of their women were doing similar actions as well. The next day, they found her lying on her husband's dead body, chewing on his flesh and sucking what blood she could get from his body. Now they do not claim that she somehow killed him. Lord knows how we women could do something like that now. They cleaned her up again, but she continued to rant in this weird language, and they sent her into Shansee to see a doctor. He sent her to me with a diagnosis of insanity. I listened to her for a while and heard her use the phrase "mammalian cells." Bethany, isn't that what the mantis called our fleshly bodies?" I nodded. "So I thought I ought to have you or someone like you take a look at her."

"Yes, I find that a highly unusual phrase. I certainly do want to meet with her. I suppose we ought to talk to Sister Natasa first."

"Okay, I'll take you to her. I have her in a room here in the palace. Follow me," Pian said. I watched as she very carefully got to her feet. I realized that it must be very hard for these women with small feet to deal with their lives now. Yet, it was either this way or the impossible Version One of Nestor's; besides, they chose to have their feet made small. Slowly shuffling along, she led us down a long hall. She had the ex-nun in a back bedroom of the palace. As we approached, another of Pian's servants bowed to her and said that she was still fine and that she had helped the nun during the last gong period. Now I knew what the young woman meant.

"I'll leave you here with her. Li here will bring you back to me when you are done or if you need something." Pian then turned around and slowly shuffled her way back down the long hall. Li bowed to us and Marco opened the door for me.

"I think it best that I see her alone first. If we all go in, she might become unwilling to speak freely," I suggested. They agreed and I entered, Marco shutting the door quietly. This was a small room with a single bed. Natasa was sitting on the bed, staring at her feet when I came in. Pian had had her bathed and dressed in a typical Tashien gown — yellow and orange silk, pencil shaped gown, of course ill-fitting around the waist. She wore the usual thin flats so common in this land. Her brown hair was thick and long. I suspected that the nuns usually kept their tied up, and seldom, if ever, cut it. She tossed her head, so that her hair moved back over her shoulders, as she looked at me.

"Hello. I am Bethany. I'm from Velona. How are you doing?"

"Natasa. I am from Velona too. I want to go home, please. I used to be a nun and worked for Cardinal Ruggerio. That was before the devil came with the plague. Now I am afraid that the Church has cast me out because Lucifer has taken over my body. I am full of unholy lust, and every few hours, Lucifer must have his lust fulfilled. If I don't have it done, I go crazy. Please, can you either kill me or take me home to Velona, where I have a brother who will kill me and free me from Lucifer's Lust."

"It is my wish to bring you back home with us to Velona. First, I would like to hear all about what you have been through," I asked. In hindsight, perhaps this was not the right thing to do now. She began telling me what had happened. She talked slowly, and I sensed that right now she was in apathy over the whole thing. She sat there utterly limp as she spoke. Actually, she added little during that hour that I didn't already know, but her slow speech consumed an hour, before I noticed that she was getting agitated. Natasa began wiggling her legs, holding them tightly together as she moved them. I sensed what was happening, and then we both heard the gongs sound.

"Please, I must have lustful pleasure now! I can't stand it any longer. I have been trying not to, but I can't stop it. Please, I have to have it now. Please, I beg you," Natasa wailed, totally out of control, her legs wiggling to find relief but not finding it. It was like an itch that one cannot itch, and it was driving her crazy or more likely insane.

I had a choice. Either I could do as she asked, after which she would probably become sane for a few hours, or I could link with her mind and see for myself what was going on. I admit now that this unexpected and highly unusual side effect had my curiosity roused. I joined with her mind.

For a moment, I too became overwhelmed with intense sexual desires, even finding myself squeezing my legs tightly together. Then, I realized what was happening. This was just our normal sexual urges to procreate in action, only the mantis had greatly enhanced such sensations. All her life Natasa had been suppressing such feelings and desires. Now that the plague had so greatly enhanced them, she was overwhelmed by them and assigning the cause of these to Lucifer or some other deity, not herself. For her, this was akin to an opium addict's intense cravings for another fix.

Natasa. Natasa. Listen to me. Yes, me. This is not Lucifer's doing. You are not possessed of the devil. There is no devil inside you. You are feeling what all women feel. It is your body wishing to mate and procreate. Your body wants to survive for the future. To do so, it must make new baby bodies. This is a natural urge that all women have. Without it, we humans would perish from the earth. Here, focus on this. Yes, that's it. It's your big toe. Now, feel the other one there. Slowly, I had her open up a sensory line to her toes and then her feet and then her ankles. That did the trick. The overwhelming urge began to dissipate and then subsided altogether. She opened her eyes and was quite surprised.

"I — I did it. I stopped it from happening. Somehow I did it."

"Yes, well done, Natasa. You are in control of your own body now. When the urge comes again, start feeling your toes, just as we just did. You can do it. You control your body, not the other way around."

"You mean there is no Lucifer, no devil inside me, lusting for such unholiness?"

"Of course, not Natasa. It is not unholy to bear children. Our future depends on women bearing children."

"But I am not married. I gave all that up to become nun and serve Lord Jehosa. Now, I am cast out of my church. Whatever am I going to do now?"

"Well, first things first, Natasa. First, you must work hard to master regaining control of your own body. Then, we will be taking you home to Velona with us. Once you are back, there are many ways that you can help the sick and needy. Let's talk with Daniela. I am sure that she could use your help. We have so many in need now. I am sure that your help will be most welcome."

"My church as abandoned me."

"What kind of a church abandons their own people in their hours of greatest needs?"

She finally smiled, "Not a very good one."

"I agree with that. Daniela has not abandoned her people, and I'm sure she can use your help when we get back. You don't have to be celibate in order to help people." I know that this was a bit of an evaluation on my part, but I wanted to get her thinking about starting a new life and perhaps finding love and thus someone to help her in life.

I left her pondering life changes, promising to return to get her when we were ready to leave. She thanked me. As we all walked back to the Princess, I relayed what I'd done and found out to the others. All were curious about how I had gotten her over her intense, insane cravings. It took a little explaining.

Once back with Pian, I had to explain it all again. "Ah, now that is a piece of very useful information, Bethany. I ought to have thought of that myself. Yes, focus the person's attention onto another part of their body until that part is real to them. Brilliant. I wonder how I can do that on hundreds of thousands of men and women? Ah well, my problem. You want to question Lin Zu now?"

We did and she had a soldier take us to where they had her locked up. They had small guesthouses joined to the main palace by a long porch with a bamboo awning over it. In the very last room as far from everyone else in the palace, we found Lin Zu. For her own safety as much as anyone else's, they had her locked in her room. A bored guard stood before the door.

The room was small, only three of us would fit, so Marco and Valerio joined me and stepped inside. We saw a typical looking Tashien peasant woman, twenty-two at most. As with most women in this land, she'd never cut her hair. It was thick, long and very black, as was her eyes. Servants had braided it after they'd cleaned her up. She was only around five-five, but very thin, probably from a near starvation diet for so many months. Still, she looked remarkably like the rest of us women. Her waist was small — red lips, dangling ear lobes, and, of course, no arms. She was not aware of our presence. Lin Zu just stared off into space, muttering to herself. We saw a bowl of rice and fish on the floor. From her face, we knew that she'd gotten down on the floor and put her face into the bowl to eat, much like a dog would.

Unfortunately, the gong sounded once more; two more hours had passed. As if on cue, she began to moan and writhe around and at last, ignoring us completely began rubbing herself against a bedpost. The fellows turned their faces away, but I continued to watch. Before long, she moaned louder, and a look of satisfaction appeared on her face. She then sighed and sat back down on the bed, as if nothing had happened. My guess was that this would be her most coherent period. I was right. She began talking, but the language was indeed strange.

Both Valerio and Marco shook their heads, indicating that neither recognized her speech. Somehow, I felt that I had heard this somewhere before, but I couldn't quite place it. Without warning, she began speaking in the Tashien dialect, "Escape mammalian cell. Escape it. Damn mammalian cell has me." That was all, she then reverted to her other unknown language.

She was using Nestor's terminology for our human bodies. No doubt about that. Where did I hear these strange sounds that she was making? Then it hit me. When I was helping the Guardian find out what had been happening during the three months he'd been unconscious, he'd reviewed all my memories. I'd finally seen and heard what the mantis was doing and saying while my three friends and I were unconscious in his flying ship. Yes, some of the sounds she was making seemed somewhat similar, though not exactly. They were being uttered by two completely different life forms. Still, the resemblance was uncanny.

"Marco, watch over me. I am going to try to touch her mind ever so gently." He put his arm around me, and Valerio took up a fighting position in front of my body, just in case she tried to attack me with her body, though how she would do that we didn't know. Yet, we had once been trained in self-defense and knew the precise points where one could strike a crippling or even deadly blow.

The one thing that I didn't want was a full contact. If it was a mantis, I had no idea how powerful it might be mentally. I put out the thinnest, gentlest, line to her mind, just barely touching it, as a goose down feather might touch one's skin as it fell.

In my opinion, each spiritual being has their own unique "feel" about them; perhaps it is a wavelength emanation or some aesthetic flow. As soon as I made that contact, I felt a being with whom I was familiar: Nestor, the mantis who had done all of this to us all! I backed off at once.

"It's him. We need to take her back with us for sure!"

"Thought so," Marco whispered. "Just feels like him, er her."

We stepped back out of the room to discuss this startling revelation further. "Yes, no doubt about it. She's Nestor, the one who attacked us and created the plague," I explained to Alexa, Flavio, and Lucianna. "You should make him undo all this," Alexa suggested, reminding me of what she'd said to me before.

I grinned. "In part, that's why we're going to take her back with us. Right now, I think it is best if we leave her alone. I have no idea how powerful he might be or even what he is capable of doing in her body, but it can't be good. Whatever you say, do not tell others that she is Nestor or was behind the attacks and plague. If someone kills her out of revenge, we might lose whatever chance we might have to get him or her to help us figure a way out of this mess." They all agreed. Since the guard didn't know our Velona dialect, our secret was safe. We headed back to Princess Pian.

Her husband, Dong Long had returned from his work. We learned that he ran a printing shop in town. He was thirty-one and wore his hair in a single, long braid. His moustache was spectacular, however. "Please, you must stay for dinner," he begged after we were all introduced. We agreed, but sent word to Luca and Marcella that we would be ready to travel when the train could get clearance to leave.

"Our beautiful daughter, Misha," Dong declared, as their ten year old daughter came shuffling into the dining room. She looked like a miniature Pian, very much like her mother, except she was much shorter. She smiled and bowed, being careful not to lose her balance because of her tiny feet. She too wore the familiar black shoes with a tall tiny heel just behind the end of her toes. Her feet were still growing, but they looked incredibly tiny. I felt a bit sorry for her having to shuffle so carefully without even arms to help herself. Alexa did likewise, seeing some of her own childhood in little

Misha.

"Our handsome son, Feng," Dong announced, as their eight year old boy followed his older sister into the room. I saw at once that he was supposed to follow her in case she had difficulty walking.

Pian whispered, "We had her feet done about two months before the plague. Awful timing, I wish now that we had waited, but she was begging us for two years to have it done." I smiled, what could I say?

We had a nice meal. This time, Pian and Misha attempted to feed themselves, so we followed suit. Normally, in Tashien the wooden bamboo sticks are used as the eating utensils. However, now that had changed. The women were forced to use the large spoons that had come with the alien package items. Still, Dong and Feng used their traditional sticks and got a kick out of showing Flavio, Marco, and Valerio how to use them properly. Yes, they had a harder time eating than we women, who also got a chuckle out of watching their struggles, especially little Misha.

After dinner, we received a message back from Luca. We were cleared to leave two days from now at ten in the morning. "Since you have two days, please, you must stay here with us," Pian insisted. Naturally, we agreed. After some servants showed us to some guest rooms, Pian and Misha showed up at our bungalow door.

"Go ahead, Misha. Ask her," Pian encouraged her somewhat reserved daughter.

Misha looked at me and said, "Would you like to come for a walk with us and see our gardens?"

"Sure, Misha. Lead the way."

"We'll bring her back in a while, Marco," Pian teased him. He lay back down on the comfortable bed.

"It's this way, but I have to go so very carefully so I don't fall down. I am now a Great Lady too, only I wish I had my arms back," Misha said. "I hope you don't mind going so slowly. Mom walks twice as fast as I do."

"Not at all. We can see more of the world when we walk slowly, Misha. You look just like your mom, two very pretty young ladies." Misha enjoyed the compliment.

"Here it is very hard to walk. Be careful, Bethany. The gardens start here. Aren't they just beautiful! In the spring, the air is filled with fragrances and pastel colors are everywhere. Mom says that you will come back for a long visit. Please, you must come in the spring and see," Misha chatted away. We spent about an hour going no more than a few hundred feet out into the garden and then back. Poor Misha's feet were taking a beating, but she was stoic about all her constant wobbling to keep her balance. Pian was somewhat better at it, though she too really had to wiggle her body to keep from falling a couple of times. Still, we enjoyed the excursion into their realm of quiet beauty.

During the next two days, I brought Pian up to speed on all that had happened to her other "sisters" of last lifetime and their parents, our close-knit family. She and Misha enjoyed hearing all the stories. I purposely didn't say anything about my recent mantis abduction and adventures. Finally, we had to leave. I had Marco sit with Lin Zu in one rik and watch over her while we headed through town back to the train yards. I sat with Natasa in another. Thanks to Pian, we timed it perfectly, leaving immediately after the eight o'clock gong and arriving before the ten o'clock gong sounded.

Luca and Marcella had restocked our charcoal and had stored some snack food for the trip. "Bringing two back with us?" Luca asked. I nodded. "Well, this time we will be going straight through. That is, we will not need to make those extended layovers. We will be part of the overall schedule of trains, so we ought to be back in four long days. Marcella will give you heads up warning of when to try to grab some meals at our stops."

As the train began to move slowly out of the yards, the ten o'clock gong sounded. Natasa bravely kept repeating, "Toes. Toes, focus. Toes." She succeeded in not losing control. Lin Zu, on the other hand, went nuts trying to get her pleasure "fix." At last, Marco took pity on her and helped her out with his hand. We looked away until he was done. I began to have some clues about the true state of these mantis beings. Poor Marco. From now on, every two hours during the day, he had to assist Lin Zu. Only at night, did he get any relief from it, as well as Lin, for that matter.

Chapter 30 Now What Do We Do

For twelve hours, we rode along southern Tashien and along the Desert of Desolation. As before, we stopped at the last station before the long haul along the edge of the desert to pick up coal, water, and a quick bite of supper. This time, we would make that long haul at night.

At ten o'clock that night, I woke up. Something was wrong, my groggy mind concluded. Ah, the train wasn't moving. Strange. It was quite dark outside and warm, so I concluded that we were still somewhere along the edge of the desert.

Quietly, I got up, slipped my shoes on, and headed out of our side door to see what was going on up by the engine. I saw two lanterns sitting on the ground near the left wheels of the engine. I moved closer to see what was the matter. Marcella was lying on the ground, her feet up in the air holding onto one of those huge wrenches. Luca had another wrench and was pushing down against her. I made a little noise trying to avoid startling them. Luca turned his head.

"Oh, I Bethany. Just a little problem here. Be up and running soon. Marcella spotted that some bolts were working loose. She's a genius when it comes to this stuff." Both groaned from the last efforts to tighten the bolts securely. Carefully, Luca held on to Marcella's wrench, allowing her to let go with her feet. She struggled to her feet, wiggling her back against the side of the engine.

"Oh my back. Stones are hard. Will that do it, Luca?" she asked.

"I believe so. I'll get the wrenches and lanterns, dear."

"You could have woken up Marco or Valerio to help you," I suggested.

She replied, "No need. It's our job, not yours. You are the paying passengers. It's all part of my job, though I wish I could at least hold up my half of the team."

"You do just fine, dear," Luca refused to let her run herself down. "Come on; let's get this train going again. Good thing that you spotted the trouble, before we lost the nuts, and had to walk back down the track to find them, dear." She smiled, yes, that had saved considerable time.

"I'll walk her back, Luca. Get the steam built up," Marcella ordered. To me, she added, "Got to make sure you are back in your car before we can start up again. Safety rules." I nodded.

"You sure know your job, Marcella. I am amazed at all you do."

"If I don't, I lose the only thing that makes life worth living for, well, now except for Luca," she grinned.

Before long, the chug-chug began once more, and I crawled back into bed. This time, I had to do some wiggling of my own and use my teeth to pull up my own covers. Soon, the gentle motion of the train put me back to sleep again.

Yes, the four-day train ride was a bit hectic on us as far as meals were concerned. While we had enough "pit stops," there just wasn't enough time at any train stop to go to an inn or diner and sit down to a relaxing meal. Rather, the fellows would dash off, grab whatever they could find, and bring it back. We did make use of our small heater-stove to fix what they could find for our meals. We were not complaining, mind you. It's just that none of us was used to traveling day and night for four days.

During our brief meal times, Natasa began to catch on to using her feet to hold a spoon. She definitely was trying to put on a brave face. Until now, she'd done nothing for herself, really. I gave her credit for trying. On the other hand, Lin Zu continued to eat like a dog. While we tried to put the bowl on the table, she merely grabbed hold of it with her teeth and managed to get it onto the floor, sometimes spilling half of her food in the process. She then got down on her knees and put her face into the bowl. After a few tries, we gave up and just put her bowl on the floor and forgot about it.

Just around sunrise on January 15, we pulled into the Velona yards home at last. Our dads and Giovanni were there to meet us, having brought our three motor-cars to pick us up. "It works, Lucianna!" Giovanni exclaimed, as the sleepy eyed Lucianna stepped off the bottom step of our work crew car.

She smiled and replied, "Of course, it would work. Now after breakfast, we have a lot of work to do to get this thing up and running." We were not back one minute before she was thinking about her inventions!

After breakfast, I contacted both Natasa's brother and our High Priestess Daniela and asked them to come over. Around ten Natasa left, now in the care of her brother. For her, things worked out well. Her brother took her into his family while Daniela convinced her that she had many jobs that Natasa could do to help the needy here in Velona.

On the other hand, we now had to figure out what to do with Crazy Lin, as Giovanni nicknamed her after seeing her eating manners and her temporary insanity bit kick in around ten that morning. We put her in our guest bedroom, but she was still oblivious to her surroundings. That she was no longer in Tashien didn't register in her mind, only hunger and the insatiable sexual urges did. Weird.

After breakfast and Natasa had left, Giovanni, Valerio, and Lucianna loaded up the LD radio gear into our motor-wagon and headed off to the DAE Enterprises. The rest of us sat down to discuss what to do with Lin Zu.

"Look, she is totally insane right now. She doesn't even know where she is at," Marco pointed out.

"Yes, but what will happen if we attempt to get her to 'wake up?' After all, if you are right and she is Nestor, what kind of powers might she have? We could be turning a devil loose on Velona," Lisa pointed out.

We all agreed that we had no idea of what kind of powers Lin might have or possess if she were pulled out of her insanity. Sergio suggested, "Well, we could send her to Isla la Roca. There she couldn't hurt anyone. Besides, if she is Nestor, she ought to pay for what she's done to us all. I say lock her up for good."

Quite a few agreed with him, but I was silent, thinking about what Alexa had suggested on several occasions. At last I spoke up, "You know, Nestor ought to be forced to make things right here."

"Well, that's true, dear," mom said, "but how can she do that now? I mean he's in a human body, not his mantis one. Besides, she's completely helpless now."

Eve spoke up, "If he knows that we destroyed his ship, he's certainly not going to cooperate with us at all and might try to kill us, Bethany. On the other hand, as he is now, he might not be worth a hoot."

"Well, he might not have recognized that it was us who downed his ship," I pointed out. "If so, if he does find out, you are right; he would probably be very angry with us and try to harm us. Makes sense."

"Besides," Marco pointed out, "those machines of his are operated by giant fifty foot mantis creatures with their weird appendages. In Lin's body, I don't see how he could possibly deal with those complicated controls of his machines."

"Maybe his mind is so twisted up now that he won't be able to figure it out," Eve suggested.

"How did he even get Lin's body in the first place? I would have thought that he would have just headed back to his home world and picked up another mantis body," Marco added.

"Even if he agreed to reverse what he's done, could we really trust him to actually do it and not turn us into something even more freakish?" asked Eve. She did have a valid point. How could we trust him not to turn us into creatures with beaks as he had first intended? While we talked some more, we really got nowhere on figuring out what to do with Lin-Nestor. Sergio and Lisa then headed off to the police headquarters to get some work done. I pondered our problem during the rest of the day.

At supper, which I made for everyone, Sergio and Lisa had some unexpected news for us. "After seeing Lin's wild antics, you know, her insane drive to pleasure herself, and your report of the tens of thousands who are doing it every couple of hours in Tashien, I decided to investigate here. We've got some men and women similar to those in Tashien right here in Velona! Mostly, they are just disturbing the peace with their crazy antics. That's why I was never called in to investigate. No real crimes are involved yet, anyway. Barti has been handling all those cases quietly, trying not to stir up the general population."

"He's got over a hundred of them locked up. According to him, the doctors have been working with them to find a cure. They haven't found any yet, but over half of them have been calmed down, are cooperating, and working on controlling their animal urges now. Barti expects to be releasing over fifty of them soon. Anyway, this phenomenon is not limited to Tashien, Bethany. I thought that you ought to know that," Sergio stated.

"Thanks, that is useful information, Sergio. Does Stefano know about this?"

"Oh yes, but he's also keeping it on the quiet as well. He's afraid that if people know about this bizarre behavior, then others may attempt to harm the poor victims or others may decide to stop fighting against such urges and allow themselves free rein on their drives as well. Neither is acceptable, he says. So mum's the official word," Sergio answered.

Lisa added her observations to the discussion, "While Sergio was busy, I visited some of them in their cells. Well, actually, I did not enter their cells, just stood outside, and observed them — you know, the hard-core ones that are not responding well to the doctor's work. They are all very low emotionally. I believe that they are all at or below undeserving emotionally. Most of those are immigrants from Tashien or New Xin. Kind of figures, doesn't it? The ones who are responding and will be released soon are all right at making amends and simply feel that they cannot withhold anything from anyone. The doctors have been working with them to get them to see that this one thing they must withhold, if they are to be a part of life and society again. They seem to be responding fairly well."

All this began to make some sense to me. If a person was so low emotionally then he or she feels it is impossible to hold back anything from anyone. That emotion is right below grief, a real solid grief. Just above this emotion, a person often becomes propitiative towards others and sympathetic beyond all logical reason. This gave me something to ponder. While the others dealt with the dishes or listened to the radio symphony hour, I sat with my after dinner tea and thought.

I reflected back on my many conversations with Nestor, via that headband which handled the translations. As I sat there, it dawned on me that Nestor was a spiritual being just as all of us. He too had a chronic emotional tone, just as everyone else had. Could I determine his? He was certainly not high; rather he was far from serene or even enthusiastic. No, he wasn't even antagonistic or angry, not even when he encountered the setbacks, such as the "accidents" that befell the little mantis creatures or even the breakdown of one of the little flying ships. Yes, he felt sympathy towards us.

That was it! He was extremely sympathetic towards us, downright propitiative actually. That's why he took our advice so readily. Emotionally, he could hardly have done otherwise! Had he been in anger, we all would have beaks right now, Version One would be worldwide. That meant he was only a shade above grief and just barely above making amends, the tone in which one simply could not hold back anything. That was precisely what Lin Zu was dramatizing; she simply could not withhold constant pleasuring of herself. She had to do it, because she had no other choice, since emotionally she could not hold back anything at all. Bingo.

I had an evil smirk on my face. If she couldn't withhold anything, then I ought to be able to get her to undo all that she had done, taking total advantage of her emotions! This was a dirty trick to play, using someone's emotions against them, but it might work. Still there were seeming insurmountable problems. Would his mind still be able to work out the genetic modifications? Would he be able to operate the machines? Would he even go along with the idea of undoing the horrific damage? Would he even remember his last lifetime as a mantis?

The biggest fear that others had about "waking" Nestor up was just how powerful his spiritual powers might be. While Eve and I were pretty strong ourselves, capable of many things, of which telepathy was only a small one, just what would Nestor's be? Could he somehow zap us, driving us into unconsciousness? He did just that when he abducted us and he'd been able to wipe the Guardian out for three months. Then, I realized that he had not done that, rather his machines had generated those energy beams, which had so wiped us out. Now that I thought about it, I'd never seen him use anything but his many machines to carry out his will. This would make sense if Nestor's emotional tone were as low as I'd estimated. If you are going to command telekinesis, you have to be very high in emotional tone, far above mere enthusiasm. I began to suspect that Nestor, as a spiritual being, had no real powers of his own anymore, having become dependent upon all his machines to do it for him.

"I'm going to do it," I spoke aloud. Then, I had to explain my reasoning. I went into Lin's room and found her sleeping for the night, sprawled across the bed. She looked as if she was exhausted, and I decided to wait until the morning.

The next morning, Marco sat a bowl of breakfast on the floor for Lin and quietly left the room. We all found her method of eating a bit too disgusting to watch. I waited until she'd finished eating before I entered, carrying a wet wash cloth and towel on the lightweight yoke. She was sitting on the bed staring off into space as I entered. Quietly, I sat down before her and used my feet to clean the food off her face. Satisfied that she looked halfway presentable, I then sat down beside her and began to work out how to best establish communication with her.

I decided to mimic her. I sat and slumped forward and stared off into space, just as she was doing. I waited. After a bit, her right shoulder twitched, so I made mine have a similar motion. Before long, she began moving her legs around, as if trying to massage her privates. I grimaced and decided to emulate her motions. Suddenly, I could see why she was doing this! I was stimulating myself. God, I hope I don't have to continue doing this, I thought to myself. Unfortunately, she only increased her motions, as the stimulation grew stronger and stronger. Damn, I thought. Yet, I continued to duplicate her actions. Oh hell, why not? I thought. She let out a moan of great pleasure and finally ceased her movements. I didn't have to pretend to duplicate her at this point.

She turned her head and looked at me. I turned mine and looked at her. "Hello," she said in the Tashien dialect. I replied in kind. She smiled; I did too. I was finally in communication with her.

"Hello Nestor. It's Bethany. We've finally found you. Are you all right?"

"Bethany? Bethany? Oh my! It is you! How are you doing? Is everything working out as we planned? Have too many mammalian cells died? I am fine," she replied.

"I and the others are just fine too. As far as I can tell, it has all worked out just as we'd hoped it would. Yes, some did die, but very few. Should I call you Nestor or Lin Zu?"

"Who is Lin Zu? I am Nestor. No, Nestor is dead." She began crying, intense grief began flowing from her.

While he had caused all of this, I still felt for him. "Okay, Nestor, please start at the beginning and tell me what has happened." I decided to run a little therapy session on him. Would our therapy work on a mantis? Well, he wasn't being a mantis any more; he was still a spiritual being.

"Oh Bethany! I have failed utterly. All is lost now. I am flying back from the southern zone that you call Tashien. All of a sudden, a meteor hits my ship from below! I feel my whole ship crack and bend! It is awful! I think the meteor then falls back down on top of my ship and it breaks into two halves. I am working my controls, but nothing is working. I see the ground coming up fast. I am going to crash. I know it! I feel a huge impact. My body is squashed. Pain. The pain is overwhelming me. Flames. Burning. I am burning, but no, I cannot feel it any more. Something explodes, and I am flying out of there with the flaming debris. I am unconscious, but still sailing along with the explosion. No, I can't see the explosion anymore, but I'm still flying along. I can't see anything anymore. I am blinded too. I wait."

He waited. I sat there for nearly fifteen minutes while he slowly moved through this very long period. I realized that he must have been unconscious for months, much as the Guardian and the others had been.

"I wake up. I am lost now. I cannot find my way home. I too am a prisoner here. No one will be coming. No one can find this planet any more. The beacons are still destroyed. I should have repaired them first, but the protocols had those to be done last. No, I'm stuck here on your planet. I must have a body! I will have to have one of the mammalian cells. I have no choice. I can't live without a body. No one can."

"I move over the land and see a village. I am lost! There are no baby bodies here! Then, I see this body lying on the ground. No one owns this one. I take it. No, it takes me! I got close to it and zoom! I am being pulled into its head. I start feeling things with this new body. I love feeling things. I see male mammalian cells eating with sticks. I panic. I don't have all those memories that you and I built into the genetic modification. Nor do I have the pile of necessary objects. I try to ask them for help, but they do not understand me."

"Then I get these extremely pleasurable sensations in the mammalian cell's reproductive system. You remember, I had to enhance these to help keep the prisoners in their cells. Oh, I am addicted to it now! I can't stop it. I don't want to stop it. I want the male mammalian cells to pleasure me too, but I cannot get them to do it. I keep trying and trying. Finally, I give up. All is lost totally. I stop paying any attention to other mammalian cells; just do what I can to get this wonderful pleasure sensation all the time. Then I see you sitting beside me. That's all. I am glad to see you, Bethany."

I had him go through it a few more times and he brightened up. "Oh, I am now speaking their language! I am aware of it now. I feel like a heavy weight has been lifted from me. Thank you, kind Bethany." I ended the official session at this point.

I decided this was the prime opportunity to ask. "Should I call you Nestor or Lin Zu?"

"I like Nestor, but it doesn't fit this wonderful mammalian cell. Perhaps we should call me Lin Zu."

"That makes good sense, Lin. I was wondering, Lin, if perhaps now we could undo some of these genetic modifications that we've made."

"Oh, I don't want to undo the reproductive glandular modifications. I am enthralled with them. I cannot live without this tremendous pleasure. There is nothing finer in the whole universe!"

"But wouldn't it be nicer if you had arms like the male mammalian cells? Then you could more easily obtain your desired pleasure," I suggested. I know, I was playing her, bribing her.

"Oh my! Yes, Bethany! You are right as always! We should have our arms back. That would make this so very much better!"

Then, her facial expression of glee crashed into a deep depression. "Alas, Bethany. I no longer have my ship. I no longer have my mantis body to work the controls. As much as I would like to do this, I simply am unable to do it for us. I am truly sorry, Bethany. Say, I would give anything to have one of the male mammalian cells reproduce with me. Can you get me one?"

"I'll have to see about that, Lin. Say. Suppose that I could get you to Chichulain and had a way for all the controls to be worked, as you need them to. Couldn't we then undo some of the genetic modifications and at least get our arms back so we can better pleasure ourselves?"

Lin's brow furrowed. I could tell that she was giving this considerable thought. After a few minutes, she finally replied, "Yes, Bethany. I believe that I can remember enough about my genetic engineering to do this. I am at a total loss on how I can possibly use the machine to develop it. Besides, I have no more ships with which to deliver the bacteria. Yet, I will try it on one condition, Bethany."

"What's that?" This sounded incredibly hopeful, yet I wondered what that condition might be.

"I need a male mammalian cell to pleasure me often. Find me one to do that, and I will go with you and see if it can be done. I cannot promise you that it can be done. If I had my old body, I could do it easily, but not while I am inside a female mammalian cell. Get me my male one and I will try. Will you pleasure me now, please rub me down there, Bethany."

"Sorry, Lin. I don't have any hands to do it for you or for me," I replied sympathetically, hiding my actual disgust. "You stay here, and I will see if I can find one for you. It may take some days."

"Oh my! Thank you so much Bethany. I know that you will try for me. I will wait." She began wiggling her legs once more, and I made a hasty exit.

"She wants her own private stud?" Marco joked when I told everyone what had happened. We were all sitting around the dinner table. Eve nearly choked on some food. Most chuckled as they heard the news. "Don't look at me, dear. I want your arms back as badly as everyone else, but there are limits on what I am willing to do, dear." We all laughed heartily.

"Say, I might have an answer to that," Sergio said quietly, after our laughter died down. "We have around fifty still locked up that the doctors have yet to reach. Perhaps we could make use of one of those men. I'll look into it."

Late the next afternoon, Sergio brought a man of Tashien descent to our house. Lisa was definitely acting as his protector; her eyes never left the man. "Bethany, this is Ning Peng, originally from a fishing village in Tan Loc. He is desperate for a wife and was jailed because he confronted too many women with his proposals and lewd actions in front of women. Like Lin, he simply cannot stop, he says, until he has a wife."

"Yes, Ning Peng need wife most badly. Ning most unworthy of wife, but promise to treat her like flower. Most kind, most loving. Ning work hard to please her. You have wife for Ning Peng?" he both pleaded and begged, most pathetically. I recognized his emotional tone right off: undeserving. Well, that part fit with the observational data we had so far.

"You promise to feed her, bathe her, and take care of her physical needs? She has no arms of course and will be totally dependent upon your care," I asked him.

"Oh yes, Ning Peng treat her okay. Feed, bathe, yes Ning most undeserving of her, but Ning do his very best to please her and care for her," he pleaded.

"Okay, let's put you two together and see how she and you get along. No promises, Ning," I suggested. I led him to her room and introduced Lin to Ning. At once, they began talking and soon were kissing. I quickly shut the door to give them some privacy.

Barely a half hour later, it was obvious that they were finished. Ning came to the door looking pleased. "Have towel and rag? Ning wash Lin Zu now. She most worthy woman." I had Marco take him to our bathroom to get what he needed while I checked on Lin.

I found her incredibly contented and satiated. "Oh my! Bethany! I am in heaven now. This reproduction is so fabulous. Thank you. Thank you. Male mammalian cell is perfect. I will try to undo our arms when you say. I feel so good!" I smiled and left her as a pleased Ning returned with a washbasin and towels.

"Well, she has agreed to give it a try. I guess that we should make plans to return to Chichulain. I will discuss this development with Stefano after supper."

Around seven, I parked my T-putt-putt near Stefano's front door and walked up, knocking with my foot. Caresa opened it, "What a surprise. Welcome, Bethany, come on in."

"Oh, hi, Bethany," Stefano appeared, entering the room. "Do come on it. What brings you by this evening?"

"We need a private chat, please. Nothing disastrous, no calamities this time, Caresa," I wanted to put her at ease. She relaxed and smiled, as he led me into his private home office. Papers were piled in stacks all over every conceivable location, including the floor.

"Terribly busy. All these things need handling. Have a seat, what can I do for you tonight?" he said, sitting down on his chair, while I took the only other chair not covered with a stack.

"Stefano, we have found Nestor. He's taken over a body of a young Tashien woman and now is calling herself Lin Zu." I began this strange tale, ending with what I was proposing. "I don't have any idea at all if this will work out, Stefano. There are so damnable many variables in this; so many things might not work out. Can she remember how to do it? Can we even work out a way to operate the machinery? Even if we can somehow manage all that, how can we deliver it? I have dozens more how do we's, but Stefano, we just have to try this. It may end up a total failure. Yet, if we can somehow pull this off, the rewards — well, we just have to give it a shot."

"I agree, Bethany. We have to try. I can donate the West Po caravel to you for as long as you need it. However, there is one major problem: obtaining enough food for such a long voyage. Stocking that much food will cause major shortages in everyone's rations. I suggest that you stop in the Southlands or the Spice Islands and pick up the large amount that you will need. You'd better take a goodly supply of gold with you; there are no Banca's on the Western Continent that I know of anyway. I can donate ten grand, will that help?"

"Thanks, yes, I will cover the difference. We'll need a crew that can afford to be gone for up to perhaps a whole year. We cannot take them away from their families who definitely need them," I pointed out.

"Yes, precisely. Let me have Vittore look into it first thing in the morning. Let's refer to this expedition as Project A, so that we don't divulge any ideas. I agree; we dare not get anyone's hopes up. A for arms, get it?" I grinned and agreed.

Back home, we discussed who should go on this very long voyage. Although Sergio and Lisa wanted to come, we all thought better of that. They were needed here to handle situations that arose in Velona. His talents as Chief Detective Inspector were invaluable to maintaining order. While Lucianna and Valerio also wanted to go, Giovanni wanted one of the two inventors to remain behind.

"Look, if anything happens to me, Lucianna, we need you to carry forward our latest ideas. It will take me another fourteen years to get a new body back into high gear. Let's take your new LD radio system with us. We can discuss things between us every day," he suggested.

"But think of the things I might learn there? I am the electricity expert, not you," she protested.

Lucianna then sighed and relented, "Well, I can see your point, though. One of us ought to be here working away. Actually, I like the idea of using the LD radio. That is a very long distance. If we can make this work, then we will be ready to put it into production when you get back. We should follow the same series of tests until you are actually there just to make sure that we both stay on the same frequency. I will need to make a more powerful remote unit for you to take along on the trip. We'd better work on that first thing in the morning."

We decided that Eve and Giovanni would go along with Marco and me. Of course, Lin Zu and Ning Peng would be with us. Now came the extensive packing and trying to anticipate what our needs would be for this adventure. We'd be sailing for at least three months to get there, three months back. How to climb to the mountain plateau was unknown as well as how long we would have to stay there. Lin did say that if we could somehow operate the machines, they would fabricate all the food that we would need while there. That sounded positive at least.

As we began our planning, none of us really dared to hope that this venture would be successful. There were just far too many unknowns and imponderables. Yet, if somehow, someway this genetic mutation could be undone, even partially, we had to try. If we women could at least have arms, the rest we could ignore. We had to make the attempt.

Chapter 31 Revisiting Prison

The sky was a bit dark, light snow fell as we headed to the docks, our motor-wagon loaded with our supplies. It was January 25, 823, colder than normal for our January. Stefano was already waiting on us; it was his personal caravel that he was lending us, the Le Envoy. We three women wore our new capes with paca fur lining and a hood, which could be pulled up over our heads. We'd already said our farewells, though Valerio, and Sergio drove us there, helping with the many bags.

"Cold day to set sail," Stefano said, as we walked up to him. "Come on. I'd like you to meet this special crew." He waved and ten men and women walked across the gangplank coming up to us. "This is your captain, Amando Armono and his wife, Allegria, who will be one of your cooks. This is Bosun Dominico Tello and his wife, Bertina, who will also be your cook. Their children are all married and living in their own homes. These six lads are apprentice seamen; all are sixteen and single, searching for some adventure." He was letting us know that these ten could afford to be going on such an extended journey. We probably would be gone a year, perhaps.

"Please to meet all of you. Captain Amando. I've brought along an additional thirty thousand gold to help with our expenses. Do you think this will be enough?" I asked.

"Yes, more than enough. I think that between Stefano's donation and yours we could supply this ship for several years," he broke into a broad smile, putting me at ease over the financial picture. "I would like to set sail within the hour, leaving with the tide makes it easier."

"Fine with us," I replied, and we all headed onto the ship. We six watched the dockhands load our things onto the main deck. The six young lads then lowered them into the cargo hold below, and then shut the hatch. I would have liked to wave to my dad. A sense of frustration struck me, but Marco and Giovanni waved for us all. While I normally liked to stand on deck and watch Velona slowly recede, it was just too chilly. We all headed inside through the poop deck sliding doors.

Here on the poop deck were the best and most comfortable cabins. The starboard cabin was double size with a large bed. The port side held two smaller cabins. At the stern was the captain's cabin. A slanted stairs led to the cargo hold where an additional ten cabins were located here at the stern. Fore of them was a large open playing area with a dartboard. Beyond that was the dining area and cargo storage. The kitchen and pantry was fore of that and the crews quarters was in the very bow, where the roughest ride occurred.

Negotiating the stairs was tricky for us women, but with caution, doable. Hence, I decided that since we would be spending a lot of time below deck, we six should take cabins near the play area. Giovanni put the LD radio invention into one of the smaller cabins on the poop deck. "I believe that you've made a wise decision, Bethany," Captain Amando complimented me on our choice of cabins.

"Why don't you let the bosun and his wife have one of these near us and also the six young lads? This is a long voyage and they would be far more comfortable back here than in the bouncing fore cabins," I suggested. He agreed, and the six teens gave us a rowdy cheer. We were a hit before we started.

"Also, we ought to lend a hand with ship chores too," I volunteered us, knowing that such would give us something to occupy the long hours ahead.

"Ah, but my dear Bethany, you seem to me to be missing your hands," Captain Amando jested. Eve and I laughed, and the fellows smiled. I liked his sense of humor already. "We'll let your lads move your gear to your cabins, then. Me and my lads will get us under way before we get snowed and iced in," he said.

"I think that you have Velona confused with Calgary," I teased him back. He saluted me with a touché sign, grinned, and headed topside, followed by the boson and the six lads. Soon, I heard orders being barked, and Eve and I began to tell Marco and Giovanni where we wanted what. Meanwhile, Ning helped Lin into their very own cabin, rather like a mother hen with her chicks. I smiled as I watched him ushering her inside their cabin.

An hour later, Captain Amando called us to his cabin, where he had a large number of navigational charts laid out. "I wanted to go over our route. Of course, the fastest route would be to traverse a great circle. However, we have only enough food for two weeks. I think the best chance of getting a good supply would be to put into Leone, Southlands, about a third of the way down the coast. If we cannot, then our next best bet would be off here at the Spice Islands. If we can obtain enough, then we can sail all the way to the southern tip of the Western Continent. If not, we must head across to Wanakan and get re-supplied there, but that will delay us significantly. We all agreed with his analysis and hoped that we could pick up all that we needed in Leone.

We stowed our things in the small cabin. While Marco and Giovanni headed up to get the LD radio setup, Eve and I wandered into the galley to chat with our two cooks, Allegria and Bertina. At thirty-eight, the short, brown haired Bertina was three years older than the short blonde haired Allegria. We found them discussing the kitchen facilities.

"Well, at least they have it setup for us. You can tell a man's been in here, Allegria. Everything's in such weird places. Dear me, we will be hours getting things where they are supposed to be," Bertina complained.

"Well, this is my first time out as a cook, Bertina. Will it be hard for us to do this on the rolling ship? Agreed, these pots belong over there and these knives ought to be in easier reach, don't you think?"

"Absolutely. Well, that's why there are these tall sides to keep things on the stoves. We have to be a bit careful and always keep things locked down. Yes, it is sometimes annoying, but I admit, Allegria, I've not tried cooking since the plague. I think that it's going to be very hard for us to manage, though manage we must. Oh, our passengers. Hello, come to check out the galley, are you?" she looked up at us.

Allegria commented, "My, I do like your earrings! So long, impressive. They must be worth a fortune, but don't they get in your way? That's why I had Amando cut my hair short. I simply could not manage it, when it was long like yours, though I admit, mine was not as long as either of yours. Not that I didn't try, mind you. Amando did like it long, but then he agrees, after the plague that is, that anything to make it easier for me is acceptable. Was it like that with your fellows?" she finally wound down. I saw that Allegria was a talker.

"Thanks. We love our earrings; they are rather old. Can we help get the galley organized? It's going to be a long trip, and it will give us something to do," I suggested.

"Only got two of these chairs, dearies, but with two pairs of extra feet, it will go quicker," Bertina replied. "I do hope that we get better supplies sooner. Why, the pantry looks as bad as ours at home, what with all this rationing going on. I do hope that crops grow fast this spring as they did last fall. Now that was something, wasn't it? We, Dom and I, planted a small garden, just like Stefano suggested. Of course, I had to have Dom's help, but we got such a bountiful harvest. Never had so many green beans before and from such a small space. Why, I've begun to put on a few pounds. I lost so many, you see, to the plague. Why I used to be quite heavyset, much to Dom's pleasure. Now he keeps saying that I'm all skin and bones. Well, with this rationing, I don't see how anyone can be anything but skinny." They chatted away, and we helped them rearrange nearly everything in their galley.

Everyone was wearing similar clothing on this trip. We wore heavier pants and cotton shirts whose sleeves were tucked inside. The serious shortage of seamstresses was still a major problem. Those who were able somehow to sew were kept busy making the new dresses that we could get into by ourselves. That was far more important than sewing sleeve holes shut. Here below deck, the heat from the galley stove took the chill off. For once, I was glad not to be up on deck were it was downright chilly, due to the unusual weather patterns.

With little else that we could do to help our cooks, Eve spotted the torque ball court. "Bethany, shall we indulge ourselves in a quick game?" she teased me. This had been our favorite game for several lifetimes. Both of us were way out of practice playing the game without arms, but we had fun.

Our long hair flew in all directions and our long earrings bounced wildly as we dove and dodged and ran about the court, kicking the ball back to the ship's side, attempting to have it hit between the two horizontal lines. Finally winded, she and I bumped into each other and used our heads to make a hug. "That was fun. I bet before this voyage is over, you and I can take on the fellows and beat them," Eve challenged.

Six days passed by quickly, as we began to adjust to shipboard life. Every morning around nine, Giovanni made contact with Lucianna to let her know that all was well and to give her our latest navigational fix. She was tracking our location day by day, in case we ran into trouble. Steadily, the weather warmed up as we followed the coastline of the Southlands. At last, we sailed into the small harbor of Leone.

Captain Amando, Marco, and I headed down the gangplank to see about acquiring a major supply of food for the long voyage. The captain led us to the largest supply store where he thought that we could get all that we needed. The Golden Zebra was a huge warehouse with a small customer ordering section up front. A burly man chewing an unlit cigar stood behind the big desk, cluttered with papers and bits of age-old, uneaten food. "Don't like to serve the likes o'thee in here. Mutants are not welcome," he growled as we three entered.

"Hello. You know me, Dan, Captain Amando Armono. We need to get supplies to hold us across to the Western Continent. Pay in gold."

He growled, "Still don't like to give out good food to mutants. Don't care how much gold yea got. Better that yea all die off. Hear your babies are mutants too. Don't take kindly to such freaks o'nature around here."

I admit that I was shocked. Captain Amando glared back. "Look, we need supplies."

"Go get them in Velona or Zargarb. Get'em from yer own kind. We don't serve mutants here." He glared back at us. I began to wonder if we would need to use force on the man. This was wild, but I began to see the fear in those who had not gotten the plague. We left, however.

"Damn! These ass holes," Captain Amando fumed as we walked back to the docks and our ship.

"Look around you. You can see all the folks staring at us," I pointed out. "You can see the fear in their eyes. They are afraid of us, probably because of the plague. This is going to be a long lasting problem, I can see that."

"Well, I heard stories that our captains were starting to run into discrimination at various ports of call. This is getting nasty," he replied.

"Have we enough to get to another port further south?" Marco asked, trying to be helpful.

"Yes, but if this bigotry is widespread, then we're not likely to get supplies there either. Maybe the thing to do is to try the Spice Islands," he suggested.

"But doesn't that take us way off course?" Marco asked.

"Aye, well, we could try a hundred miles further south at Dingo's Corner. It's not as large a port as Leone," He suggested. We adopted this as our next attempt.

Late that afternoon, the Le Envoy slipped into the small docks, where two other ships were in the process of loading supplies. Both were from Demokritos. This time, I stayed on the ship, hoping not to make our "mutant" bodies so noticeable. I watched as the two headed into the large warehouse to see about the arrangements. If I had fingers, I'd of kept them crossed.

About a half hour later, I spotted the two walking back. From their scowls, I could tell they met the same resistance. "Damn, this is getting downright nasty. The nerve of these idiots!" Amando fumed once he got onboard.

Marco growled, "Same story. Their warehouse has everything that our captain says that we need; only they won't sell it to us mutants."

We held a conference below decks to try to figure out what to do. I was fuming. This discrimination was intolerable. "Okay, Captain, you say they have everything we need."

"Yes, they have prepackaged crates. Honestly, they are very well organized here. We need to purchase at least twenty crates and a dozen water barrels. I am assuming that we can collect rainwater as we go along. I'd feel better if we had twenty barrels though. Why?"

"It's time to teach these people a lesson. Never mess with Bethany!" I said quite testily. "Wait until dark, then I will get us those supplies!"

Captain Amando didn't really believe me, but since we were his paying passengers this trip, he agreed to wait until nightfall. We relaxed and soon had dinner. The fellows kindly did up the dishes mostly to have something to do. As dusk fell, I told the captain what to do.

"Open the main cargo grates. The crates will be lowered. I'll need you and your men to move them to wherever they are to be stored. Let Marco know when we have enough aboard, and he'll relay it to me. Also figure out a fair price for what we are getting, and I'll leave it for them in the warehouse when I'm done."

"Okay, but I don't see how they are going to give us what we need or even lower it in here," he replied. Eve grinned; she had already guessed what I'd planned.

"I'll tag along and provide the light that you'll need, dear," she whispered.

We slipped away from our bodies and headed into the large warehouse. We both cast our blue light spells, and at once, I saw what the captain had meant. Crates and water barrels lay neatly stacked, ready to be loaded onto incoming ships. Provisioning ships was the main industry in this small coastal town. I set to work. Lifting one crate, I moved it towards the main doors, while Eve opened them for me. The few people who were outside saw a large, heavy crate flying through the air and then slowly descend into our cargo hold. I wished that I had a Judger with me, who could alter their minds so that they believed that they saw nothing. Ah well, I continued to move crate after crate until at last Marco said that we had enough.

Then I began moving the water barrels, two at a time. I took twenty of them. When I was finished, I noticed a large crowd of onlookers had now gathered just outside the warehouse. Eve was gently keeping them back and from interfering. Captain Amando relayed a fair price for what we'd taken and counted out the gold coins, while Marco filled a small sack with them. I then moved the bag up and out of the caravel and over to the hushed, scared crowd of people. I spotted the owner who had refused to sell to Captain Amando and dropped the bag at his feet.

I returned to my body, as the crew was shutting the cargo hold grates. "Best shove off soon," I teased the captain.

"That was unbelievable, Bethany. Had I not seen it with my own eyes, I say this couldn't have happened! We have all that we need. Thanks. Lads, to the main deck!" Marco, Eve, and I followed them. I didn't trust those on shore from trying to stop us.

That was a wise move on my part. As the crew dropped the mooring lines and began unfurling the jib, three men with long guns moved before the crowd and lined up to begin shooting our crew! "Enough of that!" Eve declared. While we watched, the three men's heads spun around in a circle; one after the other, their dead bodies dropped to the ground. Now the crowd fled in a panic. Eve grinned. "Never mess with Eve, fellows."

That was the first indication our captain, boson, and crew had that this was going to be a most unusual voyage. None of them had ever seen anything like what just happened. Unfortunately, it took them a number of calm days to cease treating us as if we were some kind of goddesses.

Giovanni relayed what had happened to Lucianna, who then told Stefano about this new discrimination policy that was springing up in the Southlands. Now he had another problem to solve. I didn't relish this one. At last, we headed out into the open seas heading across the vast ocean carefully following a great circle path.

After a few days, Captain Amando predicted that we'd make landfall on the Western Continent in about forty days. However, since our path now took us close to the old Isle of Right, we decided we'd make a stop there for fresh water. Presumably, the island would still be unoccupied. We'd make the island in about twenty days.

Soon the cold weather left us and gradually it became hot. Eventually, all of us were sweating while just sitting in the hold. The men took this opportunity to strip down to their shorts to cool off. "Damn it, I'm melting," Eve complained. "If they can do it, so can we." Soon, Eve had taken off everything but her panties. "Much better, ladies," she said. Modesty be damned, I stripped down as well, and soon our two cooks who were sweltering over the stove did so too.

"Guess the boys can have a good look," Bertina joked. "But I'm sweating to death over this stove." We had Ning Peng do the same for Lin Zu as well. Yes, the fellows gave us all a few whistles, but that soon died down. In the heat, we were all miserable, and they understood our needs, which were the same as theirs. Slowly, the days passed.

Nearly every day a squall would appear, usually off our bow. As it approached, the crew spread out collecting canvas, which funneled the fresh water into our empty barrels. As far as water was concerned, we were collecting about half of that we used, thus prolonging our supplies. After twenty days of this sweltering, we all needed a good bath. If the weather was calm and the ship not moving, the crew took turns diving into the ocean waters. However, we didn't dare to do that and continued to give ourselves sponge baths, conserving our water supply.

On February 21, we spied the Isle of Right off our port bow and headed into its northern bay. Centuries ago, this had been an experimental station of the mantis creatures. Some four hundred armless women lived in a stone fortress some distance inland, while their men lived in wooden houses down near this bay. As expected, the island remained deserted, but the beach was idyllic! We all went ashore in two long boats, bringing soap and towels with us. Objective: bathe in the warm blue waters near the shore. While we women waded out into the waters to splash and bathe, the fellows went inland in search of fresh water springs.

An hour later, they returned to fetch the empty barrels. Marco commented, "Well, the old men's houses are all falling down or rotted so badly you can't walk on their floors without them giving way. We did find a good stream. Going to refill all empty barrels." This we women found perfect, since it allowed us a good four hours on the beach. That evening as we set sail once more with all of us quite refreshed.

I must acknowledge the excellent navigational skills of our captain as well as Arsenio's inventions. We arrived precisely forty days at the western edge of the continent, within twenty-five miles of our goal. I was very much impressed with how accurate navigation had become within the last century, amazing. Most of the wild guesswork had been removed, making navigation far more accurate.

Still as we gathered around the navigational charts of the Western Continent, over ninety percent of it remained unexplored territory. Only the coastal areas contained any details and that was scanty at best, with two exceptions. Up north, Wanakan was well defined and at the southern tip lay the strange country called Konstantin, home of the amazon women, who kept armless men as their slaves. We'd have to put in at their largest port of Kostya for supplies. As we began following the coastline southwards, I mused about what would have happened to their closed society if the plague had struck them. Their policy of removing their men's arms would have left them all in the direst straights if the women lost theirs to the plague. I wondered if Nestor had thought about that aspect, though I dared not ask him now.

All told, Captain Amando anticipated that we'd need another thirty days to get to approximately where we needed to be on the eastern side of the continent. It would be a good eleven days for us to get to Kostya and we debated on whether or not to stop there for supplies. The problem was that men were not allowed to set foot on their lands, only women. Well, armless men were allowed, that is. Trading was usually done by calling out to the women manning the docks. It was always awkward to deal with these women.

"Look, we are going to be likely quite some time trying to get to our destination in the mountains and even longer once we're there," I pointed out. "We really should take on as much as we can get here."

"Well, me and the boys can go ashore and hunt and scavenge while you're gone. Surely, we can find enough fresh edible plants and animals to get by nicely," Captain Amando replied. "We hate dealing with these amazons." After eleven days of discussion, as the city of Kostya came into view off our starboard side, we agreed to dock, and Eve and I would go ashore to see what arrangements could be made.

Their small dock could now handle two caravels at one time, though ours was the only one here. Yes, there were a number of women out manning small fishing boats, though. Soon, we slid into the dock and mooring lines were tossed. Women dock hands secured them and gazed with wicked eyes upon our captain, boson, and crew. A number of amazon guards approached, three held long guns, while the others had short bows and short swords.

Eve and I took a deep breath and headed down the gangplank, watching our steps carefully. As we set foot on the wooden dock, one guard came up to us. All had stopped now to stare at us two. I heard many whispers about our lack of arms and how awful this must be.

"I'd like to discuss the purchase of fresh food supplies and water," I spoke in several languages. Eventually, they responded, speaking some dialect of Demokritos. At least we understood each other fairly well.

"Follow me; we'll take you to Queen Anastasia Toya." We fell in line behind two of them and headed into the city on foot. Frequently, we spotted armless male slaves, used much as a horse or oxen, pulling carts laden with all manner of things, even iron ore. The palace was a simple wooden house, somewhat nicer than those that surrounded it. All the guards stared at us, as we passed them by, whispering among themselves.

"Queen Anastasia, we have foreigners visiting us in search of fresh food," the guard announced as we entered a comfortable, large room.

Pillows lay scattered about the floor and flowers in ornate vases lined the perimeter of the room. The queen rose to meet us. A most surprised expression formed on her face at once.

"Good god. What happened to you? Did your men do this to you? How awful! How humiliating! I am Queen Anastasia Toya," she said. She was about forty with long, curly brown hair and blue eyes. She was pretty and had an alto voice that sounded terribly concerned.

We introduced ourselves and told her that a great plague had stuck many of the northern countries, leaving all women as we were now. She bade us sit and summoned refreshments. Unfortunately for us, we could not pick up their glasses, no handles. Two of her assistants entered and held them up for us to drink, as they often did for their men. Soon, we found ourselves telling her about the recent events in the north.

A few hours later, she summoned dinner, and again we had little choice but to allow them to assist us eating. Anastasia was a good listener and very sympathetic to us. We had no difficulty in arranging for fresh food supplies and having our ten water barrels refilled. Five hundred gold covered it all. It took two days for all of our needs to be met, during which time, the queen kept us busy having us telling her all about life in Velona.

Wearing nothing but loincloths and harnessed to small wagons, armless men pulled up beside the caravel. Strong women then emptied their wagons and they all left, while our crew brought them onto the ship and into the hold. None of us had seen such a sight. These people used their men as studs and beast of burden, little else. "What's a man good for besides breeding us and heavy hauling? They are a stupid lot, always fighting and complaining," Queen Anastasia explained to us. Creepy, I thought. We were all very glad to set sail.

On April 13, we finally hove to at the precise coordinates that Lucianna had determined where Chichulain must lie somewhere inland. Eve, Marco, and I left our bodies and headed up into the sky to locate the plateau and verify our exact location. We'd navigated fairly well; we only needed to sail fifty more miles north, before anchoring as close to land as we dared.

A bit later, we took the long boats ashore to survey the land. We saw no signs of any inhabitants. The beach looked virgin, but the sands felt good beneath our feet after so long at sea. Now the question was how to get ourselves up the mountains beyond the thick jungles of the uplands. The fellows hacked a path through the dense underbrush. As we got to the edge of the jungle, I stared at the relatively steep valleys that rose sharply upwards.

"No way can I climb that," Eve said what Marco and Giovanni were thinking. Without arms to hold on, climbing was out.

"We could perhaps rope the women to us in case they slipped," Giovanni suggested.

"Well, let's see if we can even climb a bit," I suggested without much hope that we could. Both Eve and I found this another impossible hurdle. While the fellows were able to scamper up fairly easily, we simply could not do it.

"Guys, I am simply going to have to lift us all the way up to the plateau. There is no other choice for us," I declared, and we headed back to the ship to finalize our plans. Giovanni showed the captain and the boson how to operate the LD radio and told them what time to expect Lucianna's call, around nine each morning.

Until now, we'd pretty much left Lin and Ning alone in their cabin. Occasionally, we heard their loud moaning of pleasure releases, but we tried not to listen. Now we had to have Lin's cooperation.

"Oh my yes. Yes, if we can make the machines work, they should still make us mammalian food," Lin replied. I took a gamble on this and suggested that we bring along canteens of water and a light snack. It would take us a number of hours to walk from the edge of the plateau to the main entrance of the underground complex.

The next morning, I got a real workout. First, I lifted Giovanni and Eve's bodies up in the air and then slowly moved them across the jungle and then way, way up to the mile high plateau. After gently setting them down, I went back for Lin and Ning. Unfortunately, Ning was terrified of heights and Captain Amando tied a blindfold around his eyes. A few minutes later, I sat them down beside Eve and went back for Marco and for my body. All told, it took me an hour to get us six up to this mile high plateau. Lin was very much impressed with my skill and a little terrified that I was this powerful. I had little choice but to reveal this to her, but I hoped it would not alter our bargain.

While the plateau looked smooth from a distance, in fact, it was rougher than expected, and we didn't get to the entrance until late in the afternoon. We were quite tired as we faced our first hurdle: how to gain entrance to the caverns. Months ago, when he had left to spread the plague over southern Tashien, he's sealed it to prevent anyone from getting inside.

"Okay, Lin. How do we get in?" I asked.

She rattled off something in as near to the mantis tongue as a human voice could get, but became extremely agitated and broke down crying. "I can't do anything. I can't operate the control," she wailed.

The only way I could get her back to battery was to have Ning pleasure her once more; that stopped her crying. Once she moaned in relief, she was coherent again. I had her describe precisely what needed to be done. There was a small control panel some twenty-five feet above us. A specific sequence of symbol-covered buttons had to be pressed. I gave this task to Eve, as she was the one with the finer control. Me, I just crudely lifted things. Eve floated up to the control and pressed the proper sequence. A mechanical noise resulted, and the cavern's metal doors opened for us.

Just inside, Lin pointed to another control and gave Eve the sequence to press. Now the entire place lit up brightly. We were making progress, I thought. I took charge. "We should get the mammalian food machines working and get our old living quarters operational. Then, let's fix something to eat. I'm getting very hungry."

"But I used my transmatter machine to place your mammalian cells directly into the prison," Lin protested.

"What about the service entrance that the mechanical machines used late at night to refill our food machines?" I asked.

"Oh yes, that. Well, we could get in that way, but we cannot then get back out. It has a sensor activated control," Lin again protested that we would be trapped inside.

"Well, can it be locked open for maintenance uses?" Eve asked.

"Oh my! Yes, yes of course, it can. We must enter the codes for that," Lin began acting as Nestor once more. Again, she pointed out the control box, and Eve activated the sequence that Lin described, press by press. The door rose and locked in an open position. It took Lin and Eve over an hour to program the mechanical machines to begin the manufacture and delivery of mammalian food once more. Nestor had turned those completely off when he took us back with him. Finally, with the machines bringing in freshly made food, milk, eggs, juices and meats, we six headed inside to get settled in. Since there were only two bedrooms, we let Lin and Ning have one, while we four took the other. Marco and Giovanni were forced to make beds on the stone floor, however.

"Okay, Eve and I will work on fixing supper. Why don't you two take Lin and check out the rest of the place. Make sure all is still in order or whatever," I suggested.

"Damned awkward cooking like this," Eve commented. "Sure will be glad when he gets us put to rights once more." I could not agree more fully with her.

Lin reported that all seemed as she'd left it. Ning understood nothing of what he was seeing and focused solely on pleasing Lin as often as she desired. We ate a good tasting meal and then turned in for the night.

The next day, the fellows fixed our breakfast so that we could start on the big project sooner. I made telepathic contact with Amando around eight-thirty to let him know our status, which he would then relay on to Lucianna around nine. Breakfast finished, we all gathered around the right end of the cavern where the huge genetic modifications machine occupied the entire space, floor to ceiling. While this fifty-foot monstrosity of a machine was easy for a giant mantis to operate and reach all the controls, we were dwarfed by it. None more so than Lin, who continually broke down into tears at the slightest thing that went wrong.

Thus began the long days of frustrations. We quickly discovered that Lin's emotional state was so tenuous that we could get at most a half hour of useful work from her before some slight complication arose, which caused her to break down into despair and tears once more. Only Ning's pleasuring of her could bring her back out of it, whereon we could get another half hour of production before the whole cycle began again. Day after day, this continued, frustrations only rose higher and higher.

It took us five days to get the machine fully turned on and our latest mammalian cell forms brought up on the three-dimensional display. At first, this incredible view was awesome and spectacular, but staring at it day after day, it soon lost its novelty. I discovered that the Guardian's suggestion that the process of undoing a genetic modification was not an erasing or undoing, but a re-creation of what used to be the genetic blueprint turned out to be very much the case. Even though Lin called it undoing what was done, in fact, she was re-engineering arms into our genetic makeup.

Lin moaned, "Oh Bethany, this is so hard to do like this. The tiny veins and arteries have to each one be connected up. All those nerve cells likewise have to be rerouted and joined with those on the shoulders. I just cannot make all those motions without my mantis body. This is going to fail." She broke down once more.

I began to make some estimates. Recalling the duration between the time that he agreed that Version One had to be undone and the actual introduction of the bacteria which did it, I estimated that he'd spent three days re-engineering our bodies. Based on our progress so far and considering all the modifications to be undone, I estimated that we would be here at least a year! This seemed wholly undoable.

During the next period when Lin was again lucid, I said, "Look, Lin, we all can live with the other genetic modifications. All we must focus on doing is restoring women's arms to them. If we do that, will we need to do anything to the men's bodies so that our future female mammalian cells will have arms too?"

"No, it is controlled by the female mammalian cells. Why?"

"Good. Lin, we only need to make this one modification, putting arms back on us." She brightened up, even though this was perhaps the most difficult one of the modifications to undo.

A couple days later, I came up with a brilliant plan that shaved days off the project. "Lin, can you bring up a display of our original mammalian cells before Version One?" She said that was possible. "Good. When it is up, can you somehow copy the arms, then go to our current forms, and somehow paste them into place? Will that help speed the process up?"

Lin brightened up. "Oh my! Yes, Bethany. You are right as always. Yes, that is an easier way to do this!" Okay, it took another five days for us to accomplish this, but at last, we had that process completed. Still many other details had to be worked out.

One month since we arrived here, Lin was finally satisfied that she had the new genetic blueprints exactly right. She was ready to go into production of the bacteria. However, a new problem arose.

Our food manufacturing machines began to cease delivering certain items. Milk was the first to disappear. Then eggs no longer appeared. Then fish. Lin again broke down, wailing, "The machines are running low on the basic materials from which the mammalian cell food items are manufactured. I need to use my ship to retrieve more of them and replenish the machines. Yet, it is destroyed. We have no way to get more raw minerals. Now we will starve to death. We are doomed again." Once more, she broke down completely, and I turned her over to a most willing Ning.

When she was lucid once more, I pointed out, "No need to panic completely, Lin. I can always make a trip down to the boat and bring more food up here."

"But it takes milk to help build the bones," she countered.

"Okay, we can't actually test the bacteria while we are here. I guess we can test it whenever we can get access to some milk or other foods with the right nutrition in them. Now then, Lin, how are we going to be able to deliver these bacteria to every woman in the twenty countries?"

Okay, I probably shouldn't have asked such a direct question. It brought on another wailing episode. Her flying ship was destroyed along with the little ones. The easy aerial release was out. After she calmed down, we began discussing alternate ways for the bacteria to be given to someone. The original bacteria, we soon learned, was hermetically sealed in capsules. When the ships were over an area to be infected, they released the contents slowly, allowing the air currents to help disperse it over a wide area. "So we breathed in the bacteria and it entered our bodies through our nose and lungs?" I asked.

"Oh my yes. That is the easy way. Breathe it in and it goes to work," Lin answered.

"But once you release it, it lives for only a few days?"

"Oh yes, four days tops, but as soon as it gets into the mammalian cells, it begins its work, which is completed in three days," she answered again.

Marco scratched his head and said, "You know, Lin, I don't see any other way of getting the bacteria into someone without somehow going to each individual and somehow infecting them. We can't be infected multiple times and grow lots of arms right?"

"Oh my, no. No, the mammalian cells will have complete immunity to that bacteria, once it has performed its work."

"This is going to be nearly impossible to go around and visit each woman in all these lands and somehow get the bacteria into her," Marco groaned. "We're talking millions of women. What do we put it in so that it doesn't die off in a few days? We're going to need that stuff to be active somehow for years to get to everyone. The large cities will take time, but then we have to travel to every smaller town, village, and hamlet. Worse, we then have to visit every farmstead in twenty countries. This is hopeless."

At the mention of hopeless, Lin broke down in tears once more. Ning quietly put his arms around her once more. There didn't seem to be any other possibilities for distribution. Once the sealed container was opened, it would have to be spread around within four days max. We couldn't put it in the water that folks drank or their food. I began to think hard.

When she was lucid once more, I asked her for the distribution details that she'd used with her ships. What height was needed? What speed did the flying machines need to disburse it, and so on? Lin explained that had all been computed by her machine here and uploaded into the smaller ships, that executed their flying orders.

"Look, I could lift a container to the needed height and move it about, after Eve somehow opens the container to let the bacteria out. However, I would need to know precisely all the details to somehow duplicate the needed patterns. Plus, there would always be some exceptions, such as ourselves and our cooks who might not be within the affected countries at the time of the release or who might be in transit and miss a given delivery over a city. Lin pointed out another factor. The machines also controlled the rate of outflow from the containers, large volumes over densely packed areas and thinner over the countryside. It was beginning to seem hopeless. Here we had the bacteria but no way to get it to all the women who would benefit immensely from it.

Out of ideas, I laid down on the bed. Fell back is more like it, without arms to lower myself, pulling on my hair and even jarring my earrings. I felt the apparent failure a little too acutely. My eyes watered as Marco quietly joined me, rolling me over onto his shoulders. "We'll find a way, Bethany."

Eve also felt frustrated and went for a stroll around the complex, hoping to come up with a better idea. Giovanni pushed his hands through his hair. Surely, this is just an engineering problem, he thought to himself. He watched Lin Zu for a moment and then asked her, "Say, those canisters. Is the bacteria inside under pressure?"

"Oh my yes. It most certainly is. That is why such a small container can hold such a large volume. The ship's release mechanism varies the size of the opening, controlling the amount that is forced out as the ship flies over its target zone," Lin answered.

"Is there an empty canister around here and perhaps one of release nozzles that I could see, Lin? It seems to me that all that we are facing is a proper method of releasing the contents. As long as no air flows back inside the canister, thereby activating the bacteria's four day life cycle, the bacteria inside would remain in its dormant state indefinitely."

"Yes, I suppose so. Of course, you are right, Giovanni. It has to remain dormant, because the small ships sometimes takes several days to cover a large rural area, such as in southern Tashien. Okay, let's see if there is any lying around," she suggested. The two began searching the complex, with Ning following behind her. "Oh, there might be some behind that stuff, but I cannot even move them now! I am so helpless," Lin wailed and began crying once more. Ning put his arms around his flower, gently kissing her neck, before moving to her lips.

Giovanni ignored them and began rummaging through what seemed to be a trash pile. All manner of junk lay tossed in this pile, ready for disposal later, which had not come for obvious reasons. Before long, he found two damaged containers. "Got some canisters. Now for the nozzle thing," he called out, ignoring the couple's actions. In the large open area, the damaged small flying ship still lay where it had been docked for repairs that also had never come. At least the two dead mantis babies had been removed from beneath it. He stood before it, realizing that he had no clue of how to enter it. He had to wait for Lin once more.

Knowing that Lin could only give directions, he headed off to find Eve. "Damn frustrating, Giovanni. I can't find even one idea in this entire place," she admitted defeat to him.

"Well, I need your button pushing expertise, again, my love. I am going to get inside that little ship, though I know it isn't little, not to us. Shoot, it must be a hundred feet long," he sighed. "That's a lot of ship to study. I wonder how it flies?"

"Focus on our problem, dear," Eve teased him; he grinned sheepishly. The two headed to get Lin. An hour later, Giovanni was finally studying the release mechanism buried beneath the main deck of the ship amid a mountain of wiring, conduits, and all manner of strange devices. Still, the nozzle was a mechanical device, although it's opening valve was controlled by the machinery of the ship, following the orders downloaded into it. Mechanics was something that Giovanni could handle. Eve saw that look in his eye and knew that he was on to something, just not the what.

"Lin, is there any way that we can make more of these nozzles and canisters? If so, can we pressurize a canister the way that's done when it is to hold and release the bacteria? I need to run some tests."

Four more frustrating hours passed by us with three more timeouts to allow Lin to regain her ability to focus on the problems at hand. Still, as we ended for the night, Giovanni now had two canisters pressurized and ready for his experimentation in the morning.

The next morning after we ate from our dwindling food supplies, Giovanni asked Lin if there was any way for his machinery to design and build new nozzles.

"Oh my, yes, yes," Lin replied cheerfully, but he watched as her facial expression twisted into grief once more. "I cannot do it anymore. It is so hard being like this," she wailed.

"Honestly, Lin. Even if you had mammalian arms, you would not be able to operate your machines here," he tried to console her logically, preventing her from lapsing into all out-crying once more. However, she only cried all the louder, and Ning stepped up to her side once more.

Another day went by as Eve, following Lin's orders, continued to push the symbols on the giant fabrication machine located at the other end of the vast chamber. This was the machine, which had somehow made all of our replacement kitchens and other items. Lin called it a simple replicator, which produced the objects based upon the three-dimensional models input to it. Most of the day was spent attempting to get a simple nozzle designed, one with an easy screw handle that would open a tiny hole to allow the contents to begin flowing out of the canister.

Two more days of frustrations passed before Giovanni finally had a nozzle that worked reliably. Part of the design was pure guesswork on his part. The rate of flow that was used in the flying ship would be far too great for his ideas of a release of bacteria in some building, such as a warehouse. He made a guess of a reduction of flow by a factor of twenty and went with it. If it was too slow, he could always allow more time for the space to fill up. His handle could be adjusted to make a smaller hole if the flow rate was too large.

Now he wanted a real test of the proposed solution, an inert test, mind you, but with results that he could detect visually. Another two days passed, as he and Lin concocted a harmless test gas. "Here goes," Giovanni declared, opening the valve. We heard a hissing sound and soon saw a grey mist expanding into the room. "Ah, ten seconds to fill our bedroom. Excellent. Now let's see how it does on the garden room which is ten times larger." That took all of a minute. "Final question. How many minutes will one tank last?" Much later, he concluded, "Ah ha. Each tank operates for ten hours. Now we can plan. Need some paper!" He was excited, he had some real facts that he could handle.

All told, Nestor had made close to one hundred fifty canisters which he used to dump the plague on the twenty countries. Considering that we could not reproduce his flight pattern and would have to go door to door, Giovanni suggested that we make five times that amount. I felt a bit uneasy about it.

"Look, we cannot afford to miss even one woman out of these twenty countries. If we miss one, any of her daughters will inherit her body structure. In time, the few missed will grow and multiply. I would feel more comfortable with a ten-fold increase, Giovanni."

Ten-fold it was. Giovanni's estimates suggested that we'd need five canisters for each one that Lin had used. At least Nestor's machines kept a record of the number per each zone, as the machine called them, roughly equivalent to our countries. Knowing that number, I suggested that we mark half of all canisters that we made with the corresponding country on it. These we would give to the leaders of that country and allow them to handle the actual curing of their women. The remaining extra half we would safeguard in Velona and be ready to use if a country ran out before they finished the task or if other women turned up later on who were in need of it. "Think of it as a healthy reserve in case something goes wrong."

Eve began pressing the very lengthy sequence of final symbol buttons as Lin called them out. The machine began its work, now all we could do was transport the canisters from their dispensing location at the base of the machine out into the large space where the flying machine had been stored. The machine nicely bundled ten canisters together in a wrapper. Convenient, I thought. It took another three days for the machine to get the required two thousand canisters created and filled with the bacteria cure.

I definitely got a workout! Repeatedly, I lifted two bundles of canisters and moved them across the plateau and then down the mountain to the caravel anchored in the crystal clear blue waters, just off shore. There, the crew lowered them into the cargo hold and secured them. When we were done, we had two hundred of these ten canister bundles stowed, occupying most of the cargo hold's available area. So much for game playing space on our return voyage.

On May 15, we returned to the caravel, ready to set sail for home. Captain Amando and his crew had been busy. Exploring the surrounding area, they had come across and laid in a good supply of bananas, coconuts, an exotic form of yams, sugar cane, and turtle eggs. They had been eating fresh meat all month. Our stores of dried food were therefore in remarkably good shape.

Captain Amando stated, "Bethany, I've been thinking about our return route. I am leery of returning the way we came. Without taking on a whole lot at the amazon city, we may have a real problem with our food supply and the inability to easily get more at the Southlands ports. Via Lucianna, Stefano is reporting that many of our caravels are having the same problems there. For some reason, they are unwilling to sell to us mutants, as we're now being called worldwide. We've put up enough to get us to Annelise, where they may be more favorable to selling us supplies."

"Okay, let's go that way. Plan to stop in Shansee for a week," I advised. "Gang, we need to test this 'cure,' and it looks like we can try it out in Shansee. Now the question is on whom do we try it first?"

"I think that we ought to keep the first test small," Eve replied. "Perhaps us and, well, Pian and Misha, we'll need to do them if we are going to stay at their palace while it does its thing. I suppose Lin ought to be included as well and our cooks too. If it works, then we can get Pian to begin distributing it throughout Tan Loc." I agreed and we set sail again, none too soon for the captain and crew, they were awfully bored by now.

By June 15 when we slid into the docks at Viborg, Annelise, we were all bored out of our minds. Without the cargo hold space for games, there was little to do except help the crew with routine maintenance. I was now very tired of scrubbing the decks. Only Lin and Ning seemed not to have noticed the passage of time. However, we often heard Lin and Ning talking about her becoming a Great Lady, which meant having her feet arches altered so that she could have the tiny feet of a Great Lady in their society. I hoped they knew what they were doing.

Viborg looked larger than I remembered, though the quaint white clapboard houses lining the sides of the low hills now blended with the white snow on the ground. It was winter here in the far south. After the mooring lines were secured and the gangplank fixed into place, a perfectly dressed man stepped on board. He wore the typical Annelise men's suit, made of the finest material. His white cummerbund contrasted with his black pants and jacket and stove pipe hat. He wore a velvet cape with a red lining. "Good morning Captain. I am Erik, your harbor master. Might I ask your business this chilly winter's day, sir? And your country of origin, please?"

"Captain Amando Armono of Velona. We come to purchase a goodly supply of provisions with which to make the long voyage home, sir," he replied politely. At least if he turned us down, he would be extremely polite about it, I thought.

"Ah excellent. Yes, we will be more than willing to supply your ship with what you need, Captain Armono. I presume that you are aware of our strict dress code here in Annelise?" He nodded; we certainly looked grubby according to their standards. "In this case, you have two choices. One, you may remain on your ship and provide us with your requirements and gold, and we will bring them to your ship. Two, you can be escorted directly to a fine clothier, there to purchase proper attire, in which case, you may travel the city and country as you wish. However, I am pledged to ask you, Captain Armono, do you have any women on board?"

"Aye, sir, that we do, five to be exact. Why?" he asked.

Erik's face broke into a smile before he replied, "Well, Captain Armono, this is your lucky day indeed. If you wish to visit the clothier and bring along your women as well, our finest clothiers wish to provide your women with the very latest in fashion designs most suited to their needs and at no cost to them or yourselves. Further, your suits will also cost you nothing."

"Why would they not cost us? I don't understand, sir," Captain Amando asked, tempted by this offer. It would be easier for him to visit the warehouses and pick what looked like the best quality supplies.

"I believe that they are doing this as a promotional action, but I'm sure that they will explain it more fully. What, sir, is your choice?" the harbor master asked.

"I believe that we ought to be properly dressed. Is it not said that you can tell the quality of a man by his dress?" Captain Armando replied graciously. "Allow me a minute to get them, sir." He bowed and Erik did likewise.

Lin was not interested in getting new clothes; rather she was more interested in taking them off. We chuckled and left her in the care of Ning.

The captain, bosun, their wives, and we four soon found ourselves under an armed escort, walking along the cobblestone streets of Viborg. Fortunately, it was a short walk and we arrived at a very famous clothiers. I recalled this very shop from centuries ago when we first discovered this country during our voyage of exploration.

The H & H Clothiers was both huge and plush, the finest clothing store we had ever seen. The proprietors, Hedvika and Hans Gustav IV, welcomed us warmly. We stepped into the small storefront, which was carpeted in plush red. Several suits and gowns were on display, arranged neatly in the main storefront window. The soldiers held the door open for us and we entered.

"Let us be the first to welcome Velona strangers to our city of Viborg. We have
heard of your arrival," Hans began, "and were so hoping that you would grace our fine
establishment. We have made clothes for both our kings and queens for over four generations now. Our quality is unmatched, as are our elegant designs." He was immaculately dressed as was his wife Hedvika, both of whom were probably in their late forties.

"We have heard of the horrid plague that has befallen so many northern countries. Please accept our deepest, most sincere sympathies for your awful sufferings," he went on in a similar vein for a bit. At last, he got to the point. "Here in Annelise, we have for centuries now been providing only the best in suits and dresses for the Sea Princes, Velona in particular. As Hedvika pointed out, our dresses will no longer be fitting and proper for your women. She has spent long hours designing a whole new line of elegant gowns which she hopes will be better suited for your women." She nodded encouragingly and sympathetically.

"It is our hope that we may be allowed to properly attire your lovely women today and have you take them back to Velona with you. If you find them to your liking and suited to your needs, we would appreciate your telling others that they may order similar dresses from us. Your promotion of our work will be our exchange for free suits and dresses for all of you. Will this meet with your approval and that of your fine women here?" he asked. I suspected that he was keeping his fingers crossed. Undoubtedly, we were the first of the women plague victims to set foot here in Viborg. Hence, they truly wanted an opportunity to display their new designs to the world.

"We would be delighted to show off your new line of dresses, Hans. I do hope that they will fit properly. All our existing dresses from Annelise no longer fit properly, though they can be taken in some. Still, they don't have quite the look that they originally had on us," I replied. We had not yet proven our cure actually worked. If it did not, why not see what their new dress proposals might be? We women do love our fashions.

Four hours later, we four women looked at our new elegant look in the full-length mirrors. Hedvika was ecstatic that our waists could easily manage the tight wasp corsets that reduced them down another four inches. She kept saying, "Remarkable, so many here would just die to have a fourteen inch waistline!" The long nickers kept our legs warm along with the thin cotton hose. I was surprised by the hoops, though. These were infinitely more manageable by us, being only five feet across. The drape of the velvet material was extremely pleasing to the eye and the form-fitting velvet bodices were quite warm. Her design covered our shoulders, but had a plunging front neckline, again quite appealing. Topping off our new outfits, she had designed a fabulous outer cape that draped easily over us, nearly reaching the floor. Both heavy and warm, these capes were the find of the century as far as I was concerned. They looked fantastic on us; furthermore, even if we got our arms back, these could still be worn. Although most uncomfortable in our corsets, we loved our new look. She did make a concession to us; our new boots had a manageable five inch heel instead of their usual extreme heels. She had designed for our needs, capabilities, and our elegance. Our husbands escorted four very pleased women back to our caravel. I considered this a late fifteenth birthday present.

Three days later, our hold jammed with fresh supplies, we set sail for Shansee. Yes, we went back to wearing our shirts and pants almost at once, saving our fancy outfits for more appropriate occasions.

Chapter 32 Countering the Plague

"Are you sure this will work?" Princess Pian Ling Wu exclaimed, hardly able to believe what I was saying, that our arms could be regrown. It was July 15, 823 when we docked at Shansee in the early morning hours. Marco brought one canister with us to the palace, along with the captain, bosun and their wives.

"Well, we are not sure really, Pian. We are going to have to test it on some of us. If we are lucky, it will give us back arms at least. It just wasn't possible for us to undo all the plague's effects, just our arms. It might not work at all; it might not work quite right; we might have arms that look weird or not move right. There are no end of the things that can go wrong. We hope that we got it right, Pian. The only way we will know for sure is to try it on some of us and see. If it all goes wrong and we end up with unusable appendages, I guess we can have the doctors remove them," I explained.

"Well, I'd give anything for Misha to have her arms back. Okay, what do we have to do," Pian asked.

I explained that we needed to establish nourishment guidelines, especially what our bodies needed and the quantity during the process. Pian ordered her servants to bring us whatever we asked for, as determined by what we seemed to be craving. "Ah, just like being pregnant," she jested.

Giovanni opened the valve. Eve, Pian, Misha, Bertina, Allegria, Lin, and I breathed in the invisible bacteria. He left the valve open for around thirty seconds. "Is that all? Now what?" asked Pian.

"Well, in three days we will know the results. I think that by tonight we ought to be seeing something," I said hopefully.

By that evening, we were all craving milk and cheese. Misha exclaimed, "I feel funny around my shoulders." We struggled to remove her dress. Sure enough, small arms had appeared, perhaps three inches long. Encouraging. During the three days of growth, Marco and Giovanni kept accurate records of just what we all were eating and drinking. Plenty of proteins, milk, and cheese predominated in rather large volumes.

On the fourth day, all cravings ceased. Now we seven began to examine our arms in detail. Marco checked our range of motion, while Giovanni tested our strength. Captain Amando tested our reflexes. While we were a little on the weak side, everything seemed to be normal as far as we could tell. Seven women were elated! None more so than Misha, who now could keep her balance far better while walking.

We then spent three days bringing Tashien's supply of canisters to the palace, instructing ten men on how to perform the required actions, and working out how Pian could deliver this cure to all the affected women in

Tan Loc Province. I explained just how critical it was to cure all the women and how vital the proper diet during the three growth days was to the process.

"This is a mammoth project, Bethany. If my ten men can spread the cure to say five hundred women each day, it may take us two thousand days to get to every woman!" Pian calculated. "We're going to need to double the number of men and double the number that they can reach each day in order to make this manageable, assuming we can get enough of the proper nutrition available this quickly. If so, that will cut it down to a year and a half. Golly, that is still unacceptably long."

"I suspect that the cities will go quickly, but that those isolated women in rural areas will face many months before they can get the cure," I concluded.

"What do I do with Lin Zu?" Pian asked next. "She wants to stay here in Shansee."

"Well, she helped us make this cure. Why not provide them with a home and find some job that Ning can do to support them? I would keep an eye on her, though. Let me know if anything unusual happens with her." I had no idea how Lin would do adapting to life in our mammalian bodies. Plus, I felt that I owed her something in spite of what she had done as Nestor.

On August 20, we docked in Velona. Already Velona had heard of the miracles occurring in Shanshee. Accordingly, Stefano and a hundred guards met us as we docked, safeguarding our precious canisters, which were taken to a secure location, except one canister, which we took home with us. That day, we gathered up the entire West Po clan and our families, and Giovanni opened the valve, sending the cure out into the air of our front room. Cheering and clapping, hope ran wild among us all.

Stefano had already worked out his plan of attack. Twenty men were to give the cure to five hundred women each day. While fifteen of them began working on assigned sections of Velona, the other five headed for our outlying towns and villages. Stefano wanted every woman cured in three months if possible.

We learned that he had notified the other eighteen rulers that a cure was coming. As he received more data from us in Shansee, he explained how he planned to get the cure to all the women in his sector. He begged the other rulers to get their own plans worked out and ready to be implemented as soon as their canisters arrived. On August 21, trains began to deliver the canisters to these other countries. A hundred soldiers accompanied each shipment to guarantee the safe arrival of the canisters. Stefano wanted to take no chances on these being hijacked and ransomed.

When the trains were being loaded, I made sure that Giovanni gave Marcella a whiff as they were being loaded. Three days later, she was elated to be able to shovel coal once more. As for me, I cried when mom began to play her violin again! Actually, all of us bawled like babies when we heard her playing once more.

All around the nineteen countries, men and women rejoiced. A holy miracle had come unto them. Their lives had been salvaged beyond all possible expectations. No one complained much about their dangling ears or the other minor modifications that remained. Further, Alexa now had arms for the first time, as did the remaining women who had come from Hieras Anubis so long ago.

During our absence, Lucianna had been busy working on the design of flying machines. She made a formal presentation of her ideas to Giovanni and the rest of us. She had two drawings of lighter than air flying machines lifted up by using one of the most common gases, hydrogen. She had gliders, which had no engines per se, but used wind currents and thermal convective flows to fly. Rocket engines could push a ship with wings through the air. Ornithopters came in several varieties; all had some kind of flapping wings. One looked like a fly, one like an eagle. She had a strange looking machine that moved like a jellyfish. Some had rotating propellers on top of the bodies, pulling the machine upwards. Others had top propeller that could be moved in three directions, generating thrust in all different directions. Others had propellers in the front of some wings, while others had the engine in the rear pushing it along.

The big question for these two engineers was which one of these many designs could they realistically build? Would they be worth the trouble and expense?

Trouble and expense was precisely what Stefano and the other Sea Prince monarchs were facing. Most all the Southlands ports were now refusing to resupply our ships. "We don't serve mutants" was all too commonly reported by our caravel captains. This was now beginning to cripple our shipping industry, especially since only now was our food supply getting back to normal. By this fall's harvest, all rationing was scheduled to end at last. If so, we could then totally provision our ships so that they need not have to purchase food supplies from the Southlands. They could sail around them.

Stefano's concern was what would happen if Demokritos and Megalos stopped allowing our ships to dock and resupply in their ports. We could still load up cargo and unload cargo, just not resupply. Lucianna and Stefano came up with a plan to counter this embargo and potential shipping disaster. Industrialize tenfold. By making many more powered factories, the Sea Princes could manufacture more and cheaper goods, from cloth to steamships to trains. The other countries would necessarily desire our goods and would have to pay steeper prices as long as they continued to discriminate against our fleets.

Further, Lucianna began drawing up plans for a much larger metal ocean-going ship. If she and Giovanni could design large petrol powered engines, we could potentially sail for vastly longer durations and not need to stop in the Southlands, bypassing them entirely. The goal was to make discrimination against our countries painful in their pocketbook. Vito had vast iron ore and coal deposits. Further, a few enterprising individuals had begun prospecting for the crude oil from which petrol was made. In short, Stefano began his Ten Year Plan to industrialize Velona tenfold.

Raffaella of the Church of God, otherwise Linda d'Grange, came by to visit with me a month after we returned. Already thousands of women had received their cure of the plague. She wanted to know what all I had discovered about the mantis, their future threat potential, and Chichulain.

Reflecting back upon this whole affair, I realized a curious fact. "You know, as spiritual beings, the mantis people are very low in emotional tones, very close to those in Tashien. Nestor had almost no spiritual abilities left, comparatively speaking. He and the mantis depend utterly upon their machines to do things for them. Their civilization, which at first glance, looks so impressively powerful, is in fact pretty degenerate at best. Removed from his mantis body, Nestor is only barely able to retain his own knowledge of self. We were able to get him to use his memories of how things are done, but that's the extent of his skills."

"He said that his civilization and the Grey Creatures and the Dolls have been at war with each other for three hundred plus years. If you consider that their only skills now lie in making fancy machines, all three societies must be pretty darn degraded, spiritually. I think that here on Tarra we may be well ahead of them in this regard," I concluded.

"I agree, Bethany. Before Dorota was wiped out, we were making great strides with large numbers of people. Over a hundred have really recovered a good deal of their native abilities as spiritual beings. Give us another twenty years, Bethany, to get their new bodies matured and a bit more therapy sessions, and we well may arrive at the make-break point. Of course, there is always the remote possibility that one of these alien races will send a ship here to wipe out all life on Tarra. Barring that, Bethany, I think in another twenty years, we will be unstoppable in our quest to free spiritual beings. Maybe I am being overly optimistic, but the future sure looks bright to me now, especially since you were able to work a miracle for all our women." I found this to be highly encouraging news indeed. Perhaps the best yet.
The End.

A Favor to Other Readers

How about helping other readers? Many readers rely on reviews to make the decision whether to buy a book. You can help them make their decision by leaving your opinions and viewpoint in a short review of the positive things of this book. Writing the review and expressing your opinion only takes a few minutes, and other readers will appreciate your efforts.

Click this link: Volume 12 When Worlds Collide
scroll down to Customer Reviews; click on Write a Review, and enter your review. Thank you.

Author Information

Visit My Amazon.com Author Page
Vic Broquard Author Page

Follow My Blog
Vic Broquard's Blog

Follow Me on Social Media
Facebook
Google+
LinkedIn
YouTube

Other Books by Vic Broquard

Without Warning (fantasy)

The Trident Series: (fantasy)
> Volume 1 The Trident and the Book
> Volume 2 The Trident and the Scepter
> Volume 3 The Trident and the Resurrection

The Adventures of Elizabeth Stanton Series: (science fiction)
> Volume 1 The Evolution of the Path
> Volume 2 The Great Messiah
> Volume 3 Of Kings and Queens and Troubadours
> Volume 4 Chaos in the Aftermath
> Volume 5 Power Plays
> Volume 6 Age of Exploration
> Volume 7 Abducted
> Volume 8 The Emperor and Empress
> Volume 9 A Job Worth Doing
> Volume 10 Degradation
> Volume 11 The Second Crusade
> Volume 12 When Worlds Collide
> Volume 13 Dark Ages

The Lindsey Barron Series: (fantasy)
> Volume 1 The Rod of the Apocalypse
> Volume 2 The Board of Governors
> Volume 3 The Crown of Moses
> Volume 4 Dominus for President
> Volume 5 The National Health Care Program
> Volume 6 States Justice
> Volume 7 Cross and Double-cross

Zoran Chronicles Series: (fantasy)
> Volume 1 A Dragon in Our Town
> Volume 2 Dragons, Power, Courts, and War

Planet of the Orange-red Sun Series: (science fiction)
> Volume 1 When Kingdoms Fall
> Volume 2 Dark Ages
> Volume 3 Age of the Towers
> Volume 4 Difficillis Exitus
> Volume 5 Age of the Lords
> Volume 6 The Renegade Tower

Vic Broquard

The Return of the Wizards: Twelve Companions – The Making of Wizards (fantasy)

www.ingramcontent.com/pod-product-compliance
Lightning Source LLC
Chambersburg PA
CBHW081227020726
47503CB00011B/2926